BROOKE AND DANIEL
PSYCHOLOGICAL THRILLERS
BOOKS 1-3

J.F.PENN

www.CurlUpPress.com

CONTENTS

A Brooke and Daniel Psychological Thriller

DESECRATION

J.F.PENN

"The violation of the body would be the revelation of its truth"

Andreas Vesalius, 16th century physician, founder of modern human anatomy

PROLOGUE

THE BODY OF THE young woman lies on her back, blonde hair neatly arrayed in a sunburst around her head. She looks like an angel and I bend to adjust a lock of her hair, carefully disguising the deep wound in her skull. At least I can leave her face looking as beautiful as it did in life. Her lips are still painted with wine red lipstick, slightly smudged from where she drank with me. But that mouth whispered words of disturbing truth not so long ago, and I couldn't let her unleash that reality into the world. There is too much at stake and even she was not enough to make me give that up.

I pull on a pair of sterile gloves and breathe a sigh of relief as I slip into my second skin. They make me feel safe, a barrier against the world and yet somehow heightening the sensation in my hands. I always carry a pair, and tonight they serve a noble purpose. I brush her lips with gentle fingertips, some part of me wanting to feel a last breath. But I know she is dead, for I feel the lack of her. What made her alive is now gone and I wonder if she is already on another plane of reality, wondering how she got there, questioning why this life flew by so fast. This is but a body, just another corpse, and I know how to deal with corpses.

In a medical institution, it isn't hard to find a scalpel and I pull open the drawers in the training lab until I find an appropriate one. Returning to the body I use the 22 blade to cut a line through the crimson satin dress that clings to the curves near her hips. The material bunches slightly so I have to hold it down for the scalpel to slice through, but I manage to cut away a square of material, like operating drapes revealing the area for treatment. The blade is so sharp that I can sense the layer of material separate from the firmness of her skin and I feel a rush of pleasure at the sensation.

Beginning the incision, I slice across the soft lower belly. Her flesh is still warm, skin smooth and untainted, and I envy the beauty she carried so unconsciously. The scalpel slices down, a precision instrument in my hand and a line of blood rises to the surface. Even though her heart has stopped, it is as if this body still clings to life.

I feel something, a breath of air on my cheek and I freeze, scalpel in place on her skin. I know it must be nothing, but a shiver passes over me regardless. Perhaps it is the soul of the newly deceased taking one last look around this cabinet of curiosities, trying to understand her place amongst the many dead. For her body lies surrounded by tall glass display cases, packed full of the anatomical preparations for which the Hunterian Museum is famous. Body parts line up here in a macabre apothecary's shop, strange and bizarre with colors of pus, bone and decay. It is hard to tell what lies inside the conical jars of varying sizes until you lean closer to look inside or read the brief text that refers to each specimen. Stoppered and sealed with black tape, beads of condensation have formed on the lids as if what is inside still breathes. I can almost hear the dead cry out, drowned again each night in liquid preservation, and it makes me want to emulate the master anatomist in my own work. I stop for a moment to gaze at my inspiration.

Some of the organs are flower like, petals opening and fronds almost waving in the liquid, like sea creatures of delicate, strange beauty. Ruffles like tissue paper conceal a parcel of flesh that was once part of a living human. In one container sits a gigantic foot, cut off at the ankle, swollen with elephantiasis to four times life-size. Black toenails erupt from the end of grotesque toes, skin swollen to bursting, puckered and discolored. Every time I look into these cabinets I see something new, even though I have been coming here for many years, a pilgrimage to that which gives meaning to my own work. I glimpse the trunk of a baby crocodile, decapitated with its legs and tail brutally sawn off. Next to it, the trunk of a human fetus, barely as big as my hand, limbs and head removed, the tiny chest opened up to reveal the internal organs.

There are lizards, cut open, limbs posed as if they are running away, scuttling across this landscape of trapped souls. The body of a crayfish, tail curled under, protecting thousands of tiny eggs, and next to it, fat grubs and caterpillars, the larvae of hybrid insects. Quintuple fetuses are displayed in one case, tiny bodies with mouths open in horror, like corporeal dolls the color of ghosts. For the early anatomists were allowed to use the bodies of those that died within the mother, considering them specimen before human. Nowadays I have to work in secret, wary of judgment from those who don't understand the mysteries I can solve with flesh. This body is so precious that I cannot waste the opportunity to take what might further my research.

The sounds of the party filter upwards, laughter made louder by alcohol. Returning to my work, I cut into the young woman's flesh, digging down through the layers to reveal her inner organs. I use a self-retaining retractor to hold open the flap of skin and tissue to give me better access, blood slipping over my hands as I work faster now.

My gloved fingers probe her gently, making sure that nothing is damaged. The fetus is barely nine weeks old. Dead, like the mother, or soon will be. But its existence won't be wasted. Indeed, the knowledge it may reveal could be a greater achievement than most people could even dream of. I must get it back to the lab quickly.

Noises come from the hallway at the bottom of the stairs to the museum. I freeze, listening intently as my heart pounds in my chest. I can't be caught here, not like this. The work is too important and this specimen in particular must be studied. With the final cuts, I remove the uterus, placing it in her handbag that will have to do in place of an organ case

My work completed, I move to the doorway, hidden in the shadows. It sounds as if the people on the stairs are flirting and kissing, the party lubricated by enough alcohol to release the usual inhibitions. The noises grow fainter and I slip down the stairs as the unknown couple head off into a darker corner to fulfill their desires with each other. I pity them, for they can only find what they seek with living flesh. They know not of the darker pleasures of the anatomist.

CHAPTER 1

FROM OUTSIDE, THE LAVENDER Hospice looked like a school, with bright murals on the walls, a playground with swings, wood chips to stop the children hurting themselves. But those who entered this building wouldn't leave again and their voices were silenced too soon. Jamie Brooke pushed open the gate, hearing the usual squeak. She flinched slightly, adding the count to the list in her head, totaling the number of times she had walked through it. When she had first brought Polly here, finally unable to care for her at home, the doctor had said it wouldn't be long, maybe a matter of weeks. But the gate had squeaked ninety-seven times now, twice a day, so it was day forty-nine. Jamie sent up a prayer, thanking a God she didn't really believe in but still pleaded with each day. *Let her live another day, please. Take the time from me.*

The red wooden elephant by the door was looking a bit disheveled these days and Jamie made a mental note to talk to the Administrator about it. She knew the kids adored the jolly elephant, even though few of them ever made it outside to play on him. Practical help was about all she had left to offer.

Jamie checked her watch. She had moved to a tiny rented flat just down the road from the hospice, to be here for Polly as often as she could. Her job as a Detective Sergeant with the Metropolitan Police made the hours she visited complicated, but the nurses here were patient, understanding that as a single mother with a crazy job, she was trying the best she could.

Feeling tears prickle behind her eyes, Jamie took a deep breath, fixing a smile onto her face as she pushed the door open and entered the hospice.

"Morning," Rachel O'Halloran, the senior night nurse called cheerfully, as Jamie walked through the hallway.

"Hey Rachel. How's the night been?"

Rachel's face was a study in compassion and Jamie knew how much she loved the kids in her care, some here so briefly. There were people on this earth who were here to ease suffering and Rachel was one of the best, Jamie thought, and the kids instinctively loved the nurse in return.

"We had to increase Polly's morphine as she is getting a lot of pain from her spine now," Rachel said, "and her breathing is much worse. She might be drowsy when you go in." She paused, her eyes serious. "We need to talk, hun. You can't leave it much longer."

Jamie stood silently, closing her eyes for more than a second as she fought to keep her feelings under control. Despite her compassion, Rachel was an angel of death, her gentle arms helping the children to find their way onwards. But for parents, she represented only intense pain, for there was no avoiding the future she embodied. Jamie opened her eyes, hazel-green hardening with resolve.

"I'll come by on the way out."

Rachel nodded, and Jamie walked down the hall towards her daughter's room. The children's paintings on the wall attempted to add a veneer of hope to the place, but Jamie knew that the hands that had colored them were cold in the ground and the sorrow of years had soaked into the building. Parents and staff all tried to keep the spirits of the children up, organizing as much as possible to keep them occupied. But it seemed in the end that many of the little ones were more ready than their parents to slip out of the physical body. Exhausted with pain, debilitated with medication, their souls were eager for the next chance of life.

Jamie stood to the side of Polly's door, looking through the window at her daughter, whose body was distorted by motor neuron disease. Polly had Type II spinal muscular atrophy, and she was already past the life expectancy of children with the disorder. The deficiency of a protein needed for the survival of motor neurons meant that, over time, muscles weakened, the spine curved in a scoliosis and eventually the respiratory muscles could no longer inflate the lungs. Polly was already on breathing support and despite several operations, her physical body was now twisted and wasted. But Jamie could still remember the perfection of her beautiful baby when she had been born nearly fourteen years ago, and the joy that she had shared with her ex-husband Matt. He was long gone now, out of their lives with another wife and two perfectly healthy children he could play with to forget his past mistakes. Sometimes the anger Jamie felt at Matt, at herself, even at the universe for Polly's pain, made her heart race and her head thump with repressed rage. Her daughter didn't deserve this.

Jamie knew that the cause of Polly's disease was a genetic flaw on chromosome 5, a mutation somehow created from the alliance of her own body with Matt's. Perhaps it was some kind of sick metaphor for their marriage, which had collapsed when Polly started suffering as a toddler. But however difficult the journey, Polly had been worth every second. Jamie had always told her daughter that they were an unbreakable team, but now the bonds were beginning to fray and there was nothing she could do to stop it.

Jamie glanced in a mirror that hung in the hallway, visualizing the embedded genetic flaws on her own skin. If only she could dig out the part of her that worked and give it to Polly. Her long black hair was coiled up in a tight bun and she never wore make up for work. But with the dark circles getting worse under her eyes, Jamie thought she might have to consider changing her own rules. She looked pale and young, although she was the mature side of thirty-five these days. She touched her hair, tucking in a flyaway strand, claiming the little control she had left, clinging to this tiny victory. Threads of silver ran through the hair at her temples now, but the stress of the Metropolitan Police was nothing compared to living under the threat of Polly's death. Her daughter's every breath was precious at this point and Jamie fought for time away from the force to spend at her side. She turned the handle and went into the room.

"Morning, my darling," Jamie said as she approached the bed where Polly's twisted and wasted body lay, a tracheostomy tube in her neck helping her to breathe. She kissed the girl's forehead and put the wireless keyboard into Polly's hands, turning on the tablet computer, her daughter's link to the world. Her respiratory function had become so poor that the speaking valve was now useless but that couldn't stop her inimitable daughter. Jamie stroked Polly's hair as she watched her thin fingers tap slowly on the keyboard. Mercifully, the muscle wastage had started near the core of the body and left her extremities still able to move, so they had this method as well as lip reading to communicate. Jamie knew how important the computer was to Polly, the connection to her friends and a world of knowledge online, but the speed of her typing was painfully slow compared to even days ago.

6 videos last night. 3 more to finish multivariable calculus, Polly typed.

She had been progressing fast through the pure and applied math syllabus of the Khan Academy, an online video school designed to help children learn at their own pace, since many were capable of surpassing their classroom teachers. It was part of the incredible transformation of education, from an era of treating all kids the same, to targeting their specific talents and interests. It was also a godsend for children like Polly, who wanted to devour information non-stop. Even while her frail body lay dying, her brain was desperate for knowledge, although the drugs and her increasing weakness were now slowing her down. She was kept alive by the strength of her will, but that was dwindling like the leaves on the trees in the approach to winter.

Jamie knew that her daughter was fiercely intelligent and creative, as if in some way nature had made up for her physical flaws by giving her soaring intelligence. A picture of Stephen Hawking hung on the wall of Polly's room. The scientist was her idol, and she devoured his books - even at her young age she seemed to grasp concepts that her mother found difficult. Jamie had tried to read 'A Brief History of Time', but just couldn't fathom the science. Polly had explained the concepts in pictures and for a moment, Jamie had glimpsed the far galaxies in her daughter's mind. She had felt like the child then, instead of the mother. To be honest, she felt like the child now, as if nothing could ever be right with the world unless Polly could run and laugh again. But that couldn't be. This was not a journey Polly could return from and Jamie knew she couldn't go with her. Not this time.

Jamie met Polly's vibrant brown eyes, bright with a lively intelligence.

"I'm so proud of you, Pol, but you know I don't even understand what that means. Your Mum isn't exactly a math whiz."

Jamie pushed away the fleeting thought that it was pointless to learn when the brain would be dead soon. Polly's fingers continued to tap.

I'm doing the cosmology syllabus next. I'm beating Imran.

Jamie smiled. Imran was in a room down the hall, his body ravaged with terminal cancer but, like Polly, he was determined to cram as much into his intellectual life on earth as he could before he left it. On good days, when the drugs didn't rob them of consciousness, the teenagers could compete on the levels of Khan Academy. Both were competitive and determined to win. Jamie and Imran's parents were constantly astounded at their achievements, and Jamie credited her daughter's drive to succeed with preventing her own spiral into depression at the impending loss.

Did you dance last night?

Polly's eyes were brimming with the more detailed questions that Jamie knew she wanted to ask. She didn't need to type them because the conversation was one they had played out for years. Polly's greatest frustration with her body was not being able to dance and five years ago, she had asked Jamie to do it for her. "Dance Mum, please. Dance for me," she had pleaded. "And then come back and tell me about it. I want to know about the dresses and all the different people and how it feels to move so gracefully."

Jamie had relented at her insistence and taken up tango, a dance with its roots in the sorrow of slaves and immigrants, those oppressed by society. Tango was performed with a serious facial expression, emotion held within the dance. To her surprise, Jamie had found in tango her own form of release, and now the nights she danced enabled her a brief escape.

"Yes, I went to the *milonga* last night, Pol. I wore the silver dress and my hair down with the comb you made for me. I danced with Enrique first and he spun me into a close embrace ..."

So began the telling, the ritual they went through every day after Jamie could manage a night at tango. The erratic hours of her job made it difficult to go regularly, but she did find a sublimation of grief through the movement of her body. The late nights were worth the moments of clarity when focusing in the moment let her forget, albeit briefly.

Sometimes Jamie lied and told Polly stories of a tango night she didn't actually attend, an imagined evening where she had spun on the dance floor in the arms of a strong male lead, when in reality she had been at home, eyes red with weeping. Some nights, Jamie dreamt of walking along a beach, the ocean sucked back and the sand exposed, leaving sea creatures high and dry. There was a moment of calm when the waters receded, a suspended time of complete silence and rest. But she knew the tsunami wave would crash towards her soon, destroying everything in its path. Right now, Jamie held back the grief, but when it broke, she knew she would drown in its choking embrace. Part of her almost welcomed it.

Did you dance with Sebastian? Polly tapped with impatience.

Jamie laughed at her daughter's need for gossip. It was a marvelous moment of normality, although Jamie wished she was quizzing Polly about boys and not the other way around.

"You know I can't ask a man to dance, Pol. It's against the etiquette of tango. Sebastian was there but he was dancing primarily with Margherita. She's very good, you know."

Bitch.

"Polly Brooke," Jamie scolded, "enough of that language!" But Jamie couldn't help smiling, because the twenty-five year old Margherita was indeed a talented, beautiful bitch who dominated the London tango scene. Polly had seen her regular dancing partner Sebastian on YouTube and had become convinced that he should sweep Jamie off into a romantic sunset.

Polly's face suddenly contorted in a grimace of pain and she started making choking noises, a grotesque parody of breath. Increasingly now, the secretions in her lungs became too much and she struggled for air. Jamie had heard it described as similar to drowning, the body fighting desperately for oxygen. The keyboard fell to the floor with a clatter as Polly's fingers clutched at the air in grasping urgency. Jamie's heart rate spiked and she banged the panic button on the wall, knowing that the alert would be triggered in the nurse's area, silent so as not to alert the other children. She gripped Polly's hand.

"It's OK, my darling. I'm here. Try to relax. Shhh, there now, Pol. It's OK." Jamie couldn't hold back the tears, watching helplessly as Polly convulsed in pain, trying to cough up the stickiness that was engulfing her. Rachel swept into the room with another nurse and Jamie stepped back, letting them inject Polly with a sedative. Tears streaming down her face, Jamie felt impotent and useless as she could do nothing to take away her daughter's pain.

Rachel began to suction the fluid from Polly's lungs, the noise a hideous gurgling, but after a few seconds, Polly's tense body relaxed on the bed. Jamie stepped forward to take her hand, unclenching the fingers that had tightened in pain. She stroked her daughter's skin, touch her only communication now. The body on the bed was her daughter, but to Jamie, Polly was not an invalid in pain, a wracked, twisted, physical self. She was a soaring mind, a beautiful spirit trapped here by mistake. Some days Jamie wished death for them both, to escape together into an untethered future. She picked up the cuddly Golden

Retriever puppy from the floor where it had fallen. Polly had always wanted a pet but the soft toy was the best Jamie could do. Polly had named it Lisa and kept it near her ever since, grubby now from a lot of love. Jamie tucked the soft toy under her daughter's arm.

Rachel stood close by, and gently brushed strands of hair from Polly's face.

"I know you don't want to have this conversation, hun," she said, "but sometimes it's better to let our children go. We can continue to keep Polly alive but her body is almost finished. You can see that, Jamie." Her voice was soft and calm, a practiced tone that Jamie knew she used with parents and children alike. "It's not something parents want to admit, but Polly's pain will only be over if you let her die. In any other society, she would have died of natural causes by now. We're just keeping this vessel alive, prolonging her pain."

Although appalling on one level, Jamie knew it was entirely appropriate to have this conversation in front of Polly, sedated or not. She didn't want to let her daughter's hand go in order to step outside the room, but also she knew that Polly had expressed her own strident wishes about the matter. They had talked about death and she knew that Polly wasn't afraid of it, only of the pain of passing. Jamie knew that Rachel talked about the end openly with the children and she understood the logic of that. There was an honesty at the hospice that cut through the crap of what was appropriate to discuss in polite society where the death of children was kept behind a veil of silence and denial. Here it was brutal in its regularity.

"I don't want to say goodbye," Jamie whispered. "I'm not ready yet."

"But what if Polly is?" Rachel said quietly, her voice speaking a truth that lingered in the antiseptic air.

Jamie's phone vibrated in her pocket, breaking the moment.

"It's work, I'm sorry." She pulled it out, seeing a missed call and a text. She scanned it quickly and felt her pulse quicken. Despite the desperation of Polly's illness, work was her sanity. "There's been a murder," she said. "I've been assigned to the case so I have to go Rachel, but I'll be back tonight. Just give me another day, please."

Rachel walked around the bed and touched Jamie's arm gently. "It's not me you're doing this for, hun. It's for your little one."

Tears pricked Jamie's eyes again, but she brushed them away, pulling the veneer of police business around her shoulders. Her job gave her a psychological anchor as well as paying the bills. Jamie was good at detective work, and her ability to solve puzzles and right wrongs gave her a little piece of lucidity in the face of inevitable loss. Every criminal brought to justice was another point added to her karma balance that she begged the universe to give to Polly.

CHAPTER 2

THE JET BLACK BMW motorbike pulled up in front of the Royal College of Surgeons in the square of Lincoln's Inn Fields, an area renowned for the legal profession and dominated by Georgian terraced houses. Jamie tugged off her helmet and dismounted the bike, putting her safety gear and protective leathers into one of the panniers. She had traded in her old car when Polly had entered the hospice. She couldn't stand to look at it anymore without feeling that her daughter had gone already. The bike was cheaper to run and the independence increasingly suited her. She wasn't meant to use it for getting to crime scenes but today she needed the mental space even though it rumpled her clothes. She straightened the black crush-proof trousers and tucked in her white shirt, pulling the matching suit jacket out with her handbag from the other pannier. Dusting the jacket down, she put it on and her transformation was complete. Polly sometimes called her the 'black work wraith', but Jamie preferred to wear the equivalent of a uniform to separate her professional life.

Glancing around and seeing none of her colleagues, Jamie pulled out a pack of Marlboro Menthol. Lighting one, she looked up at the imposing classical entrance to the Royal College. She smoked quick and fast, her breath frosty in the air, cheeks red with the winter cold. The cigarette was a shot of delicious poison, her own private rebellion against what she would have preached to Polly. What did it matter anyway, Jamie thought. Life is poison, drip drip drip every day until we die of whatever addictions hold us. Everything she lived for right now hung over her head like the sword of Damocles, so what difference would another cancer stick make? Besides, she needed just a little fix before facing the body that lay inside. The cigarette was a chemical separation between her home life and the professional, a space where she could squash her emotions into the mental box she kept separate from her police work.

Jamie took another drag, enjoying the mint fresh aftertaste through the harshness of tobacco smoke. In the old-school tango clubs of Buenos Aires, smoke filled the air, an important part of the culture where life was often short and lived intensely. In these brief moments Jamie recaptured that sensation in the little beats of time between her dual lives in this crazy city. She relished the start of a new case and already she was glancing around, her mind posing questions about the area. Why was the murder committed in this elegant part of town?

A gust of wind blew leaves along the road, brittle reminders of autumn tumbling over each other and rustling in the gutter. The sharp breeze bent the branches of trees in the park, a few skeletal leaves hanging on against the grey. Jamie looked up at the early winter sun, the only color in a sky that was as washed out as the commuters who walked, shoulders hunched, into the Aldwych. Winter was almost upon them and soon the British would begin their annual vigil, longing for spring as the nights arrived ever earlier. Jamie's thought ahead to Christmas, a time that Polly loved and she had always over-indulged. Would she be alone this year? Jamie pushed the thought aside, taking a final drag and pulling a small tin from inside her bag. She stubbed the cigarette out on the lid and carefully placed the end into it. The tin served as a way to monitor her habit but also to remove any evidence. She noticed there were already three inside, too many for this time in the morning.

Walking into the main lobby of the Royal College of Surgeons, Jamie gave her details for the crime scene log and put on protective coveralls and booties. A uniformed Officer directed her past the yellow tape of the perimeter to the first floor. The entrance hall was imposing, wide stairs with rich red carpet sweeping around in a curve, with marble balustrades to guide the way upwards. The hall was overlooked by extravagant paintings of the men who had once ruled this surgical empire. Artifacts from the museum were displayed in niches, drawing the eyes back through its illustrious history.

Upstairs, Jamie entered the Hunterian Museum, a place she'd never visited but vaguely knew of. It was one of those hidden treasures of London that few came to see but which changed those who did. She was partially glad of her ignorance, because she wanted to see it with untainted eyes before she polluted her instinctive impressions with fact.

Near the door, a uniformed officer sat with an elderly man, the Curator. He was agitated, wringing his hands and then rubbing his neck, repeatedly loosening his tie. Jamie recognized the body language of self-comforting and wondered if perhaps he had found the body. She would circle back to him in a bit. The officer looked up and Jamie nodded her head in a professional greeting, avoiding a smile.

She looked around, taking in the activity before her. Scene Of Crime Officers (SOCOs) were processing the area, and Jamie's eyes were drawn to a central space surrounded by walls of glass shelving that contained thousands of body parts in preservation jars. Jamie had seen many bodies in various states, but usually they were recognizably human. This was a collection of the macabre, and a strangely appropriate place for another dead body.

Jamie felt a familiar surge of excitement at a new case, a new puzzle to solve and a way to distract her from thoughts of the hospice. She registered the usual guilt as well, because for her to feel this way, a human being had to die. But Jamie was a realist and there would always be murder, violence and death. It was endemic to the human condition. She had a short window of opportunity in her life to make a difference and potentially lower the body count and it made her remarkable for just an instant. This job was not some office function where busy work whiled away the hours, counting for nothing. This work could save lives, bring justice and occasionally equilibrium to the small corner of the world that was Jamie's London. It was a chance to be extraordinary, the reason she had escaped her parents' home on the Milton Keynes housing estate as soon as she could. She had known growing up there that she had to get out of that rut or risk being trapped forever in mediocrity.

Jamie walked into the central area where a female body was laid out on the floor wearing a scarlet evening dress that had been slashed open. Her beautiful face was calm but there was a deep wound in her lower abdomen, looking more like a surgical operation than the butchery it must have been. The woman's blonde hair looked like an unnatural wig, the tresses freshly brushed and seemingly too alive to be attached to a dead body. Flashes of light from the crime scene photographer illuminated the corpse, her skin pale and posed like a model exhibit. Jamie stood still as she took in the scene. This was the moment when she knew nothing and her mind was filled with questions. Who was this woman and why did she die here last night. She noticed the red lipstick on the woman's mouth and imagined her speaking. What would she say?

"Jamie, good to see you."

Jamie turned to see Detective Sergeant Leander Marcus, his slight paunch extending the dark weave of his suit trousers, visible through the thin protective coveralls.

"Hey Lee, were you first on scene?"

Leander nodded, his face crumpled with lack of sleep.

"Keen to get off it ASAP. I've been up all night and this only came in a few hours ago. Cameron get you called in?"

Leander arched an eyebrow and Jamie gave a complicit half-smile. Detective Superintendent Dale Cameron was respected for his accomplishments but he also seemed to have Teflon shoulders, deflecting any scandal onto other ranking officers, so his cases came with a health warning. With his salt and pepper hair and a body kept trim from marathon running, Cameron had the looks of a Fortune 500 CEO and his star was on the rise within the Metropolitan Police.

He had been appointed Senior Investigating Officer for the crime, assigning Jamie to the case along with a small team of Detective Constables as an inquiry team. Jamie had clashed with Cameron before, receiving a verbal warning for acting outside of protocol. She knew that she needed to rein in her independent streak, it didn't sit well with the rules and regulations of the Force. But she also knew that her exemplary investigation results meant she was given a little more leeway. Her methods might be unorthodox, but at least Cameron trusted her enough to get the job done and assign her to this case. She needed distraction, and losing herself in work was the best way, keeping her mind occupied while her heart was slowly breaking.

"So what have we got so far?" Jamie asked.

"The deceased is Jenna Neville," Leander said. "Her

handbag is missing but we got a list from security of people who entered in the last 24 hours and she was easily recognizable after we got the names. You must have heard of Neville Pharmaceuticals?"

Jamie's eyes widened in recognition at the name.

"Of course, it's one of the biggest British pharmaceutical companies."

"Exactly. Her father is Sir Christopher Neville, the CEO, who mainly concerns himself with politics and media campaigning. Her mother is one of the top scientists for the privately owned company."

"Any indication of why she was here?" Jamie asked.

"There was a gala event downstairs last night for alumni surgeons of the college. Jenna Neville attended the event, along with her parents, who are benefactors."

Damn, Jamie thought. A medical style murder in the Royal College of Surgeons after a party filled with actual surgeons. No obvious suspects then. "How many people?"

"Around 90 guests, plus staff. The Museum was supposed to have been locked though, and it wasn't used for the function."

"Is a team on the statements already?"

Leander nodded. "There's several officers starting on it now we have the guest list."

"I don't envy them," Jamie said. " That's going to take a while." She looked up at the glass walls surrounding them, stretching two stories high and lined with specimen preservation jars. "Cameras?"

Leander shook his head. "There aren't any in the Museum itself and the ones downstairs show all those guests milling around. We need to go through the footage and see if any of them weren't on the guest list, but to be honest, there are other entrances. This isn't a highly secure building as it's not considered a security risk. There are no drugs here, or money, only old bones and bodies."

Jamie indicated a walled display of surgeon's tools.

"And scalpels, knives, hacksaws and other equipment that could be used as murder weapons."

Leander shrugged. "Of course, but the College says that these are historical objects and there are easier ways to procure knives around here. But they're checking the inventory now."

They stood in silence for a moment as a white suited figure finished examining the body. Jamie knew forensic pathologist Mike Skinner from multiple crime scenes but he barely strayed outside the boundaries of professional talk related to the case. He stood and stretched his back, then turned to them, inclining his head in a slight greeting.

"There's massive blunt force trauma to the skull and her neck's broken." Jamie could see that the head was positioned at an unnatural angle, and the hair had been pulled back from the wound. Skinner pointed behind them to an open space at the bottom of a flight of stairs from the upper level of the museum, now surrounded by crime scene markers. "There are blood and bone fragments over there so it looks she fell and hit the post at the bottom of the stairs. I suspect that the way she landed would have forced her head into hyper-extension with sufficient force to cause a fracture at the C2 vertebrae." Skinner demonstrated with his own neck, dropping his chin close to his chest. "It's a classic hangman's fracture and cause of death is likely to be asphyxia secondary to cervical injury. It only takes a few minutes. I'll confirm in the post-mortem but those would be my preliminary thoughts. Her body was then dragged to this central area and postmortem lividity shows she was on her back here when the body was cut open."

Jamie glanced down at the bloody wound, held open by a retractor. "Can you tell what was done?"

Skinner nodded. "Looks like her uterus was removed.

Skillfully done too. It's a perfect Pfannenstiel incision, a Caesarean section, and it looks like the instruments used were from the Museum's collection."

Jamie tilted her head on one side. "That implies no pre-meditation, at least for the excision." She paused, looking around the museum at the specimen jars surrounding them, an echo of the mutilated body. "Was she dead when her uterus was cut out?"

"It looks that way but I'll know for sure after the autopsy. The lack of significant blood loss around the wound suggests that the heart stopped pumping during the operation."

Jamie felt a sense of relief that Jenna hadn't felt the invasion of her body, but why had it been done?

"Any idea of time of death?"

"Between nine and midnight, but I might get some-thing more exact after the autopsy. I would say that it was certainly during the gala event. Right, I've done all I can here."

Skinner nodded at two other men, also in protective clothing and they came forward to remove the body. They bagged the woman's hands and laid down a plastic sheet. As the corpse was lifted, Jamie heard something fall from the folds of Jenna's dress with a dull thunk. She signaled for the photographer to capture it as she bent to look more closely, pulling out her sterile gloves and an evidence bag. It was a figurine carved of ivory, around four inches long, a woman laid on her back, torso opened in a detailed minia-ture dissection. The woman's serene ivory face portrayed a calm demeanor even as her body lay open and mutilated, her organs and loops of intestines painted a deep red.

"You can take the body," Jamie said to Skinner, who was clearly eager to get back to his lab. "I'll deal with this."

She waited until the body had been zipped in its bag and strapped to the gurney. Once it had been wheeled out, she beckoned to the officer by the door to bring the Curator. He shuffled over slowly, his face a mask of grief. Even surrounded by mementoes of death every day, it must have been a horrifying shock to find the newly dead body early this morning. After some brief introductions, Jamie indicated the figurine.

"Could you explain what this is, sir?" she asked, her voice coaxing.

The Curator's posture became more focused as he directed his attention to the figurine, bending down to look but careful not to touch it.

"It's an anatomical Venus," he said. "They were made from the seventeenth century onwards as a way to teach anatomy, but increasingly they became more of an attraction for the cabinets of curiosities belonging to various wealthy collectors. They wanted things that were strange or terrible, horrific or unusual, those that would provoke a reaction in the viewer."

"Is it valuable?" Jamie asked.

The Curator nodded. "Absolutely. We have some examples here but it's not one of ours. It must belong to a private collection, or a museum perhaps. Someone will be missing it, for sure."

There was a bustle of noise at the doorway to the Museum and Jamie turned to see Detective Constable Alan Missinghall enter, hunching over in an attempt to be less obtrusive. He failed miserably, his six foot five muscular frame dwarfing the other officers on scene. He was new in the department and so far Jamie was impressed with his work. Missinghall had only just turned thirty and many underestimated him, seeing in his physicality a propensity for violence. But he was gentle, his expressive face betraying an acute compassion for victims of crime and he had a way of standing that made others feel protected. As usual, he wore an understated dark blue suit, slightly too short in the leg for his height, but he still walked like a man with authority.

"What have we got, Sarge?" Missinghall said, bending to look at the figurine.

Jamie recapped what she had found out so far and he took notes on his pad, putting asterisks next to aspects for follow-up. Jamie appreciated his keen attitude, hoping that it would last, for he hadn't yet tasted the bitter side of detective work.

"This room is seriously weird," Missinghall said, glancing around at the glass walls. He walked over and stared at the rows of specimen jars.

Jamie took a picture of the figurine on her smartphone, bagged the item for processing and then followed him over. The jars looked marvelously benign until you leaned closer, until what was inside became clear. The specimens were organs grouped together across comparative species. A whole shelf contained jars full of tongues, fleshy camel, spongy lion, then a human tongue with soft palate and enlarged tonsils, wrinkled and puckered like an alien mouth. These jars of disease are evidence of our mortality, Jamie thought with a shiver, fragments of flesh and bone that once walked the earth, now imprisoned in jars of preservative, drowning anew each day.

The Curator shuffled over to the cabinets, noting their interest and clearly eager to distract his own attention from the misery of the crime scene.

"John Hunter was an eighteenth century surgeon," he said. "He introduced direct observation of the body and scientific method into anatomy, rejecting the flawed textbooks his generation used. Although his methods were unorthodox and he gained many enemies, he nevertheless changed the practice of surgery and made medical discoveries that saved countless lives."

"Is this all his work?" Jamie asked, indicating the glass shelving with a sweep of her arm.

"Most of it and more in storage," the Curator replied, "but much was lost in a fire. He worked with his brother initially, William Hunter, who specialized in medical education and gynecology. But John was the real anatomical genius, and he prepped the specimens perfectly as you can see. It became his obsession and he spent his life seeking out the strange and terrible from humanity and the animal kingdom in order to learn from them."

There was so much death here, Jamie thought, imagining John Hunter and the bodies he had cut to pieces to make this collection. It was certainly a triumph of science and reason at a time when the body was misunderstood, before anesthesia, before antiseptic, when surgery was more akin to torture and generally ended in death. But it was also a disturbing museum of the deformed and misshapen monsters that Hunter had found so fascinating. Jamie looked into one of the cabinets, staring at the face of a child with no eyes, covered in smallpox. Just a face, floating in liquid. This place was indeed a bizarre and perfect location for a murder.

"John Hunter eventually had his own anatomy school and private medical practice as well as working at St George's Hospital. He would hardly sleep, so driven was he in his studies." Jamie could hear the admiration in the Curator's voice, his respect for a lifelong obsession. "Hunter was elected as a Fellow of the Royal Society in recognition for his pioneering work and he was considered the authority on venereal disease, possibly even infecting himself to study its destructive course. He was obsessed with direct observation, hence the specimens you see here."

Missinghall leaned towards one of the cabinets and Jamie saw the grimace on his face as he realized he was staring at a set of diseased sexual organs. He shifted uncomfortably and turned back to the Curator.

"So where did the bodies come from?" he asked, and

Jamie felt her own curiosity piqued too, for there were thousands of specimens even in this one room.

"That was … difficult," the Curator said, nodding. "But they had no choice, you see. Since the time of Henry VIII surgeons had only been allowed a small number of bodies each year, usually criminals hanged on the gallows. But there were too few to use for effective teaching and the surgical schools required each student to dissect several bodies in the course of their studies. John Hunter and his brother were part of a renaissance in anatomical teaching, but they needed fresh bodies every day in the winter dissection season. Summer, of course, meant the bodies putrefied too quickly." The Curator was speaking fast now, almost apologetic for what had happened all those years ago. "So they had to work with so-called Resurrection Men, grave robbers who would take fresh corpses from new graves, from the hospitals or poor houses and sell them to the anatomists."

Missinghall's expressive face showed his distaste, and although Jamie had heard of such practices, she hadn't really understood until now that many of the bodies were stolen, taken from graves without the consent of loved ones or sold because of poverty.

"Seriously?" Missinghall was incredulous. "Wasn't that illegal then? Because it sure is now."

The Curator shook his head. "The corpse was not considered property and the Resurrection Men were careful to only take the naked body, leaving the shroud and coffin so as not to be prosecuted for stealing. They were paid more for bodies that died of exotic diseases or deformities, and Hunter also wanted to recover the bodies of patients on whom he had performed surgery to see how they had healed." He pointed into the glass bell jars at the fetuses preserved there. "These little ones were priced by the inch. There are even some claims that the Hunters bought corpses murdered to order, particularly women at various stages of pregnancy for William Hunter's detailed study of the gravid womb." He paused. "Ridiculous rumors, of course."

Jamie didn't want to hear any more of Hunter's ghoulish past and Missinghall was looking increasingly queasy, even though he was accustomed to the newly dead. What mattered right now was establishing what had happened last night, not over two hundred years previously.

"Thank you for your time, sir," Jamie said. "We may come back to you with further questions."

The Curator nodded and walked away, his shoulders tense and rigid.

Missinghall shook his head. "Let's process this freakish place and get out of here," he said. "We can look into Hunter some more back at base, but I suspect this place will give me nightmares for weeks."

Jamie nodded, walking slowly around the glass-walled cases to the bottom of the stairs. She bent and examined the blood stains there, careful to avoid the crime scene markers.

"Why was Jenna even up here during the gala dinner?" Jamie thought aloud. "The body was clearly dragged from the bottom of the stairs, so it would be logical that she fell first and hit her head before being moved."

"Or she was pushed deliberately," Missinghall noted.

"Not a very effective way to kill someone," Jamie said, walking up the stairs to the next level. "It's not guaranteed that the person will die, only be injured in some way. And these steps aren't even that steep."

"Maybe it was an accident?" Missinghall said, as they both looked down at the scene below through more glass display cases.

"Cutting out her womb wasn't an accident."

"Maybe the killer has something against women?"

Missinghall said. "Or perhaps this place just inspired impromptu surgical practice?"

Jamie ignored his black humor, understanding his need to keep a light tone with what they dealt with every day. She turned to look at the other cases on the second floor, which was focused on the history of medicine. In one was a life-size wax model of a hideously deformed victim of war, with half a face and its neck torn away to reveal the jawbone. One hand was burnt to raw pink skin with fingers missing, and there were slashes in the chest, open to bloody rib bones. In the next case, a whole series of surgical saws were displayed, all from a seventeenth century surgeon's kit. Jamie read the sign on an amputation saw, describing a time before anesthetic and antiseptic, when people's limbs were hacked off while they were tied down, dosed only with laudanum or alcohol. She turned away, before the imagined horror dominated her thoughts any further.

"We'll have to wait for the autopsy results on whether she was pregnant and we'll need the statements of the attending surgeons from last night." Jamie sighed. "So let's go talk to the parents in the meantime."

CHAPTER 3

THE STREETS OF CHELSEA were always busy but Jamie wove through the traffic with ease on her bike, while Missinghall followed in the squad car, eventually catching her up outside the Neville's residence where she jumped in beside him. The exclusive property had security cameras and the gates swung open as the police car drove up. Jenna's parents had been notified of her death earlier that morning, so they were expected.

"You're quiet today, Jamie," Missinghall said, finishing off a banana. The man never seemed to stop eating. "Do you want me to take the lead on this?"

Jamie stared out at the ornate garden as they drove slowly up the drive. The grounds were like a miniature Versailles, beautiful even in the chill of early winter, precisely ordered with not a blade of grass or stem out of place. Jamie wondered if her life would ever be this ordered. Right now, she felt it disintegrating around her, but she wouldn't share that with Missinghall, preferring to keep her distance with work colleagues.

"Sure," she said. "Why don't you talk to them first and I'll hang back a little. The father may respond better to you anyway."

"Isn't he some kind of minor aristocrat?" Missinghall asked.

Jamie nodded. "According to the case file, the family is distantly related to Francis Galton, the eugenicist, and he was in turn related to the Darwins, so they have quite the scientific background. Their pedigree plays a prominent role in the marketing for Neville Pharmaceuticals. Lady Esther Neville is the brilliant scientist and Lord Christopher is well connected amongst the aristocracy, playing high stakes business with the manners of a perfect English gentleman."

"I'm not sure how well he'll like me then," Missinghall said, emphasizing his rough East London accent.

"But at least you're a man," replied Jamie, smiling a little. "He's apparently quite the chauvinist, with the media citing his preference for much younger women when out on the town."

"Marriage issues?" Missinghall said.

"They've been married since they were at Oxford University together," Jamie said, glancing through the notes on her smart phone that had been assembled by the murder inquiry office manager. "After thirty years of marriage, perhaps that kind of behavior is normal."

"Remind me not to ask you for relationship advice," Missinghall said. "I'm very happy with my missus."

Jamie remained silent at his comment, ignoring the unspoken questions about her personal life. Her own failed marriage and her parents' misery were the only markers she had against which to measure marital bliss.

Missinghall parked in front of the main doors, which were opened by an immaculately dressed butler before they stepped out of the car. Missinghall turned to Jamie, raising an eyebrow at the unexpected service.

"Good morning, Officers," the butler said as they presented their warrant cards. "Lord and Lady Neville are waiting in the library. Please come through."

The butler held the door wide and Jamie stepped first

into the hallway. It was sparsely furnished with a few tasteful pieces, but the walls were dominated by pictures, many black and white or faded sepia. Jamie leaned close as they were led through and she caught sight of famous faces. These were ancestors of the Nevilles in classic poses, designed to emphasize the visitor's inherent inferiority in this house of distinction. There were also pictures of Christopher Neville with senior political figures, CEOs and powerful media moguls. Jamie even caught sight of one with her superior officer, Dale Cameron, accepting some award, in the days before he had risen to the rank of Superintendent. Christopher Neville was indeed well connected, she thought, following the butler further inside.

The library was straight out of a Merchant Ivory film, with tall bookcases of ebony and exotic hardwood filled with leather bound first edition books, some behind locked glass so that they couldn't even be read. It was another way to impress and Jamie felt its effect, the delineations of social class evident. She thought of her own rented rooms, cluttered with books for sure, but nothing on this scale.

Lord Christopher Neville was standing by the ornate marble fireplace, his hand resting on the back of his wife's chair. He wore a three piece suit in English tweed, the mossy color palette blending into the library backdrop, like the cover of a fox-hunting magazine. Lady Esther Neville sat like an angular statue in a cream trouser suit, staring out of the window into the distance, her blonde hair scraped back into a tight chignon. She didn't even turn her head as they entered. Jamie had the peculiar sense that the pair had arranged themselves for some effect. She noticed the tension in Lady Neville's body, her senses attuned as a dancer to how people hold themselves. It was as if the woman was arching away from her husband's hand, as if his very presence repelled her. Jamie knew that the death of a child took many marriages to breaking point, but this all seemed staged, as if this is how a bereaved family was meant to look. She wondered what lay beneath the careful veneer.

"Detectives, what can we do for you?" Lord Neville said, his voice cordial with an undertone of impatience. He was bordering on corpulent, barely hiding the evidence of good living with impeccable tailoring and his voice was the epitome of aristocracy, honed by years of conversation in the upper echelons of power. His light grey eyes were clear and piercing, and Jamie noticed that they lingered a little too long on her own slight figure.

"We're so sorry for your loss, Lord and Lady Neville," Missinghall said, with a formal tone. "But we need to ask some questions about Jenna."

Lord Neville nodded. "Of course, we'll do everything we can to help you. Jenna was our precious angel."

Lady Neville's hand flew to her mouth at his words, and a stricken look passed over her face before her mask returned as her husband's hand moved to rest on her shoulder. Esther Neville was peaky, sallow-skinned and pale, as if she spent her days away from the sun. Jamie supposed that she did exactly that, shut deep in her lab generating fortunes for the company while her husband was out enjoying its profits. It looked to Jamie as if she would have got up and run from the room, but he imperceptibly held her down. Jamie felt a pang of pity for the woman touching the edges of her compartmentalized grief about Polly. But she couldn't let her preconceptions of motherhood cloud the investigation and, at this point, everyone was a suspect.

"We understand that you were both at the gala dinner with Jenna last night?" Missinghall said.

Lord Neville nodded. "The event was to raise money for the Royal College of Surgeons and we already fund a number of scholarships there. We're interested in supporting the education of a new generation as well as saving the lives of millions through our genetic and drug research."

Jamie thought he was about to launch into some kind of marketing pitch about the company so she jumped in.

"What time did you both leave?" she asked, pulling out her notebook.

"We've been through this already in the statement," Lord Neville said, a note of annoyance in his voice. "But Esther felt unwell and left around 9.30 and I am sure I left around 11."

Jamie thought she saw a spark in Esther's eyes at that, but her face remained downcast.

"And how was Jenna when you left?"

Lord Neville frowned. "I didn't see her before I went. She had left the table earlier in the evening to dance with one of her many beaus." Jamie noted a tinge of anger in his voice and an emphasis on the word many. She would have to investigate Jenna's love life carefully. Lord Neville paused. "We had an argument actually, I'm sure others will tell you of it, so I may as well. She'd had too much wine, and she said she had something to tell us, something that would change things. But she has said such things before, and nothing has come of it. I don't know why my daughter couldn't just leave the company in peace. She took its money easily enough." He looked away and his voice softened. "I guess it will be left in peace now."

Jamie wanted to explore the conflict around Neville Pharmaceuticals further, but she wanted to find out more from other sources first. People lied to themselves most of all. Those lies could hide the truth easily, and this was a family well used to displaying a public persona.

While Missinghall began to ask questions about Jenna's home life, her studies and the law firm where she worked, Jamie looked around and began to notice how unusual the room was. Lit only by table lamps, it was hard to see into the corners, but it was as if a veneer of respectability lay over more disturbing aspects. Above the fireplace was a large painting, at first glance just a woman holding her breast to feed an infant, posed as a Madonna and Child, seated with folds of light blue fabric around her. On second glance, Jamie noticed that her belly was in fact cut open to reveal her viscera and the baby in her lap was likewise a partially dissected cadaver. Jamie couldn't help but stare as it seemed to violate all sense of what would be acceptable to display in a public room like this. What made it all the more macabre was a framed photograph near the painting of a young Lady Neville with a baby, presumably Jenna, in her arms, the pose oddly reminiscent of the painting.

"I see you've noticed our interest in anatomy," Lord Neville's voice cut through Jamie's contemplation, and she turned.

"I'm sorry for staring," Jamie said. "But the painting is so unusual."

Especially given the location and style of the murder, she thought.

"I started collecting *memento-mori* many years ago," Lord Neville said, walking over to Jamie and looking up at the painting. "Tiny sculptures of skeletons and the dead in coffins that people would use to remind themselves of the shortness of life, the inevitability of death. To see a skeleton is to behold your own death and we all need a reminder that the end is inevitable."

A soft cry broke from Lady Neville's lips.

"I'm so sorry." She stood, wiping her eyes. "You'll have to excuse me. My husband will answer any further questions you have."

Jamie watched Lady Neville leave and heard her suppress a sob as she walked briskly up the stairs. The woman was clearly distraught, and for good reason, but she would have to find out more about Lady Neville. The interview would have to wait. She turned back to the room as Missinghall continued to ask about Jenna's life. But Jamie was impatient now and she wanted to get past the preliminaries. For a moment, she let Missinghall continue with his line of questioning and then allowed herself to interrupt.

"Did you agree with Jenna's career choice, Lord Neville?" Jamie asked. She was aware from the case notes that Jenna had started to specialize in the increasingly complex legal issues around tissue and DNA ownership, animal experimentation and other areas that could directly impact the practices of Neville Pharmaceuticals. There was also some photographic evidence that Jenna had participated in activist marches against the company and others labeled Big Pharma.

Lord Neville frowned and ran his hand through his thick dark hair.

"No, but my daughter was headstrong. She didn't want to come into the family business and in fact, she seemed determined to break it apart. I know she disagreed with some of the ethics of the company, but the money paid for her education, her prospects." Jamie could hear the disappointment and anger in his voice. "For some reason, she chose to leave us and live with that awful girl in a terrible part of town, getting into all sorts of trouble. I warned her, you know …"

His voice trailed off.

"And Lady Neville, did she support Jenna's choices?" Jamie asked.

Lord Neville paused, grasping for the right words. Jamie watched as he wrestled with what to say, finally settling on platitudes.

"Esther works too hard, spends long hours at the lab," he said softly. "She's wedded to the company, but she loves Jenna and she only wanted the best for her."

"Do you have any enemies?" Missinghall asked, changing tack. "Have there been any threats against you or the company, your family?"

Lord Neville walked to the other side of the fireplace and waved his hand dismissively.

"Of course, we get so many threats that we have a full-time staff member who goes through it all and decides which ones to forward onto the police. Not that you lot ever do anything. My legal team has restraining orders on a number of individuals, but in this country, the right to protest runs deep. There are ringleaders, of course, and I'll get everything forwarded onto you for the investigation. I personally get several death threats a week related to the business, but it's *my* life, Detectives, and not something I expected to impact my daughter, especially given her activism. Do you think her murder was related to the protests against the company?"

"The violation of the body didn't suggest a crime of passion or an unskilled criminal," Jamie said. "In fact, quite the opposite. We're looking for someone with surgical knowledge. What about any disgruntled employees, people who have worked in your labs who may hold a grudge?"

"Again, I'll have the files sent on but the nature of our business attracts a fair share of crazies and psychos. To us, the human body is a treasure trove, an addiction and a fascination. The way my daughter's body was displayed was not unlike the models I have in my collection, and so I can see it as a warning of course. But of what? I have already left my body to science and it will be cut up the day I die, but for someone to do this to Jenna … It's unthinkable and I will see that person punished."

"Of course, Lord Neville," Missinghall said, a curious deference in his voice. Jamie could see that he felt the class difference keenly. "We'll be working hard to pursue the leads around the case."

"Did Jenna still have a room here?" Jamie asked. "Or did she leave any personal items with you?"

Lord Neville shook his head. "No, she was quite determined to prove her independence. Anything she didn't want to take, she gave to charity. An animal rights charity, can you believe it?"

Jamie pulled out her smart phone to show him the photo of the ivory anatomical Venus found by Jenna's body.

"Do you recognize this, sir?"

Lord Neville looked at the photo and his eyes narrowed with interest. He hesitated just a fraction too long before handing it back.

"No, but I have similar pieces."

"It was with Jenna's body, wrapped in her clothes. We think she might have had it with her that night."

Lord Neville's expression was guarded and Jamie saw a flicker of doubt there. Was it guilt or just the devastation of a parent whose child had suffered too much?

"I don't know why she would have that with her."

Jamie nodded. "Of course." She hesitated, looking at the painting of the dissected woman behind him. The similarity to the museum exhibits in the Hunterian was too much of a coincidence to pass over. "May we see your collection? It might help us understand more clearly the artistic value of this piece."

"Of course, I'll have Matthews take you through. Is there anything else, or I will see to my wife."

Jamie shook her head. "Thank you for your time. We may be back with further questions."

Neville called for Matthews, the butler, who showed them through the library and out into another hallway, then up a staircase to the next floor. He led them into a salon that had been set up as a small museum with glass cabinets and even tiny handwritten labels. It was full of old anatomical teaching devices and artwork around the subjects of death and the human body.

"I'll leave you here to browse," Matthews said. "Can I bring you some coffee or tea?"

Jamie shook her head, walking further into the room.

"I'd love a cuppa, thanks," Missinghall said, then Jamie saw his face fall as he realized that he hadn't escaped the macabre by leaving the Hunterian. She looked into the nearest case as Missinghall walked around the room, his body arching instinctively away from what he saw.

Jamie found herself next to an anatomical model of a female torso, her face turned into the room. Her perfect eyelashes lay on wax cheeks, one blue eye gazing into the distance. She had perfectly kissable lips and skin like alabaster but one side of her face was deconstructed down to bone and tissue. The jaw was opened up to display tongue and teeth, the veins in the neck exposed, and her internal organs opened to the air. The model was more disturbing because the limbs had been cut off, legs sawn through so the bones protruded through the middle of steak-like fleshy rings. Between the stumps, a vagina complete with pubic hair was expertly modeled. Like some kind of sex doll for necrophiliacs, Jamie thought, wondering where the line between teaching and pornography lay. Anatomical Venus indeed. She found herself wanting to hide the woman from view. This room was a testament to the development of science, but at the expense of human dignity.

"What do you think of all this?" Missinghall asked, his voice tinged with disgust. "I just don't get why people would want to look at this stuff?"

Jamie stared at the case with the dissected woman. Jenna had clearly inhabited a world where this was considered normal, where the human body was part of study and work. Jamie was sure that this had played a part in her death.

CHAPTER 4

LEAVING MISSINGHALL TO RETURN and process what they had so far, Jamie rode slowly through the streets of Rotherhithe towards the City Farm, where Jenna Neville had shared a flat. It was a strange suburb, a bleak, cornered world with houses crowded together, densely populated but seemingly empty. The area had missed out on the recent revival of the East End of London. Whereas the north side of the Thames had caught the imagination of the public and was now culture and party-central, this little corner of South London was concrete and unwelcoming.

Jamie parked the bike and walked to the end of Vaughn Street, looking out across the river towards Canary Wharf, the heart of London's modern financial district, and famed for obscenities of wealth. Some people lived in this area for the ease of commuting by ferry across the water but others, perhaps like Jenna, were here to protest against the high-rises and cocktail bars, six-figure bonuses and hedonism that thrived on the bank opposite. For a second, Jamie thought of Polly's impossible future, what she could have achieved in this city of potential. Feeling tears well, she sighed and pushed the thoughts away. She couldn't let her emotions leak into this investigation.

Turning back, Jamie walked down to number 15, knocking on the door of the little terraced house, unremarkable in a sea of similar properties. The door opened and Jamie showed her warrant card.

"Miss McConnell?"

Elsa McConnell was petite with a tousled head of ginger curls that she wore tied up with a lavender checked headband. Her face was clean of makeup, a few freckles were scattered across her nose and cheeks, and her blue eyes were red and raw.

"Yes, Detective. The police said you would be coming over … Please come in, and call me Elsa. Excuse me, I'm just so …"

She broke off to blow her nose as tears started to flow again. Jamie contrasted her genuine emotion with the strange stunted response of Jenna's parents.

"I know this is hard for you, Elsa, but I wanted to ask you some questions and have a look at Jenna's room, if that's OK."

Elsa nodded, stepping back into the hallway and turning towards the small kitchen. As Jamie followed her in, she caught sight of the back of her neck, crosshatched in a complicated geometric tattoo that wound beneath her clothes.

The flat was brightly lit, with all of the main lights and side-lamps turned on, almost blinding with intensity.

"I can't stand the shadows right now," Elsa whispered almost apologetically.

Jamie nodded, her eyes scanning the place for indications of Jenna's life. There were People for the Ethical Treatment of Animals posters on the walls and eclectic Indian throws over the furniture. The young women were clearly not into mass-produced goods, for the apartment was furnished with artisan products, all recycled and hand made.

"So, how did you and Jenna meet?" Jamie asked, while Elsa put the kettle on and pulled out organic peppermint tea from a cupboard.

"I've worked at the Surrey Docks City Farm for four years now, and about 18 months ago, Jenna started working there as a volunteer some weekends. She's a lawyer - I mean, she was a lawyer." Elsa wiped her eyes, sniffing. "She was so passionate about animal rights, as well as human rights. She wanted to learn more about the way animals could live within a city, and how the farm could benefit the community."

"And when did you move into together?"

"Pretty soon after we met. Before that she'd been living at her parent's London home." Elsa's voice became a sneer and Jamie sensed the undercurrent of resentment. "You must know of the Nevilles' place in Chelsea. But Jenna had become increasingly angry about the family business and just couldn't live under the same roof as her parents any longer."

Elsa passed Jamie a mug of steaming herbal tea. Jamie took it, then placed it back down on the counter top as she pulled out her notebook.

"Did she tell you any specific details of her work?"

"I know she was looking into the treatment of experimental subjects and tissue usage at the Neville labs." Elsa paused, looking a little guilty. "To be honest, I didn't pay too much attention to the detail. I'm not as - technical - as Jenna, so much of what she told me went over my head."

Jamie nodded. "Did she have a partner?"

A brief flash of anger passed over Elsa's face before she recomposed it into that of the grieving friend. Jamie noted that with interest.

"Rowan Day-Conti," Elsa said. "I guess he's her boyfriend right now. He was actually a friend of mine from way back, we were at Uni together, but he and Jenna have been seeing each other for almost a year now. They're a funny couple though, since he's so mod and she is - was - pretty vanilla." Jamie raised an eyebrow, her look clearly confused as Elsa continued. "You'll know what I mean when you meet Rowan. He indulges in body modification and believes in the use of the body for expression and pleasure. He says it's the ultimate canvas for art. Jenna, on the other hand, was pretty squeamish, despite the detailed investigations she had going into animal experimentation. I know he wanted her to start experimenting more but she wasn't keen. In fact, they had a huge argument only a few nights ago, lots of screaming and banging doors."

Jamie noted that down. "I'll be visiting Mr Day-Conti later today. Is it OK if I see Jenna's room?"

"Of course," Elsa nodded. "I haven't been in there … I was waiting for her mother actually. I thought she might come for Jenna's stuff."

"Were they close, Jenna and her mother?"

Elsa shook her head.

"Not at all. But I thought she'd come since the bitch would want to make sure there was nothing left of the Jenna she disapproved of. You know they do animal experiments at the Nevilles' lab, right?"

"I'd heard something about it," Jamie replied and added a visit to the lab to her list.

Elsa pointed to the stairwell. "Her room's the one on the right at the top of the stairs. I'll let you go up alone if that's OK. Here, take your tea, it's soothing."

Jamie took the pungent brew, and carried it carefully up the stairs. There was a bathroom directly at the top and then two rooms, one to the right and one to the left in a compact, modern design. Jamie ducked into the bathroom and poured most of the tea away, hating the hippy stuff. Give me black coffee any day, she thought, especially on days like these.

Going back out to the hallway, she opened the plain wooden door into Jenna's room, immediately noting the stark poverty of the place, despite the girl's wealthy background. Jenna evidently hadn't brought much with her, and clearly hadn't purchased much since moving in. There was a double futon with a plain white duvet and pillow, neatly made, and a white lampshade on the floor next to the bed. The dominant piece of furniture was an old wooden desk, but not the type of elegant antique you'd expect to find in the bedroom of an heiress. It looked like it had been discarded from a school and left, unwanted, at the back of a charity shop. On it, Jenna's diary and some papers were scattered haphazardly, in contrast to the neatness of the room.

Jamie put on her sterile gloves and opened the diary. It was a slender Filofax, nothing flash, something you could buy in any high street store. She flicked through the pages, but nothing immediately stood out. In fact, it contained very little for a woman who Jamie would have expected to be far more socially active. Perhaps she kept another diary at work or details were on her smart phone, which Missinghall would be processing along with the other evidence. Jamie checked the time and her stomach rumbled on cue. He should be getting back to her with something shortly.

She continued checking the papers, taking some pictures with her smart phone of the pages directly before and after the date of death. The only thing that looked strangely out of place was the word 'Lyceum' occurring this Saturday, in just a few days' time, at 11pm. Jamie wrote it down for follow-up, for there were several Lyceum theaters in London, and the word meant school in Latin, but 11pm was late for either of those possibilities.

Moving the diary, Jamie looked at the papers underneath, finding a sheaf of large artistic photos, beautiful but highly disturbing. A woman's naked torso was displayed in alabaster white, her breasts perfectly shaped, but under the right breast the body had been dissected away to show the internal organs. It was unclear whether the body was an artwork or in fact a real dissection. Jamie shuffled through the pictures and it became clear that Jenna was the model for the work. There was a photo of her lying naked on the futon here in this room, her arms provocatively held above her head. She was beautiful, her body perfectly formed and her smile was that of a lover, her eyes inviting. The digital date in the corner of the shot was only a few months ago, so perhaps the photo had been taken by her boyfriend, Rowan Day-Conti. Jamie snapped a photo of the image and wondered how Jenna had felt about artwork that had been modeled on her body, then turned into a partially anatomized torso instead of the live, warm flesh of a beloved. Was this the source of the couple's recent argument?

Turning back to the room, Jamie went over to the freestanding clothes rack which served as a wardrobe, covered with an opaque plastic sheet to keep the dust off. She unzipped the front and pulled it back to reveal a small selection of clothes. Here was evidence of the heiress who couldn't quite leave it all behind, for there were several designer dresses and jackets in gorgeous fabrics. Jamie felt a tiny pang of longing for dresses like these, that she could dance in like a goddess, but she could never afford them on a police salary.

There was a shopping bag at the bottom of the makeshift wardrobe. Jamie opened it and pulled out a shimmering blue satin sheath dress. It was gorgeous, barely there and yet would hang like a gossamer dream on a body like Jenna's. The price tag was still on it. £2400. Clearly Jenna was still taking an allowance from her parents, Jamie thought, while at the same time becoming an activist against their company. For where else would this kind of money come from?

Next to the bed was a shoebox, simple, plain white. Jamie knelt down to open it. Inside were folic acid supplements, most often taken by women planning on being pregnant or in the early stages of pregnancy. The lab results were still outstanding but this might explain why Jenna's uterus had been removed, Jamie thought. So who was the father? Day-Conti, or someone else? Jamie looked around the room again. Why was the place so empty? Did Jenna really reject everything in favor of this simple life, or was there somewhere else where she kept her personal items? This didn't look like the room of a girl who had lived here for eighteen months, a professional lawyer, an activist, the heiress to a substantial fortune.

Jamie left the room, stopping on the stairs to look down into the living area. Elsa was curled up in a big chair, staring out of the window, her eyes fixed on something outside, her face a picture of Pre-Raphaelite beauty. She looked up as Jamie came down, and there was a hint of flirtation in her eyes, a suggestion of an invitation.

"Did you know Jenna was pregnant?" Jamie asked Elsa, watching for surprise. There was none.

"I wondered, to be honest, because she'd stopped drinking last month. Said she was over the drunken nights, but then she had actually been physically sick as well. Morning sickness, I guess. But she wouldn't talk about it. I did ask her, Detective, but we lived quite separate lives most of the time."

Jamie nodded slowly. "Was she seeing anyone else apart from Day-Conti?"

Elsa looked up, her eyes piercing, showing a level of hurt that was unexpected in a mere flatmate.

"Since we're being honest here, I think she was banging her boss at work, you know, that law firm. Perhaps you should ask him about it."

Jamie came down the stairs completely and knelt by Elsa's chair, intimately close, wanting to elicit her more personal thoughts.

"You loved Jenna, and that hurt you. Am I right?"

Tears welled up in Elsa's eyes, spilling over to run down her cheeks. She nodded.

"When she first moved in here, there was chemistry between us. I know she was bisexual, I've watched her with women at the clubs, and yes, I guess I was dazzled by her perfection. But she was also principled - about the things that matter." She indicated the PETA poster behind her. "We campaigned together, we worked on the farm together, and then she chose Rowan and I would have to listen to them fucking, when it should have been me with her." Her eyes narrowed. "She deserved more than that bastard. All he was interested in was her body, corrupting that perfection into some kind of perverted art. That's all he cares about." She looked down into Jamie's eyes. "You're going to him next, aren't you? Because he was always violent. It turns him on."

Jamie saw the shadows in her eyes. "Did you have a relationship with Day-Conti too?"

Elsa paused, then shrugged.

"Sure, at Uni, years ago but it was a web of intrigue back then and we all fucked each other. It didn't mean much, but he was darker psychologically than the others, he took everything to an extreme. That's when we all started playing with body mod and I got this tattoo." Her hand drifted to the back of her neck. "But Rowan took it much further because he has such a high tolerance for pain and expects others to enjoy it too. You'll know what I mean when you meet him."

Jamie stood, and handed Elsa her card.

"Thank you for your time, and please will you let me know if you think of anything else? That's my mobile number. Call me anytime, really, I want to find who did this to Jenna."

Elsa took the card and brushed Jamie's fingers gently.

"And you know where to find me, Detective, anytime."

CHAPTER 5

As Jamie pulled up on her bike, Missinghall stepped out of the unmarked car to greet her. With the information she now had from Jenna's flat, Jamie wanted the two of them to approach her boyfriend. He would always have been under suspicion in a case like this but more so given what Elsa had told her. The press would be onto the story soon, given how high profile the case was, but Day-Conti hadn't been informed of Jenna's death yet and Jamie wanted to observe his raw reaction to the news.

Missinghall was munching on a foot-long Subway, wiping the side of his mouth carefully to keep the crumbs off his suit. Jamie's stomach rumbled but she pushed the slight nausea aside. She felt a need to punish her own body for clinging to life while Polly lay immobile in her bed.

"We got the results back from the autopsy. It was rushed through because of the Nevilles' high profile," Missinghall said, pausing to take another bite as Jamie waited with barely restrained impatience. He offered her a piece of the sub and she shook her head, wondering even as she did so why she continued to resist even the slightest offer of help. "Jenna was definitely pregnant, around eight or nine weeks. Cause of death was asphyxia secondary to cervical injury and she was dead when her uterus was excised.

There was some bruising on her hands, consistent with defensive wounds, so it's likely that she was deliberately pushed down the stairs."

Jamie nodded. "Anything interesting on her smart phone?" In so many cases now, phones provided intimate clues and almost exact time of death since people were so active on social networks or texting all the time.

Missinghall finished his last bite of the sub. "Work emails, the usual social networking with friends but nothing on her research into the Nevilles. Some angry text exchanges with Day-Conti, though."

He handed her a piece of paper with the printed texts, some highlighted. Jamie glanced through them, noting that it seemed the arguments were about Day-Conti's work but they didn't suggest a sudden escalation in violence and there were no actual threats. She frowned, sensing that pieces of the puzzle were still missing. But this was what she loved about her work, the moment where moving parts were beginning to be revealed and she needed to work out exactly how they fitted together. Her mind shuffled them around, but the edges didn't yet fit. It was a welcome distraction from the realities of the hospice, but Jamie's fist clenched as she thought of Polly lying there without her. There was a fine line between her desire to be at her daughter's side all the time, and her attempt to keep a hold on her job and her sanity.

Jamie and Missinghall walked together towards the Hoxton studio where Day-Conti lived and worked. The building was a huge brick warehouse, seemingly abandoned, but in this area of London artists were reclaiming the area and remodeling it into a trendy, creative haven. There was a large warehouse door marked Entrance that had a proper apartment door fitted into it. Jamie eyed the graffiti on the wall close by, unsure as to whether it was vandalism or art. Around here, it could be both.

She pressed the buzzer. There was no response after a minute so she pressed again, holding the buzzer down until the intercom crackled.

"Yes," a voice said, indolent, as if he had been woken from sleep.

"Rowan Day-Conti?"

"Speaking."

"I'm Detective Sergeant Jamie Brooke from the Metropolitan Police. I need to speak to you about Jenna Neville."

"Jenna?" the voice said, suddenly concerned and alert. "Is she alright?"

"Can you let us in please, sir, so we can discuss the matter."

The buzzer sounded and the door clicked open, revealing a large warehouse space. Jamie walked into the vast building, her first impression of a high ceiling, making the space light and airy. Her second was the smell, a heavy chemical preservative over the pungent stink of decay. Jamie noticed Missinghall's nose wrinkle, and she knew that he also recognized it. There was something dead in here. The huge space was bisected by great metal walls, creating a myriad of smaller rooms in the large warehouse, so it was hard to see where the smell might be coming from, but Jamie felt herself tense at the possibility of what they might find.

There was a clattering of feet down the metal stairs at the side of the warehouse and they turned to watch a man approaching.

"Is Jenna OK?" the figure called as he hurried over. Tall and gangly, he was dressed in shades of faded black that seemed to merge into his skin. As he came closer, Jamie realized that this was because he was covered in tattoos and in addition, he had small horns protruding from the front of his closely shaven head. Even his eyeballs looked different, as if they had ink on them too.

"Rowan Day-Conti?" Jamie asked, looking doubtfully from him to the picture in her hand, which showed a preppy, clean cut young man with blonde hair and a muscular body. It was a long way from this clearly modified version.

"Yes," Rowan looked down at the picture. "That's the one on file, right. It's the way my family wanted me to look, the way they try to remember me, but I haven't been that boy for a long time."

As he spoke, Jamie saw that his tongue was forked, split into two, strangely grotesque but mesmerizing to watch. Rowan's eyebrows had been replaced by the intricately drawn wings of a dragon and there was a thick spike through his nose. Missinghall was staring and Jamie was trying not to, but Rowan was clearly used to it.

"Now, tell me about Jenna," he said, "because she's not answering my texts."

As Rowan turned slightly, Jamie realized that his left ear had been carved into an asymmetrical shape surrounded by rune lines making the ear more of a spiritual offering than a facility for listening. She had seen body modification in magazines and on TV but never so close up. Those who pursued it considered the body as an art form in itself, a tool to be shaped into something new, a canvas for self-expression and a way to differentiate from the pack.

"I'm sorry, Rowan," Jamie said, "but her body was found early this morning. It looks as if she was murdered."

Rowan froze, his face falling and he sank to the floor, kneeling on the concrete in his ripped jeans. He hugged his thin arms around himself and took deep breaths, exhaling loudly to calm himself.

"No, not Jenna," he whispered, panic in his eyes. "What happened? How did she die? Oh my God. When did it happen?"

Jamie crouched next to him, trying and failing to keep her eyes off his inked skin. From this angle, she could see that around the lower half of his cheek the tattoo revealed teeth inside a skeleton's jaw, a sweep of bone towards the eye socket as if the skin had been carved away,

"We're investigating exactly what happened," she said, "but we do need to ask you some questions."

"Of course." His eyes were haunted, uncaring of their judgment. "Anything to help the investigation."

Jamie stood up and looked around the warehouse, pointing to the metal walls.

"What do you do here, Rowan?" she asked.

Rowan's eyes changed, flickering to mistrust as if he suddenly realized that he could be under suspicion.

"I'm an artist. This is my studio, my livelihood."

"Can you show me some of your art?" Jamie asked, keen to investigate the source of the smell. It was death overlaid with sterility and it certainly wasn't innocent.

Rowan stood up, crossing his arms, his posture defensive.

"Don't you need some kind of warrant?"

Missinghall moved closer to Jamie, his bulk an effective backup.

"Not if you want to show us around as visitors," he said, his voice calm. "We're just here for a preliminary chat, after all."

Rowan paused, then shook his head in resignation. "I've got nothing to hide, so look all you like. This is all legal, although you might find it a bit disturbing."

Jamie raised an eyebrow, thinking of what they had already seen today. "I've been in the Met a long time so you'll have to try really hard to disturb me."

"Don't say I didn't warn you," Rowan said, leading them around one of the huge metal walls. A human cadaver sat at a desk, flesh ripped open to reveal its inner organs, as if it had been exploded from the inside out. "This is one of my works in progress."

Jamie didn't react and she was impressed that Missinghall didn't either. They just stood there in front of the body looking inside the preserved corpse, a compelling obscenity.

"This is your art?" she said.

Rowan walked to the cadaver and stood by it, forcing them to look at him. Jamie found it odd to see this modified living specimen next to a body that had been mutilated after death. One art form presumably chosen as a statement to the world, the other displayed intimately without choice.

"Have you heard of the Von Hagens Bodies exhibition?" Rowan asked. Jamie shook her head. Missinghall looked grim-faced, and remained silent. "It was made famous by the controversy over the provenance of the bodies, because some believed they were procured from Chinese prisons and used without consent. Whatever the truth, his technique of plastination has revolutionized anatomy preservation, and has also spilled over into art for private collections, as you see here." He pointed to the cadaver. "Plastination removes water and fat from the body and replaces it with certain plastics that can be touched, that don't smell or decay. It effectively preserves the properties of the original sample but in a state that will last over time. There are several Bodies exhibitions, including one in New York, that display the cadavers in modern poses so you can understand how the bodies work."

"Why?" Missinghall asked, finally breaking his silence. "What's the point?"

Rowan looked at him with disdain, as if explaining such meaning was beneath him.

"It's the intersection of art and science, confronting mortality head on. It's like seeing your future, looking inside yourself and realizing the truth. You are just flesh and you will die. The truth can set you free, Detective."

"You like playing God, Rowan?" Jamie asked, watching his eyes narrow as she spoke. There was a spark there, a defiance.

"I enjoy the confrontation of challenging established, so-called truth, yes. Most people remain in their safe little worlds, but I like to live in a way that makes them uncomfortable. Take the way I look, for example. People judge me, expect me to behave in a certain way because I believe in the right of each person to modify their own body. But most people are incapable of seeing behind the facade of skin to the true self."

"But is it your right to modify the bodies of others, even after death?" Jamie asked, pointing at the cadaver.

Rowan shook his head. "Of course, you don't get it. I didn't expect you to. Cops are on the side of the comfortable masses." Jamie felt herself bridling against that, but she forced herself to listen. "But you have to check me out before you take any action. I have all the permits and my flesh provider guarantees that these bodies are donated specifically for artistic purpose." He looked down at the body, running his fingers gently over the defined muscles in the neck. "I don't see a dead person here. I see beauty and a tool for learning, for the illustration of truth. You see, I customize my body while I am alive but life is too short, so I modify the bodies of the dead so that they might live forever. Of course we are not our bodies, Detectives, we are more than that. But I also want to demonstrate that our bodies can live on in this fashion."

Jamie considered his words, her thoughts flashing to Polly. She realized that she believed a similar truth, but from a different angle. Her daughter wasn't defined by her broken body any more than these were actual people that Day-Conti worked on. Once consciousness left with death, the body was a mere shell, so why did this instinctively feel wrong?

She walked closer to the cadaver, bending slightly to look into the partially-exposed folds of its brain. From one angle the face was intact and from the other, the cranium was open, displaying the preserved brain tissue. The body looked as if it was in the process of being dissected where it sat, the shoulder muscles on one side partially exposed. Some of the right wrist had been opened so the tendons and veins could be seen, like a belated suicide attempt.

Rowan moved back as Jamie deliberately invaded his personal space. She had read in the file that he was the son of a family similar to the Nevilles, who were appalled at his recent life choices and the alternative world he now chose to inhabit. Eton, Oxford, and now Hoxton, Rowan had become an artist dissecting bodies while indulging in body modification of his own design. It was extreme as rebellion went, but Jamie couldn't blame him from trying to escape his past, since she tried so often to forget her own.

"What else have you got here?" Jamie asked as she straightened.

"Follow me," Rowan said, leading them through a labyrinth of metal walls, until they rounded a corner into another workspace. Jamie blinked, trying to identify what she was seeing.

"This is what we call the explosion technique," Rowan said.

It was a decapitated head, plastinated in the same way as the other cadaver, so that it was a tan-color, preserved and dried. The brain sat intact with eyeballs staring ahead, tongue poking out from a deconstructed mouth. The rest of the head was peeled away in layers, skull carved in half with teeth intact grinning outwards. The face, skin and lips were peeled further out, fanned like a flasher in a horror movie, exposing what was meant to be hidden and intimate.

Jamie stood looking at the head, examining her emotional response to it. Logically it should be stomach churning, disturbing to the point of nausea like the worst murder scenes. But it was actually so far removed from anything you would normally see that it did indeed become objectified art instead of flesh. It was clean, sterile, ultimately fake-looking. Jamie had seen the decapitated heads of murder victims, and they were never as clinical as this.

"I am driven to view the body as a receptacle," Rowan said, waiting for their response. "As a mere container for who we truly are. Our skin, bone and physical flesh is but nothing in this life, only a carrier for our soul."

Jamie turned to him. "And what did Jenna think of all this?" she asked.

Rowan sat down heavily on a wooden chair, rubbing his hand along his jaw. He sighed.

"Jenna was a lawyer," he eventually said, his strident tone now gone. "We met at a body-mod event. She was researching the legal status of human body parts, consent for medical research and how that fitted with the use of bodies for art. There was an artist in the late 90s, Anthony Noel-Kelly, who was found guilty of stealing specimens from the Royal College of Surgeons. He and his accomplice were the first people in British history to be convicted of stealing body parts, even though the trade in bodies was centuries old. The body parts were classed as property because they were preparations, so there was actual work applied to the cadavers. Ironically, it would have been legal if the bodies hadn't been worked on. Jenna was exploring those legal issues as part of her specialization. When I learned of her interest, I showed her the artistic side of the anatomical world and one night, she stayed over.

We've been seeing each other on and off for a while now, not exclusive or anything, but she was special. There was something different about her."

Rowan's voice trailed off.

"Not exclusive?" Jamie asked.

"No, we agreed to see other people, and that was fine with me, although lately I'd been thinking about her more seriously."

"Did she model for you?"

Rowan shook his head. "No, she would never do that." He went quiet. Jamie waited, aware of the photo from Jenna's flat in her pocket. After a full minute, he continued speaking. "But I couldn't help myself. I had taken some pictures of her naked. She looked so beautiful and I wanted to use them as inspiration for a new piece. A body came in, almost as perfect as hers and I posed it like she had lain for me on the bed."

"Before you carved it up, you mean," Jamie said, unable to stop herself.

"Fuck you," Rowan said, slamming his fist down onto his leg. Jamie didn't even flinch. "This is art, this is what collectors pay for. It's an evocative piece, imbued with emotion. I had a particular buyer lined up who was willing to pay a lot for it, but Jenna was furious when she found out what I'd done."

"What happened?" Jamie prompted.

"We had a huge fight, a real screaming match. She said she would find out where the woman's body had come from and make sure she was buried with dignity. She was going to stop the sale. Jenna refused to be the inspiration for what she saw as the abuse of another woman's dead body. That was two days ago, and that's the last time I saw her, although there have been angry texts from both sides, I'll admit that."

Missinghall looked up from his notes.

"Your name was down for the Gala Dinner at the Royal College of Surgeons last night."

Day-Conti nodded. "I think she wanted me to go as a 'fuck you' to her parents who were attending as well." He put his head in his hands. "I wish I'd gone now. Maybe she'd still be safe if I'd been there."

"Why didn't you go?" Jamie asked.

"To punish her, perhaps. She was disrespecting my work and I couldn't bear to be there if she was going to ignore me anyway, not when my appearance would cause such a stir amongst that stuck-up crowd. I'll admit it was a power-play." His hands clenched into fists. "But damn, she was good at winding me up."

Day-Conti must have realized what he looked like and relaxed his aggression, taking a deep breath.

"The piece she objected to," Jamie asked. "Were you were going to sell it anyway?"

"It's what I do, Detective," Rowan snapped. "The pinnacle of my art is to have it displayed in a collection, for other people's pleasure. I don't do this to have the final piece hidden away or buried, to rot and disappear into the earth like any other mundane piece of flesh. For this woman, the best way to be remembered was to be immortalized. This way her beauty won't ever fade."

"I'd like to see it if that's OK with you?" Jamie said as her phone vibrated in her pocket with a text message from the investigation team back at the station.

As Rowan led the way into another section of the warehouse, Jamie checked the text. *Day-Conti financials show that his gallery is on the verge of bankruptcy. Family have disowned him. He desperately needs cash.* Here was motive indeed, money on top of art.

Jamie shivered. It was colder down the back of the warehouse, and the lights were dim. They rounded a corner and saw a rectangular tent, made of opaque plastic, like a containment area of some kind.

"She's in there," he said, his voice hushed. "I'm still working on her."

Jamie pushed through the curtains and into the tiny space. On a lab table lay the plastinated body of a perfectly beautiful young woman, her breasts round and pert, nipples hard, with one side partially dissected, the same as the picture she had found at Jenna's flat. The woman's arms were held above her head, her legs provocatively crossed, as if tied, but willingly. Jamie could definitely see the echo of the nude picture of Jenna, but with one huge difference. The woman's head had been sawn off and the arms cut off at the elbows.

Rowan saw what she was looking at.

"I wanted her body to be the focus, not her face. This way she can be everywoman, a fantasy."

Jamie was struggling to contain her anger at such a desecration, yet she argued with herself that those feelings didn't make logical sense. This body was no longer alive, yet the callous treatment of the flesh was abhorrent to her. There was no sense of a person here, even less so because the face was missing. But it was the objectification of a woman mutilated and displayed without her consent. It was pornographic in some way, and yet how could anyone find this arousing?

"Has this collector bought from you before?" Jamie asked, keeping her voice even.

Rowan nodded.

"I don't know who they are though. They buy through a dealer, but I know this one likes vanilla skin, no mods at all. They do specify the partial dissection though, in order to see inside the bodies, always to their hearts."

Jamie shook her head, sure that the buyer would be untraceable, but her sicko alarm was blaring.

"I'll be needing all your permits, because I just can't believe this is in any way legal."

Rowan nodded. "I've been investigated before, Detective, based on a nosy neighbor's curiosity. So you've got all the paperwork for me at the local station. They know what I'm doing here and it's all legal, I promise you."

Jamie walked out of the tent, away from the disturbance of the body as Missinghall went into the tiny space after her. She heard his muttered expletives and knew how he felt. She had seen a lot of bodies, in various physical states because of violent death, but this casual arrangement of sex and death seemed much more of a violation.

She led the way back into the main gallery, then turned.

"So, apart from the fight over that piece, you and Jenna had a good relationship?" Jamie asked, trying to refocus on other aspects of the case.

"She wasn't my usual type, you know, vanilla skin and all that, but she had a fucked up mind. I'm modified on the outside, but Jenna, she was pretty mod inside. That girl had some problems." Rowan shook his head. "You should talk to her family, right. They're a bunch of screw-ups. She hated them, did you know that?"

Jamie remained impassive. "So where were you last night?"

"I was here working alone until around 10pm and then I went to Torture Garden."

Jamie raised an eyebrow.

"Seriously?" Rowan said, his voice rising an octave with annoyance and frustration. "Check it out. It's all consensual and legal. Just because it's a fetish club, you reckon something evil's going on, right? At Torture Garden, there are lines you can't cross, it's not just a free for all. Seriously, I'd expect you to be more open-minded. We just want to express our individuality and that makes us far more normal than the rest of you. If you want to find some really fucked up individuals, look at the suits and ties and those who can only express themselves after drugs or alcohol. "

"Did you know Jenna was pregnant?" Jamie asked, not giving Rowan a moment to recover from his tirade.

He looked shocked. "Shit. No." He ran his hands over his scalp, rubbing the short hair upright. "Really? You think it was mine?"

Jamie could see that he really hadn't known about it. Her inner radar was going off over many things in this house of plastinated horror, but her gut told her that he hadn't known about the baby. He needed the money and he had motive around the sale of the female torso, and he definitely had the skills to carve up Jenna's body. But if he hadn't known about the pregnancy, there was no reason to extract her uterus. She'd have to clear his alibi by checking out the cameras at Torture Garden, but she didn't think it necessary to take him in. She raised an eyebrow at Missinghall and he shook his head, clearly feeling the same way.

"Thank you for your time, Rowan," Jamie said. "Don't go far though, will you?"

He shook his head, still reeling from the news of the pregnancy. "Of course, I'll be here. Please Detective, let me know if I can help in any way. You might not approve of what I do, but I loved Jenna."

Jamie saw tears welling in his eyes as he turned away to show them out. They needed to speak to the other man in Jenna's life. Could an affair have led to her death?

CHAPTER 6

THE OFFICES OF LEIGHTON Bowen Winstone-Smyth were situated in the prestigious row of law firms on the north side of Lincoln's Inn Fields, just across the square from the Hunterian Museum. How convenient, Jamie thought, as she rang the bell on the imposing front door. Missinghall had returned to base to check out Day-Conti's alibi, so she had returned alone to question Jenna's employer and, possibly, her lover. The door was opened by an office junior, dressed in a grey suit that was just on the right side of being too small.

"I'm here to see Michael Bowen," Jamie said, flashing her badge and as she did so, a door opened further inside and a voice called out.

"Let the Detective in, please, Michelle."

A man stepped into the hallway as Jamie entered, her eyes adjusting to the changing light.

"Michael Bowen," he said, holding out his hand. "Come in, Detective. How can I help you?"

Jamie shook his hand firmly. Bowen was around six foot three, every inch of him perfectly turned out. His black skin demonstrated Afro-Caribbean roots but his cultured voice and the finely cut, designer suit betrayed his current allegiance to the City. Serious brown eyes showed curiosity at her presence but he was clearly used to dealing with the police and he displayed no trace of anxiety about being questioned.

"I'm here about Jenna Neville," Jamie said, looking around his private office at the ubiquitous bookshelves full of leather bound volumes. Even though most legal research was done online these days, places like this couldn't quite let go of the old traditions.

"Jenna?" Bowen replied, confused. "Is she alright? I'd assumed you were here about one of our open cases." He sat down, indicating a chair on the other side of the desk. Jamie sat and Bowen leant forward, placing his hands on the desk. Jamie saw the golden glint of his wedding ring, stark against his perfect dark skin and buffed nails.

"Jenna was found dead this morning, sir."

Bowen froze, one hand lifting towards his mouth and, as he turned away slightly, his dark eyes shifted from Jamie to one of the bookcases.

"My God, how?"

"I can tell you that she was murdered, but we're still in the initial stages of the investigation, which is why I'm here to talk to you."

"Of course, whatever I can do." His voice trailed off, and Jamie noticed his eyes flicking again to the bookcase. She followed his line of sight to where a few volumes looked scuffed and more worn than the others.

"May I ask about your relationship with Jenna, Mr Bowen?"

He nodded. "Of course, she was a brilliant young lawyer, perceptive, original. She was doing a private research project into the legality of using bodies and body parts in research, as well as art. She had quite the passion for it, as well as a keen legal mind."

Jamie nodded. "And what about your - more personal - relationship?"

Bowen looked at her sharply and Jamie could see that he wouldn't lie about this minor truth, suspecting he had bigger secrets to hide.

"Yes, we had an affair," he replied, meeting Jamie's eyes with no trace of embarrassment. "It wasn't long, and we finished it, by mutual agreement I would add, about three weeks ago. I was happy for it to continue in an ad hoc manner as it was mutually pleasurable, but Jenna moved on pretty fast." Bowen was twisting his wedding ring as he spoke. Jamie looked pointedly at it and he noticed her glance. "We all have our secrets, Detective, and I'm sure you have yours."

Bowen's brown eyes were piercing now, and Jamie caught a glimpse of the man he could clearly be in the courtroom, a formidable opponent. She could also see why Jenna would be attracted to such a man. There was a current of danger under the silk cravat, a tension of strength and sensuality under his refined speech. Perks of the job indeed, she thought.

"Did you know she was pregnant?" Jamie asked.

"No," he said slowly, and Jamie thought there was a hint of disappointment in his voice. "We always used protection so I know it wasn't mine. I may play the field, but I'm not so stupid as to have some bastard child when my marriage is so important to my professional life."

Jamie pitied his wife in that moment, but his steely ambition was also impressive in its single-mindedness.

"Do you know whose it might have been?" Jamie asked.

Bowen shrugged. "Maybe that so-called artist boyfriend of hers. Did you know she was investigating him secretly, trying to find out about his supply of bodies? She was obsessed by it, and she suspected something much bigger than what he was involved in." He hesitated. "Look, I think she was onto something because I received a threat in the mail yesterday."

"Why haven't you shown it to the police?"

"In the nature of our work, threats are regular occurrences and of course I know our legal rights. We have private security in the building and you know as well as I do that the police are unable to act on anonymous threats alone. But this letter was unusual."

"May I see it?" Jamie asked, unsurprised when Bowen walked to the bookshelf, pulling the worn books away to reveal a safe. With his back protecting the code, he opened the safe and removed a letter.

Jamie pulled on sterile gloves from her bag and took the envelope. The address label had been printed and stuck on and the postmark was from the Aldwych, just round the corner from the offices where they stood now. She tugged out a piece of paper from within the envelope. It was a picture from the Hunterian Museum, one of the teaching models, a torso with limbs sawn off strikingly similar to the artwork that Rowan Day-Conti had shown her. At the top was printed 'Memento Mori.'

"Remember you will die," whispered Jamie. Underneath was a short typed message. *Forget the Lyceum.*

"What's the Lyceum?" Jamie asked, aware that she had seen the very word in Jenna's diary for this coming weekend.

Bowen shook his head. "I don't know. The word means school in Latin but I've never heard of it used in this way before, more like the description of a place or a group of people." He paced across the office with agitation. "Look, Jenna was doing this whole thing on the side as a research project. She said it would bring us amazing press and some lucrative work if it paid off. She was well connected through her family, she was brilliant and I trusted her. She also continued to deliver all her other work to the highest standard, so I didn't meddle. But when this arrived yesterday, I was going to ask her about the Lyceum."

Jamie shook her head. "Unfortunately, that's not going to happen now. Could I see her desk?"

"Of course. This way."

Bowen led Jamie through a warren of offices that stretched surprisingly far back from the street. There was a focused atmosphere of tension and pressure, but perhaps Jenna had thrived on it. It certainly felt like the lifeblood of Michael Bowen's world.

"This was where she worked," Bowen said, indicating a slim desk by a window that looked out to a small interior courtyard. "I'll need to ask the tech team to get access to her computer but you're welcome to look at anything she has here in the meantime." He looked at his watch. "I need to get back to my own work, Detective, but please, dial 113 on the phone there if you need anything else from me."

Jamie nodded and he walked briskly away, his expensive shoes echoing on the parquet floor breaking the hush of the legal team working around them. She turned to the desk, which was tidy and neatly organized. She texted Missinghall to send over a tech to work with the legal firm's IT team to pull Jenna's data, but somehow Jamie thought that they wouldn't find much on her official drives. If the investigation was something that Jenna was threatened over, then it was likely she would have kept her research material somewhere safe. The question was where?

Jamie searched the desk drawers. She pulled one open to find a stack of printed material, photocopies of newspaper reports and articles. Sitting back in the ergonomically designed office chair to sort through them, she flicked the pages to check the headlines. The assortment related to multiple cases but Jamie couldn't see any common thread and nothing she could tie to Jenna's death. Then towards the end of the pack she found a sheaf of articles about grave robbery, how there was evidence of recent practice with bodies stolen from funeral homes before cremation as well as dug up from graves. Jamie pulled the piece out to read in more detail, fascinated to learn that body snatching wasn't only relegated to the past.

One article attributed the rise in grave robbery to the demand for metals that could be extracted from the bodies and sold. In an increasingly tough financial environment, people were finding easy pickings from robbing the dead. Another headline screamed cult hysteria as bones were removed for rituals and rites in communities honoring such practices. There were marks on two more articles about newly buried bodies stolen the night before their burial. Both individuals had suffered from genetic diseases that resulted in physical deformity. A yellow letter L ending in a question mark was written in highlighter at the top of these pages.

Turning the papers further, Jamie came to an article on necrophilia, only made illegal in the UK in 2003 and still legal in some states of America. Her eyes widened as she read of the erotic use of corpses and found herself shaking her head with resignation at the depths of depravity to which humanity sometimes sank. She knew that Jenna was undertaking a specific study on the legal rights relating to corpses and body parts. Were these practices also related to the mysterious Lyceum?

She took some pictures of the articles and continued searching the desk, but there was nothing personal and no more evidence of Jenna's investigation. She'd have to wait for the results of the tech team. Jamie rang through to Bowen and told him to expect them later that day. He thanked her, his voice courteous but she sensed that he had already moved on from the tragedy of Jenna's death, his mind elsewhere.

Leaving the building, Jamie stood by the park looking across Lincoln's Inn Fields back towards the Hunterian Museum, hunching her back against the freezing wind.

Her mind was trying to capture the tendrils of suspicion that encircled this case, but in these pockets of calm, she could only think about Polly and what time she might make it back to see her. She lit a cigarette and inhaled the first, perfect drag.

"You really should give it up, Jamie."

Jamie turned to see Max Nester, one of the few men from work who could wring a smile from her serious demeanor. He ignored the fact that she was a woman and treated her like a blokey mate, albeit a prickly one, and she appreciated that. Max worked on the art theft and cultural crime that happened in the capital, a huge workload, since stealing specific artworks for collectors was a regular occurrence.

"Hey Max, are you on something local?"

"I was nearby and heard you'd been assigned to this murder case." He paused. "How's Polly?"

Jamie had told Max about Polly's illness a while back and he was one of the few who knew how sick she really was. She knew his concern was that of a real friend, but she needed to keep the separation between her worlds intact. Otherwise she would just break down and bawl her eyes out here on the street.

"Not good," she said, her voice constricted. "Best distract me, rather than talk about it."

"Sure thing. I did hear something about an ivory figurine being found and thought I'd drop by to see if I could help with identification."

Jamie smiled, taking another drag, the smoke curling up into the dying day. "I get it, you want in on the interesting artifact but not the dirty work of the murder."

Max nodded. "You know me so well, but I've heard it may have been stolen from an as yet unknown collection so I think there's some legitimate overlap."

"I'd appreciate any help on it, actually. I'm not sure how

it fits into the murder, but I want to understand whether Jenna was carrying it that night and why, or whether it was left at the scene by the murderer. It could be important, but I don't know how we're going to pursue that angle."

Max took the cigarette from her hand and took a drag himself, an intimate gesture that Jamie wouldn't have allowed from anyone else. But Max was only interested in slim, younger men, so she knew his attentions were only ever out of friendship. He passed it back again in smoker's camaraderie, his face twisting into a grimace at the minty aftertaste.

"Can't you smoke something decent?" He pulled a slip of paper from his pocket. "If you've got nothing else, this guy might be able to help. Blake Daniel, at the British Museum. Here's his number, but I know he's there today if you want to drop by. He's a specialist in religious relics and figurines so I think this would be right down his alley." He paused, then grinned. "Bit of a looker, too."

Jamie smiled and took the paper. "Thanks, that's a great help." She noticed Max bite his lip. "So what aren't you telling me?"

Max sighed. "To be honest, Jamie, you'll probably think this is crazy. But he has certain - abilities - that make him unusual."

Jamie raised her eyebrows. "Sounds even more interesting. Do tell."

"He reads objects," Max said, watching for her reaction. "Some call it psychometry, or psychic reading. Blake calls it his curse and he truly is a reluctant psychic, not someone who broadcasts his skills."

Jamie considered what Max had said and weighed it against her bullshit detector. She trusted Max, even though his techniques could sometimes be a little unorthodox, and although skeptical, she had seen enough of the supernatural to not reject what he was saying outright.

"So how do you know him?" Jamie finished the cigarette and put the butt in her tin, slipping it back into her bag.

"I met him during a case at St Paul's Cathedral over a missing relic," Max said, thrusting his hands in his pockets as he jogged up and down on the spot in the freezing wind. "Blake was called in as an expert witness, but he knew things that I knew he shouldn't. I took him for a drink afterwards and he became quite chatty after a few tequilas. Talking of drinks, you coming out tonight? Streeter's leaving."

Jamie turned to go and mounted her bike.

"You know I never drink with you guys, and besides Streeter's going off to do something in business right? Which means in about three months, he'll discover he's not happy. He'll miss the justice side, the making a difference …"

"The crappy pay, the long nights, the lack of weekends."

Jamie smiled. "But we love it, Max, you know we do." She pulled on her helmet. "I'll check out Blake Daniel. Thanks for the tip."

As she pulled away, she saw him raise a hand in a wave. For a moment, she regretted not going out for drinks over the years he had been asking, but at least he continued to try and persuade her. Everyone else had stopped and Missinghall hadn't even tried, knowing her reputation for staying aloof. But her nights belonged to Polly, and sometimes to tango. There was no room for anything else.

CHAPTER 7

BLAKE DANIEL BOUGHT A venti double shot latte with vanilla syrup and added more sugar before sipping the hot liquid and crossing the road back into the grounds of the British Museum. It had already been a difficult day, and he was severely behind on his workload. A pulsing hangover had kept him on the edge of nausea most of the afternoon, finally easing to a dull ache. The sugar was helping though, and when his stomach calmed, he would go to the greasy spoon down the road for a late bacon sandwich.

He rubbed his gloved hand over the rough stubble on his jaw and chin. It was thicker than he usually let it grow, almost at the point of softness now. Perhaps it was time to let it grow into a proper beard. He knew it made him look more like a serious academic and less like the lead singer of a boy band. His hair needed a cut too. He kept it at a number one buzz-cut: any longer and it tended towards the tight curls of the Nigerian heritage on his mother's side, incongruous with the piercing blue eyes that he had inherited from his Swedish father.

Last night was a blank, yet again, but the girl he woke up with hadn't seemed to mind much when he had politely asked her to leave. No regrets, he thought, holding onto a mantra that sounded more hollow each week. The London casual scene would continue to provide escape for as long as he needed it. He took a sip of the coffee and acknowledged that he did still need it. His nights were another life, far removed from his days shut in the bowels of the Museum, examining ancient objects and creating a past for them from painstaking research, augmented with his own special brand of insight. Right now, he was working on a series of ivory netsuke, miniature carved works of art that used to hang from the kimono sashes of traditional Japanese men. He found himself lost in each one, marveling at their intricacies and the echoes of past lives behind them. For Blake read the emotion in objects, and these were steeped in layers of its rich tapestry.

Blake walked through the museum, past the crowds of tourists. Although generally immune to the classical facade of the grand entrance, the glass-ceilinged Great Hall always lifted his spirits, although today even the weak sun hurt his fragile eyes. Finally sitting back down at his desk, Blake pushed some papers around while he drank his coffee, waiting for the kick of sugar and caffeine to give him enough of a boost to at least write a paragraph on the netsuke. The grant he was working under would only last a few more months, so he needed to produce something of worth to get it renewed.

He felt the sensation of being watched and looked up to see his boss Margaret leading someone towards his desk. Oh hell, Blake thought, what can she possibly want right now? Then he caught a glimpse of the woman behind. Her hair was jet-black, tied in a tight bun and she wore an unremarkable black trouser suit. But her face was alive with expression, her hazel eyes piercing with intelligence and she walked with an assurance he rarely saw in this academic environment. She was petite, her slim figure tightly compact, but Blake could see an inner strength and knew that this woman should not be underestimated.

"Blake, sorry to disturb you." Margaret ruffled with importance. "This is Detective Sergeant Jamie Brooke from the Metropolitan Police."

"Detective, good to meet you." Blake held out his gloved hand.

Jamie held his eyes, assessing him and Blake felt an inexplicable wave of guilt, perhaps something everyone feels in the presence of the police. What did I do last night, he thought.

She shook his hand, glancing down at the gloves. "Perhaps we could go somewhere to talk confidentially?"

Margaret looked at Blake with suspicion but accompanied them through to one of the private meeting rooms, shutting the door behind her as she left.

"Call me Blake, please," he said, sitting down at the wide desk, aware of the gossip that would now be exploding back in the main office about his possible misdemeanors.

"Of course." Jamie sat down opposite him. Blake was reminded of all those TV shows people watched, and wondered what was coming next. "I've been told you may be able to help with a special investigation."

Blake raised an eyebrow. "It depends what it is, of course, and who told you."

"Max Nester recommended you." That old queen, Blake thought as Jamie pulled a package, wrapped in cloth and plastic from her messenger bag. "This is evidence, but it's been processed and we can't pull anything from it. We're trying to determine how it relates to a particular crime scene."

"And how do you think I can help?" Blake asked.

"Your specialization here at the museum is ivory carving?"

Blake nodded. "I've been working on a series of netsuke, Japanese miniature sculptures used as fasteners for pouches and external pockets for carrying personal items. The man bag of seventeenth century Japan."

His witticism didn't raise even a hint of a smile from Jamie.

"Max told me that you've helped the police with investigations before and he mentioned your - special talents - I wondered if you might consider examining this piece."

Blake cursed Max and his own big mouth. Six months ago, he'd helped with a minor investigation into stolen property and then he'd gotten drunk. Tequila was an evil mistress, and he couldn't seem to escape her addiction. Blake wanted to deny everything, wanted to shy away from helping, but something in Jamie's eyes made him nod. "I can give it a go at least, but I can't promise anything."

Jamie was suddenly hesitant. "So how does this work?"

"If you could just unwrap the object and lay it on the table. Then I'll see what I can feel."

Blake wondered if he would be able to feel anything through the last vestiges of the hangover. Part of the reason that he drank was to deaden the visions, but as Jamie unwrapped a tiny figurine, only four inches tall, he became intrigued. It was a naked woman carved of ivory, but instead of the smooth skin of her beautiful body, the flesh was open to reveal the internal organs. The woman's eyes were open, her face impassive despite the mutilation of her body. Blake had studied Anatomical Venus figures before but this was a gorgeous specimen.

"Do I need to tell you anything about the situation?" Jamie said.

Blake shook his head. "Best not to. Just put it on the table."

Jamie placed the figurine down on the white tabletop as Blake pulled the glove from his right hand, revealing crisscrossed white scars on his cinnamon skin. He felt her eyes examining them, her questions unspoken. The thin canvas gloves he habitually wore prevented the casual visions that could intrude, but now he laid his bare fingertips upon the figurine.

Sometimes the visions were hazy and he expected to ease slowly into this one but immediately he saw the body of a young woman. Her lower abdomen was cut open, her organs on display like the figurine and her body was pooled in scarlet. He snatched his hand away and the vision faded as he stood, slamming the chair back and stepping away fast. He had been unprepared for such violence, expecting something like the art theft he'd worked on with the police before. He felt a wave of nausea return and cursed his hangover.

"This is from a murder victim," he said, his voice shaky. "Her body was cut open like this one."

He saw the surprise in Jamie's eyes, and understood that she had doubted his abilities. The look she gave him was one of respect tinged perhaps with a little fear, and her reaction was exactly why he didn't broadcast his peculiar sensitivities. In fact, he did everything he could to hide them.

She nodded slowly, the barest acknowledgment that he had seen the truth.

"Can you read anything else?"

Blake felt truly sick now but he braced for a longer look. His ability to see was always tied to an object, and it was more a collection of sensations than a strictly physical viewing. It wasn't as if he could psychically spin round in a room and see everything in detail, but he could pick up feelings and particularly heightened emotions that seemed to imprint a person's experience onto the object. He felt a little uncomfortable reading in front of Jamie, but he sat down and laid his hand on the object again, breathing deeply as he closed his eyes. He felt the rush of the images and the sensations that accompanied them.

"There's anger and hatred surrounding the figure, from both the girl and another. This wasn't premeditated murder, but there was logic in the death, and emotional connection between the people involved." He paused. "The dissection was deliberate."

Blake relaxed into the vision now, feeling sensation pulse through him. The experience itself wasn't unpleasant, but it was his own reaction to it that he feared. Occasionally he could be overwhelmed, unable to keep the visions from smothering him. It was the reason why he drowned his curse in tequila most nights, losing himself in physical oblivion.

"The figurine is from a collection," he continued, deeply focused. "And the woman's body lies in some kind of museum. Her imprint feels out of place as if she was interrupted in some kind of quest. She carried the figurine with her. It was evidence of something." Blake opened his eyes and shook his head to clear it. "I'm sorry, this doesn't seem like very useful information."

Jamie tilted her head to one side. "What's it like?" she asked, curiosity clearly overtaking her professionalism. "How does it feel?"

Blake slipped his glove back on, covering his scars. He was wary about explaining but somehow wanted her to understand. He could sense a deep pain in her and recognized a spirit on the edge of breaking.

"It's a sensation of another place, and sometimes another time. I have an impression of what has happened to the object and the emotions surrounding it. Of course, objects don't have feelings, they can't see, so it's only a projection based on the people who owned them or interacted with them. If they lie in one place for a long time, I get a much clearer idea of where they have been physically. For this figurine, I sense it is missing from a larger collection of macabre items, but then these miniatures were for teaching anatomy, so that makes sense." He paused, his eyes meeting Jamie's. "There's something else."

She nodded for him to continue.

"The girl," he said. "She was pregnant, wasn't she?"

Jamie nodded slowly, then stood and paced the tiny room. Blake felt his headache returning as the hangover beat his body with a vengeance. In contrast, Jamie was a bundle of energy and he could feel her vibrations across the space. He closed his eyes, trying to block it all out and return to his own equilibrium. The problem with reading was that it opened him up, and suddenly there was an overwhelming sensation of too much, color, sound, energy. The world was abuzz, and tuning it out was a huge effort once he had become sensitized. But he wanted to know more about Detective Jamie Brooke and, for some strange reason, he wanted her to trust him.

"I don't think you're entirely confident in my abilities, Detective."

He challenged her with a direct stare and she met his eyes, without flinching. Putting her hands to the back of her head, she pulled a comb from her bun. It was a simple thing, decorated with shells and looked hand made. Jamie laid it carefully on the table.

"What does this say about me?" she asked.

Blake pulled off his glove again and closed his eyes, letting his hand rest gently on the comb. He saw dancers in a tango club, the atmosphere heavy with smoke and the extreme eroticism of close embrace. He felt a maelstrom of emotion, grief and a silent strength honed over years that had now become a cage. He glimpsed Jamie, transformed, her long hair down in waves, wearing a tight silver dress that accentuated her curves and dramatic makeup. She was stunning and as she moved, he felt her sexuality, languid but restrained, held in check by fear and grief. He felt her love for a daughter that consumed her to the extent of everything else in her life. Blake was breathless at the vision, so different from the woman in front of him.

"You're a dancer," he said, opening his eyes. "Tango. You wear your hair down with your fringe held back by this comb. Silver dress. Smoky makeup. It's a good look on you, Detective."

Jamie visibly blanched and then her face flushed. He realized that this was a part of her life that she kept hidden and he had breached a forbidden barrier. Clearly she hadn't believed that he could truly read or she wouldn't have given him something so intimate.

"Is that all?" she asked, her voice almost breaking.

"It was made by your daughter," Blake watched Jamie's eyes as the shadows descended. "She's very sick."

Jamie whirled around, yanked open the door and strode out, slamming it behind her as she left. Blake looked at the figurine on the table, wondering if she would return. He sat silently and waited.

CHAPTER 8

TEN MINUTES PASSED. BLAKE was about to get up and leave, but then the door opened again and Jamie came back in, looking a little sheepish.

"Sorry I ran," she said, shaking her head. "I guess I found your ability a little disturbing. I don't let people see that side of my life and now that I know your gift is genuine, it's slightly odd to say the least."

Blake smiled. "I understand," he said. "Truly, I have no interest in prying."

"Would you consider helping me?" Jamie asked, her voice tentative. "I'm assigned to a special task force on this case. It's high profile because the victim is the daughter of a prominent aristocratic and business family. We've kept it quiet so far, but when the story breaks, we need to have answers. I think your sensitivity could help to point us in new directions. What do you think?"

Blake looked at Jamie, visions of her dancing still running through his mind. It wouldn't be so hard to spend time with her, and perhaps this would be some kind of redemption for the dark side of his gift. If he could use his unusual talents to help solve a crime, maybe it would go some way to righting the wrongs of his past.

"Anything you need, Detective," Blake said, and he saw

hope flicker in her eyes. "I'm happy to help if I can."

"I don't have anywhere else to go with this right now, so whatever you can glean from the figurine is going to help."

Blake looked at his watch. "Reading at the site of the murder would be the most powerful. We could do it now if you like."

Jamie shook her head.

"I'll need to get clearance for that tomorrow, since it's cordoned off as a crime scene. Is there anything else you could do right now? Any leads could help at this stage."

Blake felt the figurine taunting him with its macabre history, and wanted to try and explain the process of reading.

"There are layers to any object," he said. "Especially one as old as this. Ivory is similar to bone and a strong emotional medium. When I read, I see the most resonant places first but there may be something more in times before the actual crime scene that would help provide background information."

Jamie sat back down at the desk opposite him. "Please, try what you can."

"The problem with deeper reading is that I can go under for too long and it can become overwhelming. If you see me looking faint, would you just remove my hand from the figurine?"

Jamie looked concerned but Blake was determined to get something useful for her. He looked at the figurine again, holding his hand over it, feeling an almost physical resonance.

"It's macabre, isn't it?" he said. "I can see why they wanted such things as teaching devices, but I can't understand why someone would want to have a partially dissected body as an ornament. Let's see where it's been."

**

Jamie watched Blake's blue eyes change intensity, a summer sky suddenly filled with storm clouds, as he laid his hands gently on the figurine. It was as if he was no longer present, just a shell, although he still breathed. A sigh caught in Jamie's throat, for this was the emptiness she felt in Polly's body when the drugs kicked in and her consciousness slipped away. Something was gone, the vital part of the self. But if Blake's body was still anchored here, where was his spirit?

***

Blake parted the veils of swirling shadow in his mind and sensed his surroundings. He was in a large sterile operating room, cold and drafty with high windows to provide light and air, but he was aware that no one could see inside. The walls and floor were white, and precision surgical instruments were laid out on gun-metal grey trays, with scalpels reflecting light from the windows, sharp blades waiting to cut into soft flesh. The figurine was laid across the page of a medical textbook, used as a weight to keep the pages open. The book showed the uterus of a pregnant woman, similar to the dissected innards of the figurine itself and the text was in German.

Blake's attention shifted around the room. He could hear the sound of the wind whistling through the cracks in the windows, and outside there was staccato shouting and occasional gunshots. Overlaying this was a low moaning and he slowly became aware of figures in the room before him. A woman was strapped to a gurney, her mouth gagged to stifle the noises of pain. A man stood over her in a white coat, a doctor perhaps, but Blake could feel waves of agony coming from the woman, almost a physical assault to his heightened senses. The man was operating on her with no anesthetic and it looked as if he was opening her uterus, examining its function and comparing it to the textbook.

The man made another cut with the scalpel and looked into the deep wound, packing it with surgical sponges to contain the bleeding. Putting down the knife, he reached in with gloved hands and pulled out the woman's uterus. She arched against the straps holding her down, howled into her gag and then her head lolled back, unconscious with pain. The man cut away the organ and carried it to another bench. Ignoring the woman, he started to dissect it, pulling open the membrane to examine what was inside. Blake felt the world wrench as he witnessed the tiny fetus within, a life snuffed out before it had even begun. The man began to probe at the tiny figure with his scalpel, cutting matchstick limbs and opening the chest in a miniature autopsy. As he worked, the man wrote into an oversized journal that was next to the bench. It spotted with red as blood dripped from his fingers, but he continued scratching the lines, inscribing his findings in neat handwriting. Finally he seemed satisfied, the last full stop an emphatic black mark.

The man barked an order and two women came in, faces pinched and starved, eyes blank and unseeing. They wheeled the gurney with the mutilated woman out of the room and the door swung back behind them. Blake wanted to disconnect but he felt that the emotion imbued in the figurine from this time wasn't finished yet. He needed to know, so he waited. The doctor moved the figurine from the book, turning the pages to a drawing of twins, conjoined back to back. The doctor looked closely at the figures, tracing them with his fingertip as he examined exactly where the organs were attached, as if pondering how two bodies could be bonded this way. He hummed something, a jaunty tune that made Blake's breath catch.

The doctor turned and called to the next room. The

door opened again and the women wheeled in two gurneys, each carrying a young boy, strapped down firmly. The boys were awake and alert, eyes darting around the room in fear, both gagged. The man motioned for the women to turn the boys over onto their fronts and cut away the clothes from their backs. They did so with an attitude of detachment, as if by swift obedience they could avoid being next on the experiment bench.

The man then stood between the boys and began slicing into the back of one of them. The boy's screams were high pitched and audible through the gag but the man kept cutting as he began to hum the tune again. The other child turned a deathly pale and froze, his stillness a primeval survival mechanism. Blake wanted to bear witness to the horror even as he knew he couldn't stop it, for these crimes were committed many years ago and it was too late to help the children. He started pulling away from the scene as the man reached into the first boy's open wound, his hands covered in gore.

***

Jamie watched as Blake's physical presence became stronger in the room. His skin tone paled, beads of sweat appeared on his brow and he took deep breaths to control his nausea. His eyes were wide as he struggled to return to full consciousness. Jamie reached out across the table and touched his scarred hand with gentle fingers. His hand grasped at hers and held it like a lifeline as his breathing finally slowed. After a moment, he let go and Jamie felt a moment of loss, as if the room had dimmed. Blake took a sip of water.

"I think the figurine belonged to Mengele," he said, meeting Jamie's eyes, an intensity of horror in his hoarse voice. "The Angel of Death."

Jamie frowned. "The Nazi doctor? You saw him?"

Blake nodded. "I saw what he did to a woman and then to a set of twins. It was horrific. He treated them as if they were lab-rats, to be mutilated and killed as he desired. There was something about to happen, something grotesque …"

Blake sat back in the chair and pulled his smart-phone out of his pocket. He Googled Josef Mengele and read from what he found.

"Here. Josef Mengele. German SS Officer and physician. Doctorates in anthropology from Munich and medicine from Frankfurt. In 1937, he was an assistant to a leading genetic researcher at the Institute for Hereditary Biology and Racial Hygiene. He had a particular interest in twins and it became his fixation at Auschwitz. He selected his subjects from the trains as they arrived, picking twins in particular but also collecting genetic anomalies like dwarves." Blake continued to scroll through the pages, jumping over sections, skipping through the horror until he found it. "My God, that's what I saw him begin." Blake paled, feeling his heart thumping with adrenalin as if he were still watching the crimes of over half a century ago.

Jamie took the phone from him and read from the screen. It detailed how Mengele had experimented on a pair of Roma twins, conjoining them back to back by joining their organs together. It was a particularly sick kind of evil.

"The bastard survived the war," she said, shaking her head. "He escaped to South America with the Odessa organization. He only died in 1979, despite being hunted for his war crimes. That's unbelievable. You'd think Mossad would have found him, like they got Hess."

Blake tried to sift through the visions for how this could help Jamie now.

"The figurine was with a medical textbook," he said,

"and Mengele had a notebook. Perhaps they were all kept together as collector's items?"

Jamie frowned. "The Americans and Brits spirited a lot of German scientists away after the War as well as keeping paperwork on the experiments they did. So much of what was done then has benefitted companies that still exist today, built on a bloody past." She thought for a moment. "There must be records about what happened to all the Nazi material, but it's going to take too long to track it down in time to help with the investigation. We've got to take a stab at what's most likely. The figurine was found with the body of an heiress - to a drug company - so perhaps there's some relationship to Neville Pharmaceuticals."

Blake nodded. "But was the figurine with the body some kind of threat to expose the company's connection with the Nazis? Or just a way of saying that the murder was punishment, or recompense, for the past?"

Jamie paced up and down the tiny room, then pulled out her phone and called Alan Missinghall.

"Al, can you run a check on whether any of the Gala dinner attendees were Jewish, or had any kind of Nazi links?" She paused. "Yes, I'll tell you more later, but that might help us." She hung up and turned back to Blake. "We know that Jenna Neville was working on exposing the company, campaigning for the rights of the tissue samples and bodies used in experiments. It could equally have been someone protecting the company from that exposure."

Blake sat quietly, rubbing his temples. "I want to take another look, but I can't do it today. The visions bring on migraines and I've already got a killer headache." He didn't mention the hangover. "But tomorrow, could we do it at the crime scene? That might bring more resonant memories."

Jamie nodded. "Sure. Meet me at the Hunterian Museum at 11.30 and I'll clear it. Are you sure you're OK?"

"All in a day's work." He smiled, but he could see in her eyes that she knew what the reading cost him.

Jamie picked up the figurine, carefully wrapping it in the cloth and placing it back in her bag. Blake watched her deft hands, bare of jewelry, as she put the comb back in her bun. For a moment, he had an overwhelming desire to unpin her hair and watch her dance. He pushed the sensation away as she thanked him and left.

Blake began to count the minutes until he could have his first drink of the night to drown the visions that morphed in front of his eyes. He needed to obliterate the image of Detective Jamie Brooke dancing with the Angel of Death as blood seeped from the wounds that the Doctor had inflicted on her body.

CHAPTER 9

JAMIE PULLED UP TO the hospice and sat for a moment on the cooling bike. She was late for her evening visit and she normally liked to be there for dinner time, but Blake had kept her longer than expected. His visions still disturbed her, the horror of Mengele but also his accurate perception of her dancing. She had doubted him and in doing so she had left herself open. She mentally kicked herself for being so careless with her privacy, for she had seen in his eyes a flash of pity that she resented. Despite that, she felt drawn to him, this haunted man who seemed so much older than he looked. Blake's blue eyes had the layered depth of a forest pool in an ancient wood that hid long-forgotten secrets, where the sun could not penetrate the thick canopy of twisted branches. She thought of the old scars on his hands, revealed when he removed the gloves, evidence of some kind of torture years ago. Yet he had the nonchalance of the truly beautiful, his face handsome and a body that he took for granted yet still turned heads in the street.

Getting off the bike, Jamie pushed all thoughts of Blake and the case aside and focused on her time with Polly. Being fully present was something that she tried to practice on a daily basis and it helped her separate the two halves of her life. She pushed open the gate. 98, she counted and sent up her prayer for another day. A flicker of concern nagged at the edge of her mind. Was she becoming obsessive-compulsive about her behavior? Did she really believe that her tiny actions could keep Polly away from the beckoning arms of death for much longer?

She walked through the hospice, greeting the Duty Nurse, who she recognized but didn't normally chat with. She was grateful that Rachel wasn't on duty tonight, because she didn't want to have any kind of serious conversation right now. Jamie knew she couldn't face that reality just yet and Rachel forced her towards a place she didn't want to go.

Pushing open the door to Polly's room, she found her daughter lying with eyes closed, her face relaxed in sleep or perhaps sedation. After the attack this morning, Jamie knew that the nurses would try to alleviate her suffering as much as possible and keep her comfortable. She bent to kiss Polly's hair gently and sat down next to the bed, watching her daughter's chest rise and fall under the covers. Jamie felt a rush of gratitude that she was still alive, that they had another moment together. She felt tears prick her eyes and she grasped Polly's hand softly, leaning forward to put her head on the bed covers as she concentrated on sending waves of strength to her daughter. In her practical world, in the daylight, Detective Jamie Brooke would have little patience for woo-woo energy work, but in the privacy of the night, she was just a mother doing anything she could for the girl she cherished.

After a moment, she felt a flutter in Polly's fingertips and a gentle pressure. Jamie sat up and Polly's eyes were open. The brown that had been so vibrant this morning was now dark and forbidding, a depth of mahogany that Jamie knew she couldn't penetrate.

"Hey Pol," she said softly. "How you feeling?" Polly

blinked slowly and then mouthed, 'Bad'. Jamie noticed a tension around her mouth and her forehead was creased.

"Do you want me to up the pain relief?" she asked, reaching for the pump.

Polly barely shook her head, but it was still a negative and Jamie was grateful. The drugs brought unconsciousness and selfishly, she wanted this moment of lucidity together.

'You?' Polly mouthed.

Jamie tried to smile. "Oh you know, just another day in the big smoke. Chasing bad guys. Bringing justice to the city." She paused. "Actually Pol, you'd have found it interesting, lots of medical research and strange, exotic specimens. I know you love all those gory details." Her voice trailed off as Polly's eyes drifted closed. "Do you need to sleep, my darling?" she whispered. "It's OK, you know I love you. Sleep now."

Polly opened her eyes again, and Jamie was transfixed by the naked truth in their depths. Her daughter was pulling away and Jamie felt a stab of panic in her chest at the realization that time was running out. 'Dance for me tonight, Mum,' Polly mouthed. 'Tell me tomorrow.' Jamie took a deep breath and nodded. The last thing she wanted tonight was to dance but if she couldn't talk with Polly, then perhaps it would be the escape she needed.

***

Jamie stepped into the Zero Hour milonga, one of the best on the London tango scene. Her silver dress was faded in the daylight but in this darkened space it sparkled, a contrast to the long, black hair lying loose about her shoulders. She sat down briefly and changed into her four inch heels, completing the shift from day to night. Jamie transformed for tango, even using a different name if people asked, calling herself Christina. This was a part of herself that she wanted to keep separate, for the milonga was a shifting web of complication, not fitting her police persona. In her job, she was focused and driven but when she stepped onto the dance floor, Jamie embodied the spirit of Argentine tango. Some called it the vertical expression of a horizontal desire, vicarious pleasure, an obsession that allowed the dancer to leave behind the day's trouble and dwell in the moment.

Close embrace did not presume any further intimacy and Jamie preferred it that way. She could be held, swept through the music and then be released back into the world. It was physical experience without real engagement, and there was an etiquette to tango that centered around respect. It allowed Jamie to feel safe dancing with a string of men each time. Respect for the partner, for the dance and the culture permeated the room, albeit with an undercurrent of sexual tension that only served to heighten the pleasures of restraint.

The music began to wash the stress of the day away and, as Jamie watched the couples, she caught a glimpse of Sebastian through the crowd, handsome with his olive skin and dark eyes. He favored close embrace, his body square to his dancing partner as he swept her around the room. Jamie watched his sure steps, knowing that the dominance of the male partner was part of why she could lose herself in tango. Her roles as parent and police officer meant she had to assume authority, make decisions that affected lives and take responsibility. The beauty of tango was that she could give that up, relinquish control and just follow.

Jamie waited out the tanda, a set of songs, declining several partners because she wanted Sebastian tonight. It was selfish to wait for the best dancer in the room, but her body thrilled to be next to his and she craved his peppery scent. It was a chemical attraction but they had never even had a proper conversation or met outside the milonga. The asking, and then a thank you at the end of the dance was their only exchange of words, and that was all Jamie wanted. She felt that she would break right now if anyone asked any more of her than to move with the music and she needed to sublimate her pain.

There was an emotional darkness to tango, a broken spirit inside each of the dancers. She could see it in the older couples clutching onto one other, loss bleeding from their every step. Jamie looked away, not wanting to recognize her own future in their gait. Younger dancers had different problems, but the heaviness of the world seemed to anchor their feet, giving them gravitas, a center around which to spin. The words of the Argentinian poet Borges echoed in her mind, that tango converted outrage into music. She was outraged at how her daughter was being taken from her, angry at yet another murder and crazy mad at her own impotence to stop injustice. In tango, she could rise above those turbulent emotions and just feel. But to be swept away, she needed to dance with the best.

She kept her eyes on Sebastian and as he said his thanks to his last partner, Jamie stood and walked to the side of the dance floor near him. It was brazen to look at him in this way but she felt on the edge of mania and needed the steel cage of his embrace to root her to the earth again. He caught her eye, his look a question she had already answered. He walked to her, ignoring the others who wanted him, and in the cortina, the break between the tandas, he held out his arms.

As he drew her close, Jamie felt suddenly able to exhale, as if his physical strength gave her the support she so desperately needed. The music began and they moved, bodies becoming one, pressed close against each other as she followed his lead. As they swirled, Jamie let anger and grief move through her body, willing it through her feet and into the floor, letting it charge the air between them. She breathed in the space between steps as Sebastian spun her and then held her close, swaying as intensity deepened, the music a lament for dying dreams.

CHAPTER 10

THE INCIDENT ROOM AT New Scotland Yard was still in darkness when Jamie arrived the next day. Logging on, her fingers bashed at the keyboard, hammering out her frustration by typing up the notes from the case so far. Polly had barely opened her eyes this morning when she visited the Hospice in the dark early hours. Jamie had climbed onto the bed next to her and held her daughter, listening to her heartbeat, but there hadn't even been a spark of alertness. Polly had seemed blank and unsure, even of where she was.

Jamie had whispered to her of the tango night anyway, her voice spinning expansive tales of a world her daughter would never know. She had avoided speaking to Rachel again, unable to bear the quiet question in her eyes, coupled with an acceptance of inevitability that made Jamie crazy. The injustice of it and the anticipation of grief made her mad, and even tango last night had barely taken the edge off her anxiety. Escape into the complexities of solving this crime was her best way of distraction.

Spinning on her chair, Jamie paced the length of the large open plan office, the movement allowing her space to breathe. Finally, she stood with her forehead pressed against the reinforced glass, looking out over London.

Lights from the early morning traffic flowed around the city and she could see the spires of Westminster Abbey only a few blocks away. For a moment, Jamie felt the scale of her insignificance in the world, a moment of clarity. If she disappeared, all of this would continue without her. London had thrived for over two thousand years, a hub of commerce and culture, its people surviving plagues, fire and flood. Jamie felt a pulse of passion, for she believed that it would continue to be the greatest city on Earth for many more years, whether or not she was here to see it. She acknowledged her inability to change what must inevitably come, but right now she could make a difference for the dead, and Jenna's case was still unsolved.

Walking back to her computer, Jamie began searching on one of the protected databases for any less public background on Neville Pharmaceuticals. Blake's visions couldn't be used as any kind of evidence, but if she could find something specific about the company it might give her leverage in questioning the Nevilles further. Today she was determined to speak to Esther about her relationship with Jenna and exactly why her daughter had protested against the lab.

The case room gradually filled up, the usual morning small talk ignored around her. Jamie knew that her solitary ways meant that she was considered cold and unapproachable but she still preferred it that way, avoiding difficult questions about her personal life.

"Morning." Missinghall placed his large coffee down on the desk in front of Jamie's, demanding her attention. "Anything I should know about?" He indicated her computer.

Jamie rubbed her eyes, lack of sleep beginning to catch up with her.

"Time of death has come back as between 10-11pm which puts most of the gala attendees in the building. But

I'm just not happy with Day-Conti as a decent suspect, so I'm following up on the figurine and trying to find any leads as to why it was at the scene."

Missinghall raised an eyebrow as he took a sip of his coffee. "It's early days, though. We've still got to interview some of the others who were there that night and I need to plow through all the information from the taxi companies. That should help us alibi some of them out." He looked at her more closely. "You look awful. Is there something else going on?"

Jamie thought of Polly lying in the dark of the hospice and she hesitated for a moment, part of her wanting to share what was really on her mind. She knew that Missinghall was genuine in his concern.

She shook her head. "No, I'm fine. Just a late one last night. Who else have we got to interview? I'm keen to get on it this morning."

"This guy stood out from the pack." Missinghall passed a file over the desk. "Edward Mascuria. He was on the same table as the Nevilles and he works part time at the company while he completes his PhD. Get this, it's in teratology, the study of developmental abnormalities."

Like Mengele, Jamie thought, remembering what Blake had said about the Nazi doctor's obsessions.

"I'm not sure that I can cope with more medical specimens today … but I need the distraction, so I'll go talk to him."

She picked up the file and grabbed her coat from the back of the chair.

"Do you want me to come with?" Missinghall said, taking another bite of his morning muffin.

Jamie shook her head. "You couldn't keep up," she said, smiling and walking away.

***

It was raining hard outside, but Jamie relished the wet cold as she rode through rush hour, weaving between dead-locked cars and honking taxis. The weather enlivened her senses, reminding her that she still breathed despite the anxiety that pursued her. She relished the freedom of the bike and pulled up to the address in Clerkenwell in good time, hopefully before Edward Mascuria had left for the day.

Jamie rapped on the door and rang the bell. After a minute, the door opened a crack with the security chain on and a partially obscured face peeped out.

"Edward Mascuria?" Jamie asked.

"Yes," the man said, suspicion in his tone.

Jamie held her warrant card out for him to see. "I'm here to talk about Jenna Neville. Can I come in?"

The door closed again, then opened fully.

"Of course. Come in, Detective. Anything I can do to help the investigation. I work with the Nevilles, so of course I'm devastated."

Jamie noticed that his emphatic words didn't match the coolness of his dark grey eyes, which were more like a sharks, the irises bleeding into the pupils to give him a strangely unfocused look. His eyes were too close together and his face wasn't quite symmetrical. His skin was pale, even for an Englishman in winter, and Jamie felt her skin prickle, her senses alert with suspicion just to be in his presence. She found that this happened sometimes. A person of interest could become a suspect worth investigating when the physical meeting generated a gut feeling that everyone in the police understood. There was definitely something about this man that made Jamie uneasy.

She stepped into the hallway, decorated with light green William Morris print wallpaper. There was a scent of fresh pine in the air and a cashmere coat hung by the door. It seemed luxurious for someone who was apparently a student and worked part time.

"Please, come through." Mascuria turned and as he walked down the hallway, Jamie noticed he limped and his shoulders slumped to one side. His spine looked as if it was beginning to twist and hunch, but his shoulders were powerfully muscled and his arms pumped. He certainly wasn't weak, despite his physical disability, and he further compensated with his clothes. He wore a purple striped Marc Jacobs shirt over what looked like Armani jeans. Jamie didn't know much about fashion, but even she knew this was not a cheap outfit.

She followed him further into the flat, emerging from the corridor into a large living space with an indoor garden, enclosed in glass, with a light well open to the roof. It was sparsely furnished but as she glanced around, Jamie could see that this was more from choice than budget. In one corner was an ergonomically shaped desk with an oversized Mac. There was a huge flat-screen TV on one wall and opposite it, a large painting of a minotaur. The beast-man stood looking out to sea, his muscled back and heavy bull's head seen from behind, taut with longing for escape from his island prison. One strong hand pinned a white bird to the parapet, crushing the life out of this last symbol of hope. Mascuria noticed her gaze.

"Do you know GF Watts?" he asked. Jamie shook her head and Mascuria walked towards the kitchen. "To empathize with the monster in all of us is my life's work, Detective. Tea?"

"Yes, thanks. White no sugar," Jamie said, wondering where a graduate student like Mascuria would get money for a flat like this, or for a painting that looked original.

"You were seated on the same table as the Nevilles at the gala dinner?" Jamie asked, when Mascuria returned with her tea.

"Yes," Mascuria indicated a chair and, as Jamie sat down, he began to speak from the dominant position. She rose to her feet again, not allowing him the benefit of the high ground. She knew that the body language of power could make a difference to the perception of the suspect and Mascuria clearly knew it too. His eyes were sharp and deeply intelligent, used to manipulation. "I work for the Nevilles part time, helping with lab work, but I'm mainly working on my PhD. My studies are intimately connected with the Royal College of Surgeons."

"Your specialty?" Jamie asked.

"Teratology. From the Greek for monster, it's the study of abnormalities in physiological development, due to either genetics or environmental factors." He paused. "It's of personal importance to me as I have a spinal deformity."

Jamie heard a restrained aggression behind his words, daring her to look away, the natural human response to deformity and physical imperfection. But he didn't know about her daughter and Jamie just nodded, holding his eyes.

"Did you attend the dinner with anyone?"

Jamie noticed a micro hesitation, before Mascuria answered.

"I took Mimi, sorry, Miriam Stevens. She's just a first year student, and she couldn't afford the ticket. We're not seeing each other though. I'm not … her type."

Jamie considered his words, wondering at what was left unspoken.

"Can you describe what happened that night?"

Mascuria steepled his hands, as if about to begin a sermon.

"The dinner started late at 7.25 and the speakers went on too long, as usual. People wolfed down their starter, the main course was slower and then the mingling began. The dessert course was served on platters around the room to enable people to dance. Jenna was one of the first on the dance floor when the band started at around nine. Esther said she had a migraine and left the event soon after that, I think." Jamie noticed the familiarity with which he spoke of the Nevilles. "Mimi wasn't feeling so well, I think she'd drunk quite a lot by that stage, so we sat at the table for a while. Christopher - Lord Neville - was engaged in conversation with the Dean about money. Not a surprise, the man is constantly hounded for funding."

Jamie caught a flicker of something in his eyes, but she wasn't sure what.

"And about what time did you leave?"

"We stepped out at around 10pm. I took Mimi for a walk around the square, I thought some fresh air might help her."

"And did it?" Jamie asked, well aware of what a walk around a square late at night after too much alcohol usually meant.

"Yes, we re-entered the party at around 11pm, and I saw Christopher there. But I didn't see Jenna again."

"That's a long walk," Jamie noted. "The square isn't that large."

Mascuria paused, his eyes unreadable. "We sat in the park for a while, talking. I gave her my jacket to wear as she was cold."

Jamie changed tack. "Do you know of anyone who would have wanted to hurt Jenna?"

Mascuria looked towards his glass-walled garden and his voice was wistful. "She was fiercely intelligent as well as determined. I believe she may have made enemies through the causes she was pursuing."

"Anything more specific?"

Mascuria turned. "To be honest, Detective, as part of her investigation she was going after the Royal College itself, focusing on the rights of the bodies that they have dissected over generations and trying to get recompense for the families, for victims of crimes against the body. She had probably made enemies of most of the people in that room, because she threatened their world."

Jamie sensed something more behind his words but she couldn't put her finger on what it was. She only knew that this man made her skin crawl, and looking at his thin white hands, she could only imagine what horrors he had dissected with them. Her years in the police had taught her that gut feel didn't necessarily mean the person was guilty of the crime being investigated, but it sure as hell meant something else was wrong.

CHAPTER 11

JAMIE HAD BARELY WALKED back in the office door
before Missinghall called her over.

"You've got to see this footage. It's from Carey Street, a
couple of streets back from the Royal College of Surgeons.
Not somewhere we checked on the initial sweep of the
cameras."

Jamie walked over to Missinghall's desk, pulling up a
chair so she could watch the screen with him. It showed a
dark road, cars parked close to the kerb and street lamps
casting shadows into the gloom. The impressive Gothic
architecture of the Law Courts towered above, creating an
interplay of chiaroscuro that drew the eye.

"Watch this," Missinghall said and clicked Play.

Out of the darkness at the far end of the picture walked
a man and a woman. The man was limping slightly, his
shoulders misshapen.

"That's Mascuria," said Jamie, recognizing his gait. "But
he said he was on the other side, walking in the park."

Missinghall nodded. "And the girl is Mimi Stevens. His
plus-one."

Mimi stumbled a little and Mascuria put his arm
around her waist, supporting her a little as he urged her
faster down the road. Her head slumped on his shoulder,

but she wasn't resisting. A door opened from a dark luxury car in the foreground of the shot.

"It's a Bentley Continental," Missinghall said quietly, as they watched Mascuria lead the girl to the car, pull the door further open and help her into the front passenger seat. After the door closed, he stood for a moment leaning against the outside of the car looking up and down the street. Missinghall zoomed the footage in. It looked as if Mascuria was attaching something to the car window before he stepped away. He slipped into the shadows of the law courts, melting into the darkness, but he could still be seen as a faint outline.

"He stands there for almost forty minutes," Missinghall said. "Let me fast forward."

The minutes sped past on the video until Mascuria moved again to return to the car as the door opened. He helped Mimi out, at the same time slipping whatever device he had planted into his pocket. The girl stumbled against him again, seemingly drowsy. Mascuria pulled her skirt down as he held her up.

"She doesn't remember anything at all?" Jamie asked.

He shook his head. "No, she says she has a blank for the evening after the starter course."

"Likely Rohypnol or some other date rape drug," Jamie said. "Get a couple of officers back to her place. There may still be physical evidence of assault … So who was in the car?"

Missinghall zoomed in the camera again.

"The number plate is obscured but the only Bentley Continental owned by anyone at the party belonged to Lord Christopher Neville."

Jamie slammed her hand down on the desk. "Bastard," she said. "But we don't have a visual on him. I'm going back to Mascuria's. I knew there was something up with him and I want to know what he put onto the outside of the car."

"There's something else," Missinghall said. "Look at the time." He pointed at the screen. "Mascuria alibis out during the time of Jenna's death. This video clearly identifies him in that window of opportunity and if that's Lord Neville inside, then that's his alibi too."

"But we can still get the two of them on assault if there's enough evidence. It might give us some leverage to find out what else happened that night." Jamie bent closer to the screen, examining the figure of Mascuria clutching the drooping girl. "Can you print some stills I can take back out? If he acts as some kind of pimp for Christopher Neville we need to know, and if they were out there, we don't have an alibi for Esther Neville. Can you follow up on the taxis in the meantime?"

***

Twenty minutes later, Jamie pulled up outside Mascuria's flat again, her anger at his abusive behavior barely controlled. He opened the door, a clear expression of antipathy on his face this time, every trace of his helpful attitude gone.

"Detective, back so soon. What else can you possibly want?"

Jamie pulled out the photos of him on the street, one with Mimi and one waiting outside the car. As he looked at them, Jamie was gratified to see his already pale face blanch, before his eyes narrowed. Jamie saw the warning there, but she was angry with his lies and didn't intend to back down. He stepped away to allow her into the flat and walked ahead of her into the living room.

"You said earlier that you walked around the park," Jamie tried to keep disgust from her voice. "But it seems you took Mimi to Lord Neville's car and stood waiting for forty minutes. What happened in the car?" Mascuria was silent for a moment. Jamie knew that he was calculating how he could explain this in a way that would keep him out of trouble. "Just so you know, we're interviewing Mimi Stevens again, and there may still be evidence of assault." Jamie watched his face flush, with anger, perhaps jealousy. Had he wanted to be in the car with her? She went on the offensive. "Can you confirm that it was Lord Christopher Neville in the car?"

Mascuria turned away. "You don't have anything on me, Detective. I was just walking Mimi to the vehicle for a consensual private meeting."

Jamie knew there was only a small window of opportunity to take this further and she had to offer him something. She softened her voice.

"It's an alibi for the murder, Edward. The time of death was during the interval of that video, so you now have an alibi for the murder of Jenna Neville. I want to know who was in the car so I can also rule them out for murder."

Mascuria spun round, eyes suddenly hopeful. He was a bastard, for sure, but he hadn't committed this murder, and clearly Christopher Neville would be grateful for an alibi.

"Yes, it was Christopher," he said, with defiance. "But Mimi wanted to be with him."

Jamie waved her hand, as if brushing away his words. "I don't want to hear about it. But I do want the video you took."

"There's no video," he said too quickly, but his face was clearly guilty as hell and his eyes flicked over to the Mac. Jamie walked to his desk and pulled out her cellphone.

"Have you heard of obstruction, Edward? Shall I take your computer down to the station and get it processed? What else will I find on it?"

Mascuria came very close, invading Jamie's personal

space and putting a possessive hand on top of the screen.

"You need a warrant for the computer, and you know it."

Jamie didn't back away, meeting his steely eyes with her own glare. She sensed that he felt her revulsion, but his physical deformity was nothing compared to his twisted morality.

"True," she said, weighing up her choices. She wanted that file. "But I can make a call and stand here and wait for it. I've got all day. Or you can just give me that one file right now, and I'll leave."

Mascuria stared at her, his shark's eyes calculating. Jamie felt a wave of violence emanate from him and she tensed her muscles, waiting for any indication that he would attempt to hurt her. She almost wanted him to try. After a few tense seconds, Mascuria breathed out slowly and she smelled decay on his breath.

"I'll give it to you," he said, stepping back. Jamie wondered what else he had on the laptop, because this clearly wasn't the only time he had done this, she was sure of it. Was he blackmailing Neville? Did that account for the wealth he displayed in his so-called student flat? Whatever else he had on that computer, she couldn't give him time to wipe this file.

She nodded and let him sit down at the desk. Mascuria turned the screen away from her and she stood with her back to the glass walled garden, watching him work. He plugged a USB stick into the side and quickly loaded it with a file. His eyes kept turning back to her, checking she was still far enough from him. After a minute, he pulled the USB stick out and thrust it at her.

"This had better be the right one," Jamie said.

"I think you'd better leave now, Detective. I don't have anything else for you."

Jamie saw the threat mounting in his eyes, but she held

them with her own until he looked away. She walked to the door, her back muscles tense, waiting for an attack that didn't come.

Outside, Jamie mounted her bike and then looked back as she felt she was being watched. Through the wooden blinds, she could just make out Mascuria's face at the window, his features twisted with hate.

***

Back at the station, Jamie handed the USB stick to Missinghall, who plugged it into the side of a separate desktop, disconnected from their main system in case of computer viruses.

"It's clean," he said, after a moment. "Now let's have a look at what happened in that car."

The video shot was clear but only had one angle. It started with Mimi entering the car and sitting in the front passenger seat, looking dazed and confused. In the background, Lord Christopher Neville sat with his suit jacket off, his top shirt button undone. There was no sound, but Mimi looked surprised as the seat she was on reclined. She fought to stay upright for a second but Neville leaned over and pushed her down with one firm hand on her breast.

She was mainly out of shot then but Jamie watched the movements of Neville's hands, clearly pulling up her short dress. He clambered onto her, fumbled with his hands and then began a thrusting motion, the camera shot obscured by how close he was to it.

"I think it's clear what he's doing," Jamie snapped. "This is evidence of rape, since her statement says that she remembers none of this. It's clearly not consensual."

They watched as Neville knelt up and the scene changed as he maneuvered Mimi's legs, moving a slim stiletto heeled foot across his body. He reached forward, his body jerking a little with exertion, although he seemed to be doing whatever it was with some care. Presumably he didn't want to leave marks on her skin. Jamie leaned closer to the screen to see what he was doing, and then realized with a jolt of anger.

"Bastard. He's turning her over." Jamie started to rap her fingers on the table, a staccato beat that sped up as Neville reached his climax, his face reddening as he panted on top of the prone girl. Jamie hated to watch the rape, but she felt that witnessing the crime was part of her responsibility. The anger she felt for Mimi's abuse heaped upon her pent up rage and she felt her blood pressure rising. As much as the police could hack away at the darkness, inching their way forward and bringing light to the city, behind them the shadows reformed and evil flourished in the cracks. "Can you get this to the officers working with Mimi, and I want a statement from Lord Neville."

"Sure thing," Missinghall said. "But this alibis Mascuria and Christopher Neville for Jenna's murder. Can we eliminate them from that investigation?"

Jamie shook her head. "Not yet. I'm sure there's more to this. Let me sort out the warrant for Mascuria's computer and then I've got to meet a source back at the Hunterian. If we can get the paperwork sorted on this, we can arrest the pair of them by the end of the day. I'm sure that will result in new leads for the inquiry."

Back at her desk, Jamie was soon lost in the minutiae of paperwork for the warrant. It was a thankless, but important, part of any investigation and as much as she preferred the more active side of a case, it would give her great satisfaction to be able to bring Mascuria and Neville in.

Minutes after Jamie had logged the meeting with Mascuria and the request for a warrant up to the SIO, the door of the Incident Room opened and Detective Super-intendent Dale Cameron walked in.

"DS Brooke," he called, his voice authoritative. "My office, please."

The room quietened slightly until he turned and left again, not waiting for her to follow. Jamie stood, wondering why her superior had made such a public scene. She went to his office and shut the door behind her.

"Sir. You got my update?"

Cameron stood behind his desk, looking down at Jamie, his patrician features composed. Jamie had been expecting praise at the new evidence, but his imperious tone suggested something quite different.

"Yes, and it disturbs me. I'm expecting you to focus on finding Jenna Neville's killer, not pursuing her grieving father for what was probably drunken consensual sex."

Jamie was stunned enough to stand in silence for a moment. There's no way that Cameron could have watched the video yet, so it could only mean one thing. She thought back to the photo of him in the Nevilles' hallway, the impossibility of moving on this quickly without his go ahead.

"But, Sir ..." she started.

"But nothing, Jamie." Cameron sat down behind his desk and Jamie felt like a child summoned to the head-master. "Seriously, haven't you got enough on your plate with the murder investigation without heading down some sexual assault rabbit hole that has no chance of getting any further?"

"I can ..."

"I don't want to hear any more," Cameron interrupted, his hand held up to stop her. "I'll assign another team to investigate the sexual assault claims, but you need to focus on Jenna Neville's murder. The press are having a field day with our lack of progress. What about that Day-Conti, her boyfriend?"

"He's still a person of interest, but there's no evidence against him Sir, although we're still verifying his alibi at the nightclub. I do have some other interviews lined up today." Jamie decided to omit the detail that one of those was Esther Neville. If Cameron was compromised in some way, she needed time to collect all the evidence together.

"Continue with that then, but Jamie, I will not have you anywhere near Christopher Neville unless you have some evidence directly linking him to Jenna's murder. I want the focus squarely on Day-Conti."

Jamie nodded her assent, but her eyes were cold. With such friends in high places, she could see how Cameron had earned his Teflon stripes, and she wondered what other investigations he had an interest in. But for now, there was nothing she could do.

CHAPTER 12

BLAKE LOOKED AT HIS watch for the fourth time as he paced outside the Royal College of Surgeons. Some part of him hoped that Jamie wouldn't turn up so he could go back to his research, but then he also felt she offered some kind of redemption, a way in which he could use his curse for good. The problem with being able to read the past was that you felt impotent and powerless, unable to change what had already happened. What good was an ability to see what had already failed, or died and rotted away? Perhaps this time, it would be different.

In preparation for today, he hadn't drunk anything last night, even though he had craved oblivion. Alcohol deadened the visions, shaded their vivid color and rubbed over their raw power until they faded like a mirage, and he wanted to be fully open and alert today. He hadn't read as deeply as this for a long time, and the possibilities both exhilarated and scared him.

He heard the roar of a motorcycle and a figure in black pulled up in front of him. He hadn't expected Jamie to ride a bike, but somehow it fitted her independence and need to be apart from others. As she removed her helmet, Blake remembered how she had looked in his vision of tango and tried to fit it to this leather clad wraith, her face devoid of makeup, hair scraped back as if in punishment. He realized that she had the face of a model, the kind who looked ugly in some shots and stunning in others, depending on the animation of her mouth, the look in her eyes or the way she held herself. At tango, she was a goddess, but right now Jamie's face was hard and Blake imagined that was the look that made criminals wary.

"Morning," she said, dismounting the bike. "Sorry I'm late. I had to see a man about a video."

Blake could sense her anger, the vibrations of intense emotion emanating from her.

"We don't have to do this now, you know," he said. "Maybe another time would be better."

Jamie shook her head. "If you're ready, I really do want to know whether you can shed any more light on the case." She smiled then, and he felt the shift in her, the way her attention could focus. He envied her ability to tune everything else out.

He nodded, pushing aside his own doubt. "Let's do this then. I can't promise anything but it's worth a try."

Jamie led the way into the museum, now cleaned of evidence but still closed to the public for a time out of respect for Jenna's family. Blake hesitated at the door, knowing that this place contained instruments of torture exhibited under the guise of the medical profession. There were saws that sliced bone from bodies, instruments to suck blood from flesh and knives to pare it away.

These were things he could not and did not want to touch, and he felt a wave of fear at being in such close proximity to them, a concern that he would be overwhelmed by visions of past horror. Blake took a deep breath, remembering his father's curses that had called on Hell to visit him with all its spectacles of evil to drive him mad. He felt tendrils of it in the museum and a pain began to pulse in his temples. But he felt that he deserved to face whatever was here, and only by embracing the visions could he find something to help Jamie and the murder investigation.

Removing his gloves, Blake stepped over the threshold into the Museum. Immediately he saw a wooden table laid out with a full dissection of the veins and arteries of the human body. Blake put his hand out to steady himself against the wall as a wave of bloody film swept across his eyes. He tasted a metallic tang and nausea made his head spin. He fell to his knees, hands clutched to his chest as he hyperventilated, shuddering, heart pounding. He had glimpsed the dissection beginning when the victim was still alive. In the vision, Blake saw the patient made anonymous by a hood, so the anatomist could focus on the pathology, eliminating the irrelevant human from the frame of the medically interesting, even as the body shuddered under the scalpel.

"Are you okay, Blake?" Jamie bent to him, her hand shaking his shoulder. "Blake ..."

This place was a museum of abomination. There was an ancient evil here, layered over centuries, and the deaths of many lay just under the surface of its gleaming exterior, clawing for release. Blake tried to regulate his vision, limiting the amount of sensation he was taking in at once and, as his breathing returned to something resembling normal, he tried to compartmentalize the complex web of emotion.

"I'm OK," he whispered, getting up slowly, making sure not to touch Jamie with his bare hands. He didn't want her energy swirling in this maelstrom as well, for she was alive and vibrant, her colors bold and bright. He needed to feel the edges of the palette of gray, where ghosts lingered, trapped by attachment to pieces of their unburied selves. "I need to establish a baseline for the energy of the place and then try to sift through that for Jenna. Her resonance should be greater because it's so recent." He grimaced, unable to hide his mental pain at the sensations pressing in on him. "Just give me a few minutes."

Jamie nodded, clearly worried about him but Blake knew she couldn't understand what he was going through. He was sure that part of her still thought he was a charlatan, but right now it was all he could do to hold onto the reins of his sanity. He had to face the horror head on and ride the wave into the past, and he could only do that by forcing himself to delve into the darkness.

Blake turned to a wall of glass jars exhibiting a collection of fetal deformity. Bracing himself, he placed his bare hand on the surface, deliberately exposing himself to sensation, feeling the agony of those who had suffered. In one jar was a tiny figure, with perfect arms attached to a human torso. Its head was like a lizard, taut skin pulled back over a deformed skull, slitted eyes, flat features and a gaping hole where its mouth should have been, while its legs were fused into a tail. Blake read the label, Sirenomelus, the word haunting but sweet on the tongue. He imagined the creature swimming around in the afterlife and wondered whether there was a soul out there mourning the loss of such a body.

In another bell-jar was a baby, its hair seeming to wave in the preservative liquid, its ears perfect little shells, soft as only a newborn's can be. But its face was a nightmare, with only a mouth and a gaping eye hole in its empty skull. The infant's body had been hacked open, with only crude stitching holding the corpse together for the preservation jar. Blake couldn't help but stare into the abyss of its eye, wondering at the horrors Nature could create and man could only imagine.

How could God allow these freaks to be born, he wondered. Blake knew that a woman's body would usually expel such damaged creatures, for Nature abhors malformation and human society keeps such things hidden. In times past, midwives would have been the bearers of such monsters and only some grew to adulthood, abused freaks. Now he could hear the screams of these drowned nightmares, their cries muffled by the thick preservative their bodies floated in.

In another jar, twins were joined by the face and chest and Blake's thoughts flashed to Mengele's lab. There was a macabre beauty in their perfect bodies with no faces, just a freakish pile of limbs without movement. Next to the jars lay delivery tools, a brutal pair of spiked forceps and a cranioclast, used for cutting or crushing the skull of the baby's head in order to wrench it from the mother. Blake shuddered and turned away from the violent images that flooded his mind, almost on the edge of what he could bear. But he knew he would soon reach the place when his brain was overwhelmed, fear spiked and then cool, calm would descend. He just needed to push his mind a little further.

He turned to a cabinet of diseased limbs and felt the resonance of disembodied flesh, some kind of muscle memory remaining in them, a persistent electrical impulse. Just as people with amputations felt an itch in a phantom limb, so the appendages themselves emanated a kind of psychical scratching as they were divested of the body that gave them life.

Blake walked on through the displays to a gallery of artwork. He stopped by a selection of repulsive images, sexualizing these human monsters into forbidden pleasure tinged with insanity. In one photograph a little girl, curls around her chubby shoulders, turned with an accusatory, feral glare. She crouched on deformed femurs, clutching at cloth with tight fists, as her over developed sex was exposed to the glare of the camera.

In another, a naked young woman stood, stomach

bulging, her hair done up in a complicated style, topped by a bow. Between her splayed legs emerged a third leg, angled into the air from the knee, an impossible limb. It looked as if something had been thrust up into the girl but the leg was part of a parasitic twin that had grown inside her body. All three legs wore the same boots with long white socks. Blake couldn't help but look at it more closely, and read the label, 'Dipygus tripus, parasitic twin. Blanche Dumas/Dupont'. The name served to humanize the girl but he wondered what kind of life she had been able to have, or whether it had been one of constant abuse from the people making money from her deformity.

The photos were enough to push him over the edge, and his adrenalin spiked. Blake sat down heavily, pulse pounding as the visions took over his mind, whizzing through his consciousness in a cacophony of screams and flashes of grisly horror. He felt blood pulse at his ankles and wrists as if it would burst from his body, rising to a crescendo of overwhelm. His vision narrowed to a tunnel, his hearing dulled as if under a swimming pool and panic threatened to shut his body down. Then suddenly, it broke. Blake felt the cold aftershock and his heart rate began to slow as the panic subsided. This was the moment that he had waited for, and now he could regain control.

Blake looked up at Jamie standing a little way from him, her face concerned but also intrigued by his physical reaction. He could only imagine what horrors she had seen in her job, but she only witnessed the aftermath, while he saw visions of the atrocity in progress and actually felt the victim's pain.

"Do you want some water?" Jamie said, pulling a bottle from her bag. Blake nodded and sipped at it gratefully while his heart rate returned to normal.

"I'm ready now," he said after a moment and rose slowly, his legs feeling weak and sluggish. He pushed the baseline sensations of the Museum to a separate area of his consciousness and began to sift through the eddies of energy to find a strand of Jenna Neville. His eyes were drawn to the staircase and the heavy post at the bottom. Jamie noticed his gaze.

"That's where she fell," she said, walking towards it. Blake followed and then carefully laid his bare hands on the post. He felt the extinction of life, her neck broken, the grasping suffocation of asphyxia. He shuddered as he experienced her panic and fear.

"She died soon after her neck snapped," he said. "But the baby didn't." His eyes met Jamie's and he saw a reflection of his own stricken face. "There's something about the child that explains why it was taken, why her body was violated. It feels different somehow but I can't get a clear vision." Blake grasped for a truth that was tantalizingly close and he knew that he had felt whispers of it in the cabinets. There were echoes and reflections of Jenna here and the past of this museum had come to life in the present. Jamie leaned closer, waiting for his words.

"Her baby was a miracle," Blake finally whispered. "Jenna was like one of these specimens. She shouldn't have been able to get pregnant. You need to find who created her."

CHAPTER 13

PARKING THE BIKE A few blocks away from Neville Pharmaceuticals Head Office, Jamie went into a little coffee shop. She was early for her meeting with Esther Neville and she wanted to review her notes on the case so far. Ordering a black coffee and dumping two sugars in it, Jamie considered how Blake's words had disturbed her. Although she still had some doubts about him, he had definitely been affected by the Museum and seemed convinced that Jenna and her baby were somehow special. Esther Neville would be the only person who could answer that but there was no evidence with which to start such a discussion and all of the records indicated Jenna Neville was her biological child. What did Blake even mean about the baby being a miracle? Was he just disturbed by the craziness of the Museum, filled with dead things that seemed about to wake at any moment?

Jamie examined the file on the Nevilles that Missinghall had pulled together. Lord Christopher Neville was a distant descendant of the Darwin-Wedgwood-Galton family and had been raised in aristocratic circles. After Eton, he had read Philosophy, Politics and Economics at Magdalen College, Oxford and was expected to go into Law. But at Oxford he had married Esther Galloway, a distant cousin from another branch of the same distinguished family. Esther studied medicine at Oxford and then worked in the pharmaceutical industry, increasingly specializing in genetics after DNA had been sequenced in 1977.

Neville Pharmaceuticals was started in 1979 with an investment from the family fortune and was now one of the most highly respected private genetics companies in the world. Jenna Neville, their only daughter, was born in 1985. Jamie read a couple of the articles from various pharmaceutical magazines profiling Esther Neville as a brilliant scientist, in total command of the business and scientific side of the research. Christopher Neville seemed to play a more social role, schmoozing with potential investors and clients, leaving the serious business to his more than capable wife. There was evidence of a number of affairs between Christopher Neville and young society women, and Jamie presumed that Esther turned a blind eye to her husband's indiscretions. It was certainly one way to keep a marriage of power together.

Her phone buzzed with a text from Missinghall.

Taxi dockets show Esther Neville picked up alone 10.45pm.

Interesting, Jamie thought, since Mascuria had indicated that she had left the gala dinner around 9.30. What had she been doing in that missing time period?

Finishing her coffee, Jamie drove down the road to the imposing company headquarters of Neville Pharmaceuticals. It was situated on the western edge of London, close enough to the City for ease of access but far enough out for the company to have a high rise building encompassing both official office suites and functional labs. The blue glass exterior reflected the cool winter sun as Jamie parked the bike in a visitor spot and headed in.

After the usual security protocols, Jamie was led into a long boardroom on one of the upper floors, with a giant window looking out over the city. There were a couple of pictures on the walls, magnified images of cells that were monstrous in close-up. Jamie stood, gazing out at London, considering the pulsing mass of humanity that crowded together below her.

"Detective, how can I help you?"

Jamie turned to see Esther Neville at the doorway, a tailored white lab coat cut close to her body and stiletto heels making her thin body appear like a stork picking its way through the marshes. She looked completely different in her own domain, clearly a scientist first, rather than a society wife. Her expertly highlighted blonde hair was tied back with a black clip, and under her lab coat she wore clothes of mourning black. Yesterday, at home with her husband, she had seemed timid, submissive and even fearful, yet here, she walked with authority. Jamie reassessed her opinion of Esther Neville and her position at the company, for this was an empire that she definitely would not want threatened, especially by her own daughter.

"Thank you for seeing me, Lady Neville."

Esther inclined her head and sat at the head of the boardroom table, her eyes emotionless as she spoke.

"What exactly do you need from me? I'm keen to help find my daughter's killer but I'm sure you understand I'm a busy woman."

Jamie sat down to one side and spread her files out in front of her, keeping them closed. She noticed Esther glancing sideways at them, achieving her purpose of making the woman wonder exactly what she knew.

"Can you explain a little of what Neville Pharmaceuticals does? Just for some background."

Esther inclined her head, beginning a clearly well-practiced speech.

"Our main business is genetic engineering for the

agricultural and farming industry. You must know of the increasing pressure that food production has experienced with dramatic population growth. We investigate efficient ways to feed more people cheaply, researching faster growth methods for protein sources. We also have a smaller part of the company that researches genetic mutation and how to eradicate birth defects in animals caused by environmental toxins. The exact details are protected, as the work is for the Ministry of Defense, but it's both a profitable business and an important one for the world. Do you think that the company is related to my daughter's death?"

Jamie shuffled her papers to detract from Esther's piercing scrutiny.

"What did you think of Jenna's legal investigations and protests against the company?"

A flicker of disturbance flashed across Esther's face.

"Oh, she was just going through a rebellious patch, encouraged by that man she was seeing." Esther was haughty with a tone of dismissal. "Jenna seemed willing to do anything to undermine me and her father. Although she reaped the rewards of what we do, she was determined to bring it all down and to make victims of the - very few - bodies we use for research."

"Bodies?" Jamie pushed.

Esther sighed. "The best way to learn anatomy is to dissect the human body, Detective. We all want surgeons to know what they're doing, don't we? But Jenna would never acknowledge that truth." Jamie waited, counting the beats of silence until Esther continued. "You have to break humanity before you can fix it. John Hunter knew that. He was driven by the need to understand life, and he wouldn't take accepted wisdom as truth. He would only believe the evidence of his eyes, and only by dissecting the bodies of animals and of people, could he truly understand their inner workings."

"So you objected to Jenna's legal work?"

"We argued about it, yes. But the use of the dead to benefit the living is entirely scientific. It has always been this way. It's superstitious nonsense to think that the body has to be intact for the resurrection, or that somehow we are dishonoring the dead by using them for scientific matters. There are those who would prefer not to think of this side of things, but they are also the ones who expect medical science to cure them, for their drugs to work and for treatments to be pain free. But drugs must be tested on human subjects and the surgeon must know exactly where and how to cut. What are they to practice on, if not real flesh? Of course, these days there are computer simulations but that doesn't give the proper sense of cutting into a body, the push of a blade through resistant skin. It doesn't part like butter, you know, you have to cut. Surgeons sweat as they work, it can be physically draining." Her voice was strangely wistful. "The human body is so well put together, it can be hard to pull it apart. "

Jamie looked down at her notebook to leave some silence between them, as she considered Esther's vivid words. After a moment, she looked up again.

"Can you talk me through your movements on the night of the Gala Dinner?"

Esther froze, her face stony, then slowly answered.

"I had a headache that night. I get migraines and one was threatening. I put up with that odious dinner for as long as I could, but I got up to leave as the dessert was being served. I felt giddy so I sat in the toilets for a while." She looked away from Jamie. "I don't know how long I was there. The pain was all I could think about, and eventually I caught a taxi home."

"And did you argue with Jenna that night?"

Esther laughed, a shrill sound that seemed out of place in the austere surroundings.

"Of course. I argued with my daughter whenever we spoke, Detective. That night wasn't any different."

Jamie decided to change tack and circle back on the alibi later. There should be some footage from near the bathrooms of the Royal College of Surgeons, and she could check on the migraine medication.

"What about Jenna's active membership of the National Anti-Vivisection Society? The marches against this office, against you and Lord Neville personally."

Esther rolled her eyes and shook her head. "I know she meant well, but she was misguided. Come with me and I'll show you how humane we are. I want to give you the scientific side of the story so you'll understand."

She led the way out of the lab, into a corridor and then to a lift. Esther pressed the −3 button, and Jamie noticed that there were five floors underground as well as the twenty above ground. It was an extensive facility. Esther was silent in the lift, and Jamie said nothing either. Finally, the door opened to an atrium, which smelled of disinfectant, like a vet's surgery.

"This floor is where we keep some of the animals and also where we perform legal vivisection."

Jamie noticed her emphasis on the legal basis of the research. "Can you explain to me exactly what that is?" she asked.

"In the UK, any experiment involving vivisection, where we use a live animal for experimentation, must be granted a license from the Home Secretary. The license is only given when the benefits to society outweigh the adverse effects to the animal."

"What's your definition of adverse?"

"It depends on the procedure. The definition of vivisection is that the animal is alive when we experiment but of course we use anesthesia, so there is no pain. We also have an external ethics committee."

"Why was Jenna so against this practice?"

"She believed it was morally wrong to inflict pain or injury on another animal, for whatever reason, and so any kind of animal experimentation would be unacceptable." Esther shook her head. "But Jenna was short-sighted about this, she only saw the propaganda spread by the anti-vivisectionists, and she put everything in the same box."

"What do you mean by that?" Jamie asked.

"Well, I agree that it's pointless to test household products by spraying them into the eyes of rabbits, and there are some needless experiments where positive results on animals have no application to humans. But here, we carry out genetic research, and since we cannot experiment on humans, we must make do with animals, as did the great John Hunter. Although of course, he did experiments on live animals with no pain relief."

"Which we would now consider barbaric and inhumane," Jamie prompted.

"In our culture, yes," Esther replied, her eyes curiously blank, her mouth tense. "But think of how operations were back then. No anesthetic and no antiseptic, they didn't know about germs or infections. Surgeons would go from the dissection room to the operating theatre, reusing equipment that was encrusted with the blood of the previous patient and the gore of the recently dead. The patient would be tied up or held down, then the surgeon would progress as fast as possible. Many didn't survive. Hunter became known as one of the greatest surgeons in England because he was so much better than the rest, and he was better because of his experiments. Dissection and experimentation were a means to gaining insight. It wasn't a macabre obsession, it was more about expanding his own knowledge in order to help the living."

Jamie was startled at her words, her passion suggesting

that only the law was stopping her from experimenting on humans.

"And what exactly do you do here?"

Esther led the way into the next lab, dominated by a quiet hum of medical equipment and the smell of antiseptic. One side of the room had refrigeration units with clear glass doors. As they walked past, Jamie glimpsed racks of labeled test-tubes and larger jars containing monkey fetuses of varying sizes. She couldn't help but stare at the recently extinguished lives, so similar to human babies but distinguished by tails and longer toes. It was eerily reminiscent of the Hunterian Museum, but these specimens were much more recent, and presumably modified by design.

They walked deeper into the lab to find a group of scientists in lab coats and expressionless masks surrounding a monkey. It was anesthetized and strapped to a bed, eyes shut, and Jamie felt her heart thump in her chest as she recognized a kind of kinship with the creature.

"This macaque has been exposed to specific environmental toxins whilst pregnant," Esther said. "Now we're waiting for some key stage developments, at which point we will operate and extract the fetus for further testing."

"You kill it?"

Esther looked at Jamie, her eyebrows raised as if the question was entirely irrelevant. "It was never meant to be born, so how are we killing it by extracting it early?" Jamie said nothing, but she was beginning to see why Jenna had protested against her mother's company. Esther continued in a superior tone. "Jenna accused me of being like Mengele, an animal Angel of Death. She painted me as this architect of Nazi-style experimentation, but I'm only seeking medical truth and these monkeys don't even suffer any pain."

Jamie was shocked to hear Esther mention Mengele. It

seemed too much of a coincidence after Blake's revelation. Could the book that he saw be here? She looked down at the face of the macaque, whose baby was about to be ripped from her body and she felt a wave of anger, as she supposed Jenna would have done. But had Jenna's objection been enough for her mother to have acted against her?

"I think I've seen enough," Jamie said. She spun on her heel and walked out of the lab, breathing deeply as she tried to regulate her emotions. A few moments later, Esther Neville walked out of the lab behind her.

"I didn't think you'd be so squeamish Detective, considering you must see real violence on the streets."

Jamie thought of what humans did to each other, supposedly prevented by the law, but that didn't stop the horrors that went on behind closed doors. After all, there was no license from the Home Office necessary to have a child. These animals didn't choose to be treated this way, but at least there was some legal protection in place to limit their suffering.

"Did Jenna ever come down here or visit the other parts of the lab?"

Esther nodded. "Of course, when she was younger I hoped that she might continue my work, but once she went to university and began to study ethics and law, we had to ban her. We even took out a restraining order to keep her from coming near the premises."

Jamie wondered how far the conflict had gone between the members of the Neville family. A restraining order on their own daughter seemed extreme, and surely Jenna couldn't have sat easily with them at the Gala dinner.

They walked towards the lift, and Jamie suddenly felt trapped underground in the lab, desperate to emerge into the light. Even though it was high tech and shiny, the lab felt like a dirty prison. Being kept down here in the dark and experimented on was a modern nightmare that wasn't so different to the horrors of Hunter's time.

"I'll show you out," Esther said, and Jamie thought she heard a tinge of triumph in the woman's tone.

As the lift took them back up to the lobby, Jamie decided that she had nothing to lose by testing Blake's theory.

"I need to ask a more personal question Lady Neville." Jamie waited as Esther hesitated, then nodded. "Was Jenna your natural child?"

Esther's eyes narrowed, her lips pursed and she began twisting her wedding ring, remaining silent as the lift door opened. In the lobby, Esther ushered Jamie into a small meeting room at the side of Reception, obviously keen not to be overheard as she finally answered.

"It's an ironic twist of fate, Detective, and one which sometimes seems to occur when scientists investigate an area of medical research. Cancer researchers get cancer and neurosurgeons get brain aneurysms and I have a rare genetic mutation that means I couldn't have children. It was this that led to my constant drive to eradicate mutation in animals and humans." She paused and her eyes flickered to Jamie's. "Back then, the lab was purely experimental, investigating mutations at a time when genetics was really just beginning. I worked with a fertility specialist to remove my mutation and enable my egg and Christopher's sperm to make Jenna. So yes, she is my child, but she started life in the lab. She was a miracle, because so many of the fetuses we engineered were corrupted."

"Could Jenna have had children?" Jamie asked quietly, her suspicions heightened as she realized that Blake had gleaned a truth at the Hunterian.

Esther stared out the window, silent for a moment. When she spoke, her voice was wistful.

"She shouldn't have been able to."

Jamie opened her mouth to ask more but at that

moment her phone buzzed urgently in her pocket. She took it out and checked the display. The Hospice. Her heart hammered.

"I have to take this, sorry."

Jamie stepped out into the corridor and answered the phone, a sense of dread rising within her.

"Jamie Brooke," she said and it was as if her voice wasn't her own.

"You have to come now," Rachel said. "Polly needs you."

A coldness swept over Jamie, raising goosebumps on her arms. She wasn't ready. She leaned against the wall, her hand clutching it for support.

"I'm on my way."

CHAPTER 14

SCREECHING TO A HALT outside the hospice, Jamie wrenched her bike helmet off and ran inside. The lump in her throat threatened to choke her with tears at any minute but she had to hold it together. She had to believe that this wasn't the end, not yet. Not her beautiful girl. She saw Rachel at the door of Polly's room and her face crumpled.

"Breathe, hun," Rachel said, her hand firm on Jamie's arm. "Polly's calm now, but she's drowning in the respiratory secretions and we can't suction it off fast enough anymore. She's hypoxemic, which means she's not getting enough oxygen."

"Is she in pain?" The tears came now, streaming down Jamie's face.

Rachel nodded. "She's been in pain since she was a little girl, you know that, but now her body has had enough. We've given her morphine and midazolam to dull the discomfort, but you know her wishes. We haven't fully sedated her yet, so she's just conscious, waiting for you. But, it's time, Jamie."

Rachel stood back and pushed the door open and Jamie walked slowly into the room while the nurse followed behind. It was so bright, the sun shining in from outside.

For a moment, Jamie couldn't believe that anything bad could happen on a day like this, but then she looked at the bed. Polly was lying on her back, eyes closed. Her skin had a bluish tinge and her lips were almost lavender. Her rasping breaths were harsh in the room, and every inhalation was hard fought, the sound of torment even though it was dulled with analgesia. Jamie knew that the drugs could help Polly peacefully into another place, but everything in her screamed for her to stay. She bent over her daughter and kissed her forehead.

"Pol," she whispered. "I'm here, darling. It's OK. I love you." The tears came freely now and Jamie couldn't hold them in anymore. She took Polly's hand in her own, squeezing it. Polly opened her eyes slowly and Jamie saw eternity there. In that moment, she knew that this twisted physical body was only a trap, a temporary home for the tremendous spirit that was her beloved child. More than that, Polly would go further than she ever could in transcending this physicality. Wherever she was going next, Jamie couldn't follow and she knew she would never see her daughter again. Looking down into Polly's eyes, Jamie saw that she only asked permission to leave.

With a fierce need to save her child from pain, Jamie looked up at Rachel and nodded her consent. The nurse readied a bolus of medication to sedate Polly and let her die pain-free and then injected it into the cannula.

"It's OK, Pol, you go now my darling." Jamie wept openly, knowing that Polly didn't want to hurt her but desperately needing her to find release. Trying to keep her here was only selfish. Jamie kissed her daughter's face gently. "I love you Polly," she whispered. "I'll miss you but I understand. I love you."

Rachel turned off the ventilator and stood by, a witness to the transition she had seen so many times before. Jamie sobbed, her body wracked with silent heaving, for she didn't want Polly to go with the sound of pain in her ears. She clutched her daughter's hand, pressing it to her own cheek. Jamie pleaded with God, with the Universe, anything to have her baby back. But Polly had been her gift for fourteen years, and now her time was over. The girl's rasping breaths stumbled and skipped, hoarse gasps becoming weaker.

"No," Jamie whispered. "Please, no."

She felt Rachel's hand on her shoulder and then rubbing her back, like a mother comforting a child. Like she used to do with Polly.

"I'll remove the tubes now," Rachel said, her voice choked. "Let me make her your baby again and you can hold her as she goes."

Jamie nodded, still clutching Polly's hand. It was so warm and soft, relaxing now as the pain dissolved from her face. Rachel removed the tube from Polly's neck, wiping her face carefully as her breaths became sporadic.

"There you go, hun," Rachel said quietly. "You can curl up on the bed with her now. I'll come back in a bit."

Jamie heard Rachel leave and shut the door quietly behind her. She climbed onto the bed and pulled Polly carefully into her arms, folding her daughter's head onto her chest and stroking her hair. She rocked Polly back and forth, something she hadn't been able to do properly since she had become bedridden. She felt the thin body, spine twisted and misshapen and Jamie cried silently, her tears soaking the pillow and Polly's bedclothes. She wanted Polly's agony to be over, but she also wanted to crush the girl's body to her and breathe her own life into her daughter's lungs.

Time seemed to slow down, held back by each faltering breath as the sunlight dimmed outside and night fell. Jamie listened to the evening routine of the Hospice, lives that continued even though she felt hers was over.

Finally, after a last breath, Polly's body was still, released from pain. Jamie had a sense that while her body had held Polly captive for so many years, now she was free. Her spirit had gone, and Jamie hoped that she hadn't looked back. For whatever her daughter became next, at least she wouldn't have to rely on this mess of a body to carry her there.

Jamie held Polly's body tightly against her own, knowing that these last moments were for her own precious memory. In the depths of her misery, she knew she was grateful for the years she had Polly in her life, for the joy her daughter had brought. She was grateful that the physical suffering was finished and thankful that she was able to be here to let her daughter go, that she didn't have to die alone. Although Polly's body was still warm, Jamie knew that her girl wasn't inside. She already felt the absence, the emptiness. Her daughter's pain was over now, and her own, she would bear as penance, although she felt she would never stop crying.

Polly's tablet lay next to the bed, and Jamie reached for it, wanting to see her words. Turning it on, she saw only one line of text. *Dance for me, Mum.* The tears welled again and Jamie sobbed as if she would never stop.

***

Much later, Rachel knocked at the door and came in slowly, holding a steaming cup of milky tea. Jamie disentangled herself from Polly's body and sat up.

"Here you go, hun." Rachel said as she put the tea down next to the bed. "I know you're hurting, but it was time."

Rachel's eyes were red-rimmed and Jamie could only imagine the tears that the nurse had shed for the children over the years. Jamie blew her nose, adding to the pile of wet tissues on the side table.

"Thanks Rachel." She took a sip of the tea. It was sweet, just what she needed. Rachel walked around the bed and together they arranged Polly's body, tucking the sheet around her, so she looked like she was sleeping.

Jamie took a deep breath. It seemed like it had all happened so suddenly even though the moment had been approaching for years. "So what happens next?" she asked, feeling a need to understand the process, to reach a point of completion. She had prepared hypothetically for this but suddenly her mind was blank on the next steps.

"The doctor will sign the death certificate and we'll get the funeral director to prepare her body."

Jamie nodded, remembering the difficult discussions with Polly over the choices. Her little girl had been independent minded, even about her own death.

"She wanted to be cremated, taken by fire and smoke into the freedom of the sky." Jamie's voice broke, as the tears came again. "She watched a history documentary about the Viking boat pyres … and afterwards she wanted her ashes to become part of the flowers. She loved the first daffodils of spring."

"Of course. And what about your family? Do you want me to call anyone?"

Jamie thought of Polly's father, Mark, her own parents and the fights they had engaged in over the years. She couldn't bear to talk to them and right now, she didn't even want the funeral to be for anyone else. Polly had been her life, and no one else had the right to be there as she said her final goodbyes.

But then she faltered. Of course Mark had to be there, if only for him to acknowledge their remarkable daughter. He seemed to live in denial of the miracle that they had created together, seeing primarily her disability. But Jamie knew he would mourn in his own way and she had loved him too, once. Polly's school friends would want to come as well, and a funeral was a chance to honor her memory with those who loved her.

"I can't face talking to anyone right now," Jamie said. "I need to leave all that for tomorrow. Let's just do the essentials. "

***

Much later, Jamie returned to the flat in darkness. She left the lights off, sitting on the sofa alone, for the brightness would only illuminate what she was missing. This moment had been on its way for nearly ten years but she still wasn't prepared for how lonely she felt. Polly had been her reason for everything and without her, there was nothing. Jamie's head pounded, the headache that had been growing all day exploding into her consciousness. She embraced the pain, wanting it to consume her.

The Funeral Director had come quickly to the Hospice and Jamie had wept again to hand Polly's body into their care. It was so wrong: a daughter should weep for her mother, not the other way around. Jamie rose and went to the bathroom, opening the cupboard where she kept her sleeping pills. For a long moment she looked at them, oblivion in a bottle. She twisted the cap off and tipped out two pills, then four more, then the whole bottle into her hand. Release called to her, a tangible desire to swallow these down and follow Polly's spirit onwards.

That thought made her stop, for if there was another side and Polly was there now, she would be disappointed at these self-destructive thoughts. Jamie poured the tablets back into the bottle, keeping only the prescribed two. Even in death, she didn't want to disappoint Polly, for one of the things that she had been most proud of was Jamie's job, the fact that she brought killers to justice. Jamie tried to put the two deaths into perspective. Polly had died surrounded by love, and was now mourned and missed. Jenna Neville had died violently, her parents rejecting her passionate cause, and her killer was still out there. Jamie knew that right now, across London, across the world, other crimes were being committed, other people injured and killed. If she were to stay alive, her role would be as one of those who stood against the dark tide, part of a dam that held back at least some of the monsters.

She clenched her fists, remembering the sensation of holding Polly's hand and the fierce determination in her daughter's eyes when she wanted to learn something new. She could have been the next Stephen Hawking, Jamie thought, smiling a little because every parent would say that their kid could achieve something unique and amazing. But hers could have, for sure, because Polly's mind had been special and sometimes Jamie wondered how she had brought such a being into the world.

Jamie thought of her own mother, years of not speaking creating a wall neither of them could cross. She rummaged in the back of a drawer and pulled out a card, the one that had finally broken their relationship years ago. It had a quote from the gospel of John 9:2-3.

His disciples asked him, "Rabbi, who has sinned, this man or his parents, that he was born blind?"

"Neither this man nor his parents sinned," said Jesus, "but this happened so that the work of God might be displayed in his life."

Jesus had healed the blind man and Jamie's mother had said to pray in faith that God might work a miracle in Polly's life. But Jamie could never reconcile the thought that God would have condemned a little girl to a life of torture in order to save her later. Her mother's constant acceptance of suffering as God's will was something that Jamie couldn't bear, as if the violent anguish she saw every day was condoned by the Almighty. She hadn't spoken to her parents for six years now, and cutting them completely out of her life had made the separation easier. It had just been her and Polly against the world, fighting for one more day. And now it was just her. Jamie pulled Polly's cuddly dog, Lisa, to her chest and the tears came again as she wept for an empty future.

CHAPTER 15

THE NIGHT WAS LONG and lonely. Even when Jamie managed to drop off to sleep, exhausted from weeping, she woke with a start from nightmares of Polly dying over and over again, forced to watch as she had to let her daughter go. In the end, although she knew that she should rest, Jamie could not bear lying there any longer.

Standing in the shower, she tried to think of what was supposed to happen next. Time seemed to have slowed down and her brain just wasn't functioning properly. The pills in the cabinet called to her again and she rested her palm against the wall, anchoring herself to the physical world as the wave of longing washed over her. It was all she could do to resist the pull of oblivion. Fight it for just another heartbeat, she told herself, for this too shall pass.

Eventually, she managed to drag herself out of the bathroom and started getting ready to go to the funeral directors. Jamie was dreading the practicalities and the finality, holding onto the last moments she had cuddled her daughter on the bed. That was what she wanted to remember. That, and living as passionately as Polly had wanted her to. Jamie's hand flew to her mouth and she held back a sob as the wrenching in her chest made her stop dead in the middle of the room. This was how people died of a broken heart, and even with all her years of police work, she hadn't been prepared for the violence of her own grief. She breathed into the silence until the tightness eased and she could move again.

It was still early but Jamie rang Detective Superintendent Dale Cameron anyway. He didn't answer so she left a brief message, grateful that she didn't have to talk to him because she couldn't bear his false sympathy right now. She followed up with an email to him and the HR department taking her allotted bereavement leave. She had told the Met about Polly's illness previously and given them notice of her potential need to be off work, so there would be no problem with it. Jamie felt a lingering guilt and responsibility over Jenna Neville's case, especially as Cameron had seemed to be directing the investigation away from the Nevilles. She still had her notes on Esther Neville to file, but her suspicions paled into insignificance now. They would have to find someone else to continue the investigation, because nothing else mattered anymore.

***

The entrance hall of the funeral directors was tastefully furnished with fresh flowers and cream decor, a light and airy atmosphere that seemed a respectable overlay for what must happen behind the scenes. Jamie didn't want to think about Polly's body being prepared for cremation: she wanted to remember her alive and vital, not as a shell of a corpse. In other cultures, in other times, she would have been the one washing the body and preparing her daughter for the grave. Perhaps that would have been a way to help the desolation, but Jamie couldn't bear the thought of grieving so openly in front of others. This pain was hers to bear privately.

She rang the bell, pacing the little room with barely controlled nervous energy. As Jamie waited, her phone buzzed with a text from Missinghall.

So sorry about your daughter. FYI. Day-Conti arrested for Jenna's murder.

Jamie frowned. Firstly at how her private life had been so clearly exposed but also, she couldn't understand how Day-Conti could be arrested, given the little evidence against him and the open lines of investigation still to be followed up. Jamie wondered whether her visit to Esther Neville had stirred the hornet's nest. Had Cameron used her absence to change the direction of the case? But then again, what did it even matter? She had more important things to think about right now. She pushed the investigation from her mind.

A door at the back of the entrance hall opened and the funeral director stepped out, rubbing his hands together in an awkward way.

"Ah, Ms Brooke," he said without meeting her eyes and Jamie felt her heart thudding in her chest.

"What's wrong?" she asked, sensing the man's discomfort.

He pursed his lips and twisted his hands, adjusting his tie. "I'm so sorry, we're investigating right now. This has never happened before."

"What's happened?" Jamie cut him off, impatient for him to get to the point. "What do you mean?"

"Oh, no one called you?" The man looked embarrassed and shocked. "I'm so sorry. It's your daughter's body. It's missing."

Jamie's head spun, confusion buzzing in her ears. "What do you mean it's missing? How can that even happen?" Her voice escalated to a shout. "How can you lose my daughter?"

The man wrung his hands together, clearly distressed and worried about his business.

"I'm so sorry, but there was a break-in last night and by the time security got here, her body had been taken." The man was flustered, his face reddening with every second. "It's never happened before and to be honest, we don't know why anyone would even want to steal a body."

Jamie felt a chill at his words and rising anxiety rippled through her body. It was too much of a coincidence. Jenna had been investigating the theft of bodies and was then killed, and now she was analyzing the same evidence. Was this some kind of retribution for her investigation?

Hysteria rising within her, Jamie felt a desperation to shake the man. It seemed too much to take in and she was only just clinging to the edge of sanity. The funeral director was still speaking but Jamie was no longer listening. She was thinking back to Esther Neville's clinical detachment about bodies, the horrors of Day-Conti's studio, the evidence against Mascuria and Christopher Neville. The last forty-eight hours had been steeped in dissection, mutilation and desecration. This theft had to be related.

Inside, Jamie was screaming. Someone had taken her daughter. Someone had known about Polly's condition, her death, and because of her, they had taken her body. She had to do something.

"Have you called the police?" Jamie asked, her voice outwardly calm.

"Of course, they're sending someone down to interview the staff soon."

Jamie knew this would be a priority for the Met. The theft of a body was unusual at the best of times, but when it was the daughter of a serving officer, she knew they would fast-track the case. The police had their problems, like any organization, but they certainly looked after their own.

She called Dale Cameron's office and was put straight through. She explained what had happened and her suspicions surrounding the Neville case.

"Jamie, this is terrible … unbelievable. Of course, I'll contact the officers assigned and explain the situation. We'll find Polly's body, I promise you." He paused and Jamie heard caution in his silence, before he continued. "I can't believe it's related to the Neville case, though. And, of course, you know that you can't be involved in either now. You're too close."

"But, Sir …"

"I'm sorry for your loss, Jamie, but you're now officially on extended bereavement leave. I'll keep you up to date."

Jamie's heart was thumping and her fist clenched the phone tight as Cameron hung up, dismissing her with barely concealed relief. But there was no way she could stay out of this case, especially as she was sure that the theft was related to Jenna's murder.

Looking at her watch, Jamie suddenly felt a sense of lost time. It was Friday morning and the Lyceum had been marked on Jenna's calendar for tomorrow night. It was one of many unanswered questions in this case, but she remembered the news clippings from Jenna's office, the stolen bodies marked with L. Images of the specimens from the John Hunter museum flashed before Jamie's eyes, twisted spines and diseased body parts floating in formaldehyde, torn from the bodies of their owners. She had to find Polly before she was displayed in a labeled bell-jar, her flesh carved up and trapped in liquid limbo. She would let the Met start their own investigation, but there was no time to follow the correct protocol. She needed to bring her daughter home.

CHAPTER 16

THIS PART OF LONDON was always busiest in the dark. Artists worked nights and slept the days away, and the oldest profession in the world was always active. Debilitated from grief and lack of sleep, Jamie had taken a couple of ephedrine tablets, stimulants that would keep her awake for the investigation ahead. She wouldn't rest until she held Polly's body in her arms again. With the spike in energy helping her recover, at least physically, she parked the bike and slipped along the street towards the studio of Rowan Day-Conti.

Since he was still in police custody, Jamie knew that his flat would be empty. She was determined to find out more on his sources for the bodies he worked on and the mysterious buyer for the naked female sculpture. Tugging her leather biker's jacket tighter around her, Jamie pulled a pair of thin gloves from her pocket. Slipping them on, she flexed her fingers and then rubbed her hands together. The night was cold and Jamie felt light-headed, her body fevered, running hot and cold. The tears had finally dried up, to be replaced by anger and determination. The thought of someone using Polly's body in an artistic collection of mutation made her want to vomit. It was an abomination.

She was about to commit a crime by breaking in, but

Jamie understood the risks she was taking. She could lose her job or even face charges if discovered, but right now, it felt like her life was over anyway. She would leave her colleagues to pursue Polly's case in the legal fashion, but she needed to follow the less respectable route, as time was critical. This had to be connected with her own investigation of the Jenna Neville case, and perhaps, in finding Polly, she could also bring Jenna's killer to justice.

Arriving at the flat, Jamie blocked the view of the lock with her body and, without looking around, picked it to gain access. There was no elaborate security at the studio. Why bother when no one would want to steal the dead bodies Day-Conti worked on, but then why steal Polly's body, she thought. Rage bubbled again and Jamie's face hardened with resolve.

Inside the flat she put on a head torch, the powerful beam stretching all the way to the high ceilings of the warehouse space. The hum of a generator pulsed gently in the background, keeping the remains cool. The smell of death seemed stronger now, disinfectant barely hiding decay. Jamie imagined the naked body of the decapitated young woman lying behind the panels, alone in the dark. She shuddered, imagining the flesh reanimated, body lurching blindly for a weapon to avenge her mutilation. Jamie shook away the thoughts. These bodies were dead flesh, preserved as an echo of reality, with not a shred of humanity left. What had defined those people was gone, back to the stars and the earth.

Jamie shone the torch back to the staircase that led to Day-Conti's living space. How the man could live in such proximity with the dead, she didn't know, for the smell must impregnate his clothes and his skin. Jamie padded across the floor and up the stairs, freezing as a creak echoed through the space. But no sound came after, no answering noise, so she continued upwards. At the top, she opened the door into the living area. Incense, some kind of heavy patchouli, hung in the room, disguising the smell of the dead but pungent with its own depth of scent. Jamie wrinkled her nose. Perhaps Day-Conti had damaged his sense of smell with all the preservatives. Jamie tried to imagine Jenna here, their intimacy amongst the dead. What had she been thinking? Had she been pursuing a similar goal in trying to discover the origin of the bodies and who wanted such specimens? Or had she really loved him?

Shining the torch around, Jamie could see the place was sparse and minimalist, with a basic desk in the corner and a second-hand filing cabinet against one wall. Jamie pulled it open, using her head torch to illuminate the thin folders within. One held clippings, with articles on the New York Bodies exhibition, interviews with practitioners of the plastination process and controversies over provenance of the bodies. Another file contained receipts, thrown haphazardly into paper envelopes marked with the month of spend. Jamie opened one and thumbed through the paper, looking for where Day-Conti bought his materials. The vendor of the plastics could be a lead, so she snapped a picture on her smart phone and replaced the receipt.

Jamie opened another file. In it were five separate sheets, each one an order form for an unspecified piece of art. There was only one name, Athanasia Ltd, and as the item would be picked up by courier from the warehouse, there was no delivery address. The company name rang a bell and Jamie Googled it on her smartphone. Athanasia, meaning the quality of being deathless or immortality. She took more pictures.

Pulling more files from the cabinet, Jamie discovered notes on different artistic projects, records and photos of stages of the plastination process for each artwork. She laid them out on the desk, scanning pages, and replacing each as she processed them. She flicked open one folder and stopped suddenly, appalled by what she saw. It was a child, no more than ten years old. A boy with deformities of the spine and twisted limbs was posed naked on a metal table that Jamie recognized as the one downstairs where the woman now lay. In the first picture the boy was lying, eyes closed, almost sleeping, as if he could wake up. The next picture showed the body turned onto its front, the spine dissected so as to demonstrate his deformity more clearly.

Jamie gulped for air, feeling the rise of vomit as her stomach clenched at the violation of the child. Seeing a door off the main room, she barged through it into a tiny bathroom. She fell to her knees, holding the toilet bowl as she heaved the meager contents of her stomach out, shaking with the effort as her head spun. She retched again, the sound reverberating around the flat and then she was dry heaving, her stomach spasming.

Finally Jamie lay down on the floor, placing her aching head on the cool tiles, waiting for the tremors to pass. The image of the dissected spine hovered in front of her eyes and she wished she could go back and un-see it. That little boy was tortured in life with disease and then mutilated in death. And to what end? Did the same people have Polly's body, because that close up of the spine could have been her daughter's. Jamie wished for a moment that Day-Conti was here and her hands clenched into fists at how she would teach him some respect for the dead.

Pushing herself up from the floor, Jamie took some deep breaths. She swilled her mouth out with water from the tap, and spat into the toilet, flushing the evidence away and pouring bleach down after it. She wiped the floor tiles with disinfectant and toilet paper and flushed that too.

Walking back into the main room on unsteady legs, Jamie snapped some photos of the image of the little body, trying to separate her emotions from what she was seeing. This was evidence, and this boy was dead. It wasn't torture when the body was no longer alive, was it? Jamie replaced the files into the filing cabinet, careful to put them back in the right order. She shone the torch around the room again, preparing to leave, and the light flickered on a photo in a frame next to the bed. Rowan and Jenna, lit by the summer sun, sitting by Camden Lock and eating ice-cream. Rowan's arm was around her shoulders and Jenna's smile was wide, natural and at ease. Jamie felt sure that he wasn't responsible for her murder. He might well be guilty of other crimes, but not this one, and she wondered again what strings Cameron had pulled to get him arrested while the Nevilles walked free.

Next to the photo was a diary, just a small one, easily overlooked. Jamie picked it up and opened it to the past week. Day-Conti had TG as a regular Friday night appointment and sometimes TG O. TG must be Torture Garden, the club that Day-Conti frequented, but who was O, and would they be there tonight? Jamie looked at her watch. Just before midnight. She replaced the diary next to the bed and slipped down the stairs into the night.

CHAPTER 17

JAMIE CRUISED PAST THE entrance to Torture Garden, slowing down on her bike to get a look at the crowd entering the club. Everyone was dressed up or carried bags, presumably with costumes, that were being searched by the bouncers. Parking a few streets away, Jamie used the mirror on the bike to apply heavy kohl eye makeup, and for good measure, did her lips in black as well. She let her hair swing loose. With pale, feverish skin and deep shadows under her eyes, she looked ghoulish, and black leather suited any occasion. Polly wouldn't like this look, she thought, and a lance of pain thrust through her with the realization that her daughter would never judge her outfit again.

Pushing the heaviness aside, Jamie tried to assume the persona of a sexy party-goer. She tried a smile in the mirror, knowing she had to get into the club because it was the only place she had left to go. Still no good, she thought. She pulled off her biker's jacket and took off her long-sleeve t-shirt, revealing her black bra underneath. She'd lost weight with the last few months of worry, but she still had enough cleavage to attract some attention. It would have to do. She pulled the jacket back on and strode towards the club.

Torture Garden was one of the world's largest fetish and body art clubs, a place where people could indulge in fantasy and experiment on the edge of extremity. Sex had been the last thing on Jamie's mind over the last few years of Polly's illness. There were moments in tango when she felt the thrill of attraction, pressed against a hard body and reveling in the intensity, but that ended when the dance finished. This place was a little outside her comfort zone, but then she was only here to hunt for those who might know Rowan Day-Conti. She had his more recent mugshot in her pocket, but she was aware that this wasn't the kind of place where people wanted to talk to the police. She was here as a seeker, and right now, she felt on the edge of her own sanity. Jamie looked around at the queue of people and thought that perhaps this was exactly where she belonged.

With not much more than a cursory look at her revealing outfit, the bouncers waved Jamie through. She walked into the club as dance music pumped through the atmosphere, making her heart beat in time. Jamie bought a bottled beer and stood on the edge of the dance floor, watching the crowd. There were plenty of people in skin-tight rubber, many with cutouts revealing nipples and buttocks. Couples gyrated in suspended cages, some simulating sex, others presumably doing it while dominatrixes prowled, whipping gimps in face masks. Women danced in little more than string, bound flesh poking from their bonds, but nothing was shocking about the BDSM scene anymore. Most of these people were bankers, lawyers and consultants in the city, taking pleasure in the slick darkness and then returning to work the next day with their secrets intact.

The perfection of the human body was on show, along with every variation on the spectrum of bizarre. Once the eye was used to so much flesh, nudity wasn't interesting anymore and the eye wandered. Jamie was more interested in the people who had crossed the line into true fetishism. A fat man wrapped in Mummy-style bandages stood at the edge of the dance floor, a parody of plastic surgery, dotted lines drawn over the bandages and blood seeping through the female pubic hair drawn over the groin area.

A figure close to Jamie in the full ruffles of Elizabethan dress turned towards her and she saw that the face was an alien mask, a vertical gaping mouth with razor teeth and no eyes, just purple bleeding flesh. Jamie couldn't help but shrink back as a woman in a latex SS officer's uniform pressed herself against the alien creature, her breasts pushed up, nipples revealed by artful holes. Jamie watched the figure's hand go under the woman's short skirt and begin to thrust and rub. She turned away, not wanting to watch the strange coupling as the music faded to a back-beat and then segued into an oriental track.

The crowd turned towards a central stage as the lights dimmed. A spotlight focused on a naked woman standing with her back to the audience, her hands wrapped around a shining silver pole. The bulbous head of an octopus inked in pitch dominated her back with its tentacles winding around her body. The music lifted and she began to dance. As she undulated, the octopus seemed to be moving her limbs, as if she were a puppet unable to escape its grasp. One tentacle wrapped up around her neck, entwining in her hair, another draped around her waist and dipped down between her buttocks. The work was intricate, each sucker on every tentacle finely drawn, the craftsmanship breathtaking. This was truly using the body as a showcase for art, a canvas for creation. Jamie thought how daring the woman must be, to use her body in this way, to make it a physical display and allow people to judge her.

As the woman turned in a slow dance, the full extent of the tattoo was revealed. More tentacles circled her small, tight breasts, one curving around a nipple and the other seemingly caressing the underside. The woman lifted her arms towards the audience, offering herself and it seemed the limbs of the octopus moved with her. One tentacle caressed her stomach and wound down between her legs, tattooed as if it penetrated her there.

The woman used the pole to swing her body up and then hang upside down, stretching her legs wide apart into splits. She tilted her hips towards the audience, showing that she was fully tattooed between them, her sex hairless but black with ink. Jamie could only imagine the pain that this woman had gone through to have her body marked this way, yet there was a surprising lightness in her face as she danced. She wore only pale makeup, keeping the attention on her body, but the slight lines around her eyes suggested that she was in her mid-thirties. Her hair was pixie-cropped, almost white and cut close to her skull. She kept her eyes closed, almost as if she were dancing for an unseen god instead of this hungry crowd. There was a brutal sexuality in the perfection of her body under the lights, but in her face there was only peace. Jamie felt a strange pang of jealousy. This woman was free of expectations, behaving as she wanted and empowered to use her body as she desired. The liberation must be extraordinary, and Jamie felt humbled by the gift that this woman offered, a glimpse into another way of living. Her own freedom seemed so far out of reach.

As the music rose to a crescendo, the woman draped herself away from the audience, leaving the spotlight on the head of the octopus on her back. Jamie presumed that this must be O, the name from Day-Conti's notebook and she was determined to meet her. As the music ramped up the beat and the floor thronged with dancers, Jamie edged around the club toward where the woman had left the stage and slipped into the side corridor away from the main club.

"Hey, this is private. You're not allowed here," a deep voice said, as one of the bouncers stepped from the shadows.

"I need to see O," Jamie said, taking a chance on the name. "It's a personal matter."

The bouncer shrugged, and took a step towards her.

"Sorry lady, it's off limits back here."

Jamie knew this wasn't the time to produce her police credentials, but she was so close.

"Please," she asked, with gentle deliberation. "I'm a fan, and I'm sober and clean. Seriously, I just need to talk to her."

"You're going to have to go back to the club or I'll help you leave." The bouncer sounded final this time, still polite, but dominant.

"Wait," a voice came from down the corridor. Jamie turned to see the woman peering out from one of the doors. "It's OK, Mike. I'll see her."

The bouncer shrugged and stepped back to let Jamie pass.

"Alright, but just call me if you need anything, O."

Jamie walked down the corridor a little way to where the woman stood, the beat of the club fading behind her. O's eyes were a light, cornflower blue, shining with an innocence that jarred with her naked performance of a few minutes before. An ivory robe was loose around her shoulders and one of the octopus tentacles could be seen creeping up her neck, caressing her throat.

"Why did you let me through?" Jamie asked.

O looked at her, and Jamie felt a power in her gaze, as if she could see beyond the surface. Her eyes were much older than the body she wore so well.

"I recognize pain."

Jamie paused, then nodded.

"Then thank you. I'm Jamie."

O stepped aside. "Come in. I'm just getting changed but you're welcome to talk for a while."

Jamie walked into the little space, at once a makeshift powder room for the performance artists and a storage closet. It smelled of old leather with a hint of must and a top note of sandalwood. A long mirror was propped against one wall and Jamie caught sight of her own reflection, scarcely recognizing the gaunt woman in black, harrowed features outlined in kohl. O stood behind her. With her ivory robe, almost white hair and pale features, Jamie felt that she was the demon here and O, an angel.

"Do you know Rowan Day-Conti?" she asked, breaking the momentary silence.

O's eyes met hers, as if chiding her for not asking the deeper questions.

"I heard he'd been arrested," she said, walking a few steps to where a bag hung on the wall. She slipped off the robe and reached for the bag.

Jamie was so close that she could have reached out to touch O's inked, naked skin. On her back, the head of the octopus seemed obscene, its eyes black orbs but still strangely compelling. Jamie wanted to touch it, to touch her. She swallowed. O looked back over her shoulder.

"It's homage," O said, meeting Jamie's gaze and turning, totally secure in her nudity. "The octopus is what you would call my totem animal, a being I feel kinship with."

Jamie nodded, understanding the sentiment and wanting to know more.

"Octopi are so alien to us," O continued, "so unlike our human physiology and yet they have tremendous intelligence. In my country, Norway, there is a legend of the great Kraken, a monster that will sink ships and drag men to the depths. In Japan, there's an artistic tradition depicting violent octopi raping women with thrusting tentacles. And in Hawaiian myth, the octopus is the final survivor from the wreck of the last destroyed universe. So, you see, the image has great power and resonance."

"It's amazing work," Jamie said, "but why ink your body so completely?"

"I can see you're internalizing your pain." O's blue eyes darkened. "Whereas I wear mine on my skin. It reminds me of what I am, of what I've lost." Jamie wanted to hear more, her own troubles briefly forgotten, but O turned away. "Enough of me, Jamie. Why are you here?"

O pulled her clothes from the bag, putting on underwear, a plain t-shirt and jeans. Jamie waited until she was fully dressed, using the time to try and construct a story that didn't reveal too much. Yet she also felt a strange need to be honest with this astonishing woman.

"I saw that Rowan was going to meet with you tonight, and now he's in custody. So I can't talk to him and I was hoping that you might be able to tell me anything you can about his work."

O looked curious. "What, in particular, about his work?"

"I need to know where he gets the bodies, and who buys his finished works."

"Why?' O asked, her face stony now, protecting her friend.

Jamie felt a rising frustration and the feverish headache that had been building couldn't be held back much longer. She couldn't get the image of the dissected little boy out of her mind and she had to be honest, at least about Polly.

"I'm not sure you'll believe me, but my daughter, Polly." Jamie's voice cracked and O's face fell a little, in sympathy. "She died yesterday and her body has been stolen. She bears a resemblance to some of the bodies used in Rowan Day-Conti's artwork and it's the only lead I have right now. I have to find my daughter."

O shook her head slowly, and breathed out, as if making a decision.

"Did you know Jenna Neville?" she asked. Jamie started at the name of the murdered girl.

"Not personally, but I know of her murder and her connection to Rowan. Why?"

O rummaged in her bag and brought out a key.

"I became friends with Jenna, closer friends than with Rowan really. She was investigating Rowan's supplier and his buyers too. She came to me only a few days ago and asked me to keep something for her. Come."

O led the way out of the tiny room, down the corridor away from the club. At the end was another storeroom with lockers in.

"We keep our personal items here when we perform." O explained. "Jenna came to me directly after last week's performance so I left the envelope here." As she unlocked the door, Jamie caught a glimpse of a marine biology textbook and some photos inside. O pulled out a plain blue envelope. "She said she'd received a threat to stop investigating and she wanted to leave this with me instead of carrying it with her. Just in case." O spoke haltingly. "I didn't ask enough about it. I thought she was being overly dramatic, she had that tendency sometimes. But we're used to that here, it's part of the character of the place."

Jamie knew that the envelope should be handled with sterile gloves and placed in an evidence bag. O should be interviewed at the station with proper protocol. All of those thoughts ran through her mind, but there was no time. She would get the envelope to the police in the morning but right now, she had to follow where this path might lead.

"Can you open it now?" Jamie asked.

"I guess Jenna's not coming back for it." Tears welled in O's eyes. "So we might as well."

She tore the top of the envelope and pulled out a wad of white tissue paper. Unfurling it in her hand, O revealed a key. Just plain, no special markings.

"Is there anything else in there?" she asked. "Any indication of what it opens?"

O handed over the envelope and Jamie looked inside, tearing it open for some clue, an address, something. There was nothing.

"I should give this to the police, shouldn't I?" O said. "It might help with her murder investigation. It might even help Rowan, because he can be a bastard, but there's no way he killed her."

"I know he didn't." Jamie said, wrestling with whether to tell O she was with the police. But it would change the dynamic of the situation, betray the woman's trust. Being honest with herself, Jamie wanted O to like her, to see her as an equal, someone who fitted in here. And tonight, Jamie didn't even feel like a cop. She was just another desperate seeker.

"Can I take the key?" she asked, holding her hand out. "I know someone who might be able to find out what it's for."

O hesitated. "What about the police?"

"I think we should leave them out of it for now. Please. They're too busy with the murder to worry about the theft of my daughter's body. I think this key might help."

"If your friend can't find what it's for, then it needs to go to the police," O insisted.

"Of course." Jamie nodded. "First thing tomorrow ... How do I find you again?"

O smiled, the drama returning to her eyes. "I'm a performance artist, darling, you can find me everywhere. Online, in the clubs, on the stage."

Jamie felt she had caught a brief glimpse of who O was beneath the tattoos, but now the veil was drawn again as she returned to her stage persona. But her bold example made Jamie want to ink her own pain into her skin.

"Thanks for your help, O, and I loved the show."

O stepped forward and kissed Jamie gently on the cheek, her lips cool on fevered skin.

"Come back soon," O whispered.

Jamie walked back down the corridor and out of the club, passing the freak show on the dance floor. Her heart was scarred like these bodies, her spirit just as twisted. For a moment, Jamie felt a part of them, with an understanding that the body could be a canvas, an external expression of self. She pulled the motorbike jacket tighter around her as she walked away from the club, out into the London dawn. She needed to find out what the key opened without going through official channels, and there was only one person she could think of to help her.

CHAPTER 18

BLAKE SLUNK INTO BAR-BARIAN, the unobtrusive entrance down an alleyway towards Tottenham Court Road in Soho. They knew him well enough in here, understood his habitual drinking, and didn't question his gloved hands and haunted eyes. There were dark posters on the walls of Arnold Schwarzenegger as Conan and Jane Fonda as Barbarella, their swaggering poses a declaration of confident sexuality. Fake double-edged blades hung glinting in reflected light, homage to an era when the struggle to survive eclipsed cerebral concerns. People came here to edge closer to chaos, to tame the crazy and to forget.

Rock music pumped through the bar, heavy enough to thump the heart in time. Blake found that the beat anchored him to reality and he welcomed the throbbing pulse. Seb, the barman, nodded at him and started pouring before Blake had even sat down on one of the tall stools by the chrome counter. It was always the same. Two shots of tequila and a bottle of Becks.

"Bad day?" Seb said, his voice as caring as any barman interested in his alcoholic customers could be, a tone between solicitous and encouraging so that the pounds were all spent before complete oblivion was reached. Blake used to come to the bar only on bad days, but they seemed to be happening more regularly now. He couldn't stop the visions leaking into his waking consciousness, and his ability to hold them back was weakening.

Tonight he was haunted by the mutated monsters in the bell jars of the Hunterian, their preserved flesh trapping them as undead, floating obscenities. He couldn't stop thinking of the scientific brutality of Mengele cutting into live bodies, seeking his perverted truth in vivisection. Over these nightmares, he watched Jamie dancing the tango but as she spun around, her partner was revealed as the Angel of Death, his teeth stained with blood. They were dancing over the bodies of the damned, her spiked heels piercing flesh, her eyes fixed on a horizon that she would never reach.

Blake thought it curious that his mind was spinning dark fantasy from an amalgamation of the visions, but it also worried him. Jamie was clearly affecting him, and he wanted to both protect her and push her out of his life. Helping her was dangerous, for she was already under his skin. He felt the pull of her pain, as a wrecked ship is pulled down to crushing depths.

Slamming back the tequila shots, one after the other, Blake took a pull of the beer. It chased the fiery liquid down, and Blake visualized it burning his visions and dark thoughts away. He waited for the kick of spirits, sipping the beer, now concentrating on the myriad bottles behind the bar, exotic liquids from far flung countries. Sometimes two shots were enough to chase away the demons that lurked in the corners of his mind, but tonight he needed more. The tequila buzz was dulled by years of habituation. He signaled Seb for another round.

Two more shots and another slow beer.

After a few minutes, Blake finally started to feel his tension soften and a tequila haze began to drown out the noise of his inner world. This is what tequila did for him, more of a drug than mere alcohol, changing his perception of the world into some place brighter. It swept the shadows from the corners of his mind and revealed them to be lies, planted there by the curses of his father.

Without the drink, he was alone in the darkness, sure that his true nature was a twisted, rotting thing feeding off pain and memories of torture. He struggled daily against that perception, and the tequila freed him from the chains of lies that his father had told him as a child. Blake pulled off his gloves and ran the fingers of his right hand over the scars on his left, criss-crossed lines of ivory on his cinnamon skin. These patterns intimately marked him, and he knew every stripe.

He thought back to the long nights on his knees by the altar, his father calling desperately to God for deliverance. As a child, Blake had mistakenly thought to share his visions, puzzled by the mirage he glimpsed, a tableau of the past. His father had gathered the faithful and they had held him down, forced his shaking palms out. His father had whipped his hands, prayers driving him into a violent frenzy. Blake was considered possessed, a child used by the Devil for dark purposes. "And if your right eye offend you, pluck it out and cast it from you," his father would intone, his voice carrying the authority of Christ himself.

Blake's hands were the instrument of the Devil's work, so his hands were punished, caned and whipped until they dripped with blood. His mother had wept hysterically and tried to stop the violence, tried to protect her son, but Blake had believed his father was right. He had to be. The man was a prophet in the Old Testament tradition, a figure of gravitas, strength and unshakeable faith. He was a Jeremiah of the present times, weeping for his people even as he ushered them to God's judgment. When he spoke of possession, others listened. Even Blake.

And so he had taken the beatings, clutching at his

damaged hands, silent tears spilling down his cheeks as he bore the pain. He almost relished the days afterwards while the scars were forming because he couldn't touch anything and he was freed from what he usually saw in the objects of the world. So many times he had thought the visions gone and he was blessed again, then his father would hold him close and praise God for his redemption. But days later, when the wounds were still raw and weeping, Blake would touch something and the visions would return. His father would push him down to his knees and call for the inner circle to pray again, confident in their ability to eventually vanquish the evil in the child.

Blake took another swig of his beer as the memories flooded through his mind. Perhaps the answers to his present despair lay in the past. He remembered the last time, the final escape from the cycle. He had knelt in penance at the altar, listening to the frenetic prayers of the elders, as they called down power from God in the beginnings of the exorcism ritual. As they were praying, Blake had laid his hands on the Bible that they read the lessons from in the center of the church. In a hazy vision, he had seen what these trusted men were doing, the perversions that were hidden by their veneer of holiness. They touched their daughters, they found pleasure in destructive addiction and even his own father wasn't as holy and blameless as he pretended to be. Blake saw the lies and understood that he was only punished as a scapegoat for their own sin, the beatings harder to cover their own guilt.

As the men had turned to lay their hands upon him once more, Blake had seen anticipated pleasure in the eyes of his father's most trusted minister. The man whipped down a cane and split open a recent wound, blood spotting his clothes. Blake saw excitement in his violence and as the pain lanced through him, he knew that this wasn't God's way, but only man's invention. This curse was just the reality of his life, not Satan's hand. Blake had pulled his hands back so the cane missed on its next swipe and stood to face his tormentors. His father's prayers had faltered at his son's audacity and then he began to shout. "Out, Satan. Leave my boy." But in that moment, Blake had seen eye to eye with his father. During the years of repeated abuse, he had grown into a young man and they had no power to keep him there anymore.

Blake had walked out of that church and never returned to his parent's life. His father was still preaching messages of judgment, destruction and apocalypse; his mother was still in thrall to her prophet. The visions wouldn't leave him, and so Blake had tried to live with them, adapt them to a useful life in his museum research. He had to believe that a normal life was still possible. Blake turned back to the bar and signaled Seb for more tequila.

The fifth shot.

This was the one Blake craved, because this was when the visions of reality finally left him and he slipped into memory loss. A little brain death never hurt anyone, he thought, slamming it back. Swallowing it down, he breathed out in relief, feeling the prick of tears behind his eyes, from the alcohol or his morbid thoughts, he didn't really know which anymore. He blinked the tears back, wondering where the rush of emotion had come from. He didn't want to care for Jamie, didn't want the complication of her in his life. He looked around the bar, searching for the kind of oblivion that could easily be found on a night in London.

The bar turned into a nightclub as it grew later, full of girls in tight tops, hair loose about their faces, taut stomachs curving down into fitted jeans. Blake turned on the stool to watch a girl dancing, appreciating the glimpse of soft flesh, wanting to lay his head there and forget. Young men circled around the edges, predators waiting for the sedation of alcohol to lower inhibitions. But Blake knew that there were women just as predatory, and there was a point when tequila turned him into willing prey. Women were drawn to him, the very fact that he generally avoided them was nectar that drew them in. Like cats, some women were best attracted by a kind of detachment, an inattention they had to conquer. Blake knew his bone structure helped, for sure, and despite his lack of care, his body was strong and muscular, clinging to life even as his mind struggled to escape it.

A woman danced closer and then leaned into him, her long blonde hair reflecting the spotlights. Her eyes were sultry, inviting.

"Dance with me," she whispered, placing her hand on Blake's chest. He felt a surge of desire, a need to bury himself within her and forget this day. He stood and pulled her towards him as a heavy bass rocked them. His hands slid down to cup her buttocks and tug her closer. He felt the tendrils of her life knocking against the walls of his vision but the tequila haze kept them far enough away and Blake reveled in the release.

The woman smelled of vanilla and coconut and he breathed in her scent. Then the woman's hands were inside his shirt, touching the muscles on his tight stomach and edging downwards. It was permission: all he had to do was bend to her mouth and tonight he could lose himself in her.

Lifting his head, he caught sight of their reflection in one of the barbarian blades, just another couple desperate to lose themselves for a few hours. London was full of this need, an attempt to stave off loneliness, even though in the morning there was so often regret. Under his close-cropped hair, Blake saw the shadows under his eyes, making his face even more angular. He looked haunted and there was no escaping, least of all from himself. Even the fifth tequila could not drown his life right now.

"I'm sorry," he whispered to the woman and opened his arms to let her go. She shook her head slowly but in her eyes was a crazy need and she backed into the dancing crowd. She wouldn't be alone tonight, but Blake felt that he should be.

CHAPTER 19

JAMIE PULLED UP IN front of the tall terraced houses of Bloomsbury, distinctive in this area of gentrified London. Street lamps lit the quiet streets with a glow that only seemed to accentuate the fog of chill air in the hour before dawn. The area was dotted by large garden squares, many of them locked for residents only, but Jamie could just make out the trees of Bloomsbury Square Gardens, where in the summer, students and tourists lazed by opulent flowerbeds.

She wondered how Blake could afford a place here, right around the corner from the British Museum. The area was saturated in history and academic brilliance, from the London School of Hygiene and Tropical Medicine, to the Royal Academy of Dramatic Art and the University of London. It had been made famous by the Bloomsbury Set, an influential group of British writers, artists and intellectuals including Virginia Woolf, EM Forster and John Maynard Keynes, luminaries who had lived or worked here during the early twentieth century. Jamie looked up at the blue plaques on the houses in front of her, marking places of historical significance across London, littering this district with great names from British history. Darwin and Dickens once lived here, as did JM Barrie, whose

Peter Pan visited Wendy Darling amongst these rooftops. Jamie smiled as she remembered Polly finding that out on the internet after they had read the book together. Her daughter had always wanted to know more, never satisfied with what was on the surface. The memory stung her with a jolt of grief and she caught her breath, willing it to pass.

Now she was here, Jamie desperately wanted to ring Blake's bell and get him out of bed, to plead for his help. But she knew she looked like a crazy Goth, and at this time in the morning he was unlikely to be conducive to helping her on unofficial business. Jamie slumped on the bike, her shoulders dropping as a wave of tiredness hit her. The ride from the club and the thrill of finding a clue had invigorated her, but now she felt unsure. Should she just take the key straight to Cameron and the investigation team? But then what? Jamie suddenly felt very alone.

She heard footsteps and looking up, she saw a figure weaving up the street, his silhouette familiar. As he drew closer, Jamie realized that it was Blake, and he was singing something unintelligible in an actually half-decent voice. He was definitely drunk and, as he reached his door, Jamie made a decision. She got off the bike and holding her helmet, ran across the quiet street.

"Blake," she said, as she approached. He spun round to see who it was, his face confused for a moment as he looked at her. "Hi Blake, it's Jamie."

He squinted at her, then grinned and the smile transformed his face, like a little boy proudly showing off his skills.

"Jamie ... hot Detective. You're really here?" He shook his head in wonder, like she was the fulfillment of some kind of wish. "Wow, you're looking... hot tonight. Love the black. Very alternative you."

His cobalt blue eyes raked over her body and Jamie could see his blatant appreciation, the alcohol preventing any form of inhibition. He stammered into silence as Jamie met his eyes, bemused. She was definitely stepping over the line being here with him in this state, but she needed his unique talent. If she took the key to Cameron, it could disappear into evidence for days and she needed to find what Jenna had hidden before the Lyceum deadline tonight.

"Why are you here?" Blake asked. "It's a bit late for me to help on police business tonight and I ... may have had a few drinks." He finished in a loud whisper. "Sorry."

Jamie stepped closer to him.

"I need your help, Blake, but it's not for the police right now. It's for the case but I'm investigating it separately." Blake looked confused. Jamie shook her head. "It doesn't really matter, but it's urgent and I need you to do a reading."

"Shh. Keep your voice down," Blake hushed her. "I don't like to talk about that in the open. You'd better come up."

He fumbled in his inner pockets and pulled out his wallet and key fob. His hands were bare and the scars reflected light from the street lamps. Jamie thought of the body art at Torture Garden, self-inflicted shades of pain that revealed inner lives. But Blake's weren't artistic markings, they were violent cuts, evidence of another wounded soul. For a moment, she wanted to reach out and trace the lines.

Blake managed to get the key in the lock, pushed open the door and led the way into a darkened hallway. There were a number of doors leading to inner flats and a staircase heading upwards.

"This way," Blake whispered, pointing at the staircase. "I'm right at the top."

He took the lead, swaying a little on the way up and Jamie wondered if he would be any use at all for reading. Part of her doubted it would work, but right now she would take any help she could get. At the top was a tiny landing and one faded red door.

Blake turned another key in the lock and pushed open the door for Jamie to enter. The space was small but neatly laid out with a few pieces of wooden furniture, creating a homely feel. Jamie was immediately captivated.

"It's not much," Blake said, "but I can't resist living in a real artist's garret in Bloomsbury. It's my spiritual home." He pointed to the large window. "Check out the view."

Jamie walked three steps to cross the flat and gaze out the window, over the rooftops to the moon shining above the chimneys and spires of London. Jamie thought of Polly, flying off to Never-Never Land across these skies. She turned.

"I'm sorry to come to you privately like this, but I need help with something." She reached inside her jeans pocket and pulled out the key. "I need you to read this. I have to find what it unlocks, because I think there's information there that I need urgently and time is critical."

Blake rubbed his head and then sat heavily on the bed, his eyes drooping with tiredness.

"I'd love to help you, Jamie, but this is the way I numb the visions. This is how I kill them. The finest tequila will always crowd out any demons that threaten my peace. Please don't ask me to try and pierce the happy haze." He looked up at her and Jamie caught a glimpse of the little boy again, asked to do things he didn't want to and then punished for it anyway. But she pushed aside her guilt.

"But can you?" she asked, desperate to know what might be possible.

"I don't know. I don't want to know." He shook his head. "You don't realize what my life is like. The visions come to me unwanted, unasked for. I see too much, Jamie, and this is how I numb them." He gazed out the window, speaking softly. "But it's taking more and more tequila these days. I don't know what will kill me first, the madness or the booze."

Jamie felt a surge of pity, for whatever Blake heard and saw, it was real to him. Whether it was mental illness, a supernatural gift, or a part of the brain he could access that most could not, she didn't know. But she could see that he was hurting and alone, and she recognized her own torment in that state. Part of her wanted to pull him to her, to soothe their pain together but instead, she sat next to him on the bed, careful not to touch him.

"My daughter, Polly, died yesterday." Jamie's throat tightened with emotion. She heard Blake's intake of breath but she kept staring out the window, wanting to tell him the story. "She's been ill a long time with a genetic disease, but she was only 14. Too young to die, even though we'd been preparing for it for years. I wanted to say goodbye in the way she had chosen, a cremation where she could be released to the sky and then her ashes buried to bloom into flowers. She knew exactly what would happen after she died." Jamie stopped and turned to Blake, looking into his eyes. "But her body has been stolen and I have to get it back."

"No," Blake gasped. "Seriously, what are the police doing?"

"They'll do their best, but I can't be a part of the official investigation as I'm too close to it, and I can't just sit around and wait."

Blake shook his head. "Of course ... but that's just awful, Jamie. I'm so sorry."

Jamie heard the truth of his concern in Blake's voice. Yet how could this man care so much for her so quickly? She remembered he had seen Polly in his vision of her. He had felt her pain, and his empathy scared her. This man knew her inner world and yet they had only just met. Jamie felt laid bare, part of her wanting to run out the door right now and never see him again, because she didn't let people get this close. It was the way to ensure she was never hurt again, but she couldn't run. She had sought Blake out, and she needed his help.

She stood and walked to the window.

"I think Polly's body was stolen because of what I've been investigating on the Jenna Neville case," Jamie said. "I thought perhaps you might be able to help and I can't wait until morning. This is urgent, Blake."

He considered for a moment. "Tell me about this key."

"It was Jenna's and she gave it to a friend. I only found it an hour ago and if I give it to the police, the processing will take too much time. But if you read it, we might be able to find the place it belongs to. It might lead me to Polly's body, Blake, and perhaps help me to solve Jenna's murder. They have to be related." Jamie paused, and then decided to tell Blake as much as she knew. There was nothing to lose anymore. "Jenna Neville had noted something called the Lyceum in her diary for tonight. She also had articles on body snatching at her office, marked with an L, and she was warned off investigating them. I think that what she discovered led to her death, and I think they have Polly's body too." Her voice cracked a little. "I can't stand the thought of them cutting up my daughter's body like a specimen for their cabinet of curiosities. I can't let that happen to Polly and so, I really need you, because I don't know what else to do right now."

"The specimens in the museum … the mutilation of dead bodies … Mengele and the dissections. Oh, Jamie," Blake said, his voice betraying horror at the possibilities. Even through the fog of tequila she could see he understood the parallels. "You think the same people have Polly's body? And if they do, they will …" He went silent for a moment, and Jamie saw his eyes darken. " Of course, I'll try to help." Blake dropped his head to his hands. "Shit. This is serious. I guess I can try but I've never read after this much tequila before. That's kind of the point."

Jamie nodded. "I understand, but anything you can give me is better than nothing. This is the only clue I have. Please try."

"I'm not promising anything but put it on the table." He pointed to a low table at the side of the room under the window. It was dark wood, plain, with nothing on it. "Give me a minute."

Blake stood and walked into the adjoining tiny bathroom, shutting the door behind him. Jamie placed the key on the table with some reverence, hoping like hell he could get something from it. There was a part of her that was screaming disorder at this whole process, the skeptical part of her, the police officer who at least tried to play by the rules most of the time. That part of her wanted to run out of there, hand the key over and leave it to the investigation team.

But Jamie knew the system. She knew that, however hard the police worked, there were priorities, and investigation according to protocol took time. Time she didn't have, and after all, she was Polly's mother, her protector in life and death and her daughter was not resting in peace. The image of her body on a slab, like the little boy at Day-Conti's studio, dominated her mind.

Blake emerged, his hair wet from splashing his face.

"Do you want coffee?" Jamie asked. "Would that help?"

Blake shook his head. "Not at this point. Just sit quietly while I read and note down anything I say. I can't promise much, though."

Jamie nodded and sat on the bed, a piece of paper and pen on her lap as Blake knelt in front of the table. From behind he looked like a penitent, praying at a shrine to emptiness. He breathed in and out slowly, rolling his shoulders around in an attempt to relax. He picked up the key. Jamie waited, trying to breathe quietly, not moving for fear of breaking whatever trance state he went into.

Blake was silent for nearly two minutes before he spoke. "Corinthian columns. Yellow."

Jamie frowned, writing it down.

"Looks like a church or a temple, but definitely yellow." Blake's voice was strained as if he were peering into the gloomy distance. "She's worried, afraid. She knows something she shouldn't. More yellow." Blake paused. "Green apple." He went silent for a moment and then put down the key. He turned on his knees to look at Jamie, his face distraught. "Sorry, that's it. There's an overwhelming sense of yellow. I don't know whether that helps but there's no deeper level on an object like this. It's a new key with only her imprint, but it's all so faint."

Jamie felt disappointed at what he had told her. His words seemed like impossible clues.

"Look," Blake said, "Why don't you stay here and use my laptop to do some online research. I need a couple of hours' sleep but then I can try again. Or you could go home and come back later."

Jamie thought about her empty flat, Polly's belongings reminding her of everything she had lost. "I'd like to stay, if that's OK. You've given me a few things to check out … if you don't mind."

"Sure. There's coffee and a bit of food in the kitchen. Help yourself. I'll sleep like the dead so you won't wake me with any noise." He stopped, realizing what he'd said. "Sorry, that was a stupid thing to say."

Jamie shook her head, smiling at him gently. "It's alright, seriously, go to sleep. I can see you need it."

"You look like you could do with some too," Blake said softly, and Jamie felt the deep fatigue that had seeped into her body over the long night. She shook her head.

"There'll be time for that later when I've found my daughter."

Blake logged onto his laptop and Jamie sat at his plain

IKEA desk with a side lamp on, her back to the bed as she heard the rustle of him taking off his jeans and slipping under the covers. There was a curious intimacy between them, and she felt a moment of wanting his comfort. If she went to him now, what would he do? Jamie knew that she would shatter with physical touch, grief would pour from her and the waves of desolation would crash against them both.

She pulled herself together and went to the bathroom. She washed her face, wiping off the black makeup until she was scrubbed clean. Emerging quietly, Jamie listened to the noises of the house. The pipes groaned and there were creaks, the sounds of an old area, a good house. Outside, she could hear the city waking up, buses going past and cars starting up.

At the laptop, Jamie opened Google and went to the Maps application. She went to London and zoomed in to a scale that showed where Jenna Neville had worked and where she had lived South of the river. She added in the Torture Garden Club in East London. It was a good few square miles, but not exhaustive. As she studied the screen, there was a meow at the window and a faint scratching. Jamie looked up to see a black cat with white paws and a cheek smudge pawing at the glass. On the windowsill she noticed a saucer with a little dry food. So Blake was a cat person, bonding with the independent. She smiled and got up to open the window a little way so the cat could wend its way in.

"Hello, puss," Jamie whispered, stroking as it nibbled at the food. It butted up against her hand. She smiled and picked it up, holding it close to her face, feeling its warmth. There was something therapeutic about stroking. The Lavender Hospice used animals as part of their therapy for the children, although perhaps the parents needed it more. She carried the cat back to the desk and sat down, stroking it firmly on her lap. It circled a little, kneading its paws and then settled against her. Jamie was glad for its companionship. She caressed the cat with one hand and with the other doodled on the pad where she had written Blake's words.

She tried to put herself in Jenna's shoes. She had needed somewhere to keep secrets from her flatmate, her parents, her work, basically away from anyone. Jenna certainly had a trust problem, Jamie thought, and she could relate to that. But what could be so secret that it was worth killing her for?

If it was some files, like Jenna had at work, they could be kept within a small locker. Jamie wrote down locker, then brainstormed options around that. The threat of terrorists meant that most train and bus stations no longer had lockers, and libraries and gyms cleared them out most nights. Jamie wrote down 'gym' since sometimes they rented lockers long term, but whatever Jenna was hiding might not be something so small. The key could unlock a safe or even something as big as another flat. Despite her activism, Jenna still had money, so that wouldn't have been a problem.

Jamie nuzzled down onto the cat's head.

"Too many options, puss," she whispered, stroking it and feeling its purr resonate through her.

Maybe she should just try using the words Blake had given her.

She typed "yellow + lockup" into Google.

The first results were technical errors for Ubuntu software, yellow lockups on splash pages. She scrolled down to Skull Candy yellow lockup belts and yellow transmission belts, becoming lost in the technical rabbit hole she had stumbled into. But further down, Jamie found Big Yellow Self Storage, a company with lockup space of all sizes dotted around the country and with a number of sites in

London. Jamie felt a wave of excitement run through her. It fitted, now she just had to narrow the location down. After a few more mouse clicks, she found there were a few units around the places Jenna lived and worked and also near Torture Garden.

Using Google Maps street view, Jamie started to examine the pictures of the locations. The minutes ticked by as she virtually walked the streets of London, using the technology to view snapshots in time.

Then she saw it.

Opposite the New Cross storage facility was the Lewisham Arthouse, featuring a classical entranceway with a large door framed by Corinthian columns, fitting Blake's description. Jamie virtually walked down the street a little way and found a pub called the Flower of Kent. On the sign above the door was a picture of a tree and a green apple on the ground under it, representing the tree under which Newton had been sitting when the apple fell, giving him the idea for the law of gravity. It had to be the place.

Jamie checked the opening time for the storage facility. 8am. It was only 6.40am now, so she could be there when it opened. Looking behind her at the bed, she could see a mound of covers under which Blake slept silently. She still found his ability disturbing and it wasn't admissible in court, but anything she found at the site would be. She could keep the secret of how she found the place but she could still give the key and the address to the investigation team after she'd discovered what was inside.

She wrote a short note to Blake saying thank you and that she would call him, that he was a star. He'd probably read it and wonder what the hell he'd done the night before under the tequila influence. Jamie rose and gave the cat another cuddle, relishing its warm body for a moment longer. She put it down gently on the chair, stroking it so it settled into her warm patch. Then she let herself out of the flat, pulling the door quietly shut behind her.

CHAPTER 20

JAMIE PARKED THE BIKE down a side street off the main road of Lewisham Way. There was still some time before the storage office opened so she walked down and got a takeaway coffee from a service station. She poured two sugars into it and grabbed a Mars bar at the same time. The spike of sugar and caffeine would keep her going just a little bit longer.

She sat on the steps of the Arthouse looking at the Yellow storage units, and wondered what Jenna had hidden here. What was so secret that she kept her research away from her work and home life? And would there be clues to the location of the Lyceum?

At five to eight, Jamie watched a car pull up and a woman reach out the window to key in a code on the main gate. The gate swung open and a few minutes later Jamie saw her unlock and enter the office. At exactly one minute past eight, Jamie walked across the road and rang the bell.

"We're not quite open yet. Can you wait five minutes?" The voice was hassled, clearly annoyed to be buzzed so early.

"I'm from the police," Jamie said, deciding to approach with official credentials, omitting the fact she was off the investigation. "Detective Sergeant Jamie Brooke. I need to speak with you about one of the storage units."

"Oh," the voice sounded unsurprised. "Of course, come on in."

A buzzer sounded and the pedestrian gate clicked open. Jamie walked in and showed the manager her warrant card. The woman was in her mid-forties, Asian, her dark hair tied back into a ponytail. She had the efficient air of a born organizer, and she nodded at the credentials, clearly used to dealing with the police.

"How can I help you, Detective?" she asked. "There hasn't been a break-in, not that I know of. We had one last year, but you can't be here about that."

"I'm actually investigating a murder, and it looks like the victim had a locker here. I need to see inside."

The woman looked at once appalled and intrigued. The cop shows on TV made people want to be part of crime scenes these days.

"Of course, we have strict privacy regulations here but …" Jamie could see the interest in the woman's eyes. "What was the victim's name?"

For a moment Jamie wondered if Jenna could have used a fake name, but there were so many rules around multiple forms of ID, it was unlikely.

"Jenna Neville."

The woman tapped on her computer. "Yes, I have her here. Number 714. It's a mid-size lockup, able to store a three-bedroom house worth of stuff."

Jamie pulled the key from her pocket. "Would this be the key for it?"

The woman glanced up. "Oh no, they're all number coded on a keypad, but I can let you in with the override. I'll take you right up."

As Jamie wondered what the key could actually be for, the manager led the way through the sterile complex, the bright yellow walls only serving to highlight the dead space. Full of secrets, Jamie imagined. What else might be hiding in the corners of this place? What stories would be revealed by the objects within?

On the second floor, at the very back of the complex, the manager stopped in front of one of the myriad yellow doors. She tapped a code into the keypad and the door clicked.

"Go ahead, Detective," she said. "I'll leave you to it. Just come and check with me before you leave."

Jamie nodded, wondering at her lack of curiosity about what might be inside. Perhaps it wore off after years of working here. She listened to the woman's footsteps receding down the hallway, echoing around the empty space. She imagined Jenna coming here alone, keeping the location quiet and not trusting anyone with the information inside. Blake had said that she was afraid, worried, when she held the key, and Jamie felt the same way right now. She was afraid to go in, because the contents might not be enough to give her the answers she needed. What if this didn't lead her to Polly? What would she do then?

Jamie pulled on a pair of sterile gloves, took a deep breath and pulled the door open. The space was about six foot wide, almost the same deep, with a high ceiling so that boxes could be stacked up. The only thing on the floor was a heavy metal safe and Jamie felt for the key in her pocket. She stepped inside the unit and saw that the walls were plastered with images and maps. Here was Jenna's extensive research spread out and expanded, and Jamie could see that the notes she had seen in the legal office were just a tiny part of the whole.

There were newspaper cuttings about crimes involving bodies, notes on art shows using body parts, photos of teratology specimens, historical references to John Hunter and other anatomists, as well as gruesome pictures of anatomy and quotes from legal papers on the rights of the body. On one wall was pinned the logo of Neville Pharmaceuticals and radiating out from it were all kinds of documents and sticky notes, curling at the edges. There were pictures of vivisections and animal cruelty as well as a photocopy of a very old newspaper article about the violent death of a PhD student at Oxford, back when the Nevilles were students. There was a photo of Esther Neville, looking pale and gaunt, her arm thrust out to obscure the view of the camera. It wasn't the type of picture that a daughter would usually want to keep of her mother.

Clearly, Jenna had quite a story here. Jamie couldn't quite work out all the links but it was far bigger than she expected. She couldn't keep this from the police investigation, but she could get a head start on finding the Lyceum. Pulling the key from her pocket, Jamie squatted down and opened the safe. With her heart beating in anticipation, she pulled open the metal door.

Inside were a just couple of pieces of paper. Jamie knew that she was breaking all the rules of police investigation but she was well past caring at this point. She had to know what was going on. Carefully lifting the top paper from the pile, Jamie unfolded it. A photocopy of a title deed for a piece of land in West Wycombe. Jamie frowned, not seeing any immediate significance, for there was no mention of the Lyceum.

"Found something?" The voice made her jump and she looked up, startled, her posture immediately defensive and shielding the safe.

It was Blake, holding two cups of coffee. His body was slouched against the door, languid confidence in his stance and Jamie couldn't help noticing how good he looked, all tousled and sleep-rumpled.

"Damn it, Blake," she said, "How did you find me?"

"Browser history." He shrugged. "I woke up and found you gone but your note had me hooked. Plus, I want to help you."

Jamie's eyes softened as she stood to take the coffee from him. Her fingers touched his gloved hand briefly and even through the cloth she could feel a spark between them. She realized that she was actually glad to see him.

"Thanks." She smiled up at him. "How's the hangover?"

Blake blushed a little. "I'm sorry you had to see me like that. When the visions get too much I have to escape. Tequila is the easiest, more effective way I know to tame the crazy. I hope I didn't say anything … inappropriate?"

"Of course not." Jamie took a sip of the coffee. "But I'm not sure that pickling yourself in tequila is a long-term life strategy."

"You can talk," he said, grinning. "Riding around town like some kind of vampire Goth when you should be looking after yourself."

He paused, his eyes full of compassion. "I'm so sorry about your daughter."

Jamie turned to the wall, hiding the tears pricking her eyes.

"Thank you … Well, since you're here, what do you think?"

"It's definitely yellow," Blake said. "A bit bright for me at this point."

Jamie pointed to the collage.

"Check this out. It's on body snatching, and it looks like a full-scale investigation into her parents' past and the history of Neville Pharmaceuticals."

Blake came to stand next to her, close in the small space. He smelled of spicy soap and coffee and Jamie felt a sudden desire to lean into his tall frame. She pushed away the feelings.

"Wow, this is some serious investigative work," he said. "She was a journalist?"

"A lawyer," Jamie said, "but this is personal. That's her mother and that there is her father." She pointed at the aristocratic portrait of Christopher Neville, dressed in his regalia for the House of Lords but with his head turned towards the camera in a smile. The photo was softer, more emotionally resonant, than the one of Esther. Her choice of image painted him as someone Jenna had loved. But had he ultimately betrayed her?

Turning her head, Jamie caught a glimpse of another face she recognized.

"That's Edward Mascuria," she whispered. "He works for the Nevilles."

Jenna's research wall had linked him to various projects at Neville Pharma and there was a picture of him with Esther, an obsequious look on his face as she presented him with some award. Jamie remembered how she had felt in his flat, a crawling across her flesh, the look on his face that she had glimpsed as she rode away.

"What was on the document in the safe?" Blake asked, interrupting her train of thought, his head on one side to examine the material tacked up on the other wall.

"A property deed," Jamie said. "For land in West Wycombe. I'm not sure what it means yet."

They were silent for a moment as they continued to scan the densely packed walls of information.

"I think you should look at this," Blake said.

Jamie turned to look at the montage, the word Lyceum scrawled in the center of the mass in Jenna's looped handwriting. The images circling it were cut from old newspapers and magazines, others printed from the internet. They showed bacchanalian scenes of orgies and feasting, sacrificing to the Devil, sex on altars and then in one, a corpse being cut up and dissected as figures copulated around it, faces distorted by lust. A chill crept over Jamie's skin.

"What is this?" she said, a frown creasing her brow as she bent closer to examine the pictures, trying to work out what they were about.

"Look here," Blake said. "It says that the Hellfire Club had its headquarters in caves under the hills of West Wycombe. This picture shows a map of the cave system and Jenna's research seems to point to this as the meeting place for the Lyceum."

Jamie looked confused. "I'm sure I've heard of the Hellfire Club before."

"It's infamous," Blake said. "It's been in lots of films and books, but it was actually a real club. Back in the eighteenth century, it was established by Sir Francis Dashwood under the motto *'Fais ce que tu voudras'* or *'Do what you want'* and history is rife with rumors of what they did down there in the dark, beyond the reach of the law."

Jamie looked at one image, a man carving his own heart from his chest and offering it to a laughing figure, who bent with jaws open to bite into it.

"If they met in the caves back then, maybe they still do now. So who owns it?"

She turned and bent to the safe again, removing the title deed to look at it more closely. It was registered to the Neville Foundation, one of the many holding companies of the Nevilles.

"I still don't know what's going on," Jamie said, rubbing her eyes. "But clearly Jenna linked the Lyceum to this location and her family. Maybe she challenged them about it. Maybe she threatened to expose them."

"And that may have been what got her killed," Blake said, turning to her. He was so close inside the unit and as he looked down at Jamie, his blue eyes showed deep concern. Jamie felt the weariness of the last twenty-four hours pressing upon her, the emotional exhaustion and the edge of physical collapse. All she wanted to do was lean into his strength and wait for him to put his arms around her. She could sense an attraction between them, even in these desperate times, despite her overwhelming need to find Polly.

Jamie bit her lip, the stab of pain helping her to refocus. "According to Jenna's diary, the Lyceum meets tonight."

There was a beat of silence.

"You want to go, don't you?" Blake said finally. Jamie didn't respond, staring at the images in front of her. "But I think it's time to let your friends in the police deal with this."

She looked at her watch.

"There's no time," she whispered.

Blake took her hands in his gloved ones, spinning her towards him.

"No, it's too dangerous. You can't go. Think of your daughter. She wouldn't want you to put yourself in danger like this."

Jamie snatched her hands away.

"I *am* thinking of Polly," she shouted, tears spilling from her eyes. "I'm only thinking of her."

Blake turned and banged his fist on the wall, the metallic sound echoing through the empty corridors. His face betrayed his frustration and Jamie was surprised at his vehemence, but she also felt a flicker of gratitude that he cared enough to protest.

"I need to call this in," she said. "So the police team can get round here and follow the new leads. But I know they won't be fast enough to get to the Lyceum tonight. There's too much information to process. I have to go myself."

"I'll come with you, then," Blake said, his eyes pleading.

Jamie sighed. "Thank you for your support, seriously. But I need to do this alone."

"You don't have to do everything alone, Jamie." He took a step closer to her. "Taking the world onto your shoulders will only crush you unless you let people help ... people who care."

At another time, Jamie knew that she would have leaned into his embrace, but she felt her resolve would crack if he touched her. The deep grief she was barely holding in check would break over them both and she would never stop crying. She had to keep it together, and being alone was the only way.

She stepped back, her face stony and her voice cold.

"I'm a police officer, Blake. This is my job and I know what I'm doing. You wouldn't be of any use."

He looked at her and she held his gaze, unflinching.

"Fine." Blake's voice was curt, his jaw tight with emotion. Jamie almost begged him to stay, craving his strength and support. Instead, she turned to look at the wall again, studying the images there without seeing. "I'll leave you to it then."

Blake walked out of the lockup and took a few steps down the corridor, then stopped. Jamie thought he was going to turn and say something. Perhaps that's all it would take to break her resolve. But then he walked on, without looking back.

When his footsteps had faded to nothing, Jamie took a deep breath and put her thoughts of Blake aside. She used her smart phone to carefully photograph the evidence that Jenna had collected: the title deed, the photos of key suspects and some of the newspaper cuttings. Jamie was convinced that Cameron or someone at the department was trying to frame Day-Conti, but this evidence would surely get him released and the investigation refocused on the Nevilles.

She called Missinghall, knowing that she couldn't direct this to Cameron in case he really was involved with the Nevilles. The phone rang three times before he picked up.

"Jamie, are you OK? I heard about the theft of your daughter's body. I'm so sorry."

"Thanks Al, I think it's related to the Jenna Neville case, but I need you to keep that quiet for now."

A beat of silence as her words sunk in. "Sure, but shouldn't you be resting or something? This is a difficult time for you, Jamie."

"I have to work, Al, there's no time for me to wait around, and I've found new evidence you need to get the team onto."

"Are you at the scene? I'll come over right now. Shit. How are we going to handle this?"

"Nothing to handle," Jamie said. "I'll text you the address and you get started."

"Won't you be there when we arrive?"

She was silent.

"Jamie? Where are you going? Seriously, what are you up to?"

Jamie knew her actions were reckless, crazy, but mostly she didn't care anymore. She had nothing more to lose.

"I can't tell you yet Al, but I'll call it in when I can."

"Then at least be careful, and let me know if I can help."

"Later, then," Jamie said and ended the call.

With some cleaning materials she found down the hallway, Jamie wiped any fingerprints from the key so that O and Blake's involvement couldn't be traced. She knew it was tampering with evidence but with her suspicions of Cameron, she couldn't have them under suspicion and her actions were for a greater good. She placed the key on top of the safe and then left the lockup, telling the manager on the way out that her team would be coming along later that day.

CHAPTER 21

AS JAMIE TRAVELED WEST along the motorway out of London, she felt a sense of purpose again, as if by moving she could outrun the pain of Polly's loss. She had briefly gone home to shower, change and pack a small rucksack, expecting to be away for the night and in need of a torch and other gear for investigating further. She had also downed another coffee and taken several more ephedrine tablets. Jamie felt the beginnings of shakiness from the sleep deprivation and the pills, but she was also running on a kind of nervous energy that fueled her need to go on. She couldn't rest until this was over.

The M40 motorway was busy, but her bike helped her to navigate the snarls in traffic, and soon Jamie reached the turnoff for High Wycombe. Dominated by industrial warehouses, there was still evidence of the medieval market town amongst the concrete modernity. As Jamie rode through the outskirts, she caught sight of the Neville Pharmaceuticals logo on some of the warehouse buildings: they were one of the biggest employers in the area.

She continued out of the town towards the village of West Wycombe in the Chilterns, and even this close to the motorway the English countryside welcomed her. Jamie rode under a great canopy of beechwood trees, grey-green trunks stretching high, bare branches reaching to the sky forming a guard of honor. A cool winter sun dappled patches on the road and Jamie felt a touch of its rays like a blessing.

As she entered the village of West Wycombe, Jamie realized that the Hellfire Caves were now a popular tourist attraction, and her hopes sank as she realized the Lyceum couldn't possibly meet somewhere so public. Parking the bike, she walked up to the entranceway of the caves. It was designed as a Gothic church, with tall arched windows revealing the wooded forest behind, a cathedral revering nature. Jamie hesitated at the entrance, then decided to take a tour anyway. If there was nothing here, she would have to revisit all of the evidence in the photos but why else would Jenna have the title deeds in the safe? This location had to be important.

As she stood waiting for the tour, cold air seeped into Jamie's bones, sapping her energy further. She shivered. Was this just a wild goose chase? Right now, the only clues she had that could lead to Polly pointed at these caves. There must be something down here that would help her with the next steps.

A guide gathered a group of woolen-wrapped tourists together and Jamie joined them.

"Welcome to the Hellfire Caves," the guide said. "Originally of ancient origin, these caves were extended in the 1740s by Sir Francis Dashwood. They were dug by villagers in need of employment and you can still see the pick axe marks on the walls. Here's your maps." She handed out a page. "You won't get lost, just follow the guide ropes and it's well lit. But watch out for the ghosts." She smiled, trying to inject some enthusiasm into her voice but Jamie caught an edge of boredom there. Another day, another tourist. Our lives are so dominated by minutiae, Jamie reflected, the day to day, never-ending grind. She could understand the attraction of something secret and exclusive, where people felt special and chosen. Membership of such societies was common across all cultures, but more so amongst the rich and powerful with time and money to spare. The Freemasons, and indeed, the Hellfire Club, had counted some of the most senior British aristocrats and statesmen of the time as members.

Jamie looked down at the little map, and waited until the rest of the group had gone in before she entered. She wanted to sense how the place felt without others around and she couldn't cope with the noise of tourists intruding into her thoughts. Part of her was breaking inside, desperate to hold Polly's body in her arms again, but she had to assume the mantle of the detective and focus on being objective.

She stepped inside the entranceway and began to walk down the slight incline, the ground hard under her feet. The temperature was warmer in the caves as they retained the heat and in the winter were more comfortable than the air outside. A straight entrance tunnel led to a small cave, stacked with tools similar to those used by the eighteenth century workers. Jamie looked at the picks and crowbars, wondering whether they might have seen violence beyond digging in the caves.

Walking on into Paul Whitehead's chamber, Jamie read the notes next to the grand urn and bust of the man. A steward of the Hellfire Club, Whitehead had left his heart to Sir Francis Dashwood. A mental image of the dying man suddenly came to Jamie, Whitehead's chest cracked open so his still pulsing heart could be ripped from his body. She shook her head. Where did these thoughts come from? She shivered, realizing that the temperature in the caves had dropped as she descended. Reading on, she noted that Whitehead's ghost was thought to watch over the caves, remaining with the desiccated relic of his heart.

The man had protected the club in life, even burning papers containing evidence that might have revealed the Hellfire activities just before he died.

Walking deeper into the caves, Jamie entered Franklin's Cave. The American Founding Father and polymath, Benjamin Franklin, had been a great admirer of Dashwood and his diaries revealed that he had visited the caves, although not as an official member of the Club. Further on was the Banqueting Hall, forty feet in diameter with statues of classical figures in chalk niches. In between the wider caverns, tunnels were shaped into beautiful Gothic arches, giving the impression of an underground castle. There were dark portals off the side of the main corridor, shut off with rope and No Entry signs. Jamie decided to check further into one, but just beyond the light of the lamp, the tunnel had a metal gate, heavily reinforced and locked. Jamie shook the bars, testing their strength, wondering what was in the caves beyond her sight. What went on here after dark when the tourists left?

Navigating the tunnels hacked into the chalk, Jamie finally reached a small waterway that ran through the caves. It was studded with stalactites that hung from the ceiling, twisted shapes dripping stagnant water into a stream. Named the River Styx, it represented the boundary between the living and the dead in ancient Greek mythology, where the wrathful drowned each other for eternity in Dante's Hell. It could only be crossed by paying the ferryman with coins that were laid on the eyes of the dead. At the end of the channel was the Cursing Well, where a strange mist hung over a pool, like the fetid breath of slimy creatures dwelling in the shadows. The lights flickered and Jamie felt her pulse race. She felt as if she was being watched, as if footsteps followed her into the bowels of the cave system. She looked behind her. There was no one, but she was suddenly eager to get out of the eerie cavern.

Crossing the waters quickly, Jamie emerged into the Inner Temple, where the Hellfire Club had allegedly met for celebrations of debauchery and Satanic ritual. She read that the layout of the caves was claimed by some to correspond almost exactly to the sexual organs of a woman being penetrated by a man. Given the reputation of the Hellfire Club, it seemed entirely possible that fertility rituals had been performed or that the design at least reflected the activities that went on down here beneath the earth. But were those depravities still happening today?

From the ceiling hung a great hook, presumably for a chandelier. But as Jamie glanced at it, she imagined a body hanging there, suspended above the table, tortured in front of those seated below, their eyes shining with delight. She looked away and noticed stains on the floor, as if pools of blood were seeping from the ground beneath. She blinked quickly and the vision was gone. Jamie rubbed her forehead. It must be lack of sleep, for why else would her mind play these tricks? Her imagination was clearly affected by the dissections of the Hunterian and her concerns about Polly. There was nothing here to suggest that the caves were used for anything other than tourism. They sometimes had ghost tours in here at night, but other than that the place closed at dusk. But Jenna Neville has been convinced this area was important for the Lyceum, so there must be more to it than just the official sanitized version that the public got to see.

Returning to the entrance, Jamie bought a guidebook to West Wycombe and went to a local pub to read while she ate a quick meal. Inside one of the Appendices she found a copy of a poem that referred to a secret passage running from the church of St Lawrence, intersecting at the River Styx directly below the altar. Eating without tasting, Jamie pulled up the photo of the title deed Jenna had found. The land included Hearnton Wood and the area surrounding the church of St Lawrence, so Jamie decided to head up there next.

As she was reading, her phone buzzed with a text from Missinghall.

Lockup discovery sparked a mad scramble on evidence. Day-Conti released from custody. Be careful, whatever you're doing. Let me know if you need help.

Jamie felt the ghost of a smile on her lips at his words. Missinghall was a decent man, a good officer and she felt lucky to have someone who cared enough to watch her back. She had pushed people away for so long, protecting her precious time with Polly, but now she realized how alone that left her. She looked at her watch. It was time to finish this and the church was the next logical place to investigate.

The church of St Lawrence was on the summit of West Wycombe Hill, visible from the village below. It was a brisk walk up the steep slope and Jamie found herself breathing heavily, but she pushed upwards, the pain in her legs and lungs a welcome distraction. At the top, she stood to catch her breath, gazing at the odd building behind the Dashwood mausoleum. Originally an Iron Age fort, the medieval church had been built in the fourteenth century, but little of the original structure remained. It had been radically remodeled by Sir Francis Dashwood in 1752, pieces of the new stuck onto the old, with no aesthetic sense of retaining the medieval beauty.

On top of the tall Gothic tower was a shining gold orb that caught the last of the winter sun, a copy of the Golden Ball from the custom house at Venice. Ivy climbed the walls of the mottled stone as if nature was trying to reclaim the land, but Jamie still found the church a little crass, the simplicity of faith perverted into a glorification of the Dashwood name.

The churchyard was dominated by white crosses and

the tombs of the aristocrats who had been buried here over the centuries. Jamie paused at the lych-gate and then walked slowly through the graves thinking of Polly. Somehow the lichen-covered tombstones comforted her, for death is our constant companion, walking alongside us through life. It edges closer over the years until it is all that supports us and we long to relax into its final embrace. Polly was beyond pain now, and all Jamie wanted to do was find her and let her ashes rest beneath the carpet of earth, bringing new flowers to life.

Jamie entered the church, her eyes drawn to a central panel, richly frescoed in the style of the Italian Renaissance. The walls were a mustard color with deep red columns topped by Corinthian capitals, supporting a coffered ceiling decorated with a floral pattern. Jamie walked to the altar, looking for some secret passageway or hint of Satanic ritual, but disappointment soon rose within her. Once again, there was nothing here that suggested anything untoward. It was just a slightly odd parish church with little tourist appeal. She left the church and walked back out into the churchyard. What was she missing? Jamie sensed the truth was just out of reach, but she was sure that Jenna had been killed because of the knowledge she had discovered about the Lyceum. There must be something here.

Standing on the hilltop, Jamie could see for miles around. In front of her lay the village and behind her was Hearnton Wood, a densely forested area that ended in a finger surrounding the church. Bare branches stood out against the cool sky, its absence of color epitomizing the English winter. When covered in leaves, the branches would conceal everything but, with the sparse cover of winter, Jamie could make out a shape in the distance, something cornered that broke the natural lines of the forest. She opened the map and searched for the structure but there was nothing shown in that direction. It was supposed to be pure forest. The title deeds showed that this whole area was now owned by the Nevilles, so this forest would be under their care as well. Was there something hidden within the wood?

Feeling a pulse of excitement, and daring to hope that this would lead her to Polly, Jamie took a bearing with the compass from her pack. She followed a path down from the church to the wood in the direction of what she had seen. When the well-trodden path started to circle back towards the church in a large loop, she set off between the trees, following the compass heading.

It was dusk now, the forest shielding what little light was left of the day. Jamie listened to the rustle of leaves around her, as woodland animals scurried away at her approach. She remembered when Polly had been able to run as a child, how she had loved foraging in the New Forest, finding field mushrooms for their dinner. Jamie smiled at the memory. There had never been much money, it was always a struggle, but there had been a lot of joy until Polly's pain had overtaken her and the little girl hadn't been able to run or explore again.

Jamie pushed on through the trees, letting her eyes adjust to the encroaching darkness, not wanting to use torchlight until it was really necessary. Finally, she saw something looming up ahead, a patch of darker grey between the tree trunks. As she approached, she realized that it was a wall, made of solid metal panels over ten feet tall with a sign indicating it was private land and warning trespassers to stay out. Jamie put her hand flat on the metal, as if somehow she could feel what was behind. It was cold and lifeless on her skin, and she felt her body heat leaching into it. She leaned forwards until her forehead was resting on the metal. Part of her just wanted to sink down to the forest floor and weep, but night was encroaching and she knew there was little time left to find Polly's body before the Lyceum, whatever it was, began.

Jamie listened to the night forest, straining for some indication of which way to follow the wall around. She had to find other some way in, because there was no way that she was getting over this barrier without any special gear. She could hear nothing so she went West, remembering from the map that there was a tiny lane running close to the forest. Keeping the wall on her right, Jamie picked her way through the undergrowth. She kept the torch off, preferring imperfect night sight, walking carefully and trying not to make a sound.

After twenty minutes of walking, the fence was still impervious, but Jamie heard the sound of a van in the distance. The barrier began to curve inwards as she walked, and suddenly she saw the outline of another color ahead, a darker grey indicating a change in material and finally, a gate. She froze against the trunk of a tree, waiting to catch any movement, but all was silent, so she crept forward to look at it more closely. The gate was electronic, clearly activated from the inside. There was an intercom and a camera mounted where a driver would pull up. Jamie made sure to stay out of range, circling behind to inspect the side of the gate. There was no way to climb, so she pulled back into the trees and considered her options. She could wait until much later and try to get back into the caves, or she could call Missinghall and see if the local police would cooperate in investigating this location. But she still had no evidence that anything was going on, and it would take time she didn't have.

Suddenly, she heard the engine of another truck and this time it seemed to be slowing as it drove along the road. Jamie crouched down to avoid being caught in the beam of the headlights as it swung into the short driveway in front of the gate. She quickly circled back through the trees as the truck driver spoke into the intercom. The gate swung open and Jamie ran up behind, hopping onto the back board and clinging to the material there. The truck drove through the gate and, once on the other side, Jamie jumped off again before it could speed up too much. She dropped to the ground and crawled into the trees, now on the other side of the fence. Once she was sure that the truck was out of sight, Jamie started to walk after it, her night vision slowly returning as its lights faded.

Looking at her watch, Jamie felt an urgency building inside her that crushed the exhaustion she felt. Whatever the dark purposes of the Lyceum, there wasn't much time. I'm coming, Pol, she thought. Jamie started to jog down the road, ready to sprint back into the trees if the truck returned and soon she saw lights on a low warehouse building ahead. There were no markings, nothing to indicate which company the place belonged to. It looked to be only one story, camouflaged by the dense trees that surrounded it. The truck was parked outside and a man was offloading boxes from the back onto a trolley. He wheeled them into an open loading bay area and left them neatly stacked, before reversing the truck and driving away. Jamie hugged the side of the building and slipped into the loading bay, checking the top of the box for the address slip. Neville Pharmaceuticals.

Brilliant light suddenly flooded the loading bay and a ferocious barking filled the air. Jamie was blinded, her heart pounding as fear flooded her system. She turned towards the sound, ready to defend herself, squinting into the light.

"Detective Brooke, what a lovely surprise."

Edward Mascuria stepped forward and Jamie saw the satisfied look on his face. He held a Taser pointed at her and an enormous Rottweiler stood leashed at his side, snarling lips pulled back over sharp teeth.

"You've been doing quite a bit of investigating I hear," Mascuria said. "Shame that will now have to come to an end." He smiled and his eyes were cold. "But what an end it shall be."

CHAPTER 22

JAMIE STOOD HER GROUND, holding her hands out in an unthreatening posture. She felt vulnerable but she also had nothing to lose anymore.

"Do you have Polly's body?" she asked, head held high.

"Such a beautiful specimen," Mascuria said, and Jamie couldn't help herself. She started towards him, violent fury on her face but the Rottweiler leapt forward barking, teeth snapping at her. She had to retreat before it began to rip at her legs. It stood in front of Mascuria, straining at the leash, desperate for the command to attack, salivating at the possibility of blood. She could see that Mascuria was relishing the power he held over her now.

"You bastard," she said, bile rising in her throat. "Why Polly?"

"I needed a female with her kind of spinal deformity for my teratological collection. When you came round to my flat with your - attitude - I found out more about you and your desperate family situation. But don't worry, I'm taking very good care of her body." He indicated a doorway with the Taser. "This way, Detective. You're a little early for tonight's Lyceum, but I think you might enjoy a tour. Don't even think about running. Max here will bring you down and rip your throat out on my command. He's not fed often and he enjoys the taste of human flesh."

Jamie heard the pleasure of reminiscence in his voice and imagined the poor victims that Mascuria had used to train his dog, skin shredded from their bones as screams echoed in the dark forest. She shuddered, but she didn't want to run. She was so close now and once she was with Polly's body, she could consider her options. Dealing with this bastard would have to wait, and she tried to calm her anger, shutting away her feelings and concentrating on her surroundings.

Jamie walked ahead of Mascuria through the open door. Inside was a short corridor and another door at the end with retinal scan entry. Next to the door was a waiting room with glass windows.

"In there, Detective," Mascuria indicated the room. Jamie walked in and turned to face him. "Now strip for me, and I mean everything." His eyes glinted at her hesitation. "Oh, don't worry, I'm not going to touch you - yet. Warm flesh is not really my thing, but I need to check that you're not armed before I take you inside."

Jamie shut her eyes for a moment and gathered herself. He was playing a dominance game but her body was just a body like any other. He would only take pleasure from her resistance and embarrassment.

"Sure," she said, pulling her jacket off and swiftly shedding her clothes. She steeled herself to ignore the dog's growling as her bare skin was revealed. She met Mascuria's eyes as she unhooked her bra and pulled down her panties until she was naked. She stood tall and didn't hug her arms around her body even though the cold made her nipples harden and her skin pucker. She felt a moment of victory when he broke their stare, his eyes dropping to her breasts.

"Turn," he said, and there was a gruffness in his voice. She turned slowly all the way around. "Now face the wall." She did so and he advanced into the room, the dog's growling louder now. Jamie could feel the heat from it just behind her legs. Every inch of her wanted to run and she couldn't help imagining vicious teeth tearing into her intimate, vulnerable flesh. Mascuria could do what he wanted here and she cursed her own independence at proceeding without backup.

Mascuria passed a scanner over her clothes, checking for concealed weapons and bugs. He stood close to her, and she could feel his breath against her back. He pressed the Taser against her buttocks.

"I'd love to press this button," he whispered. "I want to see you writhing in your own piss on the floor, arching in agony for the way you treated me, bitch."

Jamie realized that he was turned on by the thought of her pain and that was terrifying. She wasn't afraid of death, but didn't want to die by his sadistic hand. "But that's not enough for someone like you. You think you're so strong, but I'll break you when you watch me slice up your daughter's body."

Jamie forced herself to remain still as he whispered close to her ear. Every fiber of her being wanted to turn and beat him to a pulp. She would kill him for what he intended to do, but not yet.

"Please," she whispered, feigning submission. "Let me see Polly."

Mascuria walked out of the anteroom and the dog padded after him.

"Put your clothes back on and cuff yourself," he said, brusquely. "There's a lot to do tonight."

Pulling her clothes on, Jamie felt relief at the flimsy barrier between her and the dog, as well as respite from Mascuria's stare. She put on the plastic tie cuffs, pulling them with her teeth so that they were still loose about her hands, tucking the end between her palms. Mascuria put his eye to the retina scan and the door clicked open. He indicated that she should walk in first. Jamie held her head high and made to walk past him, but he stopped her and yanked at the tie cuffs, so they tightened and bit deep into her wrists. Jamie winced at the sudden pain.

"Wouldn't want you trying to get away now, would we," Mascuria said, and up close his breath smelled of rotting flesh. "Max is staying out here, but remember, I still have the Taser."

Jamie pulled away from him and stepped through the door into a large conference room decorated with cream colored easy chairs, potted palms and framed photographs of aspects of biological research. It was business-like and professional, clearly used for visitors to the facility, and Jamie wondered who came to this secret lab and what they were here to buy.

Mascuria made her stand to one side while he used his thumbprint to open the next door. Security was certainly tight, and Jamie was anxious to see what was inside. She kept glancing around for possible weapons, for an alternative exit but, in truth, she didn't want to get away from Mascuria yet.

Through the next door, a long corridor stretched into the distance and on either side were windows, displaying labs within. Jamie could hear noises, animal hoots and moans, and it smelled like a zoo.

"What goes on here?" Jamie asked, staring into one lab that was almost a replica of the one she had seen at the Neville Pharmaceuticals official headquarters. But here the glass-fronted fridges contained specimens that seemed on the edge of abomination, perversions of nature. In some, the creatures' skin was ruptured or scaly and others had limbs like animals on the bodies of human babies. Jamie saw one fetus with only blue eyes in its blank face, open in the clear liquid. With no mouth or nose, it had no way to breathe and her heart thudded with the desperate end it faced as soon as it was torn from its mother's placenta. In the Hunterian, the specimens had been medical history, accidents of birth, but this was deliberate experimentation. What other horrors were here, and was this what Jenna Neville had discovered?

"Neville Pharma has branched out into some of the more interesting aspects of genetic splicing," Mascuria said with pride. "We use stem cells between species. After all, it's easier to create monsters to order than to find them by chance. We've also been exploring the effects of certain drugs in populations where the governments have more relaxed guidelines on testing." He indicated a map on the wall with shaded areas in West Africa, South East Asia and even Eastern Europe. Jamie's mind buzzed with the grotesque possibilities, the lives that even now were being experimented on.

"This research is far bigger than you could imagine," Mascuria said, pushing Jamie onwards. "But what you're really looking for is much deeper inside the facility."

At the end of the corridor, another retinal scan and thumbprint opened a large metal door, this one reinforced like a bank vault with a thick outer wall. Although it was protected like a bunker from the Soviet era, inside it was just a round room, the walls lined with medical and research texts. In between the bookshelves were sculptures Jamie recognized, plastinated corpses of skillful dissection including the little boy with his spine exposed. Jamie felt a surge of pity and a rigid determination that Polly's body would not end up like this.

A wooden lectern stood in pride of place against the very center of the back wall, spotlights shining on a large notebook filled with handwritten notes and intimate drawings in a glass case. Above it was a picture of a clean cut young man in the black and white uniform of the SS, silver skull shining on his smart helmet. Jamie recognized

Mengele, vivisector and perverter of science, honored here as an inspirational role model. The spotlight also illuminated a shelf by the notebook that lay empty. Blake had seen the Anatomical Venus figurine with Mengele's notebook in his vision, so Jenna must have been here and stolen the figurine, using it as evidence to challenge her parents.

With a grunt, Mascuria turned to a panel in the wall and entered a code. A scraping noise filled the room and the large Persian carpet in the middle of the floor slid back by some hidden mechanism. One of the flagstones sunk below and sideways, revealing a staircase down into the earth.

"The real secrets are down there," Mascuria chuckled, with an edge of maniacal glee. Jamie had the impression that Mascuria wanted to show his treasures to someone with a pulse. He pointed at the staircase and Jamie stepped down carefully, trying to keep her balance with her hands still cuffed.

There were muted lights on the stairs so she could see a few steps ahead as they wound downwards. Jamie heard Mascuria step behind her, and then he must have closed the trapdoor because the darkness thickened and the lights at her feet were the only illumination.

"Just keep walking, Detective, it's not too far now, and your curiosity will be satisfied."

Jamie continued carefully down, counting nearly fifty steps until the staircase opened out into another corridor. The ceilings were carved into arches like the Hellfire Caves and down here the air was temperate, warmer than the surface. There was an earthy smell, not unpleasant.

"Welcome to the heart of the complex," Mascuria said. "It's connected to the Hellfire Caves in the opposite direction from the official tourist entrance. There's a mirror image set of caves behind the public area where the

Hellfire club really met. The fake caverns were created for delicious scandal and media interest, but Dashwood knew what he was doing."

"And now the Nevilles continue the Hellfire tradition?" asked Jamie, still unsure as to how Jenna's strange family fitted into the mix.

Mascuria laughed. "You'll have to wait and see, but right now, I want to introduce you to my collection."

He pointed at a door of ornate dark wood, carved with alchemical and fertility symbols. In the center was an ouroboros, a snake eating its own tail in a never-ending circle, representing immortality and the continuation of life.

"That is my God, Detective. Nothing we do matters, because it's all just an endless turning. But I will leave my legacy by preserving the extraordinary in nature. I will be remembered, like Hunter, as a man who appreciated the freaks." He paused, then pushed open the door. "Like your little girl."

CHAPTER 23

JAMIE'S HEART THUNDERED IN her chest. She wanted to see Polly's body but she was also terrified. She remembered her daughter as perfection but her flesh would surely be decomposed and rotting by now. Mascuria laughed, sensing her hesitation.

"Don't worry, Detective, I've kept her on ice and she's only showing a hint of decay."

He pushed her forwards and Jamie was surprised to find that the cave was set up like a morgue, with pristine floors and white tiled walls. One side was dominated by a cooling unit and drawer freezers, presumably for bodies. Opposite the dissection gurneys were racks of open shelving containing specimen jars. Jamie stared at them in horrified recognition. They varied in size from large drums on the bottom shelves to tiny jars on the higher levels and each one contained some kind of anatomical preparation.

"I am the true heir of John Hunter," Mascuria said proudly, "and this will be my legacy to the world. While he lived, Hunter was criticized and feared for his scientific methods. In the same way, if what we did here was revealed, I too would be treated as an outcast. But this way, I can perform my great work in peace, and soon I will be as celebrated as Hunter." He waved his arm at the shelves.

"I think you'll agree that I have some particularly amazing specimens from the labs upstairs."

"Where's Polly?" Jamie said, uncaring for the rest of the dead. Only her daughter's remains mattered. Mascuria's eyes hardened and he raised the Taser.

"No. Not yet. First appreciate my collection and understand the importance of my work, then you may be allowed a glimpse of my next subject."

Jamie wanted to rush him and smash one of the jars into his face, obliterating his perverted brain. She could barely contain her need to see Polly but he still had the advantage. She turned and walked towards the rack of shelving, her stomach churning as she saw what was inside. Like the Hunterian, it was both fascinating and revolting to see the freakish remains, grouped according to type, the first shelf containing fetuses and babies, nightmares that Jamie wished she could un-see.

The fluid around each was yellowish, making it seem as if they rested in a kind of amber. In one, she glimpsed a baby with a normal body but two heads, squashed onto the same neck, with skulls flattened as if the child had been violently murdered as it exited the womb. In another jar, triplet fetuses were suspended, tiny arms wrapped around themselves as if they were cold, each with a tuft of hair on its bald head. But there were only patches of skin where their eyes should be and their faces were feature-less. Next, a huge baby's head, its skin wrinkled like an old man, on top of a round body, the limbs only stumps of fingers and toes. Jamie felt an overwhelming compassion for these unborn children, but also a kind of gratitude that they had not had to endure life as monsters. She knew that the physical body didn't define the life inside, but she also understood through her daughter the pain of rejection, the instinctive human response to turn away from those who were less than perfect. But who are we to say what perfection is? And does that make the Creator a eugeneticist, choosing only those good enough to live?

Jamie gazed into other jars, wanting to bear witness to the myriad forms of forsaken humanity that were left alone here, motherless. Here was a true monster, aspects of humanity in the facial structure and arms, but the rest of its body was more like a fish. Its skin was puckered and ruptured in places, as if it had been sewn together. In the next jar was a pitiful specimen, its head perfect but the body just an abdomen with skin split open to reveal the guts within. This was dead flesh, no spark of life, for what is the human body except for us to dwell in briefly, ruin and burn, bury or dissect, returning it to the stardust from which it came.

"Were these children born here?" Jamie asked, her voice echoing round the lab. "Were they created by Neville Pharma?"

"Some were created as a by-product of the teratology research." There was pride in Mascuria's voice. "We investigate the effects of various drugs on pregnant women, to find the stage that affects the fetus the most. After Thalidomide, it became illegal to test on pregnant women but of course, it has to be done, and the money is excellent, so some are willing to be part of the research. Others are unwilling, but ... well, let's just say, they end up joining us anyway. They are from the margins of society so none of the women are missed, and they often end up part of the Lyceum, their offspring preserved forever. Who would object to such a fate?"

Jamie's head was reeling with the implications of what went on here but then his words sunk in.

"So this isn't the Lyceum?" she asked.

Mascuria's hollow laugh blurted out, the sound quickly absorbed into the shelves of fluid glass.

"Oh no, they butcher the living, but I use only the

dead. Of course, I have to prepare specimens differently, depending on their future use. Removing flesh is only one task. Here's one of their last victims."

Mascuria walked over to a huge copper vat in the corner. It was as pristine as the rest of the lab, but as he lifted the lid, the putrid smell made Jamie wince and her nostrils flared at the familiar stench of death. He beckoned her over and she met his challenge, walking to the vat, the anticipation of what she might see making her heart pound. Jamie peered over the edge, her cuffed hands on her mouth and nose to stop the gag reflex. The liquid inside was a deep brown color, with fat glistening on top. Mascuria grabbed a long handled ladle from the bench and poked it into the soup, fishing for something more solid. There were thicker, heavier parts at the bottom of the vat and he hooked one of them, dragging it up to the surface. It was a human femur, mostly bone now with just a little flesh hanging off. Mascuria smiled at her evident revulsion.

"One option to destroy flesh is to put the body in an enclosed space with flies which eventually clean the bones completely. But an alternative is to hack it into pieces and boil it in a vat until all the flesh and sinew is gone, like this. Of course, anatomy is always a sensory experience, the permanent stench of the dissection room lingers on clothes, the pervading odor of decay. Did you know that Hunter was known for tasting bodily fluids?"

Jamie grimaced as he raised the ladle towards his mouth. Mascuria laughed again.

"Come now, Detective. You know nothing human lingers here. The first time you clutch the cold flesh of a body, when you smell decay and corruption, you know it's not a person anymore. It's only entropy in action, chaos disintegrating the body, returning it to the atomic state. We're only revolted by the dead because the corpse represents the end of life, which we are meant to fear. But I don't fear it, I'm tempted by it. I only know what life truly is because I embrace the death in it." Mascuria replaced the lid on the vat and walked back to the wall units. Pulling one of the freezer doors open, he slid a gurney out, the wheels loud on the tiled floor. "Now, come and see your daughter."

Jamie walked slowly to the open freezer, as Mascuria unzipped the bag in which a body lay. Silent tears ran down her cheeks as Jamie looked down at Polly's face, her skin a lighter shade now, all color gone. Her eyes were shut and she looked more than asleep.

"How dare you?" Jamie whispered, barely controlled anger in her voice. "How dare you disturb her rest. She's suffered enough."

Mascuria reached out a fingertip and stroked the girl's cheek, running it down over her lips, then he poked it into her mouth.

"I dare what I want with the dead," he said, drawing it out again and then thrusting the finger back inside.

Jamie's face contorted with disgust at the offensive action and she whipped her cuffed hands up, striking him across the face double handed as she leaned over the gurney.

"Bastard," she screamed. "Monster."

Mascuria's head snapped back and he stumbled from the blow. Jamie rounded the gurney at speed and slammed into him, sending him to the floor as she fell on top of him, using her legs to try and immobilize him. But she couldn't hold him and he twisted beneath her, pushing her away to make a space between them. She heard the crackle of his Taser and felt pain shoot through her body. Jamie's muscles spasmed into rigidity and she lay prone as the agony pulsed through her, centering in the place where he had thrust the device. Mascuria rose and stood over her as

Jamie fought to try and regain control of her body.

"You have no power here, Detective," he said, patting himself down, dislodging any dust and brushing it off onto her. He reached down and grabbed her cuffed hands, dragging her, unable to resist, over to the wall near the door. He pulled down a meathook to lever around the cuffs and then started to winch the thick steel cable up. "This will hold you still while I work. I seldom have company when I process a body, but we have some time before the Lyceum commences tonight. Time for you to witness what I have planned for pretty Polly."

Jamie felt some feeling return to her limbs and she tried to fight the winch, but it just kept rising until she was high on her toes, calf muscles taut. She couldn't unhook herself in this position, she had no leverage. She opened her mouth to beg but only a rasp came out.

"Hmm," Mascuria said, noting her attempt. "I like quiet in my lab, so you'll need a gag." He fiddled around on a nearby lab table, producing a wad of surgical gauze. Jamie tried to move her head, resisting him but he grabbed her jaw in a skeletal grip and forced it into her mouth. He wrapped a bandage around her mouth, tying it behind her head to stop her spitting the gauze out. She tried to scream then, feeling her strength returning but it was too late and Mascuria only laughed at her tears of frustration.

He looked at the clock on the wall.

"Time to get started," he smiled at her with malice, "and just enough time to make you truly pay for the way you treated me."

He picked up a scalpel and approached Polly's body, standing on the far side of the gurney so that Jamie could see his actions. She looked at her daughter's body and in her mind, she screamed for God to help her, a God she didn't even believe in. Part of her was trying to rationalize that this wasn't her daughter anymore, that Polly's spirit was gone, that she wouldn't feel any pain at this man's abuse. But her eyes told her this was still her beloved daughter, the baby born from her blood and pushed from her own body, who had grown into a lovely young woman. Jamie couldn't hide the pain in her eyes, even though she didn't want to give Mascuria the satisfaction of seeing it.

He cupped the budding breast of the corpse with a bare hand, his fingers rubbing at the pale pink nipple. Jamie felt herself gag and had to force the vomit back down. She wanted to look away but knew she had to bear witness to his cruelty.

"Sometimes I keep the body whole," Mascuria said. "Kept frozen like this, they stay perfect for a while longer. I bet little Polly here was a virgin as well, and she will be all tight and cold inside. Perfect."

Jamie struggled furiously against her bonds, rattling the chains. She swore then that she would kill Mascuria, whatever it took. He couldn't be allowed to continue his depraved practices.

"I see the fury in your eyes, Detective, and it inspires me. I shall make Polly a perfect specimen for my collection. She will live on here amongst the monsters, labeled and tagged, her spine a source of fascination in death. And will it hurt you more, I wonder, to watch me take pleasure with her body or to see me cut her into pieces?"

Mascuria looked into Jamie's eyes and she stared straight back at him, daring him to make any move on her daughter. He laughed and reached around the body, flipping Polly over so that she now lay on her front. Her body couldn't lie straight on the table, and the deformity was clearer from the back, the twisting exaggerated. Jamie screamed, moaning into the gag, wrenching on the hook in an attempt to get to her daughter.

"When dissecting a body," Mascuria began, pointing at the corpse as if giving a lecture, "the guts are the first parts to putrefy so usually one would begin by slitting open the abdomen, folding back the flaps of skin and fat and removing the digestive parts, stomach, intestines, spleen, gall bladder and pancreas. Then one would open the chest, sawing apart the ribcage to remove the lungs and expose the heart." His fingers danced down Polly's spine, dipping between her buttocks as he smiled at Jamie's fury. "Of course, the mastery of dissection requires intricate knife skills, but also brute strength to saw through bone and hack off the parts not required for a particular preparation. Removing the limbs so that I have a nice, clean torso to work with is always a good first step, because a big part of the artist's job is deciding what to leave out," Mascuria grinned wildly as he saw the panic in Jamie's eyes. He turned and wheeled over a trolley, on which were laid out scalpels of various sizes and a large bone saw. "I think I'll start with removing her legs." He reached for a scalpel.

CHAPTER 24

THE DOOR SLAMMED OPEN, hitting the wall inches from where Jamie hung behind it. Mascuria froze, one hand holding Polly's leg and the other clutching the scalpel above her thigh. His face fell as he saw who had entered. Jamie tried to twist around but she couldn't see.

"Edward, darling," Esther Neville's crisp British vowels filled the room. "Do you really have time for that?"

Mascuria's eyes flicked to Jamie and the door was pulled back. Esther stood there, no trace of the mousey scientist, the grieving mother or wronged wife remaining. Instead she was the proud ruler of this underground domain, channeling dark spirits below while she created abomination in the labs above. Her clothes were curious, her waist nipped in with a corset and the dress an extravagant eighteenth century costume, out of place in the modern lab. Esther's serpent green eyes drilled into Jamie.

"Detective, why am I not surprised to find you here?" She stepped forward to check that the bonds were secure, nodding her head. "Good job, Edward." Jamie could see that Mascuria reveled under this compliment from his mistress. "But we already have a vivisection subject for the Lyceum tonight." Esther paused and Jamie could see that she was considering the options. "I'd like the Detective to witness her future fate, but we can get more for her at an exclusive event, for those select few who might enjoy intimacy with her kind of flesh." Esther stepped closer, her smile one of triumph. "And what do you think of the wonders we have here, Detective?"

Esther pulled away Jamie's gag, wanting to hear her speak. Jamie's mind flashed over all the insults she wanted to spit out, but she still held onto some hope that she would get out of here. Perhaps Esther could be goaded.

"You're just sick and depraved. There's no real science here."

Esther's eyes flashed with anger.

"Of course, I couldn't expect a mere police detective to understand, but this is truly magnificent work. We're developing weaponized teratology. By introducing pathogens into an environment, we can corrupt a region, making the inhabitants into monsters who will be rejected, murdered and thrown into mass graves. We can target genetically, causing extra limbs to sprout from bodies, horns from heads, perversions of nature. It will justify the killing of those groups in the eyes of those considered normal, but more than that, it becomes a judgment from God, afflictions sent as punishment for sin. Humans are so ready to slaughter those considered Other."

Jamie thought of the gas chambers of Nazi Europe filled with the bodies of the Other - Jews, gypsies, the mentally ill and those considered defective. She thought of Rwanda and the description of 'cockroaches' stacked in mass graves, seen as inhuman by people who were once their neighbors. It was terrifying to think that this lab could hold the key to unleashing atrocity on an even grander scale. But she still didn't have all the answers.

"What has the Lyceum got to do with this?"

"Why, Detective, it's just a little fun, in the medical tradition of course." Esther did a little twirl in her costume, meager breasts pushed up by the tight bodice, full skirts swinging. Against the backdrop of the bottled remains, her delight was all the more macabre. "The Lyceum Medicum Londinense is an old institution, first started in 1785 in the days of the great anatomist John Hunter to replicate his experiments, a crucible to facilitate his scientific legacy. Hunter only trusted his own eyes, so now, in turn, this is what we offer in the resurrected Lyceum. We experiment as Hunter did, exploring the very edges of human experience. Unlike you, most people don't get to see the dark side of reality anymore, it's all so sanitized. They don't get to see death or experience the end of life until they meet it themselves in some pathetic care home. But people want a taste of the extraordinary in their boring lives, they want the freak shows, the crazies. Otherwise this world is just one long dull day after another. These elite seekers are desperate for a glimpse of the other side. They crave this interaction with the dead, for it is like seeing our own future. On the slab, we are all the same."

Esther stepped closer, holding Jamie's gaze. "At the Lyceum, we remove the veneer of civilization and deliver raw truth through vivisection of the body. We want our members to see, to weep and experience deep pleasure. It matters not what they feel, only that they feel something. This becomes an addiction, an expensive one, for sure, and when we find a new member, we try very hard to find them an experience that will change them. Religion offers a way to look into the divine, but the Lyceum offers a way to look into our base physical selves. For what truth is greater than the realization that we are meat, mere chunks of flesh that can be cut away? If we dissect to the last capillary, will we find the essence of the person? No, we cannot, because it has already gone."

Jamie saw the promise of her own death in Esther's eyes, an end through flayed flesh and agony. Where Mascuria delighted in the dead, Esther was addicted to killing. It was a perfect partnership.

"Enough." Esther turned and addressed Mascuria. "Use the ketamine and dress her in something more appropriate, then string her up next to the altar. And Edward, I mean now. You can return to your - specimen - later."

Esther strode from the room, her heels clicking on the stone as she walked away. Mascuria rested the scalpel gently on Polly's back and patted her buttocks.

"I'll return for you later," he whispered, almost lovingly. He looked up at Jamie and the veil in his eyes came down, obscuring any humanity. He picked up a syringe from the surgical table and then filled it from a bottle.

As he walked towards Jamie, she began to struggle, aware that ketamine was a powerful sedative but also that it could produce a dissociative state, hallucinations and visions. She wanted to remember Mascuria's perversions and she wanted to punish him for it.

"It would have been better for you to watch your daughter's preservation than to experience Lady Neville's particular pleasures," Mascuria said. "But now, you have no choice."

He pressed the needle into her arm and within seconds, Jamie felt a heaviness in her limbs and her eyelids drooped. She forced them open again, as the winch lowered her to the floor, but she couldn't fight the drug and she slipped into unconsciousness.

CHAPTER 25

JAMIE BECAME AWARE OF the bonds around her as she woke and it took her a few seconds to figure out what was happening. Her body felt as if she were underwater, heavy and compliant, the sedation of the ketamine still in her system. She was lying on a chill stone floor, hands cuffed in front of her, wearing a mask with tiny slits for her eyes that obscured her facial features. As her senses slowly returned, Jamie realized she was only wearing a sheer black wrap over her own underwear. That bastard Mascuria had stripped her as he had the bodies of the dead. For a fleeting moment, Jamie wished to be next to her daughter on the slab. But then she remembered how much Polly had believed in living until it hurt and making the most out of every minute that we have the grace to be alive. Jamie grasped at a glimmer of hope, that she might make it out of this and revenge the abuses inflicted on Polly and the other innocent victims here.

She moved slowly, trying to take in her surroundings, fighting to clear her head. Still gagged, her throat hurt from the raw material and she was desperately thirsty. She pulled against the chain that bound her cuffs to the wall and managed to lever herself up, resting back against the stone, finally able to see. She was in a twin chamber to the Inner Temple of the Hellfire Caves, but it had been transformed into a dark cave of corrupted medical history.

The walls were hung with twisted poles wrapped with bloody used bandages, a tribute to the red and white staffs of the original barber surgeons. There were skeletons attached between them, posed in positions of torture, their limbs stretched in crucifixion. Candelabra stood around the edge, throwing an incongruous warm light into the dark space and giving off a pungent scent. Tendrils of smoke licked the walls, clouding the cave with a heady atmosphere.

Behind an altar was a long wooden pole, an intricately carved snake curled around it, forked tongue flickering to taste the air. Jamie recognized the rod of Asclepius, the Greek god of healing and medicine, but here it resembled some kind of demonic god. Around an empty central space were rows of tiered seating facing the altar where she sat. Jamie wondered who the members would be, since the original Hellfire Club had been made up of aristocrats, businessmen and politicians. Could it still be so powerful?

Jamie heard footsteps and slumped in her bonds, pretending to be drowsy as Mascuria came to check on her. He lifted her chin, and she groaned softly, playing the part. His fingers dug into her jaw.

"Time to wake up. After all, you'll want to watch the entertainment tonight and reflect on your own future." She opened her eyes slowly to see Mascuria's excited smile. But she realized that his enthusiasm wasn't for her bondage, it was for something that appealed to his darker nature, and Jamie felt a heavy sense of foreboding at what was to come. He forced her to her feet, adjusting the chains so that she was held tighter, standing against the wall, shackled by her wrists and ankles. The sheer wrap barely hid her body and she shivered as the cold seeped into her exposed skin.

"The chill is preferable to being center stage, believe

me," he said, pulling out a hip flask. "But this will warm you up." He pulled her gag away and holding her chin firmly, poured some of the liquid into her mouth. The wine was strong and some dribbled down her chin, but Jamie gratefully swallowed it to assuage her thirst. Mascuria tipped another swig into her throat, and Jamie started to feel light-headed. Mascuria saw the question in her eyes.

"A touch of hallucinogen. Altered reality will help you experience the heights of the ritual tonight, since I believe our guest is an acquaintance of yours."

Jamie's thoughts flashed to Blake, Missinghall, the nurses at the home. Who could it be? She dared hope it wasn't someone she cared about, but with the thought of what might come, she pitied the victim, whoever it was.

A drum beat started, a heavy, slow thudding that echoed around the chamber. It seemed to signify the start of proceedings because silhouettes started to enter the room, emerging through the smoky haze.

"Watch carefully, Detective, for this will soon be your fate." Mascuria whispered, slipping away from her into a shadowy tunnel at the side of the room.

Jamie watched as the figures walked slowly in, wearing buttoned long coats covered by hooded capes. Their faces were obscured but Jamie could tell by their stature that both women and men were present. Some glanced in her direction, some for a longer time than others, but she could see none of their features. Each wore the leather apron of the anatomist that Jamie had seen in the paintings of Hunter's time, and they carried small wooden cases. Some had handsome canes with finely wrought handles to complete their eighteenth century costumes. They filed into the tiered seating as the drum began to speed up, a double beat like a heart pounding.

A figure stepped from the shadowed corridor. Esther Neville, resplendent in a swirling black cape over her extravagant dress. Her hood was back and she didn't hide her face, which was now made up with gold and metallic swirls around her eyes, matching the detail on her costume. As she strode to the front of the altar, the drum pounded harder and faster and Jamie felt her heart thumping in time, jumping to the rhythm, making her blood race. She felt heady with the noise and the smoke that made the figures weave in front of her.

As Esther raised her hands into the air with a dramatic gesture, Mascuria wheeled in a metal gurney covered in a white cloth. Strapped on top of it, naked and struggling, was Rowan Day-Conti, his elaborately tattooed body arching in terror. Jamie gasped to see him restrained, and desperate to help him, she twisted in her chains, pulling against their hindrance. Bands round his wrists, ankles, waist and neck held Rowan to the table and, although he writhed in his bonds, Jamie could see that he would not escape them and neither could she reach him.

Mascuria wheeled the gurney into the middle of the space as the drum reached a crescendo and then fell silent. Esther spoke into the silence, calling out in a strange language that Jamie didn't recognize: clearly it was some ritualized welcome as the gathering responded with a chant, sipping from their goblets as they joined the words. Had the Lyceum ritualized their vivisection in this way? Was this a dark perversion of the physician's oath?

Jamie noticed that some of those present drank more heavily, perhaps gaining strength for the ritual to come. As they chanted, Mascuria moved forward and slipped Day-Conti's gag off, forcing him to drink as well. Some of the wine tipped onto the white cloth beneath his neck, staining it a deep red. He couldn't help but drink as Mascuria held his nose and tipped the stuff down his throat. Day-Conti turned his head, coughing and groaning but Jamie knew that the woozy feeling would make his limbs heavy soon enough and she was glad that something would dull the pain to come.

"Tonight we honor our medical heritage, the curiosity that has driven physicians throughout history," Esther said, her tone imperious. "For with every body we cut into, we slice into our own skin. For every drop of blood we shed, we are draining our own into the earth. For every heart that is silenced, our end is a beat closer. And every bone we break reveals our own inevitable decline."

She raised a goblet to her lips and drained it, then spun to the altar and took up the ritual knife that lay there. Holding it up to the roof of the cave, she spoke words in the strange language again and turned to the crowd. Jamie watched the proud curve of Esther's back, feeling the resonance of her power in the space, a vibration of expectation emanating from the gathering. Day-Conti's eyes were wide open, his head bowed back to try and see what was happening above and behind him, panic evident even through the haze of drugs. Then he saw her and in his eyes, Jamie understood his plea for help. Did he recognize her in the depths of his pain, or did he just see another captive bound for the same fate?

Esther stepped down to the level of the gurney and pulled a black hood over Day-Conti's head, negating his individuality. Jamie had a flashback to the artist's studio, where the body of the decapitated woman lay, waiting for the knife to etch into her dead flesh. Now the sculptor himself would feel her pain. Jamie watched Day-Conti's chest rise and fall faster, his heart pounding as he awaited his fate.

"The vivisection begins," Esther said to the gathering, holding out the ritual knife. A tall figure stepped forward, pulling back his hood to reveal a face Jamie recognized, a prominent politician from one of the more radical right-wing parties. Esther handed the knife to him and he received it reverently with two hands. Jamie felt her own heart thumping hard against her ribs, anticipating the first cut. She twisted against her bonds, desperate to get away even as the man held the knife against Day-Conti's right shoulder and sliced diagonally across his chest, the first stroke of the autopsy, the beginning of the Y incision. But this man wasn't dead yet, and blood welled up under the knife.

A hiss broke from the crowd, a forced exhalation of breath, and as one they moved forward to see better. A muffled scream came from Day-Conti as the man drew the knife across his flesh again and the drum beat began once more, muting the sounds of horror. The thudding animated the crowd and they pushed back their hoods with excitement. Smoke made their features hazy and her head spun with drugged wine and residual ketamine, but Jamie was sure she saw members of government and the upper echelons of business. The crowd parted for a second and she thought she saw Detective Superintendent Dale Cameron, his face transformed by blood lust. Jamie blinked, unable to believe it was really him, and then the robed figures swirled and he was hidden again, if it had even been him at all.

At a sign from Esther, the members pulled out their own scalpels and crowded round the gurney. They began with tentative cuts and a semblance of scientific restraint, but soon all decorum was forgotten. Their robed bodies shielded Day-Conti's mutilation from Jamie's view and she could only watch their arms as they worked. As the drum beat speeded up, the rhythm turned to slashing and thrusting as vivisection turned to dismemberment. Sickened, Jamie swallowed down the bile that filled her throat, but she refused to look away. Here was evil in the bowels of the earth, committed by men and women in power, who held sway over the lives of many. Did they consider themselves as gods, with the ultimate power of life and death?

As Jamie watched, a figure stepped from the crowd, walking towards her with a measured step. It was Christopher Neville, gore staining his robe a darker pitch and a bloody scalpel in his hand. Jamie struggled as he approached her, unnoticed by the group who were engrossed in their orgy of blood-letting. His eyes glittered in the candlelight and she sensed his dangerous arousal, remembering how compliant he liked his women as he stepped onto the altar stage and bent towards her.

CHAPTER 26

CHRISTOPHER NEVILLE LOOSENED THE chains, unhooking Jamie from them so her body sagged, pushing her to the floor out of direct sight of the crowd. As she sank down behind the altar, hands and feet still cuffed, she saw Neville place the scalpel on the edge of it, just out of her reach. Jamie felt the heaviness in her limbs, the drugs making her unresisting, but through the haze in her mind, she remembered how hard Polly had fought the deadening of her own limbs. In that moment, she surged up, trying to fight Neville's dominance, smashing into his legs with her constricted shoulders.

The drum beat hid the sound of his stumbling and the crack of his hand across her face in retaliation, but as he moved to right himself, Neville knocked the scalpel to the floor and it slipped beneath the folds of the material covering the altar. Jamie fell back from the heavy blow to her face but she saw where the blade had fallen, even as she lay dazed, her head ringing.

Neville dropped to his knees and started to paw at her body, groping her breasts. Jamie struggled to get away from him, trying to wriggle across the floor, inching towards where the scalpel lay. If she could somehow roll towards it, she thought in desperation, but Neville dragged her back towards him and she knew her attempts to escape excited him further. Jamie's breath was ragged through her nose as she tried to breathe, the gag making it hard to get enough air. She knew she couldn't stay conscious for much longer and suddenly sagged, letting her limbs go limp. Neville smiled, the wolfish grin of a predator who knows he has won his prize. He turned her body over so she faced the floor, shifting her legs up so that they were bent under her and she lay like an offering for him to take.

He knelt behind her, pulling his robes apart, and it was as if time slowed. Jamie saw him reach for the scalpel, perhaps to cut his way through her clothes, perhaps to hurt her further, but he averted his eyes from her in that second. She moved fast, rolling and twisting so her pinned arms could swing free, catching Neville's hand that now grasped the scalpel, diverting it towards his own body. At the same time, she kicked out with her bent legs, thrusting them back so that they smashed into Neville's thighs, knocking him off balance. He fell forwards, onto her, onto the blade and Jamie saw his eyes widen in shock as it pierced his neck. His eyes widened and his sharp sound of alarm was lost in the drumbeat that drove the frenzy of the room to fever pitch. Jamie could smell the metallic scent of blood mingling with the smoke and it galvanized her into action.

She twisted further, knocking Neville sideways, so he lay gasping on his back, the scalpel sticking out of his neck as he clutched at it with weakening hands, his mouth opening and closing like a beached fish. With two hands still cuffed, Jamie yanked it from him and blood pumped from his wound. Neville started to try and rise, to attract the attention of the others and get help. Jamie rose to her knees and sat astride him, some part of her wanting to use the weapon, but at the last moment she stopped. She couldn't stab the man, even though she wished him dead.

Instead, she grabbed Neville's head and slammed it back against the stone floor as hard as she could, then again and again until she saw his eyes roll back in his head and he went limp.

Maneuvering the scalpel, Jamie sawed through the plastic tie cuffs that held her feet bound and then used Neville's body to brace it so she could free her hands. The drum beat still pounded, echoing in the chamber, but Jamie couldn't count on remaining unseen for much longer. Finally free, she crawled to the edge of the altar and peered around, shocked to see that the gathering had now descended into a depraved mass of blood stained bodies, shed of their robes. The smoke was thicker now, partially obscuring the details of what was going on beneath the vapor but Jamie could see that some were engaged in sexual acts and others still crowded around what was left of the bloody mass that had been Day-Conti, hands deep in gore and faces transfigured. No-one was looking in Jamie's direction, engrossed as they were in their own drug-fueled depravity.

Jamie turned back to Neville and stripped him of his robe. He groaned and she knew there wasn't much time before someone discovered he was missing. She pulled the robe around herself and looked at the corridor where Mascuria had emerged with the gurney. That had to be the way back to the morgue area, back to Polly. She rose from behind the altar and moved swiftly to the tunnel, painfully aware of eyes on her back but hoping that somehow she would be able to escape. She had barely made it inside the corridor when she heard a shout behind her and a faltering of the drum beat. Jamie didn't turn, but ran straight up the corridor, following the most well-lit tunnels, praying that they would lead her back to the morgue.

Footsteps echoed in the tunnel behind her, before the drum beat resumed its frenzied beat disguising the sound. Moving faster now, Jamie turned a corner and suddenly saw the wooden door and stairs heading up to the trapdoor. She dashed to the morgue door, running in and slamming the heavy door shut behind her. She pushed the bolt home just as the men behind her reached it, banging and shouting at her with foul language. Jamie imagined them covered in blood, their eyes full of hatred, with a taste for murder. She knew the bolt wouldn't hold them for long.

Turning, Jamie scanned the room. A heavy cabinet with medical instruments stood in the corner and there were oxygen cylinders placed in holding units against the wall, used in morgues when decomposition was advanced enough to require breathing apparatus. Jamie opted for the cabinet, pushing it over as glass shattered inside while she bumped it over the floor to put in front of the door.

That would buy her a few minutes at least. Jamie turned to look at the gurney where Polly's body lay with her own clothes discarded next to it. She tuned out the shouts of those who hunted her and went to her daughter's side, turning her body over and gently kissing the girl's forehead. The corpse was cold and Jamie felt the absence of life keenly as she brushed a lock of hair away from the impassive face. Finally, she could acknowledge that this wasn't Polly anymore, that this shell had been cast aside while her true essence had become part of the stars. But Jamie still wouldn't leave the body to be desecrated by Mascuria.

She looked around the lab again, realizing that there was no way out. If she left the room, she would likely be taken to the slaughter of the Lyceum. The madness of that underground crypt right now meant that they would tear her limb from limb, like the madness of the Dionysians, followers of the god of all things wild. As brave as Polly had believed her to be, Jamie knew that she didn't want to die like that, but in here, she could choose her own way. She could die in here and ensure that Polly's body was at peace. Without her daughter, she was nothing anyway. The banging grew louder at the door and the cabinet moved. In that moment, Jamie saw a way to achieve a final end.

Near the shelves full of monsters was a neat pile of sacking used to wrap specimens for transportation. Jamie picked up Polly's body, cradling her little girl as she had when she was alive. She laid her down gently on the pile, using one sack to cover her nakedness and another under her head as a pillow. It wasn't quite the pyre of the Viking princess that Polly had admired in her history class, but it would be enough to take them both onwards.

Jamie moved swiftly across the room as the door rattled furiously. She opened the valves on the oxygen cylinders, twisting them to full capacity, hearing the hiss as they started to expel gas. Jamie couldn't help but breathe deeply for a second, relishing the purity as it chased away the last of the hallucinogens from her brain. She found two bottles of ethanol and hurled them to the ground, the vapor from the absolute alcohol making her cough. Turning, she grabbed one of the heavy medical textbooks from a shelf and started to smash the glass jars containing the anatomical specimens. Jamie couldn't help her tears as the liquid formalin released its contents and at the sound of breaking glass, Jamie heard the attempts of the men outside redouble in effort. Mascuria would be desperate to rescue his beloved specimens, his life's work.

Twisted body parts plopped onto the floor in a wash of preserving liquid, and dissected fetus corpses joined them in a hideous soup of human remains. Jamie stepped carefully, not wanting to damage them any more. Where Mascuria had seen the deformed beauty of teratology, Jamie saw only the worship of suffering and deliberate cruelty. Nature would not have let these poor innocents live, and now she would release them, along with her daughter.

Jamie's tears obscured her vision, as the formalin evaporated into the highly flammable formaldehyde gas. Now all she needed was a spark. Her eyes fell on her own leather jacket, with cigarettes and lighter in the pocket. She grabbed the jacket and rummaged through the pockets as the men outside broke the lock and the giant cabinet began to move. Jamie threw two of the large specimen jars at the base of the cabinet, then dropped to the floor and crawled under the sacking next to Polly's body. She leaned out and with one arm flicked her lighter open, plunging the lever and creating a spark.

The air flashed around her and as her arm burned Jamie dropped the lighter, igniting the formaldehyde and the body parts soaked in the flammable liquid. The air itself seemed to blaze and a frustrated scream came from outside the door as smoke billowed up and out. Jamie knew it wouldn't take long for the fire to reach their pile of sacking and together they would burn, a pyre of flame, just as Polly had wanted. Her heart hammered at the thought of dying this way but as she gathered Polly's body in her arms and pulled her jacket over herself, she knew it was the only way. The heat surrounded them and she closed her eyes, breathing in the toxic smoke, hoping that she might be overcome before the flames licked her body and the pain began.

A smashing came from the doorway and suddenly the men were in, but the flames had taken hold now and smoke filled the room, even as some of it billowed out into the corridor. The fire spread quickly in the morgue, amplified by the gaseous accelerants. Jamie opened her eyes, watching the vague shapes of three men approaching and she prayed that they wouldn't drag her alive from this place.

Mascuria was shouting desperately, his words barely audible over the crackle of flames, burning body parts dripping melted fat into sticky pools at his feet.

"No! My babies ... Help me."

He was picking up pieces of macerated flesh from the floor, hugging them to his chest and wailing in anguish. Jamie wrapped her arms tighter around Polly's body, pressing her face to the girl's back. As her lips met her daughter's skin to kiss it one last time, she heard Polly's voice in her head, clear as it had been when she had lived. *'Dance for me, Mum'.*

CHAPTER 27

FOR A MOMENT, JAMIE couldn't believe it but then the voice jump-started her resolve, for in that moment, she knew she couldn't just lie here and die. Polly's death didn't have to be her own end, it could be the beginning of a different life. If she died, the Nevilles could continue their sick practices and Mascuria might live to start a new collection. She couldn't let that happen.

Jamie pulled the leather jacket tighter around her, and peered out from beneath its protection. She clutched her burned arm tight to her body, the pain sharpening her senses. As the men moved further into the room, she could see a way out through the open door, as long as she could stay out of sight in the billowing smoke. She crawled away from Polly, then turned and wrapped her in the flammable sacking, pushing the precious body back towards the flames, willing it to be consumed before the fire was controlled. Jamie didn't want to leave her, feeling an emotional tug to what was left of Polly's physicality, but she knew that her pragmatic daughter would have loved being part of bringing this evil to justice.

Still kneeling, Jamie grabbed another of the bottled specimens with a piece of sacking and hurled it toward the opposite end of the room. It exploded in the air from the heat, raining glass shards down and the smoky outlines of the men turned towards the combustion. In that second, she ran, ducking low to the floor and slipping out into the corridor. She coughed, choking in the smoky atmosphere, knowing that she had to get out. Jamie ran for the staircase towards the trapdoor and the labs above and suddenly saw a figure ahead of her in the smoke. It was Esther Neville, her slight figure stepping upwards towards her escape.

Jamie shadowed her up the staircase, remaining far enough behind that the smoke would obscure her form, but as Esther emerged through the trapdoor at the top, Jamie rushed the last few steps, diving for the closing gap and rolled out into the circular room. Esther turned at the noise and flew at Jamie, screaming in anger and frustration, a scalpel still in her bloody hand. The barking of the guard dog outside the room mingled with her sounds of fury, and Jamie could hear its claws scratching at the door, desperate to join the fight.

"You bitch, you've ruined it all." Esther panted, her blade thrusts clumsy with anger. Jamie rolled away and scrambled to her feet.

"Why did you do it, Esther?" Jamie asked, as she circled, keeping her distance from the knife. Esther's face was marked with blood, highlighting her cheekbones like murderer's rouge and her teeth were tarnished burgundy. Her dress was stained with gore and chunks of wet flesh adhered to the sleeves, sticking in the folds. She stank of blood, sweat and sex and Jamie's nose wrinkled at the odor that rose in waves. The pristine scientist was gone, replaced by this base creature marred with death.

"Did Jenna find out about the Lyceum?" Jamie asked. "Is that why you had to kill your own daughter?"

She saw a flash of what might have been regret in Esther's eyes, but it was dampened immediately by her fury as the woman darted across the room, thrusting with the scalpel. Jamie spun and swatted her arm away, thrusting Esther in the direction she was moving, using the momentum to push her off balance. The knife went wide and Jamie danced away. Esther whirled around, ready to come at her again.

"Jenna was created here," Esther snarled. "A product of my lab, the perfection of my process. She lived while others died as we refined the genetic structures, so she was always mine to destroy."

Jamie thought of the monsters burning in the lab below, pieces of defiled flesh cradled in Mascuria's arms. Those creatures had been Jenna's brothers and sisters: no wonder she had wanted to rescue them in whatever way she could.

"She was going to reveal the lab's secrets," Esther spat. "She had some crazy idea that the specimens we created here had rights. She wanted to expose us, and I couldn't let that happen."

"What about her child?" Jamie tried to keep Esther talking, circling round, waiting for an opportunity to strike.

"An unexpected miracle," Esther laughed. "Somehow her genes together with Day-Conti's created something astonishing, for she should have been barren. Her death was too early, though. I wanted to bring her here for experimentation but she resisted me. I pushed her as we argued and she fell, but then I couldn't leave her fetus. It has sparked a new line of research, so you see how nature rewards my work? How can it be wrong?"

Esther started across the room again, this time holding the scalpel with a firm grip, adjusting her stance for a lower thrust. The Rottweiler was going crazy outside the room, howling and barking.

"I will slash you until your blood runs freely and then let the dog hunt you in the forest." Esther laughed again, and Jamie heard anticipated pleasure in her voice. "You aren't worthy of the Lyceum anyway, and now they're scattered, escaping the fire you have brought on us." She crouched, light on her feet. "But the Lyceum will meet again, Detective, for there is an insatiable need for its extreme pleasures in this civilized world."

Jamie watched the way Esther moved, feinting left and seeing how she adjusted her stance.

"And only you can bring them that?" she asked, keeping her eyes on Esther, watching the knife weave in the air.

"Only I am willing to, and they're happy to pay handsomely for the privilege."

Jamie let Esther advance further as she backed towards one of the plastinated corpse sculptures on the wall. Smoke was now curling up from the trapdoor and Jamie imagined Polly's body consumed by the fire, finding freedom in the flames.

"What part did Christopher play?" Jamie asked, feeling the memory of his hands groping her own flesh.

Esther's face wrinkled in disgust at the mention of her husband.

"His only use is to find appropriate people for the Lyceum within the networks of the upper class, those weary of the usual pleasures, those looking for something more - visceral." Esther's eyes glittered green, and Jamie saw that her addiction had taken her to the very edge of sanity. She felt drawn to that threshold too, feeling the battle of her police training against the vicious desire to end this woman's life. Jamie wanted to grab the knife, slash it across Esther's throat and let her stinking blood join that of the murdered Day-Conti, to hack at her body, each cut for one of the mutilated victims she had created in the labs.

Esther suddenly thrust the blade, aiming at Jamie's exposed throat. With her back against the torso of the twisted sculpture of flesh, Jamie ducked away and the scalpel embedded deep into the sculpture, leaving Esther's ribs exposed. Jamie moved, grabbing Esther's body and pulling her forward, driving her knee hard into her solar plexus, winding the woman as she let go of the weapon. Jamie pulled it out of the sculpture as Esther sank to the floor. For a moment, she wanted to yank back Esther's head and slash her throat, finishing the woman's miserable life. But something stayed her hand, some sense of what she could allow of herself. Instead, Jamie thrust the blade downwards into Esther's thigh and then twisted it as the woman howled in pain. Blood spurted from the wound, adding to the stains on her clothes. The dog barked ferociously, clawing to get in.

"That's for Jenna," Jamie said, and ran for the door, picking up the edge of the thick rug as she reached it. She pulled the rug about her body, using it as a shield for her soft flesh in case the dog tried to attack her. Esther looked up and in her green eyes, Jamie saw that she knew what was about to happen.

"No!" Esther screamed, and Jamie pulled open the door, letting the Rottweiler in, snarling and barking, teeth bared in vicious savagery. The scent of blood and gore on Esther was too much and the dog bounded across the room. She tried to get away from it but its teeth ripped into her leg by the open wound. The powerful dog began to shake her and Esther fell to the floor, the blood on her torso and face driving the dog wild. As it bit and wrenched at her exposed body, Esther's cries grew weaker.

Jamie was momentarily transfixed by the brutal savaging and the sound of the dog feeding on Esther while she still lived. The animal was deep in the blood lust of the recent kill, but Jamie knew it wouldn't be long before it turned on her. She dropped the rug and darted out through the door, slamming it closed behind her as the dog swung its head from the dying woman, baring its teeth in a bloody grimace, defending its prey.

Jamie stood shaking in the lab corridor, the pristine environment a strange juxtaposition to the unholy chaos she had witnessed down in the caves. But what had been created up here was a part of that dark underworld. Science walked a knife edge, and in the wrong hands it became a tool for evil: the legacy of Mengele still lived on in these labs. Jamie rested her forehead on the door, listening to the sickening sounds of the dog worrying at Esther's body, an agonizing groan indicating that the woman was still alive. For a moment, Jamie felt revulsion at the fate she had left Esther to. Part of her wanted to find a weapon and go in to face the dog. She had sworn to protect people, to help them, to be on the side of good. Where did her actions leave her now?

Smoke started to seep under the door and she heard the dog start to bark and whine in fear. The noise of a massive explosion came from below, followed by a rumble deep under the earth. It was too late to save Esther now, and Jamie backed away from the door, stumbling away down the lab corridor. She heard the faint sound of sirens outside, alerted perhaps by the fire that must be billowing out of the building, the flames visible from the nearby village. Jamie felt her strength break within her. The long hours of the night, what she had seen in the depths of the caves, Polly's final end, it all welled up within her and tears began to run down her face as her mind struggled to focus on escape.

She pulled open the final door, and sank to the floor in the loading bay as the flashing lights of the police and fire service vehicles filled the clearing in front of the lab. She closed her eyes against the glare of spinning red, hearing shouts as officers moved swiftly into position. She knew what she must look like, a victim of some kind of attack dressed in only a diaphanous wrap, bare legs and feet marked by ankle cuffs, her face cut and bloodied, her limbs burned and smoky black. She didn't even have enough strength to say that she was a police officer. She just let one of the uniforms enfold her in a blanket and help her to a waiting ambulance as firemen streamed into the building.

CHAPTER 28

JAMIE DREAMED OF DEFORMED bodies emerging from specimen jars, the eyes of the abandoned fetuses open and accusing as their limbs charred and crackled in the flames. They dragged their stumpy bodies across the floor toward where she crouched in the billowing smoke, moans emanating from their tiny misshapen mouths. She felt the first touch, clammy like a frog on her bare leg as one began to pull itself up her body, wanting to fill her mouth with corrupted flesh.

"Jamie, Jamie, wake up. It's OK, you're safe now." The voice pulled her from the nightmare and Jamie opened her eyes, clutching at the bedclothes with shaking fingers. Her first lucid thought was of Polly. Was her daughter safe?

Then Jamie remembered what had happened and her world dimmed and nausea washed over her. The best part of her had died and yet, after everything, she was still alive. She wanted to sink back into drugged sleep and forget, anything to dull the raw pain inside. But she remembered the voice in the flames and Polly's desire that she dance again, and she forced herself to concentrate. Dragging herself mentally to consciousness, Jamie realized that she was in a small hospital room, wearing a surgical gown. Her head ached and her lungs felt squeezed in her chest, her breath ragged.

Blake sat by the bed, watching her, his gloved hand close to hers and Jamie felt comforted by his presence, for he understood the inherent darkness within people. She had pushed him away, but he was here now and she was grateful.

"Glad you made it out," he said, smiling. "Sounds like you almost didn't."

His vivid blue eyes were intense and filled with concern. Jamie lifted a hand to touch his face, his jawline now smoothly clean shaven so he looked much younger. His eyes darkened and he leaned into her palm. She felt a connection with him, he had experienced horror and known loss and she didn't have to explain herself with him. Blake had seen her vulnerability and it was a relief to know that he saw the truth.

"Jamie, I ..." Blake started to speak but Jamie heard an edge of emotion she couldn't face right now. His kindness would break her into pieces.

"What have you heard about the fire?" She interrupted him, wheezing a little.

"Only what's on the news," Blake said, and she saw understanding of the evasion in his expression. "Fire in a chemical lab spreads to the Hellfire Caves, sparking all kinds of rumors about what was actually going on that night. But the police say further investigations are needed before they reveal any more." He raised an interested eyebrow. "So tell me the gory details, because they've taken all your personal effects so I can't read them."

Before Jamie could reply, the door opened and Missinghall entered, his face a picture of concern.

Blake stood up. "I'll leave you two to talk," he said. "You know where to find me when you're ready, Jamie."

He turned and walked to the door, nodding in acknowledgment at Missinghall, whose look of guarded interest made Jamie wonder what the two of them had talked about in the waiting area.

Missinghall sat down by the bed.

"I know you're a senior officer and everything, but seriously, Jamie, what in hell were you thinking? Going in there alone was idiotic. You could have been killed."

Jamie couldn't help but smile at his concern, and the effort made her face ache. Her body felt so beaten up, and exhaustion sapped her strength.

"They had Polly's body, Al, and I knew that the team wouldn't get the evidence processed in time for the Lyceum's meeting." She thought of Esther Neville's savaged body in the lab and Polly's remains in the morgue below. "So what happened? Did you find anything left down there?"

"It's all a big mess, and the Commissioner is trying to keep a lid on everything." Missinghall shook his head. "But we found Esther Neville's body ripped to pieces, and the remains of Edward Mascuria and several other men in the morgue downstairs. There were other body parts too, none recognizable, as well as a teenager's skeleton, mostly burned to ashes."

Tears welled in Jamie's eyes and she took a deep breath.

"That's Polly," she whispered. "That's my daughter."

Missinghall closed his eyes for a second and then let out a long exhalation. "Oh Jamie, I'm so sorry. Her remains are being looked after, and once the investigation is over, I'm sure they'll be released to you for burial."

Jamie felt a kind of relief that Polly's physical body had been committed to the flames, her Viking princess sent onward through the fire.

"What about the caves?" she asked, her voice cracking with the memory. "They murdered Rowan Day-Conti down there, Al."

Missinghall nodded. "There were several bodies in the caves, badly burned, but we were able to ID Christopher Neville and parts of Day-Conti. That's what we're trying to keep a lid on, because he had only just been released from police custody when he disappeared again, presumably abducted by the Lyceum. There are also some pretty senior people in hospital with smoke inhalation, picked up by officers in the village as they emerged from the caves. Did you see any of the others involved?"

Jamie thought back to the swirling smoke and hallucinogenic nightmare of blades and blood. Had she really seen Detective Superintendent Dale Cameron amongst the Lyceum members, or was that some mirage fabricated by her own mind?

"I might be able to identify some of them," she said, frowning. "But I was under the influence of drugs and, given the involvement of Polly's body, I was emotionally distraught. I'm not exactly a reliable witness."

Missinghall's shoulders sagged with disappointment. "Oh well, Cameron's assigned two officers to keep you safe until we wind up the investigation, just in case. They're outside the door right now." Jamie felt a prickle of concern. If Cameron had really been down in the caves, he would want to make sure that she didn't identify him. Was she safe even now, she wondered, or were her suspicions just a result of the trauma? Missinghall continued. "And of course, the investigation into the Nevilles has been blown right open."

"But they're all dead," Jamie said softly. "The Lyceum has no purpose now that it has claimed the lives of the whole family."

"But the pharmaceutical company can go on without them, so that's been kicked up into a bigger investigation. For the murder case, it's just tying up the loose ends now, and of course, the dreaded paperwork." Missinghall snorted with laughter. "Guess you'll skip that this time."

"And what are they saying about me, Al?"

Missinghall sighed, his eyes darting away as he spoke

with reticence. "Of course, your actions are being debated and some are calling for your dismissal. You committed offenses Jamie: breaking and entering, concealing evidence which amounts to obstruction." He shook his head. "Although, of course, it was understandable given the circumstances and Polly's disappearance. You also managed to find the evidence that led to the Lyceum, even though it sounds as if you used some dubious methods." Missinghall's eyes flicked back to the door where Blake had left. "Despite everything, Cameron is campaigning for your return. But with everything that's happened, do you even want to come back?"

Jamie wondered at Cameron's actions to protect her from dismissal. Was he keeping her in debt to him because of what she had seen? Part of her wanted to just turn away and never go back, but what did she have in her life now? She thought of the sleeping pills in her bathroom cabinet, the emptiness of her flat and the hole in her heart. Life without Polly was unthinkable, but without her job, there would be no meaning at all.

"I want to come back," she said. "I need to be busy, Al."

Missinghall nodded. "But for now, you need some rest. I'll visit again tomorrow, keep you up to speed on the gossip."

He rose and walked to the door, then with a smile and a wave he was gone. Jamie turned her head to look out at the grey London sky, her thoughts only of Polly. As the wind whipped dry leaves past the window, she imagined her little girl out there, her soul soaring, finally free from the constraints of her physical pain. Jamie would always be a mother, but there would never be another Polly. The child born of her flesh and blood was no more and grief was like a solid bowling ball in Jamie's gut. But her every breath was a decision to live and perhaps she would dance again, in Polly's memory.

AUTHOR'S NOTE

This book is rooted in my own fascination with how the physical body defines us in life as well as after death. Here are some of the factual details behind the story, but of course, it is fictionalized and any mistakes are my own. You can find pictures of my research at: www.pinterest. com/jfpenn/desecration/

Hunterian Museum, Dissection and Teratology

You can find the Hunterian Museum at the Royal College of Surgeons in the heart of London and I based most of my initial research around the facts of John Hunter and 18th century medical dissections. When I first visited the Hunterian, I was physically overcome with weakness and nausea at some of the specimens I saw. This visceral reaction to human body parts fascinated me and that feeling is part of what I have tried to capture in the book. Despite my initial horror, I have been back to the Museum many times and consider it a privilege to examine the specimens that have given so much to science. If you'd like to read more, I recommend The Knife Man by Wendy Moore.

For this story, I embellished the collection at the Hunterian with artifacts from other teratological collections in museums around the world. My other sources included the Mutter Museum in Philadelphia, the Wellcome Collection in Euston, the fantastic Morbid Anatomy blog and a brilliant exhibition at the Museum of London on Doctors, Dissection and Resurrection Men.

Teratology is the study of abnormalities in physiological development and it is truly a disturbing field to investigate.

Corpse art, body modification and Torture Garden

The use of corpses for art was inspired by my visit to the Von Hagens Bodies exhibition in New York, where plastinated sculptures are displayed in the exploded way described. In all my research, I couldn't find a definitive answer on the legality of using donated bodies for art. The offense of stealing or abuse of a corpse differs by jurisdiction but if there is no 'ownership' of the corpse then the lines seem blurred. So I have taken fictional liberties with Rowan Day-Conti's artwork.

Body modification by choice is an extreme form of self-expression that has a vibrant sub-culture. Torture Garden is a real fetish club in London where modification, as well as other forms of expression, are embraced. The inspiration for O's character was a painting of a man with a large octopus tattoo at the National Gallery and I'll be writing her complete story in another book as she keeps returning to my thoughts.

Psychic reading of objects/ psychometry

My obsession with the supernatural continues to be a theme in my writing. When I visited the Hunterian, one of the first things I saw was a wooden table with one of the earliest dissections of blood vessels. I imagined the person who had lain there, the rest of their flesh dissected away and that's when I wondered what it would be like to read objects as Blake does.

Police procedure

Although I have used books and expert readers to help me with the police procedural aspect of the book, I have taken creative liberties with Jamie's role. The story is less about police procedure and more about Jamie's journey and the exploration of deeper themes, so all mistakes are purely my own. The use of psychics by the Police is fictionalized.

Tango

I have always wanted to dance tango and the scene of Jamie dancing was inspired by the book Twelve Minutes of Love. A Tango Story by Kapka Kassabova. I dare you to read it and not want to head straight for a milonga.

Mengele and vivisection

Josef Mengele used human vivisection in the Nazi camps and was particularly interested in twins and genetic abnormalities. There are reports that he indeed conjoined a pair of Roma twins. The notebook and anatomical Venus are fictionalized, although there are many specimens of the latter in collections around the world.

Hell Fire Caves, West Wycombe

The Hell Fire Caves are real and you can visit to read the rumors of what went on down there in the dark nights, which I have taken the liberty of expanding into something more dramatic for modern times.

A Brooke and Daniel Psychological Thriller

DELIRIUM

J.F.PENN

For Jonathan, who accepts the crazy in me.

And for my readers, for whom I put these dark
thoughts on the page.

"Those who the Gods wish to destroy,
they first make mad."

Anonymous ancient proverb

"He punishes the children for the sin of the parents
to the third and fourth generation."

Numbers 14:18

PROLOGUE

"HERE WE SEE THE mad as monstrosities and tainted creatures."

Dr Christian Monro advanced the slide to show a vintage black and white picture: a man huddled in a corner with haunted eyes, his dirty straitjacket mottled with blood. "We must, of course, treat such as these with humanity but we must also ensure their stain does not continue into the next generation." Christian paused, savoring the moment of complete attention. "The implementation of my proposals will safeguard the future of our great nation. Thank you."

Applause filled the small room, and Christian bowed his head a little, acknowledging their respect. He had been courting this group for years now, the politicians and the religious right, as well as those in big business who funded the enterprise. He breathed in deeply, a smile playing over his lips. Finally, they were taking his work seriously, which was surely worth the sacrifice of those he had referred to the research centers.

Christian pushed the faint glimmer of guilt down as the applause ended and one of the more senior figures in the room nodded slowly at him, a promise of future favor in his gaze. Dr Damian Crowther was bald, his head angular and smooth, with one eye blue and the other brown. Despite his distinctive appearance, Crowther wasn't a man anyone stared at for long. Christian had heard rumors of the doctor's investigations into the farthest reaches of the mind, where madness bled into what some would call the paranormal. Crowther's favor was known to be a double-edged sword, but perhaps it was time to embrace the risks for the potential of a higher reward.

As Crowther turned away, Christian looked at his watch, worry gnawing at the edges of his triumph. He didn't want to rush away, but he had to make the meeting and none of these men could know about it.

After extricating himself from the late-night whiskey drinking, Christian grabbed a taxi to South London, patting his top pocket where he had the money in a cream envelope. It was a small price to pay for breathing space, but once he had power behind him, Christian would deal with the blackmailer. Handing them over for research purposes would make for appropriate recompense.

The Imperial War Museum was lit from below, a spectacular edifice, a symbol of Britain's military might. Of course, Christian had visited before, but it had been more out of curiosity for the building's past. The Bethlem Hospital had once been based here, the original Bedlam of nightmare, where the groans of the suffering were muted by thick walls. The note had told him to go around to the side gate, so Christian walked around the perimeter. It was open as promised and he walked through, into the trees at the side of the expansive park space. He strode towards the side door, gathering his confidence as a suit of armor, made stronger by his earlier triumph. Perhaps he would give this blackmailer a talking to instead. He flexed his fingers ... maybe something more than that.

The inside of the building was dark, with just a few floor lights leading inward. Christian could hear faint sounds of music down the corridor, a mournful violin, the deep notes of a cello. A door was ajar further into the museum. He walked to it and stepped inside, apprehension overtaken by curiosity.

Candles burned in the corners of the room and shadows flickered on the walls. In the dim light, Christian saw a large wooden object and he stepped further into the room to see it more clearly. A sudden movement of air and a shift of shadows made his eyes narrow. He turned, but it was too late. A needle jabbed his neck and Christian raised his hand to the wound, suddenly dizzy. He sank to the floor, suddenly faint. There was someone else here with him, but the figure retreated quickly back to the gloom, out of his reach.

"What … have you done?" Christian murmured, as his throat tightened and weakness deadened his limbs. "I have your money."

"Money you received for betraying those who trusted you," the whisper came in the dark. "I don't want it. But I do want you to remember before you die, for what you have done is just a reflection of what your ancestors once did in this place."

Colors appeared in front of Christian's eyes, morphing into the shapes of creatures that landed on the walls around him. They had tiny needle-like teeth and he tried to move away from them, but their legs scuttled fast as they swarmed onto him and he had no strength to bat them away. His skin itched but Christian couldn't raise his arms to scratch. His heart thudded in his chest. It was a drug – some kind of hallucinogen. It had to be, but knowing didn't change how he felt. Biting, tearing, tiny knives slashing a thousand cuts across his flesh as the creatures began to feast.

"Please," Christian panted, heart racing, breath ragged. "What do you want?"

The figure came out of the shadows, like a nightmare from history, an echo of the photo Christian had shown earlier that night. The man wore a dirty straitjacket, stained with blood and pus. The arms hung loose, long sleeves dragging on the floor, the straps hanging down. A black mask covered his eyes and nose, and Christian could see that the man's dark eyes were bright with intent. There was no madness within.

"You call them monstrosities, tainted blood that must be bred out. But it is you who are defective, a blemish to be erased. And now you're in here, you must be crazy. Welcome to the lunatics' ball, Monro."

The man threw his hands in the air and spun in place, the ties from the straitjacket whirling about him, creating a vortex that Christian couldn't tear his eyes from. The string instruments soared, filling the room with a cacophony of jarring noise, grating against his brain. Christian was transfixed by the whirling, as the colors shattered and the fuzzy feeling intensified. It seemed that other figures joined the man as the music played on, shadows turning into the phantoms of those who had been locked up here so long ago. A beautiful girl with bare feet whirled in place, spinning around, her thin arms held like a ballerina. She opened her mouth to smile and Christian saw that her teeth were all missing, her gums bloody emptiness – a victim of force-feeding. A hulking figure appeared next to her, his head bound with bandages around a broken jaw, moaning in a grotesque parody of joy as he lumbered to the center of the room to turn with them. Another man dragged himself across the floor towards Christian, his head shaved, electrodes still attached, drool dripping down his chin. His eyes locked on the doctor, but his stare was fixed, as if no soul dwelled behind that facade of humanity.

Christian tried to push himself up and away from the wall, but the man in the straitjacket bore down upon him.

The figures in the room dissipated and floated away as his image alone sharpened into focus once again. Had there even been any others? Christian knew the drug had a deep hold now, his mind tilted by chemical intrusion. He had no strength to fight as the man dragged him across the floor.

"Perhaps you're feeling a little stressed?" the man spat, his words bitter as he hoisted Christian onto the wooden chair, buckling straps at his ankles and wrists. Christian struggled, but it was as if he was in a thick soup and his limbs wouldn't obey his brain's command. The man bent down and picked up a padded wooden box with straps to hold the two sides together. "This should help."

Christian tried to shout, to scream, but the drugs had deadened his tongue and made it thick like a lump of liver. He could only moan as the man placed the box over his head and tightened the straps. It was heavy and dense, the darkness absolute. Christian's heart thumped in his chest as he tried to breathe through his nose, but the box was tight against his skull with only a small hole for air. He was on the edge of consciousness, panic rising as his heart rate spiraled out of control. He felt a knock against the box on top of his head and the noise of a flap being opened. A chink of light enabled Christian to see the padding inside, a dull off-white, the color of old sheets, right in front of his eyes. Then, he felt a drip of cold water on the top of his skull.

He shook his head violently, rattling the restraints that held his arms and legs. But he couldn't move far enough away and the water kept dripping, faster now. It became a thin stream that pooled under his chin, rising in cold inches against his skin. Christian closed his mouth as the level rose to his lips. He tipped his head, angling it to allow him breathing space, but he only succeeded in trickling water up his nose. Christian spluttered, trying to breathe and cough, but the water kept coming.

He heard laughter against the backdrop of music, and he imagined the spinning figures watching his torture, their eyes shining in anticipation of his end. Christian jerked and writhed, fighting to escape the stream. He moaned as panic overwhelmed him. The water level was almost at his nose now, covering his mouth. He threw himself to one side, felt himself connect with a body there, but the level kept rising.

Christian took a final breath as the water reached his nose, holding it in as he tried desperately to escape the crushing pain in his lungs. As the cool liquid touched his eyelids, he could hold his breath no longer. He choked, spasming in agony as he screamed for air, mouth opening instinctively. Water rushed down his throat, sucked into his lungs. In the moment before he died, Dr Christian Monro felt the fingers of the ghosts clawing at him, echoes of Bedlam with twisted faces, dragging him down to the depths of their Hell.

CHAPTER 1

DETECTIVE SERGEANT JAMIE BROOKE took a deep breath, steeling herself to face the crime scene. It was her first major case since her compassionate leave had come to an end, and although she craved the intellectual stimulation, part of her just wanted to huddle under the covers at her flat and shut out the world. Thoughts of her daughter, gone only three months now, intruded at every second. Jamie welcomed them, but if she let them intensify too much, she knew she would just break down. Not quite the look she favored in front of her work colleagues. Detective Constable Alan Missinghall stood outside the squad car, finishing his morning coffee and sticky bun, waiting for her to join him on the pavement. All Jamie had to do was step out and accompany him to the scene.

Missinghall had been tremendous support during the events a few months ago that culminated in the flames of the Hellfire Caves, and she was grateful for his friendship. Despite her seniority in the force, he was one of the only allies she had after years of insistent independence that protected her from gossip but left her mostly alone. Jamie pulled down the mirror and checked her dark hair, tucking a few strands into the tight bun she habitually wore for work. Her face was gaunt, cheekbones angular, and her pale skin was dull from too long inside during the British winter. *Time to get back out there again*, she thought. Jamie exhaled slowly and opened the door, pulling her coat tightly around her against the chill of the early morning.

"The body was found in one of the offices in the oldest part of the building," Missinghall said, walking slowly, as his six-foot-five frame meant his stride was double Jamie's. "This place has changed substantially since the days of Bedlam. That's for sure."

The Imperial War Museum had been built in the early nineteenth century to house the Bethlem Royal Hospital, known to history as Bedlam. Although the hospital for the mentally ill was relocated in 1930 to the outer suburbs of Kent, this place remained the hospital of the imagination, a virtual horror movie set. Jamie shivered as she glanced up at the cupola rising above a classical facade, but it was the massive First World War guns that drew her attention, dwarfing the uniformed officers already onsite. Each huge naval gun weighed one hundred tons and could fire shells over sixteen miles. Its yellow bullet-shaped ammunition stood around the gardens, each waist height. Jamie couldn't help but touch the spiked top of one of them, a testament to man's ingenuity at designing killing machines. While this place was once a supposed restorer of minds, it was now a home for weapons of mass destruction. A building in homage to war, perhaps the ultimate form of collective madness.

"The museum is currently undergoing massive restoration," Missinghall said. "They're sprucing it up in time for the centennial of the First World War, so the main galleries aren't open to the public right now."

"How was the body found?" Jamie asked.

"One of the workmen was looking for a quiet place to smoke as it was pouring with rain outside." Missinghall chuckled. "He would have needed a few more ciggies after that."

They walked towards the steps leading up to the museum entrance, passing a slab of concrete with a graffitied face and the slogan 'Change Your Life' tattooed on its tongue. Its eyes were manic, the open maw a frozen scream. Jamie bent to read the plaque, and saw it was from the Berlin Wall, a remnant of that divide between East and West Germany. This was a strange place indeed, aimed at commemoration without intentionally glorifying violence.

The sound of a little girl giggling whispered on the wind. Jamie looked up sharply, her eyes drawn to the trees beyond the memorial. Polly ran there, her blue dress caught by the breeze as she twirled amongst the early spring flowers. For a moment, hope filled Jamie's heart, but then the girl's face changed. It was another girl, alive and vibrant, where her daughter was gone. Polly was ashes now, her physical remains in a terracotta urn that sat on the shelf in her flat.

Jamie choked back her emotion and turned to follow Missinghall, who was nearing the main entrance. These moments still threatened to overwhelm her, even months after Polly's death. *Is it self-harm or self-care to want to hurt myself?* Jamie wondered. Pain is a reminder of continued life, and every day she had to make a decision about carrying on.

The craving for a cigarette was intense, her hands shaking a little at the thought. Jamie thrust one hand in her coat pocket, clutching the tin where she put the menthol butt ends, measuring her addiction. She could hardly fit the lid on by the end of the day, but right now she resisted the yearning to smoke, clenching her fist around the tin instead. She wanted to get back to the capable woman she was known as in the force. She just needed to gather her strength.

Jamie and Missinghall went through the main entrance, showing their warrant cards to the officer on the door. The crime-scene perimeter was much further inside the museum, and they walked through a warren of building works, preparation for a grand opening at the centenary of the First World War. It was organized chaos, the kind of place that would be a nightmare to process for evidence, especially with the tight deadlines for the centennial. After winding through corridors, they reached a doorway where they logged into the crime scene and put on the protective coveralls necessary to stop contamination.

The body was still in situ and a number of Scene of Crime Officers (SOCOs) worked efficiently in the room, processing the scene. Jamie tilted her head to one side, her curiosity piqued by the strange tableau. A familiar prick of interest penetrated the haze of grief and she knew that this case was just what she needed to take her mind off her own pain.

The room smelled of candle smoke overlaid with a damp, fungal aroma. A man sat in an oversize wooden chair, his feet bound to the struts and his arms strapped to the sides. His head was entirely covered by a box made of dark wood, so the victim looked more like a dummy from the London Dungeon than a real dead body. He wore a white shirt under a dark tailored suit, and it looked like his clothes were damp. The straps that held his wrists made his suit wrinkle, and his fingertips were bloody, nails cracked, as if he had tried to claw his way out of the chair. Jamie shivered at the thought of being trapped there, unable to move, unable to escape.

Forensic pathologist Mike Skinner stood against the wall, looking at his watch every minute, as if that would hurry the SOCOs. Finally the photos were complete, the device swabbed, and the body could be moved.

Missinghall helped Mike unfasten the straps that held

the box in place and together they lifted it off. The victim's head fell forward, unsupported now, onto his chest. A rush of water cascaded down and a SOCO darted forward to capture a sample. Jamie glimpsed ivory padding inside as Missinghall laid the box on the floor for SOCOs to process further. Mike unstrapped the man's arms and legs, fastening forensic bags over the exposed flesh to protect any evidence. Missinghall helped him to lift the body into a plastic body-bag on top of a waiting gurney. The man looked professorial, authority still held in his bearing even in death. He wasn't a large man, his frame short and compact, not fat but clearly more used to a lecture theatre than a gym. His hair was grey, still wet, and his lips were grey.

"First impressions?" Jamie asked.

"Drowned, I'd say," Mike replied, his curt response purely professional. "But I'll know more after I check his lungs back at the morgue."

Missinghall moved to the gurney and with gloves on, opened the man's jacket. From the top pocket, he pulled out a thick envelope and placed it in a clear plastic evidence bag, a wad of cash visible inside.

"This wasn't theft, that's for sure," Missinghall said, delving back into the man's pockets. He pulled out a thin leather wallet containing a couple of bank cards and a driver's license.

"Doctor Christian Monro," he read. "That makes things easier." He looked over at Jamie, one eyebrow raised. "Guess I'll get on with the preliminary statements then. I'll start with the security team."

A bustling came from the door, and one of the uniformed officers beckoned Jamie over to the edge of the crime-scene markers. A man stood there, shuffling from one foot to another, wringing his hands, eyes darting to the gurney inside the room.

"I'm Michael Hasbrough, the curator of the museum," he blustered. "This is terrible, terrible. You have to keep the press away. The centennial is only in a few weeks, and there's a Fun Run today, as well. It's going to get busy outside soon. You have to hurry up. Please."

Jamie put out a hand to calm the man.

"We need to process the scene properly, Mr Hasbrough. It will take some time, but of course, we'll try to be discreet."

He shook his head violently. "How can you be discreet with a damn body and all those uniforms outside?" Hasbrough seemed to realize what he had said. "With respect to the dead, of course." He glanced into the room again, his eyes taking in the scene more fully. "Perhaps I can help." He pointed towards the box on the floor next to the unusual chair. "I can tell you what that is."

"Go on," Jamie said.

"It's called a Tranquilizer. The device was used on mentally ill patients to calm them down back when this place was the old Bedlam Hospital. They were strapped in and the box placed on their head. The padding stopped any light or sound, like a primitive sensory deprivation tank. Water was sometimes poured over the head of the patient while they were in the box. Apparently it was meant to relax them." He grimaced. "Can't see why though."

"Sounds more like a kind of waterboarding," Jamie said, wondering what the victim might have done to deserve such treatment.

The curator nodded. "There are reports of people dying in the device, of course, but then much of the early treatment for mental illness was inhumane by today's standards. It was designed for control and restraint rather than rehabilitation of any kind."

"Do you have those reports here?" Jamie asked.

Hasbrough shook his head. "No, everything to do

with Bedlam is at the hospital. It has moved a number of times over its dark history. Now it's at Beckenham in Kent, a lovely campus, nothing like the cold Gothic place this would have been."

"And this room?" Jamie asked. "Was it part of the old hospital?"

The curator nodded, relaxing as he shared his field of expertise. "Yes, the museum has been substantially altered since it was a hospital but this is one of the old wings. It could have been a treatment room, but we'd have to check the old plans to make certain."

Jamie turned to look back into the room. "So where did the chair come from?"

"We still have some old artifacts in the basement storerooms, and many of them have been cleared out recently for the renovations. This chair could have been easily moved within the museum. It's not a heavy device, as you can see."

Jamie glanced around at the corners of the surrounding corridor.

"Are there any cameras in this part of the building?"

Hasbrough shook his head. "Unfortunately not. We're redoing all the security but because this is under renovation, the cameras were all taken down."

"Someone must have seen this man come in," Jamie said.

The curator nodded. "Perhaps, but we've never had any problems here before. You can't just walk off with a tank or a plane, after all."

Mike Skinner finished the initial processing of the body, covered it and fastened the straps on the gurney. As he rolled it towards the door, the wheels squeaked on the tiled floor. Hasbrough moved back, his nostrils flaring like a skittish horse, as if the mere presence of the body could contaminate him somehow.

"Can you at least take it out the back way?" he asked as the body was rolled past. Skinner ignored the man, heading towards the main entrance. "There are children out there," Hasbrough called. "Bloody half term. Always a crazy time."

"What's going on today?" Jamie asked.

"It's a charity Fun Run for Psyche – you know, that politician Matthew Osborne's thing. Advocates for equality and justice for the mentally ill, or something like that. They got permission for the event months ago. Thought it might be an appropriate place given the history here, and the new hospital is too far out for the press to bother going. But here, there will be some attention and Osborne knows the strings to pull, for sure. I think he's even running today, along with a load of yummy mummies and their brats, no doubt. There are hundreds of people due to turn up, raising money for charity. Be hell to shut it down now."

Jamie glanced down at the plans of the museum she had on her smartphone.

"It looks like the field is far enough away from the crime scene that we don't need to stop it, but we'll need statements from all the people who were here early, including your staff."

Hasbrough nodded. "Of course."

Jamie turned back to the room, watching the SOCOs go about their work, seeing Missinghall on the phone. He waved his hand at her as he began to read the registration details from the driver's license, clearly not needing her right now.

"Can you show me the outside of the building?" she asked Hasbrough.

"Sure, follow me."

Walking out into the fresh air, Jamie breathed in deeply. The sun was peeking through the clouds and it looked like the day might brighten up. Volunteers were hanging bunting around the bushes, putting up Psyche signs and big arrows pointing to the field beyond the museum where the Fun Run would be. A blast of rock music came from the speakers, swiftly muted. Heads turned briefly and then returned to staring at the police vehicles in the forecourt. Jamie had no doubt that gossip about the murder would be round the group in no time.

"There's a back way into the museum," Hasbrough said, walking left from the main building.

"What time would this lot have started setting up?" Jamie asked, counting more than twenty volunteers across the field.

"Some of them were already here when I arrived at six," he said. "That Petra Bennett is some kind of superwoman, I swear it. She was ordering the lads around, getting the stage set up." He pointed across the field towards a figure in shades of moss green and gold, the colors of the charity. Her mousy hair caught a ray of sun, and she brushed an almost-blonde strand from her face, the gesture impatient, as she bent to lift another box.

"The Fun Run starts at ten a.m., so they'll be packing up again by two. Will you have to disturb them?"

Jamie watched Petra speaking to a young volunteer, her hand gestures fast as she pointed down the field. Here was a woman who knew what was going on, and a potential suspect.

"We'll need a list of everyone who was onsite this morning, and then the team will be taking some statements." Jamie saw his disturbed glance. "But we'll try to keep it low key."

They walked on a little way.

"This is the back entrance and the one I use." Hasbrough pointed at a cream safety door. "It was unlocked this morning, but to be honest, it usually is. George, the main night watchman, comes out for a smoke now and then. You can keep time by his addiction."

Jamie clenched her fists as the wave of longing for her own cigarettes swept over her.

"What time does he usually come out here?"

"Every hour on the hour. You can check that with him, but I reckon it gets him through the nights when nothing happens. And nothing ever happens, Detective." Hasbrough paused. "At least, it didn't use to."

As they walked back to the main entrance, Jamie saw a man arrive on the other side of the field, his arms laden with bags and balancing a box in one hand. Petra ran to help him, and a smile lit his face. Jamie had seen Matthew Osborne before on TV, that slightly crooked smile flashed for the press, the gaunt jaw highlighted by an artful line of stubble. He was Secretary of State for Health, but the papers were more interested in his love life. Jamie didn't pay too much attention to politics, but she could see how this man fit right in, as he leaned into Petra and kissed her cheek. She was like a dull little bird, eager to help him, fluttering around his bright plumage. She wondered if he had that effect on all women.

For a moment, Jamie envied Matthew's easy way with people, thinking of her own inability to get close to anyone. It used to be her and Polly against the world, mother and daughter bound together, but now Polly was gone. Fighting the world alone was like standing under a freezing shower all day every day, and sometimes she was beaten to her knees by its force.

Jamie's phone buzzed and she turned from the field to check the text. Today's picture was a clear milk bottle on a red brick step, a daffodil sticking out at a jaunty angle. As usual, Blake had signed it with a smiley. Jamie grinned. For a moment, she felt the darkness in her mind lift a little. Since Polly's death, Blake had kept his physical distance, but every day he let her know he was thinking of her. That alone meant a lot, but she still couldn't see him, for he had a gift. Blake's ability to read emotions in objects meant he would feel the depth of her loss, and she was afraid she would break if he knew.

"Jamie, I've got an address. It's in Harley Street," Missinghall called as he left the museum entrance, walking towards them. "The guy was a psychiatrist. His housekeeper can let us in."

"OK," Jamie said. "Let's go check it out."

CHAPTER 2

BLAKE DANIEL SMILED AS he walked across Great Russell Street into the courtyard of the British Museum. He put his phone in his pocket and pulled his thin gloves back on, covering the scars on his hands. It pleased him to send Jamie jolly pictures each day and, although she only ever responded with a smiley in return, he knew that at some point she would emerge from her grief. He wanted to be there when she did. Jamie had become a talisman against his own oblivion, and the nights when he craved the tequila bottle were becoming ever more rare. She was worth waiting for.

Blake looked up at the facade of the British Museum, the tall Ionic columns stretching to the Greek-style pediment, a fitting entrance to the myriad wonders within. The glass roof to the Great Court was now fully repaired from the Neo-Viking attack last month, and the public were streaming in again. The day he stopped loving this place was the day he ought to retire, Blake thought.

He bounded up the steps into the tourist throng, eyes wide and clutching maps as they wondered where to start their day's adventure. Blake loved to try and guess where people came from. Those who journeyed here to stay in multicultural London had intermingled into one great family that managed to rub along together most of the time. Sporadic fights broke out, of course, for a family must hate as well as love, as in all the best Shakespeare plays. But that made life more interesting. Blake's own features were mixed, just as his cultural heritage was. He had the tight curly hair of his Nigerian mother, which he kept at a military number-one cut, and blue eyes of the northern ocean from his Swedish father. With his darker skin tone and boy-band features, he could walk with confidence in any part of London.

Swiping his pass by the door, Blake walked downstairs to the offices of the museum, where researchers worked on artifacts for the exhibits above. There was a sense of excitement here, overlaid with the calm of academia, as the minutiae of past civilizations were dissected. Blake was one of a number of researchers, but his work was supplemented by his peculiar sensitivities. It was called clairvoyance by some, or psychometry, although Blake preferred extrasensory perception, and for him, it manifested as a series of visions gleaned from an object. Their intensity was dictated by the emotions that had attached themselves to the artifact over time, so the more personal the item, the more clearly he could read it. He habitually wore thin gloves to cover his skin so as not to be overwhelmed by the visions from daily life, those gloves serving the dual purpose of hiding disfiguring scars from a childhood of abuse.

Walking through the office towards his own workspace, Blake's eyes fixed on the object that lay upon a white cloth on his desk. He had been assigned the fourteenth-century Nubian cross of Timotheus, and he couldn't get a reading on it at all. Perhaps it was a good thing – perhaps he had been relying on the visions too much, before trying to back up his claims with proper research. But his vivid writing certainly brought in the grants, as it captured the imagination of donors with his description of characters who might have been involved in the object's history. They weren't to know how much of it was truth discovered through emotional perception.

Blake sat down in front of the cross, studying the clover-leaf ends, triple hoops of iron in a simple, functional design. Maybe the passage of time had somehow cleansed the cross of its resonance, or perhaps the priests had worn gloves as part of devotional garments. Nubia had been converted to Christianity in the sixth century and had a rich cultural heritage, although the area was now split between Egypt and Sudan, both Muslim countries. This cross could give an insight into an area of Africa that had once been dominated by Christianity, with powerful empires that many would not believe of the fractious continent these days.

"How's your paper going?"

The voice startled Blake and he turned to see Margaret, his boss, standing behind him. She held a small package in a white padded bag.

"I'd like a draft by the end of next week."

Her face was pinched, but that wasn't unusual. Blake knew he skated near the edge with her, and his frequent absences due to hangover recovery had been noted. Tequila and a string of empty one-night stands had made him almost a part-time employee, but in the last few months he had been a lot more reliable. Perhaps Margaret was softening towards him.

"Of course," he said. "I'm still working on researching Timotheus from the Coptic scrolls. I found a new translation yesterday so I'll use that as part of the paper."

Margaret nodded, and held out the package.

"This came for you. But you really shouldn't have personal items delivered to the museum." She frowned. "You know what a nightmare security is with all the random objects we're sent."

Blake took the parcel. "Sorry, I didn't order anything, so I don't know why …"

His voice trailed off as he recognized his mother's sloping handwriting on the front.

"I'll leave you to it then," Margaret said after waiting a beat too long, clearly interested in what was inside.

Blake laid the package down on his desk. Why would his mother post anything? They hadn't spoken in years, and although he sent cards now and then, telling her he was OK, he hadn't mentioned his address or where he worked. Of course, Google meant that everyone was discoverable online these days: his academic papers had been in some journals and his photo was on the museum website. Blake wanted to rip off the paper to find out what was inside, but some part of him held back. Whatever this was, it drew him to a part of his life he had left behind long ago.

One of the meeting rooms was empty, so Blake took the package and walked inside, shutting the blinds and closing the door. He took his gloves off and looked at his hands, the ivory scars on his caramel skin like an abstract painting. Scars his father had inflicted in an attempt to beat the Devil from his son, believing the visions to be diabolical possession and Blake's hands a portal to Hell. But the bloody whippings had only curbed the visions until the scars began to heal, and then they returned, a curse that no amount of pain could stop.

It had been fifteen years since he had walked out on the abuse, turning away from his father and the religious community that he ruled with an iron rod, like the Old Testament prophets he had preached of in his sermons. But his mother … Blake blinked away the tears that threatened as guilt rose inside. He had to leave her, for there had been no other way. His father would rather have killed him than let the Devil take his son, or at least cut off his hands to stop the visions. And, as much as his mother loved him, she had been a devoted wife and servant, believing that it was God's will Blake be delivered from the curse by His prophet. Perhaps there was a trace of her here.

Laying his hands on the parcel, Blake closed his eyes to let the visions come. He was clean, no tequila for days, so his sensitivity was acute. He felt a rising anxiety, like a high-pitched note that hurt his ears, but under that lay a deep acceptance, a sense of peace in a faith he had no connection to. He saw a front door, the same one he had walked out years ago, and a woman's hand, older now, clutching the envelope. He wanted to see her face, wanted more than this brief glimpse into her world. Then he saw a drip, a series of medical machines, and heard a rasping gasp. He knew that voice. Blake pulled his hand away, heart pounding in his chest.

He ripped open the package and looked inside. A white cloth was wrapped around an object and there was a note, just one page. He pulled it out.

My son. There's too much to say and no time left anymore. I'm sorry. Your father has had a series of strokes. Please come. We love you.

Blake read the note again, unsure what he was supposed to feel. He wanted more from her, more than just these few lines after so long. *Why do children read so much into the words of parents?* he thought. *Why expect so much, when they are just people, damaged and desperate, just as we are?* Blake shook his head – the years apart should have given him more perspective.

The old man was dying, that much was certain. Maybe he was dead already, but the thought didn't leave Blake feeling any lighter. On the day he had walked out, Blake had sworn to dance on the old man's grave, wanting to stamp his boots onto the earth as if it had been the prophet's face. But over time, those feelings had hardened into a tight ball of anger that he kept locked up and buried within. The tequila helped soften it, helped him to breathe, but it was a bitch of a mistress that brought as much pain as it did relief.

He needed to know – which meant he had to look more closely. Blake pulled on one of his gloves, not quite ready to experience visions from whatever was in the package. He reached in and took out an object wrapped in a white handkerchief. Blake remembered how his father had always worn one, ironed perfectly into a pocket square for his suits. *A man should dress for his station*, he would say, *the Lord demands us to be our best.* An English affectation, Blake thought with a short smile. Perhaps it said more about his father's immigrant sensibilities than anything the Lord demanded.

The handkerchief was wrapped like a parcel. Blake slowly pulled the edges away to reveal his father's watch, a vintage Patek Philippe, the gold of its face tarnished and the leather strap worn, but still a beautiful piece. Blake's chest tightened and he concentrated on breathing, as a flash of memory took him back. He knelt at the altar while the Elders prayed aloud in tongues, his father's right hand slamming down the cane. Blake's eyes fixed on this watch on his father's left wrist, knowing the time it took to reach the bloody end of his penance and weeping while the seconds ticked away. He felt an echo of pain in his hands and he rubbed them, clenching his fists together as if holding hands with his past self might steel him to the memory.

The watch had been his grandfather's, and his father only took it off at night. For this to leave his wrist for any longer meant that he was seriously ill. Had he asked for it to be sent? Did his father want to see him? Or would it just be a final agony to know that Blake was still an outcast from his family, still considered to be of the Devil. Old age would not lessen the man's fundamental beliefs, but only make them more extreme. The strokes themselves would be seen as an attack from Satan, the tribulations of Job perhaps, and Blake imagined the church praying for their leader, interceding with God for His divine intervention. The reality was that his father was an old man.

Blake exhaled slowly, trying to calm his heart rate. The anxiety that gripped him even at the thought of his father seemed ridiculous now, yet still it held him fast. He wanted to touch the watch and feel something of what his father experienced, but he was also afraid of what he might see. When he was young, he had seen visions from his parents' things – he couldn't help it living in their house. But the glimmers of lust and violence from his father and the shuttered, rigid calm from his mother had frightened him. That's when Blake had first taken to wearing gloves, when his hands weren't bandaged from the beatings.

He took his glove off again and set a five-minute alarm on his smartphone. Sometimes the visions were too much, and he could be lost in overwhelming sights and sounds that left him on the brink of collapse. Sometimes Blake wondered if he should see a psychiatrist about his experiences, but he pushed away the fleeting doubts about his own sanity. These days, his reading helped to solve crimes. He remembered reading the ivory Anatomical Venus figurine with Jamie present and how she had pulled his hand away from the object, helping him out of the trance. But she wasn't here right now, and Blake wanted to see into his father's life. He needed to know whether he should go home and face his childhood fears.

Placing his hands over the watch, Blake gently laid them down, his fingertips connecting with the cool metal on the edges of the face and the smooth glass that covered it. Despite the scars, his sensitivity had only increased with age and experience. Blake let the visions come in a rush, breathing slowly as they swirled about him, glimpses of life flashing by. He sifted through the stream of impressions that assaulted his mind.

He went into the most recent remembrance, the raw emotion of a man crippled by multiple strokes, an awareness of mortality and fear of dying overlaid with too much pride to acknowledge the truth of the end. Blake looked out at the bedroom in his old house, but it was no longer the room he remembered.

The walls sprouted with black growths like nodes of cancer in a smoker's lung, spotted with dull green mold. In places, trickles of liquid ran down, pooling on the bare floorboards in patches of tainted burgundy, like diseased blood. Above the fireplace, one of the lumps moved and Blake realized it was a living creature. The hairs rose on the back of his neck as he perceived a bony spine and tail with skin like tar, the thing's face jagged and its eyes bright with lust for death. It shifted, its gaze lighting on the bed. Blake felt its stare invade his body, examining every cell for a sign of the inevitable end. He heard a moan and knew his father had made the sound: it was all he could utter. But there was no exorcism, no prayers he could invoke to cleanse the room of this filth. Hooded lids closed again as the dark creature waited. Blake sensed that it wouldn't be long now before it would feed.

He tried to see past the creatures and the corruption of the room. Was this some kind of hallucination, a manifestation of his father's worst fears, brought on by the stroke? Or could it be that he was seeing past the physical world into the spiritual realm? If that was true, then the God his father had served for a lifetime had forsaken him, for the room was filled with terror and the promise of Hell.

Blake pulled back, filtering the memories that were attached to the watch. He perceived an overwhelming sense of fear that overlaid everything, a panic barely held back by the violence of his father's fervent prayer and brimstone preaching. It was something he had never expected, for Magnus Olofsson had been the definition of strength, a watchtower the needy had run to for leadership and shelter. That fortitude had been the basis of respect in their community, where perspectives and lifestyles were held over from days long past. When Blake had walked out, he had changed his name as a final separation. Daniel Blake Olofsson had become Blake Daniel, and disappeared to a new life.

In the vision, he saw his mother's face, her eyes closed in prayer, and he felt his father's guilt as he looked at her. The emotion was so strong that Blake pulled away from the sensation quickly. He couldn't stand to know what his father was guilty of, not right now. But he held back from leaving the trance completely.

He had to go there, he realized. He had to return to the place he had run from years ago, and so Blake parted the veils of memory. He saw his own face as a young boy, kneeling by the altar in the church, tears running down as men surrounded him. He felt the righteous rage inside his father, but that anger wasn't directed at Blake, his son, it was at the Devil for taking him. Blake felt an echo of his father's thoughts as blood dripped onto the altar, *He punishes the children and their children for the sin of the parents to the third and fourth generation.*

The alarm pierced Blake's thoughts and he anchored his mind on it, pulling his hands away as he returned to the room under the British Museum again. Why was the verse from the book of Numbers in his father's mind as he labored with the cane? What sin had his father committed that God would punish his child for atonement?

CHAPTER 3

HARLEY STREET HAD LONG been noted for its private medical practices, and the very name resonated with old money and privilege. Number 37 was on the corner of Queen Anne Street, a Victorian five-story house with ornate windows. Jamie glanced up to the sculptures on the facade, displaying a laurel-crowned figure with volumes of Homer and Milton, and a reclining young man with a telescope and a star. Poetry and astronomy seemed curiously out of place on this street of medical history.

Missinghall unfolded himself from the police car, beginning his second morning pastry and offering Jamie a bite. His large frame meant he was always eating, and he chipped away at trying to get Jamie to eat more, tempting her with little morsels. Her clothes were loose around her hips now, and she often forgot to eat until she was nauseous with hunger by the end of the day. The physical reminder of her body's insistence for life was something she danced on the edge of resisting. Jamie had read that the Jain religion had a ritual death by fasting, and the vow of *sallekhana* could be taken when an individual felt their life had served enough of a purpose: when there were no ambitions or wishes left and no responsibilities remained. Some days, Jamie wanted to embrace such an end, but

Polly had told her to live, to dance, and her responsibility was still to bring justice to the dead. But was that enough of a purpose to keep her going?

It would have to be for today, Jamie thought, and accepted the offer of pastry with a smile. Missinghall broke off a generous piece and Jamie forced it down her throat, the act of swallowing almost against her will.

"There should be a housekeeper here," Missinghall said, brushing crumbs from his suit. Jamie noticed that he had red socks on today, peeking out from under his slightly too-short trousers, his way of bringing color to their dark work. "She manages the place for the practitioners."

Jamie pressed the buzzer and after a moment, the door opened. A slim woman in jeans and a Rolling Stones t-shirt stood at the entrance, her cropped ash-blonde hair belying her middle age. Jamie showed her warrant card and introduced herself and Missinghall.

"Of course, I was expecting you," the woman said. "What a business. Dr Monro dead. Well, I never." She shook her head. "Come in, come in. I haven't touched anything in his rooms, just like the officer told me on the phone."

She led them into the hallway.

"How many practices are there here?" Jamie asked.

"Four," the housekeeper said. "They keep themselves to themselves, and I look after all their rooms. Not that any of them are much trouble, you know."

"Any tension between the businesses at all?"

The woman turned on the first step of the stairs.

"Not that I would know about, Detective. But then I'm just the housekeeper now, aren't I?"

Despite her words, Jamie could see a cloud in her blue eyes. There was more here, but perhaps the rooms themselves would help set the scene before she pushed any harder.

On the second floor, the housekeeper unlocked a wooden door, inset with two half panes of stained glass featuring red and blue art deco roses.

"You can look around, and please take all the time you need, Detectives. I'll come back in a bit. Would you like tea?"

"Yes, please," Missinghall jumped at the chance. "We're both black, one sugar."

Jamie stepped into the room, pulling on a pair of sterile gloves as Missinghall did the same behind her.

She had expected a cozy nook with a couch and blankets, somewhere welcoming for private therapy. Instead, the rooms were fashioned in a Japanese minimalist style, with just two chairs and a small table in one main space and a study beyond. The walls were a light cream, with nothing to decorate the space. It was entirely blank, offering the patient no respite from their own mind.

Walking into the study area beyond, Jamie noted the filing cabinets of patient records and a general neatness and organization. There were thick medical textbooks on a bookshelf as well as a framed degree certificate, and a couple of files and a fountain pen lay on a desk of Brazilian walnut. In the corner was a small fridge, topped with a kettle and coffee plunger. On the wall, a single large canvas showed a blue ocean with white-capped waves. On first glance, the waters seemed calm, but as Jamie looked at it more closely, she noticed the darkening skies towards the edge of the painting as a storm approached. Under the waves there were shadows, darker patches of blue that could have been creatures of the depths. It was a strange painting, perhaps one of Monro's analysis tools, the shadows interpreted according to the viewer's perspective. Jamie imagined sharks there, with razor teeth to shred her flesh, but she still felt an urge to sink under the blue.

Missinghall walked to the back of the study, where

another door led onwards. He turned the handle. It was locked.

"That's his private apartment," the housekeeper said, walking in with the tea and a plate of biscuits. "I was never allowed in there. He was particular about that."

"Did he live as well as work here, then?" Jamie asked.

"Let's just say he didn't have a routine that meant he left his rooms too much." She hesitated. "I think that was a problem with some of the other partners in the building. He needed heating, electricity and other amenities at night, and never paid more than his allotted percentage. But of course, the other practices have wonderful people in them. None of them could possibly be involved in his murder."

Jamie smiled, helping her with the tea things. "Of course."

"I'll come back in a bit then, see if you need anything else."

"Thank you."

As she left, Missinghall pulled an evidence bag from his pocket, a bunch of keys visible inside.

"I thought we might be needing these," he said. "They were in Monro's jacket pocket."

Using the bag as a second glove, he maneuvered the keys, trying them against the lock for size until one fitted. He turned the key and pushed open the door.

"Ladies first," he smiled at Jamie, and she nodded her head, walking through ahead of him. It was dark inside, the windows shaded, so it was hard to see at first. As Missinghall flicked on the light, Jamie gasped at what they saw.

The room was dominated by a gynecological bed in the center, with green padded cushions and the addition of leather straps at each end, as well as stirrups and supports. Under the table was a wooden box. Missinghall lifted the lid to reveal a number of different crops, whips, eye masks and a ball gag.

"Bloody hell, I wasn't expecting that," Missinghall said, eyebrows raised. "I thought this guy was a psychiatrist, not some kind of sexual services provider."

"He was only supposed to be interested in their minds," Jamie said, walking around the bed. "But clearly, he liked to take things a little further."

She walked to a desk near the shaded window and turned on the lamp. A large leather notebook lay in pride of place, with a serpent-green fountain pen beside it. Jamie opened the book, examining Monro's handwriting within. The last page was an account of a session with a client he called 'M,' noting her response to the discipline and how many strokes she had endured. There were some musings about the efficacy of physical restraint on the mad, how they were more comfortable being punished than being left alone to get well, and how perhaps the original Bedlam had been correct in chaining the inmates. There were quotes from a Dr George Henry Savage: *I would rather tie a patient down constantly than keep him always under the influence of a powerful drug … The scourging of the lunatic in times past might have occasionally been a help to recovery.*

Jamie frowned as she flicked through the pages, seeing multiple entries over the last month, the same initials appearing several times. Were these willing participants in Monro's extra services, or did he use his position of power to coerce his clients? Was one of them responsible for his death?

Above the desk was a bookshelf with four more of the large journals. Jamie pulled another one down, finding the same type of information but with other initials. Monro had clearly been doing this for years, so it was conceivable that patients had come to him specifically for this kind of treatment. Complaints about his professionalism would have shut him down a long time ago otherwise.

"You'll want to see this, Jamie."

She turned to see Missinghall looking into a large walk-in closet. He moved aside to let her enter. A wall-size cabinet dominated the space, filled with all kinds of pharmaceuticals, some regulated substances, others common antidepressants and antipsychotics. None of them should have been kept on the premises in such large doses.

"He was dealing, as well? What wasn't this guy into?" Missinghall shook his head, moving over to check one of the filing cabinets, his gloved fingers flicking through the tabbed index.

Jamie sighed. "We're going to have to go through his list of clients, past and present. Clearly the murder was related to madness somehow, but it could have also been about sex or drugs."

"I don't think it was money, though," Missinghall said, holding up a bank statement. "His balance is unhealthier than mine."

Jamie frowned. "Which doesn't fit with the implication of selling drugs directly. So where's the money?"

There was a ring on the doorbell, and they heard the steps of the housekeeper and then her voice, faint from downstairs. The tread of two sets of footsteps ascended to the second floor. Jamie went back into the main room, pulling the door of the inner sanctum closed, leaving Missinghall to continue to go through paperwork. The housekeeper knocked and then pushed open the door to the practice rooms.

"Detective, there's a Mr Harkan here. He says it's important."

Harkan was thin and fair, with the rosy cheeks of a choirboy who had never quite grown up. He put out a graceful hand to introduce himself to Jamie as the house-keeper headed off downstairs again.

"I'm sorry, Detective, but this couldn't wait. I just heard

about the murder – the news is already out, I'm afraid, and Harley Street is a tight-knit community. I'm a solicitor. Our firm is just down the street, and we worked with Monro. He was a forensic psychiatrist as well as a clinical practitioner."

"A man of many talents," Jamie said, thinking of the room out back.

"Indeed," said Harkan, and Jamie noticed his eyes flick towards the door. Did the solicitor know what lay beyond?

"What exactly did he work with you on?" she asked.

"Forensic psychiatry is the intersection of law and the psychiatric profession, and Monro helped assess competency to stand trial. He was an expert witness around aspects of mental illness, both for the prosecution and the defense. He also assessed the risk of repeat offending."

"So why the hurry to talk to us?" Jamie asked. "You could have come down to the station with a statement."

"It's the timing," Harkan said, wringing his hands. "Monro was an expert witness for the prosecution in the case of Timothy MacArnold a few years back. A violent, repeat offender who claimed mental illness drove his actions, and Monro supported that in his testimony. MacArnold is in Broadmoor, the maximum-security mental health hospital for violent offenders."

"And why are you so worried?"

"MacArnold's case is coming up for review and Monro was trying to get him transferred to some exclusive research hospital. I don't know the exact details of that, but I do know that MacArnold has a good position at Broadmoor and if he wanted to stay there … well, he's a violent man used to getting what he wants, even inside." Harkan's eyes flicked all over the room, beads of sweat forming on his brow. His speech was hurried, tripping over his words in the haste to get them out. Jamie noted his concerns on her pad, but they would have to look at Mr Harkan more closely.

"Then of course there's the families of MacArnold's victims," Harkan continued. "They're livid at the thought of him getting even better treatment than he does now, all art therapy and counseling when he butchered their loved ones. There's a lot of anger at Monro for his support of the insanity plea."

Jamie nodded.

"We're certainly going to investigate all these angles, Mr Harkan. This is useful information, so I'd like you to give an official statement. My colleague, DC Missinghall will take you through the process and get some more details. If you'd just wait here a minute."

Jamie walked to the back room and ducked inside, careful to shield the inside space from view and closing the door briefly behind her. There was already enough gossip on this street.

"Al, can you take a proper statement from this guy? Apparently Monro was involved in the justice system, as well." She lowered her voice. "And I think we need to investigate his background, too. Seems a little too quick in assigning motive for the murder. Of course, he might just be the neighborhood busybody."

Missinghall groaned. "There's always one. Righto, but seriously, how many motives can there be for murdering this guy?" He handed a thick box file to Jamie. "You'll want to have a look through this. It's his clients, past and present."

Missinghall went out to take Harkan's statement as Jamie perched on the bed, thumbing through the cards in the box. Judging by the dates of the first appointments, they covered the last five years. There were a lot of patients, both male and female, and there were symbols on each card, perhaps a visual reference system enabling Monro to easily follow the development of treatment. But what did those symbols mean?

There were red squares, yellow triangles and a blue shape, like a raindrop, interspersed between the cards. Some had just one and others had multiple symbols. Jamie noticed that a black circle in the upper right coincided with the end of the appointments for an individual. There were also larger pieces of paper folded in between some of the cards. Jamie pulled one out to find an extensive family tree drawn in dark pen, each person labeled with a name and their mental health status. This particular patient had black circles dotted all over the page and Monro had commented in spidery handwriting on the need for intervention to stop the continuation of this family stain.

As she continued to flick through the pack of records, Jamie noticed a name she vaguely recognized. Melyssa Osborne. The card had the red square, blue raindrop and the black circle on it. Why did that name ring a bell?

Jamie got out her smartphone, removed a glove, and searched for the name. Melyssa was the younger sister of MP Matthew Osborne; she had been diagnosed with bipolar disorder and had committed suicide three months earlier. The black circle must mean deceased. Jamie flicked through the pack again and noted how many black circles there were, many of which also had the blue raindrop. Her own work was a dark business, but there was a cemetery's worth in these records. They would need to check on all the patients Monro had treated. Jamie opened Monro's diary and compared the initials to the patients in the last week. Another name leapt out at her. Petra Bennett had attended appointments every week – the same woman who had been at the Imperial War Museum for the Psyche Fun Run and who had greeted Matthew Osborne so warmly.

CHAPTER 4

BACK AT NEW SCOTLAND Yard, Jamie typed her notes up on Monro's office as she considered the new suspects they had added to the list. There was still a long list of people who had been at the Imperial War Museum to interview, and a host of other possible leads. Around it all, the miasma of madness seeped through the evidence, like the freezing fog of a London winter.

Missinghall walked up behind Jamie and placed a small square of chocolate brownie on her desk.

"It's Rory's birthday, and he insisted you eat that."

Jamie felt a wave of nausea to look at it, but she knew Missinghall meant well. Food was a constant in their working relationship, at least. She popped it in her mouth and chewed, forcing the sweetness down, willing the sugar to lift her mood. Missinghall smiled and in his brief moment of pleasure for her, Jamie felt better. At least she was beginning to make some friends in the force now, after years of being distant from her colleagues. At first, her independence had been a way to protect the little time she had left with Polly, and a way to stop herself being hurt again. Her ex-husband, Matt, had ripped her heart out when he had left her to cope with a disabled daughter alone. As the years went by, Jamie had turned her independence into a kind of armor, and doing her job well became more important than friendship. Perhaps that was changing now, since her fellow officers knew about her role in the Hellfire Caves. They also knew that somehow the glory had gone to the senior officer on the case, Detective Superintendent Dale Cameron, and there were rumors he had been offered a more senior role in the last few weeks. Jamie hoped he would move on because his presence still made her uneasy, the way his eyes followed her when she walked past his office.

Jamie still had flashbacks to that night of blood and smoke, when in a drugged haze, she had thought Cameron's face was amongst those who performed the atrocity. He had been protective of her in the aftermath of the investigation, encouraging her return to the force and then making sure she was supervised by his hand-picked team. Jamie had wondered what he was protecting her from, or whether he was merely making sure she wasn't able to report her suspicions. If Cameron moved on, Jamie might be able to breathe again as things returned to something resembling normal. Or at least what was considered normal in the homicide team.

Missinghall flipped open his pad.

"Just heard from Skinner. Time of death was likely between midnight and five a.m. Cause of death was drowning, but the Doc also found a needle stick in the victim's neck and suspects a powerful hallucinogenic drug was used. It will take a while for toxicology to come back though."

Jamie shook her head as she imagined being stuck in that box, strapped down while seeing terrifying visions. It brought back hazy memories of being manacled in the swirling smoke of the Hellfire Caves, unsure of what was real. "So it was torture as well as murder," she whispered.

Missinghall continued. "We've also got the full list

of statements from the people who were setting up the Psyche Fun Run that morning. Unsurprisingly, no one saw anything. They were all down the other end of the field because the curator didn't want kids near the flower beds so close to the reopening of the museum." Missinghall shuffled his papers, pulling out a sheaf of statements. "But Monro's financials are interesting. We got hold of his other bank account, the one he was clearly keeping separate. It shows significant payments of large amounts at sporadic intervals. The company they're from traces back to a shell organization that we can't penetrate. There's also substantial transfers for smaller amounts of money at more regular intervals. Interestingly, one of the regular transfers is to Mr Harkan, the solicitor who seemed very keen to point the finger at anyone but himself."

"Right, get him down here," Jamie said. "You can go over that new evidence with him, although killing Monro would seem to make it less likely he would get his ongoing payments."

Missinghall nodded. "I'll also get on with arranging access to Broadmoor so you can check out Timothy MacArnold, although clearly he didn't kill Monro himself. That place is a fortress."

Jamie's phone rang, interrupting their discussion. As she picked up, Detective Superintendent Dale Cameron's smooth voice spoke before she could.

"Can you come through to Interview Room 12, please?"

"Of course, sir. I'll be right through."

Her mind was buzzing as she put down the phone, and she caught Missinghall's quizzical look.

"Something up?" he asked.

"Not sure, but Cameron wants to see me – in an interview room, not his office."

"Duh duh duh, duh-duh duh," Missinghall started in with the Darth Vader theme.

Jamie pushed her chair back, standing up. "Oh, stop it. I'm sure it's nothing."

But she wondered about that night in the Hellfire Caves and what she had really seen. How much of a stake did Cameron have in her career now?

She knocked on the interview room door and went in. Dale Cameron stood as she entered.

"Morning, sir."

"Jamie," Cameron nodded, his patrician silver hair catching the harsh light. He was a striking man for his age, with the looks of a wealthy CEO or career politician. His rise through the ranks of the police was legendary, as was his reputation for Teflon shoulders when it came to avoiding responsibility for disaster.

Jamie glanced at the mirror on the wall, wondering if there was someone behind it. Why else would they be in an interview room with the ability to see in, but with no way to tell who was watching?

"This new case is sensitive," Cameron said. "Especially with the timings around the centennial at the Imperial War Museum."

Jamie nodded. "We're trying to minimize the impact on the museum, sir."

"Of course, of course … but there's something you need to know about Monro, and you need to keep this to yourself." Cameron's eyes were like flecks of diamond and Jamie looked away first, unable to meet his stare. She nodded again and he continued. "Monro was affiliated with a government program investigating ways to reduce the burden of mental health in this country." Jamie almost flinched at his use of the word burden.

"They're also interested in ways to enhance brain function in normal people," Cameron continued.

"And by normal, you mean people who haven't been diagnosed as mentally ill?" Jamie couldn't help herself.

"However you want to define it," Cameron snapped. "Regardless, I need you to communicate any evidence about Monro's research to me directly. I will be passing it on to the appropriate people concerned."

Jamie looked pointedly at the mirrored panel on the wall.

Cameron's tone softened. "Now Jamie, I know you've had difficulties coming back to work after the death of your daughter. I hope you realize I've been making allowances for your fragile mental state." Jamie wanted to interrupt him, wanted to challenge him, but she knew there was a hint of truth in his words. "Many senior officers said you should have been suspended based on your uncontrolled actions in the Jenna Neville case, but I want to continue to help you ... Do you understand?"

Jamie hesitated, meeting his eyes and seeing the blue skies of soaring ambition there. She didn't want to fly that high, especially if it meant compromising her integrity. Eventually, she nodded.

"Of course, sir. I'll report anything I find on Monro's research to you." She stood to leave, the scrape of her chair just a little louder than was necessary. "Will that be all?"

"One more thing," Cameron said. "I've heard you have a ... friend ... with skills that could be misconstrued by the press should his actions become known."

Jamie felt her cheeks color. She wasn't ashamed of Blake, but she knew how his psychic ability could be interpreted as unprofessional. She had kept his involvement quiet after the Hellfire Caves, but he had visited her in hospital, and he would have been easy enough for Cameron to investigate.

"Yes, sir. But we're just friends, and he has nothing to do with the museum murder."

"Actually, I'm interested in how we could use his skills on this case, Jamie. I don't want to rule anything out and it sounds like you had some good results from his tips before. Can you get him to have a look at the crime scene?"

Jamie was stunned, and not in a good way. Cameron's interest was never for anyone else's benefit.

"Perhaps he will be able to shed some light on the Monro murder?" Cameron continued, and it seemed he was studiously avoiding the mirrored panel on the wall.

"I don't think …" Jamie protested.

"As I said," Cameron interrupted, his fist clenching on the table between them. "I want to continue to protect your position on the force, and I'd like to hear what your friend has to say."

In moments like these, Jamie wanted to get on her motorbike and just roar away, leave all this political crap behind. But she loved the job, and she had nothing else to live for but bringing justice to the dead. Perhaps Blake would help with the Monro case, but she had to figure out what Cameron wanted with him. She nodded slowly.

"I'll get him down to the crime scene before processing is complete."

"Today, Jamie." Cameron's tone was firm.

She nodded again and walked out of the room, feeling his eyes on her back, her skin bristling with awareness of someone else watching from behind the mirrored panel. Instead of returning to her desk, Jamie ducked into one of the other interview rooms opposite and waited. She was so sure someone else had been watching, and she needed to see who it was. She pushed the door almost closed so she could see out but remain unseen herself.

After a couple of minutes, the interview room door opened and Cameron came out. He pulled open the door to the side room, and said something to the shadows. Another man strode out, taller than Cameron, which made him over six foot two. His head was completely shaved, with a skull that seemed misshapen in some way, a slight asymmetry that made Jamie want to stare for longer. His eyes flicked across to the room opposite and Jamie ducked backwards to avoid his glance, but not before she had seen that he had heterochromia, one eye blue and the other brown. What was this man's involvement with the case, and why did he want Blake to read at the murder scene?

CHAPTER 5

IN THE CAR PARK of the station, Jamie pulled on her protective gear while she considered what she would say to Blake. Her stomach fluttered and she laughed softly to herself at the faint excitement of being with him again. It had been a long time since she had looked forward to seeing a man so much. Jamie took a deep breath and dialed. Blake picked up on the first ring.

"Jamie, are you OK?"

The concern in his tone made her smile.

"I'm fine, and this is actually a work call. I wondered if you might be able to help with another case?" The silence was just a beat too long. "Blake, are you there?"

"Yes, sorry. Of course, I'm just a little distracted today. An object came in and I'm having problems with it."

"Oh, of course, if you're busy …"

"Actually, I could use a change of scene and I'd love to see you. Where shall we meet?"

"The Imperial War Museum on Lambeth Road. Just wait outside and I'll take you in."

"OK. See you there in an hour."

The line went dead as he hung up, and Jamie felt a wave of relief wash over her. Blake's abilities were disturbing, but they also meant that she didn't have to hide with him.

He had read her once through a comb that Polly had made for her hair. Blake had seen her daughter's sickness and Jamie's own grief sublimated through tango, a side of her that few had witnessed. He had laid her open and part of her craved his vision into her life. She knew he numbed his own nightmares with tequila, oblivion drowning his darkness, so they were both wounded, both struggling to survive. Perhaps they could at least fight the world together today.

Jamie sat astride her bike and pulled her helmet on. The jet-black BMW was her freedom, not meant to be used on police business. But while the long leash Dale Cameron had given her seemed to still be in effect, Jamie was determined to make the most of it. She revved the bike and pulled out into the London streets.

***

The Imperial War Museum was deliberately imposing, and as Jamie pulled up, she saw Blake standing in front of it, looking up at the great facade. His face was troubled. For a moment, Jamie realized that he had been such a support for her in the last few months, but she hadn't asked him what was going on in his own life. He clearly had his own troubles, but right now she barely had enough strength for her own.

Jamie dismounted, pulling off her helmet and putting it in the panniers along with her leather jacket. Blake stood watching her as she tidied her hair, pulling stray black strands into her fixed style.

"Hey," he said, with a shy half smile, his blue eyes striking against his dark skin.

"Hey yourself," Jamie smiled and leaned in to kiss his cheek, avoiding the intensity of his gaze. She touched his gloved hands, briefly caressing the thin material, stunned by her reaction to seeing him after so long. Part of her wanted to break down in his arms and tune out the world, for there was so much unspoken between them. But now wasn't the time.

"Thanks for coming," she said.

"To be honest, I could really use the distraction."

"Really? Anything I should know about?"

Blake sighed, shaking his head. "I'm not even sure what I'm doing about it myself yet, but I'll let you know. So what do you need from me?"

"I don't want to tell you too much, but this is a crime scene and there was a murder here, so be prepared for that. Dr Christian Monro was a psychiatrist and this place was once known as Bedlam."

Blake looked up at the giant cannons outside the museum. "It still seems to be a house of the mad."

They walked into the museum, Jamie showing her warrant card to the officer on duty. The SOCOs had finished processing the scene earlier, but the place was still secure as the investigation continued. Jamie and Blake eased past the crime-scene tape that was in place within the inner rooms. The quiet was almost tangible after the bustle of the crime scene Jamie had seen early this morning. The smell of the processing materials lingered, underneath it a note of desperation. Or was that just her imagination?

"They're refurbishing the place, so these rooms weren't being used," Jamie said. "The body was discovered by a workman."

As they entered, Blake caught sight of the sturdy chair with leather straps.

"You want me to read that? Seriously, Jamie. It looks like something from a horror movie."

Jamie stood looking at it. "It's called a Tranquilizer,

believe it or not. I understand if you don't want to read. I don't think it will be pleasant."

Blake's eyes narrowed as he looked at the device, assessing the challenge. "I'm not sure that it could be any worse than the Hunterian Museum and all those medical specimens." He peeled the glove off his right hand. "Just keep an eye on me, will you? Pull my hand away if I'm under too long." He placed his bare hand on the wooden arm of the chair and closed his eyes.

Jamie watched him, fascinated with his gift, although she still didn't quite know what to make of it. She had seen evidence that his visions were true in some sense, and they led to information that could be verified independently. His breathing slowed and there was a moment when Blake became absent, as if his life energy disappeared and there was only a body left, not a mind within. He was totally still except for a slight twitching behind his eyelids that made his long eyelashes tremble. It was hard not to study his features as he stood like a statue, a handsome god who suffered the trials of men. Jamie wondered what he was seeing.

**

There was no easing into the veils of memory this time, and Blake reeled as the noise hit him. Like an oncoming train, it started in the distance but rumbled fast into his consciousness, rising to a screech. It was the deafening clamor of people calling for help, moaning their distress, rocking back and forth with self-comforting noises. There was a rattling of chains, and a single voice, deep and resonant, singing a hymn to God, as if the Almighty could step down and open the doors of this prison like he had for St Paul.

The walls around him were damp and, in places, dripping with condensation that made the air muggy and thick. The smell of rotting flesh, of disease and shit and sweat filled the air. Blake became aware of people around him in the room. A skeletal figure, perhaps a woman, was fastened to the wall by a chain attached to a riveted belt around her waist. Her clothes were stained with blood and pus from sores as the restraint rubbed on her skin, and she held a piece of old blanket around her shoulders for warmth. She knelt in the corner, her long, dirty fingernails scratching at the plaster, making little marks. Was she trying to find a way out, or was it just the human need to record the passing of time, the transience of human existence? Another woman sat weeping in the opposite corner, her shoulders shaking with silent grief, and around her, other people rocked back and forward, their moans stifled by fear. The cell was cramped, with no separation between the patients according to their affliction. It was merely containment, preventing these rejects from impinging on polite society.

A long howl came from outside the cell, a sound from the depths of despair when words have ceased to hold meaning. The cacophony was part of the assault of this place of madness. Only the civilized are silent, or appropriate in the sounds they make, but when you were shut in here, Blake thought, how could you not cry out?

The howl came again and then the voice broke down in a scream as the noise of thudding against flesh drowned it out. Blake concentrated on the sound and found himself outside the cell in a corridor, watching as two guards beat a man with short coshes. The man was huddled, arms protecting his head, but the guards continued the beating until they grunted with exertion.

"That'll learn you, fuckin' loon," one of the men said, giving the man a final kick. "Monro don't like all that noise, especially when the ladies are getting their … exercise."

The men laughed, an undercurrent of twisted lust echoing down the halls. Blake started at Monro's name. How could the murdered man be here? These men were dressed in eighteenth-century clothing, and Bedlam Hospital had been moved from this site generations ago. The guards hauled the man back into a cell, his blood leaving a stain on the ground, and Blake followed them down the corridor towards the other half of the building.

Part of Blake's mind saw the museum as it now was, pristine cream walls with elegant paintings and no sense of the past. But the walls of this place were steeped in the suffering of the mad, the mental anguish of those chained up and force fed until their teeth broke. People would come to look at them, laughing through the windows of the cells at the craziness within. There were no witnesses here, no one to hear their screams, no one who could act to save them. So the inmates would plug their ears, singing loudly to block out the sound of collective anguish. Some believed they were in Hell, where their punishment was eternal, and now the echo of those times leached from the walls, a manifestation of the past. The air was thick with expectation, and Blake felt a psychic danger here, a darkness that longed for another soul to add to the tortured throng.

The passageways of the hospital were dark, cornered with shadow. Blake heard sounds of desperation and pain coming from the cells, but as the guards ran their clubs along the walls, the noises quieted. They came to a brighter area with two tiled rooms and Blake felt waves of agony coming from the place. He leaned on the wall as the sensations assaulted him, and then looked inside for the source.

On one side was a kind of operating theatre, but with none of the sterile trappings of modern hospitals. There was a bed with leather straps and a head brace. A tray full of medical instruments lay next to it, with a length of tubing attached to a pump.

On the other side, Blake saw a room for torture sanctioned by science. A man was strapped tightly on a board about to be lowered headfirst into a water bath by two guards. A doctor stood near his head.

"No, please no more." The man moaned, thrashing his head, panic giving him strength. But the two guards were stronger and held him tight, slowly tilting the board as excitement glinted in their eyes.

"Sshh, sshh," the doctor said, his gestures an attempt at calm. "This treatment will shock your system and restart your consciousness. We'll bring you back and you may be well again. This treatment, *usque ad deliquum*, to the brink of death, has been proven to work in many patients at other hospitals. You're so lucky we've chosen you to try it on."

The doctor nodded his head and the guards tipped the patient so his head and shoulders were fully immersed underwater. Blake counted the seconds, watching as the man thrashed around, feeling the waves of panic and pain emanate from him. The man finally stilled, his limbs going limp, but still the doctor counted on.

"Just a little longer," Blake heard the man say. "We need to make sure the shock is complete."

Blake sensed the victim's spirit lift from his body, exuding relief that this life was over, that he could finally escape. The guards tipped the board up, turned it on its side and released the man's body. The doctor thumped hard on the man's back and the patient vomited up a quantity of water that ran into the central drain. Blake felt the pull of his spirit back to physical life, the resistant despair, and then the patient was coughing and retching, gasping for breath.

The doctor nodded, writing on his chart.

"Excellent, we'll just repeat that to be sure."

The man on the floor was weak but he tried to rise at the words, attempting to drag himself towards the door as his face twisted in desperation at his fate.

"Oh no, you don't," one of the guards said, bringing his boot down heavily on the man's back, pinning him to the floor. "Back on the board with you, crazy bastard. The Doc's just trying to help."

The guard's voice echoed with the enjoyment of a man who loved to inflict pain and control, and Blake knew that this patient would only find release if they let him drown.

He tried to shift the veils of awareness back to the present time, back to the murder last night. The emotions were so weak in comparison to the people who had been trapped and tortured here long ago, who had died here. But there was a hint in the air, a need for revenge and retribution, for leveling the score on behalf of all those who were lost within these walls. There was also a clarity of thought, a strength of purpose. The mad had been beaten down and abused, judged and tortured for too long and now they had a champion, but Blake couldn't see anything of the details of that particular night.

***

He jolted out of the trance to find Jamie shaking his arm.

"Blake, it's OK. Come back now. Please."

He was lying on the floor, a cold sweat covering his body. He shivered as he centered on the present again. Blake opened his eyes to see Jamie's face close to his. For a moment, he forgot the horror of Bedlam and wanted to tilt his head and kiss her, revel in the moment and leave the past behind. But he knew it was too soon, and he couldn't bear it if she pulled away.

"Water," he whispered, sitting up with her help, leaning against the wall and pulling his gloves back on. His hands were shaking a little, the aftermath of the visions that always rocked him.

Blake drank deeply from the bottle Jamie handed him. He could smell the new paint on the walls and it seemed incongruous after what he had just witnessed. It was just one of the strange sensations of his visions, the present always so different from the past.

Jamie sat next to him on the floor, waiting for him to recover. He could feel her wanting to ask what he had seen, but she held back. After years of hiding his gift, and witnessing people's generally spooked reactions to what he saw, Blake relished Jamie's acceptance of who he really was.

"It seems your Monro was just one in a long line of mind doctors," Blake said. "Although what we would call doctors now seems hardly appropriate for what they were in those days." He pulled his smartphone from his pocket and searched for more on the Monros and Bedlam. "Here, look, the family was in charge of Bedlam for three generations, making their money from madness and hiding those considered inappropriate from society. The final Monro had to resign because he was 'wanting in humanity,' but the entire family was notorious. They prescribed treatments without even seeing patients, and back then, treatments including bleeding, purging and various chemical concoctions to sedate or shock the patient back to health." Blake scrolled down. "See here, the Georgian mad were treated as chained beasts and Monro was responsible for bloodletting, forced vomiting and blistering. Under their administration, Bedlam used chains and restraints, beating and brutality to manage the inmates. There was filthy accommodation, infected sores from chaining, gagging or bandaging of the head to stop talking, force-feeding to such brutality that teeth were missing, jaws broken and reports of rape."

Blake shook his head. "I saw some of this happening, Jamie, and the reports make it seem somehow acceptable because the medical profession allowed it. But what was reported must have been just the tiniest part of the whole."

"I think the abuse still goes on," Jamie said. "I saw evidence of it in Monro's office. The records of one girl indicated suicide after treatment that can't possibly have been sanctioned officially. But what about Monro's murder? Could you see anything about that specifically?"

Blake trailed his gloved fingertips on the patterned tiles on the floor. He shook his head.

"There wasn't much, as the dominant emotions here are the suffering of those thousands before him. But Monro's murder was certainly one of revenge, and there was no sense that the person who did it suffered from any kind of mental illness. It was as if they were clinically detached, coldly aware of what this man's ancestors had done. I don't think you're looking for one of Monro's patients."

Jamie frowned. "But surely to kill him for the sins of past generations seems like the act of someone not entirely rational?"

"Oh, I think this Monro was abusing the so-called mad as much as his ancestors had been. The murder was committed here to honor the dead, a repayment of a debt owed to those society put here to forget." Blake paused for a moment. "There was something else, almost a reckless feeling. I don't think the murderer has anything left to lose."

"You mean they're not finished?"

"If he or she, and I can't tell which, is some kind of Robin Hood for the mad, then yes, I think there will be more incidents."

"And I have no way of finding out who might be next," Jamie said quietly.

Blake took her hand and squeezed it gently.

"You can't fight death, Jamie. You can't take on every criminal in London and expect to stop the violence. Just like I can't fight the past, I can only perceive its passing …"

A buzz interrupted Blake's words. Jamie checked her phone and saw a text from Missinghall.

You're good to go to Broadmoor. All cleared. Have emailed details.

Jamie stood. "Are you heading back to the British Museum now?"

Blake thought of his father's watch, and a shadow crossed his face. "I might be going away for a few days, actually."

Jamie raised an eyebrow. "Anything you need help with?"

Blake shook his head. "I'm not quite ready to talk about it yet, but I'll text you later."

***

Blake watched as Jamie got on her bike and waved, before revving off into traffic. It made him smile to watch her drive away, all black leather and tough exterior but with so much pain and vulnerability inside. As she vanished round the corner, Blake felt the prickle of eyes on his back and he turned, scanning the road for anyone watching. A dark-blue saloon car with tinted windows pulled away from the curb just a few meters away, and Blake watched it go, an eerie sense of eyes on him as it passed.

He shook his head, the paranoia surely a hangover from the visions. He had to finish the Timotheus report, but he didn't want to go back to work now. It was time to face the past.

CHAPTER 6

BLAKE GOT OFF THE bus at the end of the lane, shivering a little in his thin jacket. Once he'd finally made the decision to come, he had left London as fast as possible and he hadn't brought his thicker coat. It was too much of a temptation to stay at home and avoid the confrontation he had feared for much of his adult life, the memory of his father looming large. Every mile he had come closer to arriving, every stop the bus had made, he had wanted to run back to London. But the room he had seen his father in through the watch haunted his thoughts, and he had to see what was really happening.

The little village of Long Farnborough was on the edge of the New Forest National Park, a train ride and then a bus from London, far enough to make it hard to visit without a car. It might well have been the other side of the world for how much he had seen his parents over the years. Blake walked slowly up the lane, the heavy weight of the past making his steps cumbersome. The scars on his hands throbbed, with cold perhaps, or with the memory of pain inflicted here.

Blake breathed in deeply, becoming more aware of the woodland around him as the birch and oak trees canopied above. Living in the city for so long, he had almost forgotten the clean scent of the forest, the ambient noise of birdsong and the rustling of woodland animals. The New Forest was actually one of the oldest forests in England, dense with whispers of the past, an echo of times when people lived closer to the earth. The intrepid walker, leaving the footpaths, could come upon an ancient monument or a round barrow from the early Bronze Age. In the past, Blake had tried to read some of the stones and trees around the burial sites, his hands flat against the rough surfaces, but he couldn't pick up any trace of those who had walked here.

One last corner. Blake steeled himself as he rounded it and saw the house his father had built with his own hands, the home he had walked away from. The place was simple, as befitted a man of God, and Blake knew his father had never cared much for the physical world, preferring to fix his eyes on Heaven. The red kitchen curtains were open and suddenly Blake saw his mother's face, his heart leaping in recognition. Precious Olofsson had married young, star struck by the prophet's dominance, and her features were still youthful, her black skin smooth. The lines around her eyes were deeper now, and she was still beautiful. Blake saw her smile light her face as she saw him and he almost wept, for there was no recrimination in her eyes, only love and welcome. *The prodigal son returns indeed*, he thought, walking faster to the door as it opened, and there she was.

"Daniel," she said, her voice soft and warm, like the bread she used to bake on a Saturday, when he would shape the dough into silly animals to make her laugh. Precious held her arms out and Blake walked into them, enfolding her.

"Oh, Mum," he whispered, eyes closed, feeling the prick of tears. Blake dwarfed her now, and he could feel how thin she was, how brittle. How vulnerable. Yet she stroked his back, her strength calming him.

"It's OK," she said, her breath warm on his neck. "I know why you've stayed away. But you're here now, and that's all that matters." She pulled away from him, clutching his hands, stroking the gloves as if she caressed the scars underneath. Her eyes shone with tears. "He's worse, you need to see him. The Lord will take him when He's ready, I know that, but the going is difficult."

Blake envied his mother's faith, an almost fatalistic view of the world. It meant she had believed his gift was God's will, but that his father's punishment was also meant to be. Perhaps it made life simpler to accept that, but Blake believed in being the author of one's own fate.

The sound of chanting came from the upstairs bedroom, rising to a crescendo and then a stream of voices praying in tongues. To some, it was the language of angels and to others, merely the expression of emotion through the vocalization of a meaningless dialect, a babble of incoherence made holy by belief.

"The Elders are with him," Precious said, her eyes shadowing. Blake tightened his arm around her. He knew how little the cabal of male Elders thought of the women in their congregation. Patriarchy was certainly alive and well in this community, a breakaway fundamentalist sect. His heart thumped at the thought of seeing the men, remembering how they had beaten him and others, how he had seen their abuse, and, God forgive him, he had never reported it.

"They shouldn't be too much longer." Precious sighed, shaking her head. "They've been interceding with God for nearly two hours. But if the Lord is calling your father, then who are we to try and keep him here? Heaven is a better place, and we must all long for the time when we will join our Savior."

Blake ignored the sense that he should answer her unspoken question. He had lost his faith a long time ago, and could no longer remember whether it was his father he had worshipped, or God himself. There seemed no difference in his childhood memories of the prophet leading the church in prayer, his deep voice extolling sermons that would leave the congregation on their knees, gasping for forgiveness.

The prayers stopped and after a moment, the Elders emerged at the top of the stairs, their voices hushed, faces grim. Blake's apprehension diminished as he noticed how much they had all aged. They had paunches, their faces sagged, and as much as they touted the poverty of faith, there was evidence of too much good living in their soft bodies. Blake stood taller, looking up at them.

Elder Paul Lemington saw him first, falling silent as the rest of the group followed his gaze.

"Daniel," Paul said as he walked down the stairs, eyes fixed on Blake. "It's been a long time."

Blake nodded, meeting the Elder's eyes, his gaze unflinching. He had nothing to fear from this man anymore, and looking at him now, Blake wondered how he could ever have been afraid of him. At the bottom of the stairs, Paul held out his hand. Blake looked at it for a moment, wanting to turn away but sensing his mother's eagerness for reconciliation.

After a moment, he held out his gloved hand to shake it. Paul glanced down and his pallor whitened a little, confronted by the evidence of his own past sin. How much did these men remember of what they had done to him? Blake wondered. How much did they still inflict on others? Blake pushed the thoughts aside as the Elders filed past him out into the dusk. It was time to face the man he'd been running from for years.

"I'll put the kettle on," Precious said. "And bring you up some tea." She pushed Blake gently towards the stairs. "Go on up to him now. He's in the spare room so I can hear him more easily."

The staircase loomed above him, like the ladder of Jacob ascending into Heaven, with his father enthroned at its height. Blake shook his head, remembering the shifting black creatures on the walls of the room above. There was no Heaven here, only his own memories to confront. He trod the first stair and strength rose within him, pushing him up the rest.

At the top, Blake turned into the bedroom, pushing the door open as the bleep of medical machines beat time with his father's heart. The walls were a faded lilac, the same as they had been when he had left years ago, and the room was dominated by a double bed. His father lay curled, eyes closed, one side of his body tightened and hunched, pulling everything towards his center. The covers were twisted around him and saliva dripped from his mouth onto the pillow. Beads of sweat stood out on his forehead, evidence of a fever or perhaps the exertion of prayer.

Blake looked down at his father and felt a strange absence, as the pent-up anxiety left him. This wasn't the man he had left behind and feared beyond all else. Magnus Olofsson, the prophet of New Jerusalem Church, had now been reduced to this pitiful state. Sitting down next to the bed, Blake looked around the room. The vision he had seen of the black creatures on rotting walls came from this spot, he was sure of it, and yet, the room smelled of antiseptic and he could sense nothing wrong here. Perhaps the visions had been corrupted by his own emotional baggage, or perhaps the Elders had truly exorcised the room, cleansing it with their prayers.

"Unnng, unngh." The noise came from Magnus and Blake looked down into his father's eyes, the brilliant blue undimmed by the destruction of his physical body. There was defiance there, an attempt at strength even from that prone position. Blake remembered the blaze in them, blood dripping from the strap on the day he had run.

"I'm here, Dad," he said, his face taut, holding emotion in check. "I've come back."

Blake felt an overwhelming desire to put his hand over the prophet's eyes, to stop the judging gaze that was fixed on him. It wouldn't take much to pick up one of the pillows and hold it over the man's face, smothering him, taking him to the arms of his God that much faster. It would be a blessing, for Magnus Olofsson's Nordic heritage was battle born, where a good death was to die fighting, with a sword in your hand, cursing the heathen.

Instead, Blake picked up the Bible by the bed, his gloved hands running over the leather-bound book, pages edged with gold. A bookmark lay within, marking the place his mother was reading from. It opened at Psalm 55, and Blake read aloud from the page.

"'Let death steal over them; let them go down to Sheol alive; for evil is in their dwelling place and in their heart …'"

Blake's voice trailed off and he looked at the walls again, trying to imagine the creatures squatting there, drawing ever closer to feed, when Magnus finally crossed over to their realm. He had seen the largest one uncurl just above the old fireplace in his vision, but now there was nothing there but a basket of dried flowers.

"I still see the visions, Dad," Blake whispered. "You never managed to beat them out of me."

"Nnnngg." An utterance of protest. Blake looked down at his father again and saw something there. Was it regret, or was that what he wanted to see?

"When I touched your watch, I saw this room through your eyes, through your emotions. I saw something here, Dad … Dark creatures."

Magnus was silent, but his eyes went to the exact spot on the wall where Blake had seen the beast curled, shifting as it waited for the end. His father's breath became ragged, as if fear compacted his chest even more than the stroke had. Blake reached for his hand, and squeezed it. He felt a return of pressure, only faint, but it was still there.

"I want to try and see them again," Blake said. "I don't understand it, but I want to see what you do. Just put your hand on the Bible and I'll try to read you through it."

Magnus moaned, his eyes frightened, as if allowing Blake to see his visions would invite Satan back in by the acknowledgement of his gift. But he was clearly desperate, because he shifted his hand a little towards the book in acquiescence. Blake lifted his father's hand onto the Bible and then took off his gloves. Magnus' eyes fell on the scars, the ivory lines a pattern of his abuse, but there was no regret there, no apology.

Blake touched the Bible and a veil fell over the room as he sifted the emotions on the book for a sense of his father's present state. The strands solidified and Blake watched the walls shimmer, shift and darken until the lilac was gone, covered only with creatures of shadow. There were more than he had seen when he had read the watch. Now they clustered on the floor as well, some slithering over each other, snake-like, leaving slick oily patches behind them. Blake lifted his feet as he felt a movement under the bed, taking a sharp breath in fright. He didn't dare bend to look, instead turning to his father.

Blake moaned, his hand almost lifting from the book in horror at what he saw.

CHAPTER 7

JAMIE PULLED UP INTO the quiet street. The bike was her sanctuary, but it had the added benefit of making her journey through the winding streets of London a lot faster. As she dismounted and pulled off her protective gear, Jamie realized she was fully engaged with this case. For the first time in months, she could feel that spark of enthusiasm, her mind processing details, eager to discover more about the key people of interest. Missinghall had remained back at the station, pursuing the leads on some of the others, while she had come to see Petra Bennett. Jamie rang the bell on the basement flat, taking out her warrant card as she heard footsteps inside and the door opened.

Petra Bennett's face had the curious look of a deep-water fish: all lips and heavy cheeks, her body drooped as if gravity pulled more heavily on her than others. But her eyes were a vivid blue, almost turquoise, and her face was alive with an inquisitive, watchful expression.

"Detective, come on in. The place is a bit chaotic as I've only just got back from the Fun Run. So much to do! But I've just made coffee if you'd like some."

"That would be great, thanks."

Jamie followed Petra into the small downstairs flat. Boxes were piled up in one corner, bunting and banners in green and gold spilling from the top. There were two large photographic canvases on the wall flanking a fireplace in an otherwise sparse room. The canvases depicted stone sculptures, rocks piled high into towers that seemed to perch like miracles on the edge of the sea. One spiraled into itself, a multi-hued grey, and the other reached to the heavens with almost impossible balance.

"What is it you do, Ms Bennett?"

"Oh, please call me Petra," she said, pouring black coffee from a percolator into a bright red mug and handing it to Jamie. "I teach Spanish to private students. Business Spanish, and some conversation. But I'm also an artist." Petra gestured at the canvases. "These are my offerings to the gods of the sea, temporary sculptures on the edge of the tide. Even with these photographs, I fear I take too much of their power. They're meant to be ephemeral, lost almost as soon as they're completed." Petra held her head to one side, gazing into the frames. "Stone is the earth's gift to us, and perhaps our ancestors were right to believe they hold the partial spirits of Gaia. When we hew them apart, when we take them for our own and shape them to our purposes, they become husks with no power, only aesthetic."

"They're beautiful," Jamie said, trying to read the complex emotion held on the horizon of blue and grey.

"I write my confessions in stone, Detective. But they're not to be understood by all."

"And what do you have to confess?" Jamie asked, eyebrows arching at the words.

Petra shook her head, her mouth twisting into something that could have been a smile.

"My own obsessions perhaps, but certainly not the crime you're here to investigate."

Jamie turned to look at the room, as she waited for Petra to speak into the silence. Pebbles of all sizes were piled in plastic boxes in one corner. Some had shapes carved into the surface, others were painted in the contours of the stone, all smooth with rounded curves.

"I've collected those from beaches all over the world," Petra said. "The figures on them represent the journeys I've taken, or those that others have traveled."

Jamie remembered walking along Lyme Regis beach with Polly, telling her stories of the dinosaurs that had once lived there, the ancient bodies that were crushed and preserved within the rock strata. Polly had been fascinated, picking up the stones to examine them for fossilized remains. She had been in a lot of pain from motor neurone disease by then, but she had remained deeply curious about the world around her. Jamie's chest tightened at the precious memory of the time with her daughter, now locked in the past.

"Most people will pick up stones when they walk along a beach," Petra continued, her voice mesmerizing. "It's a human fascination. Pebbles fit within the palm and their touch is an element we crave. My interest started when my Gran used to paint flowers on the stones she found on the beach when I visited each summer. It gave me something to watch, and then to learn, and now I create them for others."

Petra's eyes were fathomless, like the places close to land where the continental shelf dropped off to the deepest parts of the ocean. She was at once unknowable depths and light waters in the shallows. Jamie felt the woman was somehow wiser than her years – an old soul – but wisdom didn't necessarily prevent murderous rage.

"Stone is the medium that calls to me," Petra said. "Its reputation is to be hard hearted, grey and strong, building cathedrals that last for generations. But stone can be smoothed by water, its surface rubbed into something else. That same stone can be decorative, or used as a weapon, for each stone has its own message. Once I discern it, then I paint. Sometimes the message just calls to me." Petra bent to the pile and held out a small grey stone when she straightened. "Here, Detective. I think this one is for you."

Jamie couldn't help but reach for the stone, something compelling her to take it. A tiny dancer spun alone, the folds of her dress artfully rendered in just a few strokes of black paint, her passion contained within the frozen moment. Thoughts of the tango *milonga* flashed through Jamie's mind, a passion she had developed as Polly had become sicker as a way of sublimating pain and grief into the intensity of dance. Petra couldn't possibly know of this secret interest: it wasn't something she shared with work colleagues, and she even used a different name. She hadn't been to tango since Polly's death, as the thought of celebrating physical movement seemed sacrilegious. Perhaps it was time to return. Jamie held out the stone.

"Thank you for the kind thought," she said, handing it back. "But I can't take anything from you, even as a gift. As my colleague told you on the phone, I'm here as part of the investigation into the murder of Dr Christian Monro."

Petra sighed and her eyes darkened as she took back the pebble. "I can't say I'm surprised at his death. He was superior and condescending, treating patients as evidence for his pet theories. But I also needed him and his ... special brand of therapy. The man was a bastard, but he was actually helping me break through some of my own creative blocks."

"Did he handle your medication?" Jamie asked, thinking of the drugs in the large cupboard.

Petra shook her head. "I'm not on medication, Detective. I don't ascribe to the labels of mental illness or the drugs the establishment tries to control us with. That's why I work with Psyche. Some may say that I have a form of depression, but I just call it life. It's those people who look at the world and don't feel overwhelmed sometimes that I worry for. There's so much darkness, isn't it natural to retreat into despair sometimes?"

Jamie thought of the pills in her own bathroom cabinet, and how she counted them out every day, holding that deadly dosage in her hand before counting them back into the bottle. She understood the pull of oblivion all too well.

"Did you know of the room behind Monro's main office?" Jamie asked.

Petra smiled, her eyes flashing with memories that clearly gave her pleasure.

"Yes, and I went there willingly, Detective." Her tone was unapologetic. "You have to understand that some of us need restraint in order to find true freedom. In temporal pain, there is a release of pressure, a way to keep the desire for more harm at bay. Monro understood that, although sometimes I think he studied us as aberrations."

"Us?"

"Yes, of course there were others. We saw each other in the waiting area sometimes, and there were men as well as women. I don't even think it was sexual for Monro, he really did believe in restraint and punishment as an efficacious treatment for mental illness. Perhaps we deviants proved some part of his pet theory. But, let's face it, if you start offering spanking and physical relief as part of your therapy, then word will get around and certain types of people will seek it out."

Jamie raised an eyebrow. "It seems an unusual form of therapy for a psychiatrist."

"Humans are unusual, don't you think?" Petra indicated the pile of painted stones. "Each one of these is similar in some ways and totally different in others. What one person thinks is strange, another embraces. The problem with society is judgement, so much of what is experienced stays underground and repressed. Shame is another form of repression, of course, one our society excels in, and those of us labeled as mentally ill are particularly aware of that."

"Do you think others who went to him were ashamed of what they did?"

"Perhaps." Petra nodded. "But there have been many therapists who strayed into the physical realm. The great Carl Jung was rumored to have had an affair with a young client, Sabina Spielrein, and she admitted in her letters to being aroused by beatings from her father. Some think that became the basis of her sexual relationship with Jung. And, of course, the vibrator was invented by doctors in the Victorian era whose arms were tired from manually stimulating women as part of treatment for hysteria."

Jamie made a couple more notes to follow up.

"But surely Monro must have kept that aspect of his practice secret and for select patients only, so how did you find out about him?"

"Through another client of his, Lyssa Osborne," Petra said. "Of course, I know Matthew Osborne through Psyche, he's just amazing, tireless in his campaigning. I've known him a number of years, even before he was an MP. But I actually met Lyssa for the first time at a life drawing class, or should I say, death drawing, because the models were posed as corpses." Jamie raised an eyebrow and Petra smiled. "Macabre, yes, but a new way to look at the body. Lyssa was brilliant at everything she did and the lines on her paper evoked a sensuality in death that I couldn't capture on my page."

Petra's eyes focused on a point beyond the stone gateway on the wall. "In the end I just watched her sketch, the curve of the woman's breasts, the darkness between her thighs, the way Lyssa licked her lips as if she would devour what she saw. We had a drink afterwards and she told me that she was in love with death and she was seeing a psychiatrist to try and fall out of love with it, to reconnect with her physical self." Petra paused, her voice quieter now. "I too find myself drawn to death, to die perhaps like Virginia Woolf, weighed down with my own painted stones in my pockets. Monro had ways of sublimating those desires and after our sessions, I was renewed and could go another week without wanting to rush into death's embrace. Perhaps you may call his treatment some kind of perversion or abuse of trust, but I didn't wish him dead, Detective. In fact, his death brings my own that much closer." Petra laughed, a brittle sound with little joy in it. "'Beneath it all, desire for oblivion runs.' That's from Philip Larkin. Poets always say it best, don't they?"

There was no trace of concern in Petra's voice at the talk of suicide. Once Jamie would have been shocked, even appalled at the woman's words, but now she understood. Every day she woke alone in the flat without Polly, she wanted to take that one last step into oblivion. It wasn't hard to die, it was only hard to live.

"Do you know of anyone who wanted Monro dead or who threatened him in any way?" Jamie asked.

Petra fell silent for a moment, biting her lip a little.

"He would talk of suicide as the ultimate control," she said, "as the moment when you exercise the last freedom any of us have in this life. But he would also caution not to use that power lightly, for once it's used, it's finished and spent, the power is gone. For someone to murder him, it would be to take that ultimate power of choice away. He wasn't allowed to meet death on his own terms, and that would have been torture for him. But no, I can't think of anyone specifically."

"Can I ask where you were last night?" Jamie asked.

"Of course. I was here, Detective. Alone with my stones." Petra smiled. "I have no alibi, but then I really have no motive, either."

CHAPTER 8

B LAKE BLINKED, DESPERATE TO believe the vision
was wrong, but he could still see it. A creature was curled
around his father's back, its spines embedded in the old
skin, piercing through the thin gown, the visage lizard-
like and darkly scaled. Its tongue darted out, licking at
Magnus' cheek, tasting the sweat there. This thing would
be the first to feed. Blake met his father's eyes, and com-
prehension darted between them. He knew then that this
was the world his father had always perceived and that
Blake had only glimpsed the edges of.

"Daniel, Daniel, stop!"

His mother's voice intruded into the trance and Precious pushed his shoulder, jerking Blake's hand away from
the Bible.

"You know he hates your visions," she said, almost in
tears as she bent to brush damp hair from Magnus' brow.
"How could you do it here with him?"

Blake put his glove back on, looking around the lilac
room, his eyes lingering on the walls and then back at his
father's form on the bed. He could no longer perceive the
creatures, and there was no sense of anything evil here.
Was it just a hallucination, an extension of his father's
belief that there were demons in the world waiting to feed

on dying souls? Or was there some kind of supernatural reality that he had glimpsed through the eyes of a man of faith. In nearly twenty years of visions, Blake had never seen this before.

He frowned, brow furrowed as he walked around the bed to stand behind his father. He reached down and patted the bed where the creature had been curled. Nothing. He held his hand in the space behind Magnus' neck, thinking perhaps he could feel something, like a patch of disturbed air. But it was more likely the breeze from the window, open to let fresh air into this room of sickness.

"I know it's a shock seeing him like this," Precious said. "I'm so sorry I didn't send for you earlier." She sighed. "I didn't think the years would pass so fast, and look at you now." She held out a hand across Magnus' body and Blake took it, squeezing a little. The least he could do was comfort her for a moment, but he couldn't tell her of what he had seen in this room. He looked down and caught sight of a black mark on his father's back. Could this be evidence of the creature?

Blake pulled away the gown that was tied at the back of his father's neck. A moan of protest made him pull his hand away in remembrance of what the man would have done for such trespass in stronger days. He had never seen his father less than fully clothed.

"It's OK, Dad," Blake said, knowing he needed to see what it was. "I just want to look at the mark."

"It's a tattoo," Precious said, her voice strangely dull. "He would never tell me what it meant, but he has had it since I met him. He would get angry if I asked about it."

The symbol began at the very top of Magnus' spine, just below his neck, and as Blake parted the gown, he could see it spread over the main part of his father's back. The ink was faded but there was clearly a design of triple claws, overlaying each other in a knot. The thick lines were bisected with scars and welts in a rhythmic pattern, always the same diagonal down from each shoulder. It seemed his father had beaten himself as well as his son over the years, atoning for whatever sin this tattoo represented. A glimmer of understanding for the man flickered through Blake's mind. He pulled the edges of the gown up and tucked in the covers again, placing his hand on his father's hunched shoulder and tightening his fingers a little, the pressure as close to a gesture of love as he could manage. Blake's own scars were as deep as the ones on his father's back, and neither set would ever fully heal now. But there had to be something in his father's past that would explain the creatures that lurked here waiting to feed.

"How did you meet each other, Mum? You've never told me."

Precious smiled, her eyes shining, and Blake envied the simple pleasure of that memory of young love, so far from his own drunken one-night stands. His thoughts flickered to Jamie: of what could possibly be if they could face their pain together.

"It was back in London," Precious said. "I had just started college and my Pentecostal congregation in Brixton had a visiting preacher." She reached down to stroke Magnus' hair as she spoke. "Your father was a magnificent servant of God and when he spoke, I felt his words go straight to my heart. He stayed in London and soon after, we started dating, with chaperones of course. I know there have been hard times, Daniel, but you were born of love and of God."

Blake nodded. "And what about before that? Where did he live before London?"

"His family are from the very north of Sweden, almost on the border of the fjords of Norway. But he would never say any more than that, and we've never been to visit." She paused, looking down at her husband. "I don't even know their names, and that's how he wanted it. He needed to forget the past, whatever it was, and I honored that. I expect you to as well."

"But I need to know more," Blake said. "It's important, Mum. I saw something ... I can't explain, but I think Dad needs help."

Magnus moaned again, his words unintelligible, but his tone made Precious pale and Blake recognized the man's hold over her. She exhaled.

"So be it. Come, I'll show you the chest."

She picked up the Bible and walked to the door. With a last glance at his father's pale face, Blake followed Precious out the room and up the stairs towards his parents' bedroom. It had been out of bounds when he had lived here, a child's gate and later a beating keeping him away from their private space. But he had often sneaked in when they were out and he knew the huge window looked out into the forest, the bed facing the green expanse. How often had his father lain there and thought of the wilds of Sweden and the forests of his own youth?

"It's underneath the bed," Precious said, a waver in her voice. "He would never let me touch it. Even to clean. The only time he ever beat me properly was when I tried to move it." Her eyes darted to Blake's. "I know that's no comfort to you, but the nights after he beat you, he would cry in my arms. He was terribly afraid of something, Daniel. Something that he thought might come for you."

Blake knelt down, pulled the covers up and looked under the bed. A small chest sat under the side his father had slept in, the dull wood sucking in the light and deepening the surrounding shadows. He reached under and pulled it out. A thick padlock held the chest closed and the metal was rusty, clearly not opened for many years.

"He kept the key in here," Precious said, placing the Bible on top of the bed. "That's how much it means to him, for this book has been within arm's reach as long as I've known him. Even when we met it was already worn with use. I discovered the key once, years ago when we were first married ..." Her hand went to her cheek, eyes glazing over at the memory. "But I learned quickly not to pry into his past."

Blake's anger flared at her obvious remembrance of violence, but the past was done now, and all they had left was the broken man in the bed downstairs. Precious turned to the back of the Bible. A small envelope was taped to the inside of the cover, a handwritten verse on one side. Deuteronomy 28:48.

"'In hunger and thirst,'" Precious recited from memory, "'in nakedness and dire poverty, you will serve the enemies the Lord sends against you. He will put an iron yoke on your neck until he has destroyed you ...' I've pondered this many times over the years. Why link that particular verse to the key?"

She slipped the key from the envelope and handed it to Blake. He pushed it into the padlock and with a few wiggles, it finally twisted and the lock opened. He pulled it off the box and laid it down by the side as Precious knelt next to him, her breath shallow, expectant.

Blake lifted the lid, tugging a little to free the hinges. Inside was another layer of wrapping, this time a kind of oilcloth, like the type found on sailboats. It must have been cream colored once, but was now a dirty ivory. Blake tipped the chest a little and the object fell out into his gloved hand. He laid it on the floor and pulled apart the sailcloth, revealing a book bound in deep burgundy leather. A symbol was inscribed on the front, a circle in the center, bisected by four lines with prongs on either end. The lines were cross-hatched with other markings, the whole image giving the impression of a twisted snowflake.

"It's beautiful," Precious said, reaching out a fingertip to touch the leather. "But why keep this hidden?"

Blake lifted the book from its covering and opened it.

"Galdrabók," he read from the first page, flicking through the heavy book. "It looks like Swedish or some kind of Nordic language, and look at these diagrams and pictures."

"Oh, Lord," Precious whispered. "It's a book of some kind of magic, isn't it?"

Blake's fingers itched, wanting to take off his gloves and touch the book, read the chest, to see what his father was hiding in his past. But he couldn't do it with his mother there.

"I need to know more about it, Mum. Clearly it's important to Dad, but he can't tell us why. Go back down to him, and I'll check it out on the internet."

"It shouldn't even be in the house." Precious stood, her face furrowed with concern. "Leviticus 20, verse 6. 'If a person turns to mediums and necromancers, I will set my face against that person and will cut him off from amongst his people.' Goodness, what did your father do?"

She walked out the door, her footsteps heavy as she went back downstairs. Blake could hear her whispered prayers, interceding for Magnus with her Lord, and for a moment, he was envious of her certain faith. He turned the pages of the book carefully, and within its thin paper, he found a folded chart written in burgundy ink. Blake spread it open on the floor to find a genealogical history of the last few generations of the Olofsson family, written in Swedish. There were strange etchings next to some of the names, runes that marked out individuals in each generation. The symbol lay next to his own name, and that of his father and grandfather. Blake frowned. He needed to understand what this book was.

Laying it down, he took off his gloves and used his smartphone to access the internet, wanting to know more before he tried to tap into the visions. He found a reference quickly. The Galdrabók grimoire was a book of Icelandic spells with invocations to Christian saints, demons and the old Norse gods, as well as instructions for the use of herbs and other magical items. The text was a mixture of Latin, runic script, sacred images and Icelandic magic sigils, symbols of power. What was his father doing with such a text? The only way to find out was to see what visions the book could release to him. Taking a deep breath, Blake laid his bare hands on the leather.

CHAPTER 9

CHADWICK STREET WAS TUCKED into the warren of residences and government buildings on the edge of Westminster, walking distance to Millbank and the Houses of Parliament. The building was painted in shades of cinnamon and cream, with shutters around the windows giving a slightly Mediterranean feel to this bureaucratic hub of the capital. Taking off her leather protective gear, Jamie pulled a black jacket from her pannier and straightened her clothes. She redid her tight bun, winding her black hair and securing it with a clip, tucking in the stray ends. But the transformation into professionalism was wearing thin these days and the bike felt more like her real self than the buttoned-up Detective. The fragmentation of her world was seeping into the job, and part of Jamie craved a final collapse. She rang the bell.

Matthew Osborne pulled the door open within a few seconds, clearly having heard her bike arrive. He was freshly showered, his hair still wet, and he smelled of pine forests after rain. With blue jeans and a black shirt open at the neck and rolled up sleeves, he looked like he had stepped out of a weekend magazine advertising the good life of the rich and famous.

"Detective, come on in. I'm Matthew." He held out his

hand and Jamie shook it. His grip was firm, fingers smooth against her skin, and she noticed the slightly crooked tooth in his otherwise perfect smile. It was a chink of normality in his media-constructed image, but perhaps even that was designed. "I'll put the kettle on, and then we can have a chat about what you need."

"Thank you." Jamie followed Matthew inside, shutting the door behind her. She glanced around the flat as she walked into a large living space, leading to a small kitchen. The room was furnished in shades of champagne, a muted undertone, with furniture that looked comfortable but still expensive. The outstanding element was a feature wall with stripes of fuchsia, lemon and vermilion, hung with stunning pieces of modern art. In one, a woman's hand and the side of her head emerged from the canvas, as if she was trying to climb out of the wall behind. Another was a riot of color over a black tangle of what looked like neurons in the brain. It should have been chaotic, but there was a space in the middle of the pandemonium, an opening for calm.

"My sister, Lyssa, was very talented," Matthew said, emerging from the kitchen, his voice wistful. "These are just a couple from her portfolio. She could have gone so far with it, and creating the work calmed her, kept her from spiraling downwards." He paused, gazing at the woman's hand reaching out to him, as if she was calling for his help. The kettle whistled and he shook his head slightly, reverting to charm. "Now, how do you take your tea?"

"Black with one, please."

Matthew stirred in a sugar and brought it to Jamie in a blue mug with a chip in the rim. It made her almost smile to see that he was so clearly at home with imperfection. Perhaps there was more to this man than just the media profile.

"Now, what can I help you with?" Matthew asked,

sitting on one of the chairs and indicating that Jamie should do the same.

"I'm investigating a homicide that occurred this morning at the Imperial War Museum."

Matthew's brow furrowed. "Surely not at our Fun Run? It went off without a hitch and all participants were accounted for."

Jamie shook her head. "No, actually, it was within the main building, unrelated to your event. But the victim was your sister's psychiatrist."

"That bastard Monro, are you sure?"

She caught a hint of satisfaction in Matthew's eyes.

"You sound pleased."

"I am. Not to speak ill of the dead, of course, but I believe his treatment only made Lyssa worse over time." Matthew looked intently at Jamie, but she could see no hint of his underlying thoughts. With so many years of hiding things, a politician was a real match for the police. "He tried her on so many drug regimes but she was afraid of needles and the experience was always terrifying. There was no spark left in her after dosage, the drugs emptied her and left her anemic and stale. As they began to wear off, she would fill that emptiness with ideas and thoughts and color, but the cyclic regime of years wore her down. Each time the colors came back, they were more muted, pastels instead of primary shades."

Matthew pointed at the walls. "As you can see, she hated pastels, Detective. She couldn't bear baby pink and duck-egg blue. She wanted strong bold shades, like her personality. You would have noticed her in a crowd." He pointed to a picture on the mantelpiece and Jamie stood for a better look. Lyssa had been strikingly handsome, not beautiful in a traditional sense but with strong features that drew the eyes. Her hair was cropped short and dyed a deep red, and she had tattooed eyebrows in a Celtic design.

Jamie felt Matthew's analytical gaze take in her own black work-wraith uniform, her dark hair in a tight bun, her colorless skin. She suddenly felt tepid compared to this woman whose eyes were so vibrant and whose photo exuded life. Jamie felt an edge of that passion in tango, but it had become a secret part of her fractured life these days. She sat back down as Matthew continued.

"We're all coerced into uniformity but Lyssa never gave into it. Despite our lip service to diversity, society wants conformity. We frown at the misbehavior of others. That's the real reason that Lyssa was medicated ... so she couldn't be remarkable. You might think the inhuman restraint, the physical violence done to the mad is over, Detective, but the restraint has just moved from the outside to the inside, and the drugs are just a replacement for the manacles of Bedlam. Perhaps the drugs were worse because they left Lyssa without the freedom of her mind."

Jamie thought of Polly in the last days before her death, surfing the internet and learning new things, desperate to suck everything she could from life. Her body had been twisted and malfunctioning, but her mind remained clear and curious until the end.

"I'm sorry for your loss," Jamie said. She had spoken those words many times over the years, but now she actually understood them deep within. "But without the drugs, surely Lyssa may have ended up self-harming even more. Perhaps the chemical restraint helped in some way."

There was a flash in Matthew's eyes, something Jamie couldn't quite identify. He tamped it down quickly, returning his face to the politician's equilibrium.

"That's the opinion of many, for sure." His words were curt, ending that thread of conversation. "Now what exactly can I help you with, Detective?"

"I need to know where you were last night."

Matthew grinned, the charming smile that housewives all over the nation doted on.

"Oh, I'm a suspect. That's a new one."

"Not a suspect as such. I'm just following up on leads from the workplace of the deceased, and of course, you were at the museum this morning."

Matthew nodded. "Of course, it's no trouble and I'm always happy to help the police with enquiries." He took a sip of tea. "This morning I arrived at the site early, around nine, but I wasn't the first, and I wasn't anywhere near the main museum. I parked on Lambeth Walk near the London Eye Hostel, which I'm sure you can check. Last night I was out to dinner with a fellow MP. She'll certainly support that. We parted ways at around ten-thirty and I was tucked up in bed by eleven. But I do live alone, Detective, and despite what the press may speculate about my love life, I actually live a quiet, private existence. You won't find scandal here. Lyssa lived with me for a time … but of course, she can no longer speak on my behalf."

Jamie could hear the grief in his voice, and a tinge of guilt at his sister's death. She had thought life would be impossible without Polly to come home to, so perhaps Matthew Osborne felt the same. He had constructed a life that was impenetrable because of his grief, and Jamie knew she pushed others aside when they tried to come closer. She thought of Blake Daniel, and how she kept him at arm's length. Was this how Matthew Osborne behaved, too?

"I'd like to know more about Psyche," she said. "What do you want to achieve with the charity?"

"An end to the stereotypes," Matthew replied. "An admission that madness is a spectrum and we're all on it somewhere. No more us and them, just a continuum of the amazing human mind with all its complexity. We can't do a blood test and say for sure whether someone is crazy, and we can only diagnose Alzheimer's accurately after death. So is madness in the physical brain or all in the existential mind? And where is the line crossed?"

Matthew's eyes shone with passion and he clenched his fist as he spoke, clearly used to engaging hostile opponents in the political arena.

"Does Lyssa's experience drive your campaign?" Jamie asked, watching him soften a little at his sister's name.

Matthew nodded. "She started suffering a mood disorder in her teens, and I was always her champion big brother." He tapped his front tooth with an elegant fingernail. "This crooked one is the result of a brawl defending her against school bullies. I keep it unfixed as a reminder of the intolerance that the mentally ill suffer at the hands of those who don't understand them. Psyche has developed over time, an attempt to take this beyond one individual, and as Secretary of State for Health, I'm in a prime position to make the so-called mad my life's work."

"Is the word mad appropriate?" Jamie asked, wondering at the stigma of its use.

Matthew smiled. "Oh, yes. These days language is reclaimed. I support a less extreme viewpoint, but Lyssa was a member of Mad Pride, focused on taking control of madness and accepting it. The prison others build can become a fortress of strength. For that reason, Lyssa always loved the Tower of London, with all of its mad connotations. We used to stand on the arches of Tower Bridge looking down into it when we first moved here." Matthew's voice was wistful with memories of happier times. He stood and walked to the artwork on the wall, staring at it as he spoke, as if he saw beyond it to other realities. "Madness is not an aberration, Detective. It's not abnormal. It's just part of the spectrum of the human condition. Most hide their little crazy moments, but they happen to us all." Jamie's thoughts flashed once more to the pills in her medicine cabinet.

"And, of course," Matthew continued, "without the mad, Shakespeare would be without his tragic heroes who teach us so much. Surely Hamlet was clinically depressed, Ophelia to the point of suicide, and of course, there's demented Lear, howling against the storm with Tom of Bedlam for company as he raved against his daughters. The way families treat the mad is perhaps part of the truth of Lear. And look at Macbeth. Surely there was a hint of paranoia in his murderous behavior?"

"But don't some people really need help?" Jamie said. "The world is hard enough to manage for people in full possession of their faculties. The forms we have to fill in, the bureaucracy, the rules we have to obey to live in society. These must be difficult things for people whose reality is skewed."

"But who's to say that their reality is any less valid than our own?" Matthew asked.

"I guess the government, the police, the rules of our society say that a certain reality must be upheld."

Matthew threw his hands up with exasperation. "But look at this world. Every day, we hear of human depravity on the news. Of parents beating and starving their children, of countries spying and stealing secrets, of torture, mass murder, incoming disasters both natural and manmade. This keeps people on the edge of their own madness, controlled by fear of what may come if they don't obey. Surely this is why we are so medicated? The number of people on prescription drugs for anxiety and depression is out of control. Our society is wrecked, for 'those who the Gods wish to destroy, first they make mad.'"

Jamie raised a questioning eyebrow.

"Attributed to an anonymous source or sometimes Euripides," Matthew said. "The Greek tragedies were filled with the mad. My sister was delighted when she found out that Lyssa was the goddess of frenzied madness. She had been known by the name Mel all our childhood, but she embraced the name Lyssa after she studied Greek myth.

I'm not sure what came first, her name or the madness that took her.

"You're right, though. Lyssa was medicated because her mania took her to the edge of danger, and her depression took her over it." Matthew ran a finger gently down the curve of the woman's arm as she emerged from the artwork. Jamie could almost feel his touch on her own skin. "She walked the line successfully for so many years, but then, of course, she went over the edge. On the drugs she tottered like an old woman along well-worn paths, panting and wheezing to achieve anything small. Without them, she ran and laughed and danced along the cliff's edge, creating masterpieces, but she was always in danger of falling."

Matthew spun back to look at Jamie, his voice impassioned. "But isn't it better to live your life like a comet, blazing across the sky, rather than suffering this dull bus ride of normality? Of course I wanted a lifetime with my sister, but not with the dull, medicated version. She wasn't Lyssa then – perhaps she was plain old Mel, the compliant, good child my parents always wanted. Like I am, perhaps, like all who subscribe to the normal and expected way of life. But aren't the mad, the crazy, actually the ones who work at a job they hate, with people they can't stand, digging themselves deeper into debt, medicating themselves daily with food and TV and alcohol? Who's to say that isn't the more damaging way to live?"

Matthew's eyes met Jamie's, his gaze penetrating.

"Let's be honest, Detective, you don't look well. As someone who's lived alongside depression, you exude its dark energy right now."

Jamie met his eyes as she took another sip of tea. His suggestion disarmed her and his ability to see what she hid with a veneer of normality was uncanny. She wore no makeup to work, and her eyes were shadowed with dark rings. Her skin was too pale and she was too thin. Self-harming wasn't just for those diagnosed as mentally ill. She met Matthew's eyes.

"It's not your concern, but I do understand your perspective. I've lost someone too."

"And is grief a form of madness, Detective? In the DSM, the psychiatrist's manual for diagnostics, it only becomes depression after several months of suffering. Before that, grief is just grief, but then somehow it crosses some designated line and becomes something you can medicate away. I embrace it because it drives the passion for my work. When Lyssa was alive, I fought to claim her equal rights in the mind of society, and now she's dead, I work to establish the continuum of the mad and stop the abuses before they become too great.

"People forget that it was the Americans in the 1920s who started the enforced sterilization of the mentally ill based on the assumption of bad breeding. Hitler only followed their example, targeting the mentally ill before the Jews or gypsies. The mad were the first to be slaughtered, and there is still considerable prejudice against them. It wouldn't take much to tip people back into the old ways of thinking. I have my suspicions that Monro wasn't too far from those thoughts."

"What do you mean?" Jamie asked, noting how tense Matthew had become, his muscular frame taut. He paused for a moment, as if he was unsure whether to continue. "Please," she said. "It will help the investigation if you can tell us of Monro's political leanings."

Matthew nodded. "His name came up in a confidential paper distributed by RAIN. Do you know of them?"

Jamie noted it down. "No, but please go on."

"RAIN is a government agency associated with the Ministry of Defense, so it's not under my portfolio. It stands for Research into Advanced Intelligence Network, and their work is aimed at high-risk but high-payoff programs that have the potential to provide Britain with an overwhelming intelligence advantage against future adversaries. That's about all I know, despite trying to find out more. I did see a report on psychic ability and its correlation with mental health, and Monro was one of the names on it. But the agency is incredibly secretive and I couldn't find out anymore. Perhaps you can, Detective. Perhaps it's related to his murder."

Jamie remembered the raindrop symbol on some of Monro's files. It could be connected to RAIN somehow, but what exactly was Monro's involvement?

"It's ironic that RAIN are studying mental illness," Matthew continued, a dark smile in his voice. "There are studies that show that over half of us would meet the diagnostic criteria for mental disorder in our lifetimes. But we keep our thoughts to ourselves so no one will notice the throes of insanity. We maintain a semblance of normality, but who knows what violence goes on behind the closed curtains of our minds? After all, pills can now make us better than well. Why feel even slightly down if you can pop a pill and make it go away, live in happy la-la land, dulled to sensation? Why be even hurt a little when you can medicate to oblivion?"

Jamie thought of the ephedrine she used as uppers, about the sleeping pills she took to keep the nightmares at bay.

"And what do your parents think about your work?" she asked.

Matthew held his arms wide and took a little bow. "I'm their golden boy, Detective." His voice was mocking, bitter. "Their son is an MP, a respected member of the community, on the TV and in the papers. Lyssa was the more spectacular but also the more disappointing. They judged her to be wanting and took her to a psychiatrist in her early teens. She started the medication then. It was only with me that she felt safe enough to come off the drugs." He took another deep breath. "Is it just me, or are you also sick of being conformist? Why can't we all go a little crazy sometimes?"

"But suicide?" Jamie said. "Surely you don't support it."

"I support the right of an adult to take their own life if it's a considered decision. Think about it. Some days it's a surprise that we continue to live. It's much harder to keep getting up and living in this world than it is to give up and relax into the darkness. Embracing oblivion is just a choice, Detective."

"But the misery of those left behind," Jamie said. "Your own grief at Lyssa's death? Surely that would be better avoided? She could have created more, perhaps found happiness on another day."

Matthew ran his fingers along a crack that wound its way up from the fireplace to the ceiling. In any other house, it would have been plastered over, filled in and fixed. But here, it had been made a feature, and Jamie noticed the hands of tiny creatures emerging from the plaster, drawn in black ink. It was hard to tell whether they were imps from a dark place, or fairies coming forth with a blessing.

"Lyssa believed in embracing the cracks in our lives," Matthew said, his voice tinged with a sigh. "But her death was not such a simple thing."

"How did she …?"

"We rented a garage in the next street. I've never needed a car in London, but Lyssa loved to drive. It gave her a sense of freedom and escape. Sometimes she would drive to the ocean for the day, just to see the horizon in shades of blue. She loved the mad weather." Matthew laughed a little. "You know what I mean."

Jamie nodded, waiting for him to continue.

"She had been away the weekend before, some special

retreat Monro had got her into, so I didn't see her much that week. The final day, she glammed up in her favorite dress and these brilliant red, Spanish flamenco heels. She loved them. She had a bottle of champagne and one of my crystal glasses with her. Only one, mind you, because she was always going to do it alone. She blocked the garage doors, making sure they were insulated, and then turned the ignition on. She took a couple of sleeping pills with the champagne … I imagine her toasting me." His voice trailed off for a moment.

"Eventually the exhaust fumes seeped out of the garage and someone reported it, but it was hours later. I was out, just another day on the job, campaigning for her rights, and those like her. She died of carbon monoxide poisoning. She just closed her eyes and fell asleep."

"I'm so sorry," Jamie said, his loss echoing within her, but there was also a tinge of anger. Lyssa had wasted a life, when Polly would gladly have seized that spark.

"She had always talked about suicide. It was one of our frequent discussions and she agreed to the medication in order to modulate her compulsions. But she missed her bolus injection appointment that week, and she didn't tell me." Matthew's head dropped to his hands. "She was my responsibility."

"She was an adult," Jamie said. "It was her choice."

"Oh, I don't begrudge her the choice to die. It's being left behind I resent."

Jamie wanted to tell him about Polly, wanted to tell him about the pills she had in her cabinet and the struggle every day not to take them. The faint glimmer of hope that she saw in a possible future even without the glue that held her life together.

"My sister was born special," Matthew said. "Her eyes rarely met ours as a baby, but instead, she smiled at beings in another realm. She could see through the veil of this reality, Detective. We are all given a spark of madness, but for her, it fanned into a flame and I helped it grow. We see such a poor version of this life but she could hold the whole world in her mind."

"But she couldn't stand it?"

Matthew shook his head. "The world implied she couldn't stand it. If I could have kept her protected, away from those like Monro who treated her as an invalid, she would have been safe. But they drugged her and she said it dulled her world and made her into one of us."

"One of us?"

"Those who walk in darkness and call it reality. But our reality wasn't worth living for, she said. If she couldn't fly with the angels, then why bother? In my opinion, it's not the mentally ill who are dangerous, it's those who control, medicate and abuse them."

Jamie sensed the undercurrent of animosity. Had that emotion spilled into violence?

"Did you know that Monro had some more – unusual – treatments as part of his practice?" she asked.

Matthew's eyes narrowed. He knew, for sure.

"I heard rumors that he had affairs with some of his patients, but Lyssa would never have been up for that. She certainly had no trouble with sex, Detective. When she was manic, she was irresistible." His words made Jamie wonder just how close the siblings had been.

"Did she have any papers or diaries?" Jamie asked.

"She wrote a diary in the months before her death," Matthew said, his voice tired. "I can't bear to read it, but perhaps it might offer some clues about Monro."

Jamie nodded. "If you can bear to part with it for a few days, I'll see what it contains."

Matthew stood and went to the bookcase. He pulled a red Moleskine notebook from the shelf.

"Be gentle with her memory."

In his words, Jamie heard the depths of his grief, and she felt an echo of her own for Polly. The sting of tears threatened and she stood to take the book from him.

"Of course, I'll take great care with it, and return it to you as soon as possible."

CHAPTER 10

As Blake laid his hands on the Galdrabók, a rush of waters overlaid with the howling of wind filled his brain, yet he could see nothing but mist. He grasped for a tendril of emotional resonance in the haze and found only terror. Apprehensive, he followed the feeling with his mind and suddenly he was in a forest clearing at night. Stars were bright overhead and a full moon shone down on a group of men, chanting with arms raised to the skies, their backs marked by the same tattoo he had seen on his father. There was a sense of expectation in the air, a latent violence that compelled Blake to draw more closely to the group. He became aware of the stench of blood and stink of voided bowels, overlaid by the cool night air and forest scent.

Movement caught his eye from the trees behind the leader of the circle, a twitch in the shadow. Three bodies hung in the ash grove, and as he focused, Blake saw that their abdomens had been cut open. A rush of nausea gripped him; the men had been hanged with their own entrails and then wound again with rough ropes to hold their weight. One of the victims still jerked in place, his body refusing to give up the last spark of life.

"Great Odin, we call on you tonight. We relive the myth of Ymir and the creation of the world for your glory."

The leader's voice was rough yet powerful, rolling through the clearing so that every man could hear him clearly. Blake understood the words as his father had heard them all those years ago, for it was Magnus' terror he could feel, Magnus' eyes he saw through. He must have had the book with him at this occult ceremony performed on the edge of civilization years ago.

A man lay tied in the middle of the ring of followers, blood from his wounds dripping onto the grass. His eyes were closed but his chest rose and fell rapidly at the words intoned around him. The leader began a new chant, the words a repetitive phrase that rumbled from his chest. He stamped his feet slowly and the other men in the circle joined the incantation. The stamping grew faster and the repetition of the words spun through Blake's head like another voice taking over his brain. The thump of their feet resonated through the ground and his heart began to thud in time. The men drew hand axes from their belts as the chant reached a crescendo, and then they fell silent, staring at the victim in their midst.

Stepping forward, the leader grabbed the hair of the prone man.

"For you, Odin," he called to the sky, lifting his axe. Blake could almost feel the panicked state of the victim as he struggled and moaned. The leader brought down the weapon into the meaty part of the man's neck, pushing him to the floor as he hacked at the bony spine, blood spattering a dark wetness over his clothes. It took several blows to sever the head, then the leader lifted it to the sky with a primal roar as the men around him began to chant again.

Blake felt horror morph into shame, and then it struck him. His father had known the leader. This was his family; the leader was Magnus' own father. How many more sacrifices had he been involved in before he had fled this life for that of a preacher in London?

The leader gestured to two of the men, and they stepped forward with axes raised as the others continued to chant. Together the men began to butcher the body, blood soaking the earth. One of them smashed the skull so the brains ran out and made sure to separate the teeth from the jaw. It only took ten minutes to reduce a living man to body parts and gore. Blake retched, stomach heaving as he fell to his knees, unable to tear his gaze from the terrible sight. The eyes of the chanting men fell upon him as he coughed and spat, and then he saw the leader walking towards him with a determined stride, eyes wild with anger. Panicking, Blake pulled himself back out of the trance, dropping the book.

Retching and coughing, he found himself back in the bedroom, sweat dripping from his brow. He knelt on the floor, trying to anchor himself to this dimension, to this physical place. The visions had always been passive before, the very definition of remote viewing, but he had felt the eyes of the leader upon him and he had seen the intent to harm. Did that mean he could be physically hurt or even killed during a vision? Blake's mind reeled with the implications, even as the doubts about his own sanity flooded in, as they always did after a vision. Was it just some kind of hallucination, something he made up, even some kind of brain damage?

As he returned consciously to the bedroom, Blake could hear his mother praying in the room below, a singsong invocation to the God she had always trusted. In Magnus she had found a prophet, but even the great preacher must eventually stand before his God, and now it seemed, Precious had found her own voice. Blake couldn't fathom how she believed as she did, but hadn't he also seen things that proved there was more than a physical realm?

Still lightheaded, Blake reached for his smartphone and googled Odin. During the attack of the Neo-Vikings on the British Museum a while back, he had learned a few things about the Norse god, but most of his knowledge came from Hollywood, rather than the original myths. Pages of articles came up, but one in particular caught his eye. The Norse peoples had believed that the universe originally emerged from an ancient being called Ymir. When Odin and the other deities had decided to create Earth, they murdered Ymir and made the world from his body, the sky from his skull and formed the clouds from his brains. His blood ran out to form the sea and his bones and teeth were seeds for the mountains. The men in the woods had been enacting this ancient myth in order to call on the power inherent in this primeval being. Odin was the god of frenzy and violent death, and bestowed wisdom and divine inspiration on his worshippers.

Reading on, Blake found that Odin had hung from an ash tree for nine days and nights to gain knowledge of the runes that could command great power. Human sacrifices to Odin were killed in a similar fashion to honor the god and also to represent Yggdrasil, the great ash tree that spanned the heavens, Earth and the underworld. This had been his father's past, some kind of cult that still worshipped the ancient gods in a modern world.

Blake flicked open the Galdrabók, trying to understand why Magnus had kept the book all these years. Why not burn it, or leave it behind when he started this new life? He turned the pages, noting drops of wax on some and marks like blood on others. The edge of one page was heavily marked with charcoal, a substance that lifted off onto Blake's fingertips. The page contained a series of runes and Icelandic spells for charisma, for the inner power to draw people in and make them follow. A wave of anger washed over Blake, and then a deep disappointment in the man he had both feared and worshipped.

He stood and walked downstairs, the book of runes in his hand. Precious knelt by the bed praying, and his father's eyes were locked on the space above the fireplace, where the demon had sat.

"I know what you were part of," Blake said, his voice strident, accusing. His father's eyes were flint hard.

CHAPTER 11

"I KNOW YOU TOOK part in human sacrifice rituals years ago."

Blake forced the words out. There was a moment of possibility when he could have been wrong but Magnus didn't blink, didn't even flinch.

"No!" Precious put a hand to her mouth, but Blake knew she could see he spoke the truth and there was no denial in his father's eyes. Weeping, she ran from the room and down the stairs. He heard the front door bang as she left to find solace in the forest. Part of him wanted to go after her, but this was a reckoning he couldn't run from anymore.

"What else did you do in exchange for the power of the runes?" Blake shouted. "Are these demons here to take what you traded for this new life?" He stepped close to the bed. "Do you think that I was given my visions as a curse because of what you did, or perhaps a gift that you should have had instead of me? Well, I want to see it. I want to see everything. I think you owe me that much."

Magnus closed his eyes for a moment, and Blake felt the stillness of the room, waiting for his answer. When his father opened his eyes again, Blake saw agreement, and a kind of relief that he could finally share this burden. He had been holding it alone for so long.

Blake held the Galdrabók close to the bed, and Magnus shifted a little so that his limp hand was thrust towards it. Blake laid it on the book, placing his own hand next to it as he slipped into the veils of consciousness, trying to surf the waves of his father's past. Images and sounds flooded his mind, taking him back in time as the shadows circled and he glimpsed an older world of deeper forests and high mountains. He delved further, seeking the sins that haunted Magnus now.

A scream ricocheted through his brain, splintering the vision. Blake's eyes flew open at the sound. The walls bled black and the spiked creatures crept closer to the bed. The floor writhed with a mass of bodies. One hissed at Blake, clambering up the chair next to him to reach the bed. Blake tried to push it off but his hands went right through it. He was still in trance but this wasn't the past – it was right now. Another scream and then a moan and he turned to see Magnus pinned down by several of the creatures. One was sucking the air from his lips and another had a hand inside his chest, squeezing his father's heart, seeping black pus into the man's blood.

"No," Blake shouted, trying in vain to pull the creatures off his father. But his hands could find no purchase in the other realm and the creatures paid him no heed, continuing to swarm. They began to rip strips of flesh from the old body, licking the wounds and dripping blood on the sheets. The thing on Magnus' back reared up and bared its fangs, pointed and dripping with venom. Blake could do nothing as it pierced the man's skull.

Waves of pain emanated from his father. Magnus shook, his breathing a rasp as he dragged air into his lungs, even as his chest was crushed by the number of creatures swarming over him. The demon at his head crunched its jaws down and Blake could see his father's skull begin to fragment. He babbled, desperately clutching at prayers his mother had taught him from a young age, snatching at scripture long forgotten. The demons were impervious, and as Magnus convulsed, they began to bite chunks from his skin.

Magnus screamed in Blake's head but no words came audibly from his throat. Blake wept, desperately pulling at the creatures but his fingers only found air. Magnus' skull split under the teeth of the demon and his brain could be seen pulsating, the veins bulbous on the creamy surface. As the demon peeled back the bone to feed, it met Blake's eyes and he saw the promise of Hell there. With a start, Blake pulled his hand from the Galdrabók, panting with terror. He could bear to see no more.

He was back in the lilac room, the only sound the rasp of Magnus' breath, coming slowly now, each one too many seconds apart. His body was barely shaking, and there was no evidence of that other dark reality. Blake wept, kneeling at his father's bedside, his mind flooded with the echo of the visions. Even with his eyes open, the room seemed to flicker from lilac to black as if his dual perception had melded into one reality.

Magnus took a last rattling breath, the gurgling from his throat a hideous wet noise, and then his chest was still.

"No," Blake whispered. "Not yet." He took his father's hand, feeling the warmth of his skin. The hand that had inflicted his own scars over years of abuse in the name of God. Blake kissed it, pressing his lips to Magnus' palm and in his mind, he pleaded for more time. Perhaps together they could revoke whatever hold the Galdrabók had over his father. But there was no further breath and Blake sensed an emptiness in the physical body in front of him. What had been his father was gone, and although the Elders and the congregation would believe that Magnus was in Heaven with his Lord, Blake could only see visions of his father consumed by the fiends of Hell.

The door banged downstairs and he heard his mother's footsteps on the stair. Blake stood as she walked in. She saw the anguish in his eyes and pushed past him to the bed, pulling Magnus' body into her arms.

"No, no, no," she cried, tears coursing down her cheeks. "Oh my love, don't leave me."

Blake couldn't bear to watch his mother's suffering. He needed to get out of the house, for he sensed demonic eyes watching him, calling for him to return to that reality. Whatever the truth, he needed to forget, and there was only one sure way to drown these visions.

CHAPTER 12

As HER BIKE TOOK the final corner of the tree-lined road leading to the gates of Broadmoor Hospital, Jamie saw the main building looming ahead. It was an imposing structure, with red brick walls, arched windows and bands of lighter brown brick marking the floor levels inside. Bars on the windows betrayed the true nature of the place, for unlike most hospitals, people here were not free to leave. Jamie felt a sense of trepidation at going in, as if somehow this was all a trick and she would never emerge.

Broadmoor was one of the top-security mental hospitals in Britain, according to information Jamie had read that morning. It held several hundred male inmates, and had been designed by a military engineer in 1863 to house what were then known as criminal lunatics. It was originally intended for the reception, safe custody and treatment of people who had committed crimes while actually insane, or who had become insane while undergoing sentences of punishment. It had been a prison, but in 1948 Broadmoor became known as a hospital.

Jamie parked her bike and looked up at the building, its military bearing apparent in strong lines and heavy aspect. These days, its function was overlaid with medical jargon, but its residents were still the stuff of nightmares and tabloid frenzy. The Teacup Murderer, an expert poisoner; Peter Sutcliffe, the Yorkshire Ripper, and Kenneth Erskine, the Stockwell Strangler; the Krays, Ian Brady and even the inspiration for Hannibal Lecter, Robert Maudsley. In a particular gruesome incident in 1977 within these very walls, Maudsley and another prisoner had taken a pedophile into a cell, barricaded themselves inside and tortured him for nine hours, before garroting him and eating part of his brain with a spoon. Maudsley was now in solitary confinement in the basement of Wakefield Prison, in a two-cell glass cage, his furniture made of compressed cardboard. While most mental illness was considered by many to be an imbalance in brain chemistry, this level of psychopathy seemed to portray an entirely different brain altogether.

Jamie took off her bike clothes and added them to the panniers. She straightened her trousers and put on her jacket before walking to the gate. A man in a grey suit stood in the entrance hall, presumably the psychologist she was assigned to meet regarding the case. Although his suit looked a bit threadbare, the man's bearing was proudly aristocratic. Jamie had heard that Broadmoor was a highly sought location, a prestigious placement for any psychologist. It was so much more interesting than working with the general population whose troubles were mainly anxiety and depression, a banal litany of monotonous woe.

"Dr Taylor-Johnson?" Jamie asked, and the man nodded, holding out his hand in greeting.

"Welcome to our little piece of England, Detective. Let's get you through security and I'll show you around."

In the main entrance hall, Jamie put her things on a conveyor belt in the same fashion as airport security, and walked through the body-scan machine.

"If you wouldn't mind, Detective," Taylor-Johnson said. "We also need a photo for your ID card."

Jamie nodded, fascinated with the high level of security, even for a short visit.

"Of course, it's not a prison," the psychologist said, noting her interest. "This is a hospital and we care for our patients." Jamie glanced out the window at the fifteen-foot mesh fence topped with overhang and razor-wire. There were cameras on every corner, facing both ways with one opposite so there were no blind spots. Taylor-Johnson followed her gaze and visibly bristled.

"Patients are detained and they're not free to leave, but that is for their own and other people's well-being. They can't be let out, but equally we can't let them loose in a prison." Jamie could hear a defensive tone in his voice. This was clearly a subject he had to address frequently. "Broadmoor provides physical, social and mental health care with the aim of rehabilitation."

"Is this reception area the main focus of your security?" Jamie asked.

"There's the physical security, of course," Taylor-Johnson said, "but we also have procedural security, counting the patients, and regular rounds, so we always know where everyone is. We have relational security, as well, and trust with the patients so they tell us when things are amiss. We also communicate with the control room, logging everyone's movements. It's a hospital," he emphasized again, "but these methods keep everybody safe."

"You have a control room?" Jamie asked, imagining banks of computers, no doubt similar to police monitoring stations. Humans were indeed the most dangerous predators, and this place looked ready to tackle any situation fast.

"Of course, but it's all for the patients' benefit, and to prevent any kind of … situation."

Jamie was aware that there had been a couple of escaped prisoners in Broadmoor's history. In 1952, serial killer John Straffen had murdered a young girl within hours of escaping, and since then, others had made it over that security wall. There was now a network of sirens that would sound in the nearby towns and villages in case of any escapees. Jamie thought briefly of the siege of Frankenstein's castle, the terror of suburbia at the approach of the monster. But these men looked ordinary, people you wouldn't even look at twice in the street, the monster only in the pathways of their own minds.

"Patients are constantly monitored," Taylor-Johnson continued as they walked through the hospital. "Of course, psychopharmacology is critical for treatment, and the drug dosage is adjusted based on an individual's behavior and response to medication. Patients also have three to nine months of assessment by a multi-disciplinary team while a care plan is developed."

"Do you have any problems with drug use inside?" Jamie asked, thinking of the store at the back of Monro's private office.

Taylor-Johnson shook his head, pausing at a reinforced glass panel.

"This is the drug bay and you can see it's all automated. Everything is highly controlled, and everyone is searched on the way in and out."

Jamie watched as a robot arm picked a packet of pills off a shelf and dispensed it to a slot where a nurse picked it up.

"Medication is critical for dampening the immediate symptoms and behavioral problems," Taylor-Johnson continued, seemingly intent on proving the safety of the hospital. "There's a broad range of choice in antipsychotics and antidepressants these days, and we find the best combination for the patient with the minimum of side effects. Of course, the drugs may control some issues, but unfortunately they can't help with mending relationships or enabling the patient to return to real life, so we have other therapies for that."

As they continued to walk down the corridor, Jamie glanced into a side room. There were art projects laid out on benches, and a couple of men painting. Taylor-Johnson paused to explain.

"Illness doesn't get better without treatment and that takes time. Occupational therapy structures the day, so the patients have some kind of work to do, and we've found that patients engaging in meaningful activity don't act up."

Jamie could see that patients here had a reasonable quality of life. Broadmoor Hospital was now designed to care for and rehabilitate instead of functioning as a simple prison, but not all would agree that was appropriate.

"There are some people who think the men here are evil," she said. "And the things we see as police make many of us consider the world a dark place that might be better without these men in it." Jamie thought back to the drug-fueled murder she had witnessed in the caves beneath West Wycombe. "What do you think?"

Taylor-Johnson's eyes darkened, and she saw the conflict there as he considered his words carefully.

"Our aim is to care for and treat patients whose behavior could be a danger to others, in particular those with psychotic disorders. But typically these men have had traumatic childhoods and they've been punished severely in the past. They harm themselves and others as a way of managing the world. It's the only way they know. There are some here … well, let's just say that in the vast expanse of human behavior, there will always be extremes. These men exist on the very edge, so we call them insane and treat their madness. But our society can't say that they're evil, because we're rational, and rational people don't believe in evil. Do they, Detective?"

Jamie couldn't meet his gaze. To be honest, she didn't

know anymore. Being in the police certainly ground down that rationality, and with what they saw every day, it was hard to believe that there wasn't some kind of chaotic force that drove some people to the depths, twisting them from loving fathers to abusive parents, from doting mothers to drug addicts who would leave their children for the next fix. If there was no evil force in the world, then that only left human nature to blame, and the potential to harm lay within everyone.

"Let's walk on, Detective." Taylor-Johnson continued down a side corridor, pointing out the various wings as they walked. Jamie found the place fascinating, a window into a life so far removed from normality. She noticed her mind was clearer than it had been in the last months of mourning, the intellectual stimulation of the case bringing her alive again.

"There are different types of wards," Taylor-Johnson explained. "This corridor has twelve side rooms – you could call them bedrooms – and each is the same. The furniture is built into the walls so there's nothing that could be used as a weapon or broken off to self-harm. Of course, the ward facilities are what the patients need, not what they want. It's not a hotel, and we expect patients to be up and engaging in some kind of activity every day, not lying in bed for hours. It depends on their illness, and at what point they are in their recovery, but we encourage patients to keep busy. Plus, there's a range of leisure activities, music and art, gardening, computers but no internet. We monitor everything they do and report back to the clinical team on their behavior. We've found that too much empty time makes people depressed."

That was certainly true, Jamie thought, and throwing herself back into work was certainly the best therapy for her own situation. She glanced inside one of the rooms, the plastic furniture rounded, as if designed for a child. She wondered what it must be like to be watched at all times, monitored in every activity, each twitch analyzed for signs of psychopathy and then medicated, forcefully if necessary, in order to modulate behavior. If she was watched twenty-four hours a day, would these doctors perceive the dark destruction that threatened her mind? Would they see that she craved the oblivion of final release?

Jamie realized her hands were tightly clenched and she relaxed them purposefully, exhaling slowly to calm herself again. This place made her feel claustrophobic, as if all these people could see inside her head and knew her darkest secrets. She had left a woman to die, savaged by a dog in bloodlust. She had brought death to those trapped in the Hellfire Caves. Jamie glanced over at Dr Taylor-Johnson, all buttoned up and superior. What secrets did he keep, and who saw into his head? Was the line between patient and keeper so thin as to be separated by action alone?

"Did you know Dr Christian Monro personally?" she asked, refocusing on the case.

The doctor's eyes flickered a little at her question.

"Yes, of course. As a forensic psychiatrist, he was a regular visitor and returned to reassess patients over time. We disagreed on some of his cases, but professional conflict is part of the game, Detective."

"Any case in particular?"

"Well, Timothy MacArnold, who you're interviewing today, would be one example of where we clashed. I'm still not sure the diagnosis was correct, but Monro was adamant that he be cared for here, and not sent to a high-security prison."

"What do you think is wrong with him?"

"We treat him for antisocial personality disorder and he has symptoms of schizophrenia, but some days, Detective … " The doctor shook his head. "I wonder whether these men are much cleverer than we assume."

"Doesn't research on psychopathy suggest that most people with the traits also display above-average intelligence?" Jamie asked.

"Yes, and with it, incredible powers of observation, as well as the ability to charm and flatter. We're all weak, Detective, and it's easier to believe that someone is telling the truth, but lies are surely the common currency in this place. Some days, I'm not so sure that psychopathy itself is a mental illness, and of course, many people on the psychopathic scale don't ever commit a crime. Perhaps it's more of a personality scale that we will only acknowledge when we're finally ready to embrace our own darker sides."

They stopped in front of an interview room.

"Timothy is in here, but he's known inside as Diamond Mac."

"Why's that?" Jamie asked.

"Oh, you'll see." Taylor-Johnson gave a wry smile. "He'll enjoy telling you himself. He's a clever man, and there are victims linked to him who still haven't been found. He won't admit to the murders, of course, only to the theft of diamonds that went missing at the same time the bodies were found."

The psychologist pushed open the door.

CHAPTER 13

INSIDE THE CELL-LIKE room, a man sat on the far side of a thick table. He wasn't physically restrained, but two stocky orderlies stood at either side of him, alert and watchful for any sudden movements.

Timothy MacArnold wore a t-shirt that matched his eyes, the grey of an English winter sky. His features were plain, an everyman no one would pick from a police line-up – or everyone would. His left arm was a wreck of scars, with broad stitches of white tissue. Jamie couldn't tell whether it was a tattoo or some form of self-mutilation.

"It's how I was able to steal as much as I did," MacArnold said, noting her gaze and grinning to reveal perfect white teeth. "I would cut into my skin, insert the diamonds and then sew myself together again. The gems became part of me, encrusted with my blood, my pus. They became part of my body … until these bastards dug them out." He paused, meeting Jamie's eyes, and a prickle of sweat beaded in the small of her back at his cold stare. "I still feel their sharp edges when I wake alone in the dark. It keeps me focused on surviving so that one day I can feel that again. Now, Detective, please sit down."

He pointed to the chair in front of the desk, as if this was his office and he was their superior, summoning them to a meeting.

"And a good morning to you, Timothy." Dr Taylor-Johnson sat down at the table and beckoned Jamie to sit next to him. "Detective Brooke has a few questions for you about Doctor Monro."

"That bastard. He hasn't been in this week. Does that mean he's finally finished his thesis?"

"Thesis?" Jamie asked.

"He was writing about me. His pet psycho." MacArnold's tone was edged with pride. "Gonna get a book deal and everything."

"First I've heard of it," Taylor-Johnson said quickly, almost too fast. Jamie had the strange sensation that she couldn't tell who was lying anymore. This place had a force field that turned everything into double-speak and made her distrust her own gut, but there had been no manuscript at Monro's office. She pulled out her notebook.

"Dr Monro was murdered."

MacArnold laughed, throwing his head back so hard that the chair tipped slightly. The two orderlies grabbed at it, righting it gently. They had to protect the patient as well as the visitors. The laugh died quickly and Timothy's eyes were shining as he spoke.

"That's a bugger, but the bastard deserved it." He licked his lips. "How was he killed?"

"That information hasn't been made public yet," Jamie said. "No doubt it will be in the papers soon enough, but your name came up in the investigation."

MacArnold smiled. "You see the monitoring I'm subject to, Detective." He pointed up at his attentive guardians. "I am indeed a special man, but even I couldn't have escaped this prison for a night of what would have been a great pleasure, I'm sure."

"Do you know of anyone who might have wanted to harm Dr Monro? Anyone here?" Jamie asked.

"Monro got me in here, Detective, and for that I was

grateful. I'm 'rehabilitating,' and they tell me that one day
…" He put his hands together as if in prayer. "I may emerge
a changed man. For now, I embrace my own crazy line,
for it makes me special enough to be amongst the chosen
few in this place and not rotting in some stinking prison.
I know Monro had his doubts about my sanity, or lack of
it, but he said he could get me into a special government
program next and my brain would make me a valuable
asset." He paused, savoring the word. "Valuable, you see.
So why would I want him dead? Without him, these
bastards could reassess me as a violent criminal instead
of mentally ill and I could be shunted off to the slammer.
Couldn't you, Doc?"

On the streets, Jamie would have taken that tone as a
threat. At this point, she would consider calling backup,
but Taylor-Johnson shook his head gently, as if he heard
this kind of talk all the time.

"We know you're ill, Timothy. Just give it time." He
turned to Jamie. "That's the first I've heard of this special
government program."

His tone suggested doubt that it even existed, but Jamie
thought of the symbol on Monro's files and the man at the
police station. Perhaps Timothy was telling the truth this
time.

MacArnold cut in, his voice loud in order to focus their
attention back on him.

"Monro wanted to know about my hobbies, Detective.
I had just taken up taxidermy before I got caught. It's not
easy to skin an animal, you know. You have to get its hide
off like a coat and then duplicate the body in straw or
other material and then stuff that skin again. Like a turkey,
ready for roasting." He paused. "He used to ask me about
sex, too."

Jamie didn't flinch, but she felt the others in the room
tense, as if ready to stop him from speaking. She thought

of Monro's hidden room, of the edges of pleasure and pain.

"What did he want to know?" she asked.

Timothy's eyes glinted. "You want to get off on it too, Detective. I bet you like a bad boy."

Dr Taylor-Johnson pushed back his chair. "Time to go, Detective. I'm sorry for this behavior."

Jamie stayed seated, addressing herself to Timothy.

"What did Monro want to know?"

Timothy smiled, baring the edges of his perfect white teeth. He touched the scars on his left arm gently, caressing the raised welts.

"He wanted to know if this was sexual. If I cut myself for pleasure."

Jamie held his eyes. "And do you?"

"Would that make me mad, Detective? Is that what you want? What if I cut you for pleasure, eh? What if I told you it makes me hard just thinking about your blood?"

Timothy's tone was almost impassive, with an edge of challenge. Jamie didn't flinch from Timothy's gaze and held it a moment longer. His power play was impotent here.

"I think that's all I need for now." She pushed back her chair.

"I did *not* say you could leave," Timothy banged his fists on the table, rising to his feet, leaning over the table, his face contorted with rage and hate. The two orderlies grabbed him and yanked him back as Taylor-Johnson pulled Jamie to her feet and the door opened to let them out.

One of the male nurses outside advanced with a syringe as the orderlies pushed Timothy face-down onto the table, holding him still as he was sedated. The sound of shouting soon dulled to a muted roar.

"I'm sorry," Taylor-Johnson said as he ushered Jamie down the corridor. "I don't think that was much use, and I apologize for Timothy's behavior."

Jamie shook her head. "I've seen and heard a lot worse, to be honest, and there aren't usually so many people around to help. I'm curious, though. Did you ever see any of Monro's research work?"

"I know a little of what he was looking into, but he was a radical in many people's eyes, embraced by those of an ultra-right-wing persuasion. He believed physical punishment was fitting for aspects of therapy, as a way to release some of the innate tension of conditions. He apparently met with Members of Parliament, those who would support the return of harsher sentences. He was also part of the campaign to reintroduce capital punishment."

"The death penalty?"

Taylor-Johnson nodded. "It's a surprisingly popular political request, especially in these difficult financial times. Taxpayers question how their hard-earned cash can fund a place like this, where men convicted of violent crime and multiple murder have their own rooms, are well fed and get to attend art classes. There are rumors that Monro's research would have provided some kind of platform for the right-wing political agenda against the rights of the mentally ill."

Jamie couldn't see how a civilized country like Britain would ever allow the death penalty when it condemned countries like China, Iran and Pakistan, while at the same time turning a blind eye to the United States. But she also knew of the right-wing leanings amongst certain groups including the police, many of whom supported a stronger deterrent to crime. After attending the aftermath of domestic violence and child abuse countless times, Jamie found herself struggling to defend the continued existence of those who did such things.

"What do you think about it?" she asked.

Taylor-Johnson sighed. "We all have to decide where the lines are, Detective. Between those who are mentally ill and can't help their actions versus those who voluntarily choose to give in to evil impulse. The rehabilitation of the mentally ill is my life's work, so I have to believe that those with true mental illness don't actively choose their path. We need to treat them with compassion, and hope that with therapy and continued medication, they can find their way back into society again. If Monro had his doubts, well, I can understand that. Sometimes, our belief and patience is stretched. But I've seen success here, and I'm sure you've seen evidence overturned against someone you believed guilty, Detective."

Jamie nodded, knowing that as much as she and her colleagues tried, the best was sometimes not good enough and rarely, but sometimes, they got it wrong.

"Thank you for your time, Doctor. I'll be in touch if there's anything else I need to know."

CHAPTER 14

BLAKE RAN ALONG THE track towards the main road,
the Galdrabók heavy in his coat pocket. He needed to get
away from the house, from the creatures that dragged
his father's soul down to Hell, from his own memories of
abuse. Part of him knew he should stay and comfort his
mother, be the son she needed, but he couldn't face her
perfect memory of the man he now knew as tainted. The
images of dark creatures gnawing at his father's body kept
looping round his mind and the edge of desperation was
making him crazy. The need to drink was overwhelming,
and Blake clenched his fists to hold back the anxiety the
craving brought with it.

He walked towards the nearest town, keeping his
thumb out as cars passed. Rain began to drizzle down and
soon a car stopped.

"You alright, son?" The man was older than Magnus
had been, his eyes a welcoming warm brown. "Not a great
night to be hitching. Where you going?"

"Train station, if that's OK."

It wasn't far and the man seemed happy to chat with
nothing more than a few grunts from Blake in return. At
the station, Blake waved the man goodbye and looked at
the ticket office, the entrance almost obscured by the now-

pouring rain. In Britain, the nearest pub was never too far away and Blake caught sight of one just behind the car park, lights in the window promising beer and warmth. He needed the oblivion that only alcohol could bring right now, even in this shitty little corner of England. Maybe especially here.

The Bear and Staff was teetering on the edge of rundown, with old stools and wooden tables flawed by ring marks, overlaying each other through years of use. There were a couple of people drinking inside, a group of men who looked like they kept the place going with their custom, and several clearly waiting for the train. The bartender looked up with expectation as Blake walked in, smiling as he approached the counter.

"Two tequilas please, and …" Blake looked at the wide selection of ales on tap. "Two pints of Abbeydale's Black Mass."

The British penchant for exotically named ales seemed strangely appropriate given his visions, but already Blake doubted what he had seen. There was no way he could verify the facts of the Scandinavian murders quickly, and the black creatures could have been a result of the pain-relief drugs Magnus had been on. Somehow Blake's visions must have tapped into that perception, because of course, there was no such thing as demons.

The barman nodded. "Coming right up. You waiting for someone?"

He put the tequila shots on the bar, glancing down at Blake's gloved hands.

"Something like that." Blake downed the shots one after the other. The burning in his throat anchored him to this place, in this time, a physical sensation that he had never felt in any vision and helped him center with reality. The immediate rush took the edge off his craving, but oblivion had become harder to reach of late. The barman placed the beers on the bar.

"Two more tequilas," Blake said, handing over extra cash.

"Must be one hell of a bad day," the barman said, turning to pour more shots. He put a bag of salted crisps next to them. "You'd better have these, too."

The door banged and a whistle of wind rushed in, bringing a taste of rain into the dank bar. Blake glanced up as he gulped at the first beer. Two men in dark coats walked to the far end of the bar, collars turned up against the weather. One of the men looked over, piercing grey eyes raking over Blake's taut face. Could they see the twisted mass inside him, or was that just paranoia? What did it even matter? Blake thought, downing the beer in just a few gulps. He didn't care what anyone thought of him here. He only needed to blur the edges of the world as fast as possible.

His phone rang. Checking the number, he saw it was his mother. He let it go to voicemail, guilt washing over him. But he couldn't face her grief, or her unquestioning faith that Magnus would be waiting for her in Heaven.

Blake downed the next two tequilas, savoring the raw power of the spirit. Distilled from the agave plant, it survived harsh desert winds, its spiked leaves warding off predators. Blake drew on that strength now, letting the alcohol work its magic. His limbs began to feel heavy and, finally, his breathing slowed to a more even rhythm and anxiety abated.

He pulled the Galdrabók from his pocket, running gloved fingertips across the surface of burnished leather. Whatever past it represented, that was gone now, and this was all he had left to remember his father by. This and the scars. Could his gift really be a punishment from the gods in recompense for his father's sin? Or was there something wrong in his brain? That thought always teetered on the edge of his consciousness and some days he would give anything to have this curse removed. Blake took another sip of the beer … if he kept on drinking this way, he would likely get his wish.

There was one person who made him want to stop drinking for good, and Blake found a shadow of a smile on his lips at the thought of Jamie Brooke. The desire to speak to her welled up inside. Her perspective on Magnus and the visions might make everything clearer. She would know he was on the edge of drunk, but Jamie had seen him in a worse state when she had come to him desperate for help in the middle of the night.

Blake stood, placing his hand on the table to steady himself as his head spun, the pub fading in and out of focus. The group of regulars looked at him, their stares hostile, hands wrapped tightly around their pint glasses. Blake nodded at them as he walked towards the door, pulling it open with one hand as he fumbled for Jamie's number on his phone.

Outside, the air was crisp and chill. The heavy rain had morphed into that peculiarly British drizzle that barely seemed there but still soaked anyone standing in it. The tarmac was shining purple with oil marks from the car park, light from the street lamps turning the dark pools into rainbows. Blake turned towards the back of the pub and headed for a doorway with some shelter. As he heard the first rings on Jamie's phone, the door opened behind him. The two men from the bar came out, looked around and spotted Blake in the doorway. The man with grey eyes smiled, taking out a cigarette and lighting it as the other man walked wide, blocking Blake's exit to the car park.

The drunken haze couldn't hide the implied threat and Blake's heart thumped hard against his chest as the men advanced. He felt a trickle of sweat inch down his spine and cursed the amount of tequila he had drunk. His awareness was dulled, his mind heavy, his limbs sluggish.

Jamie's line went to voicemail and Blake hung up, focusing on the men in front of him.

"Can I help you with anything?" he asked. "I'm just waiting for a friend."

The grey-eyed man took a long drag on his cigarette.

"I don't think anyone's coming for you." He indicated the other man. "Except us, of course. And we're friends, really, we are. You just have to get in the car with us."

Blake looked around him, checking for anything he could use as a weapon. "I think you must have the wrong person. I don't know you."

"Oh, but we know you, Blake Daniel." The grey-eyed man took another drag and dropped his cigarette to the wet ground, grinding it into a puddle. Blake's eyes flitted to the other man, who moved like a boxer – light on his feet but with surely a hell of a punch. Blake wasn't much of a fighter, but the beatings his father and the Elders dealt in his childhood had cured any fear of physical hurt.

"What do you want?" he asked.

The grey-eyed man pulled a box from a pocket inside his jacket.

"You have a remarkable gift, and we want to help you understand it. But if you're not going to come willingly, then it's our – qualified – medical opinion that your mental health issues are putting yourself and others at risk." The other man advanced, arms stretched wide, his eyes inviting Blake to move, to resist. He clearly relished the chance to inflict pain and Blake's heart rate spiked as he saw the grey-eyed man pull a syringe from the case. "For those who may inquire, we had to sedate you in order to prevent further injury to yourself and others in the vicinity. You had to be detained under the Mental Health Act, and, of course, you will have the right to appeal."

Move! Blake's mind screamed at him, but his body was leaden, his responses dulled. He just needed to get to the car park, where someone might see him and help, or at least he might be picked up on security cameras. The men took one more step towards him. Blake ducked low and charged the gap between them.

The thump of an elbow in his back knocked him to the ground. A boot slammed into his side and Blake curled on one side, arms thrown up to protect his head as the blows thudded into his body. His phone went skidding beneath a skip in the alleyway.

"Enough." The grey-eyed man called a halt to the beating. Blake coughed and retched, gasping for air as he fought the spasms in his stomach. The stocky man grabbed his arm and flipped him over onto his back. For a brief moment, Blake felt the rain on his face as a blessing, melting away the reality of where he lay. Grey eyes came into focus in front of his face, and the man grinned as he pushed the syringe into Blake's neck. As his breathing slowed, Blake felt resignation settle within him, like a warm stone anchoring him to the earth. What could they do to him that he hadn't already faced in his visions? He shut his eyes and let the rain soak through him into the hard ground beneath.

CHAPTER 15

JAMIE PUT DOWN THE phone. She'd just missed Blake's call and he hadn't answered when she called back. Her finger hovered over redial, and then she shook her head, smiling a little. He was probably out somewhere in a noisy bar and couldn't hear the ring. With a stab of loneliness, she turned to the bookshelf where the terracotta urn sat in pride of place. She gently cupped it with her hand, the coolness on her palm reminding her that this was just a dead object. It might contain the physical remains of her daughter, but in itself, it was nothing. So why couldn't she just scatter the ashes in the bluebell woods that Polly had loved so much? Or throw them to the wind over the ocean? Why keep them here, grey dust and ashes that in no way represented the girl she had lost.

Jamie bent her forehead to the urn and knew she was still tethered to the memories. If she scattered these final grains of what had once been life, then she was utterly alone in the world. She thought of the bottle of sleeping pills in the bathroom, the oblivion that would take her away from this constant ache in her chest. Jamie breathed out, a long exhalation. The only way to deal with grief was to work. She walked to the kitchen and poured herself a large glass of pinot noir, taking it back to the sofa. Pulling out her cigarettes, she lit one and the long drag coupled with the wine gave her the tiny boost she needed. She opened Lyssa's diary and began to read.

They say it's chemistry in my brain that makes me this way. That some invisible chain of neurons has become polluted. The blackness sits in my head like a cancerous growth. In the past, they could have dug it out of my skull, lobotomized me and turned me into a loon, destroying the bad along with the rest of me.

Now, they pass electricity through my brain and try to buzz it out. With anesthetic, of course, as if that negates the barbarity. I imagine it fracturing into pieces, tiny shards of its disease spreading through the rest of my body. They say ECT is like a reset button, that I'm just a computer that needs a control-alt-delete reboot. They know best. Don't they?

But what if this blackness is just a part of me, not separate. What if it is bound into every atom of my body, making up who I am? When they try to rip it from me, or sedate it, or electroshock it away, the rest of me curls into a desperate ball, because they're destroying all of me. I am every color on the spectrum and black is necessary to highlight the bright yellow, and iridescent green, to enable brilliant turquoise to shine. Without black, there is no contrast, and without contrast, life is monochrome.

Jamie laid the diary aside. It was strange, but the overwhelming sense in Lyssa's words was life, a vibrant passion for living and creativity and an intelligent consideration of what life really was. The woman had been a dynamo, whirling through existence, and then she had crashed, ending it all. Jamie looked up at the terracotta urn. Polly had told her to dance, to continue to live, so tonight she would dance in remembrance of her daughter, and for Lyssa. Crushing the end of her cigarette into the ashtray, Jamie packed a bag quickly with her tango clothes and went out into the night.

***

Within thirty minutes, Jamie was at the *milonga*. She changed into her silver dress, the one Polly had loved her to wear. She slipped on tall heels, feeling her leg muscles elongate, the accentuation of her form. She pulled the clasp from her hair, letting the black cascade brush at her nape, as ghostly fingers of sensation ran down her spine. It was time to embrace this side of herself again, and in the dance, she could forget the complexities of the case.

The dim light in the room caressed the bodies of those who moved to the *tanda*, the grace of couples who clasped each other, some for one dance only and others for a lifetime. Jamie found divinity in the movement of human form as the *bandoneón* told of heartbreak and loss, the end of what was once perfect, but only for a heartbeat. Tango sublimated the dark soul through a repetitious beat, a singing in the blood that compelled the body to dance as if it no longer belonged to the brain. The noise in Jamie's head only subsided here, in the arms of a partner who cared only how their bodies moved together in the moment.

She caught Sebastian's eye across the room, her sometime dancing partner sensing her need. Between songs, he came to her and she stepped into his close embrace, no words necessary between them, only the challenge and acceptance of eye contact. There should be smoke here, Jamie thought, its haze casting a pall on the crowd who danced together as if the end of the world would come with the sun tomorrow. Tonight, the dancers would live as if for the final time, like the story of the rose and the nightingale, whose song was sweetest as the thorn pierced its dying breast.

Limbs were heavy until the music picked up, and the dance an automatic response to the call of the *milonga*. A primal beat, a need that must be fulfilled, an unbidden compulsion. The sound of the violin filled the room, strains of music that turned the mind from earthly pain into heavenly suffering. Surely the angels dance tango alongside pitiful humanity, and in doing so, transform their grief to something holy.

In the thrill of the dance, Jamie wrapped her leg around Sebastian's muscular one, her *ocho* a perfection of touch and release, a sensual play on the level of desire. She felt the twitch of something deep within her, a need to be touched, a need to be taken. A glimmer of it had surfaced when she had seen Blake this morning and now she recognized its significance. It was a flicker of life, when the body became music, a vessel for something beautiful that drove out the darkness within.

Tango chose me. The words came to Jamie unbidden. Tango threw its lovers together, letting them burn the flame for a pinch in time and then allowing them to slip away, burned and spent. The time in the dance was the only thing that mattered, and Jamie was already burned. Her thoughts returned to the morgue, deep underground, populated by dead babies, the remains of grotesque experimentation. That night in the Hellfire Caves, she had burned a part of herself away as Polly's body went to the god of flame in the caves. She still woke in the night with the taste of smoke in her mouth, but here she could let it all go. The color of tango was holy saffron that draped the pyres of the dead, of brilliant flame that burned the body until it was gone and darkest midnight blue, of the sky after the soul has returned to the stars.

Jamie felt Sebastian's arm around her waist and her body slid onto his, slid around it, flowing as she let herself go into the music, her *ocho* perfection. The tango connection was fleeting, the full length of the body during the dance and then the release. When the connection was broken, both must walk away, for what is perfect within the dance could only be something less if taken any further. Jamie held to this truth as the music came to an end. She walked away without looking back as Sebastian moved on to his next partner, a part of her left in the echo of his embrace.

CHAPTER 16

THE CANON CHANCELLOR, REVEREND Dr Martin Gillingham, began the slow walk around the cathedral, his ritual before leaving late each night. In the bustle of the busy daily life of St Paul's, it was too easy to forget why they all labored here. *This is the house of God, and here shall He be glorified*, Martin thought, looking up into the vast vaulted ceiling above him.

Of course, there were days when his faith wavered, as for any man, but today Martin felt a welling of the spirit, a divine refreshment that washed over him. He surveyed the holy domain, checking the corners behind the monuments, making sure the cathedral would be ready for another day.

"Thank you, Lord," he whispered, a smile on his face at how fortunate he was to work here, at the heart of Christian faith in London. He always walked this final round after most had gone home, and in the peace and quiet he could reconcile his mission with the fact that no one waited for him at his meager flat. His whole life was here, and perhaps his shade would walk this round after death, an imprint of faithful devotion. To die as a martyr for God was indeed a glorious way to enter Heaven triumphant, but Martin was content with a quiet life of service and solitude.

He passed one of the cathedral's most beloved paintings, William Holman Hunt's *The Light of the World*. A cloaked Jesus stood in a verdant wood at night, surrounded by an abundance of branches, leaves and fruit. His face was peaceful and his eyes stared out of the canvas, inviting the watcher into his world. In his left hand, Jesus held a lantern which cast the warmth of candlelight onto his face and clothes, highlighting the ruddy colors. In a cathedral that valued all faiths, the lantern reflected its diversity with cutouts in the shape of the Star of David for Judaism and a crescent moon for Islam. Martin loved the painting, seeing in it the invitation of Jesus to join him on the Christian journey for another day.

He walked down the stone stairs to the crypt, looking up at the three death's-head skulls that marked the entrance. *For dust you are, and to dust you will return*, he thought and sighed. *Every day takes us closer to the grave and every day we must live for the glory of God.* At the bottom of the stairs, Martin turned right towards the tomb of Lord Horatio Nelson, walking across the intricate mosaic of anchors, sea monsters and scalloped patterns. A huge black marble tomb dominated the chamber, topped by Nelson's Viscount coronet. The sarcophagus had originally been made for Cardinal Wolsey, Lord Chancellor during the reign of Henry VIII, but when he had fallen from favor, it had been kept for someone more worthy. Nelson was surely deserving of such high honor, Martin thought, running his finger gently along the dark stone, yet the military man would likely have scorned the marble as too grand for a soldier. Martin was glad that underneath the monument, Nelson's earthly remains lay in a coffin made from the timber of one of the French ships he had defeated in battle.

Some thought that the obsession with honoring war was too dominant at St Paul's, but Martin understood that

England could not stand without the courage of those who gave their lives in combat. This church would be nothing without military might, and Nelson's naval prowess was just one facet of glorifying God. After all, the Bible was filled with divine vengeance against those who would oppress, and this was a fitting memorial to one who brought victory for the glory of God and country.

A sharp clang sounded through the crypt, and Martin started, his hand grasping the smooth marble of the tomb. He stood still for a moment, listening, but there was no further noise. Perhaps it was one of the cleaners or security staff? The cathedral was never truly empty, but he knew the customary route of the support team and usually avoided them, moving into the spaces they vacated. After years of routine, the noise was unusual, and Martin felt a bristling under his skin, a rightful devotion for his church. Nothing must be out of place in the Lord's house.

He walked through the arches towards the Chapel of St Faith. It had once been a parish church attached to the old cathedral, and was now the official Chapel of the Order of the British Empire, where those awarded an OBE could be married or baptized. Martin's footsteps were soft on the gigantic flagstones, engraved in memory of those who had fought and died for Great Britain, the sleeping dead. The lamps were still glowing, surrounded by flames etched in metal, and the light caught the memorial of Florence Nightingale as he passed. Some had protested the inclusion of women in this chapel of war memory, but Martin found the nurse's calm face a blessing as she leaned over a dying man to give him water.

The noise came again.

Now that he was closer, Martin could tell that it came from the side chapel where the Holy Sacrament was kept. It was a sacred place, locked up tight, as no one was allowed there after the Host had been blessed in readiness for the service. Martin's heart beat faster. There was definitely something wrong here. This was not routine; this was not as it should be. He crept forward slowly. It was probably nothing, surely a mistake, but he had to be sure.

The wooden door to the side chapel was open a crack, and Martin peered through the space. He saw a man bent over the Communion wine, a hooded top obscuring his face. He seemed to be injecting something into one of the bottles. Martin frowned and pushed open the door, his righteous anger and concern overcoming any fear.

"What are you doing?" he said, stepping into the chapel. "This is a sacred place. Get away from those bottles."

The man slowly put down the syringe and held his hands up as he turned around, his face still in shadow. He said nothing, just stared, his head on one side as if considering the situation.

"It's OK," Martin said, taking another step towards the man, thinking of the security team. Their rounds down here weren't for another twenty minutes. "Let's go upstairs and I'm sure we can sort all this out." He held out open palms, a gesture of acceptance and welcome he had perfected after years of greeting parishioners.

The man moved suddenly, grabbing one of the Communion wine bottles by the neck and using it as a club. Before Martin truly saw it, the blow exploded on his jawbone. He reeled back, clutching his face, momentarily stunned. He hadn't been hit since he was a boy. Through the pain was a strange kind of relief that his physical body could still feel. But then the man raised the bottle again.

Martin stumbled backwards into the crypt, calling for help even as he knew that the thick walls would shield his cries from those above. The man came after him, arm raised, the bottle glinting in the light.

"I'm sorry," he whispered, "but this must be done. You shouldn't have come down here, but now you will serve as another example."

Martin couldn't keep his eyes from the weapon. In his haste to escape, he tripped over one of the flagstones, falling to the floor. The harsh stone stung his hands, as the words of the dead rubbed at his flesh.

"Please," he begged, his voice slurred. "I can get you whatever you need. It doesn't have to be this way."

The man stepped over to him and Martin raised his arms to shield his head. Another blunt blow smashed into his forearm and he moaned, an animal sound that barely registered as human. Scrambling now, he dragged himself towards the altar under the watchful eyes of the famous artists and scientists carved into the wall of memorial plaques.

Martin felt another blow to the back of his head and the world exploded, pain mingling with warmth and then a tingling sensation in his limbs as he fell forward. *Oh, my Lord*, Martin prayed in desperation, *let me live. I'm not ready to die. Take this cup from me.* He felt a sob rise in his chest as he gasped for breath, forcing himself to turn over and face his tormentor. The man was pulling something out of his backpack now, a silver spike and a hammer. Martin's stomach wrenched at the thought of what he might do with it. He reached his arms out to the memorials around him, Turner, Millais and William Blake, luminaries of British culture. Their stone eyes looked down upon his suffering as the man advanced. As Martin's vision began to blur, he thought he heard weeping and the rush of angel wings.

CHAPTER 17

THE SUN WAS BARELY up and Jamie gulped at her large black coffee, trying to shake off the heaviness from lack of sleep after her night at tango. Blake hadn't called back and her texts had gone unanswered, so this morning she had used the police databases to get through to his mother at the family home. The distraught woman had told her of the death of Blake's father, and Jamie had vivid thoughts of Blake drinking in some dive bar, escaping into oblivion to forget his pain. She had seen him in that state before, and remembered how she had almost crept into bed with him one night. After months of relying on his upbeat support, she was torn by guilt that she hadn't been there for him in his grief. She would have to trust that he would come to her when he was ready.

As rays of early morning sun shone on the golden dome of St Paul's, Jamie felt a rush of patriotism, a moment of pleasure and pride at working in the greatest city on Earth. There had been a place of Christian worship at this site since 604 AD, but the iconic dome had been built by Sir Christopher Wren after the Great Fire of London had gutted the church in the seventeenth century. The pride of the capital during the Blitz, the dome had not been bombed, but emerged from the smoke, still standing even as the rest of the city burned. Looking up at the magnificent cupola, Jamie wondered whether it pleased God or man more. Certainly the towering grandeur directed all eyes to the sky, but what then? Jamie felt cool rain spotting her upturned face. Then there was only emptiness, a vaulted Heaven with a God who let children die in pain. Jamie shook her head – it was time to focus on work.

Missinghall spoke with the officer on the door and they entered the cathedral, footsteps echoing in the enormous space, usually filled with tourists but now empty as the crime scene was processed in the crypt. The nave was paved with black and white marble, a chessboard representing the struggle of good and evil. Jamie remembered seeing the same motif draped over Hindu gods in Bali, back before her 'real' life had started, before Polly and the police.

She glanced to her left as they walked down the center of the nave. Two angels guarded a door, one with a sword, the other a trumpet, their wings elegantly draping the floor, faces in repose. Above the door, a scrolled parchment pronounced, *Through the gate of death we pass to our joyful resurrection.* Jamie had a momentary sense that the door was a portal: that on the other side was another world, where Polly danced. She shook her head, the brief illusion shattered. She definitely needed more sleep.

The somber atmosphere invited reflection, and they walked in silence, looking up at the intricate decoration that dominated this end of the cathedral. The ceiling of the quire was rich with mosaics of creation, so detailed that the abundance flowed into the rest of the church. Three inset roundels depicted palm trees and all kinds of land animals, an azure ocean with spouting whales and flying fish, fruit trees and birds against a golden haloed sun. In the south quire, Jamie looked up at the face of John Donne, a shrouded effigy in marble. A former Dean of St

Paul's, his writing praised the God he worshipped and his poetry was still studied in British schools. *No man is an island, entire of itself,* Jamie thought, the words echoing in her mind from lessons many years ago.

The cathedral was filled with tributes to the military might of Empire, with larger-than-life-size statues of men of war commemorated for their battle triumph. It seemed incongruous in a house of God to have such symbols of death, men who had slaughtered the ancestors of those who were now British themselves. Behind the altar was even a book of the American dead in the Second World War, its pages turned every day by the priests in commemoration of lives given in service.

Classical statues of the great men of the early church looked down upon the Whispering Gallery, and in the dome, sepia paintings portrayed the life of St Paul, transformed on the road to Damascus from persecutor to believer. Between the arches of the cupola were mosaics depicting the Old Testament prophets, Isaiah, Jeremiah, Ezekiel and Daniel as well as the four evangelists, Matthew, Mark, Luke and John. All the luminaries of the Bible were here, gazing down at believers as they worshipped, witnessing how much the simple carpenter's faith had changed the world.

Jamie and Missinghall walked down the stairs towards the muted murmur of the crime scene contained within the lower levels. After suiting up and signing the log, they entered the crypt. It was lit by small candelabra, their light shaded by metal flames, casting a warm glow into the stone space. The ceiling was low and the floor uneven with huge flagstones, which on closer inspection, Jamie realized were all tombstones of the honored dead. The usual bustle of the SOCOs was muted by thick walls and their respect for the house of worship.

The body lay at the base of a wall on the right side of a

modern altar, designed to honor those who held the OBE, and flanked by their standards. Blood stained the plaque above the corpse, and Jamie noticed it was a tribute to William Blake, artist, poet and mystic, considered mad in his lifetime. It was carved with a quote from one of his most famous poems, *To see a world in a grain of sand And a heaven in a wild flower, Hold infinity in the palm of your hand, And eternity in an hour.*

"This is a strange one," forensic pathologist Mike Skinner said as he stood and walked towards them, careful to step around the perimeter. "There's evidence of blunt-force trauma to the head and body, but then the man's eyeball was pierced by that." He pointed to a long spike with a flared end on the flagstone near the body. The sharp end was coated in blood, clearly visible as the flash of the crime-scene photographer lit up the silver surface. "There's also a medical hammer lying on the other side of the body, used to bang the spike into the man's brain."

"Would that have killed him?" Missinghall asked, his face displaying distaste at the description.

Skinner shook his head. "No, I think he may have even been dead when the pick was inserted so it's more symbolic. I'll have to check it during the autopsy, but I've seen these instruments before in medical history magazines. The spike is a lobotomy orbitoclast icepick used for severing the connections in the prefrontal cortex after insertion through the corner of the eyeball. The mallet was used to drive the pick through the thin layer of bone and into the brain, where it was rotated back and forth." Missinghall looked disturbed as Skinner continued. "Very popular in the United States in the 1930s and '40s of course, but we did enough lobotomies here, too. Brutal, nasty stuff." Skinner shook his head. "Didn't kill most patients, but turned them into vegetables."

"It's got to be related to the murder of Christian Monro,"

Jamie said. "The link to madness is too much of a coincidence." She left out the matter of Blake Daniel predicting more murders. "Al, do we know if there's any evidence of theft?"

Missinghall shook his head as he checked the notes sent from first responders. "No, the Dean has said that nothing is missing, but perhaps the Canon disturbed someone?"

Jamie looked around the crypt. "But who and why? What could possibly happen down here that would warrant murder?"

Missinghall shrugged. "Sex, maybe drugs. Something that a churchman might disapprove of."

"We need to know more about the Canon Chancellor," Jamie said. "What was he involved in that could have led to his death?"

"We'll be out of here soon enough," Skinner said. "We can secure this area for the crime scene, but we've been told that nothing stops the Sunday service, so we have to get the bulk of processing done ASAP and get out of here." He looked at his watch. "Only a few hours to go, so I'd best get back to it."

CHAPTER 18

SHADOWS SHIFTED IN HIS mind and Blake became aware of his breath, the rise and fall of his chest, and the sound of medical monitors. His head thumped with the familiar rhythm of a hangover, but it wasn't as bad as it should be. He could smell antiseptic, and his skin prickled with goosebumps from cool air conditioning.

Blake opened his eyes. The light was dim but he was clearly in some kind of hospital room. A curtain surrounded his bed, patterned with swirls that made his stomach heave to look at. He closed his eyes again, concentrating on breathing evenly as his body calmed. His ribs ached and his torso was bruised. He remembered the car park, the beating, the two men. He lifted his hand to feel where the pain centered, but it was brought up short by a rattle on the metal bars at the side of the bed. He looked down and could just make out the padded handcuffs that shackled him.

There was a drip attached to a cannula in the back of his right hand. His gloves were gone, leaving his scarred hands vulnerable to the air and, in the dim light, the ivory ropes of damaged skin seemed to glow. His fingertips felt every puff of air in the room, and it seemed that the hangover was making him excruciatingly sensitive. Blake looked around for his clothes and the Galdrabók, the only thing he had left of his father. The fact of Magnus' death resounded through Blake, the absence a finality he had been waiting for all these years. But after what he had seen in that room, he was left with more questions than closure.

Blake shook his hands, tugging on the handcuffs until his heart thumped with the exertion and pain in his head spiked, bringing a wave of nausea. Doubt swirled through his mind. Perhaps he deserved to be here; perhaps he really was mentally ill. Were the hallucinations he had seen with his father evidence that he had gone over the edge?

A sound came from beyond the curtain, a footstep on the tiled floor.

"Is anyone there?" Blake called, his voice a croak. He swallowed, trying again, pushing himself up. "Please, can you tell me where I am?"

The footsteps faltered and then continued. Blake fell back onto the pillows, tension easing in his torso as he relaxed the injured muscles.

A moment later, the light came on and other footsteps approached, sure-footed, confident. The curtain swung back and a man in a white coat stood there. In the room behind him, Blake caught a glimpse of a dentist-style chair, with heavy restraints at the wrists, ankles, waist and neck. Above it was a head brace that could be lowered down so the skull could be held still during stereotactic brain surgery. Machines with wires and electrodes and trays of medical instruments stood on wheeled trolleys near the chair. Blake couldn't help but consider why he was in this particular room. He swallowed, easing his dry throat.

"Good to see you're back with us, Blake."

The man was completely bald with a strangely shaped head, and his eyes were different colors, one blue and one brown. His smile showed perfect white teeth. His angular jaw and prominent cheekbones demonstrated a disciplined diet and he must have been over fifty, although he had the smooth skin of Botox around his eyes and forehead.

"Recovered from your night out?"

The man's voice was mocking and Blake's mind flashed back to the alleyway by the pub. He wanted to smash the metal handcuffs into the man's face, but he could only clench his fists.

"Where am I?" he asked, his voice even and calm, not wanting to give the man any pleasure in his reaction.

The doctor walked around the bed to check on the drip, adjusting the flow rate.

"You're at a private hospital for people with mental illness. I'm Dr Damian Crowther, and you're under my care. As well as providing the very best treatment for our guests here, we perform research on the outer limits of perception."

Blake felt a flicker of his own self-doubt. "I've never even seen a psychiatrist, so why am I here?"

"We've heard reports of your visions, and how they've been helpful in solving certain crimes." The doctor bent and stroked a finger along the scars on the back of Blake's hand. "You have a gift we're interested in researching …" He stood and his voice changed, an edge of hardness creeping in. "Your visions may just be an aberration we can cut out of your brain but just imagine the potential if it can be replicated." Crowther's eyes blazed with fanaticism. "The human mind is the last frontier. Those who come here add to the meager knowledge we have so far on the potential of humanity. Our remit is to pursue high-risk research in order to gain an intelligence advantage, and those who make it through the procedures have given their country a valuable service."

Blake's mind raced at the possibilities of experimentation. He looked beyond the curtains at the restraints on the chair.

"And those who don't make it through your ... proce-dures?" Blake asked, remembering Jamie mentioning a girl who had committed suicide after Monro's psychiatric treatment.

Crowther shrugged.

"The mentally ill are perceived as unstable, at risk. Their families are often relieved to have them controlled by medication and are pleased to have them incarcerated here, whether voluntary or committed. We've even had subjects delivered to our doors, the families begging for help. So, what is the real loss if the subjects pass on during testing?" He smiled, and Blake saw a glimmer of delight in his eyes. "For many of those, suicide becomes a life choice, and if we help them with that after we've learned all we can ... Well, we're just saving taxpayers money. But you're a different matter altogether."

Crowther walked over to the bench on the far side of the room and picked up the Galdrabók. "This book is full of things I want to talk to you about." He opened the pages and pulled out the handwritten family tree. "But this evidence of your genealogical history is the real gold. Do you know what the rune next to your name means?"

Blake waited a second and then shook his head, over-whelmed by his desire to know more.

"The symbol is a mixture of the runes for madness, but also for power and supernatural insight. The ancient Greeks used the same word for madness and genius, and the Nordic culture believed the same thing. The runes imply that your father possessed the same gifts as you."

Blake closed his eyes, reliving the horror of his father's last moments as the dark creatures bit into his flesh. Magnus had tried to beat the gift from his son, because he suffered from its enhanced perception himself. Tears welled up as Blake wished for the years back. Together they could have worked out what it was, together they might have found an answer. He pushed the emotion down as Crowther continued.

"It would have been truly marvelous to have you both here. I could have compared the generational effect and even split out the genetics of your line to isolate the key to what gives you this remarkable gift." There was jealousy in his voice, Blake noted. An edge of desire for that which he didn't possess. Crowther opened a drawer and pulled out a syringe and a tourniquet. "For now, we'll have to start with DNA testing and genetic markers for the more common mental health issues." Blake struggled as Crowther walked to the bed. "If you struggle, it will hurt more. It's just a little needle stick, after all. And I know you're curious about your past."

With one last tug on his handcuffs, Blake realized he couldn't stop Crowther and he stilled, allowing the doctor to wrap the tourniquet round and draw the blood. The crimson liquid filled several glass vials. Blake couldn't help but wonder whether there was something different about his physiology, and his mind reeled with the implications of his family's genetic history. There were runes marked on other branches of the tree. There were more like him, cousins perhaps, people who could see just as he did.

Crowther finished with the extraction and removed the tourniquet. A drop of blood dripped from the tiny wound and ran down Blake's arm. The ache made him want to rub it, but the cuffs were still tight around his wrists.

"You mentioned a remit for high-risk research. What do you actually do here?" he asked.

Crowther stuck a label on each of the vials of blood as he spoke.

"Have you heard of MK Ultra?"

Blake shook his head.

"It was the code name for a secret US government research project through the CIA's scientific intelligence division. The aim was ambitious – to learn about the extent of human behavior through the investigation of mind control, behavior modification ..." Crowther looked at Blake, his eyes narrowing. "Psychic ability. But alas, their methodologies meant the project was doomed once it became widely known what they were doing. They used drugs, isolation, torture and abuse on American citizens in the pursuit of knowledge. The aim was to give the USA an intelligence advantage, to create weapons that would target people's minds."

"Did they succeed?" Blake asked, tugging at his wrist restraint again, testing its strength.

"Officially, it was shut down, but of course, aspects continue under other names, other departments – using subjects that won't be missed, much as we do. But when our research found the correlation between mental health status and at least perceived psychic ability, we decided to continue investigation from another angle. What if the voices of schizophrenia are a form of extrasensory perception? What if the sensations of religious ecstasy are a form of mania? What if visions from God – or from the Devil – are just a higher function of the brain that we can all access?" Crowther's eyes were unblinking. A shiver ran down Blake's spine at the depth of his gaze, as if the man stripped away the flesh and bone on his face to see the mind within. He was no longer a person, just a vessel for a brain this man desired.

"Genealogy research is the next step, for if we can interbreed those of you with these genetic gifts, we can create the mind-soldiers of the future, those who can work in the shadows of intelligence and return our country to the glory of Empire." Crowther placed the vials of blood into a plastic box and slipped it into his pocket. "Some of my colleagues see the mentally ill as dross to be bred out, but I want to sift through you all and find the hereditary gold."

His eyes narrowed as he stepped towards the bed. Blake leaned back as Crowther loomed above him. "Your family is particularly special, Blake, and many of my colleagues are interested in trying their experiments out while you have your visions." He bent to the cabinet next to the bed, pulling out an electric razor. "But I get first crack, and we'll start as soon as the tequila poison is flushed from your system." Crowther switched on the razor, and pressed the button on the drip a few times, increasing the flow. "We'll need your head smooth for the equipment. Stay still now and this won't take long."

The buzzing filled Blake's mind and a cold sensation crept slowly up his arm from the drip. He tried to twist his head away but it was too heavy and his neck wasn't strong enough to move. As the drug-induced darkness descended, Blake heard Crowther begin to whistle softly as he worked.

CHAPTER 19

MARIE STEVENS PLACED HER leather-covered Bible on the narrow shelf in front of her, its beloved pages well-thumbed and marked with notes. She knelt on the embroidered cushion as the Reverend began to speak, his deep voice echoing through the nave of St Paul's Cathedral.

"Let us confess our sins in penitence and faith, firmly resolved to keep God's commandments and to live in love and peace with all."

Marie felt the impression of her knees snug on the cushion where so many of the faithful had knelt before, and it gave her comfort. She began the response, words she knew so well that she barely even registered them anymore at a conscious level. This was her ritual, the foundation of her week, and had been for the last forty-two years. She had sat in this cathedral with her parents, now beside God in Heaven, and she had met her husband here at one of the prayer groups. A fleeting uncharitable thought crossed Marie's mind, and she pushed it aside, offering her pain to Jesus.

"We look for the resurrection of the dead, and the life of the world to come. Amen."

Her weak ex-husband would get his just rewards in the hereafter. That was what Marie held onto during the lonely nights. That, and the touch of the Reverend's hand after the service, when briefly she felt his special blessing upon her.

Marie looked up towards the quire as the sun streamed in, a momentary glimpse of the holy here on Earth, a shimmering haze of gold dust illuminating divine miracle. In one alcove, Jesus was portrayed as crucified on the tree of life, the cross transformed by branches, leaves and a golden sun, with water running from the base in folds of blue and indigo, crested with gold. The sunlight picked out rich color on the wings of angels, the feathers of peacocks. Then, a cloud passed over and the moment slipped away.

The Reverend finished the prayers and took the Eucharist himself as the organ quietly played, encouraging a penitent calm. A line quietly formed, each waiting their turn for the Host as the faithful knelt at the altar. Marie walked slowly to the front, calming her heartbeat as she knelt again, hands cupped before her.

"The body of Christ," the Reverend intoned, placing the wafer in her hands.

"Amen," Marie whispered, meeting his eyes and then placing the wafer in her mouth.

"The blood of Christ," he said, and tipped a little wine between her lips. The chalice was cool on her mouth, and for a moment, Marie thought she felt the Reverend's fingers brush her neck.

The wine tasted unusual today, a little stronger than last week. It felt like fire down her throat, with a warming aftertaste, like a good whiskey. Marie said her silent prayer, thanking Jesus for his sacrifice. She stood and walked, head down, back to her pew where she knelt in contemplation for a moment. As she moved to sit up again, Marie's head began to spin. She reached out a hand to steady herself. She looked towards the altar and it seemed as if the gold from the mosaics had lifted off the walls and now rained down on the congregation. The painted Eden on the ceiling of the quire pulsated with energy, as if the garden would erupt with fecundity and spill down the walls, so they could dwell again with God in that holy place. It was beautiful, surely some kind of holy vision.

A single voice rang out in the quire, one of the choristers intoning a holy prayer. Unusual, but beautiful, Marie thought. She lifted her arms towards Heaven, prayers so fervent in her chest, she thought she would burst with joy. She noticed other people around her beginning to weep. Something was happening. Was this the outpouring of the spirit promised in the book of Acts?

Even as holy exultation welled up inside, Marie became aware of a malevolence behind her, a cold shadow that threatened to sweep over the congregation. She looked towards the back door of the cathedral and saw a darkness in the shadows where the sun could no longer reach. The people who sat there looked misshapen, deformed, and they were swaying and moaning. Marie sent up a prayer to Jesus, knowing in her heart that this was Satan attempting to stop the holy visions, trying to prevent the purposes of the Most High. But the Evil One must not prevail, could not prevail in this holy place.

As she looked to either side, Marie saw there were people nearer to her twisting into grotesque shapes, some bent double and vomiting as they morphed into their true demonic forms. Her eyes fell on an angel, standing with a scythe in the portico of a doorway. As she watched, it stepped down and began to swing the weapon, its face turning from heavenly contemplation into the visage of corruption, the promise of torture in its eyes. Marie knew it was a fallen one that wanted to take its victims to the depths of Hell, as company in the darkness and the agony of separation from God.

Marie watched in horror as undulations of other forms

erupted from the stone around her. The monuments to the war heroes rippled with energy and figures with swords and knives awakened to seek victims around them. With muscled torsos and strong arms, they raised their weapons to bring long-dead vengeance to this place. Held captive for so long in stone tombs, they now rose again to smite those the Lord had decided to punish. The whispered prayers of the desperate caught in the ornate decorations, decaying as they rose, stuck on their journey to an uncaring God. The cross as the route to salvation became the instrument of torture once more and Marie watched as Jesus writhed in his death agonies.

Angels launched themselves from the dome, voices like a chorus of waterfalls, crashing into explosive sound. Birds of paradise flew out from the Eden above, their wings an iridescent blue, their song turned into a souring roar by the rasp of teeth in their beaks. Their blue feathers split open to reveal rotten black, their taloned feet poised ready to rip the flesh from the faithful. The sun that had been shining down in rays of gold now turned into streams of piss, stinking and dirty, the stench soaking the parishioners who twisted under its impurity. Marie clutched her hands together in prayer, whispering to herself. "'Even though I walk through the valley of the shadow of death, I will fear no evil, for you are with me.'"

A crash came from the altar as great candles were pushed to the floor by a choir that rampaged in righteous anger, beating the young boys who had turned into demonic hosts. As flames caught, smoke filled the air, shrouding the cathedral with a thick grey mist. Warped figures thrust out of the fog, talons clawing for more flesh to rip apart. Then Marie saw the Reverend, arms outstretched to his flock, his body transfigured as he bellowed words from the book of Daniel.

"'There before me was a fourth beast – terrifying and

frightening and very powerful. It had large iron teeth; it crushed and devoured its victims and trampled underfoot whatever was left.'"

The Reverend's eyes were red and his skin crawled with maggots that burrowed into his flesh, making him an undead freak. The smell of rotting flesh filled the air, overlaid with the scent of incense as from a tomb. Marie heard a scream and realized it came from her own throat as she looked on his sickening visage, but hers was no longer a lone voice. Her shouts were part of a chorus of screams and moans that came from the thickening horde around her, as demons slithered from the cracks in the floor to torment the souls around her.

She watched two men pull a woman to the floor, one holding her down as the other pulled up her skirt. Marie could see demons cleaved to the backs of the men, their vicious mouths urging violence, long tongues licking at exposed flesh. The woman screamed, even as her mouth was smothered by a fearful creature with lizard frills about its neck and smoke rising from its back.

The organ sounded as a cacophony, polyphonic doom rippling through her skull, but it couldn't drown out the coughs of the evil ones, their throaty roars and hacking hate. Had God abandoned them to this evil? Or was this a test that Marie must overcome for Him to pour out His blessings again?

People around her had faces of demons now, their hands misshapen claws, stalking towards her to rip off her skin and eat her flesh. Marie had to stop them reaching her. She stood up on the pew, grabbing her Bible. She swung it down onto the head of what had once been a woman next to her. The thing fell to the floor, and as she opened her mouth, Marie saw a smaller demon inside, the jaw expanding to allow the fetid parasite to escape. Marie felt the wrath of God rise up inside her as she beheld the abomination of God's corrupted child. This would be her victory, this would be her offering to the Almighty. By vanquishing Satan, she would be able to sit at the right hand of God with Jesus and all the angels.

As the demon began to emerge, its body hairy and misshapen, Marie used the heavy Bible to beat at it with both hands. The wet thwack resonated through her, the weight of it sounding as a drum pulsing with the power of God. She felt the muscles in her arms tense, flooded with the strength of His army to vanquish the wicked and she heaved it against the woman's head again and again until blood and bone stained the leather Bible, a perfect sacrifice in this now-corrupted place.

BBC NEWS REPORT

THE CHRISTIAN COMMUNITY ARE holding prayer vigils throughout London tonight as nearly two hundred people were taken to hospital following an incident at St Paul's Cathedral during the afternoon service. Three fatalities have been reported, one from heart failure and two others from the brutal violence that broke out within the cathedral. Other injuries include trampling, shock, various degrees of physical trauma as well as poisoning. Five victims of rape have also been reported.

"The victims from St Paul's have tested positive for a strong psychoactive drug," Police Commissioner Malcolm Jordan said in a statement to the press. "It's thought to have been administered through the Communion wine and quickly brought on hallucinations that caused the outbreak of violence within the church."

Survivors who had not taken Communion say the cathedral had descended quickly into madness after the Eucharist was taken.

"It seemed as if some kind of collective madness took hold of most of the congregation," parishioner Eric Smythe explained. "I couldn't believe it at first, as some couples began to behave sexually and others with violence, in the middle of a sacred church service. Within a few minutes, it seemed certain that something was very wrong. That's when I called the police ... The whole thing only lasted about fifteen minutes, but I will never forget what I saw in this church today."

CHAPTER 20

THE CLATTER OF METAL instruments woke Blake and for a moment he didn't recognize where he was. His body was heavy, his mind a blur. As he remembered, he raised his arm, the restraints still locked on his wrists. Looking towards the end of the bed, he saw the chair with the head brace. That hadn't been his imagination. Crowther was setting up equipment and he glanced over as he heard Blake's movements.

"Good morning." The doctor was cheery, enthusiasm oozing from him.

"If it's such a good morning, how about unshackling me?" Blake tried.

Crowther smiled, his perfect teeth glistening. "It's actually a good morning for experimentation. For that, you need to remain restrained – for now." He licked his lips as he looked at Blake, as if about to swallow a tasty morsel of flesh. He pulled a plastic gown on over his white coat, the kind that would keep bodily fluids from staining his clothes, and then began to prep a syringe of pale green fluid.

"This will make you uncaring of shackles anyway, you'll be so lost in its embrace." Crowther tapped the syringe with a fingernail. "It's an amnesiac as well as – let's say, a mind relaxant. Something to deaden the prefrontal cortex, release the inhibitors to perception. You don't need drugs to see your visions, Blake, but this will intensify them, make them even more real. And whatever happens here, whatever horrors you experience, you'll only see them again in your nightmares." He hesitated a moment, his eyelids flickering. "Of course, some cannot separate the nightmare from reality but perhaps we can help you find some peace, Blake, some escape from the visions that torment you. But first, let's see how far they go."

Crowther advanced on the bed, and pushed the syringe into the cannula on Blake's shackled hand. Blake watched the green liquid as the plunger pushed it into his bloodstream. Part of him wanted to scream and jerk his body away, stop this drug from polluting him, but another side welcomed its embrace. For years he had wondered at his abilities. Perhaps this would help him push his ability to the limit and work out what it really was. If it didn't break his mind first.

Within a minute, the light in the room intensified. Blake could see every pore on Crowther's skin, every pixel of color in the man's heterochromic eyes. The sound of the air conditioner was heightened and he could hear his own heartbeat, steady and rhythmic. The overpowering smell of antiseptic made his nose wrinkle, and under it, he sensed a note of decay, a hint of something that had died here.

"Come and sit in the chair now. You'll find it very comfortable." Crowther unlocked the handcuffs and helped Blake from the bed into the reclining chair. A tiny part of Blake's mind saw a glimmer of escape, but it was smothered by a wonder of heightened sensation. What did his life matter when the world was so expansive, when he was just part of a grander whole? It was as if he had found his true place in the universe and he wanted to stay there forever.

Crowther rubbed a cold jelly on his shaven scalp and Blake shivered at the tendrils of pleasure that wound down his spine from the pressure. Crowther added a heavy mesh of electrodes in a skullcap. It seemed as if the world was in slow motion, and Blake felt anticipation rise in his belly at the thought of how his visions would be intensified. Crowther turned to the bench and opened a drawer. He pulled out a plain blue book, the edges worn.

"This is a family heirloom," he said, his fingers caressing the pages. "I know what it contains, but to prove the truth of your visions, I want you to tell me what you see."

Blake reached for the book, a tingling of expectancy in his scarred hands. He closed his eyes as he felt the weight of it in his palms and the veil of mist descended.

***

The smell of vomit and piss made him gag and Blake opened his eyes to find himself in a large room. A wooden apparatus was built around the walls and from it hung a chair. Strapped into the device was a young woman, her head lolling forward as she continued to puke and cough. Her clothes were dark with sweat, and between her legs, clear evidence that she had wet herself. Her hair was matted around her forehead, her eyes dull with pain. A man knelt next to her, lifting the woman's chin, making sure to avoid the mess around her mouth.

"Again," he said tersely, rising and walking away.

"No," she moaned. "Please, no."

From the side of the room, Blake heard a clack of gears and then the chair was raised. The woman lunged, trying to escape, but she was strapped firmly to it. The chair started to rotate, first in small circles and then it swung out as it revolved faster and faster.

"Another half an hour and she'll be a lot more docile," a voice behind him said.

Blake yanked his hand from the book, emerging once more into the pristine lab. He gasped, heart thumping at the peculiar torture of the woman and the implied threat of what awaited her afterward.

"What did you see?" Crowther asked, leaning close.

"Some kind of spinning device, a woman strapped into it." Crowther's smile was predatory, and Blake saw recognition in his eyes. "What is this book?"

"My ancestor, Bryan Crowther, was the surgeon at Bethlem Hospital between 1789 and 1815. The device you saw was known as rotational therapy, spinning the mad to induce vomiting, purging and vertigo. The book is his personal notebook of the experiments he did on the living – and the dead. Now, you must go back in. I want to know more."

Blake shook his head. "No, I don't want to see anything else."

He made to get up and Crowther moved swiftly, pushing him back down and using a strap to secure Blake's neck to the chair. Quickly, he secured Blake's hands to the arms and added a waist strap and ankle restraints.

"Then we'll just have to do this the hard way." Crowther placed the book under Blake's hand and wrapped a series of bandages around it, holding the pages against his bare skin. Blake fought the undertow of the visions, but the drug made his descent even faster. His eyelids flickered.

***

It was the smell of rotting flesh that greeted him this time, and Blake opened his eyes to find himself in a dark room lit only by a few candles. There were windows open to the night air but they did nothing to disguise the stench of the dead. A man was bent over a body on a gurney, focused on its head. With a knife, he cut around the forehead and peeled back the skin to reveal the skull. Blake sensed an echo of the anatomists he had encountered in the last case. He shuddered as the man picked up a saw and began to rasp the blade against the bone.

The man's breath was labored as he finished cutting through the skull and pried the bone cap off with a small flat bar, revealing the brain. With bare hands, he pulled the jelly-like organ out into a dish, cutting away the vessels that held it, and placed it on a wooden board. The man wiped his hands on his apron and scratched some notes into a book. He cut into the brain, picking up the chunks and examining them next to the candlelight. A smile twitched around his lips as he worked, and soon, the brain was reduced to mush on the bench. The man swept the pieces back into the dish, wiped his hands on a piece of linen next to the bench and walked to the next gurney. The body was covered with a sheet, only the head exposed, and Blake could see it was the young woman he had seen on the rotational device. The man picked up the knife and walked to the head of the gurney.

Suddenly, Blake saw the sheet twitch where the woman's fingers must be. The doctor stopped and pulled up the sheet, checking the straps around her wrists, making sure they were tight. He placed the knife down and returned to the bench, picking up the dirty strip of linen covered in pieces of brain. As the woman's eyes fluttered open, he wrapped the linen around her mouth as a gag. She moaned, an animal sound of terror.

"Don't struggle, my dear," the man whispered, as he

picked up the knife again. "You'll be far more useful this way."

Blake tried to pull away from the vision, tried to drop through the veils of consciousness. He didn't want to watch this atrocity, but as the doctor began to cut across the woman's face, he realized his hand was strapped to the book. He couldn't leave until Crowther allowed him to, he had to bear witness. As the doctor picked up the saw, Blake felt a scream rise up within him.

CHAPTER 21

THE GALLERY WAS TUCKED into one of the hidden squares in the warren of back streets within the City of London. As she walked, Jamie tried to put Blake out of her mind in order to focus on the case. She still hadn't heard from him and she was worried, but then he was probably just curled up somewhere with a shocking hangover. Maybe someone lay by his side, and she definitely didn't want to dwell on that thought. He would answer his phone when he was ready, and she had enough to deal with right now. The murder at the cathedral was now complicated by the drugged wine and the motive for the murder of the Canon was clearly bound up in the hallucinogenic experience. But what was the point of sending those people mad? Now there was another murder, and the pressure to find a viable suspect was intense.

Morning commuters rushed past, most not even glancing at the police presence and crime-scene tape. Jamie wondered what could penetrate the armor of self-protection that Londoners assumed about them like a cloak. To survive here, city dwellers needed to let the news roll off their backs, remaining impervious despite the proximity of disaster. Selective perception was the only way to avoid going completely crazy with worry.

Missinghall munched on his second cheese and ham croissant, brushing crumbs from his suit jacket as they walked towards the cordoned-off area.

"Posh place," he said. "Guess this lot can afford this sorta thing."

"Art not your bag, Al?"

Missinghall smiled broadly. "Only the kind on a beer label."

His humor soon dimmed as they approached the crime scene. They suited up in protective clothing and signed into the log, checking the protocol with officers present. They walked into the glass-fronted gallery to see a few large canvases, all modern art, completely bereft of any realism. Exactly the kind of work that would sell in this area, Jamie thought, for anyone could project their own interpretation onto the canvas. The city thrived on the scramble for personal success, and art was still a reflection of wealth, even in these days of supposed austerity. Perhaps especially now.

Jamie smelled the body before they saw it, resonant of roasted pork and not unpleasant if you didn't know what it implied. They walked into the back room of the gallery where forensic pathologist Mike Skinner was still processing what he could of the body in situ.

A man was firmly tied to a sturdy chair, in a straitjacket with crossed arms strapped to the opposite sides. Next to the chair was a black box with leads that connected to electrodes on the man's closely shaven scalp. There were burns on either side of his head, the source of the roasted-meat smell in the air. Blood had dried around his mouth and there were spots of burgundy on the straitjacket.

Skinner lifted his head from the examination, seeing Jamie and Missinghall.

"The body was discovered by the gallery owner's assistant when she came in this morning to open up. The deceased is Arthur Tindale, owner of the gallery." Not known for his small talk, Skinner's tone was efficient and to the point. "I'll need to check for certain at the lab, but I'd say cause of death was electrocution." Skinner gestured to the box next to the chair. "This is an old device, originally used in electroshock therapy for mental illness, but the safety levels have been altered to produce a deadly voltage." Skinner shook his head. "It wasn't a quick death." He pointed to the mouth of the victim. "The blood is from where he bit his tongue during the shocks. This man was tortured with smaller doses before the voltage was taken up so high that his heart stopped."

Electroconvulsive Therapy (ECT) had been used to treat severe depression, mania and schizophrenia since the 1940s. Jamie knew that these days it was delivered with muscle relaxants, but that there was still possible memory loss and other side effects. Despite claims of medical efficacy for major depression, the public impression was tainted by visions of death-row inmates in the electric chair and portrayals in films and literature. Indeed, Ernest Hemingway had committed suicide shortly after receiving ECT, his famous description of the experience: "It was a brilliant cure but we lost the patient." This murder was about madness yet again, Jamie thought, but what was the gallery owner's connection with Monro, or the Canon at the cathedral?

"Three makes a serial killer," Missinghall said quietly, with an inappropriate tinge of excitement in his voice. Serial killers were rare, despite the intensity of media and myriad fictional characters, and they had never had a case on their team. Jamie shook her head.

"I don't think we should go down that path yet, because of the media hype it will create. There's a connection between these murders, for sure. But they aren't random, and these deaths seem to be personal, so I don't think the general public is at risk. The question must be whether the murderer is finished yet, and what Arthur Tindale did to be targeted."

One of the Scene of Crime Officers dusted the electro-shock machine for prints, but Jamie suspected the scene would be as clean as the Imperial War Museum and the crypt of St Paul's.

"You can get those machines on eBay," Missinghall said, looking up from his smartphone. "Maybe we can track down someone who bought one recently."

Jamie nodded. "Definitely worth following up." She walked over to the desk now that the SOCOs had finished processing it. "And we need to know what Tindale's link with madness was. Can you get something on his background, Al?"

Missinghall nodded and turned away to start making calls. Jamie looked down at the papers strewn on the desk, not touching anything, just processing Arthur Tindale's personal space. It was chaotic, but clearly organized in his own particular way. This was a man who actively ran his business, and who cared about the art he chose for his space, not just the income it brought.

There was a mockup of a brochure on the top of one of the piles, and the striking front image caught Jamie's eye. It showed a giant skull, bisected so the viewer could see into compartments that made up the interior of the brain. Jamie bent to look closer at the incredible detail of each mini tableau. In one cell, a woman was gagged and tied to a pole as a man whipped her back, blood pooling at her feet. In another, a tiny girl was trapped inside a spiky horse chestnut, but the spines pointed inwards, piercing her body and holding her prisoner, each movement ripping open her bare flesh. Yet another compartment showed a sickly, albino rat cowering in a dark corner, baring its teeth. There was a man strapped to a conveyor belt heading for a crushing set of rollers. The same figure beat on the glass walls of a test tube as giant scientists hovered, ready to pour a vial of pale green liquid over their subject. Creatures crawled around the edges of the painting, some recognizable as worms and lizards, but others fantastical nightmares, chimaeras of horror, and each was biting at the skull, trying to burrow inside.

With a gloved hand, Jamie turned the brochure over. The painting was called *Labyrinth* but there was no name of the artist shown. She glanced around the gallery again, but she knew the painting wasn't there. The piece was stunning, and she would have noticed it as they walked in.

There was an empty space on the wall opposite where the body had been secured. In a gallery with so few paintings, it seemed strange that the area had been left unadorned and Arthur Tindale would have died gazing at that exact spot.

"Al, can you find out whether there was any artwork on this wall? The assistant should know."

Missinghall nodded, getting his phone out of his pocket. "She's still with a female officer going over her statement. I'll find out."

Jamie looked around the office space, but there seemed to be no obvious records of the artists and their work. After the SOCOs had finished, they would be able to process all this paperwork. She looked down again. The painting disturbed her, and she recognized something of the colors in it.

Missinghall caught her eye as he finished his phone call, his face serious.

"You're right. There was a painting in that space yesterday. It was called *Labyrinth*. The artist was Lyssa Osborne."

"We need to find Matthew," Jamie said, remembering the look on his face when he had talked about his sister. She glanced at her watch. "His Bill on mental health is due to be debated later, but if we go straight to his flat, we should just catch him."

CHAPTER 22

THE RAIN BEGAN AS Matthew Osborne reached the gates of Kensal Green Cemetery. He lifted his head to taste the first drops, remembering the tip of Lyssa's chin and her laugh as she used to do just that. She had loved the rain, and the sound of it calmed her even in the rollercoaster of mania. He had installed a skylight in her bedroom so she could listen to the rain at night, the lull of it soothing her to sleep. Now, he let the water trickle down inside the collar of his coat, wanting the sensation of cold fingers on his spine, wanting to shiver. Anything to feel again.

Matthew walked through the graveyard, accustomed to the path now, the tombs familiar sentinels on his routine visits. He wanted to talk to Lyssa once more, now that his course was set. Finally, there would be justice.

In the maelstrom of his plans and the deaths of those who had betrayed the mad, he still found peace here, a haven for the dead and the people who loved them. It was one of London's oldest graveyards, and the resonance of emotions tied to the dead remained, hovering, brooding.

Matthew looked up at the struts of the gas works behind the cemetery, like the ribs of a skinless drum, a skeleton of a building that looked down upon these many dead. He walked down the wide boulevard, past the rows of graves jostling for real estate in the crowded space. Kensal Green Cemetery was an eclectic mixture of historic graves, faded names etched with dates of years past and new monuments with garish colors and kitsch ornaments. Matthew looked down at one tomb, decorated with the wet remains of tinsel and a garden gnome dressed as Santa Claus. In many cultures, the living came to eat and party at the graveside, sharing food and wine in memory of those who had passed on. In London, those cultures sat side by side with the British sense of decorum and repression of emotion, the hidden depths of grief smothered by a downcast look and silent tears.

The newly dead still had people to mourn them, but Matthew knew that the majority were forgotten within three generations. People said they lived on through their children, but that was just genetics, nothing else. Most people left no trace upon the earth. Many didn't even know the names of their great grandparents, but his Lyssa deserved more than this silent grief, and today he would wreak havoc in her memory.

He stared at the rows of graves, a dominance of crosses against the pale blue sky, interspersed with melancholic angels. Was it all about legacy in the end? Only deeds remain, as our bodies disappear into the earth, rotting away. Whatever the truth, Matthew found peace here, as he had always done in graveyards. Back in the days when their parents fought after too many drinks, he and Lyssa used to sneak off to the nearby churchyard. He would recite to her from the graves, teaching her to read that way and the old-style lettering became her favorite font in later life. They had stayed there late into the night sometimes, curled up and sheltered from the wind by the heavy stones and cradled in the lush grass on the older graves. Sometimes they slept there, and Matthew remembered waking early one morning, in the first rays of sun. He had looked down at his sister's blonde hair, her long eyelashes against perfect skin and he had vowed to do anything to protect her.

He passed the grand graves either side of the main walkway, the most expensive plots in this fight for celestial real estate. Those inside were all the same in death, rotting corpses with memorials tattooed in platitudes. He 'fell asleep,' she 'rests in peace,' they all 'sleep with the angels.' Everyone was described in glowing terms: beloved husband, devoted wife, perfect father, true friend. There were no sinners in the graveyard, all were cleansed of individual personality, reduced to a name, a date and the relationship to those who buried them.

Matthew walked on through the riot of stone crosses, gravestones and small monuments. Nature was on the edge of reclaiming this land, tendrils of ivy growing up around the feet of the angels, moss on the roof of the mausoleum, the cracking tombstones and listing monuments, sinking into the earth. The limbs of trees stretched out like a blessing, shielding their charges from the rain above, the noise on the stones a soft drip. He passed a grave with an inscription from Revelation: *God will wipe every tear from their eyes. There will be no more death or mourning or crying or pain, for the old order of things has passed away. I am making everything anew.* Matthew felt a strengthening of his resolve, for he had only to go forward now. To pave the way for a new order of understanding, he had to destroy the old order, and God wasn't the only one who could accomplish that. He reached out to touch an angel guarding a tomb, a gesture he found himself repeating every visit. The angel stood in a modest pose, head and eyes down, wings folded, hands clasped with a wreath between her fingers. Behind its watchful gaze, his sister lay sleeping.

Her stone was modest. *Lyssa, Beloved Sister.* Nothing

more, for that defined her on this earth in his eyes. Her art had been but an outpouring of her name: mad, crazy goddess. Matthew knelt by the plain granite headstone, next to the mound of earth that marked the recent grave. He imagined her precious body beneath the dark soil, the worms that curled between her ribs, the insects that ate her flesh. It didn't matter, for her physical body had never been the remarkable thing about her. It was her mind that had soared above mere mortals.

Reaching into his pocket, Matthew pulled out a slim paperback. Lyssa had loved to read, loved to perform, so he still brought her books. There were other rain-sodden texts here, the remains of words that dripped ink into her grave, trickling through the earth to write his love on her corpse.

"Oh, for a muse of fire," Matthew whispered as he laid down a new volume, the words from Shakespeare's *Henry V*, the last play they had seen together. It had become his regular prayer, for she had been his muse, and now her light was gone. But he still had time to make others see as she had.

"It worked, Lyssa," he whispered, patting a little of the earth back into place, as he placed the book on her grave. "The drug worked, and the sane became moonstruck in St Paul's. The effects are long lasting, and my hope is that some of them won't ever return to mundanity but will stay in that other place." He bent to stroke her headstone, his voice full of regret. "You know that other place, you chose it over me after all. Now it's time to finish what I started and I'll be with you soon enough."

Matthew stood, looking down at the plot next to her. The double headstone was only half filled with her name, the space for his still empty. The mason had refused to carve it, calling it bad luck to inscribe a name while he was still living. Matthew felt an almost overwhelming compulsion to lie down next to Lyssa's grave, to coat himself in the earth that covered her. He desired only to lie in peace with her now, but there was one thing left to finish.

A massive sepulcher squatted behind Lyssa's grave, a giant stone edifice with letters carved in its side. *Dominus dedit. Dominus abstulit.* The Lord gives and the Lord takes away. The words were from Job, the story of a man tortured by Satan, while God allowed his faith to be tested. The sepulcher's main door had been sealed when the last of the family had been laid to rest here a generation ago, but in the recent storms the ground under the tomb had subsided. The strain on the door had cracked the entrance and Matthew had managed to lever it open.

Looking around to check no one was nearby, he removed the crowbar from his rucksack and went to the door of the mausoleum. Gently, he pried it open, slipping behind it into the dark. The space smelled of damp earth, and the bodies that had once lain here were dust long ago. The dead were not the ones to fear, anyway; this graveyard was far safer than the housing estates just down the road, where violence terrorized children as once it had him and Lyssa. Here there was only quiet, the soft patter of rain on leaves and stone outside, the sounds that would outlast all who visited here.

Matthew pulled a camping lantern from his pack and switched it on, the fluorescent bulb lighting the inside of the tomb. For all its exterior ornate decoration, inside was just a rack of shelves covered in the dust of corpses. A whisper of memory lingered here and Matthew was careful not to disturb what remained.

He bent down, kneeling on the floor. He reached under the bottom shelf, feeling his way to the back, and pulled out a small case, the type that could hold a musical instrument. The type that you wouldn't think of questioning in this city of ultimate acceptance. He opened it to reveal ten test tubes and two empty spots for the vials he had used at St Paul's. Plenty left for what he planned today.

CHAPTER 23

WALKING ACROSS WESTMINSTER BRIDGE, the sun warm on his skin, Matthew smiled. A champagne fizz thrummed in his veins, anticipation of what was to come. Today was the Second Reading of his proposed Bill on changes to the Mental Health Act in the House of Commons. Today, he was supposed to debate the merits of the clauses with those Ministers who cared enough to speak. But Matthew knew the truth. There was no way this Bill would go any further, no way that the media and the public would find out what he wanted, what he needed them to know. There were too many who protected their own interests, who had constituents that were more powerful, lobbying groups that wanted the mentally ill to disappear and stop being a drain on taxpayers' money. Even when most of the mentally ill were taxpayers anyway.

Christian Monro's research had galvanized support for extreme right-wing views, meaning that this Bill, generous to those in need, would be quashed by stronger voices than his. But the Bill would make the news tonight, Matthew would make sure of that, and the politicians who scoffed at the mentally ill might finally experience a slice of their pain.

He looked up at the Palace of Westminster, the cool

stone blessed by sunlight. He never failed to be in awe of its grandeur. The Elizabeth Tower, named Big Ben after its bell, towered above the Thames, its clock face marking time for the nation. Originally a medieval palace, the buildings had been destroyed by fire a number of times and the present design had been constructed in the mid-nineteenth century. The Gothic architecture was dominated by vertical lines, as if a giant beast had raked its claws down the outside of the building, anchoring the spires to the banks of the river that nurtured the great city of London. Matthew dodged around the tourists on the bridge, understanding their need to capture its architectural beauty. This was his city, and pride swelled his throat as he glanced east towards the London Eye, the Shard and onwards, imagining the Thames Barrier and the ocean beyond.

London had always been a refuge for those on the perimeter of society, and every kind of outsider could find a niche in its maelstrom. Those who didn't fit into provincial towns could lose themselves here in anonymity, those rejected as wrong somehow could be welcomed into a community. There was a place for all here, but Westminster didn't truly represent the people of London. It still stood for the elite, those who sat above the marginalized and judged them for what they didn't have and couldn't get. Matthew had tried to break through the barriers of class and attitude, but the group he represented had too many disparate voices, weakened by years of their own suffering. They were too busy trying to survive each day, and couldn't spare the energy to convince others they were worthy of higher regard. But today these men of power – and they were mostly men – would understand.

Matthew approached the Parliament entrance for MPs and other regular visitors, and pulled the small rucksack from his shoulder, readying himself for the security protocol. The area was set up like an airport, with clearance machines for bags and a metal detector to walk through. He exhaled to try and control his fast heartbeat.

"Good morning, Jen." He smiled at the middle-aged security guard who worked here most mornings.

"Is it a good one?" Jen frowned, exhaustion evident in her stance and a dullness in her eyes.

"Are you alright?" Matthew asked, part of him desperate to run past her as fast as possible, but holding himself back. He was known to be a bit chatty in the mornings, more friendly than most of the MPs who rushed by, oblivious to those who served them.

"Sean, one of my kids, is ill. I was up all night with him." Jen ran the rucksack through the detector, and Matthew tried not to pay attention to it, keeping his face concerned for her as he stepped through the archway with no problems.

"That's a shame. I hope he gets better soon." The baggage machine beeped. "Oh, I'm sorry," Matthew said, his face suitably apologetic. "It's my flask again, you know it always sets the bloody machine off."

Jen pulled the rucksack out and opened it for him. Matthew took out the metal flask, its matte silver surface reflecting a distorted version of his face.

"I don't know why you don't just use a plastic one," Jen said. "It would save all this nonsense. I swear we go through this way too often." She paused. "Unless you're just angling for some extra time with me."

Matthew laughed along with her, trying not to make her comment too much of a joke, even as he noted her grey hair and bulging uniform.

"Chemicals in plastic …"

"Get into the water," she finished for him. "Yeah, I

know." She shook her head. "As if we don't already have way too much to worry about." She handed him the flask. "Enjoy your day, Mr Osborne."

The flask was cool in Matthew's hand, an innocuous container within which judgement sat waiting.

***

Matthew walked through the grand building towards the Churchill Room. He had arranged for a reception before the Second Reading debate and as it was after lunch, he knew the Members would likely have a few drinks. You didn't become an MP without being able to hold your alcohol, and fortifying oneself for an afternoon debate was a pleasurable way to drift easily through the rest of the day. He passed a few other MPs in the hallway, nodding to them but not stopping. Matthew put on the air of a man worried about his fortunes in the hours ahead, and he knew that people wanted to avoid talking anyway. They all expected his Bill to be kicked out. After all, he'd only made it to the Second Reading by calling in some favors, and today was his last chance to be heard.

The Members' Lobby was empty, a moment of calm before the MPs arrived en masse for the afternoon debate. Matthew checked his pigeon hole. It amused him that these archaic wooden boxes were still used in an age of instant connection through email and social media. Perhaps the post boxes were only used for the romantic trysts that everyone knew went on inside the nooks and crannies throughout the palace, behind the faded grandeur. Power was ever an aphrodisiac.

Matthew turned into the Churchill Room, the paintings of previous Ministers looking down with superiority onto the long tables set out for the reception.

"Everything ready, Peter?"

Peter Jensen looked up from polishing glasses on the table in front of him, making sure there were no spots to be seen. "Just the wine to bring through, Mr Osborne."

London's hard water made it difficult to ever get glass crystal clear, but Peter seemed to manage it. He had been a steward at Westminster for many years and Matthew had fostered a friendship with him, enlisting his help for a number of events. Part of him worried about the old man today, whether he would be blamed for what would happen. He pushed those thoughts aside.

"Oh, I can get that," Matthew said, as Peter made to put down the glass he polished. "You finish the glasses. Don't let me interrupt."

"I've decanted some of the better stuff from your selection." There was a mischievous twinkle in Peter's eye, a nod to the snobbery of the wine elite.

Matthew smiled. "Thanks. I need all the help I can get this afternoon."

He slipped out through a door that led into an anteroom. A couple of the waitresses bustled around with canapés at one end of the room, but they barely gave him a glance as they were so engrossed in gossip. Matthew went to the wine table, slipping off his rucksack and pulling the flask out. With his back blocking any view of what he was doing, Matthew grasped one of the vials and poured a generous amount into a couple of the decanters. He needed to work quickly, as Peter didn't have too many more glasses to polish. The chatter of the girls continued, but Matthew was hyperaware of their presence, his heart hammering at the thought of being interrupted.

There were ten other bottles of wine open on the table, their contents breathing. He checked the labels, all excellent wines he had ordered for the occasion. Working quickly, Matthew dribbled a little of the vials into each bottle. It was a much larger dose than St Paul's, but then, that had been a dry run, and this was the real thing.

He heard the voices behind him change volume, turning towards him perhaps, wondering what he was doing. He grabbed a cloth and wiped the rim of the final bottle, slipping the material over the flask as he turned to face the approaching waitresses.

"I'll take these in to Peter," he said, voice measured. "Thank you ladies, for all you do to help."

The girls smiled and turned to go back towards the kitchens.

As soon as they left the room, Matthew packed the empty vials into the flask, put it back in his pack, and pushed it under the table. He picked up two decanters and started to carry them out into the main room, just as Peter came in.

Matthew smiled. "I was just chatting with the girls," he said, handing Peter the decanters. "You take those and I'll bring the other bottles."

CHAPTER 24

Jamie looked around Matthew Osborne's flat, remembering how she had sat with him here, an echo of the love for his sister a fleeting thought through her mind. They had been briefly united in grief, but he had used the emotion to blind her to his true plans. How could she not have seen that other facet of his personality? The side that wanted revenge and justice. The side that she had shown herself in the fiery labs of West Wycombe.

"Where should we start looking?" Missinghall asked, standing in the middle of the room, his large frame filling the space. As they both pulled on sterile gloves, Jamie thought back to the conversation when she had been here last. Matthew had indicated that she sit on the sofa and he had sat opposite in the green easy chair, its springs sagging in the middle, the once-rich colors faded.

"We need to get into his mind," Jamie said, as she walked over and sat down in the green chair. "I think he used to sit here most often." She leaned forward at an angle and put her hand down by the side of the chair, grinning as she sat back up, a worn copy of Shakespeare's *Hamlet* in her hand, its slim leather cover decorated with intricate swirls.

"'The balance of his mind is lost,'" Jamie whispered, looking at the cover, remembering a line from a long-ago English class.

Missinghall shook his head. "I've never seen it, but I presume Hamlet was mad? There seems to be a lot of that going round at the moment."

Jamie tilted her head on one side. "The play also contains the suicide of Ophelia, and the theme of madness runs through *Hamlet* like a thread of tainted blood."

"Seems entirely appropriate for Matthew Osborne to be reading it then," Missinghall said. "Perhaps he sees himself as some kind of tragic hero."

Jamie thumbed through the pages. "Look at this. It's dog-eared and some of the text is worn away towards the edges where his thumbs would rest. He was clearly obsessed with this book." She paused, shaking her head a little. "I just didn't see the depth of his infatuation with Lyssa and her suicide."

"It's not your fault, Jamie," Missinghall said. "None of us thought he was a serious suspect. He's an MP, for a start, and he has that charity thing. The guy's a model citizen."

Jamie's gaze fell on the wall where Lyssa's striking canvases hung. Matthew would have looked at them while sitting in this chair reading, a permanent reminder of his loss. What if he had something else there, too?

"Help me take those down," Jamie said, pointing at the paintings.

Together they lifted the first canvas from the wall to reveal smooth plaster behind it. As Jamie put it on the ground, she saw the back was marked by a bloody footprint and a scrawled message in looped handwriting.

"'Our vain blows malicious mockery,'" she read.

"Let me guess. *Hamlet* again?" Missinghall said as he grasped the edge of the second canvas.

Jamie nodded. "It's from the beginning of the play, when a ghost appears on the battlements of the castle in Denmark. The guards try to strike at the shade, but their swords pass through, making a mockery of their attempt

– fighting fate can only ever be futile." An echo of Polly's death rippled through Jamie, and she understood Matthew's loss anew.

"Are you OK? Do you want to stop?" Missinghall asked, and Jamie saw empathy in his eyes.

"No, let's get this done."

They lifted together and put the second canvas on the floor next to the first. There was an alcove in the wall behind, a shadowed niche. Jamie lifted a fat sheaf of papers from the space, held together by a thin, brown folder. She carried it to the table and laid it down carefully so no papers would escape. She opened the file and flicked through a few pages, noting the chapter headings.

"It's Monro's book," she whispered, looking up at Missinghall. "The manuscript he was going to publish. It's his advice to the government on resuming sterilization of the mentally ill, on aggressive restraint for those committed and the resumption of the death penalty for those convicted of violent crime, specifically the criminally insane."

Missinghall exhaled with a whistle. "That stuff would have got Monro on every talk show in the country."

"Look at the symbol on the pages," Jamie said. "The book is sponsored by RAIN." She read from the text, "'The mad are monstrosities and tainted creatures.'"

Jamie turned another page to see a picture of Timothy MacArnold's grinning face, his arm raised to display the glitter of embedded diamonds. The reflected sparkle in his eyes was calculated to make the viewer judge him as maniacal. The following pages were a handwritten scrawl of notes, quotes from Timothy that he had thought would make him a superstar, but it looked like he had been digging his own grave.

Turning the pages further, Jamie found a case study of physical punishment as a treatment for mental illness and then a series of family trees with symbols for what Monro had labeled as degeneracy.

"'Three generations of idiots are enough,'" Missinghall read from the text over her shoulder, an account of Buck vs Bell,1927, after which compulsory sterilization had been introduced in the US.

"This policy was Hitler's inspiration for his own eugenics program," Jamie said, remembering the horrors of Mengele, the Auschwitz angel of death hacking away at the bodies of his live subjects. She turned another page.

"Oh," she said with a sigh, unable to keep revulsion from her voice, as she saw what Monro had done to Lyssa Osborne. The series of photographs showed the young woman in various restraints. Her drugged eyes were glazed and staring, and a line of drool dripped from her mouth. She sat on the bench in Monro's private study, the box of sexual sadism sitting in plain view.

Jamie looked down at the canvases, what remained of Lyssa's vitality and passion for color. She thought of the vibrant woman dancing, her eyes bright with joy as she created, and what Monro had turned her into.

"I don't blame Osborne for wanting revenge," Missinghall said in a quiet tone, his large hands gentle on the page, his gloved fingers tracing Lyssa's face.

"That's the problem with this job," Jamie said. "Sometimes even murder is totally understandable. But this still isn't conclusive evidence of Matthew's responsibility for Monro's murder, and there's nothing here to link him to the gallery owner or the cathedral." Jamie was silent for a moment as she considered the options. "He's got to be at the Houses of Parliament right now, so I need you to go babysit, Al. I'll stay here and continue to go through this paperwork. See if I can find something we can clearly arrest him for, and in the meantime, you can keep an eye on him. Make sure he stays put."

"Sounds like a plan," Missinghall said. "I haven't been in the Houses of Parliament since I was a kid on a school trip. I'll text you when I'm there."

***

After a short journey across town, Missinghall quickened his pace as he strode towards the Churchill Room. The officers at the entrance had let him in based on his warrant card and a phone call to Detective Superintendent Cameron, but he was under clear orders to only observe for now. This was such a high-profile group of people that the consequences would be extreme if they had it wrong, especially before such an important Reading of the Bill. Missinghall's hand touched the outside of his pocket for the third time, checking that his phone was still there. Until there was word from Jamie of clear evidence to arrest Matthew Osborne, he would just have to wait. Missinghall looked up at the grand tapestries and the intricate wall carvings as he walked past, and smiled. This wasn't such a bad place to hang out in the meantime.

The door to the Churchill Room was open, and the hubbub of people talking spilled out into the corridor, voices lubricated by just enough alcohol to keep them going through the afternoon session. Missinghall stepped inside the reception room and stood against the wall, taking in the scene. He caught sight of Matthew Osborne deep in conversation with several Members of Parliament. There was a strange sense of recognizing these people from the media, of knowing snippets of their lives, but of course, they were just like anyone else in person. Pulling out his phone, Missinghall texted Jamie. *Am on scene at drinks reception.*

A young woman in a black and white uniform approached with a tray of canapés.

"Smoked salmon terrine, or venison carpaccio with fig," she said, offering the platter and a napkin. There was an answering pang in Missinghall's stomach as he surveyed the delicious tiny bites. It couldn't hurt to have a couple – after all, he might be here for a while and it was almost time for afternoon tea. He took a couple of each, popping one in his mouth. It was usually just a Rich Tea biscuit on the job, so these were too good to miss.

As the young woman walked away, a waiter took her place, holding a bottle of red wine with a splendid label that Missinghall knew he and the Missus would never see down their local.

"Can I interest you in this vintage, sir?"

The waiter held the bottle slightly tipped over a bulbous glass. Missinghall's mouth was full of glorious venison, so he could only nod slightly, realizing he needed something to wash down the food. He didn't drink much and it wasn't officially allowed on duty, but a few sips would surely be allowable, if only to blend into the crowd and keep an eye on Matthew Osborne. The waiter poured a generous measure, the wine swilling around and coating the sides of the glass.

"Thanks," Missinghall said, as he finished swallowing the canapé. He took a tiny sip as the waiter moved on. They had some good stuff, these MPs, he thought as the blackberry aftertaste filled his senses. He took another larger mouthful as he surveyed the room.

***

Matthew Osborne looked at his watch again. Only twenty minutes to go before they needed to move into the Chamber and only half the MPs were here. The Prime Minister still hadn't arrived, even though Matthew had followed up with his secretary this morning. At least those who were present were partaking of his generosity. They all knew the politics of the pre-debate reception, but all were disciples of Janus, the two-faced god, and they managed their betrayal with a glass of wine in hand. Matthew felt sweat drip down his back, sliding along his spine to pool where his shirt tucked into his suit trousers.

Suddenly, there was a ripple of conversation at the entranceway and Matthew saw Glen Abrahams enter the room, his trademark 'interested' face on. It drew people in and made them feel special, but for only a second before he moved on. The Prime Minister was a pro at working the room, fascinating to watch in action and Matthew couldn't help but admire the man, as much as he despised his individualist politics. Matthew walked to the drinks table, nodding at Peter to pour a glass from the special bottle of Bolney Estate Pinot Noir he had purchased especially for Abrahams. He knew the man was a stickler for all things British, part of his own insecurity as the child of an Eastern European immigrant family.

"Glen, thanks for coming," Matthew said as Abrahams approached, his eyes unreadable.

"Sorry to be late, Matthew. You know how it is. Are you ready for this debate? Great Bill, by the way. I know how much work you've put into it." For a moment, Matthew felt the effects of the distortion field Abrahams seemed to exude. Everyone did what the man wanted. Matthew held out the glass of red, his hand unwavering.

"You have to try this one. It's from Bolney Estate in Sussex, part of their new batch of pinot noir. I know Madeleine enjoys pinot, perhaps you can introduce her to a new one."

Abrahams took the glass, raised it to his nose and inhaled deeply. He waited the appropriate amount of time before giving his verdict.

"Umm, does smell good." He took a mouthful, swallowing it straight down. Matthew lifted his own glass, pretending to take a sip but barely allowing the liquid to touch his lips.

"That's so smooth. Lovely. Now, I must talk to Harriet before the debate starts. Please excuse me, Matthew, and all the best today."

Matthew saw the defeat that faced him in Abrahams' eyes, but it didn't matter anymore. He watched as the Prime Minister walked over to talk to Harriet Arbuthnot, MP for York Central, and continued to sip at the wine, draining the glass as the two spoke.

Within a few minutes the room started to clear as the MPs began to head towards the Chamber, ready for the debate.

"Good luck," Peter whispered, as he walked past with two of the empty decanters. Matthew smiled and nodded at him. It was time.

CHAPTER 25

WITH MISSINGHALL ON SCENE keeping an eye on Matthew Osborne, Jamie continued to search through the pile of papers. Amongst the typed manuscript pages, she found one in Lyssa's handwriting, torn from the notebook that Osborne had given her.

I know what Monro has done with my body. I feel the after-effects of his violation even though I'm not in myself as he does it. He's a vampire for the experiences of madness. He scribbles like he is the maniac as I speak of the things he wants to hear. If he could only see himself as he records my crazy, he would be the one under scrutiny. I've suggested he try certain drugs, to alter his own reality but he shakes his head violently, like a dog shaking off droplets of water. I don't think he trusts his own mind. As well he shouldn't, for when I glimpse the edge of my own consciousness, I realize that I'm not in control at all and shades of onyx and ebony begin to curl through my head.

Sometimes the darkness steals out of my brain at night, leaking out onto the pillow like quicksilver, and the shape shifter turns my world into a nightmare. I dream of Saturn devouring his son, the headless body clutched in bony hands as teeth tear another chunk from dead flesh. Wild hair and mad eyes fixed on my own as he swallows, ripping another mouthful, blood dripping down his chin, driven mad by the need to destroy that which he loves. Goya painted it on the walls of his own house, the Black Paintings. That is what he saw in the night, that is his legacy.

My own black paintings were formed in the house of RAIN, for now I know who they are, now I know what they did to me. Any chance I had to rise above my flawed chemistry is dashed, and they tore apart what remained. The strands that once held are now loose and broken. They said they would help me end it, that I wouldn't even have to lift my own hand. They will make it a celebration, and I welcome the finality.

But Matthew, oh, my brother. There's too much to say and not enough time. I am your smashed, damaged sister and you have forever been my champion. Your whole life has been tied to mine, like the tail of a kite, unable to escape following behind my ducking and diving. Never able to live for yourself, and defined by my broken life. By cutting us apart, I can set you free, as well as myself. Sometimes in your eyes I see a need to devour me, as if by making me a part of your body, you can make me whole. But sometimes you can't fix everything, and I'm so tired.

Jamie felt the prick of tears as she read Lyssa's final words, both for the woman who was lost and the brother intent on revenging her death. She understood the pull of violence in pursuit of justice, but Matthew had to be stopped. All she needed was clear evidence they could arrest him with and it had to be here somewhere. Jamie walked upstairs into the main office, determined to find it.

The upstairs room was spacious, a double bedroom turned into a workspace. After the riot of color on the walls downstairs, the palette here was somber. There were some hand weights and kettle-bells in one corner, and a

Swiss ball instead of a desk chair. A wall calendar etched with black marker and highlighted sections betrayed how busy Matthew usually was, but the months ahead were strangely empty, as if cleared of commitments. The room smelled fresh, notes of pine forest and spice in the air.

Jamie walked to the bookshelves, her eyes scanning for anything curious. There were a number of chemistry textbooks and journals with a thin hardback book next to them. She pulled the little book down and opened the front page. It was a Master's degree thesis on entheogens – psychoactive substances used in a spiritual context for transcendence and revelation. Osborne had once been a chemist. Jamie's mind leapt through the possibilities, the threads of the case entwining. Her heart thumped as she thought of Missinghall in the drinks reception at Westminster.

"Don't drink, Al," Jamie whispered, her voice a plea, as she grabbed her phone, dialing Missinghall's number. It rang and rang before clicking into voicemail. Perhaps he couldn't answer within the halls of Westminster. Perhaps he had already taken a sip. She texted him, her fingers mashing at the keyboard in her haste. *Osborne is the poisoner. Don't drink anything. Get security in there right now.*

She called again. No response. There was so little time, and she had to get to Missinghall. Jamie weighed up her options. Westminster was only a couple of blocks away. It would be quicker to get there herself and explain in person, rather than call and wait for the various approvals to go through. She turned quickly to head back downstairs. As she did so, her elbow knocked against another book. It dropped to the floor and a sheaf of photos fell out.

Jamie knelt down, gloved fingers pulling the pictures together briskly to tidy the scene. But something in them stopped her. They were stills of surveillance footage, showing figures entering and leaving a door under a series of railway arches, recognizable as an area near London Bridge station. One photo was dog-eared, and Jamie pulled it from the pack. The street lamps lit up the face of Lyssa Osborne, the date stamp just a few days before her death. Two men flanked her, either helping her in or making sure she entered. This must be the RAIN clinic Lyssa had referred to. Matthew had been keeping surveillance on it. Jamie flicked through the sheaf of pictures, evidence of the number of people who went into the clinic in the last months. How many of them were still able to function? How many more were dead?

Then she saw another face she knew. The image was grainy, but the features of the men were clearly visible from the street lights. The bald man she had seen with Cameron and a heavy-set bodyguard helped, or perhaps dragged, Blake into the side door of the clinic building. Blake's face was blank, as if he didn't see what was around him, his vacant expression that of a junkie in another realm. Jamie felt her heart wrench at his face, a little boy lost in the labyrinth of his mind. Someone with his kind of psychic ability would be invaluable to intelligence research. Had RAIN been targeting him since the beginning? Or was Blake suffering some kind of breakdown at the death of his father?

The photo was date stamped two nights ago. The fact that Blake hadn't contacted her meant he was either very sick or held without his consent. Jamie thought of the last entry in Lyssa's diary, the abuse she had suffered, the darkness in her mind that RAIN had amplified. She needed to get Blake out of there, but her partner needed her. Jamie called Missinghall again, the phone ringing until it switched to voicemail.

"Pick up, pick up," she whispered, her mind filled with visions of what could be happening. She knew she had to make a choice.

CHAPTER 26

As MISSINGHALL FINISHED THE delicious glass of wine, the Members started to move out of the Churchill Room and into the corridor on their way to the House of Commons Chamber for the debate. He stood to one side to let them all pass, shaking his head a little. He was suddenly unclear as to why he was here, anyway. There was a shiny edge to his vision, and like a filter on a lens, it intensified the light around him.

There was a buzzing in his pocket, but he couldn't take a phone call right now. His head was fuzzy, spinning far more than a glass of wine should make it. Whatever it was didn't matter anyway because the Houses of Parliament were stunning and he was captivated by the beauty around him. The dappled light from the windows patterned the great tapestries on the walls and made them come alive with golden rays. Sea battles raged with majestic ships that danced upon the blue ocean waves. He could almost taste the salt spray in the air and hear the cry of the sailors as they climbed the rigging, the words of *Rule Britannia* echoing in his mind. Missinghall smiled, a broad grin that transformed his face as he gazed into the tableau before him.

Then a dark cloud passed across the sun, and the light

from the stained glass cast a red glow across the room. Missinghall frowned as the waves in the tapestry began to undulate faster, their violence shaking the ships in their midst. Shadows under the waters blackened into the shapes of sea monsters, giant squid with flailing limbs tipped with razor-sharp talons. One long tentacle arched out of the water, wrapping itself around a sailor and dragging him into the water. His screams echoed through the hall and Missinghall watched in horror as the man was sliced in two, body parts floating on the waves as blood turned the sea crimson around him. A flash of silver-grey. The sharks arrived, powering through the water, teeth ripping to shreds what the monsters dragged into the churning water.

Lightning ripped through the tapestry, as storm clouds gathered above the boats, like vengeful gods punishing mankind for the hubris of happiness. Wind whipped around the boats, spinning them in the vortex of waves, casting men into the depths of the sea, at the mercy of the creatures waiting beneath. The waves churned with blood, whipped into foam by the feeding frenzy of the sharks. The purple of the angry sky bled into black at the horizon, a promise of the ultimate end. Missinghall fell to his knees, tears on his cheeks as he witnessed the destruction, desperate to save the men before him. He clutched at the tapestry, screaming into the storm.

"Sir, please. It's OK, sir," a voice came in his ear, as strong arms pulled Missinghall away. "There's nothing there. You're having some kind of attack."

"No," he roared, pushing back violently against them, his eyes fixed on the horror before him. "I have to help. Let me be."

The next moment, Missinghall was down on the ground, two large security guards pinning him down. His head spun with the sound of the ocean storm, the screams of the dying, and the words of caution spoken in his ear were just a whisper. He closed his eyes to shut out the horror and succumbed to the pull of the deep.

***

Entering the Chamber of the House of Commons, Matthew Osborne clutched his notes, looking up at the statues on either side of the arched wall. They portrayed Winston Churchill and David Lloyd George, Prime Ministers during the war years, both with one foot polished to a shine where Members had touched them for luck on the way in. He took a deep breath, experiencing a rush of pride at how far he had come, although he knew that this was likely the final time he would stand here. Behind him, Matthew heard a shout from the direction of the Churchill Room, quickly stilled into silence. Whatever it was, there was no way to stop this now. He hurried inside.

The Gothic design was stark in comparison to the Lords' Chamber, but there were touches of ornate decoration in the wood paneling towards the public balcony above. The adversarial layout, green benches facing each other, was due to the original use as St Stephen's Chapel. But there was no reverent hush here anymore, much to the appalled spectators' surprise, as Parliament was full of shouting and noise, refereed by the Speaker of the House.

Matthew watched the other Members move to their usual places in the Chamber, chatting to other MPs, alert for gossip that might be used against people once considered friends. He had played this game for years now and still didn't have the power to change things. Yet it moved him to be part of the legacy this room handed down across the years. Despite the inevitable human failings of the Ministers in the House of Commons and the House of

Lords, most of what they enacted was for the good of the nation. Matthew still believed in democratic government, but sometimes a more dramatic statement was needed to bring attention to a cause.

He looked at his watch and then up at the gallery where the TV cameras and journalists stood, pads in hand. The drug was reasonably fast acting, quicker on some than others, but he was counting on being able to at least start the discussion on the Bill before its effects were felt. The Speaker of the House sat down and Matthew stepped to the front bench as the murmur of the crowd subsided.

"Honorable Members. Mr Speaker. Today is the Second Reading of the Mental Health Amendment Bill and I will start by outlining the abuses of the government agency, RAIN, the Research into Advanced Intelligence Network."

Matthew began to read from his prepared speech, and it seemed as if his consciousness split in two. He functioned on autopilot as an experienced public speaker, well used to performing in this venue. He was confident that the text of his speech would be analyzed later, and the scope of RAIN would finally be exposed. Another part of him focused on watching the faces of the Members who had been in the drinks reception.

The Prime Minister adjusted his tie and opened his collar a little. The honorable Member for Windsor was beginning to sweat, patches spreading in semicircles under his arms as he dabbed at his brow with a hand-kerchief. The cabal of Ministers from the North looked a little confused as they glanced around the room, eyes narrowing with suspicion at the opposition. Meanwhile, the press in the gallery looked bored, junior reporters on the graveyard political shift, hoping desperately for some kind of interesting news.

Matthew moved into the contentious part of his speech, calling for greater rights for the mentally ill. The insults began to fly, the cacophony of shouting in the room growing louder as he let the sound buoy him up, allowing it to rise without trying to respond. He wanted the temperature in the room to soar. He imagined molecules of the drug bonding with neurons in the brains around him, beginning to alter their consciousness, taking their emotions to extremes, numbing their prefrontal cortex and removing their self-control. The way the establishment had stolen control from Lyssa.

***

Harriet Arbuthnot felt the prickle of sweat under her arms and her head began to swim as she listened to the drone of that idiot, Matthew Osborne. Must have had a little too much wine, she thought, refocusing on the speaker. He was such a pompous ass, like most of the Members, but of course she mildly flirted with him as she did with others. She looked at his face more closely. It was shining, his eyes a brilliant blue and his mouth appeared to speak in slow motion, like his words came from under a swimming pool, distorted and slow.

It was so hot in here. Harriet looked up at the windows at the top of the gallery and felt the radiance of the sun like a furnace on her skin. *Why couldn't they sort out the air conditioning in here?* she wondered. Her eyes drifted down to the green back-benches opposite, her usual form of meditation. But instead of the calm vertical stripes, the emerald lines began to move in rippling swells. A wave of nausea rose up within her and Harriet put a hand to her mouth, eyes wide as she stared. The benches morphed into thick snakes, their heads rising up from the wooden paneling, tongues flickering in the air. She closed her eyes for a moment, shaking her head a little, part of her understanding that she must somehow be sick. She opened her eyes again and let out a scream as the bench around her twisted into a nest of serpents. Harriet leapt to her feet.

"Help me," she cried, clutching onto the seat behind her, trying to clamber away from the snakes. She could hear the clicking of the cameras from the gallery above, but the MPs around her just stared. Harriet was shocked at the hate in their faces, their mouths twisted in grimaces and their eyes blazing with murderous rage as shouting erupted in the Chamber. She felt the slithering of thick bodies around her legs and whimpered as the snakes wound around her body, pinning her to the bench with a heavy weight as she stared down at the melee before her.

One of the Members launched himself across the room towards Osborne, fists raised as he screamed abuse. The press clamored on the balcony as they tried to get the best footage. The action seemed to disintegrate any reserve left in the room, as the two sides of the Chamber rose to their feet. Men from either sides clambered down to the middle of the room and the thump of fists against flesh could soon be heard above the din. Harriet watched the thick green snakes writhe in and out of the bodies, fangs glistening, coils wrapped around the figures below. She was crying now, desperate for this to end but pinioned to the bench and unable to move. Her heart pounded in her chest and the sound of her own pulse thudded in her head as the shouting in the room grew louder. It was overlaid by another voice, whispering spite and hate, insidious with vile suggestion that spurred the mania to a new dimension.

A scream rang out and Harriet saw two of the Members holding down Miriam Lender, MP for Banbury. She could only watch as Miriam struggled against them. Another man tugged away her skirt and a serpent slithered across Miriam's bare belly as the man between her legs began to unbuckle his pants. Harriet's screams were frozen in her throat, tears running down her cheeks as she bore witness to the frenzy around her. One of the MPs drove another man's head against the wooden end of the bench, bashing it until blood ran onto the floor. Two others kicked a third, who lay prone on the stairs, hands wrapped around his head.

Security guards ran into the Chamber, blowing whistles and dragging some of the Members off each other. But there were too few of them and the brawling men turned on the security guards, pulling them down and kicking at their heads. Harriet watched as some of the Members tried to escape, but there were so few exits in the Chamber and bodies of others blocked their path. She couldn't tear her eyes away from the maelstrom below as it disintegrated into a writhing mass of confusion.

Suddenly, someone grabbed her from behind, an arm around her neck, pulling her over the back of the bench. Harriet struggled, squirming to escape the grip but the man pulled harder, grunting with exertion. Her vision began to fade as the lack of oxygen left her gasping.

"Stay still, you bitch," the man rasped. She felt two more sets of arms and then someone lifted her feet up, helping the men to pull her over the bench. The thick green snake wound around her body tightened its grip. She couldn't breathe, couldn't see properly, but she felt their hands on her and she stared up at the ceiling, her brain screaming, her mouth frozen in silence as darkness descended.

***

As the hallucinogens kicked in and the Chamber erupted into violence, Matthew looked around for the Prime Minister, the man whose signature supporting RAIN had damned his sister, the man who justified abuse of power with no regard for the lives destroyed in the process. Glen Abrahams rolled on the floor with his Lord Chancellor, the animosity between the men finally spilling over into thrown punches and attempted strangulation. Matthew couldn't help but grin at how this would look on the evening news, the likely resignation of the man he despised, the madness of these ineffectual politicians who would have spurned his Bill today. These few minutes would have dramatic consequences indeed.

A clumsy punch slammed into his back. Matthew spun round to see the Minister from Coventry North East, eyes wide and bloodshot, locked on visions beyond the physical realm. Matthew ducked easily under the man's second punch and slipped to the floor. He needed to get out. The police would be here soon, and he didn't have to stay any longer to know his plan was complete.

Matthew dropped to the floor, and crawled around the edge of the brawling crowd. Outside in the corridor, he saw uniformed police and more security guards rushing to the scene. He stepped back to let them past, the noise from the Chamber echoing around the grand entrance hall as he left the building just before the shut-down siren sounded.

CHAPTER 27

JAMIE FOLDED THE PHOTOGRAPH of Blake into her jacket pocket and with gloved hands placed the rest of the images on Matthew Osborne's desk. This whole place would need to be processed later, but it might be too late for Blake by then. She had to get him out of RAIN, but first, her responsibility was to her partner. She turned and ran down the stairs.

***

Pulling up in front of the Houses of Parliament ten minutes later, Jamie parked the bike in the Sovereign's Entrance just as the rain started to hammer down. Pedestrians hurried past to the shelter of the underground, umbrellas raised as they splashed through puddles. As Jamie tugged her helmet off, she heard an alarm ringing throughout the building. Something had already happened. *Please let him be OK*, she thought, desperate to get to Missinghall. She had sent him here, she had put him in harm's way.

The siren wail of ambulances and police cars scythed through the rain and cars parted on the road to let them through. People stopped on the pavement to watch, the atmosphere of high drama in the air. Jamie pushed through the gathering crowd and ran to the entrance hall, where a line of tourists was being held at the security gates. She showed her warrant card to one of the uniformed police.

"I need to get in there," Jamie said. "My partner's inside, along with a murder suspect. Please let me through."

The officer bent to look more closely at her card. "Sorry, Detective. We're under shut-down protocol, and so's every government building in the city. No one's coming in here now." He shook his head. "It's chaos in there anyway, and it looks like the bastard who did this got out before we closed everything down."

Shouting burst from the corridor behind the security area and a flurry of activity turned heads. An ambulance crew wheeled out gurneys with unconscious figures slumped upon them. Jamie's heart thumped in her chest, desperately hoping Missinghall wasn't among them.

"Clear the area! Let them through."

The uniformed officers onsite pushed the tourists aside to allow the medical staff by. Jamie looked down at the faces of the victims as they passed, some recognizable from the media, all high profile. Jamie realized that St Paul's had only ever been a practice run – this was Matthew Osborne's endgame.

A gurney came past with a big man lying prone, hands manacled to the side. His head was bruised and he wasn't moving.

"No," Jamie whispered, her hand flying to her mouth. She stepped out to the ambulance crew, holding her warrant card high.

"Please," she said. "That's my partner, he's a policeman. Detective Constable Alan Missinghall. Is he going to be alright?"

One of the medics waved at her. "Get clear," he said. "We have to get this lot to the hospital."

Jamie stepped back, allowing them through. She

clenched her fists, turning to push through the crowd back to her bike. The rain was heavier now but she held her face up to it, letting it soak her dark hair. Where would Matthew Osborne go? He must know that all officers would be out looking for him, so he wouldn't return to his flat. She thought back to their first conversation, when she had realized the depth of his love for his sister. Had he said anything that would help her find him? She closed her eyes and let the rain trickle down her face and into her leather jacket as she replayed the interview in her mind.

There was one place he had mentioned. The Tower of London, and how Lyssa had seen it as a metaphor for her mind, locked down to protect the treasures within. Anything was worth a try at this point, and Jamie needed to reach Matthew before anyone else. She understood his grief and maybe, just maybe, she could convince him to give himself up. She owed Missinghall that. Jamie kicked the bike into life and roared off down Victoria Embankment.

Urgency fueled Jamie's ride as she swerved the bike through traffic along the north bank of the Thames. Darkness had fallen now and the rain made visibility difficult. She pulled off the main road into Lower Thames Street, ignoring the signage to ride along the pedestrianized area down to the walkway on the riverside. Then she saw Tower Bridge, the two halves splitting open, starting to rise up into the air to allow ships through underneath. Osborne had said that sometimes he would watch it with Lyssa. Jamie revved the bike onwards.

***

Matthew felt the vibrations of the bridge as it started to part, the two halves slowly swinging upwards on their scheduled opening. He sat for a moment absorbing the physical pulse of the structure, wedged into an access doorway at the base of the north tower. He had slipped inside as security guards had cleared the bridge, the routine operation nothing special to them. He heard voices approach and fade again and then only the sounds of machinery reverberated through the structure. It was time.

He clutched the gun in his pocket, the unusual weight of it making him feel unbalanced. He had bought the Glock 17 a few weeks ago, when he had made the decision to avenge Lyssa and punish those who had exploited her. In the end, a gun wasn't right for them, but it was a good option for what he had planned tonight.

Cracking the door a little, Matthew could see the barriers closed in the distance and the bridge all but empty. The angle of the slope was getting steeper as one half rose into the air in front of him. He needed to get as high as he could, and he wanted one last glimpse of this city of grand beauty. He took a deep breath and started to walk briskly up the ever-steepening incline, every second a chance to be alone up there.

"Matthew!" A shout came from the crowd. "Stop!"

Matthew turned, seeing a black-clad figure with the security team. She was waving at him frantically. It was the police officer who had interviewed him after Monro's death. He started to run, panting now the incline was sharper, the bridge still rising inexorably.

There were more shouts behind him. Matthew looked back to see her break through the guards and come after him. *She can't catch me now*, he thought, pushing himself harder, chest bursting. Reaching the top, he hooked his arm around the railing at the side of the bridge as the incline steepened further. Matthew looked out at the Thames, winding through the city he loved, and smiled. It was so beautiful.

"Matthew," a voice came from below. "Please wait."

He looked down to see Detective Jamie Brooke, now almost below him as the bridge rose to vertical and they both clung to the side. She climbed towards him, her hazel eyes almost amber in the lights, burning with a righteous anger.

"Stop there, Detective. Don't come any further."

Jamie paused below, but her body was tense, ready to move quickly.

"I need to know," she called up. "The drug you put in the wine – will they recover from it? My friend was in there. He's a police officer, a good man with a family. He shouldn't have been there."

"I'm sorry about your friend," Matthew said. "But there's always collateral damage, and RAIN never cared for the lives they ruined." His voice softened, and he smiled gently, shaking his head. "But I'm not like them, Detective, and the effects of the drug are temporary. Your friend will be fine in a few days, as will those bastards who deserved it. I just hoped to give them some perspective, some empathy – but I won't be here to see it." Matthew looked out across the water to the battlements lit up before them, a bastion of the British monarchy for almost a thousand years. "I've always found the Tower to be an inspiration. From the outside it's symbolic of strength, but it's really like our minds, full of rooms where nightmares and violence lie hidden. Where skeletons are buried, and evil deeds are committed in the dark. Tell me, Detective, have you stood at the place where Anne Boleyn was beheaded? There's a resonance you can feel, a mental scream that echoes through the centuries. That scream continues in the way we deal with the mad, in the way Lyssa was treated, in the way that RAIN deals with those who are different."

"RAIN will be investigated," Jamie said. "Your speech is all over the news, so you've made sure they will be held accountable."

Matthew shook his head. "I have my doubts about that, but I can't do any more. Hating means that you're still alive, but I have no hate left now. I've done what I can, but RAIN is bigger than all of us. You don't know how powerful they are. They take anyone they want and if they're not mad already, they become so in their care. They could take you, Detective, and if I'm still around tomorrow, for sure they'll take me in recompense for my actions. Those who are sectioned have no choice."

Matthew began to climb over the railings, pulling himself up, the veins in his arms bulging at the physical effort required to lift his own weight over the edge.

"Don't do it, Matthew," Jamie whispered, reaching towards him. "Lyssa would have wanted you to stay, continue your work. You said you wanted to help others."

He turned his head to look at her, eyes clear and focused. "I know this is my end, and I go happily. But what of your grief, Detective? Perhaps you want to join me. A second's jump into blackness is nothing, a moment of panic perhaps and then oblivion. Is your life as worthless as mine is without Lyssa, I wonder?" Matthew reached out a hand. "Jump with me. End your own suffering."

CHAPTER 28

JAMIE LOOKED AT MATTHEW's outstretched hand and thought of Polly's ashes on the shelf in her cold, dark flat. Part of her wanted to take this chance and step with him into blackness. Together, it would be easy, but perhaps it was the hard things that were the most worthwhile in life. She thought of Blake, held in the RAIN clinic, under the authority of the man she'd seen in Scotland Yard with Dale Cameron. She had to help him now.

"No," she said to Matthew. "I have someone who can help me live again. But I understand why you want this and I won't stand in your way. I won't make you suffer any more than you have already."

Jamie backed away and carefully began the descent to the road level of the bridge. She didn't look back, but all her senses were heightened in anticipation.

As she neared the bottom of the struts, she called on her radio.

"Suspect on Tower Bridge. Requesting backup."

A moment later, a shot rang out in the night air and Jamie turned to see Matthew's body fall from the apex of the bridge. The slip of the wind seemed to whisper 'Lyssa' as he fell, a caress as he went to meet his sister.

Jamie touched her radio again. "Suspect has jumped

from Tower Bridge. Gunshot heard, possible suicide. Requesting backup from Marine Police and a river search team."

The Marine Police boat arrived quickly, its search-light sweeping the dark water for Matthew Osborne. It didn't take long before they dragged a body from the water slightly down-river. Jamie found herself holding her breath, wanting him to have found his escape. The police on deck pulled a body bag out and Jamie knew that Matthew was gone. She was grateful that fate had not been so cruel as to leave him here.

Jamie stood for a moment looking down into the river, the eddies in the current reflecting her indecision. The Detective Sergeant side of her knew she should return to the police station and report on everything, be a part of the Westminster case gathering the evidence. She pulled the photo of Blake from her inside jacket pocket, her fingertips trailing across his haunted face.

CHAPTER 29

THE ARCHWAYS OF LONDON Bridge were only a few blocks away. Jamie cruised the back streets of the area, her eyes scanning the passages underneath the branching railway tracks, fanning out from one of the biggest stations in the city. The sheer blue sides of the Shard towered over her, a symbol of wealth in this rejuvenated part of London. She pulled into one street, recognizing the looming structures of Guy's Hospital. The arches opposite looked familiar, so she ducked the bike down a side alley. Stopping to pull out the picture of Blake, Jamie could see that this was the place.

The clinic had a professional facade, with opaque glass over the front and discreet signage indicating it was a mental health practice. There were some lights on but no movement or shadows inside. The next two archways had no signage and only the last one had a door on it with just a keypad. Did the clinic stretch further inside the structure?

On a nearby corner, a twenty-four-hour greasy spoon cafe was still open, advertising all-day breakfast for a few pounds. It was the type of place that did so well next to a bastion of health, as people craved comfort food and sweet tea when faced with terrible news. Jamie parked the bike and headed into the cafe, ordering a mug of tea and sitting in the window, so she could watch the clinic.

As she sipped the tea, Jamie thought of Blake, lost in his nightmare visions and how she had done Cameron's bidding by involving him in the case. She was responsible for Blake being in there, so she needed to get him out. Lyssa Osborne had died because of what RAIN did to her in there, amplifying her internal anguish, making her believe there was no point in living. Jamie didn't want to lose Blake in the same way.

The progression of night changed the types of people walking this area from professionals scurrying home late from the office, to those seeking oblivion from the day's stress. There were nightclubs under some of the arches, their doorways hidden by graffiti elevated to the level of street art through vivid detail and color. The clubs drew seekers and Jamie wondered whether the clinic found some of its clients from those who had lost the path completely.

This area of Southwark, south of the river, had been the red-light district, the entertainment area for much of London's history. The Rose Theatre of Marlowe and Shakespeare's Globe had once stood here, the reconstruction of the Globe just minutes from where she sat. The pilgrims from Chaucer's *Canterbury Tales* met in the Tabard, a pub on the thoroughfare on the route to Canterbury near here. Just a street away, there was an unconsecrated graveyard known as Cross Bones for the outcast dead, the prostitutes and their children. The paupers had been forgotten in their own time, but now the place bloomed with flowers, left there by those seeking the favor of the dark shades.

There were a number of nurses walking home as the shift ended at Guy's, and several passed the window of the cafe, some laughing together, some with faces fixed in anxiety edged with desperation. Jamie knew that look from years of dealing with the public, of trying to serve those in need and being abused verbally every day and physically far too often. One woman in a nurse's uniform caught her eye, as instead of walking past the cafe, she turned towards the door of the clinic.

Jamie ran out the door and across the road, reaching the clinic as the door shut behind the nurse. Jamie banged on it, hoping that the woman would think she had dropped something.

The door opened a crack. Jamie showed her police warrant card.

"Good evening, I need to speak to whoever is in charge. We have reason to believe you have a murder suspect here."

The nurse looked suspicious, her eyes narrowing to examine the card.

"We're not open, Detective …"

"Brooke," Jamie finished for her. "That doesn't matter. I need to speak with your night supervisor immediately."

At the authority in her tone, the nurse opened the door a little more.

"OK, but you'll need to wait here while I get him."

She pulled open the door and Jamie stepped into a waiting area, just like any up-market clinic, with piles of magazines and even a bowl of sweets on the countertop. The nurse indicated a chair.

"Please wait here. I won't be long."

Jamie picked up a magazine and looked away slightly, turning back to watch as the nurse entered a number on a keypad by the door and stepped through as it buzzed. Four, six, five, two, nine. Jamie repeated the numbers in her mind and before the door shut, she moved swiftly to stop it closing. As she listened to the woman's footsteps clacking down the hallway, Jamie's heart thudded in her chest. She couldn't wait for whoever was in charge to check on her warrant card, especially if, as she suspected, Dale Cameron was involved in Blake's admission.

She heard the nurse go through another door and Jamie slipped into the corridor behind her, closing the outer door firmly. There were several more doors off to the side but for now, Jamie just needed to hide. There was no time to find Blake now, so she needed to wait until they thought she was gone.

Jamie tried a few doors. The first was an interview room, just a table and some chairs with nowhere to hide. The second was dark, so Jamie pulled out her tiny flashlight. It was an office suite with computers and a bank of old-fashioned filing shelves on one side, with winding handles to make more space. She ducked inside, pushing the door quietly closed, and wound the shelves partly open, squashing herself down the back, away from the view of the door. Seconds later, she heard voices in the corridor.

The angry, low tones of a man interrupted the voice of the nurse, but Jamie couldn't hear what they were saying. She hoped they wouldn't check for her, assuming she had left the building out of the main door. After they had gone back into the front office, she heard raised voices in a discussion and then they faded away down the corridor again.

Jamie waited, concentrating on her breathing for ten minutes, twenty, then half an hour. How long would it be until they had forgotten her and just continued with the routine of the night? She looked around at the files on the shelves, realizing they were medical records, inpatient folders and test results. Jamie pulled one off the shelf near her, holding the tiny flashlight in her teeth to read. There was little to indicate anything wrong here, but the sheer volume of records was overwhelming.

She looked at her watch. It was nearly two a.m., and the adrenalin of the day was wearing off. She was tired, which meant that the people on duty must be, as well.

She couldn't go in with guns blazing, she didn't even have a weapon, but she had to try and find Blake. She stood, stretching her limbs.

Pulling open the office door a little, Jamie listened, but all was silent and the corridor was dark. Her tiny flashlight illuminated the hallway, so she advanced slowly, trying more doors along the way. There was another office, then an examination room with nothing untoward in it. It looked like an outpatient clinic, perhaps somewhere to screen those that RAIN might be interested in. The door at the end of the corridor looked more hopeful, but it had a keypad on it.

Jamie tried the numbers she had seen the nurse use. Four, six, five, two, nine. The door buzzed and she pushed it open slowly, expecting to see one of the staff but once again, there was just a corridor with doors leading off it. By the angle, it stretched far into the building next door. Jamie stood listening quietly for a moment. There was a faint beep of medical equipment coming from the rooms around her, but no sound of movement. She kept trying doors, until she came to one set up like a hospital ward. Jamie held her breath, not daring to move, her heart pounding as she realized there were bodies in the beds, chests rising and falling rhythmically.

Nobody moved, no alarms went off. Jamie swung her flashlight around the room. There were four beds, with a person in each, but all were hooked up to drips and seemed to be deeply unconscious. Was Blake one of them?

She quickly checked each one, all young men, but no Blake. Jamie frowned. It was strange that they would all be sedated, but perhaps it was a way to avoid extra staffing. There were no charts on the beds, but there was an empty nurses' station. Jamie bent to the desk and shuffled through the paperwork. The sheets for the four men were stamped with 'Transfer,' but beneath them was a procedural document on managing insulin coma. Jamie pulled it out, reading the words but not quite believing them. It seemed these men had been 'recruited' locally from the homeless population and were now being used as test subjects for a new form of insulin coma therapy. Popular in the 1930s, insulin was injected to decrease blood sugar causing the subjects to descend into seizures and eventually a soporific coma that could be revived through intravenous blood sugar with the aim of shocking the system into recovery. The notes on this document implied they were being given the treatment in combination with ECT, and they would be transferred to the long-term RAIN facility the next day. Jamie took out her smartphone and snapped a couple of pictures of the paperwork and the bodies of the men in the beds illuminated by torchlight.

She replaced the documents and edged out of the room into the corridor again. The next room was a similar ward, but this time with a curtain obscuring the back half. Jamie tiptoed closer, hearing the rhythmic breathing of a person behind the curtain. She peered around to see Blake's face on the pillow, his head closely shaved. Her heart leapt.

"Blake," she whispered. "I'm here. Wake up."

No response. Jamie stepped behind the curtain and leaned down to his ear. "Blake. Wake up." She touched his shoulder. Still no response.

His face was calm in repose but there were dark shadows under his eyes and even in the few days since she had seen him, he had become gaunt and thin. His arm was hooked to an IV and Jamie pulled the tubing from the cannula, hoping that the sedation would stop and he might come round. There was no way she could get him out while he was unconscious. She saw the shackles on his wrists and knew then that he hadn't come in willingly.

Jamie looked around the back half of the room, noting a chair with restraints and a head brace. What had they done to him? Jamie leaned down and stroked Blake's forehead, his skin dark against the white pillow. He moaned a little, his face twisting.

She had to get the cuffs off him. Jamie walked to the chair and saw the trolley next to it, with medical instruments in a neat line. There was a key in the perfect line of implements, as if placed there by an OCD torturer. Picking it up, she unlocked Blake's cuffs, gently freeing his scarred hands. She tucked them into the sheets as she waited, hoping the drugs would wear off enough that he would wake soon. Meanwhile, she needed to find evidence of what this lab was for.

At the back of the room was a white workbench, with a closed laptop and paperwork filed neatly next to it. Jamie looked through the pile of papers, finding a thick brown file with Blake's name on the front and an old book, bound in burgundy leather. She opened the file to find a sheaf of photos, taken over a period of years by the looks of them. There were some images taken more recently, at the Imperial War Museum a few days ago and some of an older man, his face similar to Blake's. Putting the photos aside, she scanned the papers, finding two versions of a family tree – one handwritten on thin paper and the other a typed medicalized version, similar to the one she had seen at Monro's psychiatric practice. The two had some differences, but both were clearly of Blake's extended family. Jamie turned to look back at the bed, Blake's wan face on the pillow. RAIN clearly wanted to understand his genetic history, but how far would they go to get it?

Suddenly she heard a sound in the corridor, the squeak of wheels and the slow footsteps of someone approaching.

CHAPTER 30

Jamie slipped round Blake's bed, ducking down behind the curtain, folding herself out of sight of the door. She heard a rush of air as it opened and the steps of someone coming into the room. Her heart pounded in her chest, her pulse racing. They couldn't find her now, not when she was so close.

The wheels of the trolley squeaked closer. If it was a nurse with night meds, they would see very soon that the IV was unhooked. They would know she was here. She had to move. Jamie grasped the handle of her tiny flashlight, ready to use it as a weapon, and braced herself to jump forward.

"I know you're here, Detective." A smooth voice filled the room and Jamie started at the unexpected sound. "You might as well come out and we can talk. I know you're worried about your friend, but perhaps I can explain his treatment. This is a hospital, after all." The man sounded reasonable and Jamie stood, unfolding herself from the folds of the curtain.

It was the bald man she had seen with Cameron at the station, his head a strange asymmetrical shape. His dual-colored eyes were sharp and focused.

"Detective Brooke, my nurse said you were looking for

me. I'm Dr Crowther, and I would have shown you the facility if you'd requested it. But now you're here, you can see that Blake is fine. He's restrained for his own good – we had to stop him self-harming after the death of his father."

"I want to talk to him," Jamie said, keeping her eyes fixed on Crowther. "I want to know that he's consented to be here."

Crowther frowned.

"You know he's mentally ill, don't you? He supposedly sees visions of other dimensions, of the past. All evidence of insanity, which we can help him recover from. I can tell him you were here when he wakes up tomorrow, and we can arrange for you to visit at a more … sociable time of day." He gestured towards the door. "Let me escort you out."

Jamie hesitated. Crowther was being so reasonable, implying she could visit Blake easily tomorrow. She thought of the men down the hall locked into insulin comas with transfer papers. But perhaps Blake wouldn't even be here if she came back later.

Crowther's eyes narrowed as if he could see her hesitation and his hand slipped into his pocket. Seeing the movement, Jamie shoved the bed with her leg, smashing the metal frame into his knee, as he whipped something from his pocket and sprayed it directly in her face. Jamie felt the sting of pepper, her eyes streaming, and she began to cough, her lungs seizing up. She dropped to the floor, bending over and heaving as she tried to draw air into her lungs. Crowther's boot thudded into her side and she rolled sideways, pain exploding through her body, panic descending as she fought to breathe.

"You silly bitch," he sneered. "You think you can just walk in here and take my prize specimen away?" He kicked her again. Jamie gasped, fighting for air. "You have no idea who's involved in this. Your boss, Cameron, he knows,

461

and you'll find you have no place in the police now. Not ever again." He reached down and grabbed Jamie's arm, dragging her up and into the chair. "Now, why don't we try and send you a little mad? I hear you're close to the edge already and the main facility is always happy to get fresh brains to play with. No one's going to miss you anymore."

The chair was hard against her back and as she rubbed her eyes, Jamie felt her other hand clicked into place, manacled to the arm of the chair with a metal cuff. His words resonated through a haze of pain. Perhaps he was right. Without Polly, without Blake, no one would miss her. Missinghall would try to find out something, but he was hospitalized for now. She would be left inside whatever hell Crowther wanted, a lab rat for the mind, an experimental subject with no identity, just a label they decided on. In the past, women had been sent to Bedlam for nothing more than questioning their husband's authority, and now she would be sent there for challenging the supremacy of those in control.

"Let me go, you bastard. Help!"

Jamie shouted, twisting against the man, throwing her head back to try and hit him with her skull, reaching round with her arm, her eyes still blinded by the pepper spray.

"There's no one to hear you. No one who cares, anyway." He laughed, his voice further away now. "We just need a little sedation, and then you won't be able to speak. You won't remember anything but the nightmares that emerge in your sleep, when you wake covered in sweat, fear dripping from your pores." He fought with her, his higher position and strength giving him just enough leverage to click the manacle onto her other wrist. "You think you've seen the depths of what humans can do in your work, Detective, but what I show you in here, strapped to this chair, will send you right over the edge."

Jamie's eyes were clearing now, tears streaming down her face as they washed out the pepper spray. She could see the hazy outline of Blake in the bed. Crowther filled a syringe with green liquid, a smile of triumph on his face. She twisted her body, shaking her arms, pulling at the restraints, desperate to get away. Once she was drugged, she would be out of control, and she would truly be whatever he wanted her to be.

He turned with the syringe in his hand.

"Now, if you hold still, this will be more pleasant for both of us. Or, I can restrain you even further. Regardless, you will be sedated. This particular concoction also has amnesiac side effects."

Behind the doctor, Jamie saw Blake move his head towards the sound. His eyelids were fluttering. She tried not to look at him, willing him to wake up fully.

"Surely it would be more fun for you to torture me without sedation," she said, trying to keep Crowther's eyes on her. Behind him, Blake opened his eyes.

The doctor smiled. "Who said anything about torture? This is research, Detective, a scientific endeavor that gives this country a competitive advantage. Think about it. If we can find ways to turn off empathy and regret, our soldiers will be more effective in the field. If we can find a way to kill sexuality in the brain, we will no longer have sex offenders. If we can find a way to make people commit suicide, we will rid the world of those hangers on, the drain on society that means we all pay so much in benefits. If we can control behavior and emotion, then we will truly be the most powerful country on Earth. To learn all this, to test all this, we need subjects. You should consider your participation to be the ultimate in service to your country. You would have joined the police for similar reasons, surely, Detective?"

Crowther took another step towards Jamie, syringe

held ready. Behind him, Blake was slowly sitting up, realizing his limbs were unshackled.

"I chose the police in order to make a difference," Jamie said. "But my actions within the force were my own choice. The people you experiment on come to you for care, and you abuse their trust by treating them as test subjects. Your research would be banned if the public ever knew of it."

"The public?" Crowther snorted. "They couldn't give a shit about the mentally ill. They just want to be protected, defended and made well again. Those half-assed liberals still want the best for themselves and their own children, and our research will give them that future." He took another step forward. "And your sacrifice will help."

CHAPTER 31

BLAKE REACHED FOR HIS IV stand. As he did, he brushed the metal cuff on the side of the bed. Crowther turned at the clanging sound and dropped the needle in his haste to reach the panic button on the side wall. As he moved, Jamie kicked out, knocking him down. Crowther scrambled to his feet but Blake was up now, swinging the heavy IV stand down to smash onto the doctor's back. He moaned, but still crawled forward.

"Hit him again," Jamie shouted. They couldn't let him press that panic button.

Blake shifted his grip, his face set in a grimace. He slammed the IV stand down again, the metal bottom smashing into the side of Crowther's head. The doctor slumped to the floor, unconscious. Blake stared down at him, his eyes still vague and hazy.

"He won't be out for long," Jamie said. "Blake, look at me. You need to get me out of these shackles. We both need to get out of here."

Blake looked up, his face twisting with anguish. "I don't know what's real anymore. What I see and what he made me see. Am I really crazy, Jamie?"

"Come here," Jamie whispered, longing to hold him. "Just breathe and listen to my heartbeat." He walked forward and laid his head on her stomach. She wanted to stroke his head, like she used to do for Polly, but her hands were still shackled. "That's what's real. I'm real. You're real. And we need to get out of here."

After a moment, Blake stood up straight again, his eyes clearing of clouds, the blue sharpening as some of the natural color returned to his face.

"You're strapped down," he said.

Jamie smiled. "Good to see you're paying attention. The keys are over there, I think." She indicated with a nod of her head to where a number of implements lay next to the doctor's laptop. Blake found the key and unlocked her cuffs, his movements unsteady.

Jamie rubbed her wrists and then swung her legs off the chair, adrenalin fading as tiredness washed over her. "We have to get out of here, right now." Blake leaned against the chair, clutching at it for support. "Can you walk?"

He nodded, his eyes determined. "I'll manage."

She grabbed the file with Blake's notes from the sideboard, shoving it in a large specimen bag. She added the syringe of green fluid, putting a plastic cap on to shield the needle. It was evidence of something, even if she didn't know quite what.

"That burgundy leather book as well," Blake said, his voice almost breaking. "It was my father's."

Jamie pushed the book inside the bag, then turned to help Blake towards the door. There was a doctor's coat hanging there. As Blake pulled it on to hide his patient's gown, he sighed heavily.

"Are you sure I'm not meant to be in here, Jamie?" He looked unsure. "I saw things when my father died, things that made me wonder whether something is wrong in my head. And my visions here …" He shook his head. "I just don't know what to think."

Jamie squeezed his hand. "If there's something wrong,

we'll find it out together. We'll get help on your terms. People come in here and disappear into the system. Some of them die, whether by their own hand or helped along by RAIN. I won't have that happen to you."

Her voice betrayed her emotion. For a moment, Jamie thought Blake would kiss her and she longed to feel his lips on hers. Just a moment of connection. But his eyes shadowed again and he nodded.

"Thank you. Let's go."

Jamie slowly opened the door of the room, listening for any other noise, but it was all quiet. They shuffled out together into the dark corridor. Blake leaned heavily on her shoulder, his breathing labored as they walked. Jamie relished the warmth of his body next to hers, her arm wrapped around his waist. She could feel the muscles under his skin, realizing it was the first time she had really touched him. Their steps were slow but it wasn't far to the main exit. Just a few more minutes.

Red flashing lights suddenly illuminated the corridor in a silent alarm. A door slammed, and a roar of frustration echoed down the hallway.

"We have to run now," Jamie said, tightening her grip on Blake. "Crowther must have made it to the panic button."

Blake picked up his pace, but his legs were weak and he stumbled. His weight was too much for Jamie and he fell to his knees, coughing. His face was pale and haggard, the after-effect of the drugs pulling him back towards oblivion.

"You … go on," he wheezed. "Leave me."

"After all this?" Jamie said. "I don't think so."

As she began to help Blake up, Crowther charged around the corner. Blood ran down his face from the wound on his head, and his eyes blazed fury. In the flashing red lights, he was a staccato nightmare. He threw himself at Jamie, knocking her to the floor, his weight pinning her to the ground. Blake slammed against the wall, knocked off his feet. The specimen bag fell open, its content skidding across the floor.

"Bitch," the doctor bellowed, drawing his arm back to smash into Jamie's face. Her police training was automatic and she bucked her hips hard, throwing him off balance as she turned sideways, raising her elbow. She slammed it into him, screaming her effort as she struck him in the side of his head.

Using the momentum, Jamie rolled fast, pushing Crowther away from her. Blake grabbed the doctor's neck in a headlock from behind, grimacing as he used every last ounce of energy to hold the man. Crowther fought, his fingers scrabbling at Blake's arms. In the flickering red lights, Jamie saw the rage in Blake's eyes, his intention to repay the torture he had undergone. Next to him, she caught sight of the syringe.

Grabbing it, she pulled the cap off and sat on Crowther's chest, pinning his arms down with her knees, while Blake yanked the doctor's head back, exposing his skin. Jamie thrust the needle against the doctor's neck, watching it pierce his flesh. She pressed down the plunger and he groaned, eyes fluttering in horror. Crowther struggled for a few more seconds and then went limp. The sound of panting breath filled the corridor as the red light still blinked its silent warning. Jamie met Blake's eyes and saw her own exhaustion mirrored there.

"Now, we really have to get out of here," she said. "He said that drug had amnesiac properties, so perhaps he won't even remember what happened here."

"I wanted to kill him," Blake said, his voice dull, as he looked at the unconscious body.

Jamie helped him up. "I know, but we can't leave a dead body here, and I don't think they'll come after us now. This is an organization that lives in the shadows."

She filled the specimen bag again, taking the empty

syringe along with the book and papers. They left a lot of evidence behind, and RAIN could easily find her and Blake again, but somehow, she thought that they might find easier targets after this encounter. Her own involvement in the Matthew Osborne case was high profile enough, and if she was called to give evidence in court – well, she knew enough to worry the higher echelons of the organization.

Together, they hobbled down the corridor and out into the street, emerging between the arches of London Bridge station. The sky was bright with shades of pink and orange, heralding the dawn across the city. It was quiet and peaceful, as if nothing could possibly have happened here. These doorways held dark secrets but within hours, this area would be teeming with people working normal jobs, oblivious to what lay beneath.

"It's not far to my place," Jamie whispered. "You need to rest."

Blake nodded, his eyelids drooping as she helped him on the bike as a pillion passenger. His arms tight around her waist, she drove through the streets back to Lambeth. The events of the last days whirred through her mind, and she knew there was one more thing she had to do.

CHAPTER 32

Leaving Blake in her bed, passed out from exhaustion, Jamie roared back towards New Scotland Yard on her bike. She registered the heaviness in her limbs as the adrenalin of the last few hours subsided. There was an anticlimax after action but the highs and lows were what drove her back to work. A mundane office job would never suit her; she needed this edge.

***

As she walked into the station towards her desk, a voice stopped her.

"Detective Sergeant Brooke. My office, please." Dale Cameron's voice had an edge of steel. He rarely called people by their full rank unless a dressing-down was on the way.

"Yes, sir." Jamie changed direction and went into his office, her heart thudding.

Cameron slammed the door shut.

"The Prime Minister and a load of MPs are in hospital, Missinghall's in there too, and you let Osborne jump," he barked. "Why?"

"I … he … I couldn't reach him," Jamie stuttered. Of

course no one would understand the grief she had shared with Matthew, but who wouldn't let someone in that much agony find relief?

"You were captured on police helicopter cameras, and the video phones of spectators below. You know how powerful citizen journalism is nowadays and you're clearly shown leaving him to shoot himself as he jumped. There's evidence at his flat but his arrest and confession were paramount." Cameron paused and walked around his desk to sit in his chair. "Jamie, it's been a rough few months for you, but you've repeatedly flouted regulations. You've sent your partner into danger. God knows where you've been overnight when you should have been here working the case." Cameron rubbed his forehead, and exhaled slowly. "You're just not a team player, and I can't trust you anymore."

Jamie heard his words and it was like witnessing a slow-motion car crash. She could see what was coming, but she couldn't stop it. "I have no choice but to suspend you pending investigation. You're relieved of duty effective immediately."

Cameron's blue eyes glittered with triumph. By discrediting her and removing her from the task force, Jamie knew she would have no strong position to question his allegiance to RAIN or to make sure the organization was investigated in detail. Perhaps Cameron had been waiting for this opportunity since the Lyceum and the Hellfire Caves, the night she thought she had seen him in the murderous crowd.

"If you don't make too much of a fuss about this, I'll see you're just demoted and there'll be a decent position outside London. Perhaps it's time for a change, anyway. It might do you some good."

Jamie's heart thumped against her ribs as she repressed all the things she wanted to say to the bastard. Men like

Cameron would always emerge unscathed from trouble and in this male-dominated hierarchy, his kind would always win. But the thought of leaving London disturbed her, for this was her home and memories of Polly lay across the city like an emotional map. She could trace their journey together in the tides of the Thames. Jamie took a deep breath, fighting back her angry words.

Finally, she nodded, unable to trust herself to speak, and turned towards the door.

"It's a shame, Jamie." Cameron shook his head. "I had high hopes for you."

She walked out and slammed the door shut behind her.

Jamie stood for a moment in the corridor, trying to hold back the tears that threatened, but she would not cry here, not where anyone could see her. Jamie thought of the day she had left her parents on the Milton Keynes housing estate, telling them she would be part of the Metropolitan Police, that she would be someone, she would make a difference. All she had ever wanted was to be remarkable and now, they were pushing her out. She had lost Polly, and now it seemed she would lose the job she loved as well.

Jamie closed her eyes for a moment, focusing on breathing, trying to remain calm. The rush of the last few days swirled about her. She saw Matthew Osborne's face before he jumped, Missinghall lying prone on a gurney, Blake unconscious in the hospital bed under the archways of London Bridge. She had a feeling that the investigation into RAIN would be stonewalled from higher up, perhaps the clinic was being emptied even now. Matthew Osborne's actions in Westminster were tainted by the murders he committed, and, as there could be no trial, he would soon be forgotten.

The hubbub of the police station surrounded her, sounds she had always associated with her place in the world. But suddenly Jamie knew it was time to move on.

Her old life had died with Polly, and the police held too many memories. There were people she couldn't trust anymore, and Jamie knew she couldn't change it from the inside.

She turned and pushed into Cameron's office again. He looked momentarily surprised and then angry.

"I thought I told you ..."

"I resign," Jamie interrupted, her voice strong, with no hint of hesitation. She pulled her warrant card from her pocket and put it on Cameron's desk, her hazel eyes holding his. He broke the gaze first and she could see he understood what she knew. She spun on her heel and walked out of his office, down the corridor and into the day, a lightness in her step.

She steered the bike down to the Thames, parking near Tower Bridge where Matthew Osborne had ended his life. Jamie looked out over the fast-flowing water, feeling the breeze on her face as she gazed at the Tower of London on the north bank. Its strong walls had stood there while the inhabitants of London had gone about their mad lives for centuries, and it would continue to stand when she was gone.

This life was a puzzle and sometimes the pieces didn't fit, but the attempt was still worth it. Sometimes pieces were lost, as Polly was lost to her, but London was all about reinvention and rejuvenation, and tomorrow could be another life. She thought of Blake, asleep in her bed, and a smile flickered across her face. Jamie inhaled deeply, feeling more alive than she had for months.

AUTHOR'S NOTE

The themes of *Delirium* were born years ago when I studied psychology at the University of Auckland, New Zealand. I took classes in neuroscience and clinical psychology, as well as learning about issues of gender, individual differences and the history and abuses of psychiatry.

The motif on the title page and at the beginning of the chapters is a Rorschach ink blot, a psychological test where the individual interprets the image according to their own perception, used to diagnose underlying thought disorders. What do you see in the image?

You can see a collage of ideas for the book on Pinterest.com/jfpenn/delirium

History of mental illness

The Tranquilizer chair used as a method of murder in the Prologue is a real device. The person's head was encased in the padded box to block out light and sound, the legs and arms were pinioned and then hot and cold water applied to the head and feet. The other treatments mentioned are also historically accurate, although the story is, of course, fictionalized.

Bedlam, as Bethlem Hospital was known, moved to

different locations over time. It was once at the site of the Imperial War Museum as described and is now in Beckenham, South East London. I visited the museum at the current hospital, and it's a lovely, leafy campus with an art gallery as well as a cafe for visitors. The *Labyrinth* painting in the gallery scene is based on William Kurelek's *The Maze*, which I saw in the museum.

Three generations of the Monro family ran Bedlam, during which time it acquired its reputation as a kind of hell. For more, read *Undertaker of the Mind: John Monro and mad-doctoring in eighteenth-century England*, by Jonathan Andrews and Andrew Scull (2001). Bryan Crowther was a surgeon at Bedlam in the eighteenth century, rumored to have dissected the brains of dead inmates and to have donated their bodies to the resurrectionists, whose anatomy work I covered in *Desecration*.

I wanted to have a scene in Broadmoor because it's as well known in Britain as Bedlam once was. The men incarcerated there are extreme cases and in fact, very few people with mental health issues actually harm other people. They are far more likely to harm themselves, or commit suicide, than hurt others. You can learn more about Broadmoor through the NHS videos here: www.wlmht.nhs.uk/bm/broadmoor-hospital/about-broadmoor-hospital-video/

Research into Advanced Intelligence Network (RAIN) is based on the Intelligence Advanced Research Projects Agency (IARPA) www.iarpa.gov. This real American agency "invests in high-risk, high-payoff research programs that have the potential to provide the United States with an overwhelming intelligence advantage over future adversaries." I'm sure the British must have an equivalent!

Personal note

I have the utmost respect for people who are on the diagnosed spectrum of mental illness, and for those who care for them, and so this book is more about the exploitation that has dominated the history of psychiatry. Whenever we consider people to be 'the Other,' there will always be abuse.

I also believe there is a spectrum of madness in all of us, it's just a matter of degree. We all have moments of craziness, inspired by life situations or through the influence of drugs, illegal or prescribed. Like many of us, I have caught glimpses of what some would call mental illness in my own life. I share these thoughts honestly, as a mentally well person living happily in society. I hope to demonstrate that the continuum is a slide we all move up and down, and perhaps help you reflect on where you sit. Here are some of my experiences:

If I drive at night, I want to steer into oncoming headlights. I have an almost overwhelming attraction, perhaps a compulsion, to smash into them. I have to tighten my hands on the steering wheel to stop my desire to turn into the path of death. For this reason, I don't drive at night unless I really have to.

When my first husband left me, my anger and grief caused me to want to self-harm. I wanted to hurt myself so badly that he would be driven back to me out of guilt. (That was years ago and I am now happily married again!)

I sometimes feel untethered from the world, as if my physical body is nothing and I could just leave it behind. I have moments of detachment where I don't care for anyone. I feel like an alien put on this planet and nothing matters. I look around and it could all disappear and I wouldn't care.

When I write, I sometimes read my words later and I

can't remember writing it. I didn't even know I thought those things and I don't know how they arrived on the page.

I have experienced religious conversion, spoken in tongues and I once believed the world to be teeming with angels and demons. Perhaps I still do.

All these moments have passed over me in waves. They are seconds in a life of nearly forty years as I write this, and UK statistics show that one in four people will experience some kind of mental health problem in the space of a year:

www.mentalhealth.org.uk/help-information/mental-health-statistics/

I'm not on any medication and I don't think I'm 'crazy', whatever that means. I move up and down the spectrum and I expect to continue doing so during my allotted span.

My biggest fear in terms of mental health is to become demented and for my brain to die before my body does. Fantasy author Terry Pratchett's descent into early-onset Alzheimer's started my investigation into the choice to die. It is a writer's responsibility to think about the hard issues and suicide is certainly a contentious one. I support the charity Dignity In Dying, campaigning to change the law to allow the choice of an assisted death for terminally ill, mentally competent adults, within upfront safeguards. You can read more about it here: www.DignityInDying.org.uk

If you want to read more on the themes of this book

Bedlam: London and its mad – Catharine Arnold

The Locked Ward: Memoirs of a psychiatric orderly – Dennis O'Donnell

What is Madness? – Darian Leader

Mad, Bad and Sad: A history of women and the mind

doctors from 1800 to the present – Lisa Appignanesi

Failed by the NHS – BBC documentary with
Jonny Benjamin

Touched with Fire: Manic-depressive illness and the
artistic temperament – Kay Redfield Jamison

(Life:) Razorblades Included – Dan Holloway

Poetry by Sylvia Plath and Anne Sexton

A Brooke and Daniel Psychological Thriller

DEVIANCE

J.F. PENN

"Do not conform to the pattern of this world …"
Romans 12:2

"You were wild once. Don't let them tame you."
Isadora Duncan

CHAPTER 1

THE TRAIN RATTLED ALONG the tracks on the brick bridge above their heads, lending a rhythm to the words spoken below. London was never completely dark, the city lights lit up the sky at all hours, but tonight it seemed that the darkness was deeper, the space between the stars an all-consuming black. As the nearby church bells tolled midnight, the small group gathered together. Candles flickered, casting a halo around their heads, bent in respect to those lost here.

They stood in front of a pair of tall gates, closed and locked to segregate this small area of scrubland in the heart of Southwark, a stone's throw from the river and affluent Borough Market, at the junction between Redcross Way and Union Street. The dull metal struts of the gates were alive with multi-colored ribbons, each inscribed with a name. They represented those whose remains lay under the earth of Cross Bones Graveyard, names gathered from records of history in an attempt to personalize the dead. Their shades walk these streets still, a sliver of their memory in the hip-swinging walk of sex workers, their song in the local pubs, their laughter in the late-night bar crawlers.

"I was born a goose of Southwark by the grace of Mary

Overie, whose Bishop gives me license to sin within the Liberty."

The words of local poet John Constable rang out in the night air, his poem a tribute to the women who had once plied their trade here under the authority of the medieval church. They were known as Winchester Geese, controlled by the Bishop of Winchester and their taxes filled the coffers of the church. But in death, these women and their bastard children were outcasts, denied a burial in consecrated ground. Tonight these Outcast Dead would be honored in the memories of those who walked in their footsteps centuries later.

A young man with a guitar played a mournful dirge, his voice clear in the night air. His blond hair reflected the light from the candles, a blue streak through it giving him a rakish look. Jamie Brooke stood on the edge of the group listening to his song. She held a candle in both hands and gazed into the flame as her thoughts shifted to the memory of her own daughter, Polly, who had died six months ago from a terminal illness. The ache of grief still made her breath catch on days when her guard was down, but here, amongst these other mourners, the memory was tender.

A smile played across her lips. Polly would have loved this group of colorful people who lived outside the conformity of the city suits. These were no mourners in dull black. There were several women from the Prostitutes' Collective, holding a banner high. They honored their sisters and brothers who had died servicing society, courted and loved in secret while rejected and hated in public. One woman wore a belt of a skirt, tall spike heels revealing killer legs. Jamie caught the woman's face in profile, realizing that it was a man in drag, or perhaps someone transgender. Not that it mattered here, in the city where all could find a place.

As the group joined together in song, Jamie recognized a woman in the crowd, her pixie-cropped ash-blonde hair shining almost white in the candlelight. Known to Jamie only as O, she wore light makeup, her petite features making her look like a teenager, wrapped tight in a black denim jacket and skinny jeans. But Jamie knew what lay beneath her clothes. She remembered her first glimpse of O, dancing naked at the Torture Garden nightclub, her full-body octopus tattoo undulating as she moved. She was certainly no teenager.

A woman started crying silently and O put her arms around her, solidarity clear in the gesture. Jamie noticed other signs of a tight-knit community as people held hands, love evident in the way they looked at each other. For a moment, Jamie wished she had that kind of community. But her years as a police officer and caretaker of her sick daughter had meant little time for friends.

What would my ex-colleagues think of this gathering? Jamie thought. This patchwork of personalities held together by respect for the dead and perhaps, by a hope that they could transcend the bleak future of those gone before. Jamie knew that many here would go out tonight and trade their bodies for money in the hotels and backstreets of Southwark. It ever was and ever will be. She looked up at the stars, which had witnessed lust in these streets since Roman times. Human nature didn't change. There would always be sex and death, drinking and drugs, peace and war, violence and love. There would always be light in the dark too, and Jamie hoped to be one of the bright ones in this borough.

"Tonight we march along the same streets as the Outcast Dead, in memory of those who came before us and the sisters and brothers we have lost along the way."

The strident voice echoed through the street, an Irish lilt evident in her tone. It belonged to the leader of the event and one of the personalities of Southwark: Magda Raven.

That's what she called herself anyway – no one seemed to know her real name. She was tall, built like a pro netball player, her long limbs muscled and toned. She wore a tight black t-shirt and black jeans, both arms displaying full-sleeve tattoos that covered them from shoulder to wrist.

One arm was tattooed like a stained glass window, with the figure of Mary Magdalene kneeling in front of Christ in the garden of Gethsemane. The other arm was a riot of ravens, wings beating in a tornado of wind and nature, as if they would lift from her skin. Jamie had heard Magda called an urban shaman, that she walked the city with a vision of the other worlds it contained, and she had heard of Magda's campaign to turn the graveyard into a memorial park. The woman was seemingly unstoppable, a hero to the local people and a thorn in the side of developers who wanted to make a tidy profit from this valuable land.

The cemetery had been so full of human remains in the late nineteenth century that it was closed as a health hazard and became an urban myth over time, a legendary graveyard for the forgotten dead. Thousands were buried here, and the land remained locked in dispute.

"Let us honor their memory now by tying ribbons in their name."

Magda's last few words were drowned out by the rising sound of a hymn and feet stamping to a rousing chorus.

A group of people rounded the corner at the end of the street. They were mostly middle-aged, more women than men, their voices strident as they sang. They carried banners embroidered with scenes of pastoral perfection and emblazoned with slogans. *No sin in Southwark. Hate the sin, love the sinner.* At the bottom of the banners, their allegiance was printed in black: *The Society for the Suppression of Vice.*

Magda pointedly ignored the singing and continued with the service, indicating that those present should come forward and tie new ribbons to the gates next to the faded ones from previous months. O walked forward, kissing a pink ribbon before tying it to the gate, her head bent in remembrance.

"Dirty fucking whores."

The shout came from behind the Society for the Suppression of Vice, and some of the singers turned, faces shocked by the language. But others glared at the group gathered by the gates, supportive of the words that condemned those they considered unclean. Emboldened by the harsh words, the Society singers took a step forward as if to push back the people who offended them with their mere existence.

They filled the width of the street, their dark coats and muted colors a dull contrast to the bright clothes of the sex workers and their supporters. Jamie noticed that some of the girls pulled hoods up, shielding their faces in fear of recognition.

Magda Raven stood silent for a moment, looking towards the Society group with fire in her eyes. She attached her own ribbon to the gate and lifted a candle towards the sky.

"Mother Goddess, virgin and whore, from whom all life comes."

A low hiss came from the Society at her words, and they took another step towards the group.

"May we who remember the Outcast Dead be blessed on this night and protected on the nights to come."

Magda poured some of the wax from her candle onto the bottom of the gates, marking it in remembrance. Then she walked through the crowd and began to lead the sex workers along the street, down Redcross Way towards the river. The Society walked behind, matching their steps.

Jamie lingered towards the back of the group alongside some of the male sex workers and local campaigners. Her senses were alert to the possible threat here, honed by years in the police. Most of those who marched under the banners of the Society were harmless middle-aged women from Southwark Cathedral who thought they were doing good by denouncing sin on the streets. Their eyes were guarded, their fingers gripped their banners tightly, armor against being polluted by the sin of the fallen.

But Jamie saw hate and fanaticism in the eyes of some of them. She had seen that same look in the eyes of racist thugs, religious fanatics and, once, in the smoky Hellfire Caves of West Wycombe, where she had almost died.

At the end of Redcross Way, Magda led the group into Park Street and then Stoney Street. The bars of Borough had mostly closed, but there were still a few people in the streets, laughing as they headed home. Some noticed the two disparate groups, the calm slow steps of the colorful sex workers, followed by the tramp of the Society.

"Come 'ere, darlin'," a man shouted across the road at one of the younger girls. "I've got somethin' that'll put a smile on yer face ... or *somethin'* on your face at least." He guffawed and his mates collapsed in laughter as they staggered off down the road.

O took the hand of the younger woman and they kept walking, faces set in respect, some looking down at the candles they held. Jamie knew that they must hear such words often. It came with the job, but that didn't make it right.

The group approached the end of Stoney Street near the medieval Clink prison, where old warehouses had been turned into luxury apartments overlooking the Thames. Magda turned right, leading the group towards the ruins of Winchester Palace. The monthly vigil always culminated at Southwark Cathedral just a little further on, where they would leave a symbolic wreath in memory of the unconsecrated dead.

The great rose window atop a high stone wall was the only thing that remained of the original twelfth-century palace, illuminated by spotlights at night. This was where the Bishops of Winchester had lived until the seventeenth century, rich men who often held the post as Chancellor. The coffers of the church in this, the Liberty, were filled from the proceeds of the stews, the brothels, the Clink prison, gaming, theatres and all manner of pleasures suppressed in the City across the river. This was where London used to sin – and where, perhaps, it still did. Jamie remained at the back of the group, a buffer between the working girls and the protestors. She felt the eyes of the Society members on her back as she walked, and she wondered briefly what they thought of her.

As the first of the group passed into the light of the Winchester Palace ruins, a scream rang out, a long shrill note that pierced the night.

CHAPTER 2

Jamie started forward, her body instinctively reacting from her police training, her pulse racing with adrenalin. Her eyes scanned the scene. There was no obvious danger.

"Stay back," Magda's strong voice called out. "Move away now."

Jamie pushed through the throng even as the group surged forward to look. Human nature was ever to gaze at whatever horror lay beyond. Some of them pulled out their phones to take pictures.

She reached the edge of the railing that protected the ruined foundations and looked down. In the middle of the courtyard, a man lay spread-eagle on his back. Jamie automatically processed the crime scene in her mind, as she had always done in the police, scanning the area and noting the details of the body. The man's arms were a ruin of bloody flesh, the skin flayed off with a very sharp knife by the look of the clean wound edges. He wore the remains of a shredded cassock, slashed around the torso, the white collar still visible. His mouth was stuffed with white feathers and more lay around him, stained by his own blood.

"Call the police," Jamie shouted, her tone authoritative. "We need to secure the scene."

As Magda pulled her phone out, Jamie ran down the steps towards the man. The blood around him was fresh and he could still be alive. Stepping carefully so as not to disturb the area too much, Jamie bent to feel the pulse at his neck. There was nothing, but there still might be hope. She had to try.

With the cuff of her sleeve over her fingers, she tugged the feathers from his mouth, the goose down stuffed so deep into his throat that she couldn't get them all out.

After a moment, Jamie stopped. There was no way this man was alive. His face was frozen in agony, his eyes bulging and bloodshot. His thick dark hair was shot through with a streak of white. Jamie was aware of the lack of life in him. His body was still warm but the essence of it had gone, leaving only this ruined flesh. It was now more important to preserve the scene for those who could look into his death and bring him some kind of justice.

Jamie wiped away the prick of tears, frustration at another wasted life and the fact that she would not be on the police team that would investigate his murder. Her statement would be taken, as she had once taken them, but she would be on the outside this time.

Who was this man and why was his body left here? Was it a statement to the community and, if so, which part?

Jamie looked up at the faces staring down at her. At one end, the frightened faces of the sex workers and at the other, the hard expressions of the Society for the Suppression of Vice. Sirens rang out in the London night as the police arrived on the scene.

***

Dale Cameron stood in the shadows of Winchester Square, his heart pounding as the rush flooded through him. The sense of almost being discovered gave him an added thrill. He knew he should leave but he couldn't bring himself to move just yet. The initial scream of panic at discovery of the body had given way to a low hubbub. He could hear someone weeping. He breathed deeply and let the sounds sink into his consciousness as he savored the aftermath of violence.

He clutched a dark blue waterproof bag in his fist. It was designed to keep things dry while kayaking on the river, perfect for the collection of his trophies. It was heavy now, weighed down by the bloody skin inside. He stroked the outside of the bag with tentative fingers. The kill was nothing compared to the harvest of his bloody keepsakes.

Sirens burst through the noise of the disturbed crowd. Dale snapped out of his reverie. The sound belonged to his other self, his daytime self, and his phone would soon be ringing with the news.

A slow smile crept across his face.

As a Detective Superintendent he could even stay and help process the crime scene. The officers on duty would respect him even more for doing grunt work far below his station. Part of him was tempted by the idea – part of him wanted to skate so close to the edge that they might even suspect him. But no … He shook his head. There was too much at stake now and he was so close to his goal. These small purges were nothing to what he had planned for Southwark. For now, he needed to get away from the scene before it was locked down.

Dale walked through the back streets of London Bridge to his car with a confident stride. Not too slow, not too fast. Nothing that would draw attention to himself. He placed the bag in the trunk and got into the driver's seat, giving himself a moment before completing the final phase of his ritual.

He leaned over and opened the glove compartment,

then reached in and pulled out a pot of Ponds Cold Cream. He unscrewed the top and lifted it to his nose, closing his eyes as he inhaled the floral scent.

Dale smiled. His mother had had such beautiful skin, with the translucence of Egyptian alabaster. He used to watch her as a boy as she smoothed cream into her arms and hands, massaging it slowly until it had all disappeared, leaving only a trace of scent in the air. One day, she had turned to him, the sunlight from the window a halo around her golden hair. *Come here, darling. Let me put some on you.* He had stood between her knees as she took a dab from the fragrant jar. The lotion was slick on her palms as she rubbed it between them and then she took his arm and touched him with cool fingers. Goosebumps rippled over Dale's skin at the memory, the sensation clear in his mind, a moment of happiness. But then … his face darkened and he screwed the top back on the cream, slamming it back into the glove compartment. He would not sully the perfect memory tonight.

CHAPTER 3

HIGH CEILINGS OF PANELED glass supported by the
green pillars of Borough Market allowed the light to flood
into even the inner corners of the building. There had
been a food market here since the eleventh century, but
these days it was aimed more at the high-end restaurants
and well-paid foodies of the city. Jamie walked past an
artisan baker, who piled sourdough and spelt loaves next
to tempting sticky fudge brownies. She inhaled the smell
of fresh bread and baked sugar goodies, sweetness lingering on the back of her throat. Her stomach rumbled in
anticipation, but the problem with Borough was the sheer
volume of choice. It was hard to know what to choose
when every stall contained another tiny world of culinary
pleasure.

Jamie was exhausted from last night. The police had
arrived quickly and taken statements from those people
who remained, although many had vanished into the
darkness when the body had been discovered. Because
of her history and contacts, her own statement had been
processed quickly. She had been able to leave before the
others, but she couldn't get the image of the man's face out
of her mind and sleep had been hard to come by.

She weaved her way through the market, navigating

the early shoppers, glancing at the abundance of produce as she passed. One stall was covered with baskets of mushrooms: wild, golden chanterelles and purplish pied bleu lying next to the thick trunks of king oysters. There were butchers with fresh game, carcasses of ducks and deer hanging down outside the shops where men with heavy hands served packets of paper-wrapped choice cuts. Proud chefs sold specialized wares – cider from a local orchard, honey made from urban Hackney bees, cured prosciutto from the happiest free-range, acorn-fed pigs. There was also a row of street-food stalls and coffee carts at the back near Southwark Cathedral, and Jamie wound her way through the crowds in that direction.

She was beginning to find her way around after moving into Southwark last month. Her old flat in Lambeth had become unbearable after Polly's death, memories slamming into her whenever she walked in the door. Jamie had wept in the empty room before locking it for the last time, but her daughter was free now and Jamie needed to live as Polly had asked her to. She had handed over all her old cases after resigning from the Metropolitan Police, and closed that door as well. But she couldn't bring herself to leave London. The city held her tightly, curled itself within her.

Jamie caught sight of Detective Sergeant Alan Missinghall at the edge of the throng, his six-foot-five frame dwarfing the people around him. He was struggling to hold two coffee cups along with several bags brimming with pastries. Jamie grinned as she hurried through the crowds towards him, happy that some things never changed. Missinghall always made food a priority.

"Let me help with that," she said. He turned at her approach.

"Hi, Jamie. Good to see you."

Missinghall handed her the pastries and bent to kiss

her cheek. Jamie was slightly bemused by the affection, something he would never have shown on the job. They had worked together on a number of cases and he had been junior to her at the time, as a Detective Constable. He had covered her back during a couple of dangerous investigations and was probably her closest friend in the Met by the end.

"Let's go sit in the churchyard with these," she said, leading the way through the gates and into the grounds of Southwark Cathedral, where they found a free bench in a patch of sun. They sat in comfortable silence for a moment sipping coffee as the busy market bustled behind them and the calls of the market traders echoed across the little square.

"How's business then?" Missinghall asked, as he started into the second cheese and ham croissant. He leaned forward, making sure the crumbs fell to the pavement below. Pigeons came pecking within seconds and cleared up his scraps. This area was teeming with bird life, drawn by the rich pickings from Borough Market.

"It's quite a different side of the city, that's for sure." Jamie smiled. "But it's interesting work so far, especially round here. I got a few clients within days of putting up the new website. Thanks for putting the word out."

Missinghall grinned. "Recommending you is good for my reputation. You're quite the celebrity, to be honest. And that pic on the website is a hit."

Jamie blushed a little. She had used a picture of herself in black leather, standing with arms crossed against her motorbike, black hair loose in the wind and the City of London in the background. Her gaze was no-nonsense and capable, with a hint of challenge. It was a look she had never been able to fully embrace when she worked as a Detective Sergeant, but now she worked as a private investigator, she could do whatever she liked.

It was hardly idyllic, however, and Jamie pushed down her guilt at lying to Missinghall. Her new business as a private investigator was only just paying the bills, and the cases were dull and repetitive. Prenuptial investigations and matrimonial surveillance were not quite as fascinating as homicide cases. It seemed that the pull of death was in her blood, echoing the pulse of the city. She missed the all-consuming cases in the way that an addict missed a fix – with the sure knowledge that it was killing as she indulged. She missed the camaraderie and the sense of doing something good for the community – though she didn't miss the paperwork, or Detective Superintendent Dale Cameron.

"And what about you, Al?" Jamie said. "How's life as a DS?"

"The promotion's alright and the missus appreciates it. But to be honest, I miss the way we worked together. I guess I'll get used to it soon enough. Nothing stays the same in this city …" Missinghall's voice trailed off as he looked up at the Gothic cathedral in front of him. "Well, nothing except the architecture anyway. I'm glad we can still meet up though, and you know I'm happy to help out if I can."

Jamie took another sip of coffee, letting the hot, bitter liquid soothe her tired brain.

"Do you know anything about the homicide that happened here last night?"

Missinghall chuckled. "I thought you'd want to know more about it when I saw your name on the witness statements. We off the record?"

"Of course. I'm part of the community here now and I was there, so …"

Missinghall nodded.

"Turns out that the murdered man, Nicholas Randolph, worked here at Southwark Cathedral. He was part of the community outreach team, working closely with the toms. There have been suggestions that he used to be a sex worker himself, but not confirmed as yet. You might be able to find that out more easily than we can. People round here are pretty tight-lipped about that kind of thing."

Jamie frowned. "What about his arms? They looked flayed."

"We got some pictures from the next of kin. Randolph had full-sleeve tattoos that revealed quite a bit about his past. A combination of religious iconography and gay-pride images."

Jamie raised an eyebrow. "You can see how some might have objected to that. Any suspects?"

Missinghall shook his head slowly. "You know I can't talk about that." He paused and looked up at the sky. He took a deep breath and Jamie waited, taking another sip of coffee and allowing him the silence.

Finally, his dark eyes met hers and she saw concern there. "Look, tell your mates round here to keep an eye out." He paused. "Off the record, this isn't the first homicide with this MO. There've been two other bodies found recently in Southwark – undesirable characters by some definitions. They also had flayed parts of their bodies where tattoos had been excised. But they were illegal immigrants and this is the first high-profile case. A man of the church, whatever his past. Even the Mayor has gotten involved. With the run-up to the election, he'll be antsy to get this solved."

"Is Dale Cameron really running?" Jamie asked.

Missinghall grimaced at the name. Dale Cameron was a rising star in the Met with the looks of a corporate CEO and the slippery shoulders to match. He had been their superior officer on previous cases, and crossing him had directly led to Jamie's resignation from the police. When she'd woken from nightmares of smoke and burning body parts, she'd been sure that he had been in the drug-fueled haze of the Hellfire Caves.

"Yes," Missinghall said, shaking his head. "He's got a good chance, as well. Loads of the top brass want someone with a hard line on crime in the Mayor's seat. And Cameron is a hard bastard, that's for sure." He sighed. "But whatever we think of him, he certainly gets results. Crime's down across the city. He's cracking down on immigrants and he's moving the homeless and mentally ill out of the central areas."

"That's what people want, I guess," Jamie said. "As long as it doesn't upset their own lives in any way."

Missinghall looked at his watch. "I've gotta go, sorry." He stood up and brushed pastry crumbs from his suit. "Do this again sometime?"

Jamie smiled up at him. "That would be great. Thanks for coming, Al. Stay in touch."

Missinghall turned and walked away but after a few steps he came back, his eyes serious.

"There's also been a rise in reported missing persons around here," he said. "Prostitutes, illegal immigrants, homeless addicts. You know we don't have the resources to pursue all the cases in detail, especially with people who move on so quickly. But it's worrying, so stay out of trouble, Jamie."

Jamie put her hand on her heart and gave him a look that made him grin before he walked off into the crowded streets. But she knew she couldn't let it go. The police would do their investigation into the murder, but there was something wrong in Southwark and after last night, she was already involved

Jamie stood and walked to the cathedral door, her eyes drawn to the flint cobbles embedded in the walls on either side. She reached out to stroke one of the rocks, its surface smooth and almost metallic to the touch, the colors layered like the center of the earth. Then she pushed open the door to Southwark Cathedral and walked inside, determined to find something of Nicholas Randolph here.

The Gothic cathedral was a mixture of the architecture of ancient faith and a modern sensibility, appealing to tourists and the faithful alike. A series of medieval bosses were attached to the back wall, fastened there as remnants of the fifteenth-century church. One of them portrayed the Devil devouring Judas, its face blackened by fire and time.

One of the stone tombs caught Jamie's eye. It had *Thomas Cure 1588* written above it, a memorial for a saddler to the Tudor King Edward VI, Queen Mary and Queen Elizabeth. With a prominent ribcage and skeletal bones with an over-large head, it looked nothing like the tombs usually seen in churches. Instead of a representation of the man in life, this was a cadaver effigy, a decomposing body, a direct *memento mori* to remind people that our physical remains will soon be as this. Jamie shivered a little in the cold of the stone church.

"May I help you?"

Jamie turned to find a bright-eyed older woman, leaflets clutched in her hand and a 'Volunteer' badge pinned neatly to her lilac knitted sweater. Jamie smiled.

"Thank you, that would be great. I'm doing some research about the area and I've heard that the medieval church here was involved with the brothels. Is that true?"

The woman frowned, her face showing distaste. "As much as many of us would like to erase the past, it's the truth. The church used to be St Mary Overie and it was owned by the Bishop of Winchester. He licensed the stews, as they were known, in Southwark for four hundred years. But of course, that was a long time ago and we are now actively working to clean up the community, to rid it of that dirty past."

"I'm interested in the work the church does with the community," Jamie said. "Is there someone in particular I could talk to about that?"

The woman smiled, clearly relieved to be focusing on a more suitable topic. "Well, we're all involved," she said, pride evident in her voice. "Was there anything in particular you wanted to find out about? Volunteering perhaps …" She looked Jamie up and down, in the way only an older woman could. "We have rehab groups, too."

At her words, Jamie became more aware of her appearance. She'd lost weight recently, eating only for fuel these days. Her cheekbones stood out against pale skin. She rarely wore makeup and she tied her dyed black hair into a tight bun most days. But drug-addict chic was not really the professional look she was aiming for.

"Did you know Nicholas Randolph?" Jamie asked.

The woman froze, her breath catching at the name. She put a hand against the wall, her head drooping a little. Tears glistened in her eyes.

"I'm sorry," Jamie whispered. "Were you close?"

"He was Nick to us," the woman said. "And he was a good man, despite what some said about his past." A hard edge came into her voice at that. "But the Lord forgives and washes our sins whiter than snow. The darker spark within us may lapse into old habits but even that can be forgiven. Repentance is a daily practice after all, and I'm afraid that Southwark more than most is testament to the dual nature of sinner and saint. Nick was both, as are we all."

"Was his community outreach program supported by all in the church?"

The woman hesitated and doubt flickered in her eyes. "Yes, of course, we're an inclusive church. We have an altar for the victims of AIDS … Although, of course we cannot ignore what the Bible says about sexual sin. Nick was more

tolerant than many, for sure, and he worked with some ..."
She paused and shook her head. "Well, let's just say that
I'm not sure there's anyone who can replace Nick in that
particular part of the community outreach program." The
woman shuffled her leaflets and then handed one to Jamie.
"Here's some information about the church windows and
the main tombs of interest. I'll leave you to continue alone."

The woman turned away to greet a family of American
tourists who would be unlikely to ask such difficult questions.

Jamie walked towards the middle of the church and
paused in front of a stained glass window portraying
characters from Shakespeare's plays. This had been the
playwright's borough, back when theatre was part of the
pleasure bank of the Thames alongside the prostitutes,
bear baiting and gambling dens. The replica of the Globe
Theatre stood a few streets away, and the stained glass
honored the greatest of the Bard's plays. Prospero com-
manded the tempest with Caliban at his feet, Hamlet
stood contemplating the skull of Horatio and the donkey-
headed Bottom cavorted with pixies, while around them,
all the world continued to be a stage.

At the very back corner of the cathedral, Jamie found
the chapel to the victims of AIDS. A young man knelt
on an altar cushion, his eyes closed, lips moving in silent
prayer. There was a noticeboard set up by the side and
Jamie walked closer to see what the church was involved
in.

There were pictures from community events, people
smiling at sausage-sizzles under rain-soaked skies, children making origami animals to accompany Noah into the
ark. In one picture, Jamie spotted Nicholas Randolph, his
dark hair recognizable with the streak of white. He looked
younger in life, his face relaxed and happy. He wore a shirt
with sleeves rolled up, revealing a rainbow on one arm, the

promise from God not to destroy the world again and now a symbol for acceptance. Next to him, her face alive with laughter, was Magda Raven.

CHAPTER 4

BLAKE DANIEL TRIED TO concentrate on the document on his screen. He willed his brain to conjure the next sentence and strained against the need to get up. He swallowed and clenched his fists under the desk.

Just one drink and the anxiety would subside.

This need for alcohol was a permanent thudding in his blood. His father's recent death and the discovery of a dark family history had sent him back into the tangled embrace of the tequila bottle. But now he was determined to pull away. Jamie managed her grief at the loss of her daughter and she was much harder hit than he was. Coffee would be a better remedy – at least for now.

Avoiding the critical eye of his ever-watchful manager, Margaret, Blake walked upstairs, out of the research area of the British Museum into the Great Court. It was a stunning marble courtyard with glass panels overhead that allowed the sun to touch every corner, a magnificent setting for the treasures within. Blake loved his job as an artifact researcher at the museum and every time he walked these halls, he marveled again at how lucky he was to work here.

He grabbed a coffee and a cupcake from the posh bakery in the forecourt, then found a place to sit so he could look out at the crowd. He popped a couple of headache pills and then sat for a moment, watching the people go by. He tried to guess the nationalities of those who walked past, a game he often played here in the city where all could find a place. Blake felt at home in London, where his own mixed-race heritage was a cultural norm. His mother was Nigerian, his father Swedish, and his caramel skin and blue eyes were less unusual here than in either of their native countries. Not that he had been to either. He listened to chattering voices around him, most in languages he couldn't even guess at, let alone understand. Perhaps it was time to visit.

Blake sipped his coffee, holding the hot brew between gloved hands. The thin leather hid deep scars across his skin from years of abuse. His father had tried to beat the Devil from his son, intending to destroy the ability to read objects and see visions from the past, or even another realm. But the beatings hadn't worked and the visions still came – sometimes as a gift and sometimes a curse. Blake had reconciled himself to his scars years ago, but now he was almost glad of them, a physical reminder that his father had even existed at all. After years of hating the man, his death hadn't brought peace, only more questions.

A gaggle of chattering schoolchildren caught Blake's eye, their laughter a welcome remedy to his melancholy. As they walked past, the shifting crowd around them parted for a second and Blake saw someone in their midst, a craggy face with a hint of familiarity. The man's eyes were a piercing blue, his features sculpted by northern winds, a scar across his nose like a mountain gulley. His body was like a menhir carved from ancient rock. He was still, his limbs tense. It was as if he waited for something – or someone.

Blake shivered, his skin goosebumps as he remembered the vision of the bloody rite of Odin, a human sacrifice to the gods of the north that he had glimpsed through the Galdrabók, a grimoire of Icelandic spells. His father had kept the powerful book under lock and key, but now it lay wrapped in sailcloth under Blake's own bed. He sometimes looked at the runes within, his gloved fingers tracing the angular lines that marked out his name as gifted, wondering about the others whose names were etched in a similar fashion. For the men who renewed the sacrifice of Ymir were his kin, and he saw an echo of them in the man here now.

He stood, trying to see the man more clearly even as the tourists whirled about, sweeping him out of view. Blake walked quickly towards the place the man had been standing, but he was gone. If he had even been there. Blake rubbed his forehead, urging the pain to subside. Could his visions be bleeding over into the real world? Or was he just seeing his father's face in the visage of another old man?

Blake walked back to the research area and pushed the glimpse of the man from his mind. His supervisor, Margaret, gave him a stern look, as she always did when he took too many breaks for her workaholic sensibility. She beckoned him into her small office.

Time to go on the offensive, Blake thought. He smiled, meeting Margaret's eyes with a direct gaze that made most women blush, a hint of promise for pleasures after dark. He had the look of a boy-band singer after a night partying, perennial stubble and close-cropped dark hair, and Blake knew he could turn on the charm when needed. He walked into Margaret's office, a mischievous smile on his lips.

"I've had some ideas about what we could call this new exhibition," he said, seating himself on the side of her desk, leaning towards her a little, his posture deliberately relaxed.

Margaret was the archetype of a middle-aged museum

researcher, a little wide in the hips, no makeup, greying hair. But Blake liked that in an academic. One of his idols was Mary Beard, a professor of classics at Cambridge who brought Roman culture to life with her down-to-earth ways, uncaring of what the world thought of her looks while she stunned the public with her brilliant mind.

"You know that's up to the marketing team," Margaret said. "They're trying their best with the – unusual – material."

"How about the Las Vegas of Londonium," Blake said with a cheeky smile. He indicated the clay sculpture of a phallus lying on Margaret's desk. "Or Cocks of the Capital."

Margaret's mouth twitched.

"Cock of Ages?" Blake added.

She couldn't help but laugh at that. The musical, *Rock of Ages*, played down the road from the museum and was popular with tourists.

"Hmm, not sure that will fly," she said. "Although it looks like we're going to have to make it over-eighteens only."

"Better for marketing anyway," Blake said. "After all, the British Museum does have one of the largest collection of pornography in the world. Bless those Victorians."

Few were aware that the British Museum had the Secretum, founded in 1865 after the Obscene Publications Act, which preserved a chronology of pornography from the era. Blake stood up to leave.

"Can you shut the door a minute?" Margaret said, her voice suddenly serious. Blake pushed it shut, and the click of the door echoed in the pit of his stomach.

He sat back down on the chair opposite her.

"How's your paper coming along?" she asked, her voice losing all trace of flirtation now. "You seem to be behind … again."

Blake looked away. "I know. I'm sorry – my father's death …"

"I'm sorry about his passing, but we have a hard deadline on this exhibition. You know that. I need researchers who can deliver on time, and you've been repeatedly absent or late this last year." She paused. "Sometimes when you come in, I know you've been drinking, Blake." She pulled a paper from a folder next to her computer. "This is a formal warning about your behavior. It goes on your record and it means you're on notice."

Blake took the paper, but he couldn't read the words. They swam in front of his eyes, a mixture of legalistic terminology and HR gobbledygook. If only he could just have a drink. It would help his concentration.

At heart, he knew the discipline was deserved but it felt like he'd been slammed into a wall. His life was a balancing act, for sure, but he had thought he was managing it well enough. This job was stability even as his personal life was in shambles. He couldn't lose it.

"Blake, do you understand what this means?" Margaret's voice was a little softer now.

He nodded.

"Yes, I … I need to get back to work." He waved the paper, attempting a smile. "Lots to do."

Margaret nodded. "I'll expect an update at the end of the week."

Blake left Margaret's office and went back to his own desk, a little corner haven in the bustle of the museum. He sat down heavily and stared at his computer screen for a moment. He ran his gloved fingers along the edge of the desk, considering the possibility of just walking out.

The craving for a drink was overwhelming, but he had removed the flask of vodka from his bottom drawer last week in one of his attempts to go cold turkey.

There was a bar across the street, though.

He only had to walk upstairs and over the road and he could soothe the crazy and focus again.

He took off his watch and laid it on the desk next to him. *I don't have to stop drinking forever*, he thought. *Just another ten minutes.*

He opened the file on his computer and focused on what he needed to do. The research team had a lot of objects to sift through for this exhibition, searching for the ones that would be the most effective to convey the desired message. It was about the sexual history of London, a daring subject that skated near some difficult truths about the capital's past. But history didn't have to be portrayed as dry and dusty.

Blake's visions enabled him to see the real people behind the objects, and his job was to help others see them too by putting together insightful curated displays. He loved to bring history to life, giving a glimpse into a past that might inspire others to learn as he had. What better place than the British Museum to do this work? There really was no substitute, so he couldn't lose this job. He just couldn't.

He started typing up his research notes, making suggestions for his specific area. The idea for the exhibition stemmed from the remains of a substantial Roman temple discovered to the south of Southwark Cathedral, with stone foundations and tessellated floors. A jug inscribed with *Londini ad fanus Isidis* – 'In London, at the Temple of Isis' – had been found nearby in 1912, a relic from Roman times.

Southwark back then had been outside the defended area of the Roman city, a no-man's land where any sin could be indulged. There was evidence that Isis, Apollo and Hermes had been celebrated in wild processions culminating in frenzied public orgies on the same land where the cathedral now stood. Every night was Saturday night in Roman Southwark, and alcohol played just as much a part in the lives of the Romans as it did for contemporary Londoners.

Blake forced down his itch for a drink, checking his watch.

Another ten minutes.

He rested gloved hands against a *spintriae*, a Roman brothel token with lists of services for purchase. He wondered what he would see if he tried to read it with bare hands. Would he glimpse the life of the Roman red-light district? Did he want to?

There was a room in the museum that few knew of where he would go to read sometimes. Not read with a book, but with his bare hands, to see into the past of the objects he researched. As much as he considered the visions a curse, he also craved them. Just like the tequila bottle. Was it the lure of the unknown, a break from stifling normality? When he drank, and when he read, Blake didn't know what would happen. Was it about loss of control?

Blake pulled his hand away from the object. He wasn't strong enough to witness what this token might show him this morning. The Romans understood appetite in all its forms: food, sex, violence. All were celebrated to excess in the Roman world. *Perhaps our time is not so different,* Blake thought. *There is such a thin veil of civilization over our animal nature, after all. It takes little to let our teeth show.*

The face of the man upstairs flashed into his mind, and then a memory of the vision in the Nordic forest. The groans of the dying strung up in trees, the grunt of the men who hacked at the corpses, the moon on the dark blood that soaked the earth.

Blake shook his head, banishing the images. He began to search the database for details that would add color to the description of the *spintriae*, attempting to balance the truth with language that would educate but not offend. He tried several different descriptions, chuckling to himself as he wrote, trying for a balance of double-entendre that skirted the edge of acceptability.

As he delved into the archives, he discovered the lists of sexual services were not only displayed on tokens. There were women, known as *bustuariae*, who worked the cemeteries lining the roads out of London. They used gravestones to advertise their services, chalking up their specialty and prices during the day and liaising with clients after sunset. Sex and death were intimately wound together and this could add a new angle to the display.

Blake pulled up the records from the Pompeii exhibition from a few years back, one of the most popular for the museum. The ancient city was the ultimate combination of sex and death, with art depicting satyrs raping animals and gods abusing maidens, where myriad clay penises were dug from the ruins and wall frescoes depicted scenes of orgies. Blake leaned in to type more quickly, the thrill of discovery suppressing his cravings, at least for now.

CHAPTER 5

JAMIE LOOKED MORE CLOSELY at the photograph on the church wall. Magda was clearly a friend of Nick's, their easy camaraderie caught on camera. Jamie knew she should let Missinghall know about the picture, but perhaps this wasn't anything important. After all, both of them worked with people in the community. But maybe it was time to meet Magda Raven officially. Jamie walked back down the nave towards the exit and out into the sun.

Magda wasn't hard to locate. She was a photographer and artist with a studio address listed on her website a block away. Jamie walked down a small alleyway, past the place where the Tabard Inn once stood, where Chaucer's pilgrims had met in the Canterbury Tales. Jamie smiled as she passed the blue plaque marking the spot. It was surrounded by scaffolding from building works in an area that was forever being reincarnated, with layer upon layer of history and life. This was one of the charms of living in London. Every square inch was saturated with history and the echoes of the past could be felt in every footstep.

The building ahead was an old warehouse converted into studio flats. It looked to be mixed industrial and residential, a working artists' haven. The main door had buttons with labelled names and businesses. Jamie rang Magda's bell, and a minute later the intercom crackled.

"Magda's Art. Can I help you?"

"Hi," Jamie said. "I'm new to the community and I was on the walk last night. My name's Jamie Brooke. I wondered if I could talk to you about it."

There was a pause and the sound of a brief muted conversation, before Magda replied.

"Last night was terrible. I don't really know what to say about it, but of course, come in."

The door buzzed and Jamie pushed inside. The corridor was bare, concrete walls presenting a neutral face to the outsider. There were sounds of banging upstairs and the faint tinkle of a piano. A door at the end of the corridor opened to a bright space beyond. Magda Raven stood in the doorway, a tentative smile on her face. She wore a black t-shirt with butterflies all over it and blue jeans over bare feet.

"Come on in," Magda said. "Kettle's on."

The studio was spacious, with a high ceiling supported by metal beams. A row of rectangular windows allowed light to penetrate the space. A stepladder with a wide platform stood underneath one open window, a pair of binoculars and notepad resting on top. There were doors at the other end of the room, one open to give a glimpse of a kitchen. On one side of the studio, white panels separated part of the space, with cameras on tripods and distinctive silver umbrella flash lighting set up. Jamie could see a shadow moving in the space beyond.

"I'm in the middle of an impromptu photo shoot but we're on a tea break right now. Why don't you have a look around?" Magda said. "Would you like tea or coffee?"

"Coffee would be great," Jamie said. "Black, one sugar, please."

Oversize prints covered the studio walls, grouped by theme. Faces of Southwark residents captured in stark black and white, an old woman with wrinkles as deep as scars, a Rastafarian with dreads swinging, smoke wreathed around his head. A young woman leaned against a brick wall, cigarette in her hand, figure-hugging dress revealing slim curves. Her posture invited attention, but her eyes were haunted and cynical.

Birds dominated the next set of prints. Some whirled above the backdrop of the City, silhouetted against the stark outline of the Tower of London. A murmuration of swallows swooped above Stonehenge, a cloud of synchronized beauty in the beginnings of a storm. Then there were close-ups of the ravens Magda had tattooed on her skin, their feathers glossy blue-black, eyes bright. The final panel contained a series of prints in full color, scenes of the Borough streets that brought a smile to Jamie's face with their optimism. Red balloons against the white backdrop of the Globe Theatre. Street performers outside the Tate Modern striking poses for the passing tourists. The silver arc of the Millennium Bridge across the Thames with St Paul's haloed by a sunbeam. The multi-colored ribbons tied to the gates of Cross Bones Graveyard.

There was a corkboard next to the prints, covered in fliers about local events: a masquerade ball, the London Tattoo Convention, and exhibitions coming soon at the British Museum. Jamie's mind flashed to Blake and she wondered what he was working on at the moment.

"See anything you like?" Magda said as she handed Jamie a mug of hot coffee, waving her hand to encompass her prints.

"They're all beautiful." Jamie pointed at the picture of the ribbons. "Cross Bones must mean a lot to you."

"Last night …" Magda shook her head. "Well, I hope that last night wasn't the last memorial there, but the trauma of seeing what we did might mean we have to cancel it for a while." She looked at Jamie more closely. "You're the woman who went to the body."

Jamie nodded. "I used to be a police officer, so I'm used to crime scenes." Jamie noted that Magda's body stiffened at her words. "But I'm a private investigator these days and I'm not involved in the investigation into the murder. That's with the police now. I recently moved to Southwark, so I'm keen to get to know the community. That's why I came along last night."

"I'm sorry your first experience here was so memorable for all the wrong reasons. But this community is a rainbow of people, which means we have dark as well as light on the spectrum." Magda pointed at the wall of images. "It's not possible to have life without the shadow side."

"Did you know –"

Jamie's question was cut off by a voice from behind the screen.

"Where's my tea, Magda? I'm parched."

O emerged from behind the screen, pulling a sarong around her body to cover her nakedness. Her elfin features were highlighted by dramatic eye makeup, as black as the tattoo under her clothes and emphasized by her ash-blonde cropped hair. Her eyes widened as she caught sight of Jamie.

"I remember you," she said, coming closer. "Last year when Jenna Neville died, you came to the club. What are you doing here?"

Jamie was disarmed by seeing her there. O had broken through her defenses that night at Torture Garden. She had helped with a clue to the case, but also saw through Jamie's professional veneer to the pain beneath.

"I … I've moved here actually. I was there last night. I wanted to see if there was anything I could do."

O came closer, her eyes fixed on Jamie's. "Does death follow you, Jamie Brooke?" O whispered. "Or do you seek it out?"

Jamie couldn't speak. The words were too close to her

own thoughts. O broke the moment with a dramatic half turn.

"Why don't you stay while we finish the photo shoot?" she said. "We're trying to counter the images of death with life. Magda is a fantastic artist."

"Only because you're such a great model to work with," Magda replied with a laugh.

O walked back to the set, unwound her sarong and dropped it to the floor, completely at ease in her naked state. Jamie had seen her tattoo before when O had danced at the Torture Garden nightclub, but in the daylight, it seemed more unusual. Her back was inked with the head of an octopus with tentacles that stretched out to wrap around her slight frame. As she walked in front of the camera, the octopus moved with her, part of her spinal cord.

One tentacle wound up onto her skull, the black visible under short hair, another wrapped around her waist and dipped down between her buttocks. O turned to face the camera and Jamie couldn't help but gaze at how the tentacles of the creature roved across her body. Her breasts were encircled, with one nipple caressed by the creature, while another tentacle wound down between her legs, touching her hairless sex as it penetrated her there. The detail was exquisite and it was incredible to consider the hours of work involved in the entire piece. O was a work of art and her body the canvas. She stamped her originality on the world with her ink, and Jamie wondered if she could ever be as brave herself.

"How do you want me, Magda?" O asked, and there was a trace of flirtation in her voice. Magda walked round in front of the camera and turned O, her fingers lingering on the woman's shoulder, caressing her skin.

"Look up towards the window. We're going for angelic in the next shots."

"A fallen angel, perhaps." O laughed, her cornflower-blue eyes bright. She composed herself and stood as a statue while Magda clicked away.

Every few seconds, O shifted her posture slightly, changing the angle of her head or her limbs. Her dancing at the Torture Garden had been explicitly erotic, an invitation to sin in a venue that celebrated the physical and the unusual. But here, her body was an embodiment of creation, of human perfection, and the tattoo seemed only to emphasize her vulnerability. Jamie wanted to know why O had chosen this design. Now their paths had crossed again, perhaps she would be able to find out.

Eventually, Magda put the camera down, her face relaxing from the taut posture of the concentrated artist.

"We're done," she said. "There are some great shots in there."

O looked up out of the window, suddenly pointing.

"Look, Magda, the ravens!"

Magda spun quickly and climbed the stepladder up to the high window, gazing out at the birds above, transfixed by their flight. She pushed open the window and began to whistle, soft notes that lilted with a Celtic refrain. It would seem impossible for the tune to be heard above the din of the city and the wind that swept Southwark, but the ravens began to wheel closer.

Magda's song was like a silken cord, drawing the birds to her, and soon there were hundreds of them flying close to the studio windows, their dark eyes fixed on the woman who sang within.

There was a vibration in the air, a heightened sense of connection to the natural world, something Jamie hadn't felt so strongly before in London. It was as if the wild had been brought in here, the rhythms of a far older world reasserting themselves in this cornered civilization. Magda finished her song and threw her arms wide on the final note, the ravens cawing as they winged away and the sky was clear again.

"The ravens are my totem," Magda said, her eyes dark as she descended the ladder. She pulled up her sleeve to reveal the tattoos on her arm in more detail. "They are on me and in me, and they channel my deeper connection to the city."

"I've heard you called an urban shaman," Jamie said. "Is that to do with the ravens?"

Magda smiled. "If I see beyond the skin of the city, then my sight is from the birds. But mainly I live in the world of the practical and human. Like last night."

"Did you know the victim, Nicholas Randolph?" Jamie asked.

"I didn't recognize his body at first. I didn't know it was him …" Magda sighed. "Nick was a friend and we worked alongside each other. He used to work the streets himself years ago, before finding the church. He was gay and spent a lot of time helping the young male prostitutes. He didn't judge them, but helped them with health issues, education, even with places to stay when they were desperate. He visited them in hospital if they got beaten up. He bought their meds. He was a bloody saint and he didn't deserve to die like that."

"But despite his good works, people judged him as they judge the rest of us," O said. "Especially the Society, those bastards who marched behind us last night." She shook her head. "Suppression of Vice – it's a crazy aim, especially around here. The sex trade has been in this borough since Roman times, through medieval London and up to today. The Society tell themselves that they're trying to save us, but they're really trying to get us to conform."

O pulled on her clothes. Skinny jeans and a man's shirt soon covered her tattoo and she could easily pass for an art student on the street. Then she turned around sharply, her face set in determination.

"Tell her, Magda," she said quietly.

CHAPTER 6

MAGDA SIGHED, HER FACE suddenly looking much older.

"Nick's murder is just the latest in a series of worrying events. There've been a number of people going missing round here recently. Sex workers, illegal immigrants, homeless people. Not exactly the cream of society, but people from our community." Magda paused for a moment to take a sip of her coffee. "Of course these things happen everywhere, but this area is under development and many in power want us gone. Since the Shard was built, prices have shot up and there's a lot of money to be made round here," she said, referring to the 87 story skyscraper in Southwark that opened in 2012 and was still under construction. "If only they can get rid of the deviants, the misfits, those of us who don't fit their idea of the future borough."

"If we're gone," O said, "then they can pretend it's all hipsters and expensive coffee and build luxury flats over the sins of the past."

"What have the police been doing about the disappearances?" Jamie asked.

"We report all of them," Magda said. "But missing persons aren't unusual in these transient lines of work, apparently."

Jamie nodded, understanding the other side. The police didn't have the resources to tackle every MISPER in London.

Magda looked at her watch. "I've got to head along South Bank for a meeting at the Tate Modern. If you want to walk with me, I'll show you where some of the people disappeared from as we walk."

"I'll come along too," O said. "I'm heading in that direction."

They left the studio and walked back towards Borough Market, turning down Southwark Street and then into Maiden Lane. Neat terraced houses were interspersed with old converted warehouses as they approached the river.

"This was one of the main streets for prostitutes," Magda said, "back when the Globe and the Rose theatres were the center of the red-light district. Bankside was the Elizabethan Soho. If you look at maps of London, you can tell the areas where sex was for sale, although the street names are changed to something more genteel now, of course."

They walked down to the Anchor pub on Bankside, now flanked by a Premier Inn. The budget accommodation seemed appropriate to the history of the area, a place that a modern Chaucer's pilgrims might stay. Magda pointed to a service doorway round the side of the Anchor.

"A friend of ours, Milo, used to sleep rough here," she said. "He disappeared about a month ago. He preferred sleeping out to the hostels where he'd just get bothered." She smiled, her features soft in reminiscence. "He had the face of a fallen Greek god. I've got some photos of him back at the studio."

"He also had a gorgeous back tattoo," O said. "We compared ink one time. He loved dragons and they flew over his skin, scaled in hues of purple and orange flame."

"And you've never heard what happened to him?" Jamie asked.

Magda shook her head. "He's not the only one, and with Nick's murder, I'm worried that Milo may have ended up the same way." She pointed up at the Anchor pub. "The location echoes with Nick's murder, too. The Anchor used to be a brothel and a tavern, a popular place near the bear-baiting pits round the corner in Bear Gardens."

"The Stews," O said. "That's what they called this area. And it's only a block from here to the Palace of Winchester, where the Bishop who licensed the whores sat in luxury. For four hundred years, it was the Bishop's right to exploit the brothels here, and many of London's most attractive architecture is built on the proceeds of the sex trade."

Magda laughed, a hollow sound that reflected the irony of the past. "For all its official line on celibacy and prudery, the church turned a blind eye to prostitution, believing it to be something that would always be part of life. As Saint Augustine said, 'Suppress prostitution and capricious lusts will overthrow society.'"

They walked down a little further to stand on the banks of the Thames. The waters ran swift today, in hues of grey and brown. A working river for trade and commerce, as fast as the city itself, taking goods to the world.

As they continued on, Magda gazed over to the towers and high-rise office blocks on the north bank.

"Look at the City over there. A square mile of conformity, where they slander us by day and then come to play here by night."

She pointed up at a carved stone head with two faces, one pointing east towards the sea and the other west towards the interior of England.

"It's Janus, the god of two faces," Magda said. "A perfect metaphor for London."

Jamie understood the dichotomy. London was both sinner and saint. It was glamorous and gorgeous, a rich and intoxicating pleasure garden. But there was also dirt here and darkness and the stink of rotten dead, the wretched mad and crazy drunks lying in its gutters.

Magda turned to face Jamie, her eyes soft. "This is where the women of the outcast borough have always walked, where men have sinned upon them through sex and lies and judgement. But the earth beneath us and the river that flows through here has nourished us for generations. Someone or some group is trying to move us on, trying to sweep the darkness under the carpet and pretend we don't exist. That's why people are disappearing. But we're not going anywhere."

They continued west along Bankside, the south bank of the river, a popular path with tourists and locals alike. Every time Jamie walked here, her love for the city was renewed. She had been offered a job in the police far away from the city after Polly died. But this was her home now and what was happening in Southwark made her even more sure of her place here. London could rip you up and spit you out and leave you with nothing, but then you wanted more of it. And Jamie craved that edge.

A violinist played in the underpass under Southwark Bridge, the sweet strains of music filling the confined space. O gave a little twirl and put some change in the violin case, blowing the young man a kiss as she did so. There were posters for a masquerade ball pasted along the underpass walls, emblazoned with coquettish eyes peering out from colorful masks.

"You must come to the ball, Jamie," O said. "We're all going and it's going to be such fun. It's a fundraiser for cleaning up Southwark and a number of the Mayoral candidates will be there."

Jamie thought of her nights at tango, a side she had kept away from her professional life in the past. Perhaps it was time that she integrated both into her new life.

"I'll be sure to get a ticket," she said.

They emerged out of the underpass into the sun and

walked a little further to the replica of Shakespeare's Globe, a magnet for tourists who snapped pictures against the backdrop of the round, white theatre.

"This was a popular place in medieval times to pick up customers," O said. She flashed a flirtatious smile at a handsome young tourist. "Perhaps it still is …"

Jamie still wasn't certain what O did. The police side of her was ready to ask, but another part wanted to encourage friendship. In the end, curiosity overcame politeness.

"Do you …"

Jamie's words trailed off but O picked up the meaning.

"Sell sex?" O said, her eyebrows raised. She appraised Jamie for a moment, as if weighing trust. "Does it matter?"

Jamie shook her head. "No, not at all. I've seen you dance and I would think you'd have people queuing up after that."

Magda grinned. "That she does – but you're picky, aren't you, O?"

They stood for a moment looking out at the Millennium Bridge, a silver parabola that spanned the Thames between the Tate Modern and St Paul's in the City. Tourists walked over it, their footsteps and happy laughter filling the air.

"I used to do a lot more," O said, "but most of my income is from dancing and modeling these days. I still have a few regulars and of course I campaign for better safety. The situation is crazy right now. It's legal to buy or sell sex, but it's illegal for women to join together in a brothel. So we can't practice safely together, we can't get security to protect ourselves from the nut-jobs who inevitably try it on. Sex work is just another kind of work after all, and we should all be safe in our jobs." Her face softened. "Most customers aren't too bad, though."

Magda stretched out her tattooed arm displaying the image of Mary Magdalene kneeling in front of Christ in the garden of Gethsemane. The reformed prostitute as the devoted servant of God.

"Many of my previous clients wanted to cuddle," she said. "To be touched by another person. They were lonely."

"Why did you give it up?" Jamie asked.

"I'm called for other things now," Magda said. "But I know how it feels to be treated the way these women are by a society that can't do without them. It's important for our community to accept the freak and the stranger." She touched the face of Mary on her arm. "The sinners."

"Who is the sinner, anyway?" O said, indicating St Paul's with a nod of her head. "Did you know that the lanes around there are some of the best pickings for the boys?"

O looked at her watch. "Right, I've gotta get to the Kitchen or I'll be late for my shift. When can I see the photos, Magda?"

"I'll have the edits for you tomorrow morning if you want to come over then?"

"Great." O leaned in and kissed Magda on the cheek.

"Can I come to the Kitchen with you?" Jamie asked. "I've heard a bit about it, but I've not been down there yet."

"Sure." O smiled. "We're always in need of a helping hand."

CHAPTER 7

THEY WALKED A COUPLE of blocks into a warren of streets near Mint Street Park, finally reaching a rundown warehouse in a cul-de-sac.

"It's not much, but we try to look after our own round here," O said as she pushed open the back door and stepped into the Kitchen. Jamie followed her inside to find a storage area, shelves stacked high with tinned goods, all labeled and ordered by date. Many were over the sell-by date and O caught Jamie's sideways glance.

"We get a lot of the tins from supermarkets when they go over date," she said. "But there's a period when the stuff inside is still fine. The food bank gives out specific rations, but then we let people take what they want from the over-date bin. Sometimes that makes all the difference." She pointed at a tin of sticky toffee pudding. "I mean, come on, what's not to like about that?"

O laughed, a silvery sound that lifted the dank atmosphere of a place set up to feed the increasing number of poverty-stricken Londoners. She led the way into a commercial kitchen area where several other women had already started work. They called greetings to O as she passed.

"Can you help Meg with chopping vegetables? We've

got to get the stew on." O pointed Jamie towards an older black woman with dreadlocks tied back in a blue patterned scarf. She stood by a large sink with a mountain of potatoes in front of her and a box of carrots and other mixed veg next to it.

"Of course." Jamie headed over and introduced herself, grabbed a peeler, and started on peeling the carrots. Although tentative at first, Jamie was soon into a rhythm. There was a meditative state in food preparation, a repetition that left the mind free to wander.

"This stew is for the evening run," Meg said. "It's best to cook it for a long time to soften the offcuts of meat that we get, so we have to start cooking it soon. We get a load of regulars every night and then we take any leftovers out into the parks round here." She smiled and Jamie saw that her teeth were crooked and bent. The wrinkles in her skin were deeper than a woman of her age should have and there were faint scars around her neck. Meg put down her knife and Jamie noticed her hands shaking, perhaps a symptom of long-term alcohol abuse.

"For some who sleep rough, it's their only meal of the day." Meg pointed to a number of round mixing bowls on the side, covered in tea towels. "That's bread, too – we make it ourselves. We have an allotment out east. That green veg is from our garden." There was a quiet pride in Meg's voice and Jamie wondered about her past. Her own tragedy was just one voice in a city of hurt and sometimes it was good to get some perspective, to realize how much others suffered too. Everyone dealt with life in their own way.

O's laugh rippled through the kitchen area and Meg looked up.

"She's magic, that one," she said. "Keeps everyone's spirits up, even when we're overrun. She can bring a smile to the most depressed of our clients, and I've seen her face down a huge man high on meth. She's fearless."

Jamie watched O as she organized the various teams with a smile and a personal touch that left people beaming. She made them laugh with light remarks, always remembering their names. Jamie thought how different this place was from the police, how isolated she had been there. Her own independence had been partly to blame, but as a woman in a male-dominated environment, she had definitely felt left out. But here she might find a place in a community that really seemed to care for its people.

"Time, everyone," O called out and went to the front door, unlocking it to allow a stream of people into the front area, set up with long tables and benches. They had clearly been queuing outside and they knew the drill. They were quiet as they came in, taking a bowl and lining up for thick porridge liberally doused in white sugar.

One woman with cardboard pieces tied around her body hefted her plastic bags into one corner and stood silently in line.

An old black man shuffled forward with little steps, his gait evidence of Parkinson's, his hands shaking as he reached for a bowl.

A waif of a girl slid through the door, a dirty denim jacket over a short dress, her arms wrapped around herself for warmth. Her eyes were black with kohl and darted around with nervous energy, her movements jerky and jolting.

The smell of unwashed bodies pervaded the cooking area, but no one reacted to it. Jamie supposed it was nothing unusual here. She finished the carrots and began chopping the bunches of green leafy veg. Meg pulled two huge saucepans from a rack and began browning onions and garlic, her shaking diminished as she concentrated on working.

O served strong instant coffee from a big vat, handing

it to each person with a smile and a welcome. There was no judgement in her eyes as she looked at them, and Jamie saw that her respect gave the homeless more dignity. They walked to the benches a little straighter in posture, their humanity restored even for a brief moment. Jamie had seen the other side of poverty in the police: the crime and domestic abuse that often resulted from money problems. She had seen these people as criminals, but O and her team saw them as people needing food, warmth and a community.

After everyone had been served, O went around the benches, speaking in low tones to each person. She carried a bunch of leaflets, clearly trying to help with advice as well as food. The waif-like girl kept her head down as O approached, turning her face away. But O sat down next to her, whispering soft words and after a few minutes, the girl reached out a hand and took a leaflet about the sexual health services she could access.

The breakfast service soon finished and as each person left, a young man on the door gave each one a brown bag. He had a blue streak in his blond hair and Jamie recognized him as the guitar player from the Cross Bones memorial. Some people snatched the bag away without thanking him, but others were effusive in their gratitude. One woman had tears in her eyes as she left, clutching the bag close to her chest as she walked out into the day.

"Right, let's get the benches to the side and start weighing out today's rations." O rallied the team as Jamie helped Meg add the meat to the pans and begin to brown them, adding some oregano and other herbs. A delicious smell began to waft through the warehouse, drowning out the unwashed stench that still lingered. The smell of cooking reminded Jamie of the opulence of Borough Market, where food carts overflowed with amazing produce at prices only few could afford. This place was just a few streets away and yet here, they were scraping the barrel to feed the hungry.

"We can't give people anything they want," Meg said, noting Jamie's interest in the rationing preparations. "There are rules for the food bank and we have to weigh out rations for people who come to make sure there's enough for all. We give them three days' emergency food based on the stamps that they bring for themselves and their families." Meg shook her head, a look of despair on her face. "Problem is that some days we don't have enough food here to feed all who come. Makes you wonder, don't it?"

O organized the packing of boxes, some with more perishable food in them than others. Jamie knew that some families didn't even have a way to cook, so there was a balance of tins to whatever fresh food they could get hold of. O made sure to add a couple of apples to each box and Jamie noticed her frown as she surveyed the room, a shadow crossing her beautiful face as she calculated what they had left.

Meg crumbled some stock cubes over the meat, added salt, and poured in a kettle of hot water on top of each pan, then covered them with lids.

"We'll let these simmer for a while now," she said. "I'll get the bread on. Why don't you go help pack boxes? I can manage here."

Jamie walked through the kitchen area and joined in the packing production line, finding a place next to the young man who had been on the door.

"First day?" he asked Jamie, as he added a tin of beans to a box before passing it on to her. Jamie added a packet of macaroni cheese and passed the box to the next woman.

"I guess so," Jamie said, realizing that she would come back here. Looking at the Kitchen made her doubly grateful for what she did have, and she knew that it was only luck and circumstance that put her on this side of the fence.

"We have our ups and downs," the young man said. "Some days we win and we feed everyone. Other days one of our regulars doesn't show up and we hear of suicide or death in the streets. But Southwark is our community and this is our way of caring." He smiled at Jamie. "This place saved me, that's for sure."

O stepped up to the table, a broad grin on her face.

"Ed is one of our regulars. He's a superstar." Ed blushed under O's praise and Jamie saw a glimmer of the unspoiled youth beneath his harder exterior. O brought that out in people. "How are you finding it, Jamie?"

"I'm amazed at everything you do here," Jamie said. "I had no idea, honestly. I'd love to come and help again."

O smiled. "We'd love to have you back." She looked at her watch. "Ten minutes," she called across the room and everyone on the line speeded up their box packing. "Hungry people incoming. Let's feed them all today."

CHAPTER 8

"WE HAVE TO SHUT down that soup kitchen," Mrs Emilia Wynne-Jones said, clutching her designer purse to her chest like a shield as she stood to speak. "It's a danger to the schoolchildren who walk that route every day. And all those homeless beggars …" She shook her head. "One of them might harm a child, because they're probably sex offenders, you know. It's criminal to let them sleep there."

"Not to mention that it's affecting the house prices in the area," one of the older men in the hall said with a grunt, thumping his walking stick on the ground for emphasis.

The church hall echoed with murmurs of assent as the gathered crowd shifted on their seats. The tabled agenda had been finished and now they were onto Any Other Business, which usually consisted of a litany of complaints.

Detective Superintendent Dale Cameron nodded, his face serious as he met the eyes of the complainants. He always enjoyed the meetings of the Society for the Suppression of Vice. They were full of his kind of people, those who were ready to take the hard decisions necessary to make the city great again. After years of focused ambition, his day job was finally taking him into a position of real power.

He looked out at the crowd in front of him – the older

stalwarts near the front, middle-aged men and women who voted to get rid of immigrants and return Britain to the white paradise they believed could exist in a multi-cultural world. Towards the back were a younger group, men with shorn heads and thick-soled boots, hands deep in pockets and wary eyes. They brought physical energy to the old who gathered to complain every week. They were the ones Dale Cameron really aimed to inspire. Men who only looked for a leader to give them permission to act.

Dale nodded at the discussion, his face set with concentration as he listened with one part of his brain even as the other dissected the crowd. He was aware of the impression he made on them. He exuded confidence and control, and years of studying body language had given him an ability to change his behavior to manipulate any situation. With his salt and pepper hair and trim runner's body, he looked more like a corporate CEO than a senior police officer. Not that he expected to be in the police for much longer. He was running for Mayor and fully intended to win.

As the discussion tapered off, he held up his hand for quiet. His authority silenced the room in seconds.

"You all know that I stand for cleaning up the city," Dale said, his voice strong and well measured. "That includes moving the homeless out of the central areas and into communities further away. There's plenty of council housing up north, if we can only get people to accept it."

"Ungrateful little –"

"What are you going to do about the sex workers?"

"When are you going to develop Cross Bones?"

"How will you deal with the drug problems of Southwark?"

Dale held up a hand again, calming the barrage of questions.

"I share the concerns of the Society," he said. "But I can only act with a mandate as Mayor. City Hall is around the corner, so it makes sense that my first acts will be cleaning up my own borough."

"Hear, hear," someone shouted, and Dale smiled out into the crowd. He made eye contact with many of them as applause rang out around the church hall. As they clapped, a ray of sunshine split into myriad colors on the floor, filtered by the brilliant stained glass windows above. Jesus fed the five thousand in one window and healed the blind on another. Dale found himself thinking of Borough Market round the corner. These days, Jesus would probably have to feed the hungry with multigrain spelt bread and wild salmon, that's how entitled they all were.

"You can help drive out the sex workers and the drug addicts," Dale said, and his eyes met those of the hard men at the back. "Report them to the police. Make it difficult for them to work. Make life more unpleasant for them and they will move on – or go back to their own countries."

The applause began again, and then it was time for tea. A queue formed in front of the dais of those who wanted a little one-on-one time with Dale. He would give them all the time they wanted, understanding that every individual connection was one more vote for him in the Mayoral election. His campaign manager was right – it was all about 'high touch.'

As his team organized the line, Dale accepted a china cup of tea from a frail old woman. Her liver-spotted hands shook as she handed it to him. Her eyes were rheumy and her skin sagging around a face that had witnessed the cultural change of the city since the Second World War.

"It's good that you're here, love," she said. "None of those other politicians understand that we have to reclaim what belongs to us before it's too late. It's time to stamp out the cockroaches and you're the man to do it." She patted Dale's shoulder and shuffled away, leaving him to ruminate on the surprising nature of some of the members.

The Society for the Suppression of Vice had been started in the nineteenth century to promote public morality, a successor to the Society for the Reformation of Manners. Dale liked the overtones of the word reformation, but manners were something few cared about and didn't quite have the dramatic ring to it. But who could object to the suppression of vice, a word that conjured all the nasty, dirty things that went on under cover of darkness. Surely no one could openly support those making money from vice – the prostitutes, the drug pushers, the criminals. Who would stand for them? Of course, Dale thought, as he took another sip of his tea, such obvious vice was merely the thin end of the wedge. He wouldn't rest until the city was clean in all senses of the word.

His idea of a future London centered around the temple of Salt Lake City, a beacon of shining white against a backdrop of blue. Not because of faith, but because of those who looked to it as the pinnacle of good behavior and of perfect obedience.

Whereas London … Dale shook his head as he stirred his tea. Well, London had been a melting pot of multiculturalism, artistic expression and personal freedom for far too long. The Society sought to redress the balance and take back the city for morality – pushing a right-wing agenda that would move the poor on benefits out of the city, clean up the streets of hookers and drug pushers, scrub the stain of graffiti from the walls of Shoreditch and Hoxton and renew a sense of pride in the city.

One of the younger men from the back approached and Dale waved him forward. The man sat opposite him and leaned closer. His jaw was much larger on the left than on the right, an asymmetry that Dale tried not to stare at. The man smelled of tobacco smoke and fried bacon. The thought of a breakfast fry-up made Dale's stomach rumble.

"There's some of us that want to help with your campaign," the man said. "We work out at the boxing gyms in South London and there's a lot of support for what you want to do. If you need us, give me a call. Here's my card."

The man handed over a business card with frayed edges and a blue boxing glove in the middle. Dale took it, noting the scars on the man's knuckles.

"Thank you, I appreciate the offer. There will definitely be leafleting to be done over the coming weeks." Dale met the man's steel gaze and saw that they understood each other. "I'll have my office call you."

They shook hands and the man walked off without looking back.

A well-preserved middle-aged woman sat down next, her designer outfit coordinated in shades of camel and ivory. She placed her knees together, her slim legs and high-heeled shoes tucked under the chair. She placed her hands in her lap, manicured nails with a hint of natural color. A large diamond sparkled on her left hand alongside a gold wedding band. Dale noticed how soft her hands looked and he wondered briefly how they would feel on his skin.

"Detective Superintendent –" she began, her eyes darting to his.

"Dale, please," he said, putting a hand briefly on her knee. She colored a little and raised a hand to her neck, touching the pulse point there.

"Oh. Dale, then." She smiled and he saw opportunity in her gaze. Flirting was always a good way to get another vote.

"I'm part of a group within the church," she said. "We're trying to encourage the sex workers into an abstinence program. We've had some success, but we'd like to get official backing from the Mayor's office. Perhaps even some funding?"

Dale smiled, pouring sincerity into his gaze.

"Of course, that's the kind of program I'd like to encourage. Once I'm elected, I'd appreciate it if you could submit your proposal to my office. I will personally make sure it gets the proper attention."

"Thank you," the woman said, her smile wider now. "Our aim is to honor what the original Society intended."

Dale knew that the Society had been formed by William Wilberforce in order to stem the immorality so rife in the Georgian period, when prostitution added almost as much to the economy as the thriving London Docks. It aimed to ban public drinking, swearing, lewdness and other immoral and dissolute practices, as well as ending the obscenity of pornography and disorderly pubs and brothels. It was a good model for the modern Society. But in Dale's opinion, they had made one mistake that still rippled through the strata of Britain. By banning what they called 'obscene publications,' they had also stopped the distribution of contraceptive advice to the working classes, giving rise to more births amongst the poor.

One of Dale's intentions was to introduce a substantial one-off payment to any woman who underwent sterilization, which would encourage those worse off in society to stop breeding. *About bloody time the class balance was redressed*, he thought. Once the dregs of society were dealt with, then he would start trying to get the right sort of people to have more babies. They would need a working group on how to influence more intelligent women to stop pursuing aggressive careers. It was an unfortunate correlation that the more educated a woman was, the fewer children she had.

"May I have your autograph?" the woman asked, pulling a pad from her handbag. "Once you're Mayor, you'll be far too busy."

She bent forward and Dale caught a trail of her scent in the air. Ponds Cold Cream. His breath caught in his chest and he was back in that room with his mother. As she stroked the cream into his skin, the door had slammed open. His father stood in the doorway, still wearing his police uniform, his face red from drinking after his shift. *You little faggot.* His father's voice had been a growl, an animal sound as he stepped towards them with fists clenched.

He always rolled up his sleeves before he began, revealing the tattoos on his forearms. One arm displayed Justice as a beautiful woman holding a sword in one hand, her weighing scales in the other, blood dripping beneath from her blindfold. The other arm was inked with the words his father lived by: *When justice is done, it brings joy to the righteous but terror to evildoers. Psalm 21:15.* Dale understood his father's right to discipline his family – it was how he felt about London now. After all, spare the rod, spoil the child.

"Are you OK?" the woman asked, her eyes concerned.

"Of course." Dale smiled and refocused on her. "Sorry, it's been a long day already." He pulled a fountain pen with a silver fox-head cap from his inside top pocket. He signed his name with a flourish, realizing that this was likely just the start of such events. Perhaps he would even take a book deal once he was Mayor.

The woman walked off the stage, her hips swaying a little more than was necessary. Dale felt a familiar stirring. He took another sip of his tea and waved for the next person to come forward. He would stay here until he had given them all a moment of his time, but later tonight he would indulge his own particular brand of release.

CHAPTER 9

JAMIE SAT AT HER tiny desk, scanning through the financial records of a husband whose disgruntled wife was sure he was having an affair. Her new office was the size of a large cupboard, rented in a shared office space on the edge of Southwark. She had tried working in her new flat, but surprisingly, she missed having colleagues around. She had never been the chatty type, preferring to keep quiet and rarely drinking with the other police, but there was an energy in having other people around.

The shared office space was a way to get some normality back into her life, the routine of getting out of the flat, looking presentable enough for others not to notice her. The office space was generally quiet, with the tapping of keyboards and low voices making phone calls. She nodded to the other people she saw in the lobby and little kitchen, but she could see reservation in their eyes. She wondered how fast the turnover was round here. Perhaps when she had been here for a while, they would accept her as part of the community – and she did intend to be here a while.

Jamie returned her attention to the records in front of her. From what she could see, the man was having much more than an affair. She'd tracked him to another house and it looked like he had another family altogether. Jamie shook her head. She had barely managed a relationship with one person. Two marriages would be a hell of a lot of work.

She added the last pieces of information to the file, attaching photos of the man's second family. The woman had essentially paid to destroy her marriage, to break apart the status quo. Part of Jamie didn't want to send the information to her client, but perhaps the woman knew already and could use this to move on. Or perhaps she would find strength in her children. A sudden rush of loneliness took Jamie by surprise. She missed Polly every day, but the grief had subsided to a dull ache most days. It was a back note to her life, but this spike was something new. She completed the file, resolving to avoid marital cases if she could. She preferred missing persons – at least they had some chance of a happy ending.

Her mobile phone buzzed and she saw Magda's name on the screen. She picked it up.

"Hi, Magda."

"Jamie." Her voice was broken with concern. "You have to help. You need to come quickly."

"Of course. What's wrong?"

"O's missing. I went over to her flat to show her the photos from yesterday. She didn't answer the door or her phone, so I let myself in with the spare key. Her bed hadn't been slept in. I don't think she's been back here since we were with her yesterday."

Jamie thought of O's dancing at Torture Garden, and her admission of occasional sex work. O was a beautiful woman and there were plenty of possibilities for where she could be.

"Perhaps she was working?" Jamie said.

"No." Magda was emphatic. "We have a check-in system for when she works. If it's sex work or dancing or anything potentially risky, she texts me. Even when it's something fun and casual, she always lets me know. She wouldn't miss that, Jamie. She knows the lifestyle risks and that's how we manage it." Magda's voice was high-pitched with desperation. "She's been taken, I know it."

"Did you report it to the police?" Jamie asked.

"Yes," Magda said, "but I know they're not taking it seriously."

"It's not really been long enough yet for them to consider it a missing person, but I know some people," Jamie said. "What's the address? I'll be there as fast as possible."

After getting the information, Jamie jumped on her motorbike, weaving through the streets until she reached a Victorian terrace behind a park. Magda stood outside smoking, her fingers shaking as she sucked on the cigarette. Her face was pinched with worry. Bare of makeup, she looked much older.

As Jamie put her helmet in the pannier, Magda wiped a tear from her cheek.

"I keep thinking of Nick's body," she said. "Whoever it was cut his tattoos off. Maybe Milo too. What if they have O?"

Jamie thought of how much of O's perfect body was inked, trying not to imagine her skin covered in blood.

"We'll find her," Jamie said. "Show me the flat and then I can call someone. I still have friends in the police."

Jamie followed Magda up the stairs of the terrace into a second-floor flat. The door opened into a large living and dining space, with one side separated into a tiny kitchen. There was a separate small bedroom and postage-stamp-size bathroom. Framed prints decorated the cream walls, all of sea creatures and dominated by octopi. There were several erotic Japanese prints, clear evidence of the inspiration for the intimacy of her tattoo.

The flat was minimalist, in keeping with O's Japanese interest. A futon with white linen and a red pillow dominated the bedroom. It felt empty, and Jamie was sure that Magda was right. O had not slept here last night.

"Do you know where she was going after her shift at the Kitchen?" Jamie asked. "When I left, she was still there."

Magda shook her head. "She mentioned meeting someone to discuss a potential modeling contract, but it was in a coffee shop somewhere, nothing seedy. Her ink sets her apart and she has photographers flocking to take her picture these days."

Jamie went to the window, looking out at the back of other houses in the area. She called Missinghall.

"Al, it's Jamie. Have you got a minute?"

"This murder case is crazy but of course, I'll help if I can."

"It's about a MISPER, a friend of mine. Olivia Ivorson."

There were sounds of typing as Missinghall searched for any notifications.

"Another one in Southwark." His voice was grim. "It's not a great place to be at the moment, Jamie. When did she go missing?"

"Sometime last night. After ten p.m."

More sounds of typing.

"She's a sex worker by the look of it. She's been cautioned before. Maybe she's out working?"

"I know she isn't, Al. And I'm concerned because she's heavily tattooed."

"It's not unusual these days, Jamie. You know that. Most of bloody London has ink now."

Jamie saw O's perfect body in her mind, the alabaster skin claimed by the octopus that encircled her. Jamie shuddered at the thought of a blade drawn over that flesh.

"You said yourself that Southwark isn't a great place to be right now."

Missinghall sighed. "Look, everyone is focused on the Winchester Palace murder right now, but I'll see what I can do."

"OK, thanks, Al. I'll keep looking this end and I'll text you with any updates."

Jamie ended the call and turned to Magda. "I don't think we're going to get any help from the police at the moment. She's got form."

Magda put her head in her hands, her shoulders slumped in defeat.

"There might be another way," Jamie said. "I have a friend who might be able to help. Do you mind if I call him?"

Magda looked up, a glimmer of hope in her eyes. "Please, anything you think. Maybe he can come over?"

Jamie scrolled through her contacts for Blake's number. Her heart raced a little at the thought of his voice and of seeing him again. They had both been through a lot since the events surrounding the murder of psychiatrist Dr Christian Monro. Jamie had seen Blake at his weakest then, and she knew he still struggled to put the mental torture of what he had seen during that case behind him.

Her own decision to leave the police and start a new life meant she had been busy, and they had both kept away from each other. But Jamie knew it was more to do with an instinctive desire not to be hurt. They were both vulnerable, and there was a spark between them that could devastate them both if they gave into it. She remembered the night she had gone to Blake's flat – the night Polly's body had disappeared. He had been high on tequila and she had wanted to lie down next to him, let him sink into her. But he was dangerous. His gift both frightened and intrigued her, but perhaps now it could help her new friends.

She dialed his number.

"Jamie?"

Blake's voice was smooth, and Jamie couldn't help but smile. She had missed him and from his tone, he was pleased to hear from her.

"Hi, Blake, how are you?"

"Busy prepping for a new exhibition," he said, a smile in his voice. "You know the world of academia never stops its frenetic pace. How's your new business?"

"Actually, that's why I'm calling. There's been a disappearance and I could use some help. Any chance you could come have a look?"

There was a moment of silence, and Jamie could picture Blake's handsome face as he wrestled with the decision. The last time she had asked for his help, Blake had ended up drugged and tortured for his gift by men who intended to break his mind and send him into oblivion. She understood his hesitation.

"Is it a murder?" Blake asked, and Jamie heard a note of trepidation in his voice. She turned away, hoping Magda hadn't heard the words.

"I hope not," she said. "A friend has disappeared and the police investigation will be too slow for my liking. But I'm really worried. There have been other disappearances that haven't ended well round here lately. I could really use your help, Blake."

"Where are you?" he asked.

"Southwark," Jamie said, giving him the address.

"I'll come over in the next hour," Blake said. "Extended lunch break."

***

Blake arrived as Jamie made Magda a fourth cup of tea. O's flat had nothing stronger and Magda didn't even drink anymore. Reformed in so many senses of the word, Magda's strength had seemed boundless, but it was clear from her hunched shoulders and staring eyes how much O meant to her.

The doorbell rang and Jamie went down to open it.

Blake stood in the doorway, two coffees in his gloved hands, his blue eyes bright.

"I figured you could use some," he said. Jamie stretched up to kiss his cheek, her lips brushing his stubble. He smelled of sandalwood soap and she wanted to lean in to him, feel his arms around her.

"It's good to see you," she said, stepping away.

"You too," Blake replied, and his eyes said all she needed to know.

She took one of the coffees.

"Come on up."

They entered the flat and Magda got up to greet Blake. He indicated the coffee.

"Sorry, I didn't know there was someone else here. Would you like my coffee?"

Magda smiled weakly, worry breaking through her resolve. "If you can help with this," she said, shaking her head. "I'll get you all the coffee you need. What can I do to help?"

Jamie knew Blake would be reluctant to talk about his unusual gift with someone he didn't really know.

"To be honest, Magda," she said. "I think maybe you should go and have a rest. O might even show up at your studio for those photos. We'll be here a while."

Magda nodded. "You're right. I should go." She handed over the keys. "Let me know if you find anything, or if you have any questions." She left the flat, her footsteps heavy on the stair, leaving Jamie and Blake alone.

For a moment, the silence lay between them. There was so much to say and yet, none of it really mattered. Jamie knew the attraction between her and Blake was dangerous, and she needed his friendship more than anything. The balance was difficult to manage, but perhaps this time they could walk the tightrope.

"So, what happened?" Blake asked.

Jamie told him about O and the other disappearances in the area, as well as the murder from the night before.

"We're worried about her," Jamie said. "Her tattoo makes her fit the profile of the other victims."

Blake looked around the flat.

"So you want to know where she might be?"

"Anything you can help with really. Perhaps there's something in here that might give us some clues as to where she is."

CHAPTER 10

Blake looked around the small flat, traces of a woman he didn't know yet in the furnishings and pictures on the walls. He usually read objects where the memories of those entwined with them were dead and gone, the civilizations they came from crumbled and fallen. But this woman, Olivia, might come home any minute and it made him anxious.

The last time he had read a living person, it was the day of his father's death. He had seen demons consume the frail body and that had sent him over the edge into his own madness. But that's why he was here. He still owed Jamie for rescuing him from the delirium of the RAIN experiments. If she needed to know what was going on, then he had to help, even if it put his job in jeopardy.

He looked at his watch. He could still get back within the hour if they were quick.

While Jamie began to search the living room area, Blake walked through into O's bedroom and sat down on the futon, looking around the small bedroom for a sense of what O valued most, for what might give him insight into her life.

He looked down to the side of the bed at a low table with a lamp on it. There was a jade greenstone pendant lying there, shaped in a Maori *manaia* design. With the head of a bird, a human body and the tail of a fish, the *manaia* was the messenger of the gods, representing spiritual power and a guide beyond the physical realm. The frayed leather cord tied around the neck of the bird indicated that O wore this often. Something about it called to Blake and he could almost feel the smooth stone in his palm.

He took off his gloves and picked up the pendant with bare hands. The crisscross network of scars didn't prevent him from feeling the coolness of the jade and the contours fitted into his hand perfectly. His heart raced a little in a combination of fear at what might come but also exhilaration at glimpsing into another's world. He closed his eyes and let the visions come.

The mists of memory swirled about him and Blake sensed many emotional threads tied around this one pendant, but there was one that was particularly strong. He let himself sink into that layer of consciousness and opened himself up to the sensation.

He was weightless, floating in a blue-green ocean, experiencing a scuba dive as O had done one day when she had worn the pendant. Blake heard the rhythmic sound of her deep breathing through the regulator, watched the bubbles float away and, for a moment, he understood why people craved time underwater.

He could feel O's calm, her almost meditative state as she finned above a rocky bottom. It was cool and he could feel the thickness of the wetsuit she wore. These were temperate waters, not a warm coral paradise. Mats of thick kelp covered the walls and rocks around, swaying in the surge. Wrasse in shades of purple and green darted in and away, curious of the diver, while blue two-spot demoiselles clustered in the shelter of the kelp.

O leaned forward, tipping over to descend, exhaling to

empty her lungs. Her buoyancy control was natural and her body relaxed, as if she were part of this aquatic realm, unhindered by the heaviness of the gear she wore. A hole in the rocks appeared as she descended and she finned towards it, heading into a sea cave.

It was dark inside but Blake sensed no fear in her. She added a little air and then floated, neutrally buoyant.

Blake felt another presence, something substantial, something powerful. His eyes adjusted to the dark and shapes appeared in the cave. There were boulders on the bottom, lumps of grey stone covered in soft coral, big-eye fish clustering at the edges of view. Something stirred in the shadows and then moved towards them in the water. O's excitement was palpable but she stayed motionless, waiting for it to come closer.

The octopus ascended, its tentacles hanging below, curling slowly in the water. It was large and covered in nodules, its bulbous head as big as a watermelon. Its eyes were pools of black in the semi-darkness but Blake sensed an intelligence and a curiosity for the creature who entered its territory. It glided past towards the cave entrance and O turned to watch it silhouetted against the light, following slowly after. Its movement was mesmerizing, each tentacle a separate dexterous limb twisting in the blue.

It swam out of the cave and O emerged after it, eyes fixed on its strange beauty. It was inescapably alien, a body with no backbone that could squeeze into the tiniest hole and yet, out here, it was glorious. Blake tried to fix the moment in his mind, the sun shining down through the water patterning on the octopus' skin as it turned in the water to examine the diver in the light. The second stretched on and Blake felt the connection, understood why O was so fascinated with the creature. It was wild and free in this wide ocean, something a human could never be.

The sound of a boat engine rumbled through the water and the octopus shot away incredibly fast, all eight tentacles thrusting, turning its body into a torpedo that sped out of sight. Blake felt O's loss at its disappearance, the moment broken, perhaps never to be repeated. As the intensity of the experience dropped away, the mists of memory began to swirl about him and he reached for tendrils of pain associated with the pendant that were bound to another time and place.

As he fixed on the new vision, it crystallized into a tattoo studio. O lay on her back, the pain intense as the tattoo artist inked a tentacle on the skin under her exposed breast. The man looked up, his brown skin marked with a full facial Maori moko.

"Just say the word, O, and we can take a break."

"I can do another ten minutes," she said, clenching her fists. "We've got to finish it. I'm moving to Europe as soon as we're done."

"I'm going to miss my finest work," the man said, bending his head again. "But maybe I'll see you at the tattoo convention sometime. I've heard they have a good one in London."

The buzz of the tattoo machine started again and Blake could feel the nuances of pain as it inked O's skin. There was a sense of being fully present in her body, a crossing over into a place where thought was secondary to physical sensation. It was an initiation of sorts, where pain represented the crossing of a threshold into a new world. Once crossed, there was no way to remove the mark.

Blake understood now why O wanted to have the octopus on her skin. It represented camouflage and the ability to transform its body in movement. It was grace and intelligence and, ultimately, escape. It had marked her that day in the sea cave and now it would mark her skin until death parted them.

That thought ripped Blake from the vision, for he felt no sense of O's end in the strings of memory. He didn't really understand what the visions meant or how they worked, but he had learned to trust his instinct. O was alive – at least for now.

***

Blake pulled his hand from the pendant and sat for a moment, breathing deeply as he reoriented himself to the surroundings. He looked up at the Japanese octopus print on the wall and smiled. The vision he had seen was a privilege, a glimpse into a world he might never see with his own eyes. Sometimes his psychic ability was a curse, to be drowned in tequila until he could no longer feel. But this was a glimpse into something wonderful, and now he felt such a connection with O that he was determined to help Jamie find her.

He stood up and went back into the living area. Jamie flicked through a pile of papers on a bookshelf and looked up as he came in.

"Find anything?" she asked, then frowned. "Are you OK? You look pale."

Blake held up the pendant. "I read this and at least now I understand her obsession with octopi. I had a brief tattoo experience, as well."

Jamie raised her eyebrows. Blake knew she had been skeptical at first, doubting the veracity of his visions. But after the last two cases they had been involved in, she accepted what he discovered without need for further explanation.

"Did you see anything that could help us find her?"

Blake shook his head. "Nothing concrete, but I think it would make sense to connect with the tattoo community in London. Her ink had deep meaning for her and might bring us closer to finding out where she was last night. Her tattoo artist was Maori and I think I'd recognize him if I saw him again."

Jamie shuffled through the papers on the desk. She held up a printed flier for the London Tattoo Convention and smiled.

"This is a multi-day event and it went on late into last night. Maybe O was there? We could head over now and see what we can find out. Can you spare the time?"

Blake thought of the caution that lay on his desk back at the British Museum, of Margaret's stern expression. He should get back and spend the rest of the day in research. But when he was with Jamie, his craving for alcohol lessened and surely the focus on finding O, a living woman, was more important that investigating those dead and gone.

"I'll file the time under research," he said, with a smile.

***

The Tobacco Dock was an early nineteenth-century warehouse of sturdy brick and ironwork that had once housed imported tobacco. It was in that part of East London described as 'up and coming,' still underdeveloped and affordable but on the edge of turning fashionable. It wouldn't be long before the artists had to move even further out of the city.

"I've thought about getting a tattoo, you know," Jamie said as she and Blake entered the gates into the venue. "I can't decide what I'd want to have done though." She thought of Polly and how her daughter would have liked to help choose the design. There were so many possibilities. But in the end, Jamie knew that her own body carried the memory of her child, her own flesh and blood now turned to dust.

"I'm considering it too," Blake said, pulling Jamie from her thoughts. "When I read O's pendant, I had a glimpse of what ink meant to her and why the octopus is her totem. I'm convinced there will be people here we can ask about her."

The venue separated into several spaces around open courtyards overlooked by a second tier of rooms. There were booths hung with flash, tattoo art displaying the style of the artist from traditional naval styles to curly feminine floral motifs, Chinese dragons and darker tribal marks. A rock band played to a lively crowd, overlaying the sound of buzzing from the tattoo machines. There was sizzling from the barbeques and the smell of roasting meat, hot chips and coffee hung in the air.

A generation ago, there would have been stereotype attendees to these type of events – fat and balding Hell's Angel types, gang members, sailors and prostitutes. A freak show of outcasts, considered deviant by decent people. But now the crowd was mixed, beautiful young women wandering amongst middle-aged rebels sipping Pinot Grigio, and, of course, a healthy dose of leather-clad men, from male model to grandfather. Some art was discreet, a single image on a patch of skin. But others had gone all in, art personified, their bodies a canvas of meaning.

A man walked past wearing plain black jeans and boots, the simplicity setting off his bare torso. There was no patch of skin unmarked by dense tattoos, the images ranging from the head of the Devil at his navel, to a huge dragon around his ribs that wrapped into steampunk wings on his back. His head was shaven and his skull and face were tattooed in strong black geometric shapes.

"With so many inked bodies and tattoo artists, how are we going to find those connected to O?" Blake wondered aloud.

They continued walking through the maze of booths. The buzz of tattoo machines was a soothing backdrop, like bees on a summer's day. Many of the clients lay relaxed under the skilled hands of the artists, trusting their skin to strangers.

"Why do you think tattoos have become so popular these days?" Jamie asked, as they stopped to watch one artist ink script into a man's shaven skull.

"Marking skin is nothing new," Blake said. "The oldest human bodies found in glaciers have tattoos, showing allegiance to a tribe or gang, or to God. Perhaps that's the point. We've lost that sense of meaning in our secular society so we go through ritual behavior in the ultimate pursuit of individualization. Tattoos are only the start – I've read that there's also a rise in piercings, scarification, branding and implants."

Jamie thought of Rowan Day-Conti's extreme body modification from the Jenna Neville case, and his obsession with how the body could be used in life as well as in death. He had been her first connection to O.

The rock music finished and the roar of the crowd subsided. In the brief lull, Jamie heard music that reminded her of the night at the Torture Garden when she had seen O dance.

"This way," she said, heading off in the direction of the music, through the crowds of people as Blake tried to keep up.

CHAPTER 11

THEY EMERGED ON THE second floor overlooking a stage area with a raised dais and a pole that stretched up to the ceiling. A mixed-race woman in a leather bikini hung upside down and as she spun around, Jamie saw her back was a tattooed garden of exotic flowers that curled and bloomed across her skin. It was beautiful, complementing her curves and, judging by the flash of cameras in the audience, much appreciated.

Blake's eyes were fixed on the dancer as she slid around the pole in an acrobatic and sensual display of strength and flexibility. Jamie understood his fascination, because the woman was stunning. She knew that her own release came in tango. She wondered if Blake would look at her like that if she danced for him. But that was a side of her life that she kept private – for now at least.

The music finished and the dancer stepped off the dais to be mobbed by fans asking her to sign photos. Jamie found it interesting that most of these fans were women, many in plain clothes. Perhaps they wanted to find the courage to expose themselves as she did, to ink their skin and be proud of their bodies.

They finally made it to the front of the queue and Jamie introduced herself and Blake.

"We're looking for a friend of ours who has gone missing," she said. "You might know her as O. She has a –"

"Octopus tattoo," the woman said, cutting off Jamie's words. "I know her. She was meant to be here today, part of our performance team, but she didn't show up. There are plenty of girls ready to take her place but she was missed by the fans. She has quite the following from Torture Garden."

"Do you know if her tattooist is here?" Blake asked. He smiled and Jamie watched as the woman melted in the face of his charm. She had to admit that a tiny part of her was jealous, but if they could use his good looks to find O, it was worth it.

The woman leaned closer.

"He is here, actually. All the way from New Zealand. I'm on my break now, so I could take you to him and maybe show you around a bit." She brushed her hair back from her face and touched Blake's arm, looking up into his eyes. "I'm Minx, by the way."

Of course you are, Jamie thought, managing to keep quiet as Blake accepted her offer of help.

Minx led them through a central area reserved for artists engaged in more traditional tattoo methods. A Polynesian man used a small hammer to drive a stick into a man's shoulder. Each stroke was deliberate and the man underneath looked as if he was barely coping with the pain. Yet he remained unmoving, determined to go through this initiation as generations before him had done.

"The word tattoo comes from *tatau* in the Polynesian language," Minx said. "It means to strike and mimics the sound of the hammer hitting the stick. Modern tattooing uses machines, of course. They can do far more pricks per minute than tattooing by hand, but it's all so clinical these days."

Winding through the halls, Minx stopped at a booth

dedicated to implants. The walls were covered with objects that could be put under the skin. The man running the booth had a row of beads in his skull, raised bumps like a dinosaur spine. A raised cross implant with bulbous ends sat in the middle of his bare chest, skull tattoos erupting with flame on his pectoral muscles.

"Hey Zee, d'you know where Tem Makaore's stall is?"

Zee turned and his eyes were kind, soft brown like a puppy and Jamie instinctively warmed to him, despite his unusual looks. He bent to kiss Minx's cheek and smiled at Jamie and Blake.

"He's down the back of the vaults 'cos he booked late."

Jamie leaned closer to examine some of the items on show. There were different sizes of horn from little bumps to several inches, as well as thin batons and rings. Zee noticed her interest.

"Skin is remarkable," he said. "You can stretch it over things and it will accommodate. So you can embed a small object at first, a round marble, for example, and the skin will stretch around it. Over time, you replace the small object with a larger one. Or you can have silicone injected to stretch it slowly into shape."

Blake pointed at a row of long metal spikes for skull implants.

"How can you possibly sleep with those in?" he asked.

Zee smiled at the question, keen to talk about his art. "The implants in the skull are actually metallic studs so the spikes can be attached by day and removed at night."

"That's pretty cool," Blake said. "Not sure how well it would go down at the office though."

"People are trying all kinds of things these days," Zee said. "Braille implants for example, to enable blind people to enjoy body modification. There's also a rise in magnetic finger implants which act like another sense. The wearer can feel magnetic fields, from portable electronics to invisible magnetic fields. Split tongues are requested more in these days as dragons have seen a resurgence in interest.

"Ultimately, I'm a skin artist, and the bodies I work with are temples to my god. I create the implants that result in a changed shape. I carve away excess flesh to leave an artwork behind. I restructure to create." He pointed at a photo of an ear reshaped into that of a cat. "Individuation is the point. To be set apart from mundanity. I mean, look at our developed world. How many people are trapped in lives of quiet desperation? I help people escape that through embracing their power. I match the outer body to the inner vision of self."

"It's fascinating," Jamie said. "I hope we have time to come back later."

They walked away from the stall, heading down the stairs towards the vaults.

"Zee's lover died a few years back," Minx said as they descended. "He had the ashes put into that hollow cross and implanted them over his heart."

Her tone was respectful, both of his choice to implant and his method of remembrance. Jamie understood that need to have the dead so close they could not be forgotten, even for an instant. Ashes could be made into glass and diamonds now, turned into tribute jewelry. She had also heard that they could be mixed with ink and used in a tattoo. That thought actually appealed to Jamie. Polly had understood the attraction of the macabre and would have laughed about it.

The vaults level had an eclectic range of stalls ranging from tattoo inks and equipment to a cabinet-of-curiosities shop, selling animal skulls, taxidermy, and art made from human teeth. The buzzing of her cellphone caught Minx's attention and as she answered, she pointed Jamie and Blake towards the back of the vaults, waving them away.

"Maybe you can say goodbye after her next show,"

Jamie said with a smile as they walked down the corridor.

"I don't think I could keep up with her," Blake grinned. "This place is amazing, though. I keep wondering how much of this will end up in the British Museum eventually, part of British civilization in the twenty-first century. Future academics will be musing over the tribal markings and obscure implants from this age, as they do over ancient peoples."

Several booths hung with Maori and Polynesian designs sat in the corner of the vaults, the distinctive use of white space highlighted in bold black to create *koru* spirals and geometric shapes. It was quieter down here, the sound of the bands muted by thick walls and flooring.

Three men stood near one of the booths, drinking bottles of beer. They turned as Jamie and Blake approached, their faces marked by tribal tattoos, their body language aggressive. Jamie took a deep breath.

CHAPTER 12

"We're looking for Tem Makaore," Jamie said, although Blake was clearly looking at one of the men more intently. He had distinctive facial moko, the blue-black ink curving around his chin and jawline, bisecting his nose with geometric shapes, sweeping up from his eyes like the wings of the dawn. His lips were fully tattooed and the fierce markings made him look like a warrior from another time, incongruous against his black t-shirt and jeans. Jamie had a fleeting desire to see if the ink continued on the rest of his tightly muscled body.

"I'm Tem," the man said, his face breaking into a smile. The warrior persona dropped away. "Kia ora. What can I do for you?"

"A friend of ours, O, is missing. We wondered if you'd seen her?"

Tem frowned.

"Of course, I know O. I'm super proud of her ink and I don't get to do such extensive work too often. We met for a drink last night about eight and she was meant to come by today, but I haven't seen her since then."

"We're worried about her," Jamie said. "Did she tell you anything about where she was going after you met?"

"No, but I wouldn't expect her to. But she wanted to

talk about new ink, which means something has happened in her life. Something has changed. You see, the soul can't speak in words." Tem smiled, his eyes wistful, and Jamie wondered at the bond between tattoo artist and the skin he worked on. "The soul can only speak in symbols and patterns and every person will choose something different. Or, if they choose the same symbol, the meaning will be different."

"What did she want done?" Jamie asked.

Tem gestured for them to come closer and see some of the designs on the wall of the booth.

"She only had vague ideas and it's bad etiquette to ask the meaning of someone's tattoo," he said. "It's possible that the person themselves won't know what it really means." He pointed to his facial moko. "To try and put these markings into words will lessen their power. But you have to understand that to tattoo or modify your body is to embrace the shadow side of yourself. That's why many can't do it.

"Most people cannot bear to look into that darker side, preferring to keep the mask of normality. But to repress the shadow for too long will mean it eventually has to escape in other ways. Into compulsions, into chaos." Tem looked at Jamie, his dark brown eyes as tangled as an ancient wood. She saw secret things hidden in those depths, a glimpse of an older world. "I think O's octopus has been dominant for too long and to change, she has to ink something new. But I can't tell you what. She wanted to know how long I was in town as we'd need several sessions. But she was ready to walk through the fire again."

Jamie tilted her head to one side, his words puzzling her. "What do you mean by that?"

Tem pointed at the tattooing instrument on the bench. "That is for pain but also for change. After all, nothing worth doing is entirely painless. Friendships fade, marriages break apart, families splinter, but your body is yours until the end. What you do to it will be with you every day until you breathe your last. So you mark your skin to mark the path through the fire of life, and after the change is complete, the wound is bandaged and you can heal."

A picture on the wall drew Jamie's eye. A woman stood side on, her arm lifted to reveal a tattoo that opened up the inside of her body as if she were clockwork. Behind broken ribs, cogs and wheels turned, pistons pumped and over them lay a network of bones and skin. It was a macabre optical illusion of a steampunk hybrid. Next to her was a woman with blonde hair, her dark eyes staring into the camera from a face of blue and purple swirls, her whole body encased in ink.

"She was born with a skin condition," Tem said, noticing Jamie's gaze. "Her skin blistered and scarred so she started tattooing as a way to claim her skin back. If people were going to stare anyway, she decided to have them stare for good reason. This is the outward expression of her inner self, an alchemy of her physical curse and the archetypes within her mind. We are embodied souls, after all."

"What happens at the end?" Jamie asked, thinking of the implant of ashes they had seen upstairs. She pointed at Tem's heavily tattooed forearms. "When your body dies, is that the end of the meaning to the images?"

Tem looked serious. "In my culture, yes." He nodded. "The spirit lives on, but after death the body is buried, returned to *Papatuanuku*, Mother Earth." Tem paused for a moment. "But others revere the physical form. I've heard of specialists in skin preservation, those who work with the bodies of the dead to keep tats for family or gang affiliation. I've also heard rumors of a skin trade, a black market for inked skin. Fetishists mostly." He shook his head. "But after what I've put onto people's bodies, nothing surprises me these days."

Jamie thought of the missing and the dead so far. All were inked.

"Do you know where we could find someone like that in London?" she asked.

Tem shook his head. "Really not my thing. I prefer live bodies to work with, skin I have permission to ink." Tem pointed along the corridor. "Go see the taxidermists. They have their own little community." Tem looked at Jamie, meeting her eyes. "And come and see me when you make your decision about what you want inked."

Jamie blushed under his gaze, wondering what it would feel like to have his strong hands inking her skin. Part of her wanted to find out.

"Thanks for your help," Blake said, breaking the moment. He shook Tem's hand. "We really appreciate it."

They walked away from Tem's stand towards a corner of the convention hidden amongst the arches. Here were the cabinet-of-curiosity shops where strange objects were sold alongside herbal remedies, and taxidermists displayed their wares. The people who sat on the stalls generally wore black, many were tattooed, and Jamie wondered at the crossover between the groups. Was it a fascination with death or just with skin?

They walked around, trying to get a sense of who to speak to. One stall displayed beetles and spiders, butterflies and frogs pinned on boards, their remains spread out for viewing. The vibrant colors of the shiny carapaces and wetness of the skin made them look like they had recently been caught and mounted. Jamie was reminded of Damien Hirst's *Last Kingdom* piece, which placed dead insects in exact rows, a rainbow of colors of the dead. Was it all just *memento mori*, Jamie wondered, to help us remember that we are all animated dust waiting to return to the earth?

Blake wandered over to an area with pieces of furniture that had been modified to incorporate taxidermy animals. He bent to a red wingback chair to examine two young foxes, stuffed as if they were playing and mounted into the hollow back. Jamie turned to another stall nearby.

It had animal heads mounted on wooden bases, but they weren't in the style of hunting lodges where old men boasted of their kill. These heads were embellished with colorful beads and jeweled flowers, embroidered silk and ribbons. Each piece turned the animal into a celebration of life. Jamie stopped to look more closely and a young woman came out from behind the table. Her hair was ash blonde, tied back from her pale face with a garland of flowers. Her eyes were intelligent, slightly wary, as if she expected criticism for her work.

"Hi," she said, her voice timid. "Can I help you?"

"These are beautiful," Jamie said, and she found herself meaning it. The initial revulsion of these dead bodies had been replaced by fascination for the beauty of the objects.

"Thank you," the young woman said. "I mostly make custom taxidermy for collections and private museums, but my passion is turning the dead into flower gardens." She pointed at a deer's head. "And of course, no animals are ever killed for the purpose. I only use roadkill."

Jamie thought of this young woman walking along the edge of a quiet road in the countryside, waiting to stumble upon dead animals.

Blake wandered back over from the chairs to join the conversation.

"Can I ask what your fascination is with taxidermy?" he asked. His attention made the young woman bloom a little. Her eyes darted away from his handsome face and back again. *Must be tough to get a date when your house is full of dead animals*, Jamie thought.

"Ultimately, it's about respect for the animal and for life itself," the young woman said, her voice growing stronger as she talked. "You can get closer to it than you ever could in life. I study anatomy so I can get the dimensions right and make sure the muscle shapes are clear. And it's also art, creating something that will make people think. Perhaps it's the ultimate blend of science and art, chemistry and sculpture."

"Is there much of a community in London?" Blake asked.

The young woman nodded enthusiastically. "Oh yes, we have meetups and classes. It's quite a scene. The tattoo conventions mostly have a section for us as well, so we get to meet new people all the time."

"We're looking for someone," Jamie said. "He – or she – works with human tattooed skin, preserving it after death. Do you know of anyone like that?"

"There is a man …" The young woman hesitated, her eyes guarded. "He doesn't really advertise but I've been to his place once – a while ago. He might not be there anymore."

"We'd really like to try and track him down," Blake said. "Can you give us his address?"

"It's more of a squat than a residential place," she replied. "Out by Limehouse Cut."

Jamie pulled out her smartphone and opened a map application. The young woman showed her an approximate area.

***

As they walked out of the convention, Blake turned to Jamie.

"That place was not what I expected, but it makes me want to mark my skin." He touched his gloved hands together gently. "With something more than scars." He thought about the runes in the Galdrabók, how they would look on his caramel skin. Would inking them on his body help him to claim their power or perhaps even tame his curse? He looked at Jamie. "What about you?"

"When we came in here, I was still unsure. But now I have a clearer idea. I want birds on the wing." Jamie touched her neck on the right side. "Maybe here, down my shoulder onto my back."

"Escape? Freedom?" Blake said, thinking that tattoos on Jamie's skin would also be damn sexy. "A desire to transcend this physical life, perhaps?"

Jamie grinned. "It's rude to ask the meaning of someone's tattoo."

"Even one that doesn't exist yet?"

They walked to Jamie's bike and she pulled a second helmet from her pannier. "Can you come?" she asked, offering it to him.

Blake hesitated. Every hour he was away from the museum was another nail in the coffin of his research career. He looked down into Jamie's hazel eyes and saw that she needed him. Her friend was missing and perhaps he could still help find her.

"Of course I'm coming," he said. "I work in the museum with a load of mummified remains. I can't miss out on meeting a real-life skin preserver."

CHAPTER 13

THIRTY MINUTES LATER, BLAKE shook his head as he pulled off the motorbike helmet, running his gloved fingers over his buzz cut.

"That is too much fun," he said, handing the helmet back to Jamie. "Even if I have to ride pillion."

"One of the pleasures of life," Jamie said. "Not really enough open road around London though."

She looked up at the sixties concrete block in front of them. It had been a technical college once, later abandoned and now inhabited by an eclectic group of artists, many of whom also lived in the building. Some might call them squatters but in this part of East London, turning a derelict building into something this productive was akin to a miracle. Rejuvenation of the old Docklands was happening slowly and the artists were often the first to move in.

"Nice place," Blake said with raised eyebrows as he stepped gingerly over a bare needle on the broken concrete path.

"Let's take a look inside," Jamie said.

She pushed open the front door to reveal a neglected corridor strewn with the detritus of people living rough. Cardboard boxes and string, a folded blanket and old tins of beans. It smelled of stale sweat and sweet marijuana smoke. Music thumped through the building and they followed the noise along the corridor to the back of the structure. It had a deafening bass that Jamie recognized as "Closer" by Nine Inch Nails. A hymn to finding God in desecration and violation, a song to bring alive the crazy in anyone. A song she remembered playing as a teenager bent on escaping a mundane existence, desperate for something more than suburbia. Strange to hear it again here.

A metal door barred their way. Jamie rapped on it, but there was no chance that anyone would hear them inside with that racket. She pushed at the door but it was firmly locked from the inside. She hammered with her fist as the song came to an end, but no one came to let them in. The bass kicked in on the next song and their knocking was drowned out once more.

"Let's go round the outside," Jamie said, and they walked back out.

The building was on the edge of the Limehouse Cut, a waterway that ran from the River Lea down to the Thames. The sun sparkled on the slow-moving water, bringing a moment of beauty to this urban junkyard.

"Come look at this," Blake said, as he walked towards the side of the building. A ramshackle houseboat was tied up there, its moorings rusted and weed-covered from its long-term berth. He pointed at the name of the boat, the paint chipped and faded but still clearly visible.

"Pyx?" Jamie said. "I don't get it."

"It's one of the oldest doors in Westminster Abbey," Blake said. "Anglo-Saxon and over a thousand years old. What's more interesting is that it has panels of skin upon it that some believe were from the bodies of flayed criminals, left there as a warning to those who would attack the church."

They walked along the narrow path behind the building. Huge windows dominated the back section and a door stood open a little further on. A man stood on the back step blowing smoke rings into the air, his eyes closed in bliss as the bassline pumped from the studio behind him. He was tall and thin, his body held with the slumped posture of one who worked hunched over most of the time and often had to bend in the presence of others. His limbs were long and gangly, as if he had never had the nutrition to help him grow into them. His skin was pale, his head closely shaven and smooth, reflecting the sun.

His eyes flicked open at their approach and he quickly stubbed out the cigarette.

"Please wait," Jamie shouted, waving at him.

The man stepped inside the studio and Jamie ran to the open door, reaching it as he tried to force it closed. She wedged her foot into the crack.

"Please," she shouted above the music. "We only want to talk to you."

"I don't have anything here. No money, no drugs," the man pleaded, his face desperate as he tried to push Jamie out. Blake stood behind her.

"We're not here to take anything," he said. "We're looking for a friend and we heard you could help."

"I'm a private investigator on a missing persons case," Jamie added. "Please just talk with us for a second."

The man's features softened as he realized they weren't there to steal from him. Jamie could understand his anxiety in this part of town.

"Alright," he said, moving back from the door. "Let me turn the music off."

Jamie and Blake stood by the door as the music quietened and the man returned.

"Great album," Jamie said. "I always loved Trent Reznor."

"Forgive me, I don't get too many visitors in this part of town. Most are here looking to score." He took a deep breath. "I'm Corium Jones." The man's features softened and he held out a hand. The skin was red and raw with evident chemical burns but Jamie shook it without flinching, meeting his eyes as she did so.

"I'm Jamie Brooke and this is Blake Daniel."

"What can I help you with?" Corium asked.

"We were at the tattoo convention," Jamie said, "and heard that you provide an unusual service for those with body art."

Corium nodded, a wry smile on his lips.

"Yes, people pay me to preserve their tattoos after death," he said. "It's a growing industry. After all, they may have paid thousands to emblazon their skin with meaning in life and so they want to pass that on somehow. Their lifetime stories are inked into their skin, and they don't want it to rot away. They can't imagine the worms devouring it, or the fire consuming it. Skin preservation is an ancient art with few of us left. And, of course, much misunderstood."

"Can we have a look?" Jamie asked, glancing behind him into the dark of the studio.

Corium paused and Jamie felt the intensity of his gaze as he assessed her and Blake. Perhaps he sensed the death around them both, because after a moment, he stepped aside and waved them in.

The room had several workbenches with tools lined up neatly on one side. There was a vat of salt in one corner and a skin pegged out on a frame in the shade of an open window, the faint blue lines of a tattoo barely visible on the opposite side.

The smell of chemical preservative hung in the air, reminding Jamie of the studio of Rowan Day-Conti, the artist who had worked with the plastination of dead bodies. She shuddered when she remembered how the Jenna Neville case had ended for Rowan, trying to keep an open mind about what they might find here.

"How does your service actually work?" Jamie asked. "Do you cut from the bodies directly?"

Corium laughed. "I don't deal in bodies, only in skin. My clients pay for services, the skin arrives, usually rough cut in medical boxes. I prepare it, mount it as directed and then return it to the specified address. There's actually no personal contact – except with the skin, of course."

He stepped to a bench and indicated a piece of what looked like leather.

"This one is ready for mounting." He stroked the edge of it, his face showing pride in his work. "You can touch it if you like. It's very soft. Young skin, I think."

"So you don't actually know where the skin comes from?" Blake asked.

"Not at all," Corium said. "It's not my job to ask, either. I merely act as the preserver."

Jamie shook her head slowly. The man's words seemed logical in one way, and he was just a leather worker of a kind. But how could he touch these skins and not feel that they were once a thinking human?

"Can I ask what body parts you work on?" she asked.

Corium went to a row of shelves and pulled out one of the large photo albums stacked there. He laid it on the table and flicked it open.

"These are some of my favorite works," he said, a note of pride in his voice. He turned the first page. "These are the most common. Full-back tattoos which result in a rectangular finished piece, or two longer panels, depending on how close to the spine the skin was excised. There are also cross shapes where the shoulder and arm pieces have been saved."

Jamie swallowed her revulsion as she looked down at

the pages, but the pictures were artistic, the skin turned into something beautiful. There was incredible skill in the ink and the colors: a waving riot of flowers that seemed to grow across the skin with blooming roses and curlicues in a feminine design.

A gigantic pair of strong angel wings, each feather inked in detail, the size of the skin indicating it came from a large man.

A tiger prowling through a verdant jungle, its eyes staring out at the viewer.

There were quotes, too. In one, calligraphic handwriting flowed across the skin: *I'm the hero of this story. I don't need to be saved.* It seemed terribly sad that the hero was no more.

"Then there are the full-sleeve tattoos which result in a long tapering shape," Corium continued. "Very pleasing to the eye."

He indicated a lion's head in profile, its mane rippling over what had been muscles in life. A school of hammerhead sharks swimming over a submerged ancient city.

A list of coordinates with passport pictures and snapshots of faraway places.

A kaleidoscope of galaxies and stars in hues of cobalt blue, luminous greens and pinks.

The variation was incredible and Jamie could see how preserving these works of art was as much of a skill as inking them.

"I also have a number of head tattoos, which are more or less oval in shape, although it can be hard to get the edges right on those. They're the main ones," Corium raised his eyebrows, "but now and then I get some more intimate parts. Quite unusual, I must say."

Jamie looked at the shelf of photo albums.

"How long have you been doing this?" she asked.

"Since I was a child," Corium said, and the look in his eyes spoke of the deep loneliness of the misfit. "It started with taxidermy of small animals and tanning of found hides, but then one day a dying friend asked me to help preserve a part of himself and I couldn't say no. My reputation spread in the tattoo community and here in London these days there's no shortage of preservation work. There are also people who are willing to pay a lot of money for human leather products, from unmarked and inked skin."

Corium ran a hand across his smooth head. "I want ink myself of course, but I suffer from the tyranny of choice. After all, I have all these examples of fine art and I can't decide what I want on my own canvas. We have such a small amount of space and to get it wrong would be ..." He shook his head and sighed. "Well, I can't abide the thought that my own legacy would be inferior to the skins I work on all day."

While Corium spoke, Jamie could see that Blake had wandered down to the far end of the studio to a tall bookcase. He bent more closely to look at the books, and then turned to call back to them.

"Could you tell us about this particular book?"

Corium's head snapped round and his eyes narrowed. He had the look of a man who would protect his domain at any cost.

"It's an early edition of Francis Galton's *Hereditary Genius*. For a very private client." His voice was cold as he stalked down the studio, Jamie following close behind.

The shelves were mostly filled with photography books of tattoos and body art, with others on taxidermy and skin preservation. But one shelf had a thin book bound in soft leather. The pattern inked on the skin looked like dragon scales in hues of purple.

"Is it bound in human skin?" Blake asked.

"Anthropomorphic bibliopegy is a great tradition," Corium said. "Anatomy texts bound in the skin of cadavers, judicial proceedings bound in the skin of murderers –"

"Lampshades made from the skin of murdered Jews …" Blake whispered, looking more closely at the books. "Where do you draw the line?" He turned back to look at them and Jamie saw his blue eyes were steel-hard. "May I touch them?"

It wasn't a question. Corium nodded slowly. Blake removed one of his gloves and reached out to touch the book.

CHAPTER 14

Blake could sense vibrations on the surface of the skin through his fingertips, as if it held within itself the energy from the dead soul it had once bound in flesh. The veil of consciousness clouded his vision and he dipped into memory.

He found himself in a basement with high ceilings, the walls and floor tiled so they could be more easily hosed down. There was a copper smell in the cool air, the bitterness of blood. Empty meat hooks hung in a line on a railing above. There was an animal shriek in the darkness, a sound of terror that echoed through the empty space. Blake shuddered and tried to move, but the body he could see through was chained to the wall and couldn't escape.

He heard footsteps coming towards him and a whimper of fear echoed in the basement. He wanted to pull out of the trance, but he needed to see who was there. A man came out of the darkness, a skinning knife in his hand, his face obscured by the mask of the plague doctor, hooked beak swaying as he approached.

As panic escalated, Blake pulled himself from the trance, ripping his hand away from the book and collapsing to the floor. His breath came fast, his chest heaving as he tried to calm himself.

"It's OK, Blake," Jamie whispered, stroking his forehead. "You're safe now."

She gave him some water and he sipped at it, slowly recovering his breath. Corium Jones stood looking at them, his eyes narrowed in interest but not judgement or doubt. Blake supposed that the man was used to the odd in his line of work. But how much did he know of the provenance of the skin he worked on?

"The skin was taken," Blake said after a moment. "This person was murdered for it but the man who did it hid his face. He wore one of those Venetian plague doctor masks with the long beak for herbs to prevent the smell and decay from reaching them."

"Do you have some kind of psychic ability?" Corium asked, fascination in his voice.

Blake stood up and put his glove back on.

"You could call it that," he said. "I can read the emotional resonance of objects."

Jamie pointed at the book. "Who gave you this skin?" she asked, her voice soft but insistent.

"I can't possibly divulge information about my clients," Corium said, turning to walk away from them towards the door. "I think it's time for you to leave now."

Blake took a quick step forward, his blue eyes blazing with anger.

"Don't you understand? This skin is from a murder victim."

"You have no evidence of that," Corium said, pulling open the door.

Jamie picked up a vial of chemicals from a bench next to the bookcase. She put the book of human skin next to it.

"What does this do?" she asked, waving the bottle. Corium's face fell as she pulled the stopper out and held it over the book.

Corium put his hands up in a gesture of supplication.

"No, please. That will burn the skin. It will ruin the book."

There was fear in his eyes, whether for the object itself or the person he made it for, Jamie didn't know. She tipped the bottle a little, splashing the bench next to the book. It made a sizzling sound and the smell of bitter berries filled the air.

"No!" Corium shouted, rushing across the room. Blake stepped in front of Jamie and pushed the man back, a rough shove in the middle of his thin chest.

"Tell us who the client is," Jamie said, holding the bottle over the book again.

Corium's body drooped, his shoulders slumping in defeat.

"I'll give you what I know," he said. "But it's not much." He walked to a filing cabinet in the corner and pulled out a thin cardboard file. "Here, that's everything. Now please, leave the book alone."

Blake checked the file quickly and nodded to Jamie. She put the stopper back in the bottle and put it down next to the book on the bench. Corium rushed to it, cradling the book to his chest like a precious child as he sank to the floor, sitting with his back to the bench as he watched them with hollow eyes.

Jamie pulled out the pages in the file. "There are regular payments here," she said with surprise. "How many of these have you done?"

"Six so far," Corium whispered. "But it's an ongoing contract. I'm expecting more skin in the next day or so and then I produce a book within the following month."

"There's barely any useful information here," she said. "Just a PO Box for the return address."

Blake pointed to the bottom of the page. "But the book is overdue for delivery, so maybe we can stake out the pickup?"

They turned back to Corium.

"Package it up," Jamie said. "We'll deliver it for you."

He clutched it to his chest.

"You don't understand," he said softly. "This is not a man you want to meet in person. He's not someone I want to cross, either. Please, don't do this."

Jamie walked over to him. "A friend of ours is missing," she said. "I don't want to see her skin on your bench." She held out her hands for the book. "If you won't package it, then I will. But we're taking the book."

Corium clutched it tighter. "He'll know if the package is done incorrectly," he whispered, his eyes darting around the room. "If you must take it, I'll do it for you."

He stood and placed the book gently on the bench, preparing the package and wrapping it in bubble wrap, then brown paper. A normal-looking parcel hiding a macabre object inside.

"There." He handed it to Jamie, his voice cold. "Now, get out."

"Gladly," Blake said, as they walked to the door and back out into the sunlight. Corium slammed the door behind them as they headed back along the Cut. Jamie held the package carefully in both hands.

"Did you get any sense of the person when you read?" she asked.

Blake shook his head. "Only the sheer terror of being chained up in what looked like an old abattoir – and the knowledge that the end was coming." He sighed. "I've felt that before. It's anticipation of the inevitable, but of course, those I read have not gone quietly or at peace."

"I'm sorry I involved you in this."

Blake reached out and pulled her to him. They stood for a moment in the sunlight, Blake's arms wrapped around her. Jamie relaxed into him, relishing the moment of connection.

"I'm not sorry," he said. "I want to help you, Jamie. And now I want to help O, too. The research I do at the museum doesn't change anything, but with you, I have the chance to make an impact on the living." He pulled away a little, looking down at her. "Now, let's go catch this crazy skin collector."

Jamie laughed and the moment lifted her spirits. She had begun to despair of finding O, but now they had a real lead. She wanted to call Missinghall and involve the police, but she knew that Blake's vision was inadmissible as evidence. Even if they raided Corium Jones' place, she now had the book of skin. It would take days to test and they would lose the chance to catch the collector when it was delivered.

"Do you know what Corium means?" Blake asked, checking his phone as they headed back towards the bike.

Jamie shook her head. "I just thought it was an unusual name."

"It's the Latin for dermis, one of the skin layers and also a term used for the thickened leathery part of an insect wing."

Jamie sighed, shaking her head. "Only in London," she said.

***

An hour later, Jamie walked into a post office delivery center further east in Plaistow and dropped the package off with a bored clerk on the front desk. He typed the information into his computer and gave Jamie a delivery receipt. As she turned to walk out of the office, he picked up the phone but Jamie couldn't hear his words. She walked back outside to find Blake standing by a lamppost opposite with two takeaway coffees.

"Tell me that you have some kind of useful tracking mechanism," he said. "You've stuck a sticker on the package and we can track it with our phones, right?"

"Of course, my private investigator budget stretches to all kinds of Bond-style gadgets," Jamie said with a grin. "But since we're here, we might as well stake the place out. I think the clerk made a phone call about the package, so we might not be waiting too long." She took a sip of the coffee and looked at her watch. "I'm worried about it being another night before we find O. Corium's workshop looked exactly like the type of place some sick bastard would send her perfect skin to be turned into a book. Did you see anything else in the vision that might help us?"

"Only the abattoir setting," Blake said, pulling out his phone. He opened a map of the area. "Meat processing is mainly done outside the city these days, but an older map might help us with where the abattoirs once stood." He was silent for a moment and then showed Jamie the phone. "Look how close we are to the East London Crematorium," he said. "If you had to dispose of body parts, this would be a good place to do it."

"We could split up," Jamie said. "You can stay here and watch for anyone collecting the package and I'll go to the crematorium and see what I can find."

Blake raised an eyebrow. "Seriously? You want to go alone to the crematorium?"

Jamie shrugged. "The dead don't bother me. It's the living I worry about."

The buzz of a motorbike grew louder as it came up the hill and then pulled to a stop outside the post office. It was a courier bike with the logo of a well-known firm on the side. The leather-clad figure dismounted and then entered the delivery office.

"This must be it," Jamie said. She pulled on her helmet and sat astride the bike. "You coming?"

Blake grinned. "You really know how to give a boy a good time."

He pulled her spare helmet over his head, sitting behind her and wrapping his arms around her waist. The delivery man emerged with the brown paper package under his arm. He put it in one of the side panniers and headed off down the road. Jamie pulled out behind him, keeping him in sight as they drove further east.

The shops changed into housing estates, evidence of homelessness and job seekers in the rundown yards and people hanging out on the corners. Jamie stayed well back, but with the volume of traffic even this far out, it was unlikely the courier would be suspicious. He was only doing his job.

It wasn't long before the courier turned into an industrial estate with only one road in and out. Jamie pulled over at the edge of the road and watched as the bike turned out of sight around a corner towards what looked like a derelict warehouse. The courier opened a roller door, put the package inside, pulled the door back down, and then drove back out of the park. He glanced at Jamie and Blake as he turned from the estate, but with the nonchalance of live-and-let-live London, where anything goes.

As the courier roared away up the street, Jamie drove down to the warehouse, turning off the bike's engine outside the roller-door. Blake dismounted and pulled his helmet off and Jamie followed suit, pulling a flashlight from her pannier.

They stood for a moment, listening for any sound. All they could hear was the noise of the city. There was nothing from inside the building.

Blake reached down and pulled up the roller door to reveal an empty loading bay. The package sat inside the entrance.

"Leave it," Jamie whispered as Blake reached for it. Her

years of working for the police had honed a sense of when something wasn't quite right and this place made her skin crawl.

There was a door at the back of the loading bay. Jamie pointed at it and Blake nodded. Together, they walked quietly towards it.

CHAPTER 15

THE DOOR WAS DOUBLE padlocked, but that didn't deter Blake.

"Misspent youth," he explained as he picked up a short metal pipe, swinging it a little to heft its weight. Wielding it like a hammer, it only took a few sharp blows to smash off the padlocks. The sound of the metal clashing resounded in the loading bay, and it would definitely warn anyone inside of their presence.

The door opened silently at Jamie's push, evidence that it had been oiled recently which seemed out of place in a derelict building. It was dark inside, but she could sense a wide space in front of them and the sharp lines of machinery loomed from the shadows. A metallic smell pervaded the air. As Blake stepped in behind Jamie, he grasped the door frame, his knuckles white with tension.

"This has to be the place," he whispered. "I recognize the smell of old blood."

As her eyes adjusted to the darkness, Jamie realized the machinery was for meat processing and packaging. Chains and hooks, winches used for heavy carcasses, blades for cutting, crushing weights. She shivered a little, imagining the place spattered in the blood of dead animals. She turned on the flashlight quickly and the beam reflected off shiny surfaces within. The equipment was spotless and left pristine, although a thin layer of dust had settled over it, evidence of time passing since the last animal was processed here.

"This isn't the slaughter room," Blake whispered. "We need to go deeper into the factory."

If she had still been in the police, it would have been well past the time to call for backup, but Jamie knew they wouldn't come for an empty, disused abattoir with a bad feeling about it. Her rational side understood the craziness of following a hunch based on Blake's psychic vision, but he had been right before and they had no other leads on finding O.

She shone the torch around the large processing area, finally locating a door behind one of the machines.

"That way," she said, walking with light feet across the warehouse, her senses alert for any sound. It was so quiet here, too quiet. Blake's hand found hers and squeezed gently as they crossed the space.

"We'll find her," he said, but his voice was shaky.

What had he seen in the vision that had affected him so much? Jamie wondered. And would they face it again in reality behind this door?

There were signs next to the door indicating a cold zone and the safety equipment necessary to enter the slaughterhouse rooms. Jamie pushed the handle down and the door swung open.

She shone the beam inside with her arm outstretched, panning it around the long room. The floor and walls were tiled and meat hooks hung down on chains from the ceiling. A long metal table stood in the middle with grooves down the sides and a drain underneath. Jamie couldn't help but imagine the table running with blood, crimson circling the drain as life ebbed away.

A dripping sound echoed through the space.

"That's water from a cooling system," Jamie said. "If the place is deserted, it shouldn't be on."

She stepped into the room and walked past the table heading for the shadows at the far end. Blake followed close behind, his breath coming fast. The silence was oppressive, as if the walls of the building were closing in on them, ready to crush them into pieces. Jamie couldn't stand the quiet any longer.

"Olivia," she called, her voice echoing in the chamber. "Is anyone here?"

As the echoes died away, they waited in silence but no noise came back except the dripping of water. They walked to the back of the space and found two enormous fridge doors. There was a low buzzing noise, evidence that the fridges were running.

Blake pulled at one of the doors and it swung open, an automatic light coming on inside.

"Oh no," he whispered as he saw what was within.

"What is it?" Jamie yanked the handle, pulling the door fully open so she could see inside.

A metal table sat against one side of the fridge. On top of it were several pieces of flesh, each covered in a tattoo. There were two long strips, one tattooed with a rainbow that Jamie recognized from the picture of Nicholas Randolph. She pushed down the nausea that rose within her. She had been at so many crime scenes, but there was something macabre about this one. The pieces of flesh were clinically clean. But for the tattoos, they wouldn't have known this had once been a man.

"I have to call it in," Jamie said. "This is a police matter now."

"What about the other fridge?" Blake gestured towards the other door, his face sickly pale in the harsh light. Jamie gulped down her hesitation and yanked it open, ready to face whatever horrors might be within.

As the automatic light flickered on, Jamie saw the thin figure huddled in the corner, arms wrapped around herself, head drooped to one side, features pale with a blueish tinge.

Jamie rushed inside and pulled O into her arms, feeling for the pulse at her neck. There was a faint beat there, but it was slow and unsteady. Blake blocked the fridge door open and together they carried O's unconscious form out into the main slaughter area. Blake pulled off his jacket and wrapped it around O's body and head, pulling her close to his warm frame as he rubbed her arms.

Jamie pulled out her phone and called for an ambulance and the police.

***

Several hours later, Jamie and Blake sat in the Royal London Hospital emergency waiting room. They had given detailed statements to the officers in charge of the scene, and after Jamie had spoken to Missinghall, they'd been allowed to leave.

Jamie tapped her foot on the floor, a rhythmic sound of impatience.

"They'll tell us when she's awake," Blake said, putting his hand on her arm. "There's nothing more we can do."

"I hope she remembers the bastard who took her." Jamie stood up and paced the floor. "Missinghall said the abattoir was clean. No prints. Just a lot of bleach. Whoever it was knew police procedure."

A nurse poked her head around the doorway.

"Olivia's awake. She wants to see you, Ms Brooke."

Jamie looked over at Blake and he nodded his head.

"It's OK, I'll stay here and wait for you. She doesn't even know me."

"I'll make sure she understands about your part in finding her," Jamie said. She followed the nurse out of the room and down a white corridor to the ward area. The smell of antiseptic reminded Jamie too much of the morgues she had frequented as part of the homicide team. It was a smell that masked disease and decay in her mind, not a scent of health and wellness. The nurse pointed out a tiny room where a police officer stood outside the door.

"Ten minutes," she warned. "Then she has to rest."

Jamie gave her name to the officer, and after he had checked her ID, she stepped inside. O lay curled up in the bed, wrapped in warming blankets around her body and over her head in a hood. Her eyes were bright blue against her ice-pale skin, but her lips had a pinkish hue now. She would make it.

"How you doing?" Jamie asked, sitting by the bed.

"Better than earlier," O whispered, her voice hoarse. "Thank you."

The words were simple, but Jamie understood the edge of death. She had come close to it herself in the Hellfire Caves and she knew what it meant to come back from the brink.

"Do you know who it was?" she asked.

O shut her eyes for a moment and then sighed. "I wish I did. I was walking back to the flat late last night. I'm not afraid to walk in Southwark – it's my patch, you know." Jamie nodded for O to continue. "As I walked under the arches at London Bridge, a figure came up behind me and covered my mouth with a cloth, holding me tight, and then it was only blackness. The next thing I knew I was shivering in that fridge." She fell silent for a moment. "But I heard a knife being sharpened, Jamie. That metallic repetition as the blade is drawn over and over on the lodestone … and later I heard screaming."

"I believe you," Jamie said. "There were – packages – in

the fridge next to yours, but no fingerprints or anything in trace evidence to help us find whoever did it."

"He came in once," O said, her voice so quiet that Jamie had to lean in closer. "He wore black clothes and a floor-length black apron, and a mask on his face with a long beak."

"The Venetian plague doctor?" Jamie asked.

O nodded. "Yes, I've seen similar ones. The mask gave me hope because if he didn't want me to see his face, then he was going to let me go. But then he told me to strip. It was so cold, but I did what he asked. He told me to spin around and show him the extent of the octopus tattoo. I couldn't see his eyes but I felt them on my body. It was like he was measuring me up for something. It was the first time I've wanted to scrub the ink from my skin." Tears glistened in O's eyes and one rolled down her cheek to the pillow. Jamie reached forward and took her hand, waiting for her to carry on. "As I turned, he said that it was a shame I wouldn't be dancing at the masquerade ball. Then he told me to dress and that he would be back."

"And then?" Jamie asked.

"Then I tried to stay warm … and then you were there."

There were voices outside the room and then the door burst open. Magda rushed in, her face stricken, arms outstretched. Jamie stood and let her take her place by O's side, the tears of both women mingling on the pillow as they whispered to each other.

Jamie walked to the window, looking out as they talked for a moment in low voices. She remembered waking up in hospital after the Hellfire Caves, how Blake had been by her side, his hand near hers on the bed. A flicker of a smile played on her lips. It made all the difference having someone who cared enough to be there. She thought of him waiting for her a corridor away. They were both such damaged people, but perhaps there was hope that together, they could transcend their history.

"Thank you, Jamie," Magda said. "If you hadn't found her when you did …"

"I don't think this is the end of it," Jamie said. "We didn't find the man responsible, and if O's right, he could be targeting the masquerade ball next."

"So many of the people going have ink," O said. "Lots of my friends from Torture Garden are attending. Any excuse to dress up extravagantly."

"I need to call my contact at the police and let him know about the threat," Jamie said. "Is there anything else you need?"

O smiled and squeezed Magda's hand. "I've got everything I need right here."

Jamie left them together and emerged back into the corridor. She called Missinghall and he answered quickly.

"Damn it, Jamie," he said. "Those tattooed body parts reminded me of those specimens from the Hunterian case last year. You always seem to find the weirdest crime scenes."

"It started out as a missing persons case, Al. Things just got a little crazy."

"Well, it's definitely got the notice of the big guns around here. Dale Cameron is heading up the case himself now, taking a personal interest in the murders and also pursuing the tattoo angle. He sent a handpicked team to the abattoir. You know he's running for Mayor, right?"

"You mentioned it," Jamie said. "So I guess he's heavily invested in finding whoever's involved."

"Exactly," Missinghall said. "His slogan is 'clean up the city,' so he's trying to make sure that starts now."

"There might be more trouble coming," Jamie said. "I've spoken with Olivia, and she told me that the man who abducted her mentioned the Southbank masquerade ball."

"That's tomorrow night at the Tate Modern," Missinghall

said. "We can't shut it down at this stage, but it will be full of the city's finest, including the Mayoral candidates. Let me get the information to the security team and I'm sure they'll assign more security. We'll get this bastard, Jamie."

CHAPTER 16

LEAVING O IN MAGDA'S care, Jamie walked back along the corridor into the waiting room. Blake stood as she entered.

"How is she?" he asked.

"Alive – and grateful." Jamie smiled and for a moment it seemed as if everything was right with the world. She walked into Blake's arms and hugged him, her arms wrapped around his strong back, the warmth of his body against hers. She inhaled his masculine scent and they stood together, just breathing. The seconds ticked past and what had started as a friendly hug between friends morphed into the edge of something more intimate.

Jamie's heart beat faster as she felt an overwhelming desire to lift her mouth for his kiss. He was a beautiful man, and his scars and wounded soul only made him more desirable. She wondered what his bare hands would feel like on her skin. Would he be able to read the desire from her body as he read objects? She took a deep breath. This couldn't happen, not now. Perhaps not ever.

She stepped back, exhaling slowly. Blake's eyes were cobalt blue and she saw her own desire reflected there.

"I need to go," she said, too aware of his proximity. "It's late."

Blake nodded. "It's been a long day."

They walked together out of the hospital, the silence between them no longer comfortable but heavy with unsaid words. When they reached Jamie's bike, Blake refused the pillion helmet.

"I'll get the Tube back," he said. "I know you prefer to ride alone."

Jamie couldn't tell him how much she had relished his arms around her waist as they had zoomed around London together. How his heat against her back had made her feel again. How she longed for more.

She put her helmet on, needing its protective shield to stop her words from escaping.

"Thank you for coming today," she said. "You're the one who really found O."

"We did it together," Blake said. "We make a good team." He reached for her hand and squeezed it. "Sleep well, Jamie."

He turned to leave, but she called him back.

"I'm … going to go to the masquerade ball tomorrow night," she said, her words hesitant. "O told me that the man mentioned it, so perhaps he'll be there. I need to find him, Blake, and Southwark won't sleep easy until he's caught."

The corner of Blake's mouth twitched in a slight smile. "So it's more of a stakeout then," he said. "Definitely not a date."

"Definitely not," Jamie said, but she couldn't help but smile back.

Blake nodded. "I'd better sort out a costume then. I'll look forward to seeing you tomorrow."

As he walked away through the car park, Jamie roared off on her bike, back through East London towards the south. As she rode, she felt the crazy rise inside her. When she felt like this, she needed speed and escape.

She wanted to drink and dance, to stamp her claim on life and shout to the world that she was alive.

Finding O felt like a chink of light in the darkness, a triumph that she needed to celebrate. Life was so short and dark men could cut it shorter still. Or illnesses like the one that had taken her daughter from her. Death is inevitable, the only question is when and what can be done with this life as the seconds tick away. While blood still pumped in her veins, Jamie felt the need to snatch these moments of pleasure and revel in them.

She rode back to her flat, grabbed her tango bag, and headed back out into the night.

The tango *milonga* was a place of transformation. No one questioned anyone's identity outside, because only the dance mattered in here. It was the early hours of the morning now so only the hardcore remained, those with the stamina to dance for so long, those with the addiction to movement.

Sebastian was there, dancing with a young woman whose body seemed molded to his. He saw Jamie come in and nodded at her. He was always the one she wanted, the chemistry when they danced together was as close to sex as she could get without taking her clothes off.

Jamie put her tall heels on, letting her hair out of the clasp so it fell in dark waves down her back. She shook it out and stepped to the edge of the dance floor as the music faded and Sebastian left his partner to come to her.

There was no need to speak. Their bodies were all the conversation necessary and as the bandoneon began to play, Jamie surrendered to the movement. This was the loss of control she craved. The male role was dominant in tango, he led and she followed, bending to his touch and spinning at the pressure of his fingers on her flesh.

Sebastian had the perfect arrogance necessary in a tango partner, but with an edge of tragedy that filled every step with meaning. Jamie sublimated her desire into the steps, arching into him. She looked up into his eyes as he held her in close embrace, bending her backwards and pressing himself down upon her. She sensed that he would take this further if she gave assent. But dancing with Sebastian would change if they took it any further.

The pleasure of tango was in frustrated desire held in check, not the release. The fantasy of how it might feel to be possessed by him was more erotic than the taking would surely be. But Jamie was glad of the spark, glad that she was not defined only by the loss of her daughter or her work. As a dancer, she was a desirable woman, and the darkness she faced outside didn't matter right now. Here was only life.

CHAPTER 17

THE FIGURE WITH THE skinning knife took another step towards him, bending over his prone form. The blade flashed as it caught the light and then it descended, cutting into his flesh. The touch was gentle at first, a caress along his chest followed by a bead of dark blood. But then the pain began as the man pressed the knife deeper.

Blake twisted, trying to get away from the blade, but he was trapped, tied down, unable to move. His breath came in ragged gasps.

The man laughed and Blake saw the scar that marred his nose, the craggy features of the man he had seen in the museum.

He woke with a start, pulling himself out of the twisted bedclothes. He sat up and deliberately calmed his breathing as the sounds of London waking came from the window. The light was dull, grey clouds scudded past and the wind whistled through the chimney pots in the roof above. Blake took a deep breath. These were the sounds of his flat. He was safe.

He reached for the silver hip flask next to his bed, his hand hovering over it for a second. *Just a little*, he thought, taking a quick swig. Tequila was better for dulling the visions, but this early in the morning and before work, vodka was a better choice.

Feeling calmer now, Blake turned and sat on the edge of the bed, reaching underneath it for the package wrapped in dirty ivory sailcloth. His bare fingertips brushed it and Blake pulled away, reaching instead for the gloves by his bedside. This was a book he dared not read again with bare hands, since the visions had been so bloody and violent on the day his father had died.

Blake pulled the gloves on and then reached back under the bed, pulling out the tightly wrapped book. The Galdrabók. His father had used rites from the grimoire to summon powers of persuasion and charisma to lead his extremist Christian sect. In the last moments of his life, Blake had seen him consumed by demons come to claim what he had bargained for earthly power.

Or at least he had seen a vision through his father's eyes of what he'd *believed* was there to claim him. The visions were so tightly bound to the people he saw through, Blake was never sure how much could be considered objectively real. He smiled, shaking his head. Could demons ever be considered truth?

He pulled open the sailcloth to reveal the Galdrabók, its cover of deep burgundy leather inscribed with a circle bisected by four lines ending in prongs. Each line was cross-hatched with other markings, each a form of controlled chaos, like a deformed snowflake that had missed its natural perfection.

Blake opened the book, gazing again at the pages of Icelandic spells, invocations to demons and Christian saints. There were symbols and images for calling on the Norse gods and instructions on how to use herbs for visions of the otherworld. There were runes and symbols of power, Icelandic magic sigils, Latin texts and sacred images within. It was a dense bible of pagan belief, but Blake didn't really know what to make of it.

The museum researcher part of him wanted to take it

in for study, to academically discern the meaning of the symbols and words within. The book could be a lifetime of research, perhaps a way for him to discover the Nordic half of his family tree and give his academic life some deeper meaning. His mind skipped forward to conferences in the icy north, tweed jackets with elbow patches, book signings with bearded colleagues.

But the other part of him, perhaps the Nigerian half from his mother, perhaps the part that allowed him to see visions through time – that part wanted to read the book with bare hands laid upon it and speak the words within. His mind flashed to the vision of the ash grove, the human sacrifices to Odin, the power that hummed through those present. There was a world a long way from London, up in the dark forests of the Arctic Circle.

Blake closed the book and traced the symbol on the front with gloved fingertips. He thought of the man he had seen in the museum, the man who now haunted his dreams. Had the book really belonged to his father, or had he stolen it? Blake placed his hand flat on the burgundy leather. Was the stranger here to take it back?

***

An hour later, Blake walked up the steps into the British Museum, his close-cropped hair still wet from the shower. The Galdrabók was tucked safely beneath his bed again, the decision on what to do with it put off for now. Blake felt spring fever in the air, a sense that something was changing, and if he didn't move with it, he would be left behind.

He walked into the Great Court, looking up at the glass panels above, the sun streaming through. He descended to the research area and waved at Margaret in her office as he sat at his desk to work on some of the text for the exhibit. To his consternation, she stood and walked towards him.

"Morning," Blake said, his voice jolly as she approached.

"You weren't here much yesterday," Margaret said. No small talk today. "Even after our discussion."

"I was actually researching the sex trade in Southwark," Blake said. "To add some color to the exhibition."

Margaret raised an eyebrow. "Interesting. Well, your research might come in handy, as the curator needs a hand constructing the exhibition space. I'm volunteering you for the job since you can't seem to sit still down here."

"But –" Blake protested, but Margaret held a hand up.

"I actually think you'll enjoy it," she said with a smile.

Blake walked back upstairs towards the exhibition space, right in the middle of the Great Court. There was a security guard on the door to keep out the tourists. Blake showed his pass and then went into the central space. The walls were black and could be shifted around to bisect the space into various sizes, all the better to display the objects within. Spotlights lit the glass cases and Blake could see that the curator was aiming to entertain as well as educate.

The first case contained an array of phalluses – from the stone carvings offered to the gods for fertility, to the wind chimes of winged penises from first-century Roman London used to ward away evil spirits. It was a comical display, setting the tone for a tongue-in-cheek ride through erotic London.

A clanging noise came from further in.

Blake followed the sound into a larger space, where a petite blonde woman struggled to maneuver a leather stool onto a stage area. Her long hair was tied back in a simple ponytail and her plain blue jeans and black t-shirt gave her the air of a graduate student.

"Let me help with that," Blake said, helping her to lift the stool up. Once in place, he ran his gloved hand over the metal rivets at the edges. "Well made, isn't it."

"Yes," the woman said, a cheeky smile on her face. "Britain makes some of the best spanking stools and bondage gear."

Blake pulled his hand away quickly and the woman laughed.

"I'm Catherine Agew," she said.

"You're the guest curator for the exhibition," Blake said. He had assumed that the curator would be older ... and not so good-looking.

"You must be Blake. Margaret said she was sending someone up to help me with the lifting and shifting."

Blake raised an eyebrow. "Lifter and shifter at your service." He turned to look at the stage area. "So what's this going to be?"

"Flagellation was a popular sexual service, especially in Georgian London and particularly amongst the nobility," Catherine said. "Brits have always enjoyed a good spanking."

She pointed at a wall filled with images of Victorian pornography, some of the more acceptable pictures from the museum's extensive collection. A black and white illustration showed a bewigged aristocrat bent over by a window, a woman beating his behind with birch twigs.

Blake found his eyes lingering on one image where a young woman lay over the knees of an older man, her blonde hair hanging down as he raised his hand to spank her. He turned away to find Catherine looking at him, curiosity in her eyes. He swallowed. Suddenly it seemed stuffy in here.

"So," he said. "What do you need me to do here?"

Catherine smiled and pointed out some of the other items to be placed on the stage, creating a tableau of a boudoir in one of the high-end establishments. Blake began to move the furniture, trying to push the lewd images from his mind.

Catherine's fingers lingered on his arm as he moved the final piece into position and Blake understood the possibility implied there. Before he had met Jamie, he had been living well in the promiscuous London singles scene, fueled by alcohol and a desire to forget. He had never had any trouble finding willing partners, but he struggled to take anything further than a one-night stand. Questions about his scars and doubts about his own demons had stopped him. But Jamie had given him hope that he could give more of himself, and tonight he would see her at the masquerade ball. Perhaps tonight they would be more than friends.

He took a step back, away from Catherine's touch.

"It looks great," he said. "I like that you've added humor to what could be a – difficult – exhibition."

"I'm glad you think so, but I also wanted to portray the darker side," Catherine said. "Whores who got on the wrong side of the law were sent to Bridewell house of correction and whipped in public. There were many who enjoyed watching and who paid for the privilege. Who were the real sinners after all?"

Catherine's eyes hardened and even with her small stature, Blake could see how much this exhibition meant to her.

"It's good that you're the curator," he said. "It's almost a feminist take on the sex trade, something that many wouldn't have considered."

Catherine's face softened and she sighed.

"Thank you. It means a lot to me to reclaim some of the myths. Of course the sex trade had its horrific side, but there were also women who made a lot of money with it. If they didn't die of disease or violence, they could live more independently than ever. Profits from the sex industry actually financed the development of huge swathes of the city. It was one of the most valuable commercial activities in the eighteenth and early nineteenth century, as important as even the London Docks."

Blake shook his head. "It's one of the paradoxes of London. Some of its greatest achievements come from the shadow side."

"Of course, it's difficult to know where to draw the line," Catherine said, the cheeky smile returning to her face. "The truth of London's past is often hidden for good reason." She pulled out some old street signs. "I want to put a couple of these up around the exhibit. What do you think?"

She shuffled through them so Blake could read the texts: Maiden Lane, Love Lane, Codpiece Lane, Gropecunt Lane. He put a hand up to stop her, laughing a little.

"I think that last one would bring in a raft of complaints," he said.

"It became Grape Street and then Grub Street over time," Catherine said. "But I quite like the original name. At least you knew what you were going to get there."

They worked with an easy camaraderie for the rest of the afternoon, the exhibition taking shape around them. Blake enjoyed watching Catherine work, her strong sense of what she wanted to portray commanding the space. Flirtation aside, she inspired him with the way she could use an exhibit to make people laugh and think, to make them feel. He understood why Margaret wanted him up here. He was reminded once more what a future in the museum might mean, what he could do with his gifts. He could bring the past alive and the thought enlivened him.

Blake looked at his watch. He still needed to pick up the tuxedo from the rental shop before heading to the Tate Modern for the ball.

"I've got to run," Blake said. "But I can help you tomorrow if you like?"

"I'll look forward to it," Catherine said with a smile that promised far more.

Blake emerged from the central exhibition space into the crowded Great Court. Tourists and families thronged the space and the noise of the crowd rose in waves. A lone figure caught Blake's eye. The man with the scar on his nose stood by the door of the Enlightenment Room, his piercing blue eyes fixed on Blake.

Blake's heart thudded in his chest as he recognized aspects of his father in the man's face, and the promise of the north in his eyes.

He took a step forward.

The man ducked into the Enlightenment Room behind him. Blake followed, expecting to find him there, wanting to challenge him. The room swirled with people, but the man was gone. For now, at least.

CHAPTER 18

THE VAST EXPANSE OF the Turbine Hall at the Tate Modern was transformed for the masquerade ball.

High ceilings were crisscrossed with thin wires at one end and acrobats walked with long poles over the crowd. Trapeze artists swung across the expanse, tumbling across the space to be caught before the long drop to the concrete floor. Long silk ribbons hung down in another area and four lithe women wound themselves up before letting themselves spin towards the ground, plunging in barely controlled descent. The acrobats wore close-fitting, almost see-through body suits with artfully placed embroidery and crystals reflecting the light. Their limbs were etched against the black roof, the embodied perfection of human art in this temple to creation.

Jamie stood for a moment, looking up in wonder at the kaleidoscope of color and movement above. The sounds of a live jazz band accompanied the performers, although the dancing would start in earnest as the alcohol flowed more freely. Jamie remembered the night she had taken Polly to Cirque du Soleil, a circus that celebrates the extremes of the human body, communicating story through movement and music. Polly's body had been ravaged by motor neuron disease by then, but her eyes had been alive with joy that night.

With a smile on her lips at the memory, Jamie walked towards one of the bars. Tempted as she was by the multicolored cocktails, she chose a small glass of white wine and took it to stand on the edge of the dance area, scanning the crowd.

Most wore masks, some attached over their faces while others held them on long poles in the Venetian way. Those who wanted to be recognized held their masks casually, but most were incognito.

A couple spun past on the dance floor, the woman in an ice-white dress, her face masked in branches of icicles, her lips painted blue. Her partner was a Green Man, his face obscured by the leaves of the pagan god. There were men in the crowd with the long nose masks of the Scaramuccia, a rogue and adventurer from the Venetian Commedia Dell'Arte. The wearers had a swagger that matched their characters. Two women walked past in steampunk half-masks of copper and rivets, cogs and wheels, extravagant Victorian dress with bustles and petticoats. The flash of photographers captured everything, some attendees striking coquettish poses and others turning away from the light.

The masquerade ball was the society event of the season and Jamie was aware of how her outfit was nothing compared to some in the room. She wore a black chiffon dress with layers that flowed around her legs, with a bodice in a peacock feather design. A matching butterfly mask hid the upper part of her face with its gauzy wings. It fitted well and although extravagant on her budget, Jamie looked forward to wearing the outfit at tango another night. The feeling of the dress swishing around her legs as she walked made her want to dance, but tonight she was here to watch.

A man walked past in white tie, his black suit tailored to perfection, the lining bright scarlet. He turned and

Jamie saw that he wore the mask of the Devil, his face half perfect angel, the other half a demon with twisted features.

She knew the one she sought wouldn't wear such a mask. His peculiar fetish for flesh made him a demon in her mind, but he would no doubt be as mundane as other criminals she had encountered in her years in the police. Yet she wanted the man to come tonight, and she wanted to face him in the darkness.

Jamie found it easy enough to spot the police and security guards in the crowd, their bodies alert, eyes scanning the people before them. Some had no masks, their earpieces marking them out in an obvious fashion, but there were others who wore plain black masks and tuxedos in an attempt to blend in.

A couple spun past as the music sped up. The man wore an eagle mask, its body between his eyes and up onto his forehead, its wings stretching up to meet above his head like a prayer. A woman wore a ragged blue dress, ripped off one shoulder and stained with blood. Her mask looked as if it had been carved from her skin, wet and dripping. In any other setting, Jamie would be rushing to her aid, but the woman's dark smile as she turned heads made it clear she was dressed to win one of the costume prizes for the night.

Jamie understood this craving to be both seen and disguised. It was how she felt at tango, a separate being from her daytime self when she could let the wild side out and not be restrained by society. Masks are used to de-individuate, so the person behind is lost and they can behave as they might want to in a world with no consequences. There were masks that revealed and there were masks that concealed, and as the night darkened and wine flowed, it became evident why some chose concealment. As the alcohol loosened inhibitions, the dark corners became havens for couples locked together in momentary escape.

Jamie had arranged to meet Blake under the trapeze artist, so she made her way through the crowd. It parted for a moment and she saw him, looking up at the performers. His suit was understated, a perfect tailored fit showing off broad shoulders and wide chest. His mask was black leather and it looked soft enough to touch. He turned, sensing her presence. His stunning blue eyes met hers, framed by the leather mask, and Jamie couldn't help but go to him.

"You look lovely," Blake said softly, bending to her ear so she could hear above the band. Jamie beamed, twirling her skirts a little.

"Glad you like it," she said. "You don't look bad yourself."

"Shame it's not actually a date then." Blake smiled and Jamie blushed a little, staring out into the crowd, avoiding his gaze. "How do you want to manage tonight?" he asked, changing the subject.

"There are plenty of security guards here for any obvious trouble," Jamie said. "But I want us to focus more on potential victims. I'm sure the man will be here tonight. How could he stay away?"

Two women walked past, their low-backed dresses framing their tattoos – one a stylized tree growing out from her spine, and the other of bright fish splashing in a pool of blue.

"Any skin fetishist is going to get off tonight, that's for sure," Blake said. "So we just walk around and keep an eye out?"

"I guess so," Jamie said. "I don't even know what we're looking for." Her voice trailed off as she gazed into the throng, the myriad colors and textures creating ever-shifting patterns in the great hall, a moving work of art.

They walked together around the edges of the crowd as the band wound up its final song of the set. The bass made Jamie's heart thump in time and she could see that Blake longed to get out there and dance. Part of her wanted to forget the case and let loose together, darkness and music and collective energy freeing them from daylight responsibilities. Neither of them had any reason to hold back from each other, did they?

Applause erupted as the band finished up and the lead singer left the stage. Then the lights dimmed and a young black woman walked out, her silver dress sparkling as she moved. She took hold of the microphone and began to sing, her voice rich and powerful as she told of rivers running deep and forsaken love. Couples merged together as her accompaniment joined in, the song lifting the emotion of the crowd.

Blake turned and leaned down, his breath against Jamie's ear. She shivered at the sensation.

"Will you dance with me?" he whispered, his gloved hand taking hers, moving so close that all she had to do was take one tiny step and she would be pressed against him. Jamie's heart thumped in her chest. He smelled of pine needles and spice and all she wanted was to be in his arms.

A moment's hesitation and then she took that tiny step.

She wrapped her arms around his strong back, her cheek against his chest as he held her. One of his gloved hands cradled the back of her head against him, the other stroked her lower back slightly above her buttocks. The song intensified and they swayed together. Jamie pressed her full length against him and she heard him catch his breath.

She looked up and met his eyes. They were dark and intense, filled with a stark need that matched her own. Jamie tilted her head slightly, lifting her mouth to his as he leaned down to kiss her.

CHAPTER 19

A FLICKER IN HER peripheral vision made Jamie stop and pull away.

Through a crack in the crowd she saw a man in an ivory plague doctor's mask on the opposite side of the room. The long beak had been filled with herbs when the sixteenth-century doctors had treated the plagues, but the nightmarish figures reeked of death. The man wore a long black cloak that billowed behind as he stalked through the crowd. Jamie thought she recognized something of his walk, but she couldn't quite grasp who she was reminded of.

The moment was broken and Blake turned to see what she was looking at. Jamie felt the loss of his touch but pleasure would have to wait.

"There," she said, nudging Blake to look across the room, but the man had slipped away in the crowd.

"I don't see anything," Blake said. "What was it?"

"A man in a plague doctor's mask," Jamie said.

Blake's jaw tightened as he scanned the crowd.

"Let's go in opposite directions around the perimeter," Jamie said. "See if we can spot him again."

Blake looked down at her, his face in shadow but his concern evident. He stroked her cheek with one gloved finger. "Don't challenge him, Jamie. Please. Get one of the security guards if you find him first."

"Don't worry," she said. "We don't even know if it's him. It is a masked ball, after all, and the plague doctor is a commonly used mask."

"I'll meet you back here then," Blake said, turning and slipping back into the crowd, his posture resolute.

Jamie began to walk slowly in the opposite direction, scanning the crowd.

***

The mask was heavy but the freedom of anonymity was worth the pain. Dale Cameron stalked around the perimeter of the ball, his eyes flicking over the skin of those dancing close by. There was plenty to tempt him tonight.

In the whirl of the dance, he saw the glazed eyes and wide smiles of intoxication. In the corners of the hall, couples were already indulging in the pleasures of the flesh and on their skin, the marks of the tattooist's trade. But he couldn't stop to admire the body art of the deviants right now. He had other plans for this masquerade. He looked at his watch. It was almost time.

He had been down earlier to inspect the security procedures as part of his day-job role and had brought the bag in then. No one would think to question a Detective Superintendent, after all. Now it was under his cloak and all he had to do was position it, then leave.

***

The band reached a crescendo and the excited crowd screamed and whistled their appreciation. Then the lead singer pointed up to the roof above. The main lights went out and spotlights lit up a net of black and white balloons above.

"Ten ... nine," the crowd shouted.

The countdown to midnight had begun, when the balloons would be released. Inside were all kinds of prizes, tickets to other events, luxury gifts and getaways. Jamie anticipated craziness on the central dance floor as people dove for the balloons, and she moved as far to the edge of the crowd as possible. There, she stood next to one of the huge pillars that supported the main hall.

"Eight ... seven."

Her leg brushed against something and Jamie looked down to see a black package resting against the pillar. Cold sweat prickled across her skin. She looked around quickly for a security guard. Something was very wrong here.

"Six ... five."

She shouted a warning to move, but the attention of the crowd was on the balloons above and the band played so loudly, it was impossible to hear anything. She couldn't see any of the security team near her, but there would be a team by the door. Jamie slid around the back of the crowd, making for the exit as fast as she could.

"Four ... three."

In the flash of the spotlights sweeping the room, Jamie spotted the man in the plague doctor mask walking towards the main exit in front of her. One of his hands reached into the pocket of his cloak.

Jamie pushed her way through the crowd after him, her heart hammering in her chest.

"Two ... one."

On the final count, the crowd screamed in excitement and drums beat faster as the balloons dropped and the scramble for prizes began. The spotlights swept around the room faster now, whirling in crazy patterns with strobes that took the atmosphere to an edge of hysteria.

The man turned, surveying the room, his demeanor that of a judge pronouncing a death sentence.

Jamie emerged at the edge of the crowd. He saw her and met her eyes as she took another step towards him. Jamie felt a spark of recognition as the man turned away and walked swiftly out the exit, as a blast shook the building and the screams of the excited crowd turned to terror.

CHAPTER 20

SCREAMS ECHOED ACROSS THE darkness of the Turbine Hall as another blast boomed, followed by the crash of falling masonry.

The explosions were concentrated at the back of the hall right by the stage, where the crowd was the most dense. Jamie was torn – she desperately wanted to pursue the man in the mask, but Blake was back there in the darkness along with hundreds of other people. This was her community now.

She turned back into the hall.

The shouts of the security team could be heard above the din of suffering and those who could walk began to stream for the exits. The dull green emergency lighting cast sickly shadows on their skin, the masks turning them into escapees from a demonic realm. Sirens wailed outside as police and ambulances arrived, the central location at least guaranteeing a swift emergency response.

Jamie joined the security team, helping people to the exits as she searched in growing desperation for Blake at the back of the hall.

Body parts lay strewn on the floor amongst pieces of rubber from the balloons, some limbs perfectly intact but ripped from their owners. The bombs had contained tiny ball bearings which acted as bullets in the blast. Jamie brushed back tears as she stepped around the edge of the horror.

She had to find Blake.

In triage mode, Jamie stepped through the bodies. Some people were groaning, clutching bloody limbs, others were silent, staring straight ahead. She reached down to check one woman's pulse, her face painted white with dust, her eyes open but unblinking. This one was dead. The couple Jamie had seen dancing earlier lay entwined together a little further in. The top half of their bodies were intact, his eagle mask still perfectly placed and nestling into her neck. But their torsos had separated from their legs and they lay in a pool of blood.

Jamie pushed aside her desire to run from the horror, calling on her police training to face what lay head. She focused on her search for Blake, checking bodies, rapidly becoming inured to the dead and dying. Around her the paramedics worked quickly and bodies were stretchered away. London was ever ready for disaster, but it had been years since it had visited the capital in such terrible carnage. Jamie's resolve hardened every second, for every body she checked, for every life that was taken. She would find the man in the mask.

At the very back of the hall, Jamie found a huddle of people behind the stage. The metal structure had shielded them from the airborne missiles and they weren't seriously injured. Blake lay amongst them, blood trickling from the side of his mask to the floor, his blue eyes dazed. Jamie rushed to him, gathering him into her arms, tears coming at last as she lay in the dust at his side.

"Oh, Blake," she whispered. "I thought …"

He pulled her into his arms and she heard his heartbeat against her cheek.

"It's OK," he whispered. "I'm not going anywhere."

***

She had been in too many hospitals lately, Jamie thought a few hours later. She sat in another waiting room drinking crappy coffee, watching the minutes tick by until Blake could be discharged. He only had a concussion but she was well aware of how much more serious it could have been.

A TV in the corner played the early-morning news on a ten-minute repeat cycle, images from the aftermath of the explosion cut together with smartphone footage shot earlier in the evening and uploaded by eager partiers. The parade of beautiful faces in glorious gowns, smiles under their masks, made the after images of body bags and billowing smoke even more shocking. The media was already calling it the Bloody Masquerade.

The news came on again and this time, the images were live. Dale Cameron's patrician face was somber as he read from a prepared statement by the police.

"This morning we mourn the sixty-four people lost last night in the tragedy at the Tate Modern. Over one hundred remain in hospital, some critically injured. My team is processing the crime scene and we're confident that we will be able to bring the terrorists responsible to justice in the following days." He looked directly into the cameras. "We *will* clean up the city, and that's a promise I personally intend to keep."

The camera flicked back to the newsreader.

"That was Detective Superintendent Dale Cameron, who is heading up the task force for the masquerade attack. He's also running for London Mayor in the elections early next week. His main rival, Amanda Masters, was critically injured at the masquerade ball which she was attending as patron of the arts in Southwark."

Jamie's eyes narrowed as she looked at the screen,

focusing on Cameron's stance. There was something there, a camouflage of respectability, a hard edge that people wanted but that she knew hid a dangerous side. That kind of strength attracted people and made him a pillar of society, but how far did he take his crusade to clean up the city? Jamie thought back to the night in the Hellfire Caves when she had thought she had seen him in the smoke, part of those who dismembered a man in the darkness. And he had definitely been connected to RAIN, a group who used the mentally ill for their own research ends, uncaring of the human cost. Could Cameron be the man in the mask?

The waiting room door opened and Blake came back in, a dressing on the side of his head. There were dark shadows under his eyes and she saw exhaustion there that reflected her own. She went to him and took his hand.

"I'm taking you home," she said. "By taxi, not by bike."

He smiled. "Thought you said it wasn't a date."

Jamie gave a sharp laugh. "Guess that concussion isn't too bad then."

***

After a short taxi ride, Jamie pushed open the door to Blake's flat in the historic Bloomsbury area. The early-morning commuters were walking through the streets, but it was still quiet in the square. Many of the tall terraced houses were affixed with blue plaques commemorating the famous names who once lived here: Darwin, Dickens and even JM Barrie, who created Peter Pan. As Jamie helped Blake inside and up the staircase, she considered that he was a kind of Lost Boy, his beautiful face wracked by pain from past lives that were not even his own. He mounted the stairs slowly, gripping the bannister with his gloved hand.

Blake's rooms were at the very top of the building, a small studio flat nestled in the eaves with a view over the rooftops of London. It was sparsely furnished with a few pieces of wooden furniture. Jamie had been here once before, when she had been crazy with grief and Blake had been out of his mind on tequila. He had looked after her then, and she would help him now.

"Shall I make tea?" Jamie asked, as Blake sat heavily on the bed.

"You don't have to stay, you know," he said. "I'm only going to sleep."

Jamie smiled. "You have concussion, you idiot. I'm staying while you sleep so you don't suddenly die. After all that trouble finding you after the explosion, do you think I'm going to let you out of my sight now?"

Blake managed to return a smile that turned into a grimace as pain crossed his face. He lay back on the bed and closed his eyes, exhaling slowly.

Jamie crossed to the little kitchen, searching in the cupboards for teabags. She found a mostly empty bottle of tequila next to the Tetley. As she made the tea, she noticed another empty bottle of spirits in the recycling. She knew Blake drank, but she hadn't really realized how much until now. He was damaged, but then so was she. They just coped with their grief in different ways.

She carried the sweet milky tea back to Blake, putting it on a side table within his reach. Jamie sat down on the edge of the bed for a moment, looking down at him. The soft morning light from the window touched his face, his caramel skin smooth and unblemished, his stubble almost a beard now. His chest rose and fell rhythmically but every breath was controlled, forced through the pain of bruising to his chest.

If he had been in a different place when the blast went off … Jamie couldn't think of losing Blake that way. After all, he'd only been there because she'd asked him to be and she had put him in danger before. Images of broken bodies came to her mind, the Turbine Hall full of smoke and the bloody corpses of those who had been celebrating only moments before. The full force of the tragedy began to settle upon her now. It seemed surreal, the sensation similar to how she had felt after Polly's death. The realization of obliteration, how fragile we really are on the face of the earth, how easily ended.

Blake opened his eyes and the deep blue was intense as he gazed up at Jamie. He raised one gloved hand to her cheek, touching her face softly.

"Will you lie down next to me?" His voice was soft with a note of vulnerability. "You must be exhausted too."

At his words, Jamie felt a wave of tiredness wash over her. The last few days had been crazy and the events of last night had almost broken her. This was not how she had imagined them being together, but right now, they both needed a human touch.

"As long as you don't think this is a date," Jamie whispered with a half smile, but she felt the prick of tears in her eyes. She lay down next to him, putting her head on the crook of his shoulder, her hand on his broad chest. Blake smelled of smoke and antiseptic and underneath, his own musky scent. Jamie nuzzled closer, he put his arm around her and they slept.

CHAPTER 21

Dale Cameron breathed a sigh of relief as he walked through his front door and shut it firmly behind him. He was alone at last after the hours of media frenzy that followed the explosion at the Tate. He was still very much awake though – the exhilaration of running rings around the whole lot of them made sure of that.

He stood on the brown welcome mat and took off his brogues, adding them to the shoe rack against the left wall, making sure that they were aligned correctly. He put on his inside shoes, a soft pair of leather moccasins that molded to his feet and allowed him to walk silently on the wooden floors further inside. He hung up his overcoat, adjusting the sleeves so they draped nicely on the peg. He put his keys in the red bowl on the dresser, enjoying the jingling sound as they fell.

Entering his domain was a ritual he relished, especially after a day in the grime of London. When he had cleaned up the city to the point where it was as perfect as his house, his job would be done. And he had made a good start to that in the last twenty-four hours.

He paused by the two portraits that hung side by side in his hallway. His mother's beauty had been captured in a candid shot when he was a child, his own smiling face next to hers as she hugged him close. He had been eleven when she had died of internal injuries sustained after falling down the stairs. He knew what she had been running from, but the police looked after their own and back then, fewer questions were asked about injuries in the home. Dale lifted a finger to her face, as he did every time he came home.

Next to it was a picture of his father, taken in uniform at the height of his career, his face confident. "I have already surpassed you," Dale whispered. Once he was Mayor he would go to that stinking old people's home and spit the words in his father's dying face. That day would come soon now.

Dale smiled at the thought and padded into his study at the back of the house. It was the very model of what a Detective's room should look like, with leather wing chairs, a large oak table and bookshelves with all the latest forensic tomes as well as older first editions behind glass panels. A cigar box sat on the desk and Dale adjusted it so the edges lined up perfectly with the tabletop edge.

He walked to the drinks cabinet and poured himself a generous measure of 62 Gun Salute, one of the best of the Royal Salute whiskeys. Tonight he deserved to celebrate. The list of the dead included noted homosexuals, social justice campaigners, tattoo artists and liberals of every kind. If only that bitch Amanda Masters had died in the blast, but then, perhaps that would have made her some kind of martyr.

He padded behind the desk to one of the bookshelves. He pulled out an Arthur Conan Doyle volume and typed a code onto a hidden keypad. There was an audible click and Dale tugged on the bookcase, revealing a door behind. He pulled a key from around his neck, one he kept hidden under his clothes and on his person at all times. His heart beat faster as he inserted the key in the lock and twisted it slowly, prolonging the pleasure of the moment.

Keeping this place was risky, but a man had to have a way to commemorate his successes and relive his pleasures. Dale needed a sanctuary away from the world, when he could be his real self. It was a tremendous effort balancing the demands of the police with his real agenda. There were those he worked with on other plans, but the group had been damaged in the wake of the Hellfire Caves scandal and the investigation into RAIN had further weakened the inner circle. But now he was close to power and soon they would rally again.

He pushed open the door and entered the small room, flicking a switch to turn on the lights that illuminated certain parts of his collection. One wall was dedicated to masks and Dale reached out to touch the plague doctor's hooked beak. He had replaced it after his success at the masquerade ball. The city was infected with a plague and it was time to weed out the weak and the needy, those who were a burden on society. Nature knew how to cull the herd, he only helped the process with his bombs.

Next to the mask were his knives, some ceremonial and precious for their monetary value. But others … Dale walked to the display and caressed the gleaming edge of the skinning knife. This one held greater pleasure than much of his collection, but now he would have to rest it for a while. He would soon give up control of crime scenes as Mayor and no longer have the ability to disappear evidence. The knife would have to remain on the wall, at least for now.

He ran his fingers over the books of human skin that were placed on their own bookshelf, flesh against flesh as their covers touched. Each was a slightly different size, all the better to allow the tattoos to be fully displayed on the covers and spine. There was space missing for the book he would have had made from the skin that had been found at the old abattoir. It was in the evidence room now, but perhaps there would be a way to get it back once the noise had died down.

Owning a Cabinet of Obscene Objects had once been fashionable amongst aristocratic families. So many of the treasures of antiquity portrayed sex and debauchery that special rooms were created to protect the eyes of the more sensitive members of society. Dale thought of this place as his own cabinet, where only the strong could stomach what was within. Not that he ever allowed anyone inside. The bachelor life suited him just fine.

He turned and bent to his prize possession, his pulse racing as he placed his hands upon the box. It was carved with images of carnal depravity, one of those objects that the public would complain of while secretly craving a look. As part of the police task force on pornography, he had overseen the seizure of millions of photos and videos over the years. He had kept a selection of it to add to his own collection, not for his own pleasure of course, but to galvanize his desire to stamp out the perverts who made them. Only by understanding their mindset could he seek them out and destroy them.

He had also kept copies of crime scene photos, finding a beauty in the colors and poses of corpses. He opened the box, his hand hovering over his pictures. He wanted to allow himself the time to sit and gaze at them, to find his own pleasure in the descent into depravity. But he had more work to do today. He pulled out four new photos from his jacket pocket. Each one was a close-up of a corpse from the Turbine Hall, three women and a man, each body ripped apart but their faces intact. Dale liked beauty with an edge of darkness and these epitomized his particular fascination.

He sat down on the single chair in the room, an antique he had purchased from the estate of Sir Francis Galton, the esteemed eugenicist, a man who had known about culling the weak. Dale liked to think he could channel the great man here somehow. He breathed deeply and took another sip of his whiskey. Now that he had the mandate of the city to pursue those responsible for the Masquerade Massacre, it was time to send a stronger signal. He had been preparing for this day for a long time and finally he could act with public support behind him. In the next week, he would rid London of its dregs and take the Mayoralty on a surge of public support for strong-armed action.

He thought back to the Turbine Hall in the moments before the explosion. He had turned to fix the masquerade in his mind, seeing the hall through the slits in his mask, framed as a tableau of revelry. The proud before the fall. But someone had seen him. There was no way Jamie Brooke could have recognized him in the mask, but he had felt a moment of connection between them.

She had been a thorn in his side for too long now. Her interference had brought down the Lyceum that night in the Hellfire Caves and she had stumbled into the plans RAIN had for the mentally ill. Dale remembered their confrontation after that case. He had wanted her reassigned somewhere she would be kept busy and out of the way, but she had resigned and started her own investigation service. She couldn't be allowed to threaten his plans, but there were ways she could be dealt with this time and it might help rid him of the others too.

Dale pulled out his wallet and riffled through it, finding the business card with a blue boxing glove on it. He picked up the phone and dialed. He would start with Southwark, his own rotten borough. If he picked off the leaders, the rest would fall.

CHAPTER 22

THE SMASHING OF GLASS woke Magda from a deep sleep. Her heart beat fast at the unusual sound, panic rising in her chest. She untangled herself from O's sleeping form and pulled a robe around herself. She walked quickly into the studio area to find flames spreading from a broken bottle of accelerant, glass all over the floor from the broken window.

The fire caught on some of the flammable paint and flames spread quickly towards the stack of canvases in the corner.

"Olivia," Magda shouted. "Get up, quickly. We have to get out." She grabbed at some of the canvases nearest to her, dragging them out of the way of the flames, but she knew it was too late. The fire was spreading too fast.

The high-pitched squeal of the smoke alarm pierced the air, a note of danger and desperation. Magda beat at the flames with a fire blanket, sobbing as she watched her canvases catch and burn.

O emerged from the bedroom and rushed into the kitchenette to grab the fire extinguisher. But Magda knew that it was only meant for a small fire and sure enough, it was soon empty, the flames still spreading. She called the emergency services, giving the address in a calm voice and explaining the situation, even as her mind struggled to fathom the destruction around her. The soothing voice of the operator assured her that the fire brigade was on its way, but Magda knew it would be too late.

"We have to get out." O tugged at her lover's arm, covering her mouth to block some of the smoke.

"I can't leave it all," Magda whispered in desperation. "This is everything. I'll be ruined."

O put her hand on Magda's cheek, turning her face and looking into her eyes.

"*You* are everything, my love. This stuff can be replaced, but you can't. Haven't we learned that over the last days?"

Magda looked around at the flaming studio, her canvases, her equipment on the way to ruin. This was her life's work, her sanctuary. The flames roared as they accelerated through a pile of packaging material.

"We have to get out now." O pulled on her arm and Magda's resolve crumbled. With tears in her eyes, she stumbled out of the studio and into the courtyard outside. Groups of people stood looking on, tenants from the flats above weeping as the flames climbed higher and they were pushed back towards the road beyond.

The sound of cracking and buckling beams could be heard from within as an upper level collapsed down through the ceilings to the ground floor. The creaking protests of the building were like the groans of the dying.

Magda stood as close she could, the heat from the fire almost burning her skin. In other circumstances she would have reveled in these flames, an element of destruction that allowed rebirth. She had thrown her own past on flames like these, destroying what was spent and rotten to enable the new to arise. But now … everything she had built here would be destroyed. She swallowed, fighting to hold back the tears.

The sound of sirens filled the air and fire engines

arrived along with police to control the scene. Tenants and onlookers were pushed further back, urged to move away but Magda couldn't leave. She watched as fire hoses began to soak the flames, their powerful jets raining down on her studio. Whatever hadn't been lost in the fire would be destroyed by its opposite element. Perhaps there was a lesson in that.

O slipped an arm round Magda's waist, leaning her head on her lover's shoulder.

"There's nothing we can do here," she said. "Why don't you come back to my place? Have a drink. We'll come back when it's all under control."

But Magda couldn't tear her eyes from the flames.

"I need to stay," she said, her voice quiet. She turned and looked into O's eyes. She was so lucky to have this woman in her life, but there were times when she needed to be alone. "But maybe you can go get some supplies. Hot chocolate would be good. Maybe something stronger to go with it."

O leaned up and kissed her full on the mouth.

"Of course, I won't be long."

O turned and navigated through the crowd away from the scene. Magda walked to the edge of the perimeter and sat down on a step, exhaling deeply as she looked into the flames again, holding out her hands to the fire so she could see the full length of her own tattoos, silhouetted against the orange-red of the flames. The marks on her skin were both the end and the beginning, she thought, remembering the past. Had it all been worth it?

She had left Ireland twenty-two years ago now – strange that it had been so long. It seemed like a different life.

Back then, her name had been Ciara, for her dark hair and for the saint who saved a village from fire back in the seventh century. Raised in a strict Catholic home and sent to a convent school, her world had been shuttered and controlled by rules. Any question deemed wrong for a girl to ask had resulted in punishment, and she had spent a lot of time recovering from the birch in the struggle to be silent.

Boys were forbidden and exciting, although she had sensed more of an attraction to girls even back then. The nights she had escaped the convent and spent drinking with the local boys had turned into something more, and when she discovered she was pregnant, her world turned. She was called deviant and possessed by the Devil for following the path of sin. Magda remembered how confused she had been back then, how angry that fumbling and pain had resulted in something that turned her into a pariah. Even now, she could still recall the hate in the Reverend Mother's eyes as she had been cast out.

They had sent her to a house for unwed mothers to await the arrival of the child, but Magda knew she couldn't stay. She had felt an overwhelming sense that she would die there if she remained. The eyes of the other girls were hollow and haunted, rumors of a pit out the back where hundreds of babies and young mothers were buried, taken back to God.

That night she had run from the place, escaping over the fields and heading cross country, eventually reaching the coast. There she had used her body to bargain for a ferry crossing, the pregnancy not yet far gone enough to put the man off. She didn't care for the sexual act, but she certainly understood what it was worth.

Once on English soil, she had found an abortion clinic. When they asked for her name, she found herself saying Magda. The harsh syllables were more European than Irish and yet Mary Magdalene had always been the saint she had loved the most. The sinner who Jesus had loved, the woman whom he chose to reveal himself to first in the garden after his resurrection.

Magda looked down at her tattoos. The ink reclaimed her body, but it had taken many years to get to the point where she accepted all of herself. Sex was the only trade she had when she arrived in London, and she had become the very sinner that the nuns claimed she was. But the sex was mechanical, and never meant anything except cash to live on. It was work, and easy enough. There had been some bastards but most were lonely men who needed to be touched, and she had understood their need for love and acceptance.

Perhaps she had always loved women, but she hadn't even known it was allowed until London, the city that welcomed all. She had found her tribe here, the sex workers, the junkies, the pagans, those who society had labeled deviant but really just didn't conform. A cast of antiheroes against the backdrop of the greatest city on earth.

The Magdalene had been her first tattoo, embodying both sinner and saint in her many incarnations. She was also separate from the Mother figure, the Mary who Magda could only pity. The Mother had no identity apart from her relationship to the Son and Magda couldn't ever see herself living like that. But the Magdalene – now there was a woman worth admiring.

The flames were dying down now, finally under control by the fire service. Above her, Magda heard the cawing of the ravens. The birds wheeled high in the sky but Magda could still feel her connection to them. Sometimes it was as if she saw with their eyes. Her other full-sleeve tattoo was for them, her totem birds, and for the Morrigan, the Celtic goddess of battle who roamed on the wings of ravens, choosing those who would die and those who would live again.

On the day the tattoos had been finished, Magda finally felt her own transformation had completed. She tied herself to her Irish-Catholic roots in one way, but her own truth was bound up in the strong female goddess. On that day, she had walked away from sex work – but not from sex workers. This borough was her home now, and her work as an urban shaman was to bring that sense of the otherworld to the physical. But was she too attached to what she had created here, and was this a way to leave it all behind again? Was it time to turn her back on London and seek peace somewhere new?

There was a deep booming sound as thunder rolled across the night sky and it began to rain. Magda turned her face to the sky, letting the drops wash her tears away as she sent up a prayer to the goddess of the dark, she of the moon, the Maiden and the Crone.

"Help me," Magda whispered.

Ash ran in rivulets around her feet now, remnants of her art mingling with the structure of the building. It would soon flow into the Thames, the droplets becoming one with the great river that kept the city alive. Magda smiled. Her own ashes would be scattered there one day. It was a reminder that all would perish but this city would stand, whatever came.

As the rain began to hammer down, Magda huddled back into the doorway. Some of the crowd dispersed while others put up colored umbrellas, their faces in shadow. O returned, juggling an umbrella and a bulging paper bag. She crouched on the step next to Magda, sheltering them both from the downpour.

"Here," O said, pulling out two steaming cups of hot chocolate. "Sugar makes everything better." She dug back in the bag and pulled out a large chocolate brownie. "Overdosing on it must seriously help." Magda gave a half smile as they broke the cake in two and shared the pieces, watching as the firefighters finished dowsing the flames and the rain dampened any last embers. The sweet taste in her mouth made Magda focus on that moment, how grateful she was to be alive, to have O by her side.

"Thank you," she said, turning to kiss O's cheek. Her words contained a promise for a future, whatever that would look like.

"We'll take it a day at a time," O said. "You'll create new work soon enough, and you can stay with me until we find you a new studio. The insurance will cover it, although I know the money won't replace your art." She paused, gazing into the ruins that lay before them. "What do you think they'll do with this site? Rebuild the studios?"

Magda stiffened as realization dawned. "This block is owned by the same corporation that has been trying to turn the social housing into luxury flats. They've been trying to get us out for years. Now there'll be no more annoying tenants to deal with."

"You don't think –" O's words trailed off, her blue eyes clouding. "Oh no – what if this isn't the only place under attack?" She dug through her bag. "I haven't been checking my phone." She pulled it out. There were ten missed calls and texts.

O stood up, her face pale. "I need to get to the Kitchen."

CHAPTER 23

They came before dawn, black balaclavas over their heads to hide their faces from the ever-present CCTV cameras and matching black clothing with no identifying marks. One of them carried a baseball bat, another one hefted a tire iron, banging it against his palm. The other two held no obvious weapons, but their meaty hands were clenched into fists. They all wore thick-soled work boots. "The uniform of the militia," their leader called it. They were working together to clean up the city and as long as the police powers were curtailed by bureaucracy, this was the only way the deviants could be dealt with.

They were silent as they approached the Kitchen, their steps deliberate, single-minded. One of them jimmied the lock, breaking open the door and allowing them into the space. The smell of roasting meat hung in the air, a homely smell that made one of the men briefly reconsider what they had come to do. The leader took charge, gesturing as he spoke.

"You and you – get to work on the cooking facilities. I want everything destroyed so it can't be easily fixed. No fire here though, only damage. You – with me out the back."

Two of the men got to work in the kitchen. One unplugged the chest freezer, opening the lid to reveal containers of stew, cuts of meat and bags of vegetables. He grabbed a huge bottle of bleach from the cleaning supplies and poured it over the food. *No dinner for the dole bludgers*, he thought. Then he turned to the double fridge, swinging the baseball bat as he walked. *Time to break some shit.* The man smiled with pleasure.

Another man began to systematically destroy the inner workings of all the equipment in the large kitchen. With his electrical and engineering background, he understood it wasn't about brute force and smashing things. It was about twisting wires and cutting supply lines and melting specific elements that were hard and expensive to replace. It would take them weeks to get this place running again.

In the storeroom, the leader opened the back doors to reveal the small truck they'd arrived in.

"Everything needs to go," he said, pointing at the shelves full of canned and packaged food, boxes of fruit and vegetables. "Empty the place and we'll dump it all on the way home."

They began shifting the pallets, loading them into the truck as sounds of muted destruction came from the kitchen.

It soon began to rain, the overcast skies breaking. The leader looked up at the clouds. It would be heavy enough to help firefighters calm the flames from the studio they had torched earlier.

"Let's get a move on," he said. "We need to get out of here."

As they finished packing the last of the boxes into the van, a young man rounded the corner, approaching the entrance to the Kitchen. He was blonde, with a blue streak through his hair. He had his hands in his pockets and a half smile on his lips.

The men in the shadowed parking area stood still as he approached. The leader held his hand up, waiting to see whether the young man would pass on, just another local out for a morning walk.

But he stopped at the door of the Kitchen and pulled a set of keys from his pocket. As he reached for the lock, his face fell. He saw the broken lock and reached for his phone.

The leader nodded at two of the men.

They burst from the shadows with no words, only heavy footsteps thumping on the pavement. The young man looked up and saw them, dropping the keys and sprinting away.

The first man was on him in seconds, pushing him to the ground.

"No you don't, you little fag."

He kicked out viciously, slamming his boot into the young man's stomach.

The beating was swift and deliberate, the men knowledgeable on the various subcategories of assault, battery and grievous bodily harm. Within a minute, the young man was unconscious, his beautiful face a bloody mess, his body curled in on itself in pain.

They left him there and ran back to the van, jumping in as it roared off down the road. The rain pooled around the young man's body, washing the blood from his broken skin.

***

O jumped out of the cab and ran towards the door of the Kitchen dodging the puddles. Magda paid the driver and followed her, shielding her face from the heavy rain. As she approached the door, O slipped, dropping her bag. Magda bent to pick it up and as she did so, she saw the body on the pavement further down the street.

Magda dashed to the young man's body, O running after her. Magda felt for the pulse at his neck. It was weak and sputtering. She pulled out her phone and called for an ambulance, giving them the location.

"It's Ed," O said quietly, kneeling by his body, uncaring of the puddles. "He works the morning shift." She bent to his ear. "Hold on," she whispered. "We're here now and help is coming. Hang in there, Ed – please."

Magda reached out a hand and laid it on the young man's chest, willing life into him. Above her, a flock of crows began to gather and circle, their feathers dripping in the rain. Their harsh cawing joined Magda's whispered chant of ancient power as O looked on, her eyes fixed on Ed's pale face.

Within minutes, a yellow and green motorbike swerved around the corner, the distinctive shades of the ambulance service marking it out. In central London, they were mostly on scene faster than the larger vans. The single responder grabbed her bike pack and knelt by Ed's side. As Magda lifted her hand and moved back, the crows settled in a nearby tree, silent now as they watched the scene with narrow black eyes.

"We only recently found him," O said, as the paramedic expertly assessed the wounds, calling on her radio for a full ambulance crew.

"We can't move him," the paramedic said. "And I'm worried about internal bleeding after an assault like this. The police will be here soon to take your statements."

Magda held O's hand as they watched her work. The ambulance arrived and they soon had Ed on a gurney and in the van.

"Where are you taking him?" O asked.

"St Thomas," the paramedic said. "But it will be a while until he comes round."

The police arrived as the ambulance drove off. Two officers emerged from the patrol car, gesturing to O and

Magda to stand in the shelter of the nearby houses.

"Didn't we see you earlier?" one of the officers said. "At the fire near Borough Market."

Magda nodded.

"It's been a busy night."

"How about we do the statements inside the Kitchen?" O said. "We can get out of the rain."

They walked back down the street. The door was open a fraction.

"That's unusual," O said. "It should be locked, unless Ed opened it."

One of the officers bent to the lock.

"It's been broken," he said. "We'll go in first."

Magda and O stood back as the officers pushed open the door and proceeded inside. The smell of rancid meat wafted out to them, overlaid with the stink of shit and piss.

O's face contorted with pain and she rushed inside, Magda following.

The police officers stood looking at the wreckage of the place. Every piece of furniture was smashed, every item in the kitchen destroyed, food all over the floor topped with human excrement. The walls were spray painted with graffiti, the black paint dripping globules onto the floor.

Whores. Fags. Deviants. Get out.

The hateful words burned in Magda's mind, somehow worse than the destruction that lay about them.

O fell to her knees, tears streaming down her face. Magda knelt next to her, wrapping her arms around her weeping lover. After a night of staying strong, this final offense had broken them.

CHAPTER 24

IT HAD BEEN A long day.

Blake walked slowly along the crowded streets from the museum back towards his flat. With each step he felt the jarring of the pavement through his bruised body and each breath hurt his lungs. He really should be in bed, but the exhibition opened at the weekend and it was all hands on deck to finish the last pieces of work. He wanted to be part of it.

After the blast at the Tate, Margaret had agreed on time off, but Blake wanted to complete his part of the display, and working alongside Catherine wasn't so difficult. He turned away from the flat and headed for Bar-Barian. Alcohol was the best way he knew to quiet his mind and dull the pain of his injuries.

A couple of drinks to take the edge off.

He walked into the bar, its familiarity a comfort. He didn't have to pretend here, because he was surrounded by people like himself. People who found truth and solace in drink.

"Usual?"

Blake nodded and Seb the barman poured two shots of tequila and grabbed a bottle of Becks from the fridge. Blake downed the shots, letting the golden nectar seep through him, bringing a calm he could reach no other way. He sipped at the beer, checking out the after-work crowd who gathered in Soho to find love for the night, acceptance in the arms of a stranger. Drinking alone in his flat meant that he had a problem, but here he was just one face in a party that went on at all hours in this part of London.

After another couple of shots, Blake sensed the heaviness that would let him slip into dreamless sleep. He wandered home slowly, the few blocks taking longer than usual as he lingered, watching the faces of the passersby. This was the floating part of being happily drunk, a well-being that buoyed the spirit.

Maybe he should call Jamie, Blake thought. Maybe she would come over and they would be together. Or he could call Catherine for something altogether less complicated.

He shook his head as he pushed the key into the lock on the front door. Probably best to go to sleep. He walked up the stairs, his steps heavy.

Then stopped at the top of the stairs. Something was wrong.

The door to his flat was open a few inches. Someone was here. The drunken sensations subsided as Blake focused. He clutched his keys in his hand, pushing one through his fingers to use as a weapon if needed.

He pushed open the door.

The man from the museum sat on his bed holding the Galdrabók in his strong hands. It was open to a page of Icelandic spells, the man's lips moving as he read them quietly.

He looked up at Blake, his eyes the color of northern oceans that would freeze a man to death in seconds. The scar across his nose was deep, the flesh livid around the edges. He was a stranger, but once again Blake saw a hint of his father in those features.

Blake stood in the doorway, ready to run.

"What are you doing here?" he asked. "Who are you?"

"I've been wanting to read this book again for a long time," the man said, with a slight Scandinavian accent. "Your father stole it from us many years ago."

Blake knew he should give it to the man and let him leave, but he felt a strange possessiveness for it, a need to keep it under his bed like a talisman. His father had used the book and Blake was curious as to whether he could use it himself.

"You don't look much like him." The man smiled, baring teeth that had been filed in the way of the Vikings. "But then I heard Magnus married as far from the north as he could."

"Who are you?" Blake asked again.

"Your uncle," the man said. "Allfrid Olofsson. One of your northern kin."

He held out a hand to Blake, holding it there, waiting. His other hand rested on the Galdrabók, claiming it.

After a moment, Blake reached out with gloved hands and shook. Allfrid looked down at the gloves.

"You have the sight, then."

His words were matter of fact and Blake reeled at the implication. It was the first time that anyone had been so accepting of his gift, treating it as mundane.

"What do you know of it?" he asked, coming into the room now and shutting the door. Allfrid was a threat, of that he was sure, but he also wanted to know more.

"You come from an ancient line of seers," Allfrid said. "But your father wanted none of it. He was scared of the visions and what was demanded of those who could renew the pact with the gods."

Blake sat down heavily in his desk chair.

"My father had visions too?"

Betrayal washed over him. The years of beating, the

curses, the claim that Satan had entered him. All were just a way for his father to deny his own gift.

"He was one of the strongest among us," Allfrid said. "At least when we were young. But he left before he understood the true meaning or how to control it."

Blake looked at Allfrid, the words sparking something within.

"Yes, boy." Allfrid understood the look. "You *can* control it. You don't need those gloves if you know how to separate the visions in your mind from reality. You've never been taught the right way."

Blake pulled the gloves from his hands, revealing the crisscross scars underneath.

Allfrid shook his head in resignation. "Your father?"

Blake nodded. "He tried to beat the curse from me. And yet he kept the Galdrabók and used it to draw people to him. Even my mother, I suppose."

"We all have to manage our addictions," Allfrid said. His piercing gaze rocked Blake to the core, as if he could see the alcohol wrapped around his soul. "It's a struggle we each walk alone." He traced a finger over the pages of the book. "But this can help you, as can your family."

He thrust the book towards Blake.

"Read me through it, I know you can do this. Let me show you the north."

Blake hesitated. He had read his father through the book and witnessed a human sacrifice that left him retching and weak. Was he safe in this room, in a city so far from that wilderness?

He sensed a hard edge to Allfrid, a blade's breadth away from savagery, but here in the city it remained cloaked. If he opened his mind to the man, would he be able to return?

But curiosity drove him on. This was the first time anyone had explained his visions as an integral part of him, and now he knew he wasn't alone.

Blake put his hand on the book and closed his eyes.

There was no sinking through the layers of memory this time. There was a pure jolt of energy and he gasped with the cold. Blake opened his eyes to find himself standing in freshly fallen snow surrounded by birch trees. The tinkling of a stream pervaded the glade and a light rain fell on his exposed skin. Above the trees he could see mountaintops.

Blake inhaled deeply. The air was fresh and clean, filling his lungs as a sense of freedom expanded within him. There was nothing of human manufacture in sight, the sounds and smells only spoke of what had been here for millennia.

There was a crunch in the snow behind him and Blake turned to see Allfrid smiling at him.

"This is only the beginning," he said. "But I wanted you to see the place I come to be at peace." He looked up to the mountain. "Your father and I climbed that peak as boys. Back then, he understood the power of the place. But he left and when you're far from nature, you lose touch with its strength."

Blake could hear his own heartbeat in the still of the glade. He could feel the pulse at his neck, his wrists, and he felt a connection to the earth here. He wanted to jump around in the snow, lie back in it and look up at the sky. It was far from the wild, dark places of the New Forest where he had grown up.

Allfrid cupped his hands around his mouth and called into the woods, a harsh sound, the words as raw as the land they stood in.

A few minutes later, faces appeared in the trees and figures crept through the wood, darting between the sheltered spaces. There were children amongst the group as well as older people and those Blake's own age.

One little girl peeked out from a tree close by, catching his eye. She giggled at him and Blake smiled back. He must look odd to them with his dark skin and city clothes. She took a step out into the snow, her hand held out to him in greeting.

As she came closer, Blake reached out to touch the girl's fingers.

A whoosh of cold wind swept snow into his face.

He gasped, opened his eyes, and he was back in the attic flat again. He grabbed the desk with both hands, trying to orient himself into the physical space again.

Allfrid laughed, shaking his head. "You need training, boy, if you're to use your gift properly."

"They could see me," Blake said, his voice shaky. "Those people, they could see me and touch me?"

"Our tribe live with closer ties to outer realms. What you see as a vision, others experience as part of their usual world. You differentiate but that's only because you haven't truly accepted that part of yourself. But every time you read, you take a step towards us. Each time you sink into memory, it also seeps into you. Beware of doing this without the proper training, boy. Come to us and I will show you."

Allfrid rose to his feet, the Galdrabók in his hands. "Now, I must go and I'm taking this." His head almost touched the ceiling in the tiny flat and he bent a little, the posture of a man who was always leaning over others. "The grimoire belongs with the family – but you are one of us."

He pulled a map from his pocket and handed it to Blake. It was marked by lines and runes, with a clear red X in a patch of green in northern Sweden. "The glade is marked. If you come to us, we can teach you of your gift and how to use the book." Allfrid looked out of the window, over the rooftops of London. "Or you can stay here, wearing those gloves to hold back the visions, using alcohol to deaden their power, wondering how you fit into the world." He looked down at Blake again. "It's your choice."

Allfrid turned and walked out of the flat without a backwards glance, leaving Blake sitting on a chair, shaken by the experience of the vision. He heard his uncle's footsteps tramp down the stairs and then the bang of the door onto the street.

CHAPTER 25

JAMIE PUSHED OPEN THE door to her tiny office and picked up the mail from the mat, juggling her coffee cup in the other hand. She wanted this space to keep her work separate from her personal life but once again, the two were mingling. *Perhaps work was life*, she thought. For some people at least. The need to work certainly drove her, and she never wanted to stop. Retirement seemed an outmoded concept from a different time and the day her brain checked out was the day she would stop working. But it was more than the love of the job that kept her going today. After Polly's death, she had lost purpose but there was a glimmer of hope that she might find it again in this community.

The news from Magda this morning had made Jamie determined to dig into the ownership records of the buildings in the Southwark area. Who would stand to gain from the destruction of the studio apartments and who would want the Kitchen closed? Ed was in a stable condition in hospital, but it seemed like the community was being attacked on all fronts.

She opened her laptop and began to search the council databases that held the area's property records. There were layers of holding companies but the trail would be there,

Jamie was sure of it. She knew how to investigate into the directors and shareholders of companies from her days in the police and it was only a matter of patience to sift through the levels down to the originators. She sipped her coffee as she searched, copying and pasting lists of names, cross-checking against the Companies database that held the legal records for each UK entity.

After a couple of hours lost in data, Jamie had a broad sense of how many companies were vying for the valuable property in Southwark. Many were registered overseas, but there were names that tied them together. There was a crossover of interest between projects as varied as the Shard construction to Guy's and St Thomas' hospital development and renovation of some of the older warehouses. One name kept coming up: Vera Causa Limited.

Jamie did a quick search and discovered that the Latin words meant True Cause. She began to delve into what she could find about the company, quickly discovering that the shareholding lay in bearer shares. These were physical stock certificates where the owner didn't have to be registered in any way and dividends were disbursed to whoever held the shares. The setup was designed to hide ownership and legislation was currently being debated that would make it illegal. But for now, the owner of these bearer shares could stay hidden. Jamie frowned, taking a last sip of the now-cold coffee.

A sudden commotion and banging from the outer offices broke her concentration.

Jamie emerged from her office to find one of the other tenants shouting at a man in the hallway. The official wore a pinstriped suit, standing with back straight as he taped a notice on the door.

"My contract clearly says that the lease is six months," the tenant exclaimed, waving paperwork at him.

The suit handed a document to the gesticulating man.

"You missed the clause for pest control," he said. "Everyone needs to be out of here within the next two hours and then fumigation will commence. You won't have access for at least a week, but you'll be contacted when the building is available again."

The tenant continued raging, his protestations useless against immoveable bureaucracy.

Jamie ducked back inside her tiny office, packing up what little paperwork she had started to accumulate into her backpack. There was a nagging doubt in her mind about the timing of the pests and no evidence of them that she could see.

Walking downstairs ten minutes later, she stopped to read the notice from the landlord on the way out. The company name at the bottom was one of those that she had tied back to Vera Causa.

The sun was out as she emerged onto the street. The units were away from the main tourist strip along the Thames, but close enough that she could be amongst people quickly. Jamie appreciated anonymity in the middle of a bustling city. Small communities might protect in some ways, but they also curtailed originality and punished nonconformity. The city allowed all to flourish and anyone could find their niche here, but could it be that Vera Causa was trying to make Southwark compliant in some way? A test case, with the rest of the city to follow.

Walking helped her to think, so Jamie emerged onto the riverside near the Anchor pub and turned west. The grey of the Thames was like quicksilver in the sun, the waters high and lapping against the strong pontoons that held it back from the city. Jamie passed a busker in the Southwark Bridge underpass, the jaunty guitar tune bringing a smile to her face. She dropped a couple of coins into his case, nodding a thankyou. The buskers and street entertainment flourished in the city as the sun came out, the summer months bringing tourists from all over the world. And here in Southwark, busking kept artists from the food banks and brought music to the streets. Doubly wonderful, Jamie thought.

A little further on, she reached the Tate Modern. The old power station with its one tall chimney stood proud on the south bank facing the Millennium Bridge, with the classic dome of St Paul's beyond. But today, the crime scene tape held back curious tourists and the gallery was closed until further notice. Most of the structural damage from the masquerade attack had been at the back of the large Turbine Hall, out of sight from the north view, but Jamie knew what it looked like inside.

Images from that night flashed through her brain, the dead and the dying, her frantic search for Blake.

Her breath came fast and she moved to the edge of the pavement, sitting down on a step for a moment as the dizziness passed. A part of her mind witnessed the panic her body felt. Strange, because she had never experienced this in the police, even as part of the homicide team.

Jamie let the waves of anxiety roll over her as she sat looking out at the ever-shifting waters of the Thames. Perhaps it was precisely because she had no team that she was feeling out of control. She certainly missed having backup and resources. She thought of Missinghall and his enthusiasm, the respect she had earned in the police. Had she been too quick to resign? Could she consider going back?

Feeling calmer now, Jamie walked back to her little apartment complex. If she couldn't work at the office, she'd have to make a space in the flat because the job was really too private to work in a public coffee shop.

Her street was tightly packed with close terraced houses, each one up against the next in a racially mixed community. Jamie spotted a few people standing outside her building. She frowned. That was unusual.

As she approached, she saw the same eviction team that had been at the office building. But this time there were a couple of enforcer types with the suits, gorilla men with thick biceps and heavy foreheads. The crowd of tenants from the building had been joined by several of the other street residents. Some were angry and others shook their heads in resignation.

"It's temporary," the suited man was saying, his hands held up apologetically. "But you have to be out before midnight. You should be able to get back in within the next week. We'll notify you all."

"What about compensation?"

"You can't do this –"

"My kids need –"

"Where are we meant to go?"

"The faster you get out and we can start the fumigation process, the faster you can all get back in."

Jamie stood on the edge of the crowd. There was no way this was legal, but it would take a lot of energy to fight the powerful corporation that stood behind the eviction notice. It seemed Vera Causa Limited had a long reach, and this definitely felt like it was turning personal. Years in the police had given Jamie a sense when all was not quite as it should be, and she was getting that vibe on overdrive right now. She needed to find out more on Vera Causa, but she couldn't do it here.

She elbowed her way through the crowd.

"I'm in Flat 9," she said to the man on the door.

He grunted and let her through.

Up in her flat, Jamie grabbed a rucksack and filled it with some clothes, grabbing whatever was clean. Looking around, she realized there wasn't much she actually cared about here. Her life wasn't defined by things anymore, but by memories. She picked up the photo of Polly by her bed, her daughter's laughing face captured in a moment without pain. She smiled. She would have done anything to save Polly, but at least they had experienced happy times together in the short time they had. She wrapped the photo frame in a t-shirt and put it gently in her pack. Vera Causa could take her home and her workplace, but they couldn't take her memories.

Jamie pulled bedsheets out of the cupboard and spread them over the furniture. She was doubtful that they were actually going to fumigate the place but might as well make it look as if she believed the story.

It was getting dark when she emerged outside. The gorilla men stood by the gate and they ticked her name off a list as she confirmed her cellphone number.

"We'll call you as soon as it's all done," one of the men said. "Should be a week at most."

Jamie didn't bother to reply. She headed down the road away from the flat, back towards the center of Southwark.

She had a feeling of being untethered, unsure of what to do next. She could just keep walking. She could get on a train and head to the coast, get on a boat and go to France and on through the continent, or even fly somewhere new. She thought of the freedom she felt dancing tango. South America had always been somewhere she'd wanted to visit. Now she was free to go and the opportunities suddenly seemed endless.

After all, there was no real reason to stay. Was there?

Blake was damaged, and perhaps she had imagined their connection. Establishing her business was an uphill battle and she was only on the edges of the Southwark community right now. They wouldn't even notice she was gone. The thought was freeing but also slightly disconcerting. Jamie knew her independence had kept her from being immersed in a community when she was caring for Polly, and her life was poorer for it now. But the double eviction seemed like a pretty big sign that she wasn't wanted here.

Could she commit to this place when everything seemed to point towards leaving?

Jamie walked down to South Bank and stood looking out at the Thames. The waters ran swiftly towards the ocean, the eddies making patterns in the current. Flotsam and jetsam, pieces of the discarded city, caught on the boats moored in the central channel. They were pinned for a moment, crushed against the metal and then dragged under or whipped around the side by the fast-moving river. Then they drifted on towards the sea.

Jamie exhaled slowly, then pulled out her phone and dialed.

CHAPTER 26

O ANSWERED ON THE second ring.

"Jamie, are you OK?"

Jamie smiled at the caring note in O's voice. She did have friends here, and right now her friends were hurting too.

"Actually, I've been evicted."

"What the hell is going on?" O's frustration echoed Jamie's own. "Why don't you come over here? You can kip on the couch, if that's alright. Magda's here too."

"Thank you," Jamie said. "I'll be there in twenty minutes."

***

O's flat was chaotic. Magda stood in the middle of the living area surrounded by the few canvases that hadn't been destroyed in the fire. She held out one of her crow photographs to Jamie, the edges of one corner burned and curled, the black bubbled up beneath the feathers.

"I think I might have found a new technique," Magda said, her laugh with an edge of mania. She shook her head. "But this is all I have left from ten years in that studio."

O swept out of the kitchen, a large glass of red wine in either hand.

"You have your wonderful mind left, my love." She handed one glass to Magda and the other to Jamie. "And you both have my flat. What's not to like?"

She turned back into the kitchen, emerging with her own large glass and the rest of the bottle.

Jamie couldn't help but smile at O's optimism. In the face of everything they were going through, it seemed she still saw a positive side.

O looked at her watch.

"Quick, turn on the telly. The announcement about the Mayor should be on any minute."

The familiar sounds of the BBC news jingle filled the flat and they watched in silence as the announcement was made. Even O couldn't summon anything positive to say as they watched Dale Cameron step forward to accept the position.

Jamie felt a stone settle in the pit of her stomach, a heavy sense of dread. Riding high on a right-wing ticket of cleaning up the city, Cameron's patrician face was all smiles and promises, but part of her knew that he was entwined in some of the darker corners of government.

"Shit." Magda took a large swig of her wine. "There goes everything we've worked for. That bastard is in the pockets of the building development companies. Southwark will become a rich man's playground now he has a say."

O stood and downed her wine, then began to open another bottle of red. "Surely he won't have the power to change things so substantially?" she said.

Jamie sighed. "He has the mandate of being elected on his policies to clean up the streets, so he'll be able to act pretty fast."

"And with Amanda Masters in hospital ..." Magda shook her head. "Maybe we should give up, leave London altogether. We can start again somewhere new. I can find a studio somewhere else."

O put down her glass and hugged Magda close, her pale arms stark against Magda's dark clothes.

"Don't say that," O whispered. "If we leave, they will have won. I won't let you go. This is your place, Magda. Your ravens are here, your people are here. Cross Bones needs you." O looked over at Jamie. "Tell her, please."

Jamie took a sip of her wine.

"It certainly seems as if we're being pushed out – arson, violence, evictions, all targeted at one part of the community." She frowned. "But if we go, then this area will be poorer for losing its diversity. You two are figureheads, leaders of the community. Tomorrow, we should start organizing for protest, contact the press and start taking control of the story."

Jamie's voice was stronger than she felt. A few hours ago she had considered leaving herself, and she knew the power that Cameron had on his side. It wouldn't be easy to go up against him.

O stroked Magda's tattooed arm.

"Sleep helps," she said. "Everything looks better in the morning."

Magda nodded and got up slowly, walking into O's bedroom, leaving O and Jamie to make up a bed on the couch.

"Are you sure this is alright?" O asked, patting the pillow.

"It's amazing," Jamie said. "I … don't have many friends."

O leaned forward and kissed her cheek.

"You have us now. Sleep tight."

Jamie lay down and pulled the blankets tight around her. Somehow, despite everything, she felt hope.

***

Jamie woke to the early-morning sun peeking through the curtains. She unfolded herself from O's couch, her body aching from the uncomfortable night, but her mind felt refreshed and clearer now. They could make a plan to mobilize the community and take back what was threatened.

She heard the buzzing of a mobile phone in the next room.

Moments later, the door opened and O stepped out. She wore a plain white t-shirt that ended at the top of her thighs. Her hair was tousled and her face stricken.

"It's Cross Bones," she said. "There are bulldozers on site. They're beginning construction today."

"Bastard," Jamie said. "Cameron must have had this all lined up. And I bet I know which company is involved." She thought of Vera Causa and how much they stood to gain in the area by raising housing prices. That tiny patch of land was worth millions.

Jamie rolled out of bed, quickly pulling on her clothes. Magda emerged from O's room, tucking her black t-shirt into her jeans. Her eyes were puffy as if she'd been crying, but the angles of her face hardened as she made coffee for them all. She texted furiously as the kettle boiled.

"We have a text chain," she explained to Jamie. "Friends of Cross Bones. I'm telling people to get down there ASAP."

Downing their coffee, the three of them headed out into the early morning, through the streets of Southwark down to Cross Bones Graveyard.

***

Jamie could hear the sounds of trucks and heavy machinery as they neared the square and they quickened their pace. Rounding the corner of Redcross Way, the scale of the project was immediately evident. A whole construction team stood waiting at the gates of Cross Bones. There were two bulldozers ready to demolish what was left standing on the derelict ground and diggers idled on standby to begin excavation.

The building site foreman argued with two people who stood in front of the beribboned gates, their arms wrapped around the railings. Jamie recognized one of them – Meg from the Kitchen, her dreadlocks bouncing as she gesticulated at the graveyard.

"You can't come in here," Meg shouted. "This is sacred ground."

"We have the permits," the foreman said. "It's all been cleared by the Mayor. You have to leave or we're calling security to forcibly remove you."

O ran forward to help, Magda following behind.

"Please," O said. "You can't do this."

As O and Magda argued for more time to present their case to the council, Jamie took up a place next to Meg, winding her arms through the gate railings. The metal was cold, and Jamie shivered a little. Clouds gathered overhead, grey skies threatened rain and storms were forecast for later today. Jamie only hoped they would have reached a reprieve by then.

More people from the community arrived. One by one, they stood silently against the railings, backs to the graveyard, hands touching the fence behind them as if part of the structure. Some brought bike chains and padlocks, attaching themselves physically to the barrier.

The air of rebellion was palpable and Jamie found herself thrilled to be a part of it. As a police officer she had only ever been on the other side, viewing protestors as standing in the way of law and order. But now she had a very different perspective. If the graveyard fell to developers, it would be an end to old Southwark. The enrichment of corporations at the expense of the lively, diverse community. But they had this one chance to stop it.

More and more people arrived as O and Magda kept the foreman talking. Soon, the whole length of the side road was lined with people protecting the graveyard, living flesh and blood standing guard over the bones of those who came before.

"Shit," the foreman finally shouted, spinning away from the two women in frustration. He turned to his team. "Bill, get security down here to move this lot on. We have to break ground today. Until then, time out, everyone."

The workmen turned off the vehicle engines and stood in a huddle away from the site, smoking and drinking coffee. A gentle rain began to patter down and the protestors pulled out raincoats and umbrellas, the colorful arcs echoing the multihued ribbons on the gates. Some shared their shelter and soon people were chattering in groups, the tension broken for now. But Jamie watched the foreman on the phone, wary of who he was speaking to. She knew all too well how the upper echelons of power could skirt round regulations.

A couple of guys from a local independent cafe brought down a tray of red velvet cake and took orders for hot drinks. They had elegantly waxed mustaches and wore black and white striped aprons, part of their funky branding. Jamie couldn't help but smile – only in London could protestors get a hand-delivered double shot vanilla latte.

A young man with a guitar began to sing. At first the protestors and workmen watched him with bemused expressions, but as he sang more bawdy songs, they began to laugh. He played tunes that people knew and some protestors began to sing along. Even a couple of the workmen joined in, and for a moment, Jamie wondered if this might be resolved peacefully, that somehow, the community could save this plot.

Then two white vans turned into Redcross Way, parking next to one of the bulldozers.

The doors slid open and five big men emerged from each.

They were all dressed in security uniforms, impeccably dressed, but Jamie didn't think they would mind getting a little messed up. In fact, they looked like they would welcome it. If she had still been in the police, she wouldn't be scared of this lot. There was a hierarchy of authority and the police trumped security, but here, these men held the higher ground and she saw how much they relished it.

The young man stopped playing his guitar and went to stand against the fence, his hands wound protectively around his instrument. Around her, Jamie sensed the unease of the protestors.

She reached for her phone, turning towards the gate, and quickly called the local police station, reporting trouble. Then she texted Missinghall, advising him to get people down here. It was all she could think of to do.

The rain began to fall harder now, spattering the dirt of the graveyard into murky puddles. The foreman stepped towards the gates, a swagger in his step now he had security backup. He held a golf umbrella above his head with the words of the company emblazoned on it.

Vera Causa.

O and Magda walked forward to represent the protestors, ready to go into verbal battle again.

"We have the correct permits," the foreman said, his voice icy calm now. He thrust the appropriate paperwork at them. "You all need to leave immediately so we can start our work. If you don't, you'll be removed by security."

The big men walked down the line of protestors, their eyes fixing on each face, the promise of violence in their posture and clenched fists. They didn't touch anyone but their message was clear.

Jamie watched one tower over an old lady in a moth-eaten fur coat, a remnant of Southwark's past. She lifted her chin at him in defiance and clutched the railings even harder at his sneer. The people of Southwark were indeed a hardy bunch and Jamie wondered where the woman's strength came from.

"We're exercising our right to protest peaceably," O said, her voice strong. Magda stood at her side, her face stony. "You can't use force to remove us. We've called the press and we'll report our story and stop this development."

The foreman shrugged and signaled to the workmen.

Two of them got back into the bulldozers and started the engines, revving them hard. The other workmen began to gather their equipment, ready to move into the graveyard.

The protestors looked at each other, shaking their heads, not knowing what to do.

"Hold still," Magda shouted above the din. "They're trying to intimidate us. They won't touch us."

As the rain hammered down, the security men spread themselves down the line opposite those huddled against the fence. At a signal from their leader, they took a slow, deliberate step forward.

CHAPTER 27

JAMIE SAW THE MENACE in their eyes, but she didn't believe they would be able to touch the protestors. They were relying on brute intimidation, waiting for the crowd to crack. And it looked like it was beginning to work.

One middle-aged man stepped away from the fence, raising his hands in surrender.

"I'm sorry, O," he called out as he walked away. "I didn't sign up for this."

His defection caused a wave in the group and more began to drop away, heads down against the rain as they retreated. But a core group remained, clustering in front of the main gate, their resolve hardening.

The foreman's phone rang. He answered it and smiled.

He signaled to the head of security and Jamie didn't like what she saw in his eyes. They couldn't touch the protestors – unless someone was protecting them, unless someone would be able to spin this story and stop the police from getting here or preventing charges. It had to be Dale Cameron.

The security men surged forward at the signal and pulled the protestors forcibly from the gates, dragging them kicking and screaming, pushing and shoving hard enough to hurt but not injure too much.

One woman ended up face down in the mud still clutching ribbons from the gate. A security guard stepped on her hand and she screamed. The man smiled and pressed his boot harder.

Jamie moved to help and the man turned to grab her, his meaty fist high. She ducked under and used a knife hand to jab into his throat. He gasped, clutching his neck, his eyes surprised at her retaliation.

Jamie bent to help the woman up, then turned to see two more of the security men walking towards her.

"Feisty little thing, aren't you," one of the men said.

"I'm a former police officer," Jamie snarled at them, standing her ground. "You're all in a lot of trouble for this."

The men laughed. They lunged at the same time and Jamie realized this was no time to fight. There was no way she could come out of this well. Not here, not against these men. She put up her hands and took a step back but the men were already fired up.

They bundled her to the floor, dragging her hands up behind her back, grinding her face into the muddy tarmac.

"Now you stay down," the man whispered, forcing her hands up higher until Jamie felt her shoulders crunch. She let out a whimper and the man relaxed his grip, clearly delighted by her acquiescence.

A roar came from one of the bulldozers. It began to move towards the gates, revving its engine to scare the last protestors out of the way.

It was moving too fast for such a small area, but the man driving was encouraged by the cheers of his co-workers. The rain obscured his vision, hammering down on his windshield as he drove inexorably towards the gates.

Suddenly, Jamie saw O twist out of the grip of one of the security guards and run towards the gates. Magda turned too late to grab her and for a split second, Jamie saw O standing in front of the bulldozer, her body the final obstacle. But the bulldozer didn't stop.

The crunch of metal against gates.

The thud of the vehicle against a body.

Magda's scream.

It all came at once.

The man holding Jamie down released her and she sprang up, running towards the front of the bulldozer. The other workmen were shouting now and the vehicle reversed away. Jamie caught a glimpse of the driver's stricken face. This had all gone too far.

"Call an ambulance," the foreman shouted.

A little group gathered around a fallen figure. O lay against the gate, hands clutched at her belly, eyelids fluttering over a startled gaze. Magda wept by her side, her arms cradling her lover.

"Olivia," she whispered. "Stay with me."

As the rain spattered the ground around them, Jamie heard sirens coming closer. O had stopped the developers today, but at what cost?

***

Jamie leaned her head back against the wall behind her.

Somehow, she had been spared again. In the midst of death and destruction, she walked unharmed. Even though she had begged whatever god there might be to take her instead of her daughter. Even though she had been in the burning caves and near the explosion at the Tate. Did she have some kind of gift like Blake? Or could it be called a curse to watch those you love hurt while you continued to breathe?

Magda sat in silence next to her, staring ahead, her hands clasped so tightly together that her knuckles were white. This waiting was driving them both crazy.

"I'll get us some more coffee," Jamie said. Magda nodded without meeting her eyes.

Jamie walked through the corridors to the hospital coffee shop, navigating by the multicolored department signs. Sterile white walls with the occasional poster encouraging hand sanitation could have been any hospital anywhere. London's complexity disappeared within these walls, individuals reduced to injured body parts.

O lay in surgery with multiple internal injuries from the crush of the bulldozer. The expression on the doctor's face when they had taken her in made Magda weep afresh.

The building work had stopped after the accident, but Jamie knew that it would start again. If not tomorrow, then perhaps the next day or the next. The leaders of the community had been taken out and the rest would now weaken and give up. It was inevitable. The last few days had been about breaking them so they would give up without a fight. Or at least only a pitiful one.

Jamie bought two double shot coffees, some chocolate bars and bananas and headed back to Magda.

"Here you go," Jamie said when she arrived back to find her friend in exactly the same position. "She'll likely be hours yet, so you need to keep your strength up."

"I can't lose her," Magda whispered, turning to Jamie with haunted eyes. "It took me so many years to find someone who accepts all of me."

Jamie took her hand.

"She's not going to die." Jamie put all her hope into her voice, claiming the words as truth as if somehow it would protect O. "She didn't die at the hands of the skin collector, she made it through that and she *will* live now."

Magda nodded. "Yes, you're right. She's a survivor."

"And we have to think positive," Jamie said. "Send her your strength."

Magda took a sip of her coffee.

"The company that wants to develop Cross Bones," she said. "They'll try again, won't they?"

Jamie nodded.

"They have the permits. It's only a matter of time." She paused, thinking of Vera Causa and how entwined they were with the property market in Southwark. Perhaps there was a way. "I do have an inkling of who might be behind it all, though. Perhaps I might be able to find evidence against them. It might help us keep the protest going, get some media attention at least."

"They've taken so much in the last few days, Jamie. If you can find out anything, it might help us keep the community together."

Jamie nodded. She looked at her watch. It was after nine p.m.

"I'll go now. I have a few leads to follow up. Text me or call if you hear anything."

Jamie headed out into the evening, her mind made up.

She had the address of the Vera Causa offices from the research she had done in the last few days. It was time to go to the source and see what she could find.

Getting onto her bike, she rode through the familiar streets, considering what she was about to do. Breaking and entering wasn't new to her – she had broken into a Hoxton studio during the Neville investigation, but Vera Causa was cloaked with secrets. Would she rouse a more powerful force by entering their domain?

She drove along the street where the office was situated. The area was split between residential buildings and new office space. The Vera Causa address was nothing special and there was no sign on the door, no way to know whether this was really the right place. But at least the lights were off.

Jamie parked a little way from the building and then walked back, hands in her pockets. She passed a pub at the head of the street. A couple of smokers stood outside with pints, engrossed in a political argument. The office was at the quieter end, so Jamie walked straight up to the door. Deliberate action was less obvious than hesitancy. *Confidence inspired confidence*, she thought, echoes of her police training resonating even in this less-than-legal situation.

The door had a numeric keypad, so she wasn't getting in this way without specialist equipment.

Jamie walked around the back of the building. There was a fire escape staircase leading up to the second floor. Stepping lightly, she mounted the stairs, examining the windows and doors on each level as she ascended. They were all locked and alarmed.

She turned to look out over the nearby buildings. The Shard towered above, a beacon of blue light announcing its majestic presence. *It was beautiful*, Jamie thought. *A testament to the power of human creativity and drive. If it can be imagined, it can be created.* That's what she used to tell Polly about the world. *Everything around us first existed as an idea in someone's mind*, she would say. Then they made it happen.

Of course, that was just as true for destruction as for creation. Someone's mind was set against the community of Southwark and Jamie felt a renewed desire to seek them out.

She turned and looked at the upper-level windows. They were all locked. Her eyes scanned upwards onto the roof. There was a skylight built into the tiles and it looked as if it might be open an inch. Jamie glanced down. It was a long way to fall.

She began to climb, pushing herself up with her legs and pulling on the tiles above. *Don't look down, don't look down.* The words a mantra in her mind as she inched her way to the skylight.

It was open a little and she slipped her fingers under, pulling it up slowly. It pivoted and opened with only a tiny creak. It didn't look like it was alarmed.

Jamie turned her body, dropping feet first into an attic space. She stood for a moment, breathing quietly, letting her heart rate return to normal as she listened to the building. It was still, silent, and she sensed it was empty, at least for now. But she didn't want to stay too long.

She clicked on her pen torch.

The attic space was cluttered with piles of boxes. Jamie opened one to find stacked rental agreements from the surrounding area. Another was full of sales receipts from a shop with a local address. With so many boxes and not much time, she couldn't hope to find anything up here.

Jamie walked down the stairs, pausing as one creaked underfoot. Her heart raced, but there was no sound of anyone else here. She continued on.

The first floor had an open-plan office space and a conference room with glass walls. The decor was magnolia and shades of blue, a relaxing professional place. She walked around the desks and checked the computers, but all were password protected or logged off. There were some papers on the desks, all evidence of a real estate management company. Nothing untoward. Jamie's heart sank as she looked around. Clearly Vera Causa was very good at navigating the right side of the law, even if their ethics could be questioned.

At the back of the open-plan area was a separate office area, the size of the space indicating it was for senior management. Jamie pushed open the door and glanced around. It was immaculate, chrome surfaces gleaming. It looked to be entirely paperless, no filing cabinets, no documents left out.

Then she saw something glint in the torchlight. Something that could make all the difference.

CHAPTER 28

IT WAS ONLY A fountain pen, but Jamie recognized it as belonging to Dale Cameron. Its distinctive silver fox-head cap was rare and she remembered him using it to sign paperwork back when she was in the police. It had also been in his top pocket when the news of the Mayoralty was announced. Now, the pen lay on the desk, perpendicular to a clean A4 pad of paper.

With her sleeve over her hand, Jamie picked up the pen, wrapped it in a sheet of paper and put it in her jacket pocket. The pen was useless to her, but perhaps Blake would be able to read something from it that would help.

Jamie walked quickly back up to the attic and climbed out of the skylight, making sure to leave it at the same angle it had been when she'd entered. She slipped down the roof tiles onto the fire escape and then quietly walked away from the office building. The pen seemed to burn in her pocket and she saw Dale Cameron's face in her mind. Like a puppet master, he controlled so much behind the scenes, and she wondered how far his influence stretched. How much further he could go as Mayor.

She roared away on the bike, heading towards Bloomsbury.

***

Blake stood in the kitchen holding an empty tequila bottle. It was the last of the batch and there was no other alcohol in the flat.

Perhaps he would go to the corner store and get a small bottle of vodka. That's all he needed to take the edge off. Or he could go down to Bar-Barian and buy his way into oblivion. In many ways that would be preferable, because right now he didn't know what else to do.

The choice his uncle had offered was a gold chalice laced with poison. He wanted to know about his gift, he wanted to meet his extended family, yet he had seen what they did in the forests of the north in a vision of blood and madness. He should forget the Galdrabók and embrace his life here.

But what life? he thought.

He and Jamie skirted the edges of something but were they both too damaged to take it any further? Without her, there was only casual sex, and with his job under threat, would he even have the choice to stay?

Blake clenched the bottle in his hand, knuckles white. Perhaps he shouldn't fight the addiction anymore. Perhaps it was time to just let it play out. He put the bottle next to the bin, picked up his keys, and grabbed his jacket.

The doorbell rang.

Blake frowned. He wasn't expecting anyone, certainly not this late. He clicked the intercom button.

"Hello," he said.

"It's Jamie." Her voice was soft. Blake's heart leapt in his chest. He put down his jacket and pressed the open button.

"Come up," he said.

Blake pulled open the door, listening to her footsteps climb the stairs, and then she was there, looking up at him from the stairwell. Her dark hair was tied back and there were shadows under her eyes.

"I'm sorry for coming this late," she said.

"It's fine." Blake smiled. "Are you OK?"

Jamie walked up the last few stairs. "It's been a hell of a day, to be honest."

Blake saw the vulnerability in her eyes and pulled her into his arms, hugging her close. She was stiff for a second and then she relaxed, exhaling as she returned his embrace.

She explained what had happened at Cross Bones, about O, the Kitchen, her eviction and the threat to the community.

"That really is a hell of a day," Blake said. "Coffee?"

She stepped away. "Yes please, and then I need your help with something."

He saw the question in her eyes.

"No, I haven't been drinking." He smiled again, this time with an edge of embarrassment. "Although if you'd come ten minutes later, things might have been different."

He wanted to tell her of his uncle's visit, of the possibilities of his gift. But she needed his focus on her now, not on his own dilemma.

Blake put the kettle on and made fresh coffee, carrying the mugs back into the main room. Jamie stood at his window looking out over the rooftops, her eyes fixed on the horizon like she wanted to fly out into the night.

She turned and placed a silver fountain pen wrapped in a piece of paper on his desk.

"I need you to read this," she said. "I don't know what else to do. I'm hoping that you'll see something that could help."

Blake considered his uncle's words, how every time he read strengthened the link between him and his kin. How he opened his mind to the other realm each time and that the *drip drip drip* of darkness would inch into him. He shouldn't do it. But this was for Jamie.

"OK," he said. "But you know I can't promise anything."

She nodded. "Please try anyway."

Blake sat down and took his gloves off. He placed both hands over the pen and lowered his fingertips to the silver, letting the cool metal connect with his skin. He closed his eyes and let the swirling mists rise up in his mind.

He felt an initial resistance, but then he gave into the sensation and dipped through the veil.

The pen was dense with memory, the emotions imprinted upon it holding fast to the metal. Colors swirled about him as Blake began to assume the mantle of the man who owned it. He picked a thread and opened his eyes within the vision.

He looked out at a sea of cameras, of smiling faces, a moment of triumph captured against a backdrop of the City of London. It was the pinnacle of the man's life so far. Blake felt a surge of power, the man's heart pounding as he accepted the position of Mayor. But behind the triumph, there was something darker, a pulse of rotten black that Blake saw as a visible stain. The man gloated over those he looked down upon, for they didn't know his true face.

Blake plucked the darker strings, following them down into a hidden place, closing his eyes again.

He had rarely followed these deeper emotions, preferring to skim on the surface of vision. But this man – Blake's breath caught as he glimpsed a corrupt core under the gleaming surface. The power he wielded was greater than the police, greater than the Mayoralty. He believed he had the power of life and death, who would rise and who would fall in his city. The sense of arousal was strong and as much as he didn't want to, Blake followed that thread.

He opened his eyes within the vision again and saw the chains and hooks of the abattoir above him.

He smelled the metallic hint of blood and machinery.

His hands felt sticky.

Blake looked down through the eyes of the man to see a body that lay on the slab before him, the skinning knife in his hand. A dragon in shades of purple flew across the man's back but there was no life in him left, only his skin would outlast his mortality. The knife hand hovered above the body. For an instant, Blake wanted to pull away in revulsion and drop out of the vision. He stopped himself, controlling the nausea, testing his own limits to stay within.

The man began to cut around the edge of the tattoo, dipping down into the layers of flesh. There was precision in his work and Blake experienced deep concentration and pride. The compartments in the man's mind enabled him to separate his public and private selves. *We all have these two sides*, Blake thought, *but some are more deeply separated than others*. There was no sense that the man saw the body in front of him as a person, only as an artwork in progress. And a way to exercise power against those who cluttered the streets.

But none of this would help Jamie. They needed proof, a way to stop the man.

He let the veil close over the scene and reached lower into the man's emotions. There was a rich vein deeper still in consciousness, a hidden box within the layers the man cloaked his life with. Blake let himself sink into it, and opened his eyes again.

He was in the man's study.

A pair of brown leather wingback chairs sat at oblique angles to a large oak table. Bookshelves lined the walls with an eclectic mix of tomes, from first editions to the latest forensic journals. The man was secure here but there was also a latent excitement, an expectation that went beyond what this room offered.

The man reached for a book on the bookcase and typed in a code, pulling a hidden door open. His arousal was heady and Blake fought to keep himself separate from this man's dark psyche. He understood the temptation to vicariously experience – the visions could allow him that – but like ink into water, it would taint his soul.

The hidden room was a trophy cabinet, Blake could see that immediately. He saw the beaked mask of the Venetian plague doctor, the books of human skin and framed tattoos, skin stretched and pinned into place. The skinning knife, clean and shiny, its blade glittering.

The man opened a safe and pulled out some papers. Blake glimpsed stock certificates with the name Vera Causa on them. The man pushed them aside and reached for a box carved with obscenities. He opened it and pulled out a sheaf of photos. Blake caught sight of a child's face and felt a spike in the man's arousal. He pulled away quickly before the images imprinted themselves on his mind. He had seen enough.

Blake opened his eyes and lifted his hands from the pen. The room swam a little as he refocused on the present, anchoring himself again to the physical world he inhabited. He let his mind scan over his own body, sensing he was back and had separated from the tendrils of the evil he had briefly touched.

Jamie handed him some water silently.

Blake drank several big gulps, letting the cool liquid slide down his throat, latching onto physical sensation. He took a deep breath and turned to face Jamie.

CHAPTER 29

"I think the pen belongs to the new Mayor, Dale Cameron," Blake said. Jamie didn't look surprised. "OK, you knew that."

Jamie nodded. "But I think he's more than that."

"You're right," Blake said. "I saw the abattoir, the beaked mask from the ball. He has a box full of photos – children – but I pulled away then."

Jamie reached for his hand and squeezed it. "I'm sorry you had to see that," she said. "But now we know."

Blake shook his head. "But it's inadmissible, you know that. The visions mean nothing without physical evidence."

Jamie's eyes glinted in the half light. "I know that, but I have contacts in the police. I can get this to the attention of the right people."

Blake put his head in his hands. The desire for alcohol had subsided, but his head pounded with the aftermath of the visions.

"You need to rest," Jamie said. "I know how much reading takes out of you. Come lie down."

She patted the bed next to her, pulling the covers open for him.

There was a part of Blake that wanted to lean down and kiss her right now, to stroke her bare skin with his scarred hands. Could he read her past? Could he take her pain from her?

But now wasn't the right time. It never seemed to be the right time.

He lay down and closed his eyes. He felt her breath on his cheek and then her lips touched his face in a light kiss. Her weight shifted a little as she leaned down.

"I need to make some calls and then I'll come and rest with you," she whispered. "Sleep now."

Blake wanted to hold onto that moment, he wanted to wait for her to come to bed, but he was exhausted. His mind and body spent. He let go of wanting and slipped into sleep.

***

Jamie heard Blake's breathing change as he fell asleep. His face relaxed and she watched him for a moment. He was a beautiful man and part of her wanted to curl around him and kiss his caramel skin, taste his body. He would wake in the night and they would finally take things further. All she had to do was slip into bed next to him.

But his vision had shaken her and Jamie knew she wouldn't sleep now.

Dale Cameron had been her boss in the police, but she had glimpsed his darker side several times. She had tried to ignore her suspicions before, but now she was sure that it must have been him in the smoke of the Hellfire Caves, covering up the scandal for his aristocratic friends. He procured the victims for the RAIN agency and now he was cleaning up the city in a much more personal way.

Jamie picked up her motorcycle helmet and gloves. She looked down at Blake's sleeping face once more, fixing his image in her mind.

This wasn't his responsibility. She had to do this alone.

She picked up the pen and put it in her pocket. Then she slipped out of the flat, mounted her bike and roared back towards Southwark.

The Mayor's new office was in the Shard, the tallest building in Europe, a tower of glass that rose above the ancient city like an angel's spear pointing the way to Heaven. Jamie parked below it and looked up. It was beautiful, a fitting place for Dale Cameron to survey his new domain. Jamie thought of the temptation of Jesus in the desert when the Devil had taken him to a high place and offered him the world if only he would call on the angels to lift him up. It seemed as if Cameron had already taken his deal with the Devil.

It was late, but she knew Cameron's habits from the police. He often worked late into the night, and in the first few days of his Mayoralty it was likely that he was still at the office. She also still had his mobile number.

She stood at the main entrance, closed and locked for the night. Jamie dialed Cameron's number.

It rang once, twice, three times. Her heart sank as she realized that she might not have the reckoning she craved tonight.

"Jamie Brooke." Cameron's voice was calm and assured. "I'm a little surprised to hear from you, especially at this late hour."

"I'd like to talk to you," Jamie said, her heart pounding. She didn't really have a plan as such, but her anger had carried her this far. She had to see it through now. "I remember how you used to work this late in the police." She paused. "I miss those times."

There was a moment of silence and she wondered if she had laid it on too thick.

A click and a whirr and the door slid open.

"Come up. Take the right-hand lift."

Jamie walked in, her footsteps echoing on the marble slabs underfoot. This place oozed wealth and power. No wonder Cameron liked it here.

The lift made her feel slightly queasy as it zoomed upwards. She took her phone out and activated the recording app, slipping it back into her pocket as the doors pinged. Jamie stepped out to find Cameron standing at the doorway to his office, a bottle of burgundy in his hand. He wore a grey suit that looked like it cost more than Jamie's motorbike. He was clean shaven and she could smell a hint of cologne. Enough to woo the senses, not overpower them.

"Drink?" he said, holding up the bottle. The movement revealed a Patek Philippe watch on his wrist. "I was about to have one myself and after all, it's not something we ever did when we worked together."

Jamie nodded. "That would be great."

He turned and she followed him through the open-plan workspace into his office. There were piles of boxes everywhere, paperwork strewn over desktops and pictures still in bubble wrap.

"We're still moving in," Cameron said, pouring the wine into two Riedel glasses. His eyes twinkled with excitement. "Lots to do. Exciting times for the city."

Jamie felt the edge of his charisma as she sipped the wine. He had the ability to make people feel special, his gaze a sunbeam of energy, like they were the only person in the world to him.

"It's good to see you, Jamie," Cameron said softly. "You were a great Detective, and I'm sorry you left when you did. I apologize if I made things hard for you, especially when you were coping with the death of your daughter."

Jamie let him talk. He was still a smooth bastard, that was for sure. No wonder the city loved him. But now she knew what was underneath that facade and she just had to draw it out.

"I need people I can trust now and as Mayor, I can make connections for you," Cameron continued, his voice confident. "You could come and work for me. Or you could go back into the police if you want, perhaps even at a higher level. I can make that happen. Or I know some people in private security, where you could earn more money than you ever have before, doing the work you love."

She pulled the silver pen from her pocket.

"I actually came to return this," she said, laying it on the desk.

His grey eyes narrowed a little as he reached for it.

"I wondered where that had gone." He looked at her closely. "Where did you find it?"

"I've been doing some private investigation work on behalf of the Southwark community since the murders. We've had difficult times in recent days."

"I'm sorry to hear that," Cameron said, his response almost automated, trotted out in interviews to display compassion. But the words were empty, his eyes suspicious.

"The company behind the evictions and the security company at Cross Bones is called Vera Causa. I found your pen at their offices."

Cameron raised an eyebrow. "I've been doing a lot of community work for the Mayoral campaign. I must have left it there. Thanks for returning it." He paused for a moment, leaning back in his chair. The shadows shifted and for a moment, he was shrouded in darkness.

He pointed to a staircase in the corner of the room. "Let's go up to the roof. There's something I want to show you. Something I think you'll appreciate with your love for the city."

He pushed his chair out and walked up the stairs without looking back.

Jamie sat for a moment. Cameron was dangerous and following him was a risk, but she needed evidence to stop him. She grabbed the silver pen from his desk and slipped it back in her pocket before following him up the stairs.

CHAPTER 30

BLAKE WOKE IN THE darkness of his room. His heart pounded as he emerged from a nightmare of gleaming knives and blood.

Jamie.

She had been here when he had fallen asleep and now she was gone. A coldness swept over him as he realized that she must have gone to meet Cameron. After his reading last night, she had decided to face him alone.

Blake jumped out of bed and grabbed his phone, dialing Jamie's number quickly. It rang and rang and then switched to voicemail.

"Damn it, Jamie," he whispered. He needed to get down there, but he needed local help.

"Magda, it's Blake Daniel. We met at O's flat earlier this week. I'm sorry to call so late."

"Oh, not at all." Magda's voice was dull. "I'm back at the hospital and O is recovering from surgery. Maybe Jamie told you?"

"Yes," Blake said. "It's about Jamie. I need your help."

He explained about his reading, his suspicions that Jamie had gone to meet Cameron.

"I'm coming," Magda said, her voice stronger now, galvanized into action. "This has gone too far. I will not have another of our number hurt tonight. I'll meet you on the corner of Stoney Street next to Borough Market."

***

Jamie emerged from the stairwell onto one of the very top floors of the Shard. The view was stunning, a 360-degree panorama of London with the river a dark ribbon running through its heart. This level was still under construction with glass panels enclosing three sides of the structure, but the east side and the roof were partially open to the elements, with only a safety barrier blocking access.

A gust of wind whipped through and Jamie pulled her jacket close about her shoulders. The metal girders creaked a little and the glass rattled, the sound of the building shifting in the sky.

Cameron stood looking north over the city, his nose inches from the glass. He turned at Jamie's approach.

"Isn't it amazing up here?" His grey eyes shone with passion. "This is where I come to get some perspective, and I hope that you will be able to see as I do." Jamie stepped slowly towards him, needing to get closer to record his words. He pointed out, sweeping his arm in a wide arc. "This is London, as far as you can see. The city is not just Southwark, it's not just your Kitchen or Cross Bones Graveyard. It's millions of people who deserve a city where they can thrive. A city that has been cleaned of those who don't deserve to be here. Like a cancer, they must be cut out so the healthy body can survive."

Jamie looked down into the streets of Southwark. She thought she could see Cross Bones Graveyard below them, a patch of dark in the bright orange spectrum of streetlights.

How insignificant our lives are, Jamie thought. The

Shard was built upon the ground of an ancient borough and the blood of two millennia had been spilled here. Now the anger of the Outcast Dead rose up, the shades of those buried by the advance of the rich and powerful over the years.

She placed a hand on the glass.

"I don't see the city as you do," she said softly. "I see people who need help, communities that need leaders who will stand up to your plans." She turned. "Like we did at Cross Bones."

"And look how that ended for your friends," Cameron spat as he walked behind her and stood at the top of the stairs.

"I *will* clean up London, Jamie," he said, his eyes cold, a steel grey as hard as the girders that surrounded them. "I have powerful backers who have the money and power we need for rejuvenation and redevelopment."

"But you'll destroy the diversity that makes this borough a unique historical community," Jamie said.

"Local color is overrated." Cameron chuckled. "People would rather have more wealth. They've demonstrated that in the way they voted and it's time your 'community' moved on. I'm only helping them move on faster."

Cameron cocked his head to one side, regarding her as if she were a problem to be solved. Jamie tensed, realizing how much of a mistake she had made in coming up here.

She darted sideways, ducking under his arm as she rushed for the stairs.

He caught her arm, swinging her back around. Her phone fell out of her pocket, the case smashing on the concrete floor as it spun towards the open edge of the building.

She struggled against him, bringing her arms up fast to break his hold. But he was quick and strong, punching her in the solar plexus sharply with a broad fist.

Jamie dropped to her knees, winded and gasping for breath.

"You should have died that night in the Hellfire Caves," Cameron hissed as he grabbed her hair. "You should have burned alongside your daughter's body."

He dragged her over to the open east side as she struggled against him. Cameron kicked her phone out, sending it spinning into the void.

"You won't be needing that anymore."

In the split second he watched it fall, Jamie grabbed his fist with both hands, forcing her thumbs into the pressure points and twisted hard.

Cameron grunted, releasing his grip for a second. Jamie turned away on her knees, scrambling for the exit, trying to get up.

His boot crunched down on her ankle and strong hands grabbed the back of her jeans, tugging her towards the opening.

"You're only leaving one way," he said, yanking Jamie over and then kicking her in the stomach, his face contorted in a snarl.

She curled inwards, trying to protect herself, pain shooting through her. Her fingers scrabbled for the pen in her pocket, clutching it in one fist.

As he kicked again, Jamie grabbed for his foot and pulled it towards her, tugging him off balance. She scrambled on top of him, using the pen to stab him in the groin. Once. Twice. He howled in pain and doubled over.

She took her chance. Jamie got up and ran for the exit.

A crackle behind her.

A burning pain in her back.

The shuddering agony of electricity shot through her and she crumpled to the floor, limbs jerking. Jamie's mind was screaming even as her body was frozen by the shock.

Cameron stood over her, the police-issue Taser in one hand.

"It's been so hard for you lately, hasn't it?" He straightened his tie then bent to her feet. "First you lose your daughter, then your job, then you're evicted. Your community is crumbling around you. It's no wonder you had to end it all. But at least you chose to jump from somewhere with a great view."

He picked up Jamie's feet and dragged her paralyzed body across the floor towards the east opening.

CHAPTER 31

JAMIE COUNTED IN HER mind, knowing that the complete paralysis only lasted a few seconds. She could start to feel a tingle in her limbs again but she remained still, only hoping that she would get her strength back in time.

Cameron dropped her feet and swept aside the safety barrier. The wind was stronger now, buffeting them as he dragged her closer to the edge.

"Bracing, isn't it?" He grinned, and Jamie saw a mania born of addiction to power there. Cameron was used to getting everything he wanted, destroying lives in the shadows while he stood squeaky clean in public. He bent to pick up her feet again.

Jamie felt tingling in her arms and legs. *One more second*, she thought. *Don't move too soon.* The gaping hole in the building was only a meter away now and she struggled to relax as Cameron dragged her closer.

Then she saw it.

A blowtorch ready for the next day's welding. It was within reach, but she only had one chance.

"I'll make sure the papers write something good about your death," Cameron said. "Perhaps I'll even do the eulogy at your funeral." He turned and smiled. "Fitting, don't you think?"

Jamie lunged for the blowtorch as she kicked out with both feet.

Cameron fell backwards, teetering on the edge. He grabbed for the side girder, pulling himself back in.

Jamie pressed the switch on the blowtorch, sending a spurt of flame into his face.

Cameron screamed in rage and pain, protecting his face with his hands. The smell of singed hair and burned flesh filled the air. He charged her, bellowing his anger, blocking her path to the exit as he ran at her like a bull.

Jamie dropped the torch, ducked away. She just needed to stay out of his reach.

Thick metal girders led up to the next level. Jamie ran for them and began to climb, fixing her eyes on the rivets in front of her, trying to ignore the sheer drop beneath, one thousand feet to the ground below.

"Come back here, bitch." Cameron's voice was rough and he breathed heavily as he pulled himself after her.

Hand over hand, Jamie climbed. She reached the next level only to find the floor hadn't been finished and there was no way to get down again. She could only go up.

The Shard tapered as it rose into the night sky, the girders getting thinner the higher she climbed. Jamie could hear Cameron's breathing below her. Her arms shook with effort as she pulled herself up another inch.

***

Blake arrived at Borough Market to find Magda gazing up at the Shard through binoculars.

"The Mayor's new office is up there," she said, focusing the lenses on the upper levels. "If Jamie's up there, we might be able to see her."

Blake stood, his fists clenched as Magda slowly

scanned the building. Every part of him wanted to be with Jamie now. He'd been crazy to sleep after telling her about Cameron. He should have known she would take action.

"Oh no." Magda's voice chilled Blake with its dark intensity.

"What is it?" he said, grabbing the binoculars from her and training them on the upper levels.

"Look at the east corner," Magda said. "That must be her."

Blake could make out a lone figure clambering up one of the exposed metal girders on the open east side of the building.

Behind her, another figure climbed with strong movements, gaining on her quickly.

"Jamie…" Blake whispered. "Hold on." He spun to Magda. "How do we get up there?"

She shook her head. "There are so many levels of security. We won't get in that way." Her eyes narrowed. "But there might be something."

"Anything," Blake said. "Please. We have to help her."

"You have your gift," Magda said. "I have my own."

She pulled one of her sleeves up, revealing the tattooed ravens that whirled on her arm. Pulling a small penknife from her bag, she cut a symbol into the feathers of one of the birds, tracing three whorls into her skin. A bead of blood welled and dripped down her arm to the ground.

As it splashed on the earth, Magda began to whistle.

The tune was soft at first and then stronger, the notes a Celtic refrain of growing power.

The wind changed and the cold made Blake shiver as Magda called on the Morrigan, the shape-shifting goddess of war, fate and death. She who roamed the battlefields in the shape of a raven, choosing those who would live and who would die.

As Magda whistled into the wind, her hands held high,

Blake heard the beat of wings on the air. A flock of ravens appeared out of the night and flew overheard, wheeling about her. They were strangely silent, their beady eyes looking down on the one who called them.

Magda turned towards the Shard and her whistling song switched to a harsher refrain.

She pointed at the top of the spire and the birds streamed away from her, cawing loudly now, a jarring cacophony that drowned out the sound of the city.

They flew up and soon a dark cloud obscured the top of the Shard. Blake could only pray for the outcome above.

CHAPTER 32

Jamie's arms burned as she tried to haul herself up a little further, inching away from Cameron into the highest reaches of the building. The wind buffeted her and she clung to the metal, heart pounding as she hung above the void, vertigo making her head spin.

She looked down to see him inches below her foot, his hand stretched out to grab her.

"I will see you fall tonight," Cameron said. "So give in to it, Jamie. Lean out and you will see your daughter again."

Jamie stamped down on his grasping fingers.

"Polly never gave up," she said, panting with the effort of holding on and trying to kick him away. "Neither will I."

Cameron grabbed her foot and twisted it. Jamie gasped in pain as he forced her leg sideways off the side of the girder. Off balance for a second, she grabbed for another hold and slipped down a few inches.

Cameron reached for her and Jamie saw her death in his eyes.

As his hand stretched out, a stream of ravens swirled up in a vortex into his face, beaks and claws ripping at his skin.

Cameron screamed, his arms waving at them, trying to beat them off even as they pecked and shredded his flesh.

Jamie put her hands over her face, clinging to the girder as the birds dive-bombed Cameron, bodies repeatedly thunking against his. Individually the ravens were nothing, but together, they forced him from the girder inch by inch.

Two birds landed on his hair, claws ripping it away in bloody chunks. He raised both his hands, losing his grip, and for a moment he teetered on the edge of the girder.

The flock wheeled, and together they pounded into him.

Dale Cameron plummeted off the Shard, his dying scream drowned out by the triumphant cawing of the ravens.

***

Jamie couldn't move.

She clung to the girder, eyes closed, as the wind whipped about her. The birds were gone, Cameron was gone, but she was still at the top of the building, hanging above certain death. Her strength was fading, her limbs ached, and she only wanted to close her eyes and let it all go.

Climbing down seemed like an overwhelming impossibility – but perhaps she didn't have to. With Cameron gone, the circle could be closed on the cases she'd been involved with. She could be with Polly if she just relaxed. The end would be swift, she knew that.

But then Polly's voice came to her in the wind. *Dance for me, Mum.*

Jamie held on. *One more minute*, she thought.

***

It seemed like a long time later when she heard a voice calling her name.

"Jamie," the voice called softly. Blake's voice. "It's OK. You can come back now. It's safe. Please, Jamie. Look at me."

He was here.

Jamie opened her eyes and looked down through the girders to the platform below. Blake stood there, his hands outstretched towards her. Behind him, Magda stood like a dark guardian angel.

"Inch back down towards me," Blake said. "Just a little way and then I can reach for you."

Blake's voice was soft, but in his tone she heard a promise. "Please, Jamie."

Slowly, she stretched out a leg, her muscles shaking as she gripped the metal with all her strength, easing backwards down the girder.

She inched her way down as her friends called encouragement, every step a huge effort.

Finally, she felt Blake's hand on her foot.

"I'm here," he said. "A little closer and then I'll help you in."

She pushed herself with every last bit of energy she could summon. Then his arms were pulling her into the safety of the tower, into his embrace.

CHAPTER 33: A WEEK LATER

A TRAIN RATTLED ALONG the tracks high on the over-bridge, the rhythmic sound a back note to the folk band playing below in Cross Bones Graveyard. Jamie strolled through the open gates, still hung with ribbons commemorating the dead but today flung wide to welcome the community. Towering above her, the Shard rose into a blue sky, its glass panels reflecting the sun like a beacon for the city.

Families walked around the flowerbeds and Jamie watched as one little girl bent to smell a pink rose, her little face lighting up with pleasure as the petals stuck to her nose. Jamie smiled. *Polly would have loved it here*, she thought, but the pang of grief for her daughter was more a dull ache than a sharp pain now. It was settling, she realized. This community and the purpose she had found here gave her something to live for.

Applause rang out across the green as the band finished one song and then launched into a reel. The dancing began again, bare feet pounding the ground where the dead lay beneath. Jamie thought that the women and children who rested under this earth would relish the celebration. Perhaps they had danced here long ago, a moment of pleasure that connected across the generations.

Magda and O spun together in the crowd, laughing as they danced. O wore a flowery summer dress that floated around her and Magda was her dark opposite in customary tight black jeans and t-shirt. Jamie looked around and realized that she knew many of the people there. This was her community too now.

O spotted Jamie and walked over, her blonde hair shining in the sun. She grabbed Jamie's hands and spun her around to the tune.

"Isn't this wonderful?" O said with a delighted laugh. "Everyone has come out to celebrate. Finally, Cross Bones can be an official memorial garden."

The last few days had been crazy. Dale Cameron's death had officially been ruled a suicide after the contents of his locked room had been leaked to the press. His part in the Southwark murders was still being established, but Jamie had heard from Missinghall that there was evidence from years of criminal activity to go through and the scandal had rocked the upper echelons of power.

The new Mayor, Amanda Masters, had opened her first week by giving Cross Bones Graveyard to the people of Southwark and providing new funding to the Kitchen. The community rallied, and together they were making this a sanctuary for those outcast in life as well as death. Magda and O were leading the development team and Jamie would join them in the next week. It was time she used her skills to build and nurture instead of clean up the aftermath of violence. It felt good to be part of something new, something vibrant.

Magda walked up and kissed Jamie on the cheek, her smile wide as she surveyed the happy crowd.

"Thank you for coming, Jamie. We really couldn't have done this without you." She put her arms around O, pulling her tight against her body. O giggled and nuzzled against her. "And I might have lost Olivia without you."

"Get a room," Jamie laughed, pushing them away, and they skipped back to the reel.

"Fancy a dance?" The voice caught her by surprise and she turned quickly.

Blake stood there, holding a bunch of purple tulips. He ran a gloved hand nervously over his buzzcut.

"I … I hope it's OK that I came. I brought flowers for the memorial."

"They're gorgeous," Jamie said.

She reached out and touched his arm, her fingers caressing his caramel skin before linking her arm with his. He smelled of pine forests after rain.

"I thought you were going north for a trip," Jamie said. "Did you change your mind?"

"That can wait," Blake said, his voice soft. "I have more important things to focus on here."

Jamie looked up and met his eyes. She saw a promise there, something they could build upon, a new beginning.

"We can lay the flowers together," she said.

AUTHOR'S NOTE

As with all my books, this one is based on real places and then spun off into a new direction for the story. For images relating to the book, check out the Deviance board on Pinterest: www.pinterest.com/jfpenn/deviance/

Cross Bones Graveyard

Cross Bones is a post-medieval burial ground, that much is true, since excavations found an overcrowded graveyard during the construction of the London Underground Jubilee Line.

John Constable, a Southwark writer, is responsible for the interpretation of it as an unconsecrated graveyard for the Outcast Dead, women who were licensed by the church to work as prostitutes and their children, their sin used to fund the lifestyle and buildings of the clergy. John is an urban shaman under the name John Crow, who also channeled a Winchester Goose to write *The Southwark Mysteries*. He also leads walks around the borough. You can find more about his work here at www.SouthwarkMysteries.co.uk

The character of Magda Raven was influenced by John Constable/John Crow, and also by the book *Pastrix* by Nadia Bolz-Weber.

When I first started writing the book, Cross Bones Grave-yard was under the threat of development by Transport for London, but in Jan 2015, Bankside Open Spaces Trust was given temporary planning permission and a three-year lease for a memorial garden.

You can find videos and more information at
www.crossbones.org.uk

Tattoos

If you want to know more about the meaning of tattoos and body modification, then check out *Pagan Fleshworks: The Alchemy of Body Modification* by Maureen Mercury.

You can see tattoos I love on the Pinterest board and yes, I am intending to get ink!

Octopus

The scene that Blake reads in O's pendant is from my own scuba diving experience at the Poor Knights Islands in New Zealand years ago. A huge octopus swam by, stopping for a moment to hang in the water and check me out before swimming on. I've seen a lot of octopi in holes and crevices but this is the only one I've seen in open water. I had the sense of something so alien, yet also intelligent. I've seen the same look in the eyes of dolphins when swimming wild with them.

This fascination with octopi led to the emergence of O's tattoo in *Desecration*, so I wanted to write about its origin story here.

Sex trade in London

It's fascinating how much of London is shaped by the history of the sex trade. The main books used for my research were *City of Sin* by Catharine Arnold and *The Secret History of Georgian London: How the Wages of Sin Shaped the Capital* by Dan Cruickshank

ACKNOWLEDGEMENTS

For DESECRATION

First and always, thanks to Jonathan, for understanding my fascination with death and the macabre and not being freaked out by my consistently dark obsessions. And to my readers, who I write for.

I also have a great team who have helped me to shape the book. A huge thanks to: My Mum, Jacqueline Penn, for her line editing and consistent encouragement; My Dad, Arthur Penn, for his honest appraisal as a crime reader which helped reshape the procedural aspects of the book; Doctor Denzil Gill and Doctor Kim Gill, dear friends who helped me with the medical aspects of the book including Polly's illness and death; Garry Rodgers, author and ex-coroner for answering my morbid questions about methods of murder and anatomical specimens; Clare Mackintosh, writer and ex-police officer, for her expertise and suggestions on procedural aspects; New York Times bestselling authors David Morrell and CJ Lyons, for their feedback, encouragement and mentorship. And to Rachel Ekstrom, my agent for a time, for her hard work on my behalf and suggestions that improved the plot.

Thanks also to my production team: Liz Broomfield, at LibroEditing.com for the proof-reading; Derek Murphy at Creativindie for the cover design; Jane Dixon Smith at JDSmith-Design.com for the interior print design; Suzanne Norris of www.sakurasnow.com for the brilliant interior cabinet of curiosities artwork.

For DELIRIUM

Thanks to Dan Holloway, for writing so eloquently on aspects of mental illness, for answering my questions and for being a superb beta-reader and helping me improve the story. And to Garry Rodgers, ex-coroner, for checking my death scenes.

Thanks to Jen Blood, my editor, for her fantastic work in improving the text, and to Wendy Janes for excellent proof-reading.

Thanks, as always, to Derek Murphy from Creativindie for the fantastic book cover design. And to Jane Dixon Smith for the interior design.

For DEVIANCE

For Jonathan. Thank you for joining me on sex tours of Southwark and indulging my weird obsessions at the Tattoo Convention.

Thanks to Jen Blood, my fantastic editor, to Wendy Janes for proofreading and thanks to Jane Dixon-Smith for cover design and interior print formatting.

MORE BOOKS BY J.F. PENN

* * *

Brooke and Daniel Psychological Thrillers

Desecration #1
Delirium #2
Deviance #3

* * *

Mapwalker Dark Fantasy Thrillers

Map of Shadows #1
Map of Plagues #2
Map of the Impossible #3

If you enjoy **Action Adventure Thrillers**, check out the **ARKANE** series as Morgan Sierra and Jake Timber solve supernatural mysteries around the world.

Stone of Fire #1
Crypt of Bone #2
Ark of Blood #3
One Day In Budapest #4

Day of the Vikings #5
Gates of Hell #6
One Day in New York #7
Destroyer of Worlds #8
End of Days #9
Valley of Dry Bones #10
Tree of Life #11

* * *

For more **dark fantasy,** check out:

Risen Gods
The Dark Queen
A Thousand Fiendish Angels:
Short stories based on Dante's Inferno

More books coming soon.

You can sign up to be notified of new releases, giveaways and pre-release specials - plus, get a free book!

www.JFPenn.com/free

If you loved the book and have a moment to spare, I would really appreciate a short review on the page where you bought the book. Your help in spreading the word is gratefully appreciated and reviews make a huge difference to helping new readers find the series.

Thank you!

ABOUT J.F.PENN

J.F.Penn is the Award-nominated, New York Times and USA Today bestselling author of the ARKANE action adventure thrillers, Brooke & Daniel Psychological Thrillers, and the Mapwalker fantasy adventure series, as well as other standalone stories.

Her books weave together ancient artifacts, relics of power, international locations and adventure with an edge of the supernatural. Joanna lives in Bath, England and enjoys a nice G&T.

You can follow Joanna's travels on Instagram
@jfpennauthor and also on her podcast at
BooksAndTravel.page.

* * *

Sign up for your free thriller,
Day of the Vikings, and updates from behind
the scenes, research, and giveaways at:

www.jfpenn.com/free

* * *

Connect with Joanna:
www.JFPenn.com
joanna@JFPenn.com
www.Facebook.com/JFPennAuthor
www.Instagram.com/JFPennAuthor

* * *

For writers:

Joanna's site, www.TheCreativePenn.com, helps people write, publish and market their books through articles, audio, video and online courses.

She writes non-fiction for authors under Joanna Penn and has an award-nominated podcast for writers, The Creative Penn Podcast.

Lightning Source UK Ltd.
Milton Keynes UK
UKHW041346270123
416070UK00004B/377